REUNIONS

REUNIONS

A NOVEL

DAVID ADAMS
CLEVELAND

GREENLEAF
BOOK GROUP PRESS

This is a work of fiction. Names, characters, places, and incidents are either the product of the author's imagination or are used fictitiously. Any resemblance to actual persons, living or dead, or actual events is purely coincidental. Reference to any real institutions, including universities, is made for fictional purposes only and does not imply any affiliation with or endorsement by those institutions.

Published by Greenleaf Book Group Press
Austin, Texas
www.gbgpress.com

Distributed by Greenleaf Book Group

For ordering information or special discounts for bulk purchases, please contact Greenleaf Book Group at PO Box 91869, Austin, TX 78709, 512.891.6100.

Design and composition by Greenleaf Book Group and Mimi Bark
Cover design by Jason Bohr

Publisher's Cataloging-in-Publication data is available.

Print ISBN: 979-8-88645-369-0

eBook ISBN: 979-8-88645-370-6

To offset the number of trees consumed in the printing of our books, Greenleaf donates a portion of the proceeds from each printing to the Arbor Day Foundation. Greenleaf Book Group has replaced over 50,000 trees since 2007.

Printed in the United States of America on acid-free paper

25 26 27 28 29 30 31 32 10 9 8 7 6 5 4 3 2 1

First Edition

As always, for Patricia, Carter, and Christopher,
whose love and support have made everything possible.

We consider the process of reversing and overcoming the dangerous progression of disease as a war. As in any war it is important to mobilize all the means of intelligence and weaponry . . . By adopting such multipronged strategies for each disease process and each aging process, even baby boomers like myself can remain in good health until the full blossoming of the biotechnology revolution . . . Biotechnology will provide the means to actually change your genes: not just designer babies will be feasible but designer baby boomers.

—Ray Kurzweil, *The Singularity Is Near*

PROLOGUE

College reunions, except for the most stalwart or starry-eyed, tend to be a mixed blessing, since time is suddenly compressed, merging one's youth and advanced age in often agonizing proximity, as the ambitions and foibles of student days are placed under the magnification of maturity. And there, amid campus scenes barely changed, as through a glass darkly, we glimpse the limitless vistas of those early days, aspirations long-foundered on injustice or neglect, those vaunted gifts that died aborning. Not that there aren't many pleasures to be found in such a juxtaposition of past and present: friends and roommates, teammates and lovers seeking to reconnect, old flames toying with second thoughts, and, dare one admit, competitors and even enemies fallen by the wayside, out of the game or simply lost to memory, whose presence or sad absence offers the chance of healing.

But what of those lockbox secrets that will out or not, things best left to the obscurity of unremembered dreams?

For time is the great equalizer and comforter. The years count for and against.

Early reunions are a cinch; even the most hardened and cynical can weather the fifth and tenth, even the fifteenth, when most are cruising along with grad degrees and first jobs and first marriages, with successes notched—and failures that can simply be chalked up to the arbitrary caprices of life's crapshoot. But the later years, the last years when we plod the upland path, when the next five-year cycle of reunions no longer seems like a sure bet—what of those? Can we still bluff our way back to those halcyon days, that not-so-golden age once ours and ours alone, which newly minted historians and pundits are already picking over for misbegotten excesses and pathetic failures, rearranging the shards of what had once seemed a glorious whole, as seamless and omnipresent as the hum of summer cicadas. How could those splendid days of righteous certainty against war and inequality (marching for civil rights, women's rights) through which our lives passed be called into question? When did those inspiring and heartfelt causes become such brittle and unrealized things in the eyes of younger generations, faded snapshots fraying at the edges? Hadn't it still been a vital stream bearing us along at fifteen and twenty years out, as we reached for the glittering prizes still hovering at our fingertips?

And, good Lord, what are we to be left with when one has reached the farther hills that line the upland path, those rugged milestones thirty to forty, even fifty years out? When we have fought most of life's battles, hopefully won more than lost, when the carousel of reunions slows to a canter, the shadows lengthen, the smoke from abandoned campsites disperses, and the distant valley below sprouts strange new tributaries and byways. Where are the woodlots and stone walls that once provided resting places, that sylvan landscape we thought impervious to time, as comforting as the illustrations in our children's favorite storybooks, picturesque as a sunstruck watercolor by Salvator Rosa.

And so, decked out in gaudy Reunions gear, we arrive back on campus sporting our confident faces, crackling with bonhomie as we drink in the familiar landmarks of student days, somewhat resigned, by our fortieth, to find we have become who we are, done what we came or hoped to do. The evidence writ as well in the greetings of our contemporaries, faces—some almost unrecognizable—strangely lined and sagging in the dappled shade of the elms and maples that seemed, once upon a time, mere saplings.

Our nostalgic gaze out our home or office window has retreated, leaving behind our well-ordered desk, and with a fair wind at our back, we seek shelter once more in the arms of our alma mater, hopefully not for the last time, murmuring all the while orisons to deliver us from creeping regret. There to meet up with our band of battle-scarred brothers and sisters, if not the specter of our younger, more ambitious selves. And, if the gods be willing, with children in tow. There, under the stately elms, in the cloistered shadows overseen by gargoyles—bloodless, stony-faced, sardonic—we gather again under the kindly eyes of our contemporaries, hoping they might yet extend to us the benefit of the doubt, and so allow us, for a few blessed hours, to live once more as we were. Our larger-than-life selves: the one who caught the winning pass in the corner of the end zone, who hit the three-pointer at the buzzer, still the gifted pianist, artist, and dancer with the packed résumé that got us here in the first place. Perhaps, a parallel universe for the physics-minded, even as we, in our heart of hearts, can't help wondering what ever happened to that splendid fellow burning the midnight oil as he finished his thesis on medieval troubadours, that gal with the perfect figure who danced on the side with Paul Taylor, that inseparable couple (whose wall-banging bedstead provided a fifteen-minute study break each and every night of senior year) whom everyone assumed, given all the practice, would marry and produce a passel of kids.

Phantoms glimpsed in others' eyes.

And who could have hoped to live up to such expectations anyway?

Confounded too by the long shots who surprised everyone, including themselves.

All are climbing the same dusty trail, as the foothills reach the mountains, as the valley below recedes into dusk, as we pause for breath . . . and our steps begin to falter. And so we learn to harbor our remaining reserves, trying to put names to familiar, yet greatly changed faces, hoping the name will come to us before a greeting or the prompting of a name tag in a wobbly hand, searching frantically for some clue—that dance, that song (Amy, whacha wanna do), that soft halo of blue light at the senior dinner-dance, a fragrance of perfume or aftershave, the taste of sweat or semen, even a brief searching kiss—that will allow the memory to rise once more before us and transport us back to when we were most alive, when we could still so easily indulge our essential selves.

Such epiphanies, such privileged moments of vision, were first enumerated by Augustine in his *Confessions*, where he describes the return of such memories as sparks of spiritual enlightenment, which arrive, as he writes, "with the flash of a trembling glance." When labyrinthine memory gives birth to things past that are yet present, things present that are not yet past, and a future transforming all as it comes into being. Or, as Einstein would have it, the relativity of simultaneity.

When we believe that our fine aspirations of long ago, despite all, may indeed outlast time in the guise of our extratemporal selves, in loyalty to our class and the university we loved, our family and children, or perhaps in the miracle of a perfect metaphor to be penned in that novel we always meant to write, that now we will finally have the time to begin. Recording that first kiss, the scrumptious taste of cold pizza and warm beer, the song of katydids in the tall grass as we gazed at the fixed constellations, the scent of firs and lilacs in a moonlit garden. When our imaginative selves may again take flight over that far-off Brueghelian valley. Or glimpsed in a memorial service for those among us who have passed on, when that familiar patch of ruby light high up in the poets' window causes our breath to catch in wonder, where those tiny, haloed figures hover in pure space . . . there indeed to be reunited with our better angels before the hourglass spills its last. Or even compelled, like the Old Testament's Jacob, to wrestle a final time with one's destiny in the guise of an angel: the kinder, more loving person we always knew ourselves to be. That secret sharer in the stained glass who returns our stare as if it were their own.

A miracle . . . waiting to happen.

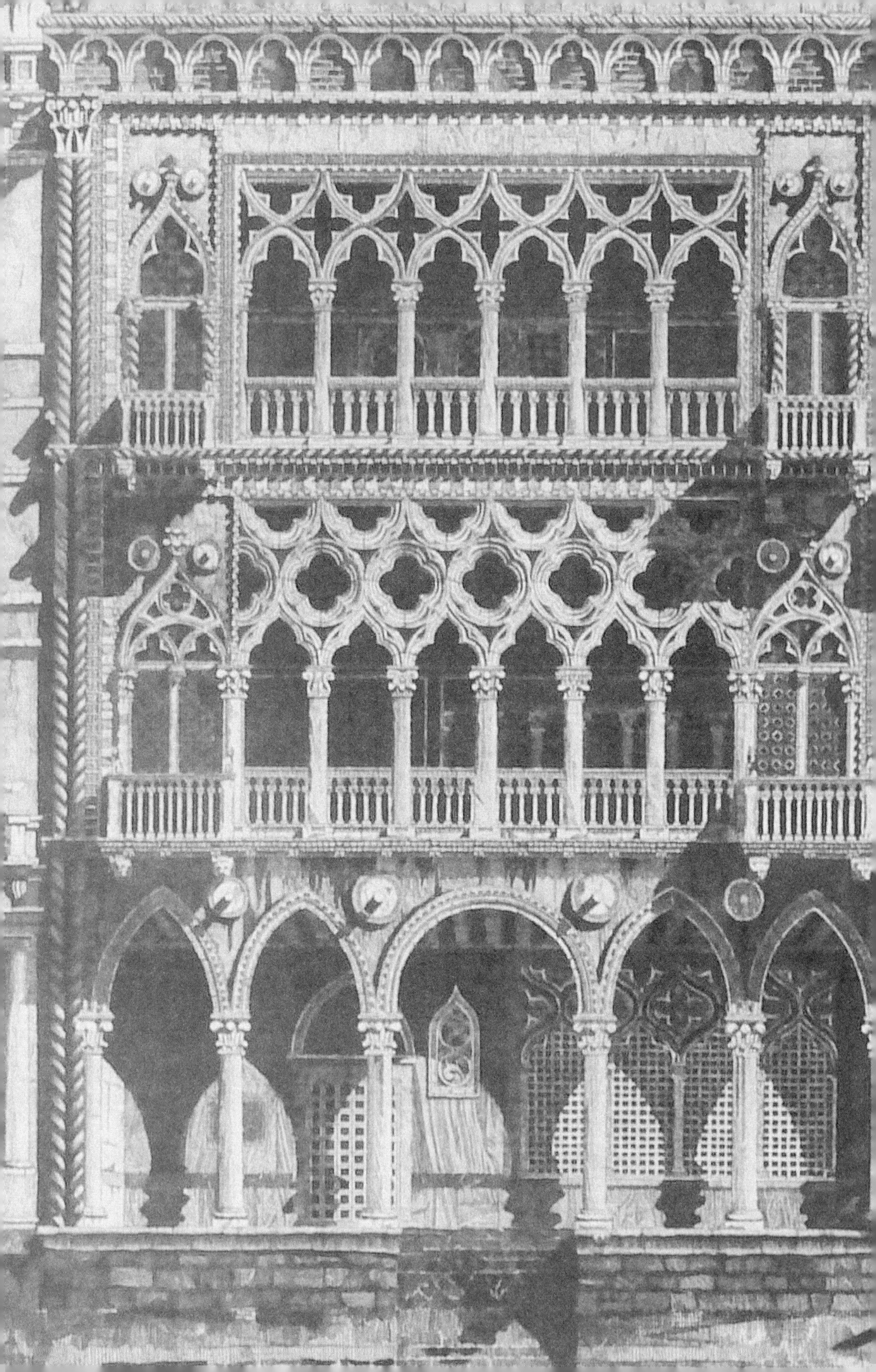

CHAPTER 1

She carried within herself a great fund of life, and her deepest enjoyment was to feel the continuity between the movements of her own soul and the agitations of the world.

—Henry James, *The Portrait of a Lady*

Ginistrella Wingate was much pleased with herself as she checked the blue hands of her father's art deco Rolex. Not only was she actually early for the Friday luncheon kicking off their fortieth college reunion, but she'd beaten out her three teammates (four-time Ivy League tennis champs), who were now volleying in texts like the possessed as they converged on the Gothic splendor of Holder courtyard bathed in late-spring sunshine. At a corner table under the huge tent, she found it advantageous to pretend she was busy returning office emails on her iPhone when she was surreptitiously taking notes on the ambulatory disasters on view at every turn of her elegant neck. Just days before—the cure for all that ailed her—she'd resolved to take up again the novel, her prize-winning senior thesis, no less, that she'd long ago vowed to rewrite and update for publication. Less about herself—God forbid (the first woman editor in chief and CEO of a major publishing house, neatly following in the steps of her late husband and father) than a meditation on her life and times, with a nod to her fellow Stoic, Marcus Aurelius. Who better placed in her class to write the story of their generation? Under her inspired leadership, Tandem Press had been driven to greater profitability and prestige, with two of her authors recently winning Pulitzers and another a National Book Award. For twenty years, she'd been a power player in a cutthroat industry (elbowing the old boys into well-deserved early retirement), with a discerning eye—"Maxwell's eye," as she thought of it, for her editorial hero, Maxwell Perkins—for quality fiction, and Reunions had quite suddenly sparked a reassessment of things left undone—that first novel for one, her relationship with her graduating daughter, Erma, another.

Which was why she opted to stake out a corner table, so avoiding classmates with books to pitch her (the publishing forum tomorrow would be challenging enough!), while contemplating how best to approach her difficult daughter who was graduating in five days. Gini had let her honey-blonde hair grow longer in the last year and now wore it down over her broad, still-powerful shoulders, less to look like her girlish self of decades before than for her daughter's sake, to approximate the approachable inner-hausfrau she suspected Erma had lacked growing up. She'd even dispensed with her usual comfortably sleek and elegant Armani work attire for something matronly, a floral-print poplin cotton dress, which she knew would appeal to Erma, her science kid, who, when not identifying wildflowers over summers at West Chop, had dissected horseshoe crabs and bluefish on their front veranda. Something cool and breezy for the tropical New Jersey humidity, a gathered waist, and a few inches above the knee that at least showed off her svelte figure and long legs. (How some of her classmates had let themselves go to seed!)

But something was off, something to do with the young man who had just caught her eye, dispensing with a white lab coat and taking up a chair at the sign-in table across the cloistered courtyard. Who hadn't been there when she'd checked in half an hour ago. Glancing up from her phone again and removing her reading glasses, she noted him in animated conversation with members of the student Reunions team, going down a checklist on a clipboard, pointing out things on the sign-in table, and then again taking a seat on a folding chair at a slight angle to where she sat. The short, brassy hair was somehow wrong as well, even as the regular-featured face with prominent brows and alert, curious, watchful eyes was oddly familiar. As were his swimmer's shoulders, barely contained by his orange-and-black tee shirt with a list of some kind—victories, perhaps, on the front—that recalled a similar shirt worn by her daughter. Had she seen the young man at one of Erma's diving meets? (She'd gone to two or three swim meets, but Erma had always discouraged attendance, complaining that her mother's presence made her too nervous.)

For a glorious moment, she saw her daughter suspended in thin air in a twisting, forward dive, every muscle, every line a thing of perfection.

As the young man stood to greet one of her classmates, she was struck again by the flicker of bemused intelligence about the eyes, a curious smile—just look at the expression of startled recognition in that woman's face! Her heart raced as she squinted, finding herself squirming in her seat. Handsome, sure, but unremarkably so in what was certainly a most remarkable young man; otherwise, he wouldn't be here. Unlike members of her class, filled with plenty of unremarkable souls—okay, somewhat talented, even earnest in their attempts to end the Vietnam War and march for civil rights, but not in the league of these kids today, like her daughter, whose intellectual bandwidth so often put her mother to shame.

Could it be? "Jake's son . . ."

With this whispered incantation, a spell broken, a gust of wind, a stiff breeze suddenly swept through the tent, blowing sun hats and orange napkins like a rain of confetti off the luncheon tables. As she raised a hand to batten down her place setting and hair, she turned her curious blue eyes to the stately quatrefoil arcades of the residential college shimmering in leafy shadows, silvery, lilac, lemony green—an impressionist palette. What sea change did this portend? For just the barest instant, she thought she detected the scent of brine, burning wax, or even dope, or perhaps mold, as in the old sail locker for their long-defunct Vineyard 15. She drew another deep breath as if to fully release her imaginative grasp, closing her eyes and opening them, a reboot, a Lucretian calmness, just the right distance to fully allow that waking dream to unfold backward . . . as her daughter slipped beneath the surface. Poised on this welcoming threshold, she raised her eyes to the soothing blue cradling of the quad's gargoyle-picketed roofline. "Whitman . . . ," she exclaimed, as if reciting just the right line or two might ease open the cracked door, whispering under her breath like a soothsayer's prophecy: "If you want me again look for me under your boot-soles . . . Failing to fetch me at first keep encouraged, missing me one place search another, I stop somewhere waiting for you."

Her heart beating to the cadence, she found herself staring at the trampled grass and muddy footprints of the quad just beyond the plywood platform under the tent; it had rained much of the previous week. Then came a distant drumroll drawing nearer, the cry of trumpets, the moan of tubas as the motley Princeton University marching band straggled into Holder courtyard to drum up nostalgia in the luncheon crowd. Fight songs to invoke glory days past. The band leader and the color guard, a striking Asian American woman, were dressed in white swallowtail jackets and trousers with orange tiger-striped piping. While the band members, a distinctly diverse crew, sported orange-check jackets or beer jackets, some with straw boaters, some with caps, some bareheaded, some in black pants or just jeans above Nikes or flip-flops. Such lack of strict uniformity had been de rigueur in their rebellious student days, and she was delighted to see that this motley informality was now a beloved tradition verging on caricature. All in keeping with the high jinks and tomfoolery of Reunions.

Irony. She wondered: Had that supremely ironic, if not sarcastic gaze been the defining character of her generation after the fight for civil rights? Irony that allowed a thousand quirky opinions to flourish, a freedom of expression largely lost on the young of today.

Her gaze, possibly reinvigorated, focused again on the sign-in area, where that closely cropped young man stood to greet more members of the great class of 1976, animated, talkative, captivating those passing in review as he handed out Reunions swag. Was he wearing a slight beard, a goatee and mustache? That didn't quite fit the long-haired image so firmly fixed in her mind's eye, but then so many athletes were wearing strange facial hair these days. Still, something about the rather ordinary but recondite face, nicely tapering nose, and thin but kissable lips . . . hardly wildly attractive.

"Yes, it has to be . . ."

Her heart began racing, so much so that she found it necessary to pretend a rapt fascination with the marching band as it swung around the back side of the tent, trumpets blaring, drum section fired up as if desperate to engage a still-preoccupied audience, more focused on greeting friends and the sumptuous buffet. Why so flummoxed, she scolded? Why the teenage angst? The shame of a voyeur caught in the act. She clamped her hands over more napkins as that welcoming breeze started up again, as if to settle in her mind such pesky near memories and so better indulge the convivial pleasures still in the offing. Placing her phone over a pile of napkins, she turned her scrutiny to the age-old and still comforting calluses on her right palm, the one on the heel a bit sore, showing abrasions from her recently increased workout schedule (in preparation for the charity tennis match tomorrow). For a moment, she contemplated her gold wedding band. "Fast fish . . . loose fish . . . fast fish . . ." She'd worn the wedding band for Erma's sake, to celebrate her graduation as her father, Bill Cheshire, would have celebrated. Her thick eyebrows tightened in a pang of free-floating guilt, as if she was being surreptitiously shadowed. Her gaze shifted to the agitated tree forms flickering across the thick grass of the courtyard, lifting to the lanky boughs of an immemorial elm where it sheltered Holder's buff-gray and brown collegiate Gothic stonework, layer upon layer of stratified limestone, as if in deft mimicry of geologic time. Where ageless bowers of gnarled wisteria slithered skyward, skirting sunlit windows of leaded glass.

Having secured as many napkins as possible under her phone, she gave her full attention to one of these ropey lavender staircases, her eye led upward, as if from digital gloom to something possibly more propitious, only to be met by a band of gibbering gargoyles perched along the roofline, glumly peering down upon the faithful. How had she failed to canvass these fantastic oracles from her student days? Two dolphin-like creatures rising off a cresting wave (somehow familiar) leaped skyward from one shadowed cornice, while another, caught in a slant of sunlight, now drew her gaze: a grotesque, ancient, lizard-like face with bulging eyes behind round spectacles examined an upheld beaker grasped in a skeletal paw. A devilish alchemist, so it struck her, seeking to turn ordinary matter into gold, virgin's piss into wine, or perhaps turn back the clock with some elixir of youth. Or was it that warning shout over the rooftops of the world, as she would one day write: run, girl, run as fast and far as you can.

"Run . . ."

The faint murmur of her own perplexed voice, oddly enough, instead echoed forth an image of crazy youth: naked youth, hairy, goose-bumped male backsides, seventy or more—not that she was counting. Thoroughly inebriated young men and a few women shivering in the Holder courtyard, only sneakers between them and a frigid February. It was the first of the annual Nude Olympics, inaugurated by her junior class in the savagely cold winter of 1974. Now, if she recalled right, officially banned by the university (lest someone sue for unwanted touching). When she and two of her teammates, Bianca and Apolonia, had joined the guys (not to be found wanting in the true Princeton spirit of raucous devilry), while discreetly keeping on their panties as they jogged around campus. And yet that image of pale half-moons, shivering, pimpled male asses, one more familiar than the others, now looped in a long-unremembered conversation, sparked by a favorite line of Shelley.

"Thou lovest: but ne'er knew love's sad satiety."

"Who's that—not our sad Allosaurus?"

She and Jake Burrage had been sitting on a wooden bench in the candlelit near darkness of Guyot Hall—probably the fall of 1975, while devouring hoagies and contemplating the toothy dinosaur skeleton tethered by metal rods in the geology department's exhibition space.

"If you spent more time reading instead of poker and pool." She waved to the dingy quatrefoil windows, where feeble lamplight barely penetrated. "And why we need to have dinner al fresco in this chamber of horrors is beyond me. And Boris, over there"—she pointed to the display cases of Egyptian mummies—"is the pits."

"Why, not upmarket enough for you?" Jake reached down and adjusted a candle on a paper plate at their feet.

"When we could be having a cozy meal at Cap, where all my friends adore you—my science-distribution-requirement ringer—even if you take all their money at poker."

"What shall we call him, our chewy mascot?"

She paused, hoagie in hand. "Jabberwocky . . ."

"Who?"

"'The jaws that bite, the claws that catch'—I'll put it on your reading list too, along with Whitman and *Moby Dick*. My brainiac who thinks he's going to survive the next mass extinction."

"Au contraire—how's my pronunciation? As soon as you ask why there is something instead of nothing, you have gone beyond science."

"I thought your science had the answers to everything. Even if, as Huxley complained, it removed the obscuring veil of mystery from so many things."

"My science! And you the obscurest Stoic—or is it a Jamesian thing, along with the veiled mystery of cancer and dementia . . . Huntington's."

"But not our Jabberwocky."

"Listen, even the physics jocks can't get past the singularity of the big bang. All their equations around relativity break down and become meaningless in the first instants of the universe, because that magnificent event transcends space-time, and so the reach of science. How's that: mysterious enough for you?"

She held up her Dixie cup of cheap Almaden to his.

"And dear Jacob, just for the record, I have no intention of growing old, even if Seneca considered birth and death the indispensable realities of a good life."

"My dear Isabel, my Jamesian heroine, that's the kind of imaginative optimism I love about you. That, of course, along with your wisdom, courage, and temperance—and that lovely goose-bumped rear end in Holder entryway. What's not to love?"

"Not my backhand?"

He put his arm around her shoulder and squeezed tight. "Yes, with my upgrades, Wimbledon will be a cinch."

Standing with her classmates, she now joined in singing to the marching band's scrappy version of "Old Nassau," fist over the heart, extending outward . . . something of that freezing February night of a mere forty-three years before still captivating her mind, tongue exploring her lips as if they might be chapped, almost sure she could taste the two or three or four vodka-and-pineapples they had downed, antifreeze and Dutch courage to run in the Nude Olympics. Their tiny band of sisters, who had pretended not to look at the men as they streaked the campus that night. The men, who pretended not to look at the women, with Bianca's magnificent breasts, thankfully, drawing most of the covert scrutiny.

She regained her seat just as a dreadful vision of what the Nude Olympics might look like, if run now, flickered darkly in her imagination.

She took a deep breath, almost giddy with relief to feel the return of June humidity caressing her body through her thin cotton dress, prompting a last look at that cozy stretch of pale blue beyond the leafy branches where lazy clouds chased one another. While at sign-in: raised voices, laughter, guffaws . . . could it really be—Jake's son? Refocusing her gaze once again on the sign-in table, she spied one of her teammates, Dr. Apolonia Baranski, waiting in line. Surely AP would provide the tip-off to confirm the identity of the now achingly familiar face, the badass kid handing out Reunions gear as he exchanged smart-alecky banter. Yes, short hair parted on the left . . . the same cleft right eyebrow?

"Like father, like son . . . ," she murmured to herself.

This improbable probability triggered a desperate need to reexamine her own face in the glass of her phone, a grimace and forced smile, that hadn't done at all badly compared to some of the horror stories now filling up the tent. Some loose rigging around the eyes and along her long chin, but nothing Botox couldn't fix if she ever got desperate—like now. Hadn't Candice, her favorite beautician, and Rafik, her longtime hairdresser, both assured she looked barely out of her forties? Hadn't she been effortlessly able to crank up her tennis sessions to three times a week at Sutton East—red clay, thank God—over the last two months to prepare for the charity match tomorrow? Okay, the right knee wasn't exactly happy, but Serena Williams complained of aching knees too, after a three-setter. Not that she'd ever let on to anybody about aches and pains, especially not her ageless roomies—such a Shirelles thing.

She glanced around and, slipping her hands under the orange tablecloth, eased off her wedding band and deep-sixed it in her beige leather Cuyana backpack.

"Loose fish . . ."

Ginistrella Wingate offered up a guileless smile to the gathering, determined to be in the moment (Erma's complaint about her mom's zero mindfulness), and watched as Apolonia—"girl god" to her secret lover and confederates—slowly edged closer to the end of the line at sign-in, eager to see her reaction to the young man who had definitely been attracting the curiosity of others. Becalmed classmates who stood for moments slightly spellbound, heads canted, nervously laughing, vigorously shaking the young man's hand as they moved on to the buffet luncheon. For a few moments more, she sat in expectant silence, only to whip out her phone and dash off a glowing text to her daughter, who'd been keeping strict radio silence. A perfect excuse to run by Erma's dorm and hand-deliver her graduation dress, where, presumably, she was sleeping off a hangover from senior festivities—God knows her mother had, stumbling through her own graduation half-stoned and reeling from her breakup with her boyfriend of three years, Jake Burrage. How the hell had she gotten through her salutatorian address . . . ?

Dr. Apolonia Baranski, bleary-eyed, still on Jackson Hole time (screaming baby on the Denver–Newark red-eye), had been cruising though the check-in line, preoccupied with an age-old heartache, when brought up short by the appearance of a young man handing out their Reunions gear. Could it be? She fumbled on her reading glasses and shook back her locks of somewhat unruly brown hair (a few notes of distinguished gray carefully deployed). She nibbled at her lower lip, a look of wonder and intense curiosity in her hazel-eyed squint as she sought to make a diagnosis. *Jacob ("Jocko") Burrage '16*, according to the name tag hanging off his left pectoralis major, looking for all the world like his old man minus the long hair, ratty jeans, slide rule, and jangling key fob attached to a belt loop. So Jake had managed to reproduce; who knew? Waiting as the classmate ahead of her in line gathered in his swag (baseball cap, sports shirt, and nifty water bottle emblazoned with their class logo of a tiger hanging from a star: *Stars and Stripes, Still Brilliant*), she found herself fast-forwarding through her long-stashed memories of this gorgeous kid's old man. Jake, ever on the make, curious as a cat, perched on the hillside overlooking the courts tracking Gini's tennis matches—he was the love of her life, even if their ever-resolute queen Agrippina would never admit it. She bent and picked up some windblown paper napkins skittering across the flagstones, seeing again Jake's pale blue eyes, reddened and sleepless, rising to meet hers from the smoky circle of a poker table.

And yes, to her eternal shame, he had been assigned to her by the chemistry department for tutoring chores, as she had failed organic chemistry not once, not twice, but three years in a row. To give the devil his due: he was as patient as Job. Without Jake's tutoring, encouragement, and moral support, she'd never have made it to med school. But how was it that Jake Burrage's son—couldn't need the money—was the student "manager" (in bold letters on his name tag) of their class-reunion site when his old man was a gazillionaire? Hadn't Dad just recently given a new science building? Not a week went by without Burrage Pharma reps breaking down her dispensary door with the latest drugs du jour to lower cholesterol and high blood pressure, to treat arthritis, kidney disease, even dementia and prostrate issues. Anything to keep the grim reaper at bay.

"Hello, Jacob, you must be Jake's son."

"Hey, Dr. Baranski . . ." He laughed, an expression of mock surprise and genuine pleasure as he stood to shake her hand. She noticed her name had already been checked off on his list of those who would receive Reunions gear. "I see you're still in the same size sports shirt as the day before yesterday."

"And what size exactly is that, Jacob?" she asked, trying to go with the flow (her bedside manner), even as his facetious tone grated.

"Same old scrub tops and lab coat."

"Oh, that . . . And how's your dad—my spaceman—doing, Jacob? Haven't seen him around these cloistered halls since we graduated."

"Same as ever. Nothing keeps him away from the lab." Young Jacob smiled easily as he rummaged for the right size in the boxes by his chair. "But you, AP, girl god, a Patriot missile through med school and now Jackson Hole doc to the rich and famous."

For an instant, she was quite flummoxed by his knowing overfamiliarity: her nickname, the friendly if flippant tone winging her back to a thousand barely remembered conversations. Hesitating briefly, her eyes swimming over his face: the gorgeous, lush eyebrows—the right with a sexy cleft corner just like his old man, and warm, long-lashed, off-blue eyes, the bulge of biceps at the sleeve of his swim-team tee shirt. She offered her most sympathetic smile (who knows how these social-media-obsessed kids think—her two, for instance) as somehow the scruffy template of remembrance made a match.

"Just call me Apollo 11."

"The moon and stars."

"Oh, do you think it's pretentious"—she tapped her name tag—"including the D-R before my name?"

"Hell no, everyone should be damn proud; I know my father is."

This perfectly acceptable reply caused her to tilt her head with relief, her bemused lips set in a judicious grin. "Not without the help of your dad, who got me close to the finishing line; I finally broke the tape at a summer session at Georgetown. I still have his congratulatory postcard somewhere."

"Organic chemistry," he proclaimed with a wicked eyeroll, then glancing toward the next in line as if slightly miffed at having to rush their chat, "not for the faint of heart."

She took his outstretched hand and offered a knowing crease of her brow. "Hey, thank Jake from me, and let him know I'm now a true believer in Burrage Pharma's latest cholesterol-lowering drug—or my patients are."

"Correptin?" he shot back with a taut grip of her hand, snapping up this data point with alacrity.

"That's the one."

"So, they're pleased—and no troubling side effects? Muscle pain, upset stomach, that sort of thing."

"Minimal, and I don't mention the side effects to avoid, you know, the 'nocebo' effect. You'd be amazed how many times when you mention a symptom to someone—next day: Geronimo."

His face lit up as he gave her the thumbs-up. "We have liftoff."

"See you later, Neil."

"Armstrong, Neil Armstrong." Two thumbs-up.

"Andromeda or bust."

"Hey, AP . . ."

She turned back to find his eyes still fixed on her with something akin to a fondly puzzled squint. "How did it all go: orgo, med school, doctoring—I mean, are you happy?"

How to respond to that crazy inappropriateness in five words or less? "Just fine, thank you—just what the doctor ordered."

Not a little touched, possibly unnerved by this quirky parting note, this disjointed collision of past and present (no one but her closet confederates knew her as AP or girl god), she quickly gathered up her Reunions gear and tried on her tan baseball cap, modeling it on her iPhone with a bit of a swagger, as was her wont, adjusting her orange paisley scarf to go with her black tennis dress and tiger-striped leggings. Hardly the attire of a GP running a moderately successful practice, but heck: even as she'd now spent most of her life hanging out with the wealthy and upwardly mobile, she prided herself on never trying to disguise her blue-collar, Manayunk, Pennsylvania, roots. Or, if pressed, that she could still beat most of her male patients on the court, while skiing rings around all but her two children.

Standing just behind the band's tall tuba player, nicely screened from the festive scene, she caught sight of her distorted reflection in the brass bell, her face stretched wide like a rubber band, while in the blue above, two leering gargoyles stared down from the rooftops. The tuba player, a gorgeous mixed-race woman (Chinese, Japanese, Indian, Javanese?) turned in place as the band prepared to exit. In fact, on closer inspection, the band members looked to be a mixed bag of the word's nationalities, so unlike in her day, when her pure Polish roots made her something of an exotic among Gini's WASP crowd. As the band clattered with a drumroll toward the exit, she took the opportunity to neatly deposit her handful of collected paper napkins and United Airlines seat stub in the side jacket pocket of the tuba player, a display of dexterity and sleight of hand—surgical precision, she liked to think—honed over years of slipping non-sugar lollipops into the pockets of her child patients.

Still vaguely disconcerted by her interaction with young Jacob, even as her mind drifted back to a more long-standing and immediate preoccupation, she looked for Gini across the luncheon scene in the familiar confines of Holder courtyard, where her orange-and-black-clad classmates were huddled around orange table settings with orange flower arrangements (never enough orange) or eagerly jostling at the buffet, which, she noted, was loaded with healthy salads—whole-wheat pasta no less. How unlike the wretched food of her day. Seeing Gini standing and talking to a classmate in a far corner of the tent, her smile quickly turned into a look of disbelief. A sundress? How unlike her elegant doubles partner, whom she hadn't seen for three years since Gini and Erma's last ski trip to Jackson Hole.

Checking her email for any important patient messages, she prepared to enter the fray when she was brought up short by the tolling of the chapel bell, instantly recalling her agonized trepidation of recent weeks, the dreaded moment fast approaching: the two o-clock memorial service for Princeton's recently deceased and greatly beloved fifteenth president, John Proctor. And there—could it be?—staring at her, hung in effigy between the Gothic arcades, along with the oversize heads of other Princeton luminaries—John Witherspoon, Woodrow Wilson (in years to come excised from institutional memory), Albert Einstein—was the caricatured face of John Proctor, uncannily capturing that same boyishly scrappy bang of hair over one eyebrow, that adorable dimple and slightly crooked beak of a nose, and those brilliant auburn eyes, forever glowing with the witty intelligence she had once so desperately wanted to make her own.

"Oh, John . . . ," she exclaimed, instantly aghast as if the hundreds of faces under the tent had now turned her way. How many knew or had suspected their long-running affair, that tightrope of scandal and disaster she'd walked in her undergraduate years and after? And by today's standards, it would be downright bizarre, if not unhinged. How had she been driven to such foolhardiness, much less survived the constant fear and risk of discovery? She breathed deeply, inwardly quailing as that creepy likeness amid familiar surroundings cascaded bittersweet memories. How she'd endangered not only her scholarship and John's career but also his family and the university they both loved. As the tolling bell drifted off, to be replaced by the murmur of hundreds of nostalgia-sparked conversations, she found the intimate, scholarly confines of Holder (those same quatrefoil arcades a reminder as well of their romantic week in Venice and the Scuola di San Giorgio) echoing her lover's voice as she'd once known it: bookish, intimate, fiercely discerning and eternally wise, and steeped in a fiery desire for reckless unbridled sex—anytime, anywhere, and everywhere—that had daily risked their immolation. That crazy thing, that still-crazy lingering flame, the crazy love of her life, now further stirred back into being by one Jacob Burrage's channeling his father's wicked intelligence (the only mind that had ever come close to matching John's). It was enough to freeze her blood as she fought back tears and the tremble in her jaw, replaced by her game-on face as she headed into the fray.

"You look like you've seen a ghost," said Gini, squeezing her arm.

"Oh, it's nothing. I'm just having apoplexy over John's memorial service."

"Oh dear," consoled Gini, admiring Apolonia's sporty Athleta tennis dress and tiger-striped, past-the-knee tights—and not a wobble of flesh on her nicely muscled arms. "Are you going to go?"

Apolonia speared some rigatoni, famished, eyeing her teammate a moment and cocking her head. "Golly Miss Molly—Gini, you're the spitting image of your mother at graduation in that country club floral from Brooks Brothers."

"God forbid!" Horrified, a turned-out palm to her brow. "I'm only doing it for Erma's sake—you know, a warmer and cuddlier mom." Gini gazed fondly on her onetime doubles partner, again admiring her casual comfortable outfit and her powerful calves and nifty Nike running shoes. "Trust you to be already togged out for the charity match tomorrow."

"It must be your hair—wonderful! I haven't seen you wear it down like that since it was one long pigtail hanging down the back of your white tennis dress as I was about to serve."

"Tell me something."

"Yes, it's Jake's son, isn't that just wild? Out of the blue. Who knew?"

"Really—you sure were chatting with him long enough. So, what's the story?"

"Yeah, it was a little odd, like the long-haired seventies version has been upgraded to the clean-cut, purposeful millennial version—2.0 on steroids. That spaceman had some kinda jacked body."

"Spaceman?"

"My nickname for when he tutored me in organic chemistry."

"Really . . ."

"The really weird thing was I had this . . . fantasy, I guess you'd call it, that it was Jake returned to earth after visiting Andromeda, and he'd remained the same, minus the long hair, while we had all aged."

Gini's brows knitted, holding up her phone to Apolonia with arrival texts from their two roommates, Bianca and Annette. "You've been reading too much science fiction."

"No, it's that movie my Christopher dragged me to, *Interstellar*: gravitational time dilation." Apolonia caught the note of apprehension in her roommate's face and reached out a comforting hand. "Very down to earth. Swim team, sleek facsimile of Michael Phelps. But surely Erma—how is my goddaughter, by the way?—must know him from poolside."

"She hasn't returned my texts for at least two weeks. I'm just assuming she knows about Reunions and that she's graduating in five days."

"Hey, tell me about it: graduation was such a blur. I only hear from my two when something's wrong or they need money, or their father needs a referral for rehab—and they're still living with me. But what the hell?"

Apolonia wolfed down more pasta and went on. "They're gainfully employed, licensed ski instructors, and now sous-chefing for their father most of the year. Tony, his highness with an unbroken track record of never having paid a cent of child support, even as the kids still sleep in *my* house. But hey, they're *my* kids."

"Erma had a thing for Christopher when she was in high school: *her* ski instructor."

"Damn, I should have invited him to come." Apolonia, carefully spearing her arugula and a tiny pearl of mozzarella, held up her fork. "He kinda freaked me out, young Jacob, his father's probing wit, non sequiturs—you know what I mean, always leaving you wrong-footed."

"You look incredible, by the way. I guess there's nothing like long winters on ice and plenty of sex. Whatever happened to that snowmobile manufacturer?"

"You mean, as I was just reminded, catering to Jackson Hole's rich and skinny, talking them out of dodgy plastic surgery and unlicensed yoga gurus (spine-breakers), fad diets and picking up the pieces after black runs, and dispensing medical marijuana like jelly beans."

"Ah, you were always the marketing genius among us," said Gini, remembering back fondly to when AP ran the student racquet-stringing agency, their suite bunkered with Adidas shoeboxes next to her stringing machine. "How's pot for ailing knees?"

"Let's not go there . . ."

"What's the matter?" Gini put a hand on Apolonia's shoulder, catching the tremor at the corner of her eyes. "John's memorial service, of course. Oh, AP, are you okay?"

"Being here—back on earth—that kid's weird knowingness . . ." Apolonia glanced at the sign-in table, where roommate number three was in line, and then again to the quatrefoil arcades hung with effigies of famous Princetonians, ready to be carried in tomorrow's P-rade. "I mean, to think John gave twenty years of his life to this place, and it all comes down to a papier-mâché face, a memorial service"—she gave a troubled if loving smile—"and his kids are sure to be there. And me, the ancient mariner."

"*Ehilà, Bianca, comme sta?*"

The familiar voice caused Bianca Macaluso, aka Big Mac, to freeze in place where she waited in the sign-in line. For a split second—crazy jane—she found herself back in Venice (she'd been staring at the quatrefoil Gothic arches of the quad) before recovering her senses and searching for the source of that oddly familiar voice. She lowered her sunglasses and peered over the top of the dayglow-orange frames, squinting, just able to make out a seated figure as a classmate in front of her moved off with her gear in hand.

"Holy mother of God," she gasped, crossing herself as she moved forward. "Jake, is that you?"

"Jacob. How are you, Big Mac?" He reached up a hand from where he sat before a pile of sports shirts and baseball caps.

Stowing her sunglasses in the neck of her spandex top, she took the outstretched hand in hers, confused, taken aback, leaning forward to read the name tag as she brushed back strands of strawberry-blonde hair dancing over her eyebrows.

"Jacob," she read. "Of course, you must be Jake's son. My error. I just had my eyes checked yesterday, dilated, and they're still not back in full working order." Putting on her reading glasses, she examined the front of his swim-team tee shirt emblazoned with a list of wins from an undefeated Ivy season below the moniker *Making Waves.*

"The one and only."

"Do I have to read your entire tee shirt to get my loot?"

"Only the first two lines." His sparkling eyes flashed with mirth as he seemed to hesitate a moment, looking up from where his finger had found her name on his clipboard, possibly admiring her muscled arms and long neck as if double-checking for the right measurements, then handing her a cellophane-wrapped sports shirt and cap.

"How is your old man, by the way?" She tried on the cap, fumbling to adjust the Velcro strap at the back to accommodate her wide brow. "Whom I haven't laid eyes on since"—she caught herself and then threw caution to the wind—"he washed up on my doorstep in Venice in, what, fall of '79? I was doing graduate studies. And he was just finishing up his PhD at Stanford."

"The Scuola Antiqua, wasn't it? You provided front-row seats for concerts at the Scuola di San Giorgio and the Scuola Grande di San Rocco."

She cocked her head in a mock double take. "He mentioned all that?" she exclaimed. This a guilty secret she'd never breathed a word of to anyone, lest it get back to Gini.

"Venice was a kind of secret language around our house when I was growing up on Sheridan Place. Prints of palazzos lined the staircase, Italian cuisine for many dinners, a Carpaccio reproduction of Saint Augustine over my parents' bed, in honor of their honeymoon."

"No way," she huffed between an abiding melancholy and faint incredulity.

"Hey, at sixteen, after my parents' divorce, I was sent off to Venice for two weeks, all expenses paid. Get me out of the pool, as my father put it, and instead of chlorine, soak up a little art and culture."

"*Dio mio*, that sounds just like him. How's our most brilliant one doing?"

"Your guess is as good as mine." He handed her a water bottle, now with a distant stare, as if she might have simply evaporated right before his eyes. "Busy, eternally busy."

"But there's your graduation?"

"Yes, so I have it on good authority."

"And Reunions?"

"Why would he sully a perfect record?"

"Good point . . ." She held up her water bottle in an admiring gaze, singing out: "'Catch a falling star and put it . . .' Well, there's always hope, always the forty-fifth and fiftieth reunion to come."

"Why not the hundredth?"

"Hey, let's go for it. Tell your old man congrats on producing such a fine specimen of boy wonder, and Bianca sends a big kiss. Ciao, Jacob."

Quite disarmed, if not disconcerted, Bianca slunk back into the shadowy arcades of Holder courtyard as if still needing to gird her loins for an onstage appearance. And speaking of loins, she felt a sharp pain in her solar plexus, quite unlike anything in recent post-menopausal memory, a pain that now seemed to slither upward, pressing on her chest, gripping her fast-beating heart, then echoing in her ears with an odd ringing sensation that, even more oddly, transposed itself into a tenor voice, that of Orfeo from Monteverdi's *Orfeo*—"*Tu se' morta, mia vita, ed io respiro?*" Was some kid practicing in the arch, an open window? She found herself mouthing the words, as she had all those years before accompanying the singer in concert at the Scuola di San Giorgio (yes, with Jake Burrage in the first row), hearing the voice in all its soaring rapture, calling her upward, calling her out of herself . . . summoning her soul's recantation. So enraptured, her eyes straying skyward as she moved out into sunlight, she caught sight of a gargoyle projecting from the roofline, two sinuous dolphins leaping astride a wave or possibly a ship's prow. The sculptures returned her for a moment to a stonemason's workshop in her working-class neighborhood of Venice during her three years studying seventeenth-century music performance. And a curious Jake Burrage, seemingly stranded on the threshold like a pillar of salt, inveigled by the stonemason's art.

"Get a grip, Macaluso," she scolded herself, annoyed at letting that somewhat sardonic (so she decided) young man throw her for a loop. She redeployed her strappy shoulders, took three deep, cleansing breaths as she swept locks of her once-brown hair, bleached and toned to a strawberry blonde, under her new cap, and waltzed out into the sunlit tent, weaving her way past packed tables, stopping here and there for quick hugs and comic repartee (her student specialty) and easy, off-color banter, and so avoiding the painful subject of her shamefully much-reduced post-divorce life: her ongoing gig as an Upper West Side dog-walker, personal trainer for aging hippies, and piano teacher to some of the snottiest untalented kids in all God's creation, just enough to keep paying the rent on her Ninety-Third Street efficiency. Finally, breaking away with self-deprecating asides from still-worshipful fans of Shirelles days, she made her way to her roommates' table. She was almost as tall as Gini, and her large, broadly featured face and Roman nose lifted with pleasure to be back once again with the ever-faithful, her sister Shirelles. Her olive-brown, heavily made-up eyes beamed, her long lips sporting tangerine-hued lipstick twisted into a sardonic smile as she and Gini and Apolonia came together in a three-way hug.

"Get a load of those biceps," admired Apolonia with a squeeze, pulling back from their lingering embrace. "What are you lifting these days, you animal?"

"Well," she scissored her prominent jaw, eyeing Apolonia's nifty outfit, "let's just say I can't match my best bench press of 198."

"When did you do that?" asked Apolonia, genuinely impressed.

"Back in my early thirties, in my monster days. Clearly why my husband eventually up and left—when I first wore out his johnson and then my welcome." Bianca grinned wickedly. "How do you like the hair?"

"Delicious." Apolonia smacked her lips.

"What man in his right mind," said Gini, fluttering her eyes, "would give up on a woman with those dark and sultry Modigliani features?"

"Oh, my ex attributed all my deficiencies to my peasant stock—as if that schmata-faced, ex-orthodox Polish Jew should talk. Besides, I get all my best traits from my Sicilian—God rest her soul—grandmother: the Jewish nose (he married me for), the Arab eyes, the Norman chin, and possibly the Byzantine smarts geared to deception (so the fucked-up men in my life complain), along with my foul mouth and viper's tongue, which only real men can appreciate."

"Hey," said Apolonia, "it sure didn't keep all those lost boys from lining up outside our entryway door for four years: sexual healing, if I remember."

Bianca sighed, glancing at her plate of buffet foragings. "Ah, weren't those our salad days, ladies—all the good breeding studs to be had. Not that I'd trade them in, considering how I managed to produce my darling son and heir, Matteo, who just happens to be playing a gig here tonight with his trio, opening for the Grease Band. A little jazz à la Coltrane for the sophisticates in the crowd. Did you get my email? The Shirelles are on for Saturday night after dinner."

"Not the Shirelles," said a more than a little flustered Gini. "I haven't sung in years, and there's no time to practice."

Bianca laughed this off while showing off their signature arm movements, pumping left and right and left again. "It'll all come back to you ladies in a flash; it always does. The best days of our lives, you never forget."

"Like Jake Burrage," said Apolonia, with a glance at Gini. "We saw you chatting up the kid. Isn't he adorably shorn and sculpted?"

"Ah, you too, so it isn't just my poor old eyes deceiving me."

"What were you gabbing about?" asked Gini.

"Oh, nothing," she lied. "I was wondering why his old man refused to show up for Reunions. Maybe he's just too filthy rich for his old crowd."

"And . . ."

"Busy. Like father, like son, huh? Never leaves the lab."

"Did you get a peek at that body?" said Apolonia, her gaze drifting back to the sign-in table.

"Adonis in tiger stripes. Hey, Gini, doesn't Erma know him? She's on the swim team."

"Diving team."

"He seemed a little dismissive of his old man, but then, what kid isn't?"

Apolonia added, "Did you notice he has Jake's slightly angelic but nefarious smile? You remember what he was like—like he knew something you ought to know but wasn't letting on."

"Pot calling the kettle black," exclaimed Bianca, tapping an accusing finger on Apolonia's name tag. "Talk about scandalous misbehavior."

"Yeah, well, we got away with it. Which is more than I can say for some people around here," and she poked a finger in Gini's shoulder. "Young Jacob is lying about something."

"Don't look at me—why?" asked Gini.

"Doctor's intuition. Young guys will always lie about their alcohol consumption, their drug abuse, or how many sexual partners they've had."

"Well," sighed Gini, glancing toward sign-in, "that's hardly something *we* need to concern ourselves with."

"Worst luck," added Bianca. "Celibacy refuses to grow on me."

"Hey, look," exclaimed Apolonia, "there's Annette and Matt at sign-in, talking to the scion of Burrage Pharma. Like long-lost buddies."

"Didn't Jake work for Matt on tour one of those summers after graduation, tracking his matches?" asked Bianca.

"Since when?" Gini shot back.

The day had not started off well for Annette. There had been an early-morning brouhaha about a recent sermon from their new female minister, though feminism was the least of the issues. Then a disconcerting call from her son, Arthur, expressing "deep reservations" about speaking at an alumni Reunions panel of the Princeton chapter of

Athletes for Christ, of which she was a founding member and on the board. Goodness knows what was going on in Arthur's Goldman Sachs life. And in the rush to the Jacksonville airport, she'd failed to download her daily Gospel lesson with commentary. Waiting in the sign-in line with her husband, Matt, she'd accessed that lesson on her phone: "These things I have spoken unto you, that in me ye might have peace. In the world ye shall have tribulation: but be of good cheer; I have overcome the world." No sooner had she raised her eyes from this comforting text than the classmate in front of her had moved off and she'd found herself face-to-face with a young Jacob Burrage, who didn't hesitate a moment to welcome her and Matt like fast friends.

"Annette—so how am I doing today?"

It was an expression his father had used each morning on tour. For a moment, she was rendered speechless, doing a mental double take, until she spotted his Reunions badge with his name and class and, printed in capital letters, *manager*. With an uneasy laugh, she'd reached to his extended hand and felt his firm fingers carefully enclose hers as he stood, lingering a moment before shaking Matt's as well. For a minute or two, while wife and husband got their gear, they had engaged in a delightful, if slightly awkwardly SO familiar conversation, the aftereffects of which now glowed behind her eyes, filled with joyous memories of that one glorious summer, from Roland-Garros to the US Open, when Matt had rounded back into winning form, when Jake Burrage had saved their marriage. When she had hung on Jake's every word, every intonation, every flickering expression that flashed out from the molten blue of his ever-amused eyes.

"I can't believe you kept that from me all these years," complained Gini with a swig of her white wine, trying to tone down the hint of bitter reproach in her voice.

"Oh, darlin'," crooned Annette (sporting a faux-Southern intonation that now grated on Gini) as she patted her husband's hand. "We weren't trying to keep anything from you, dear—right, Matt?" She returned to devouring her lunch, her plate piled high with chicken salad and arugula, bunkered with three bananas, and a dessert plate crammed with cupcakes slathered in orange icing.

"It was kind of a secret at the time," said Matt, raising his long, tawny, sun-beaten face, his kindly silver-blue eyes brushing Gini's. "Jake was my ace in the hole—not that the sports press didn't pick up on it pretty quick when my ranking began to skyrocket after my quarterfinals win at Roland-Garros. He was so ahead of his time, the things—shot selection, placement, winners, percentages, stats, data points—that IBM or whatever now churns out on broadcasts of the US Open."

Annette added with a perky nod: "Jake was AI before AI. He used to talk about going to Cubs games at Wrigley Field with his dad, who taught him to keep THEIR scorecard. That's where he got the idea of doing the same, tracking tennis. Not that I'm telling you anything you don't already know, Gini dear."

Gini turned to Annette with eyes in a laser-beam focus (all news to her), her co-captain on Princeton's winningest women's tennis team, onetime rival (the one woman she couldn't beat, at least not twice in a row to claim the number-one spot), and still the same petite, gritty blonde who now lay her head affectionately against her famous husband's shoulder.

Gini stared off a moment, catching sight of Gareth, her freshman-year boyfriend. "Come on. You didn't think I could handle it."

"Hey, darlin'—you, who were unwilling to share Jake and his match tracking in our heyday."

Matt added between mouthfuls: "Jake used to say that Ernie Banks's five hundredth home run was the biggest thing in his childhood."

Gini shook her head. "You know he only had the bandwidth to work with one player at a time."

"There you go-o," sang out Annette, her point made. "And it all came about through the power of prayer," she added a little dreamily, with another glance at her phone, where she'd been reading further commentary on her daily Gospel lesson. "Right, dear, overcoming tribulations—that and visiting the Carpaccios."

Matt patted his wife's hand. "Our faithful Borzoi."

"Carpaccios?" queried Gini, as if yet another proprietary redline had been breached.

"I mean, part of the problem," Matt went on between a mouthful of his pasta salad, "was that Jake just couldn't keep his mouth shut, especially to certain players, who shall remain nameless, on the women's tour."

"Oh, my Lord," said Annette, naming names. "Chrissie Evert was so-o fawning over him."

"The thing is: I was just so impressed with the way he raised your game, Gini,"

Matt went on in a consoling mode, holding up his wineglass in tribute. "Remember, I was on hand when you helped land that fourth of four Ivy crowns with that win over Harvard's number two—a freshman ranked twenty-one in the country. Your improved shot selection, the way you mixed up your serves, and your winning percentages. What's not to like?"

"*Sports Illustrated* did a piece on Matt and Jake's tracking system. We can hardly be accused of keeping it from you," said Annette.

"Why, for the life of me, would I have not wanted to know?" pouted Gini. "I was his guinea pig, his lab rat for developing his damn tracking system, honing it—me, body and soul—over three grueling years."

"Soul . . . well," mused Annette.

Gini sighed, poking at her plate of wilted arugula, as she struggled to regain her composure around the luncheon table, as the conversation sped on without her, as her mind reeled like a whirligig down a rabbit hole of once-discarded memories. She tried to resist stealing panicked glances toward the sign-in table, where Jake Burrage's son now presided as a shaft of sunlight crept his way, ushering in more late arrivals while getting them kitted out in baseball caps and whatnot. Momentarily, the presence of Jake's son had distracted her from coming to terms with her somewhat fraught mother-daughter relationship of recent years. As if (ridiculous, of course) his presence in her daughter's class—on the swim team, for heaven's sake—had been just another bit of information withheld by her distant, diffident Erma, along with a boatload of unspoken, unspecified blame for her husband's death eight years before. A laundry list to go along with a detailed chronology of soul errors (her father's Stoic expression) that had lingered in Erma's accusing stare. Perhaps if only they'd managed a brother or sister for Erma, to counter the loneliness of an only child. God knows, she and Bill had talked enough about a second, a son, perhaps.

"Oh, for heaven's sake . . . ," she muttered under her breath, trying to keep tabs on the table conversation, where the greatest hits of their four Ivy League titles were being rehearsed. Yes, that Harvard freshman had gone on to a world ranking as high as twenty-six and reached the quarterfinals of Wimbledon. She glanced again toward the sign-in table. How could she have just walked away? Walked away from the man who'd revolutionized her game, who'd sparked the best, most alive years of her life. Years when she'd felt so overcaffeinated, so intoxicated with love and ideas, that every blessed morning was a revelation, that saw her flying out of bed (his bed, her bed) to make the most of the day's few remaining hours. Days that had found her ranked thirty-eighth nationally when she graduated summa cum laude, days sped on by her lover's Hermes-winged heels (erection nodding in the breeze), a life (Wimbledon, her discarded novel) that might have been, the better person she might have been: better mother, wife, and lover.

She turned over these phantom regrets in the reflected light and laughter of her teammates' eyes, now joined by faithful Gareth (as well as her first-year boyfriend, he had been Jake's best friend), hoping to be disabused of such wobbly notions as an alternate life, which had somehow been spurred into existence by that frisson of doubt, weighted by the shapeless, free-floating anxiety that Erma's if not exactly hatred, then lack of respect, had lain on her shoulders.

She saw again her daughter's tearful face turning to her in the halogen-lit corridor of Memorial Sloan Kettering. "Mom, all you really ever cared about was what was in your authors' books."

Proof of innocence, as if she needed as much, was to be found in the fondly animated faces around their table, or even in the many respectful glances in her direction (classmates still in awe of her on-court prowess, many more who would corner her in the publishing forum tomorrow) crowded under the sailcloth-filtered sunshine, in the hum of twice-told tales embedded in a lifetime of friendships, of couples grown old together who had had a lot more to work with than she and William Cheshire. She, for one, had always prided herself on her loyalty—courage, spurred by curiosity, that would have her face up to the unknown and unknowable. Precisely the virtues Jake had always espoused, which, truth be told, she and Bill had somehow passed on to Erma, her brilliant science kid.

She smiled at her neat summation to the jury, as if repurposing the upbeat table conversation might re-ballast her ship even as she bailed with excuses: We soldier on, we do our best, and hopefully life expunges our defeats from the record. After all, Jake had never really complained about her Stoic principles . . . okay, around the edges, after she got him reading Lucretius, after she finally shamed him into reading Whitman and Melville.

"You live your life more out of your books than life," he had once complained, staring her down across a table in their favorite corner of the physics library. "I'm stuck with long days in the lab, student jobs, tracking your matches. Some of us just don't have the time."

A series of soft clinks from a nearby table (plates being gathered up?) had shunted these memories to another obscure siding, where an expanse of green felt sped the passage of pool balls to find their pockets. And there, squint-eyed above his cue stick, was Jake's rapt face as he patiently explained Lucretius's atomism shot by shot, pocket after pocket—the poet who refused any concern for death or dying.

"You see, just the slightest swerve, a fraction here or there, and the atoms are off in another direction—another lifetime, if you will—and so Lucretius's sublime indifference that renders us immune from pointless anxieties. Once you likewise learn to control a tennis ball, you'll be in control of your opponents and then your fate. Leaving us free to evolve as needs be. Your Whitman, correct? 'The smallest sprout shows there is really no death.'"

Yes, she'd finally got him reading Whitman, a beautiful Modern Library edition for his birthday. But his smart-alecky banter had always pissed her off: appropriating her poetic license to bolster his insane claims. And when exactly had that conversation occurred? Sophomore year, junior, senior? How annoying not to be able to pin down anything anymore, the thing she never ceased demanding of her proofreaders and fact checkers.

"There is no such thing as past, present, or future according to Einstein—just our subjective experience as opposed to the eternal now. The rapture of now . . ."

As she struggled for a rejoinder, a counterargument, she could almost feel his arm tighten around her shoulder, steering her through Prospect Garden, scene of so many scuffles with his insufferable cockiness, if not his "perennially blooming" cock, where her mind had once unleashed itself like a fast-running stream—yes, yes . . . yes, as her mainsail filled with the scent of those majestic firs and California lilacs, the yellow roses that somehow fascinated him in the first flush of night, that soft, satiny moonlit yellow: "This is thy hour O soul, thy free flight into the wordless, away from books, away from art, the day erased, the lesson done."

"You say something?" asked Apolonia.

Bianca wagging an accusing finger, "Doubtless—yes, admit it, oh queenly one—a bookish sneer at our plot to go slumming at the singles mixer tonight. Not that Gini would demean herself to put in some face time at such a gathering of two-time losers."

Gini smiled serenely, stretching out a hand to the floral centerpiece of orange geraniums, bending over to breathe in their scent. "Hard to believe these are for real."

"Is that a blush of lust on your face?" Apolonia asked. "Remember—my first-ever operation—when I had to extract those thorns from your bare ass?"

"You, court queeny, can hardly complain," pursued Bianca, with one of her obscene Italian hand gestures. "You who made Prospect Garden infamous in our day—mulch sex."

But Gini's mind was already elsewhere, foraging backward, trying to remember—how could she not remember?—when they'd first met. In some ways, she felt like she'd always known Jake . . .

The rattle of cutlery on the tray of a server summoned forth yet another untethered image, barely freed from a more general impression. "Keys . . . ," she whispered to herself. That huge fob of keys hanging from the belt loop of his perpetually lab-stained jeans, jingling keys that seemed to unlock forbidden doors all over campus, acquired or purloined while Jake, that brilliant scholarship kid from Evanston, was doing campus jobs, sporting his long, disheveled (rarely washed) hair that streamed back from his broad shoulders as he ran—jogging everywhere, a science nerd so unlike her crowd of classics-English-art history majors, friends of the art museum, that tony band of New England aesthetes and intellectuals who suffered mightily, complained endlessly at the imposition of a science distribution requirement. Perhaps the last generation that really took the humanities seriously: learning for learning's sake, how to live a well-lived life.

She closed her eyes, intent on her quarry, until she'd run the specific moment to earth, that familiar bark of a voice breaking free of the conversational hum.

"It's simple, if you'll just let me demonstrate. It's all in the numbers: probability theory."

She could almost smell the clay of the Har-Tru court, the scent of sweat and crushed leaves by the fence where she always hung her towel, as she picked apart her diligent but predictable Harvard opponent from Braintree, whom she had already beaten half a dozen times in the juniors . . . and there, perched on the hillside overlooking the courts, a figure with notebook balanced on one knee: intent, unswerving, meticulously entering data, translating her every breathing moment into numbers.

"You see," Jake continued, pointing with his chewed pencil to the lines of figures on the graph paper, "here are your placements, winners, unforced errors, all of which can be broken down into percentages, which tell you what needs improving."

Nothing about congratulations—great match, how she'd destroyed that pesky little bitch in crimson.

"I promise you—it's a cinch, how you can do even better."

Probably the sexiest opening gambit she'd ever heard from a man.

She turned her gaze back to the table, only to catch the pensive stare of Annette's husband, Matt, that prince of a guy who somehow combined a demonic competitive drive with a gentle nature—a Christian thing? Matt gave her a knowing look from his sun-battered face, the man who'd stared down the tantrums of Alex Metreveli in a thrilling, five-set Wimbledon finals win, still sporting that crisp boyish smile, signed up by his wife to umpire their charity match tomorrow morning.

"Do even better," she mouthed, and winked at Matt. How those few, pitch-perfect words summed up Jake, perhaps their whole stupid affair: one-upmanship on steroids. For a moment, she closed her eyes, as if better to see that eternal optimist dashing off to yet another student job, a hustler exploring all the angles, seeker after the undiscovered, the unseen, leaning into all the incredible scientific advances of the seventies that would culminate in the genetic engineering and biotech revolution—all those promised cures for cancer (none of which had saved poor Bill Cheshire), heart disease, and every plague or infirmity known to man.

As if needing to cover her tracks, she found herself drawn back into the table conversation by echoing one of Jake's favorite lines: "There are tortoises and bowhead whales that live into their hundreds. Eliminate disease, rejuvenate and replace aging cells, and we're home free."

"What was that?" asked Apolonia.

"Oh, just one of my authors on the prospects of aging gracefully."

"I thought we were talking about wives," said Bianca. "A thousand days . . ."

"A thousand?" said Gini.

"Yes, *your* thousand days," accused Bianca with a frothy, knowing wiggle of her strawberry-blonde head. Quickly going on, covering her tracks before Gini could respond: "Or was it Ann Seymour, days of wine and roses (not the Jack Lemmon and Lee Remick version), before Henry hacked off her head? Except AP and I will be on the chopping block tonight in the boneyard of a fifty-and-over dating scene. A shooting gallery"—she tapped her class name tag, hanging on her ample bosom, with an orange-nailed finger—"what with our sell-by date front and center."

"It's Anne Boleyn, Henry's second wife," Gini corrected. "Jane Seymour was his third."

"Wasn't there a movie?" asked Annette, devouring everything on her plate. "*Anne of the Thousand Days*, with a gorgeous Richard Burton."

"You don't look a day over thirty-five," assured Gareth, putting an arm around Bianca's shoulder.

"Just the compliment I've been looking for. It's all one can do to keep up with Gini, not that Agrippina would ever stoop to such self-abasement, not with your faithful Gareth to keep you out of trouble." She reached across the table to grab one of Annette's orange cupcakes. "Even you," she sang out, "can't eat all those cupcakes."

Gareth, his graying hair neatly cut short on a balding head, laughed and patted Gini's hand. "Forever young, forever true . . ."

"I stopped counting at forty-five," offered Apolonia. "I still think I'm the best-preserved whippersnapper at any social gathering, and I can beat women half my age on the court and ski rings around their husbands. And the good news"—she flicked at strands of her just-graying hair—"patients like their doctors to show the wisdom of the ages."

"Droopy tits, that's the deal-breaker," said Bianca. "Trust me on this. Why the best-looking guys always gravitate to the jailbait, even if she's as dumb as a dildo—was that Darwin or Doolittle? Like my geriatric ex, Hannibal Lecter, who traded me in for a shiksa straight out of Stuyvesant."

Gini drifting off . . . remembered the movement of Jake's hand over her breast, the stirring of his long hair across her face, blotting the fir boughs against the stars. "Don't you see, there is a grandeur in this view of life, Gini. A grandeur . . . almost as exciting as sex with you."

Whenever she played badly, whenever she was down before her period, or after a spat—"just think of it, the grandeur." And he'd hand her a bouquet of yellow roses pilfered from Prospect Garden.

"Hey, Agrippina, court queen," said Bianca with a wave, wolfing down her cupcake, "just get over it, girl. Go on, introduce yourself to that gorgeous young hunk and get it over with. And while you're at it," she muttered, licking orange icing off her fingers, "see if you can get out of him why his pappy is such a no-show."

Gareth laughed. "I already drilled the poor kid on that score. I mean, what a streamlined, turbocharged, Microsoft-whatever version of Jake." Gareth held up his phone. "Captain of the swim team, two Ivy league records in the 100- and 200-meter freestyle, with an invite to the Olympic trials for Rio."

"No way, José," exclaimed Bianca. "Why are we bothering with the over-the-hill gang tonight with kids like that around our tepee?"

"Ever the cradle snatcher," groaned Apolonia.

"Hey, sister—look who's talking, our very own X-rated snatchee who almost lured our El Presidente to his doom in her misbegotten youth? You can hardly complain about us seventies babes keeping our hand in with the young fry, unstirred and with an olive—keep the tubes limber and the orgasms flowing."

"Now you're embarrassing Annette and Matt," scolded Apolonia. "Not that Gareth hasn't endured all your free-association crap before. And let us ladies at least be left to bask with dignity in our post-menopausal bliss."

Gareth grinned. "Here's the thing: young Jacob truly is a dead ringer for Jake, at least the last time I saw Jake—oh, I guess about twenty years ago now, give or take; groomed, fit as a fiddle, ageless, dressed in a suit and tie when he showed up to pitch our firm, looking to raise capital in the early years of the biotech boom."

"You never told me that," said Gini.

"My father's firm back then. We still have stock in Burrage Pharmaceuticals & Health, like buying Apple at 100. You guys know, right? He gave the new biochemistry lab by the stadium; it's stunning, palatial, cutting-edge, the most beautiful building I've ever seen."

"Well, there you go, Gini," scolded Bianca. "You could've been married to a biochemistry lab. Just like I thought I was marrying the king of Upper West Side real estate until Lehman went under."

"But you did," Apolonia corrected. "You and Anne of the thousand days just didn't count on a real estate bubble and the headsman."

"Matt and I," said Annette, "couldn't believe our eyes when we first saw Jacob; took us right back to that fabulous summer of 1980."

"I," Bianca raised her hand, singing out, "was such a star on every concert stage in Venice that summer."

"I was lucky," said Matt. "We caught him just between finishing up at Stanford and his postdoc at Chicago."

"Now don't go on pouting," said Bianca, making a face at Gini. "We all told you; you should've gone on the tour after graduation, especially after winning the NCAAs."

"Shoulda, woulda, coulda—I had a living to make."

Annette reached a consoling hand to Gini. "You were probably smart; take it from a veteran of twelve years on tour with Matt—right, dear? Not for the faint of heart. And Arthur, who's here for his fifth reunion, turned down the pros for Goldman Sachs. So there you have it: Art couldn't be happier."

"And I, in all my fading glory, get to umpire on number-one court tomorrow," said Matt, reaching out a huge, still-callused right hand to pat his wife's as he eyed her cache of orange cupcakes.

"Hardly." Annette's face lit up: proud wife. "Adidas just signed him to another lifetime sponsorship deal."

"Hey, I'm a shoe—an old shoe. Who woulda thought it?"

"The most popular name-brand sports shoe in the world."

Gini, turning an earnest look to the happy couple: "How well did it work for you, Matt—Jake's data points, tracking, turning your sweat into wine?"

"The game was changing so fast that I figured there was nothing to lose: it was Jake or retirement. What really helped, actually, was tracking my opponents' matches to find default patterns, weaknesses."

"Ranked below one hundred in the world, he skyrocketed back to the top ten. If it hadn't been for Björn Borg . . ." Annette shrugged.

"Who had no weaknesses," her husband concurred.

"Well," piped up Apolonia, "talk about name brands, I can tell you Jake's sales reps are relentless, forever knocking on my door about the next elixir of youth."

"Our eternal Borg," sighed Bianca. "Am I the only one who dreams about Federer's backhand—Oh, Roger—"

"Stop leering at the waiters, Big Mac," said Apolonia. "Young sluts are bad enough."

"I did my Borg upgrade almost twenty years ago," said Gini.

"Hey," Bianca laughed, "too bad you didn't upgrade your stock portfolio with Burrage Pharma shares at the same time. Looks like we all should've."

Gareth, now sporting a gray mustache to go with his graying hair and large, silver-framed glasses (his mother was a fifth-generation, Philadelphia-born and -bred African American), had been scrolling on his phone when not flashing glances Gini's way, as if in hopes of deciphering the distracted look in her slightly bloodshot eyes. "That's my BPH—Burrage Pharma & Health—stock talking." He laughed and handed his phone around with the latest quote on BPH shares.

"Do you suppose Jake's unrequited love for Gini has kept him away all these years?" asked Apolonia with a straight face, as if to repress any hint of a facetious tone.

"Give me a break," said Gini, waving off the remark.

"Hey," corrected Gareth, "nobody and nothing scared that boy, who kept me in penury at the poker table. I never knew anyone who made losing money seem if not inevitable, at least a worthy cause."

"You," Bianca crowed, "of all people, Ginistrella Wingate, should've kept tabs on that bad boy Croesus. I'll never forget our senior dance: how you danced the night away with Jake, tears streaming down your face. Tears of happiness, so we all thought—right, girls? We were all crying with you, for you. What fools, believing you'd cashed the check on the best years of our lives. For a few wonderful hours, we thought we were witnessing the most poignant display of romantic sensibility ever. Our own Agrippina, no less. And then you had to go spoil it all—gone girl. Jake too, like all those years together had amounted to nada, squat."

"Sorry I disappointed everybody." She drained her wineglass. "Believe me, it was not . . . not"—she waved a flattened palm by her cheek—"the way I planned it. Nor my falling-down-drunk mother at our senior dinner-dance, either."

"Your dad was a prince of a guy at our graduation dinner," said Apolonia, trying not to glance at the effigy of John Proctor where it hung, sunlit, against the shadowed walkway of the arcade. "My parents were kept in stitches, and then when they got onto the subject of a possible Phillies-Yankees World Series matchup—a love fest."

Bianca pointed to her wrist: "My dad loved that art deco Rolex your dear father wore, even if he was a Mets fan. Not that he ever got over the Dodgers abandoning Brooklyn."

"While I was tasked to deal with my mother spitting nails at the far end of the table."

Bianca nodded brightly. "Seriously, we all thought it was going to be wedding bells, to go along with Annette and Matt's."

Gini surveyed the table as if quite gutted by the subject of their graduation dinner-dance, the raw details long banished to fathomless obscurity. She waved blithely. "We went to see *The Way We Were* out on Route 1 the night before the senior dance. As the kids say: *Totally*, it was *so-o* our story." She looked to the faces turned to hers and shrugged unconvincingly. "Irreconcilable differences."

"But Streisand was an idiot to give up on Redford," offered Apolonia.

"I don't get it," said Annette. "Which one are you? I mean, Redford just had that something, that effortless aplomb."

"Hell," countered Bianca, making one of her goofy faces, "he sold out his talents, while Streisand stuck to her guns—encouraging him to be all he could be." She reached out for a high five from her roommate. "I'm with Gini on this—the not-selling-out part."

"Hubbell, Hubbell . . . ," sighed Gini, "toil and trouble—and my mother: a cyclonic disaster zone."

"The Jake I knew never gave up on anything—ever." Gareth indicated his phone once more, declaiming. "BPH, dedicated to the 'transhuman future,' in which humans may prolong life, delay or limit aging and cognitive dysfunction, banish"—he raised a finger—"banish, it says right here, cancer and heart disease through bioengineering and gene therapies."

"Hah," Apolonia spouted, "sounds just like spaceman Jake, who tutored me in organic chemistry: forever reinventing a future that only he could see. Scary then, maybe not so scary now."

Gareth again raised a finger as he read: "Nanorobots repairing cells . . . immortalists."

"Is that a word?" asked Gini.

"Hallelujah: He is risen," cried Bianca, raising her arms in supplication.

"Come now . . . ," scolded Annette.

"Snake oil," said Apolonia. "Just talk to my cancer patients."

"Hey, don't knock immortality unless you've tried it," said Bianca.

"Hey," echoed Gareth, "he's got Bezos and Elon Musk invested."

"Dick pics and all—huh." A lascivious smile from Bianca. "Tiger, tiger, cis, boom, bah—who has the fairest cock of all."

"What?" asked Annette.

"Don't ask," Matt said.

"We just grew apart, that's all," murmured Gini with an unconvincing wave of her hand.

"Fuck him," Bianca exclaimed. "Big swinging dick didn't deserve you. You could hardly have done better than producing my fabulous goddaughter, Erma—you and the sadly departed Bill."

"There you go," added Annette, "all part of God's plan. The proof is always in our children."

"Not that my two even applied," sighed Apolonia.

"They're brilliant—wonderful," Gini was quick to note. She'd taken Erma on many ski trips to Jackson Hole, where Apolonia's eldest, Christopher, had taught Erma to ski.

"Hey," suggested Bianca, "you don't suppose young Jacob's got webbed toes, like Kevin Costner in *Waterworld*?"

"Oh my God," Apolonia groaned, "what a terrible movie."

"I'll take Kevin wet or dry or with a lemon peel." Bianca chortled and casually passed her Red Roof Inn key card across the table toward Gareth. "I remember snogging you a few times when you'd finally given up on the grand Ginistrella Wingate. And you weren't a bad kisser, either. Well, I'm back in the gene pool, and the water's fine. And you'd get to be stepfather to my darling Matteo—Columbia class of '11, with a summa in neuroscience—who, if I didn't already mention it, is playing with his jazz trio tonight at dinner."

"Same year as Arthur," noted Annette, wolfing down her third cupcake.

At this, Gareth stood and bowed to the ladies, tapping the proffered key card while throwing a kiss. "We have a date tonight; bring your dancing shoes. I'm off to catch up with my graduating daughter at lacrosse practice; they play the NCAAs next week."

"Jeest," scolded Apolonia as Gareth moved off, "do you have no shame? He's a widower—what, four years now?"

"Hell," replied Bianca, nodding at Gini, "she's a widow too, and he's been putting the moves on her all lunch with his soulful Harry Belafonte eyes. Besides, I'm dying to know if he used the race card to get his daughter in."

"Ladies, ladies," said Annette in her cool, calming alto voice, which she'd once deployed to great effect as captain of the women's tennis team. "I'd like to propose a toast in remembrance of Gini's husband, Bill, whom I miss terribly, who graced these gatherings for many years: a wonderful man, a loving husband, the most perfect father."

They raised their wineglasses, and Gini thanked them, wiping a stray tear from her eye.

"Oh, we're just jealous," said Bianca. "All the best guys were in love with you, Gini."

Annette and Matt exchanged quiet, knowing smiles.

"Of course," Bianca went on, with a raised glass in an irreverent salute to the celebrity couple, "Annette had the Christian fellowship and Athletes for Christ to land her big kahuna."

"Remind me to bring my surfboard next time." Matt winked.

Bianca now on a roll: "Of course, AP over there, our own girl god and Jackson Hole's Pot Doc, was playing in a league all her own, jousting with Superman, which left me to pick up the scraps, the loose ends, the Snuffles on their hind legs begging for their dog biscuits."

"Fie on you, Big Mac," Apolonia cried. "You cut a swath through the men in our class like Sheridan through Georgia."

"Sherman," corrected Gini.

"You were fucking more guys—thankfully before the advent of AIDS—than I could count. Every week there was some new dude lurking around our entryway, whose performance issues you dissected in clinical detail with nothing left to the imagination. Who needed med school when I had such an in-house expert on male anatomy for a teammate? Or should I say a sister Shirelle, since you had every callow kid in the arch sings swooning to your oh-so tender, come-hither voice."

"Obviously, I wore them out—or maybe corrupted their naïve souls, because they never show for Reunions now, when I need them. At least I never almost broke up a marriage or threatened the powers that be with nuclear winter. Not that I too wasn't propositioned by certain to-remain-nameless members of the faculty. And there wasn't a night when we girls weren't terrified there'd come a knock on the door—the proctors, to take you away."

"The SWAT team, more like it!" Annette, who'd been hanging wide-eyed on every word, sighed.

"You knew too?" exclaimed Apolonia in horror.

"How could I not? You know the walls of our suite were paper thin."

On the soft spring air came the desultory tolling of the chapel bells.

"Oh my God, how many others knew as well?" Apolonia glanced apprehensively around the gathering under the tent as she rose from her seat. "Well, girls, I'm off to pay my respects to John. Wish me well. The campus proctors may arrest me yet."

CHAPTER 2

With the chapel bells now pealing elaborate changes, Ginistrella Wingate began a discreet reconnaissance with all the feminine guile she could muster, terrified of being taken for a stalker (everyone had to be wondering about her reaction to Jake's son). Carefully modulating her cool, domineering charm, she edged closer to the sign-in table while chatting up classmates, possibly to gather intelligence on young Jacob, while still basking in wisps of her own celebrity from tennis days past or even comments from Shirelles groupies. She deftly parried inquiries from aspiring, over-the-hill authors, handing out business cards with only her office email and telephone number as she homed in like a heat-seeking missile on her quarry, bunkered on three sides by emptying boxes of Reunions swag.

To her dismay, she couldn't help being reminded of a now-deceased member of her class who had run for class president as El Deuco Perverto wearing only a trench coat, boxers, and sunglasses at campaign rallies, a flasher in the mold of John Belushi, whose antics and ribald appropriation of the lyrics of their youth (cum, cum, cum till her daddy takes her dildo away . . .) brought a helpless smile to many weary faces during that frigid winter of junior year.

She handed out another card to a lovely man with steel-rimmed glasses and two gray front teeth who had been in her short-story-writing seminar with Richard Ford. "Do come to the publishing forum tomorrow for some insider tips on where the industry is headed."

She'd been the star of the seminar, with Richard Ford taking her aside at its close and predicting a great future for her as a fiction writer.

She sighed and shook back her hair. The Perverto ticket, she pondered: Was that what her generation would be known for? Irony, sarcasm, a sardonic thumbing of the nose at tradition and order after the chaos of burning inner-city neighborhoods, assassinations, and a disastrous war that had marked her youth? Sometimes it had felt that only she and Jake had stood their ground—she with her steadfast Stoic belief in the classics, the healing powers of great literature, and earnest Jake, with his faith in science to set the world on a better path by the numbers, and so evolved for perfection. But how to get all that into her upgraded novel when she'd so blithely dismissed—refusing to be dependent on Jake's tracking system—the chance to play the women's tour, which might have provided her such rich material—Billie Jean King, for one—on the early struggles of women athletes claiming their just due.

Stealthy side-glances only accelerated her heart's tattoo as young Jacob came into better view, a figure neatly adapted and upgraded to current grooming standards, if not swim-team chic, something she knew a little about from Erma's eleven years as a competitive diver. His blondish-brown hair was clipped just above the sleekly flattened, streamlined ears—gorgeous ears—no piercings, ears hardly ever glimpsed in the original except when lying abed when she'd indulged herself in sweeping back Jake's long hair to kiss the side of his face and tongue the swirling hollows, as if a royal pathway into that fevered mind. And long, luxurious eyebrows . . . could it be, the same cleft right eyebrow? Was such a thing genetic? Not a little freaky.

She had now merged herself into the rear of the check-in line, catching glimpses of young Jake's eyes as he flashed toothsome smiles at arriving classmates, eyes green or turquoise or off-blue, just like his father's, which always seemed to change color in various lights. Becalmed in the slow-moving line, she noted the pleasant surprise on many of her classmates' faces as they reached young Jacob, her gaze drawn to the sumptuous curve of his left wrist, where he held a cheap ballpoint between long, tapering fingers. A lefty too. She noted how he was checking off names on his clipboard long before the person even arrived at his station to announce themselves, before their name tag was visible, like a big-name actor gamely going through the motions of a minor role. A stand-in much in keeping with that winning or possibly amused smile shared with her classmates. And his tee shirt was indeed the same as she'd seen Erma wearing out sailing on Vineyard Sound. *Making Waves* . . . clinging to his muscled torso like a second skin but somehow lacking anything of the jacked show-off. Even his biceps seemed only to demurely bulge his sleeves, as if tastefully leaving most of his sleek athletic build to the imagination.

"Thank God," she murmured out of earshot, no tattoos in sight, no chest hair either, to go by the clean swath of skin below the collarbones—de rigueur for her daughter's generation, she knew from her occasional hacking of her daughter's laptop to check what porn sites or dating apps Erma frequented. She feigned a studied fascination with the bulletin board: Battle of the Alumni Bands, Triangle Show at McCarter (*Inconvenient Sleuth*), various exhibitions at the art museum.

The peal of the chapel bells was slowing, now a single, mournful tolling, fading, recalling to mind the bells of the Gesuati on the Zattere, as her gaze settled on the blue hands of her father's art deco Rolex, and his serene voice as he led her through the narrow streets of Venice at seventeen.

"The splendor is in how little has changed in centuries, while we, it seems, change moment to moment. Like your mother and I."

She grimaced and checked the time on her phone, ever comforted by the perfection of his vintage Rolex.

Nothing from Erma.

Young Jacob stood to rummage through a box of sport shirts. She observed over the top of her iPhone his long black shorts to the knee, where swirling calves tapered elegantly in flip-flops. A stray shaft of humid May sunlight had found its way between the overhanging elms to reveal a sheen of sweat on the young man's cheeks and tanned forehead, a touch of gel on those godly locks, and yes, a sprinkle of soft whiskers on his upper lip and half-dimpled chin. Another generational grace note and possible upgrade from the Jake-of-ages who cared so little about personal hygiene, not that she'd ever complained or even let on to her roommates, who cannily noted the grooming shortfalls of so many of the males who frequented their entryway. How could she possibly have complained since, for a busy nonathlete, Jake had somehow stayed in superb shape, jogging everywhere, insisting she join him in the weight room of the gym to work out, long before that had been standard practice for female athletes. He'd convinced her to work out three days a week with free weights to increase her power from the baseline and serve. As with so much else, ahead of his time.

Again, she turned to her phone as if to escape scrutiny as another classmate moved off the line, gear in hand. Closer now, she could, with a squint, make out his Reunions name tag: *manager: Jacob ("Jocko") Burrage '16.*

"Jocko . . . Jocko," she whispered, happy to have a descriptive to ponder, eager to conjure any possible literary allusions. Perhaps a Navy SEAL, a fearless halfback, or some aggressive AK-47-toting Marvel action figure, heroic, indomitable, intrepid, with sexual prowess to burn. For Jake, a science nerd, such an appellation would have been laughable, a behind-the-back banana shot in the side pocket.

A last tolling of the chapel bell (how she felt for poor Apolonia facing that memorial service as a virtual outcast) fading on the air, like a Sophoclean chorus quieting to leave only the two actors in possession of the stage. Some clueless woman gabbing away at the front of the line, clasping her Reunions stash to her flat chest.

How his very gestures, expressions, invoked Jake; his low, exacting tone so familiar, forever pleading with the uninitiated, desperate to portray that invisible time to come, bringing to life ideas beyond the grasp of ordinary minds.

Yes, his large hands, swimmer's hands plying that crystalline, three-dimensional realm—boundless as the fourth: time itself.

"Gini, don't you get it?" There had been a shaft of intense moonlight shadowing his expressive gestures where he knelt on her dorm-room bed. "Our life, all these moments we share are cumulative, like sedimentary rock, Indiana limestone maybe, set down layer upon layer in the seas of our lives, layered like our memories, like the tiny marine fossils you find embedded in building walls." And he'd cupped her breasts as if to demonstrate, working up the nipples with his thumbs until she cried out in supplication. "And this—this moment too will find its place and nestle down with the others until reawakened, a cockleshell, a worm casting . . . who knows when or where our voices may call it back again into life. Sad but magnificent, this view of things, don't you think?"

"Had we but world enough and time . . ."

"But you'll always be my missing link, my wonderful girl."

"And you my marvelous boy."

She had to stifle a cry of alarm at this startling instant of perfect recollection, as if this personification of her devotion had the effect of distorting time—a balm dispersing the years, just as that shaft of spring light now elicited her contrition, that warm, wisteria-scented light, like a tender palm stroking her cheek and lips, smoothing out the lines in her brow, tender fingers pressed into her fizzy hair, a whisper in her ear. Time's luxurious concoction, the essence of which, an admixture of freshly mown grass and trodden earth and fresh sweat, came suddenly pinwheeling back as if to exalt her soul.

Aghast, she turned from her quarry, raising her blue pencil, convinced this blurring of the years might be better confined to her revised novel, noting the nodding bowers of wisteria sunning themselves on their limestone ledges, their lush purple carillons reflected in the leaded glass. She took a deep breath, ready to dismiss these absurdities, overseen by the leering gargoyles chorused above, when a familiar voice erupted out of her past, greeting this eager-beaver coed disguised for all the world as the most matronly of Brooks Brothers mothers in her floral-print dress.

"Well, it's about time: Ginistrella Wingate, I was wondering whatever happened to you . . ."

Her head snapped around as if that voice, once infinitely far, had suddenly blared in her inner ear. She blinked, feeling the blood pounding in her brain as her dry mouth found a professional smile that hinted at bemusement.

"How's that . . . ?"

He laughed and pointed to her class badge, where everything was explained by her crisply printed name, now residing at a slight tilt upon the upper curve of her left breast, replete with azaleas and apple blossoms.

"And you, of course, must be Jake's son?"

"I think that can now be definitively established by any number of conversations with your classmates." He held out a powerful arm and welcoming palm. "How are you, Gini?"

She felt his fingers close on hers, tight, assured, proficient.

"I'm good—and you?"

Their handshake lingered a moment more than required.

"Pumped, excited. It's an honor and pleasure to see so many legendary members of your class—half the NIT championship team of '75 so far."

"Oh, well, I guess four-time Ivy champs in women's tennis doesn't quite rate on that Richter scale."

"More than registers, since I've already had the pleasure of meeting your returning teammates and the truly legendary Matt Collins in the bargain."

This was said with precisely the cadence and tone that Jake had always used when calling out some gaff, some peculiar Gini-ism that defied all logic and scientific explanation, and so setting up an ambuscade of counterpoints and final checkmate.

Feeling more than idiotic, she sputtered: "I was hoping I might exchange my cap for a larger size."

"It's one size fits all. Here, let me adjust the Velcro for you, Ms. Wingate."

"Ginistrella—Gini, please."

"Straight out of James—*Henry James*," he said in perfect imitation of 007, the Sean Connery version. Now a twinkle in his eye.

"Of course. And how's your dad? How is Jake? I hope he's coming back for Reunions?"

"Not that I know of. He's incredibly busy this time of year—dozens of marketing meetings, our annual investors' meeting, pending FDA approvals. Much in demand in an already inflexible schedule. Rarely lured from his lab bench."

"But surely"—a slight pause as she pondered a discretionary riposte—"he'll come back for *your* graduation on Wednesday?"

"Time will tell."

"And your mother?"

"They're divorced, and not happily."

"Oh, sorry to hear that"—an eerie echo of her own parents' disaster—"well . . . but surely, for your graduation?"

"If she showed, he wouldn't." A careless shrug. "A Mexican standoff."

Rising from his folding chair, he stood appraising her for a moment, his voice calm as he motioned her forward with the adjusted cap in hand. She bent across the table and he reached out, deftly fitting the cap like a crown of laurels, even tucking a few strands of hair behind her ears, their faces inches apart as she breathed deeply for the scent of him, clean sweat and deodorant, elixir of youth.

"There," he said, leaning back at the picture before him. "Good as new."

She was about to mention her daughter—a diver on the swim team, his class; heck, a biochemistry major, graduating as well on Wednesday—but something in his overconfident appraisal triggered caution, his deeply lashed eyes, mirrored in hers, blinking out a warning.

"How is—thank you, Jacob—your dad? We were pretty close once—once upon a time in a galaxy far away." This allusion, conjuring Apolonia's *Interstellar* theory, sent a quiver of helpless wonderment down her spine, which she disguised with a show of adjusting her cap and then canting her head in a sporty gesture, her face helplessly aglow.

"Insanely prosperous"—he flicked a patient look at the next in line—"and you've got a charity tennis match tomorrow."

For some reason, this reminder caught her off guard, or perhaps the swoon of pleasure at the chance to show off her tennis game quite confounded her; sweat trickled down her arms, and every muscle in her body tensed as if preparing to return serve. She pulled herself up straight, standing her ground.

"How did you know?"

"Annette invited me. I even got my old man to kick in ten thousand." His brows furrowed as if recognizing the spark of joy flushing her cheeks, which seemed to impel him to reach out and gently gather her ringless right hand in his, where he turned it palm up, a flicker of wildness in the glittering blue-green of his eyes. "And hard-won calluses, no doubt."

"Oh, that—well, hardly ladylike, but once upon a time I was a ranked player."

"Thirty-eighth in the nation."

She checked the awkward instant of shock at this familiarity with a swallow, along with any temptation of a show of bravado as she stared at her shaking palm in his. Temptations, which her Stoic beliefs (passed down from her father) discouraged for cool equanimity. *Speak little and well—show virtue but don't speak of it.* So crucial in the dog-eat-dog publishing fraternity.

"Hard to believe . . . ," she got out, tempted to reach out to his bicep, his shoulder, as if to bridge the gap of the years, only to squeeze his hand with a tepid laugh and withdraw hers.

"Who turned down a qualifying slot at Wimbledon from Donald Dell."

This almost sunk her: a thing so completely repressed that it almost seemed untrue.

"How did Jake . . . ?"

"When I told my father I'd be managing your reunion"—his eyebrows shot up as if sighting the Holy Grail—"you'd think it was his idea all along."

"Really? Well, you see, he was fascinated by the game, by the strategy, what seems, now, like the dark ages before it all went professional, when keeping your amateur standing still mattered—BB, before Borg." She tried to repress the pleading, almost apologetic tone in her voice. "It was almost like he saw where the game was headed: strategy, training, his tracking system that you can now download to your phone. But it frustrated me too, because I reacted badly to the idea that numbers, probability, percentages could be so easily translated into the human. Maybe because he wasn't an athlete himself."

At this near-confessional flood, an enigmatic smile floated up on the face before her, animating those long eyebrows, the cute cleft space on the right that she'd once loved.

"But he was. He was captain of the swim team back at Evanston High; he always liked to boast that he got into Princeton on a swimming scholarship and never swam a stroke. Which was not strictly true, of course, since he was a standout on the swim team freshman year."

At this—*not strictly*, this almost bland tone contrasting her cluelessness—she found herself struck dumb, bewildered. Had they been talking about different people? How could she not know this? You don't sleep with someone for almost three years and not know this. And yet, there he was, his son, standing at ease, hands on narrow hips where his black shorts hung to his flexing knees, head cocked sarcastically just like his father, a hint of mockery, of exploding your expectations by uncovering yet another nugget of truth that had been staring you in the face all along if you'd just been diligent enough to dig for it. She smiled into the deep-set eyes, sparkling with earth tones and just a hint of green—yes, turquoise.

"Freshman year, yes, of course. I guess I'd forgotten."

A more-than-patient classmate in line behind her let his presence be known, and she realized her time was up.

"The trick," he offered in a consoling voice, "is to prioritize your goals."

"So wise," she replied graciously as she began to move off. "I'm glad you've somehow managed to find the time to excel at so much."

"Hardly. It's never easy," he replied and nodded to her classmate moving up in the line. "Studying on the bus to and from meets, finding someone to monitor your experiments in the lab. But the team, the guys and girls, the time together," he shrugged, "makes it all worthwhile."

"Wow, good luck on that—and the Olympic trials," she added, throwing out this nugget from Gareth as a way of holding her own. "Oh, and remember me to your father."

"I'll do you one better"—and he gestured with what she took as a chivalrous, perhaps half-humorous bow of the head—"I promised him a dance. Until tonight, Isabel."

The deployment of this last most private of private endearments, the name of that obdurate heroine of her early life, had her scampering out of the hot sunlight into the cooling shade of the courtyard arcade. There, pressed by an instinct as old as the hills, she turned her face skyward, only to find that fiendish gargoyle with his beaker raised against the blue: "Eureka!" she blurted. Or, as she would one day pen it: a salute—and some, to kingdom come . . .

CHAPTER 3

The envelope—"By Hand to Patton 44. Apolonia Baranski"—had been slipped under the door of their suite that glorious spring of junior year. Letterhead, office of the provost on very official-looking heavy stock stationery with a single sentence typed in capital letters: *PLEASE CALL THE PROVOST'S OFFICE IMMEDIATELY TO ARRANGE AN APPOINTMENT.* She was panic-stricken but did as she was told, telling nobody, not even Gini or Bianca, not a peep to John, whom she assumed was kept in the loop on such delicate matters.

It had been one of those warm, bracing April days that put paid-in-full to an already remote, bitterly cold winter. The aroma of newly mown grass mixing with that of heady dope. Every expanse of green dotted with pale bodies released on parole. Azaleas and rhododendrons gaudily bunkered the entrance to Prospect Garden. A splendor that she was nearly oblivious to as she hurried up campus so as not to add tardiness to her other crimes. Her executioner awaited. Never once had she darkened the door of stately Nassau Hall, just barely recalling the student tour guide's description on her first campus visit about the Battle of Princeton, something about a cannonball leaving a dent in the dun, ivy-clad stonework. Nor seen the inside of the president's office, when she'd seen just about every other room John had frequented, either staring at the ceiling or down into her lover's face.

The provost's waiting room seemed unbearably stuffy, the air permeated with the odor of damp plaster and ancient oak paneling, as she struggled to catch her breath.

Neatly arranged black Windsor chairs, embossed with the university crest in gold, were arranged in a semicircle, as if awaiting the return of jurors and a verdict. On the ceiling, a liver-colored water stain made a sharp turn at a wall, only to disappear between a row of antique prints of the university. She took a seat and nervously rearranged some issues of the alumni magazine on a side table, then thumbed through a dated course catalog. A door creaked, and an officious secretary wordlessly ushered the sinner into a spacious office overlooking Cannon Green, where the provost sat behind his desk, head bent to a document. She glanced out the large window fringed with waving fronds of ivy—creepy green leprechauns, so it struck her, peeping toms leering for a glimpse before the guillotine fell. She could smell the sharpened pencils on his desk, which stood at attention in an orange-and-black mug with a broken handle, imprinted with his name and *Princeton Sociology Department* in gold lettering. The provost's bald, clean-shaven head remained bent, as if desperate to decipher whatever was contained in the document before him, making quick check marks in the margins. Bald, bald, Kojak bald was all that came to mind: Who loves ya, baby? Definitely no lollipops on offer. A thin razor cut on his pinkish-white cranium was the only sign of imminent violence she could detect; otherwise, a studious, rotund face glowed like a baby's bottom with protruding ears. He finally waved her to a chair before his expansive desk and only then met her eyes as she sat.

"How are you, Apolonia?"

Blue, eyebrowless eyes aglitter with what she took for icy malice.

"Doing just fine, sir."

"You're playing as well as ever. Do you think you'll take the Ivies again this year?"

"If we all avoid injuries, sir."

"Injuries—yes. A cracked vertebra freshman year, wasn't it?" How did he know that? "I perfectly understand. The very thing, the reason I called you in." His bald head swam forward and back in a slant of light through the high windows, where the ivy continued nodding from the peanut gallery. "Injuries, of course, come about through risk-taking, when you push something to its limit, beyond its design specification: the pressure, the torque, the impact—what have you."

"Or endurance, exhaustion—"

"But you get my point." And he bent forward, tapping impatiently with a yellow pencil, squinting eyes riveted on her fearful face, dark hair hastily pulled up with a rubber band in a messy chignon. "You must understand my role, as a friend to you—to both of you . . . and John and I are close friends, I assure you. I'm bound to warn you that you hold not just the life and career, a marriage, a family, wife and children in your power to do great injury, but this university as well. John was instrumental in bringing women, co-education to Princeton, increasing minority admits; he personally championed that fight on the board, took huge risks. This thing, this *folie à deux*, could destroy everything—just imagine . . . not just his life and career but yours as well. The scandal will engulf you and tarnish all your days. If you bring him down—such a fine, well-meaning . . . a beloved man—nobody will ever forgive you."

Apolonia stared, not a little mesmerized, at where the tapping pencil met the cue-ball head reflected in the dark patina of the desktop.

"And yes"—the pencil hung suspended—"as I said, John is a friend of mine. I implore you—as I've implored him as well, both of you—to call it quits, while you can."

"What does he say?" She couldn't believe she'd choked this much out.

"Think of his wife and children—the destruction of a family."

"Actually, I think about that every day—especially . . ."

He bent forward, his shiny nose and wide lips posed in a question mark: "*Every day . . . ?*"

"I didn't mean it quite like that."

"If *I* know—think about it; if those closest to him know, imagine how many others know: how close—only a matter of time—to the line of disaster you've come; your toes are poised on the edge of the abyss."

She was weeping, speechless.

"Middle-aged men sometimes go off the rails sexually; history is rife with examples. It goes with the territory of high ambition and then burns itself out." He shook his head at this aside and then waved a piece of notebook paper with lines of scrawled handwriting in black ink. "And this arrived a week ago, unsigned, but clearly an undergraduate, threatening to spill the beans if ROTC isn't thrown off campus. Blackmail."

She squinted as the evidence, the not-unfamiliar handwriting, was carefully replaced in a manila folder.

"Give it up, and I will see that your scholarship is fully funded, including allowances, so that you won't have to do any student jobs, so you can focus on your tennis and academics. God only knows, premed is challenging enough, even for the brightest kids." He sank back in his wide leather chair and raised his hands as if to confer a blessing. "Otherwise, we may have to consider revoking your scholarship entirely, requiring your parents to pay the full freight—if you should still want to matriculate."

At this, at the threat to withdraw financial aid—the money thing—something had snapped inside her brain, and the kid from the streets of Manayunk had lashed out.

"He'd never let you do that . . ."

The provost had smiled quixotically, a meaty tongue wetting his lips. "Of course not, but that's the point. Forcing him to do that may be the only thing to bring him to his senses."

As the chapel bells reached a crescendo, easing off into a long, final, desultory tolling, Dr. Apolonia Baranski shook her head in disbelief. What had allowed her to stand up to such threats, to pursue such a folly in the first place, to risk everything? How she longed for the fortitude and absolute love of those earlier years.

"You mean besides your delicious honeypot and cunning little breasts and those wily Manayunk sex moves—what's not to love?"

She smiled at that soft purr of remembered endearments, a voice comic, biting, as super intelligent as it was down-to-earth, who had worshipped so brazenly at the altar of her young body. Always, relentlessly building her up, fortifying her confidence. Wiping a tear, she patted the protruding red sandstone shoes of one John Witherspoon, where the berobed and bewigged figure stood glowering from his niche in Pyne Hall courtyard, that iron-willed Presbyterian sixth president of Princeton to whom John Proctor often laughingly compared himself. "A niche in Pyne saves time."

Was that a piece of pink chewing gum someone had affixed to John Witherspoon's shoe? She grabbed a tissue from her backpack and removed the offending thing and disposed of it in a nearby waste can.

Meeting Jake's son had her somehow spooked. Years of debriefing patients gave her the distinct impression of a young man pretending to a maturity way beyond his years or, even more strangely, an older man acting the role of a precocious kid. And that now-remembered letter on the provost's desk, the somehow familiar handwriting . . .

"Abyss . . . ," she murmured to herself as she took another peek around the corner of Pyne archway at the nearly empty steps of the chapel, ready to make her move as soon as the coast was clear and zip unnoticed into the back of the nave for John Proctor's memorial service. She checked her face in her phone, adjusting any stray locks of hair that had escaped her straw hat. Her black tights and tennis dress and orange Nike running shoes were hardly appropriate, but hey, at least she wasn't like Gini, stalking (when last seen) that virile young man, demeaning herself by chasing after phantoms, the son of the man she should've married. And to think—a blue-collar kid from Philly's own Manayunk—she had once actually envied her teammate, if not her Grace Kelly looks and breeding, certainly her sophistication. And face it, AP, her brainpower—and Jake's too. And for that matter, John Proctor's in spades. And yet she'd married a chef who'd never cracked the pages of a book—except cookbooks—in his life. How many times in that distant, obscure event horizon of her mind, fucking away with the love of her life, filled and about to be filled, had a glimmer of heat lightning not sparked the prayer: Dear God, just give me a bit of John's intelligence, if not in me, in my offspring.

"No fucking way, AP—you're a doctor—and a good one, not some wacko." She squinted, eyeing a tall blonde woman lingering by the front door of the chapel holding the hand of a young boy. She was wearing a trim black dress and orange scarf . . . John's eldest daughter—granddaughter!

Why did everything seem such a struggle? Unlike Gini, who had effortlessly aced her academics, who always beat her on court while hardly working up a sweat. Gini, so-o like all those privileged women she'd kowtowed to at the Merion Cricket Club, where she'd first ball-girled. At thirteen, in the summer between junior high and high school, she had talked her way onto the housekeeping staff cleaning the women's locker room, a ruse to get some court time, picking up a few bucks here and there as a hitting partner for some old grande dame or a last-minute fill-in for a lady's doubles match. Then she'd started stringing racquets in the club's pro shop, while further honing her scrappy game by cadging pickup matches in FDR Park with local hotshots, hustling five-dollar bets while navigating the cracks and potholes in the ancient courts, clawing her way up the regional and then national girls' rankings, even as her roofer father, a diehard Phillies and Eagles fan, had washed his hands of her and that "sissy rich kids' sport." Getting into Princeton on an athletic scholarship had done little to dampen her father's low opinion, and she soon found herself underprepared for the academic load and nearly leveled by the premed requirements. First Gini (editing her freshman essays) and then Jake had saved her. Jake's tutoring in math and science had crammed just enough into her brain for her to graduate, even as it took two years of summer school to finally pass organic chemistry, and finally—"finally"—get into med school.

"Apolonia, for a girl god, you sure have a few nutty ideas that I've tried and failed, it seems, to correct." Jake's spartan dorm room. Smell of unwashed laundry. Framed photographs over his desk: Einstein and Johnny von Neumann and Marie Curie and others—his heroes. On his standard-issue desk piled high with journal articles and computer printouts, snapshots of the kid with his father, fishing along Cripple Creek.

And there again, that uncanny echo as if from an hour before at the sign-in table.

"We—two blue-collar kids—are not descended from apes and chimpanzees. We share a common ancestor, which means we are cousins, of a sort, since their line of evolution broke off from ours way before we became wholly human, a half million years or so ago, by present best estimates. An evolutionary fitness that should be on full display in the Nude Olympics tomorrow night. Hey, I'll bet you ten dollars you can't talk Gini and Bianca into running. Not to mention living up to their feminist ideals."

She had needed the ten bucks. Bianca was easy, Gini took some convincing, along with a few shots of vodka for antifreeze. Feminists, crazy as the guys—crazier! Of course, Bianca wanted to dispense with their panties as well, but that's where Gini drew the line—so, Bianca complained, having her miss out on the "Best Bush" prize (when bushes were still in season), which she'd have won hands down with her glorious red thatch. She smiled to herself: how memories of their bouncing, beautiful tits still drew vivid sighs of appreciation from the old guys in their class.

Again adjusting her broad-brimmed straw hat and putting on her sunglasses, she took a deep breath and prepared for her final assault on the chapel, as the tolling now consisted of a single tenor bell, speeding her—oddly, in a day of oddities—back to that one glorious week in Venice, visiting the Carpaccios, the happiest week of her life, when she and John actually had time to themselves, without fear of discovery or recognition, when the last tolling, tallying bell of the Gesuati echoed over the Giudecca, where she watched the canal-reflected light on the ceiling of their room, orgasm after orgasm after orgasm. A tallying of a tallying (a thousand orgasms deep)—was that John's phrase or Gini's, in her Whitman phase: *"With the twirl of my tongue"—you cunning linguist—"I encompass worlds and volumes of worlds."*

"Yes, a thousand and one deep . . ." And she, truth be told, had probably doubled his tally, all tolled by the time they finally parted ways during the years of her residency.

As the tenor bell faded on the blue cloudless sky, she made a dash for the rear side doors of the chapel.

Yes, yes, she chided herself, of course she should have had her son, her Christopher, join her for Reunions—now, right at her side; it was the least she could've done.

And to think it had all begun so innocently, so earnestly. A pickup tennis game with an older, knobby-kneed guy, then still in his forties, who just happened to be Princeton's fourteenth president, who also just happened—who knew—to be the first in his family to go to college, who had actually played tennis, like her, on his high school team, who had married too young to his high school sweetheart, a lovely woman who simply had nada for a sex drive: a total deadbeat in the sack. To be honest, his sex drive was off the charts (fifteen lean years of marriage). Not that hers wasn't exactly the Daytona 500, even with all the young fry—five guys to every girl—begging to sample her charms. And Jake tutoring her once a week in his cozy study. Let's face it, AP: you were one horny bitch in heat; the two of you fuel to the fire—Marilyn Chambers's *Insatiable* was kindergarten stuff: incandescent, incendiary, white hot!

As she reached the side door to the chapel, more giddy memories of long-ago trysts spilled across her mind as if in defiance of those stalwart Presbyterian spires ranging above, the bell tower a last, quieting stillness, a final echoing cry against the silencing of such a great man, her lover, her best friend, whose singular preoccupation during her student years was where to fuck, when to fuck, and was there any way to prolong their fucking. When the fucking logistics of their secret fucking was such an obsessive preoccupation that she was often forced to finger paint just to get the subject off her mind. Except for Venice—thank God for the Carpaccios. She opened the chapel door, suddenly bathed in the cool shade of the ambulatory as a Bach cantata playing on the organ halted her in her tracks by memory's force majeure: her backside sloshing against the olive-green linoleum floor of the Proctors' kitchen, Bach playing on the living room stereo, yet again unable to make it to the bedroom.

The mourners—no, celebrants—were compacted nearest the altar and choir stalls, where Bach's cantata "Wie Schön Leuchtet der Morgenstern," John's favorite, swelled and filled the huge, soaring, crystalline nave. She had the rear seats almost entirely to herself—the scarlet woman, Lady XXX. She breathed deeply to calm her heart's tattoo, a flow of sad joy washing over her, along with the smell of beeswax mixing with the floral scents from a score of carefully deployed flower wreaths, garish lifesavers mounted across the nave. She slumped into a seat, keeping on her straw hat and dark glasses, fighting the frisson of fearful daring as if her ass were still sliding across that kitchen linoleum.

How could all that lovely tally come to this? A grand life reduced to a few burning altar candles and a scattering of wreaths. And the crowded pews in front looking like a geriatric ward, forgotten by the young, fading for the old. And it wasn't as if he'd been exactly good-looking, with that crooked nose and the incipient jowls, when last they'd been lovers, just out of his forties. And yet a face, a voice—God, yes—a mind overspending with the keenest observations and insights, as worlds after worlds had been opened for a young woman, page after page on economic theory, not to mention art and architecture and the ferocious politics of building the future of a great university. A man with unerring judgment about everything under the sun except keeping his libido in check, who predicted the future—faculty votes, board votes, referendums—with unerring accuracy, and yet couldn't keep his fly zipped in the moment. Not when faced with this kid from Manayunk who could thrash him on the tennis court, who could time her orgasms to his, and then trump him with dizzying solo flights.

What exactly had been the aphrodisiac? His mind or the sex or the explosive fusion of their conjunction? How she ached to have found something approaching that incandescent love over all the intervening years. A life on half rations.

Had it been that his wife, the long-suffering poor Betty Anne, had never been able to come? Even the sex therapist they'd gone to hadn't been able to help. Or the sheer danger of a double life? A wager with death and eros, as he liked to say while quoting Byron from memory as they wandered the streets of Venice. Lust as an antidote to death and development economics (his academic specialty) and fear that his ambition led to a blind alley.

"Love in full life and length, not love ideal, No, nor ideal beauty . . . something better still, so very real . . . that you would purchase, beg, or steal."

And steal they did as she savored these lines from Byron like a worshipper called to her private devotions. How she alone of all womenkind had truly rung John Proctor's bell, had traded in the academic for a lothario, for the transient pleasures of carnal love, moved to ecstatic wonder by Carpaccio's Augustine, to tears by the cry of a boatman, by the flickering enchantment of that Venetian light caught in her lover's fervent gaze. A tally of love unavailing even to a retrospective gaze—that fugitive essence of life all the more real for its vanishing, like those early-morning mists from their balcony overlooking the Zattere.

"Oh, John . . . ," she sang out over the organ.

His supple voice that had lingered on long after their final parting as lovers (her first-year residency at Denver's Saint Joseph Hospital), beginning with long, reflective letters and then emails and then, finally, years later, in care packages delivered by FedEx of annotated copies of his favorite books (downsizing after his wife's death) on Venetian art and architecture, on Byron and Ruskin, well-thumbed tomes on Carpaccio and Vivaldi, Bellini and Scarlatti, arriving like missives from a fair and bountiful isle, the creased and underlined pages still full of that same longing, as if that week overlooking the Rio San Vio had only been yesterday.

Each book inscribed to her with a line from Byron.

"One of those forms which flit by us when we are young, and fix our eyes on every face . . . whose course and home we knew not, nor shall know, like the lost Pleiad seen no more below!"

Yes, she repeated to herself, yes, I should have brought Christopher.

A regret that oddly brought to mind (as the last notes of the Bach cantata trembled and fell away) Gini's rapt face across from hers in her cozy Jackson Hole living room after a long day on the slopes, when Christopher had taken Erma out clubbing in town, when the eternal subject was once again broached between these two veteran conspirators, when she put on her best bedside manner and confessed the weight of it.

"The good sex *was* the love, don't you think? When it's so good, you simply lose your mind to the madness, to the sickness, the recklessness, and become the other person—the beloved . . . until death do you part."

And she'd caught the echoed spark in Gini's soft blue eyes: the recognition that such a truth, such a loss had branded them as sisters for the ages.

CHAPTER 4

Ginistrella Wingate headed down campus at a brisk clip, not fleeing a ghost exactly, but close enough that she felt the need to aerate her brain before her head exploded. Perfectly ridiculous, of course, so she scolded herself—an overreaction to a very ordinary chat with an extraordinary young man who just happened to be the son of a onetime lover. But his look of retrospection, the trembling depth of his eyes, that seeming fathomless recognition of her younger self had her unnerved.

Rather than being panicked, she should be celebrating the fact that Jake, like herself, had made it through the early trials of this life with flying colors, siring a wonderful son, as she had birthed a wonderful daughter. Yet, she was frightened, needing familiar scenes, familiar faces to calm her jittery nerves. There had been something uncanny—a seasoned knowingness about the young man's conversation, there in the vibrating lower registers of his voice. A searching quality, a pensiveness that locked onto hers, penetrating that airtight seal on a past done and gone that now threatened to spill into the moment.

"Better to have loved . . . ," she murmured to the sky, as if flinging overboard clichés might somehow rebalance her listing bark.

A familiar jingling noise brought her up short at the entrance to the Dillon gym pool. Once the arena for swim teams past, the old pool had long since been superseded by a dedicated natatorium (how she loved the Latin) on the far side of campus where she'd gone to watch Erma dive. She shook her head. Some old memory had snaked its way behind her eyes, but she was damned if she could make it out before her reverie was interrupted by a gaggle of tenth-reunion goers (garishly dressed in Hawaiian-themed outfits replete with surfing tigers and dancing pineapples) elbowing up campus to their Reunions site. Her eye was caught by a gorgeous thirty-year-old woman who gave her a gracious smile—tiger earrings agleam—before hurtling past, probably aghast at her elder's insipid sundress. For an instant, struck by their gossipy tones, she caught wind of a moment at her own tenth reunion, when she'd first invited her husband to be, William Cheshire, the senior science editor at Tandem Press, as her guest. Although a Harvard physics PhD, Bill had gamely participated in the self-reverential festivities, even as he busied himself visiting colleagues in the physics department and even recruiting potential authors in the astrophysics department (the Hubble telescope was the new-new thing in the field). It had been a test run, a proving ground for Bill, ten years her senior, who came through with flying colors: he was adored by her roommates, enough that she'd barely noticed Jake's absence even as memories of their escapades seemed imprinted a thousand times over whenever she'd dared revisit their old haunts.

Even as their haunt of haunts had been erased from memory's map, the old university tennis courts now replaced by Whitman (not the poet) College, a huge new collegiate-Gothic dorm named after its eponymous donor, a woman in her class who had made it big in the tech world.

"Keeping tally with the meaning of all things," she recited, as if by closing her eyes for a moment she might yet recall the smell of that Har-Tru green clay after rain, the aroma of matted grass rising off the earthy hillside where Jake (along with hundreds of spectators) had sat to watch her matches. "Yes . . ." And the way the fall leaves whirled down the breeze from the line of shady maples along the path above, their ranks marshaled against the chain-link fence where she hung her lucky Charlie Brown towel.

"Of course you can make it to Wimbledon." She had been protesting his Darwinian explanation for the increase in record-breaking times at the Olympics. "And evolution simply means design modifications over time. Look at you: tall, fast, supple, strong—self-selected; the mechanisms of success are right at your fingertips: better training and coaching—that's me. And the ultimate reward of having fulfilled your biological destiny. All you need is some weightlifting in the gym and increased topspin to give yourself more margin for error, and so unleashing your full potential as an athlete. Take a look: the numbers never lie . . ."

"The hell you say," she now retorted, remembering how his voice had faltered and his gaze turned inward.

An odd, almost puzzled look had crept over his face, a look she would come to know all too well in the coming years, the circumspection of one who had shoved the tiller to port upon sighting a distant squall line scooping waves before it. "Numbers . . . never lie," he repeated, even as his mind careened around yet another corner. "I just realized how all science will eventually be data-driven as opposed to hypothesis-driven; it's just that we don't have the computational tools yet—or I don't. Getting time at the computer center is almost impossible. And yet, working with you, the future comes alive in my bones."

Well, that future now sang out in her hurried steps down campus as she began scouting out the new tennis center (all hard courts, a lean and spare tennis pavilion, plenty of bleak grandstands—efficient but hardly lovable), where she and the Shirelles would take the court tomorrow in a "celebrity" match, teamed up with the young fry to raise money for one of Annette's Christian charities. The women's team, ranked nineteen in the nation, was working out in preparation for the post-season NCAAs. She lingered a moment by the litter of tennis bags courtside, breathing in the ambrosial scents of fresh tennis balls, sweaty socks and towels, and sunscreen before taking a seat in the stands and putting her new Reunions baseball cap to good use. As she watched intently, every nerve in her body began to vibrate with desire as the tall and strong women sheathed in orange-and-black uniforms were rocketing the ball across the net in rallies that went on forever. Any one of them would have made mincemeat of her in her prime. Athletes at the height of their powers—the literalness and mystery of total absorption in the moment of being. That absence of doubt and introspection and ambiguity that had once been hers. "Oh my God . . . yes!" she exclaimed at the utter clarity of the epiphany before her: the future Jake had predicted, perfectly evolved specimens who epitomized his theories: bigger, faster, stronger, and playing the percentages, with huge topspin shots off either side, balls exploding off their racquets in tortured yet glorious arcs, well over the net and well inside the baseline. These were the upgraded models first pioneered by Chrissie Evert and Martina Navratilova, followed by a deluge of amazons out of Eastern Europe and the Williams sisters.

"Biological destiny . . . ," she murmured. A destiny she'd proudly dismissed out of hand at the end of her senior year, along with her lover.

Her throat constricted with a longing she could barely contain, yearning to be one of those women drilling on the court, every iota of her being striving to recast itself in homage to a Wimbledon crown that might have been hers, even as her Stoic principles warned against just such a fantasy—the ephemerality of gold and silver trophies, the crown of laurels.

And it wasn't as if she'd foregone or dismissed the new techniques that had revolutionized the game. Twenty years before, she'd switched to the new topspin strokes, the Björn Borg game, with a semi-western grip on the forehand and a two-handed backhand, seduced into it by the new young pro, Oskar, at the West Chop Club on Martha's Vineyard. Whatever it took to make sure she remained the number-one woman on the island as the younger women began to gain on her. A recalibration that had allowed her to hold that number-one spot in women's singles for another ten years before some young amazon out of Stanford finally relegated her to the senior ranks. Oh, Oskar, Oskar from Poland, with that wiry body and winning, insouciant smile, seductive green eyes and foreign accent; otherwise, she'd never have made the transition. Oskar, who made her feel like seventeen again, worked with her for a month, every day for three hours, until she'd mastered the modern game. At least tomorrow, taking the court, she wouldn't look like an antique tennis racquet tumbled out of the hall closet.

"Take a look at these stats: service placement, returns, unforced errors and winners, your success on break points—nudge these up by twenty percent and you'll be on your way to Wimbledon."

"Jake, have you ever played tennis?"

"Nope."

"Is this how you pick up all your women?"

"It seems to work with you."

"You see that woman on court five—my teammate, Annette, our number one."

"She's a beautiful player."

"Her mother's a tennis pro, her younger sisters are ranked in the juniors, her father played on the team here before the war—good genes, huh? Her national ranking is higher than mine. And she's played mixed doubles at Wimbledon, where she got to the third round and lost to Billie Jean King and Clark Graebner (of course, it helps to have a partner and boyfriend ranked in the top ten in the world). If your system can get me past Annette, you've found your girl."

On the way up campus to her daughter's dorm, she was once again waylaid, near the pool entrance of Dillon gym, by a telltale rattle of car keys against her phone in her backpack purse.

"His keys, his goddamn keys!"

Jake was never without a fistful of keys, hung on a metal fob from the loop of his ratty jeans; they jangled whenever he turned suddenly or sat abruptly. Mostly keys to access facilities for his student jobs, keys to the biology and chemistry labs, keys to dining areas in Wilson College, the student center—but how he'd purloined the rest remained a mystery. Hardly on the up and up, if possibly illegal.

It had been late, making their way back from the physics library, where they'd been studying, and he'd suddenly grabbed her arm and turned her around, his keys jingling in the moonlight.

"Why not a swim before bed?"

"Don't be ridiculous. I've got a killer test tomorrow in Latin poetry. It's closed anyway."

A pregnant pause, a finger to his lips, and a moment to sort through that palm-wide bunch of keys, until, locating the right one, he waved her on.

As if obedient to this specter out of her past, she found herself, as though in a trance, descending the steps to the pool's spectator gallery, her trepidation heightened only by her self-ridicule. She pressed the push bar on the door, her nostrils assaulted by the close, humid smell of chlorine, sensation merging with memory, as that long-ago midnight hour returned in the flickering lamplight through the windows high above the viewing gallery. It was enough that she closed her eyes for a moment as if to better make out the red *exit* signs in the darkness, reflected on the buff-toned tiles of the viewing gallery, and then in wavy, scarlet geometries over the aquamarine glitter—uneasy, disturbing, claustrophobic—of the empty pool. Her curious eyes widened with trepidation as she began to scout the back wall of the viewing gallery, lined with framed photos of swim teams past.

She'd shuddered at the sudden grip of her hand. Less reassurance in the face of danger than a kind of umbilical cord to viscerally share the experience of one of his more fantastic whims: that detour to the wild side, that crazy escapade, that rapid tumble into the rabbit hole. They moved like phantoms through the viewing gallery and down another staircase to the dark, musty changing rooms and through to the pool deck. Panting, reeling in the pitch-black until her eyes adjusted to the vague lamplight flickering beyond those high windows and the eerie, fiery glow of the *exit* signs, triplicate reflections stitched into the opaque membrane of the Olympic-size pool.

"How about a skinny dip to wash our disagreements—or is it sins—away?"

"What, a coin for Charon? Besides getting us kicked out for trespassing?"

"Did anyone ever tell you that you have an uncanny habit of worrying about nothing most of the time, while not giving a damn about stuff that really matters?"

"You have the even worse habit of never quite telling the truth or, worse, doctoring the facts to suit your purposes."

"Ah, do I detect your favorite lament that mankind—womankind, sorry—saddled with unequal talents and brains, is forever stuck in first gear? Or is it that we have inequality thrust upon us by an oh-so-uncaring universe?"

"You think it's all a joke: women's rights, civil rights, human rights."

"I'm only saying that hierarchies"—he gestured like a necromancer about to cast a spell upon the dreaming waters—"at least on this bank of the River Styx, happen naturally because as individuals, as groups, as a species, we're stuck with status consciousness. It offers us comfort to follow someone we respect, to bow to their expertise; otherwise, it's chaos. A pileup of wildebeests in the shallows."

"Ergo, those, like you, with all your superior knowledge, make the rules."

"Knowledge is power. None of us, ambition's spawn, got here by being shrinking violets."

"Ain't that the truth."

"Listen, we all want the same thing: to build and grow and have our achievements outlast the ages. Hierarchy is how evolution guarantees the persistence of life over time, which means freedom to reinvent ourselves on a dime, like you do every day on the court, like . . . here, where everything is a game of matter and light."

Without another word, he'd stripped and kicked away his jeans and sneakers—the fob of keys ringing out on the pool deck—and dived through the translucent surface, reappearing dolphin-like as his back and shoulders surged forward, knifing the water, his wake touched by a fiery red contrail. She stood gazing in awe, taken out of herself, as if at the discovery of a creature suddenly released into its natural element. Had she detected the speed? The perfect form? A perfection that only gained momentum, putting on more speed at each turn—flicking through turns, four hundred meters, until coming to an abrupt stop before where she stood rooted on the near shore. He swept back his long hair, a young, oh-so-virile Poseidon, and gazed up at her with that galling expression of disdain and sardonic pleasure as he awaited her reply to the thrown gauntlet.

"Water's fine . . . ," he prompted.

"Shouldn't you have showered first?"

Why had she not recognized the nature of the beast in that moment? The twisted bond, the temptation to eternity? That they were more alike than she dared admit.

Sheltered in the near darkness, she'd gone to a bench, and slowly, exactingly—timid soul—undressed and unshowered, with a little scream of daring, had dived in lest she allow this nervy merman to trump her pretense to caution and good sense. She had swum a leisurely lap or two to demonstrate she was no slouch, that she was still the alpha female in this relationship, when he'd caught hold of her and roughly pulled her backside against his chest, taking her in a kind of body lock as his mouth explored the nape of her neck, biting her ears, fondling her breast, while one encircled hand began a dexterous play on her clit. Then his erection was nuzzling the crack of her ass, probing lower and lower, until her thighs spread, uplifted by one arm, and he suddenly slipped into her—deep, deeper than deep, as those agile arms and hands continued their orchestration, a delicious rhythm in counterpoint to the hungry waves against the side of the pool, urging on every exposed nerve in her body. The freakiness—surprise, wonder, the weightlessness—had been such that time itself seemed suspended, one skin sloughed for another. Finding herself swept away by one orgasm after the next, her body electric, radiating energy as much within as without, breached and birthed on the very tides of her being as she hung in her lover's arms.

"You okay?" he finally asked as they stood embracing in the shallow end of the pool.

This, yet another demonstration of his insidious power over her, leaving her shaken, abashed, crying tears of rapture and joy, even as she worshipped at this baptism of defeat. For long moments, she feared for her sanity. And only when her convulsions had quieted, her breathing stilled, did she again recognize herself. She finally nodded numbly to the grinning figure in the shallows, shaking his hand where she'd bitten his finger.

"A sex wound," he laughed and lifted her to the pool deck. "The mark of the beast within."

She now sank to a seat in the spectator gallery, heart pounding, sweat pouring from her armpits as she tried to calmly disinter this long-lost interlude that had so buried itself in her flesh as to become a silenced witness to a life foregone, as if one arc of existence at the flip of Charon's coin had seamlessly merged with the next. Suborned by her first multiple orgasms, her Stoic soul had been put to flight, as pure pleasure had trumped prudence, much less condom-protected sex, not that it mattered much in the halcyon days before AIDS when she'd been on the Pill.

"You okay?" he asked again, his shadowy eyes brimming in triumph. Her hand was clamped over her pubes where she sat panting on the poolside.

"I never—I dunno . . ."

"Yes, primal—the soup from which we first sprang. Makes sense—yes?"

"You scared the daylights out of me."

"You should see your eyes, so big and round, like a Tarsier."

"A what?"

"A cute little nocturnal animal with huge, owl-like eyes. It sees by moonlight, starlight, and twilight. They don't even have a tapetum lucidum, a kind of mirror behind the retina, which gives the retinal pigments an enhanced way to intercept faint light. They just have wide eyes."

"Yes, stars—I was seeing stars." She looked down at her hand. "You came inside me."

"I know, I'm sorry, but it's a big pool, lots of chlorine."

"That's so gross."

"Nobody will know unless one of the girls on the swim team gets pregnant."

"That's not funny."

"Do you still love me?"

"Well, I'm a little beyond love right now—my right mind even. I'm a little beyond everything."

"But isn't that the whole point of being alive?"

He laughed and pushed her legs apart and put his mouth to her vagina and sucked out the rest of his semen. Then, springing out of the pool, he flicked her lips with a kiss and went over to a water fountain and spat into the drain.

No man before or since had ever done anything like that. She'd never known anyone so unfazed, man or woman (not even Apolonia), by bodily secretions. He'd go down on her whether she was ovulating like mad or had her period. Anything human was of fascination to him. Everything connected. How one moment in time, one hard-won insight inevitably led to another, leading on to that undiscovered country that he kept firmly in view. How one discovery or observation always suggested another in an endless cycle of wonder.

Or as AP had once noted to her by her Jackson Hole fireplace: "You know, Jake would have made a great doctor's doctor. He was so curious, always so into what makes you tick, what was on your mind, how you felt. Everything that has the makings of a great bedside manner."

"What makes you tick as well, so it seems."

"I was taken, but you had the inside track, leading by a mile."

"Foolish girl . . . foolish girl," Gini sang in mock regret. But in that moment, by the crackling fire, she realized that Apolonia, given half a chance, would have traded in John Proctor for Jake, if only to break the fever of fear, the terrible damage that discovery of their affair would have brought down on her lover's head. A terror that had so darkened her college years.

She rose unsteadily, dazed, from her seat in the viewing gallery, knowing in her heart of hearts that yet more of that unfinished novel was yet to be plumbed, her fingers itching for the keys of her laptop—to tap into this alluring alternate universe: tantalizing, ripe with possibilities. Why not write about their college days? Why not have her heroine enlist Jake for the women's tour? She knew plenty enough about the early days of the women's professional tennis tour to write with authority. Why should Annette get all the benefits of Jake's tracking her husband's matches on tour?

She went to the double row of framed photos of swim teams of yore (prompted by Jacob's casual remark at the sign-in table) and, putting on her reading glasses, worked her way back to her freshman year. And there, clear as day, the face of one Jacob Burrage posed in the first row in his tight-fitting Speedo and tee shirt—the short-haired version so neatly mimicked by his son at sign-in—mirroring the threadbare remnants of her obstinate, incurious pride and a potentially revised story line. As if, once again, her perfectly edited life had been thrown into disarray, as her secret author closed one unfinished chapter, only to begin another.

CHAPTER 5

Apolonia found herself uneasily humming the last strains of Bach's cantata "Wie Schön Leuchtet der Morgenstern" as John's daughter prepared to take the pulpit and give her eulogy. Of more immediate concern was a rogue shaft of rose-tinted light from the poets' window relentlessly seeking her out in the back of the chapel, where she cowered beneath her straw sun hat. She berated herself for being such a shrinking violet—so unlike her assertive, take-charge self, John's "Morning Star," as he liked to call her—and not waltzing up to the front of the nave to add, at the very least, a note of color to the gray-suited denizens of the economics department, mostly ancient faculty huddled like a dovecote. Neil, John's bald-as-a-billiard-ball provost and friend, had long since passed on.

In the subsequent silence, a tall, heavyset woman dressed in somber gray silk wavered on the first step of the pulpit, dark hair twisted up neatly off the back of her neck, leaving a husband and older children in the first pew.

"I could be your daughter, John." How many times muttered in postcoital despair?

"A statistical anomaly—surely."

She toyed with removing her Reunions name badge—scarlet letter—just in case the daughter in the pulpit had telescopic vision, as that shaft of rose-colored light inched ever closer.

"My father loved this chapel, as he loved poetry"—and the daughter gestured upward to a resplendent window down the nave—"not because he was a believer—far from it—but because of its grandeur and connection to both the university's past and the past of European culture, an edifice that had served as the fountainhead for the transmittal of knowledge across time, the essential idea and ideal of the university."

Good God, she even had her father's cadences down, the way he canted his head and raised his eyebrows for emphasis, not unlike her Christopher.

"Why he loved the poets' window best, embodying in light the transmission of poetic inspiration from King David to Virgil to Dante, Shakespeare to Donne—and my favorites, Emily Dickinson and T. S. Eliot."

Apolonia shifted uneasily in her seat, wiping tears, her mind racing as she sought to channel again some of John's vital energy. "Now let us sport us while we may, and now, like amorous birds of prey . . ." She found herself needing to grip the back of the chair in front of her, lest she rise and shout out joyous praise, possessed by a phantasmagoric image: how they had been more like vultures tearing at each other's vitals, panting screams and groans, not unlike those that had flooded her head during an episode of postpartum psychosis after the birth of her first child, Christopher.

"His brilliance and humanity, champion of civil rights and affirmative action for women and minorities, his public life writ large in the lives of thousands of graduates and the splendid new science buildings dotting this campus—especially the life sciences, for which he was the essential champion and fund-raiser. There's not a single brick of new architecture on this campus built in the last thirty years that my father didn't have a hand in when it was on the drafting table."

Ain't that the truth, Apolonia thought as she found herself swept back to the soaring brick architraves of the Frari in Venice, as John had explained in stunning detail all the elements of Gothic architecture.

And what about his playfulness, irreverent laughter, his extravagant humor and off-color puns—good God, and his slow hands and easy touch.

Strangely, she found herself reminded of Gini's aghast face burning into hers, standing in that same chapel pulpit as class salutatorian, gesturing in John's direction where he sat dressed in splendid academic regalia (like a personage out of a Bellini portrait) as she referenced Dido's lament not once but three times: a queen, a demigod ditched at the last by her faithless Aeneas, another slut who'd wormed her way into the graces of a brilliant man and so paid the price.

Slut to MD: My Story. Perfect in today's tabloid climate, if not for Tandem Press, so Gini had once joked gathered around the blazing hearth during one of her Jackson

Hole ski vacations. The tell-all victim of a powerful man, who offered any number of times to divorce his wife and a lusterless, lustless marriage. How appropriate a tale for this newly enlightened age of female empowerment. What tantalizing details she could provide, from the color of his kitchen floor to the contents of his bathroom cabinet or the thread count of the sheets on their marital bed.

But the sex wasn't the true story, just the tip of the remembered iceberg. No, something else . . . a mind on fire.

Now the son took the place of the daughter in the pulpit, a stocky, well-built man with regular features, looking nothing—a frisson of relief washed over her—like his father, perhaps more of poor Betty Anne, already in his midfifties, almost a decade older than the age at which his father, a human dynamo, had bedded her at nineteen. The son stalled twice at the opening remarks of his eulogy, his voice breaking, wiping away tears.

Almost worse than Gini's relentless upbraiding or Bianca's big mouth and radar for illicit trysts between faculty and students had been Jake's nagging questions about her neglected sex life—and her refusal to ever admit the circumstances.

Jake sitting back from his desk: "I don't get it, AP; you've got guys parked around the block, hanging out at your stringing machine, even your own fan club during tennis matches cheering you on—even Gini doesn't have such a following. They worship the court you walk on. And you can't be a lesbian, even if there's a whiff of the tomboy about you."

"What kind of whiff—am I leaking engine oil?"

Had Jake known something, tipped off the provost?

"Unless, of course, AP, you're a chimera."

"A what?"

"Well, in mythology, a chimera was a lion, with the head of a goat protruding from its back, and a tail that ended with a snake's head. But with you . . . it's more like there's another life lurking behind the simmering smile and sexy nonchalance."

"Thanks, Jake, just the thing to help me pass orgo." She pointed out a newly framed black-and-white photo, a rather dour Marie Curie, to go along with his pantheon of Einstein and Johnny von Neumann, along with others above his desk.

"Gini kept asking me: Aren't there any great women scientists?"

"Listen, I'm just trying to pass organic chemistry here and get into med school."

"Did you by any chance have a twin brother?"

"Not that I know about, Jake. How about you?"

"You see, in biology, a chimera is an organism that has inherited not just genes from its mother and father, but also genetic material from either a male or female counterpart in the womb, where, like twins, they share the same placenta. This was first noticed in cows—freemartins they were called—which had sexual characteristics of both sexes and were infertile."

"Oh great, so now I'm a hermaphrodite."

"In humans, human chimeras, as they're known, sometimes have two blood types."

"Okay . . ."

"It's just your name, Apolonia—a lovely name, so rich in associations, don't get me wrong, but a male god nevertheless (fair-skinned, beardless, and hairless chest—a smooth man, like my namesake, Jacob, in the Bible) with powers of prophecy and healing—like you, an aspiring healer. And, of course, god of light and music; you do have a lovely voice as backup in the Shirelles. And considering his father, Zeus, and his twin, Artemis, goddess of the hunt, well, Apollo was a pretty nifty fellow around the ladies."

"My father named me after some dude in a famous Polish cavalry unit, the winged horseman. And, of course, he wanted a son." She tapped the photo of Marie Curie and crossed herself.

Jake persisted: "You *are* something of an enigma."

"Okay, let me get this straight: you're telling me I'm a clean-shaved lesbian, and I suppose—women athletes and all—me, Gini, Bianca, and Annette are a coven of dikes, and you're the little boy with his finger in . . . Well, where the hell is this going?"

"Apolonia, you just radiate sex appeal like a homing beacon. Where are your soul mates, your Olympian bedmates, your fraternity brothers, lovers of light and the wild fandango?"

"Are you coming on to me, Spaceman?"

"You don't need to hide in Gini's shadow, girl god; you have the power to make the ordinary come alive and resonate with the heavens, even if your math leaves something to be desired. Just wondering: Who's getting the benefit?"

"Speaking of benefits, how about tracking *my* matches? Then we'll see."

Bathed now in a shaft of rose-tinted light, "Benefits," she whispered, her heart beating faster as she recalled once again Jake's son at sign-in, sending a chill down her spine, something not right that she couldn't put into words, even as that face, so curious, so intent, omniscient, invoked elusive, possibly erotic memories long consigned to oblivion. So much so, she found herself fanning herself with the memorial service program while repeating under her breath, like a mantra, a prayer for the dead learned at the knee of her Catholic mother—"Eternal rest grant them, O Lord . . ." Praying that his kids were never clued in on the truth—whatever the truth, a truth that, had it gotten out, given the present day's increasingly poisonous political climate, might well have chewed a hole in the space-time continuum, and so put the kibosh on this splendid service, which might well have never been had they married.

Gini, being Gini, had probably put it best: "You're playing with Armageddon here—know it: for him, for you, for the Shirelles—and they'll run you out of Dodge long before they run him out."

John Proctor's son looked up from the pulpit: "Dad was so charming and attentive, taking me aside on my wedding day when I was too nervous to speak, and assuring me that everything would be all right, that we'd have a long and happy marriage just like him and Mom. He was so much more than just a great father; he was a life coach, a cheerleader, a comforter when our first child was born with Down syndrome."

"Dear God . . ." And she lowered her face into her hands.

"Well, look who's here," chirped Annette, standing in the chapel aisle, leaning into her husband's arm.

"How could I resist?" Apolonia blinked from under her sun hat. "I was just remembering your chapel wedding."

Matt laughed. "Yes, we heard the chapel bells, and it took us right back."

"To Venice, actually," interjected Annette. "A very special moment in the Scuola di San Giorgio—right, Matt?"

"What's with this pilgrimage thing—visiting the Carpaccios?" asked Apolonia, as if she was immune to such nostalgia.

"Saint Sebastian baptizing the Saracens . . . ," said Annette, her perfectly groomed blonde hair swishing her shoulders as she graciously smiled at the retreating mourners. "How sad, a grandson with Down syndrome."

"Here—there's a test for that now—come sit with me a moment." Apolonia indicated the seats on either side. "Bodyguards."

Annette's eyebrows crinkled sweetly as she sat and patted Apolonia's hand. "Do you remember? John Proctor gave such a nice toast at our wedding dinner—not a little in awe of Matt at the time."

"He was such a fan of women's tennis," said Matt.

"How could I forget?"

"He couldn't take his eyes off a certain bridesmaid," her husband laughed.

"Hey, a bridesmaid who felt like she'd been inducted into the tennis hall of fame."

"Gee willikers." Matt smiled nostalgically. "Bob and Clark and Arthur and I were still playing, hardly Hall of Famers yet."

"Well, you're in it now, dear, and still playing," said Annette, waving as one of the last mourners made his way down the aisle. "Matt's off to a workout with Art and the men's tennis team—an honorary member. And speaking of offspring: how are your two?"

"Christopher and Margie, still sous-chefing for their dad, still teaching skiing—the tennis gene never took, thank God." She patted Matt's knee. "And to think you had a friend and competitor like Arthur Ashe."

"I was praying for Arthur just now," said Matt, staring up at the glorious array of stained-glass windows lit by a westering sun. "Not a day goes by when I don't miss him."

"What was that song when we were kids . . . ?" inquired Apolonia. "The good die young."

"Yes, the Lord seems to take the best early," said Matt.

"Well, that explains why I'm headed for a ripe old age." Apolonia yawned, now eager to change the subject. "I'm exhausted, my hippocampus in overdrive."

"Hippocampus?" Annette's lips softened into her always endearing little pout.

"The part of our brain"—she could almost hear Jake's voice in hers—"that integrates all our five senses and forms memories. Why I'm kinda dreading your charity match tomorrow. Who needs to be shown up by our younger, better selves?"

"Oh," said Annette, "I've been soundly beaten by my kids for years. Art was beating Matt since the kiddo was sixteen."

"Hey," her husband said, quick to note, "try the pro tour, where, as each year goes by, you face more and more hungry young faces across the net."

"Yes," Annette said and nodded, "an ordeal by fire Gini couldn't face, no matter how much Jake bullied her."

Apolonia turned to her teammate: "Bullied, you think?"

Annette looked at her husband with an uncharacteristically flummoxed pinch of her eyebrows. "Odd, wasn't it, honey, how Jake's kid at sign-in seemed, besides being the spitting image, to be channeling his dad's—right word?—savoir faire. Like he just stepped out of the players' box at Wimbledon and wanted to debrief Matt."

"Uncanny," her husband added, staring up at the glorious light from the stained-glass window as if possibly seeking an inspired explanation. "Just a few minutes conversation and I felt that glorious summer season on tour fill my heart and soul. Like the kid cast a spell. I've been walking on air ever since."

"Matt and I were just saying how often during the tour that summer Jake liked to ease the conversation around to Gini."

Matt laughed. "The poor guy spent all his spare time watching the women's matches . . . dreaming of what might have been, I suppose."

"Remember, Matt, what he called her—what was it? The perfect phenotype for tennis."

Apolonia had to smile, recognizing the allusion, which now came to her with ease. "Yes, sounds just like him: a phenotype is the sum result of the interaction of a genotype with its environment, the observable features that distinguish it from all others."

"Yes, how did he put it, Matt? The beaver's flattened tail and sharp incisors are to the creation of lakes what Gini's forehand and serve is to a Wimbledon champion."

"There you go." He laughed, as if slightly amazed that his wife too had fallen under that same spell of geared-up memory. "I guess these days it's Roger Federer's backhand—a work of art."

Annette pressed a hand to Apolonia's shoulder as she rose to go: "Not that he ever offered to share his tracking system with the likes of us when he was working with Gini."

Alone now, as the chapel emptied, Apolonia—not a little under the spell of Jake's son—spent a few minutes more bathed in the tinted light from the stained-glass windows, seeing again the vast interior of the Frari in Venice—or no, perhaps the sacristy, where Bellini's Madonna and Child resided on an intimate altar (Mary's bereaved, tearful stare) as she listened intently to the voice of John Proctor explaining the history of the Renaissance triptych. Having just heard so much about the legacy of her onetime lover, she was prompted to wonder about hers (doctor to Jackson Hole's rich and famous), especially in the eyes of her classmates, her sister Shirelles. Would all her good works (her sabbaticals to Africa to treat the truly needy) be eclipsed by her one great folly: the woman who had been mistress to a Princeton president and lived to tell the tale. Or worse, dare she think it! How John's true legacy, his invisible legacy, resided in her and her alone: a Byronic energy summoning poetic insights into the unseen, the barely imagined, where past and present merged into a life of cosmic rapture. The same energy poured into fund-raising and the building out of the life sciences infrastructure to make Princeton a leader in a half-dozen fields.

CHAPTER 6

Bianca wasn't entirely sure where she was headed, or whether it was grief or resentment or possibly a jealous rage that consumed her: the way Gini, always Gini, prompted first by Annette and then Apolonia, had gone on and on about Jake's son, as if those three, abetted by Gareth, had a proprietary piece of the kid. When it was she—yes, she who had been there in Venice for Jake. Saved him—saved him from drowning in despair and disappointment at Gini's no-show. Not that she'd ever breathe a word—their thousand-day wager—much less take credit for throwing him a lifesaver.

That beautiful kid at sign-in, looking exactly like his father when she'd first discovered him sitting sad and dejected in the Scuola di San Giorgio, had her spooked. She took a deep breath, her life in playback mode, when every turning, every face reminded her of a stardom foregone, first at Princeton, then studying and playing concerts in Venice.

And her one unforgivable sin . . .

She stopped her wandering, her aimless cantering, looking up, sniffing the air as she caught sight of the quatrefoil windows (hijacked from a Venetian palazzo) of the art museum just ahead.

And irony of ironies: Why was it she had always acceded to the role of man-killer among the roommates? Who hadn't even liked Jake, who never resented his tracking of Gini's matches like Annette and Apolonia. Could she help it if her star power attracted men? Dreamy-eyed boys, artistic types more interested in a platonic love affair, even if she tended to brag to her roomies, exaggerate to keep pace with Gini and Apolonia.

What was it that had her more than a little freaked out? Something about that sweet, seemingly innocent but insouciant greeting of young Jacob at the sign-in table. The heart-stopping familiarity of his gaze, how his memory-softened, blue-green eyes burned into hers—that same kidding but tender voice, forever curious, intrepid, in the same way his dad liked to turn a phrase, turn a key, to explore a starburst of possible meanings in the most ordinary things.

And those eyes, a burnished blue mirroring hers.

Her tongue lolled against her long lips as her face lit up at the minty taste of orange lip gloss. She sensed a following wind energizing her long-limbed strides, her handsome Roman nose riding high and proud as she finally set course for the Woolworth music building (scene of so many first-concert triumphs).

She paused again, as if still needing to take her bearings; she could almost swear to the scent of brine in the air, of crumbling plaster on the cooling breeze, even the faint stink of cat piss. So conjuring in her mind the image of a high green door, slightly ajar, where, on the lintel above, two marble dolphins presided over the entrance to the Scuola di San Giorgio, which the last tolling changes of the chapel bell seemed to sear into memory. "Holy Mary, mother of God," she exclaimed, hearing the lapping of waves against the embankment of her tiny Corte Contarina, her home of three years off in the wilds of Castello, the echoing cry of a boatman—or was it her joyous scream when she'd thrown back the bedclothes upon waking, crossing herself, only to find her jetlagged lover fallen like Milton's Beelzebub from out of the blue, still on Stanford time.

"*Santa Maria, madre di Dio . . .*" She blew a parting kiss to the Gothic quatrefoils high up on the pink façade of the art museum, this looming evocation of the Ca' D'Oro further sealing her return to her glory days enrolled at the Scuola Antiqua for her doctorate. Not that she'd ever be so presumptuous as to affix "Dr." before her name: such the exclusive right of Apolonia. She'd immersed herself in Renaissance and seventeenth-century performance practice, even mastering the intricacies of period costumes and dialect. Days when the lagoon city had been plastered with handsome posters of her face, touting her starring performances at the Scuolas di San Rocco and San Giorgio, San Marco, and twice at La Fenice—with side gigs at

Florian! A reprise on steroids of her Princeton years when *she'd* been the heartbreaker among the roomies, the musical prodigy, founder of the Shirelles, while playing the number-four slot on the tennis team, the "Rosie Casals" who got no respect but who, more times than not, provided the decisive 4–3 winning margin (grinding out her three-setters) and saving the day. Just like she'd ended up saving that poor shipwrecked boy washed up on her shore at the Scuola di San Giorgio.

"Yes," she exclaimed, crossing herself as she left those glorious quatrefoil windows behind in her haste for the ivories. "It's all true, dear God. I swear it on my mother's grave."

The young man she remembered, hers and hers alone, just finishing up his Stanford PhD in record time, curious as a hungry lynx, and first drawn to the city's flora and fauna, its history of plagues and suffering, its eating habits (olive oil and fish), until its artistic treasures and their lovemaking finally shifted the balance of his imagination elsewhere.

"Aren't they spectacular?"

On that first day, they'd wandered like lost souls, barely able to say the obvious, loath to reference their time at Princeton just three years before (a thousand days), to touch on the painful truth, even as their hands occasionally jostled, as she dared grab his hand to lead him on to yet another of her favorite haunts. They'd gotten as far as the fish market at the Rialto when she'd had to halt their steps for a return to her apartment and a change of clothes for her concert that evening—just as his eyes had lit up like beacons at the zoology textbook on ice come to life.

"What? Oh, but they're so creepy—all those claws."

"Don't you just love the names: *stoccafisso, cappesante, cappelunghe, gambero rosso, scampi, seppioline* . . ." Jake's jetlagged face had turned to hers from a fish stall just off the Rialto Bridge.

"Ugh, you can have the squid. I'll stick with Charlie the tuna."

A smile lit up his face, the first smile of that first day.

"No, no, they're all so fascinating, to think they're our ancestors, when we were all swimming around in the Silurian sea."

"Silurian—oh, of course. I mean, like any good Roman, I'm more comfortable on dry land."

"Four hundred and forty million years ago, when the teleosts, ray-finned fish, evolved after the near-death extinction of the Ordovician freeze."

"Well, certainly nobody here I want to bring home to mother."

"No," and he'd smiled that winsome smile she so well remembered. "You've come a long way, baby." He'd kissed her gently, gratefully, on the cheek. "Thank you."

"For what?"

"For being here, now." He'd gestured to the icy stalls of the fishmongers and then to the broad sweep of the Grand Canal, lined with a cavalcade of palaces, and sighed. "Einstein would have loved this *now* because you can almost imagine it conforming with his objective sense that in physics, in space-time, there is no such thing as the present, neither past nor future."

"How can that be? Your pals on ice around here swimming around in ye old Silurian sea would surely object."

"Oh, even Einstein could be wrong. We have memory, our fabled subjectivity, to help us distinguish the gut experience of living inside time from the timeless nature of mathematics we use to describe it."

She sang out, channeling, Bob Hope's "Thanks For the Memories"—"sentimental verse, nothing in my purse . . ."

"Yes, and your Augustine . . ." He had tried to smile but, failing that, had been about to go on when she'd taken his hand and hurried them back to her tiny apartment to change for her concert date.

She glided safely into port at the Woolworth music center, upgraded since her student days with a new performance hall, a place ringing with past glories for a music-scholarship kid from Queens, even if that echo out of her past sounded a hollow ambivalence as well: the long-running bust of her music career. Thankfully assuaged by her prodigy of a son, her wildly talented Matteo, now on tap for the evening's festivities. She walked the halls and practice rooms, opening doors for a peek to see if any of her favorite pianos remained—not, alas, unhappy to find most of the department bigwigs of her day long retired and so relieved of the prospect of any uncomfortable chats. "Ah," she smiled, her wide-apart, gray-blue eyes finally lighting upon an old friend through the open door. She entered the practice room and settled herself on the nicely padded piano stool to take the familiar Steinway grand for a spin. Happy to laugh away recollections of inappropriate touching, casual fondling, ass-clutching hugs, and sloppy kisses from various instructors and professors, just as long as it stayed within bounds, just as long as her own agenda was inched forward.

Those were the days, her phenom days, when she was the best pianist on campus, with a hand size and reach to equal most of the guys, with a reputation as a loud-mouthed, tall, and rangy Italian American (often imitating her even louder-mouthed Sicilian grandmother from Agrigento) from a blue-collar enclave of Ozone Park, who talked fast and slangy, with a gift for gab, who, oddly enough, was turned off by romantic opera, to the despair of her blessed mother, an amateur singer who idolized Renata Scotto, and Transport Workers Union lawyer father who spent every Saturday afternoon listening to the Texaco opera broadcasts live from the Met. But an early love for Scarlatti and Vivaldi and later Mozart had buoyed her young life, so that by age nine she played the piano with a tenderness and nuance unusual for her age—a thing even odder in a tomboy addicted to tennis, who by sixteen had won almost every girls' tennis tournament in the city (six months younger than Gini and so having a year to herself at the top of the fourteens, sixteens, and eighteens-and-under), and then New York State in her age bracket, only lacking the funds to compete out of state and so get a national ranking like her archrival from the city, Ginistrella Wingate.

Maybe that had been her problem—piano and tennis: never enough hours in the day to practice both, even as she'd given up serious competition upon graduation, which had been like the amputation of a limb, woken from that dream state of moving on the court like a dancer on stage—that glorious opening of the body on the backhand, the thwack of the ball off the strings, when winning was simply a by-product of a deep aesthetic pleasure. She lacked Gini's killer instinct, Annette's relentless focus, Apolonia's street smarts and grit, in the end opting for the ovation of an intimate audience and the rhythmic drumming of her heart at the conclusion of a Mozart concerto as she stood to take her bows.

And by sophomore year, she had acquired yet another claim to campus fame as the lead singer for the Shirelles, with Gini, Apolonia, and Annette singing backup in uncanny renditions (her own arrangements) of the Motown group's greatest hits, "Will You Still Love Me Tomorrow" quickly becoming their theme song. On party weekends, when not off at away matches, the four roomies would perform their act at arch sings and eating clubs, further solidifying their friendship and camaraderie, marking her, in many admirers' eyes, for future fame, a fame that peaked in her Venice days, when the Italians adopted her as one of their own. When she was admired, even idolized, for her deep-souled beauty and spirited interpretation of the Baroque repertoire, if not for her broad expressive features, zaftig boobs, and long, red-tinged auburn hair, which she'd worn up high on her head to accent her supple neck and shoulders, angular cheekbones, and expressive mouth, especially when wearing her daring, low-cut performance gown of blood-red silk.

She smiled to herself as she finished playing her favorite Scarlatti sonata, the G minor, Kk. 8, with its poignant sense of resignation and loss, recalling the Viennese cadences of her thesis adviser senior year, Herr Braun (a Jewish refugee who'd escaped Hitler's clutches), who wrote all her recommendations to Juilliard, whose puffy fingers would beat time gently on her shoulder and somehow manage to stray to her thigh when the tempo needed a little picking up.

"*Mein Gott*, Bianca, you have zuch beautiful, zuch perfect long hands for the keyboard. Of course, a bit more width wouldn't hurt, but zuch strength and delicate touch. But these blisters on your right hand—are you sure, dear, playing tennis doesn't affect your dexterity or lead to muscle cramps? I hardly think you'd want to risk your feel and touch on the treble keys with the brutal physical exertions required by zuch a sport."

A legendary performer, a world-famous composer, whose long white hair and sensitive mouth were almost enough to excuse his occasional groping, who had landed her grants and scholarships to Juilliard and, later, the Scuola Antiqua in Venice; later still, he had connected her with Caspar Davidov, her first and only agent. But her playing of Scarlatti now was not to honor her onetime mentor, who had passed on two decades ago, but to raise the spirits of that young man in the first row as she played the upper chamber of the Scuola di San Giorgio, a jetlagged face streaked with tears, possibly consoling tears, healing tears, even on-the-rebound tears.

"Hey, Gini," she chided the Steinway at her fingertips, "bet you never brought tears to his eyes."

And again, she began the Scarlatti, closing her memory-softened eyes to that young boy's face at sign-in, as, with a slight jolt, the overnight train from Venice to Vienna began to depart: her appointment hastily arranged with a clinic of super Teutonic efficiency and discretion.

She let the notes fade beneath her fingers as she bowed her head to the keys, whispering: "*Perdonami, Padre, perché ho peccato.*"

Regaining her composure, she opened her eBag and took out a folded piece of paper, a color-copy enlargement of two manuscript pages displayed in Carpaccio's *Vision of Saint Augustine*, two sixteenth-century compositions, one a religious hymn, the other a secular tune (City of God, City of Man), which she now began to sing, accompanying herself on the piano, her contralto sometimes approaching the echoing quality of Gregorian chant, and so bringing again to life, as the green door swung wide, the damp glittering waterways of the sixteenth-century lagoon city. Scene after scene rose now before her, tinctured with the sweet scents of daybreak, freshly baked ciabatta and cappuccino, fresh roses in the flower seller's stall, damp plaster and brine . . . time's eternal tally. And there too, in the curious eyes of the aged Augustine turned to his window, and in the press of a hand in hers as they hurried back to her tiny room above the bakery in Corte Contarina.

CHAPTER 7

"He who is without sin among you . . ."

Annette, wandering, a little lost, her footsteps headed in the direction of Prospect Garden, found herself pondering the unfinished admonition left dangling from the lips of John Proctor's daughter moments before she'd slipped out of the pulpit—more an aside, hardly a judgment, or just possibly a half-humorous afterthought flung down the nave on the sly after her fulsome praise of all her father's good works. A hinted sarcasm, perhaps, that had seemingly gone right over Apolonia's head, given the careless nature of the conversation just ended and her slovenly attire. Even as this arrow shot in the air—knowing the good doctor only too well—had to have lodged itself like a nettle in her heartstrings. A daughter's farewell words that strangely echoed their new pastor's tirade against original sin just last Sunday at Amelia Island's Grace Episcopal Church. "Laureen, Laureen . . . ," she muttered. Cause of heated emails to the nomination committee, which in turn added to her anxieties over her son Arthur's early-morning email—without warning, without explanation, "pulling out of tomorrow's Athletes for Christ panel." For a flickering moment, as the cool shade of Prospect Garden beckoned, it felt like sin was everywhere on the prowl after that unsettling meeting with young Jacob Burrage, as if feigned insouciance was simply the devil's invisible cloak. A whispered call to the disinterment of long-buried transgressions.

Transgressions, pesky sins, which the stunning appearance of Jake's son had somehow blown back into life. Unlike her husband, who only had grateful memories of when Jake had joined them on tour, hers were of a different order, mostly heart-wrenching and, even with the distance of years, disturbing. It was not that she'd hated Jake; she'd just hated how he had Gini in erotic and intellectual thrall, had insinuated himself as her private coach, with a bull's-eye on her spot as the number-one player on the team. She respected Gini's tennis and smarts too much to be jealous of her, or Jake . . . but the third-rail temptation Jake embodied, even after her marriage, rankled her soul. Intellectual brilliance certainly had its attractions, given that Gini dismissed her as a lightweight Christian.

"Fortieth reunion," she muttered, to distract herself as if searching for some alternate source for her unease, half in disbelief that such a number could be pinned over her heart. Weren't the children of Israel compelled to wander in the wilderness for forty years after rebelling against Moses, who had fasted for forty days before descending with the stone tablets, doubting that the Promised Land could ever be theirs? And hadn't the rains poured down on Noah for forty days and forty nights to collectively punish humanity for its sins? "Forty years, dear Lord." Like any good Christian, she knew her sins to be manifold, envy of Gini and her career in publishing being the bugbear of the moment. The problem was to fully identify and then purge the little monsters.

Again, her thoughts gravitated to young Jacob at sign-in, speeding her back to when Jake had joined them in Paris at Roland-Garros in that glorious spring of 1980, when Matt had begun his meteoric rise in the rankings. Something too in Bianca's face across the table, that shifty, breathless unease when Big Mac was sitting on a piece of juicy gossip, just dying to hatch an earth-shattering revelation, whatever she needed to get off her big chest. Usually something to do with men.

And then there had been something Matt had said on the way over to the chapel: "Speaking of Venice, I was just thinking about when I called Jake from the phone booth at the Pensione Seguso."

"To ask him if he could take the summer off to join us on tour."

"I hadn't realized how much spadework you'd already done in Rome."

"Oh that . . . just to see if he might be available."

"He said something funny, something about: did I have to kick all the cats out of the phone booth."

"He said that?"

"Yeah, you remember how all the stray cats off the streets hid out in there?"

"It stunk."

"Turns out, he'd only recently stayed at the Seguso."

Ah . . . she thought as she fingered the shooting stars on the lapels of her class-reunion jacket as Bianca's sultry smile took on shape and substance in her mind. She tapped her name tag as if to make sure it was securely fastened—why had she never thought twice about taking her husband's name when all of her roomies had kept their maiden names?—while bathing her eyes in the approaching riot of color and scent, where the ancient guardians, those stalwart cedars and oaks, stood their solitary ground at the upper entrance to Prospect Garden, while beyond, on the downward slope of the gardens, casting bewitching shadows, a rampart of pointed firs made for an intimate setting. Breathing deeply, pursing her lips, she hoped to dismiss the low-level panic attack that in recent years had increasingly caught her unawares when confronted by her own inadequacies (a career of her own), her failures to do the right thing. And so-o unlike her feisty self, raised by a no-nonsense uber-mother, a national champion and tennis pro, who dismissed all excuses for failure.

"It's a competitive world, little orphan Annie. So you've just got to try that much harder."

Arching her back to gain as much height as possible, she turned for a reassuring look at the chapel's soaring towers. She should be relishing this hour on her own, out from under the shadow of a famous husband. Even now—she looked down—she wore his Adidas tennis sneakers with their distinctive green heel guard and name inscribed: an iconic retro brand sold worldwide. A celebrity shoe that she was contracted to wear on all public occasions, prompting a few skipped steps like the carefree child she suddenly recalled holding her father's hand—could it be?—fifty years ago. When her faith had set her apart as a schoolgirl, as an athlete, provided her with the edge to make it through the torturous seventies with her sanity and marriage intact.

Not without a little help from the devil himself, Jake Burrage. A scaley shiver slithered down her spine as she saw again the face of young Jacob at sign-in rise before her, that same discordant, flippant, all-knowing grin that had greeted them each morning on tour, as he presented his numbers crunched overnight, just daring you to contradict his pearls of wisdom—his "ten commandments"—contained within the pages of his creased, coffee-stained notebook.

"Going down the T on your serve, Matt, in either the deuce or add court, always gives you a winning percentage, since your opponent is often jammed and doesn't have the angle down the line on your first volley."

Once, just once, she'd asked Jake to kneel and pray with her—a favor, a gesture—in hopes of bolstering her troubled faith that she'd resorted to bringing an avowed atheist onto their team. They had been visiting Sainte-Chapelle, near their hotel on the right bank. The only time she'd ever seen a mildly flustered expression on Jake's face, eyes bathed in soft, transcendent tones, his voice nearly breaking.

"Faith, faith . . . well, sure. But I must tell you, my faith is in the numbers, what my eyes can see, what I can touch, what the algorithms tell me. A faith a lot less dangerous to the soul than the faith-based ideologies that have hardened into killing machines."

"Faith created this, Jake, this, this—God's gift of light and color."

That had been during the early rounds of Roland-Garros, early days, very close matches, when Matt just managed to reach the round of sixteen as he began to adapt to Jake's system. When Matt and Jake became best pals. When Matt began looking to Jake for guidance in all things. And she a mere appendage.

She scowled in self-chastisement, muttering: "Little girl—you competitive bitch, overly competitive, eternally competitive. Okay: comes with the territory."

"Little orphan Annie . . ." Her mother's withering scorn. "Get a grip, young lady," yelled while smashing tennis balls at her daughter where she cowered at the net. "You play through the pain of Eve's curse; run off the cramps—God doesn't give us any more pain than we can endure."

One thing she'd learned at her mother's knee during Bible study was that everything in life was predestined, just like Christ's ministry and teaching, death and resurrection were foreshadowed by Isaiah in the Old Testament. The faithful, as her mother always said, just had to keep their eyes peeled for portents along the path: "Young lady, you grab that main chance."

She worked her right arm, a touch of tennis elbow from her increased workouts (not that she'd ever admit it) in preparation for the charity match tomorrow.

Perhaps her jitters were much ado about nothing, just Reunions jitters. Maybe she was simply unused to having more time to herself as each of her homeschooled kids had fled the nest, busy wife to the director of the Amelia Island Tennis Academy, consumed by her charities and church boards. "Laureen," she groaned, feeling the iPhone in her jacket pocket vibrate with more emails and texts of protest about their new pastor's recent tirade against the "male dominance hierarchy." Well, it wasn't her vote on the nominating committee that provided the margin. Laureen, who had preached a radical attack on both Saints Paul and Augustine and how these "spiritual brainiacs" had foisted the doctrine of original sin on the shoulders of womankind. "Like it's our fault, Eve's fault, always our fault—right, sisters?"

"The Lord be praised . . ." At least Arthur wasn't around to hear that. While her increasingly apathetic husband, who now mostly slept through early-morning services, had shot her his wicked smile and shrugged the whole thing off: "Dear, hoisted by your own petard . . ."

Maybe that was why she hadn't shared Arthur's email with his dad, who had left her to go off and hit with his son and the men's team at a Reunions get-together. She'd always prided herself on never inflicting her faith on the kids, choosing to simply set an example in her own life, a life bathed in the love and sacrifice of Jesus. Just as she'd said not a word when Arthur had foregone a chance to play the pro tour for an offer from Goldman Sachs. Like Gini, maybe he had made the smart move, certainly financially. The pros were ten times tougher now than in their day. And her dad, as Arthur never stopped reminding her, had been a financier with a seat on the New York Stock Exchange. Her dad, a sweet, loving, if sarcastic soul now recalled by the white rhododendrons couched in glossy green along the garden path, which had grown in profusion in her childhood home of Oyster Bay. A serene smile edged up her pensive lips as she recalled her father, class of '36, marching in his orange-striped jacket in the P-rade, tiger tail attached, followed by his three daughters, each holding the tail of the one in front, who had never failed to encourage her tennis since age four when she'd first picked up a racquet. "Why I married my tennis pro," he always liked to tell his cronies as his daughters won every junior tournament in the mid-Atlantic and New England, where she'd first clashed with Gini. She nodded her sun-bleached face to a cooling breeze just filtering through the line of stately firs parading the southernmost perimeter of the garden. Promise of low humidity for tomorrow's charity match.

"Dear Lord . . . ," she said and bowed her head. A mother, two younger sisters (who didn't make it into Princeton and were coaching women's college teams), a husband, a son . . . so many lives sacrificed to the game they'd made a living by.

Or perhaps her lingering discontent had more to do with the look on Gini's face when it had slipped out over lunch that Matt had hired Jake to track his matches over that long-ago summer of 1980, Roland-Garros to Flushing Meadows. Well, hardly a lie; at worst, a sin of omission. A white lie. An innocuous sin (to spare the afflicted of heart), the specifics of which Laureen had spelled out in her sermon even as she disparaged the patriarchal sexist theology behind that monstrous disaster of original sin. Something—the sins of others—that, as team captain, mother, and wife, she'd always prided herself on not condemning outright. Always resisting stirring up old hurts, ruffling feathers. It had been her policy to accent the positive, believe the best of people, and steer her family away from criticizing competitors, a hardened shell she'd had to develop over donkey's years cheering from the players' box (pros acting like spoiled brats, the McEnroe thing). And then there had been the interminable weekends and afternoons spent carpooling her kids to tournaments (when cheating on line calls was rampant), flying up from Amelia Island to watch Arthur play while still homeschooling the rest of her brood. Something, she knew—if secretly, behind her back—that Gini, Apolonia, and Bianca rolled their disapproving eyes at: selling out her life and career to concentrate on her husband's career, while bringing up good Christian children. Barely disguising their vague embarrassment at such self-sacrifice (the steely cross of Miss Goody Two-Shoes). Even if, to her face, they'd go on and on, oohing and aahing about her celebrity life, twice invited to sit with Lady Diana in the royal box at Wimbledon, married to a onetime world's number one.

Overheard more than once through the paper-thin walls of their dorm room: "Just imagine the children she'll produce married to Matt Collins." "Yeah, and if she's lucky, they'll get his height as well."

If only they knew . . . She sighed as she walked the winding gravel paths of Prospect Garden, trying to identify the more exotic "denizens" (Jake's expression) as a way of distracting herself from Gini's accusing glance at lunch when Matt had let the cat out of the bag.

She smiled. "Cats out of the Seguso phone booth."

Yes, Jake had been different (the haircut certainly helped) when he'd arrived in Paris, eager to get to work but somehow chastened, down-in-the-mouth—still not over Gini, which, so she and Matt had figured, constituted the first real failure in his life. Something had changed—"evolved," in his parlance. Content to join her in their few spare hours off from the tournament to visit churches, the Musée de Cluny, and the Louvre, where they'd tracked down Carpaccio's *The Sermon of Saint Stephen*. Even with a biochemistry PhD now in his pocket, he displayed more and more interest in art, referencing literary texts in his conversation: the all-around Princeton guy Gini had tried to mold in her own image.

"Matt is Starbuck to Borg's Ahab. We've got to give him a plan, a default pattern that's statistically sound to counter the kid's monomania and the clones coming up in his wake."

She could hardly be accused of betraying Gini in doing everything in her power to support her husband.

Just as Laureen had justified Eve's transgression.

"Didn't Eve have the right—asserting her agency and so partaking of the tree of knowledge—right, ladies? Far from betraying Adam—pissing off the Almighty—she was only demanding what any woman should expect: the right to choose what's best for her own mind and body—and yes, to find pleasure in the act of sex, not just a vessel for sin-spinning procreation."

"Pleasure . . ." A searing image came to mind: long ago, woken by Gini's interminable moans of ecstasy at two a.m. and heading to the bathroom in their suite, when she'd run into a stark-naked Jake headed the same way: Jake sporting a full erection! Who, instead of covering himself or turning away, had, satyr-like, grinned and bowed and waved her on—"Ladies first is my motto." It was the first she'd ever witnessed such a thing before her marriage.

"Sin!"—who was Gini to talk, given her scandalous behavior in Prospect Garden? "Prospecting," and she grinned while pondering the ropey bronze flanks of a flute-playing Pan, centerpiece of the spouting fountain around which the garden paths wove their floral tapestry. And if anything, Apolonia and Bianca's sexual shenanigans were even worse—not that she'd ever condemn them. And to give Gini her due, she'd remained faithful to Jake for three whole years—and why not, given the added benefit of Jake's tracking and coaching as she relentlessly tried to knock her out of the number-one spot. Only to cruelly dump Jake on the one-yard line, along with her chance to make it on the WTA tour. Unforgiveable, really—with all her God-given talent, that steely, insane hard-heartedness at Gini's core.

Well, at least Gini knew how to dress properly, unlike Apolonia at the memorial service. Gini, who, consciously or not, had always tried to undermine her faith in their student days, what with her repeated, if absurd, claims that Seneca could just as easily have written Jesus's pastoral ethics in the Gospels.

None of them had any inkling of what it was like to accept God's plan in your life, to feel His love in your heart and so direct your life in the fulfillment of His glory, whether being a stay-at-home mom, endlessly raising money for the church and its various local charities, much less standing by your husband from the first years of marriage as his ranking relentlessly plummeted, month after month, year after year (except for that one miraculous summer when Jake Burrage joined them on tour). Even when it meant forever toasting away in the stands, relegated to the sidelines, rooting for another's performance: tennis wife, tennis mother . . . tennis widow.

She breathed deeply of the scented air as she strolled the garden paths, as if some fragile serenity might yet be returned if only by giving name to the exotic array of blossoms everywhere on display. Even atheistic Jake, in his manner, had an ethical compass: "naming the world," was how he put it. "By giving the flowers names we truly bring ourselves into existence." Jake, who would have been able to identify every last petal, anther, and stigma, just as he had when they'd walked through the Wimbledon gardens while waiting for Matt's post-match press conferences to end.

"These denizens have us at their beck and call—not we them. By putting on such brilliant finery and wearing their finest Lanvin, they invite us to their garden party." Jake had glanced around the gardens of the All England Club and snapped off a yellow rose and handed it to her. "That which we call a rose by any other name would smell as sweet."

She paused, brows compressed, as those audacious eyes of so many years before merged with young Jacob's piercing eyes at the sign-in table. "And folks, don't forget to check out Prospect Garden—spectacular as ever."

And thoughtless Apolonia—the nerve to attend that memorial service dressed like a tennis slut, when her lack of self-control, then as now, might well have shattered the afterimage of a marriage, desecrated the memories of a grieving family, brought down the condemnation of an entire university community on the tennis team she'd once led to four Ivy titles! Even Laureen had kept adultery in the necessary-sin category to protect the family. John Proctor's daughter had probably recognized Apolonia under that stupid straw hat. A doctor, no less—a home-breaker. Not that she'd ever accuse AP of such a thing. For four long years—and forty more—she'd kept her silence over the goings-on of her roomies, celebrating their questionable marriages, their poor choices. Just as she had as team captain, only drawing the line at drinking and late-night sex before a match.

And God only knows what Arthur was getting up to, wining and dining Goldman clients at the Four Seasons, playing golf in Palm Springs, and skiing at Jackson Hole. A mother could only do so much.

She bent her face and pulled down a spray of purple-blue lilacs ("California lilacs . . ." so there), the perfume a liquid balm to her soul, bringing a smile to her face as she nodded at passing reunion goers in their gaudy attire, one proud father with a newborn in a bright orange snuggly bending low so his child might smell the flowers. How lovely to be a nondescript older woman, safe in her anonymity, no second glances by complete strangers—those of a certain age, who recognized her tall, blond husband: familiar face, TV—the taller of the Smothers Brothers perhaps—("Aren't you famous?"). Some still insisting on autographs, but most these days just asking to pose for a selfie.

Oh, the luxury of compassing her own simple soul! To reprise her student days blissfully free of doubt, when the strength of the Lord had allowed her to beat all those she should beat and only fall short when her opponent was the better player. The faith that had allowed her to hold her own against Gini—never losing twice in a row and so toppled from her number-one spot . . . even if Gini had all the size advantage and the raw physical talent, her Stoic pretensions. "Seneca, my ass." And Jake's tracking to give her the edge. Gini, who was going to write that first novel about the early days of the women's professional tour, who'd promised to include accolades about her teammates, thinly disguised characters, and so immortalize their student years. Abandoned, just the way she'd abandoned Jake due to her bloody-minded pride.

And again, she found herself frozen in her tracks by that dagger's edge in Gini's accusing glance over the luncheon table, as if a jackdaw had rummaged her purse. Okay, perhaps there'd once been a time when she'd been a tad jealous of how Jake had favored Gini exclusively, unwilling to share his tracking system with anyone else (bogusly claiming that he could only focus on one player at a time), when Gini's improved performance placed her in the crosshairs. But all that had nothing to do with her phone call from Rome, pleading (her husband would be too proud) with Jake to take off that summer between Stanford and his Chicago postdoc to work with Matt. Galling too, when Jake, like Gini, was such a godless pagan at heart. Maybe that was what she'd immediately recognized in young Jacob's face at the sign-in desk, that same intolerant, slippery brilliance—admittedly enticing, a kind of airy agnostic canniness, yet full of absolute certainty when in furious pursuit of the prize: that science and the numbers would rule that future City of Man.

"My faith"—and he'd waved on that long-ago day bathed in the light from the resplendent stained-glass windows of Sainte-Chapelle—"is in the data—the hard facts to the exclusion of superstition; the muddy vesture of this world as it is, not the transcendent, forever disregarding the conclusions of reproducible research." And he'd taken her hand. "Even God has to do the math."

And yet it had worked, as if, like some sorcerer's apprentice, he'd thrown that cloak of a pagan dream around their marriage, catching them in his net and drawing them into the crucible of his new order. It had nothing to do with getting back at Gini, as her husband had more than once suggested: she'd been at her wits' end after Matt's terrible loss in the first round of the Italian Open to an Argentinian teenager. For two days, Matt could barely rise from his bed at the Rome Hilton, his nerves shattered, his faith in himself, his God, his marriage: gone.

"I'm not exactly free. I've committed to lab jobs over the summer. Journal articles to write up. And I'm still a penniless student." There had been a long pause on the overseas line. "On the other hand, I've been tinkering with my tracking system ever since Gini." Another pause. "And the opportunity to work with a player of Matt's stature—what does he think of the idea?"

"He'd be thrilled!"

An outright lie, even if it hadn't taken much convincing to bring Matt around once she'd steered her husband off to Venice to get him away from the tour for a few days. A second honeymoon, a second chance.

Yes, that was the thing she'd seen in the face of young Jacob—the superiority of a life where every instinct had led to success, where ambition had chalked up every prize going. She couldn't help wondering what that brave new world looked like from such a pinnacle of scientific accomplishment. From the uplands of research into reinvention and rebirth, the banishing of disease and infirmity (how he'd endlessly gone about such things in the players' box): that misbegotten conviction in the perfectibility of man, of some eternal life in the here and now. A kind of glittering reprise of those glorious months shimmering on in that young man's face—May through August, Paris to London to New York, only faltering in a five-set loss in the quarterfinals of the US Open.

"Dear God"—remembering how she'd immediately slipped that pilfered yellow rose at Wimbledon into her bag (partner in crime)—"Annette, you're losing your mind."

Yes, a small sacrifice to false gods, now common as ditchwater, that had allowed them a winning season and a way back to a sustaining faith and enduring marriage. Putting her in mind of Christ's plea in Gethsemane, his sadness and fear as he asked the Lord to let this cup pass from his lips. Facing the abyss, as she had too, kneeling by the window of their hotel room in Rome, high above the ancient city where Peter and Paul had been martyred, her prayer had been answered. She'd heard a voice, a man's voice, soft and scholarly and urbane, speaking Italian or Latin, she wasn't sure which, when the face of Carpaccio's Augustine had come to her—Gini's Carpaccio, as it had hung on the wall of their suite over all four years, prompting a memory of how the Shirelles, returning from a party near graduation, had once proclaimed their everlasting solidarity, a pledge to be confirmed by a visit to Venice and the Carpaccios. And in that moment in Rome, that drunken pledge of years before reverberating in her ears, she had sensed another's voice in hers. If not Augustine's, then Jake's: the chance of redemption. God's little miracle come to her in a vision through a window.

Perhaps it was something of that selfsame miracle she'd witnessed at the sign-in table, a hint of that ancient pagan magic now touched with a literary flair—a recrudescence in Jake's son, old wine into new. Children. And just maybe her own son, Arthur, who seemed to be going through a rough patch, a crisis of faith, could use some of Jake's magic. Whatever it takes. We're only human. And if need be, she'd take over at the Athletes for Christ forum tomorrow and knock 'em dead, even if flying on the fumes of a once-youthful ardor, just as she'd taken a leap of faith to suggest to her congregation that their new minister should be a woman—that they must move with the times (not that she was in any way a radical feminist).

And hadn't Laureen shaken things up in a good way (not unlike Jake), preaching that digging deep into the Bible's message—testing their faith—was the best way to strengthen that faith: "Chip away at the old paint, rub mightily with solvents, and see what might be hiding below the surface." Even if last Sunday she'd lowered the boom on original sin—a "typically" perverse male obsession. Laureen's entering wedge was to undermine the very Gospels she sought to extol, especially the accounts touching on the nature of Christ, as if the demolition job on the foundations of their faith was the only way to lay waste to that all-male preserve of white privilege.

"Notice, ladies, how the Gospel accounts on the nature of Christ are so different from those of Paul: worlds apart. How can we trust Paul on Christ's nature when he'd never met our Savior, even if we accept the encounter on the road to Damascus? Is Paul's identification of Christ with God definitive, laying the groundwork for Augustine's Trinity? None of the Gospels go that far."

Annette paused on the gravel path as she neared the looming line of tall firs, where a wall of pink rhododendron blossoms enticed her eye, seeing again their young minister's impassioned eyes, the color up in her broad cheeks, fresh out of New York Theological Seminary, sweeping back a lock of her golden hair as she reached out to her congregation and then placed her hands over an ample bosom.

"Can we take on board—take to heart—the manifold inconsistencies in the New Testament and simply accept them for what they are: God's words passed down in an oral tradition for at least the first hundred years after the death of Christ, and so naturally prone to such inconsistencies—as the epics of Homer display inconsistencies emerging from an epic tradition of oral poetry? When a close analysis of Paul's letters and writings leads us to conclude that seven out of fourteen are problematic: not written by Paul at all, who would have been steeped in both a Hebraic tradition and Greek philosophy. And don't forget, in Paul's time, the pagan gods were still dangerously active in daily life and worship. Zeus often appeared in the guise of a human or animal, to have his ways with mortal women, while the Emperor Augustus had only recently been proclaimed a god by the Roman Senate. Even our fellow believers in the Old Testament God, those of the Hebrew faith, have plenty of examples of divine personages come to earth, angels and spirits and other godlike intermediaries between man and God. And don't forget, Jacob wrestling with his angel . . . is not Jacob an example for all of us?"

Laureen had paused for dramatic effect and to make eye contact with her congregation, who were stirring uneasily in their seats.

"Who here has not had to wrestle with their better angels?" She nodded knowingly. "How we like to pride ourselves on our New Testament God, who is so-o unlike His spiteful, grumpy, curmudgeonly, and vengeful Old Testament self: a God full of light and love and forgiveness. But a close reading finds that it isn't always so. Just as the nature of Christ is open to interpretation: as God is God, a Holy Spirit, or Son of God (and don't forget the Trinity is found nowhere in the Bible). That was mostly Augustine's doing—taking Paul's lead, not to mention the good saint's notion of original sin passed down the generations from mother to child. Good Lord, ladies: Are we to be accused of giving birth to sin? So"—and Laureen had bent forward over the pulpit with glittering blue-green eyes to hammer home her point—"do we go by the Gospels, or Paul—both so reverential to the powers that be of the Roman Empire—supporting slavery, and so rife with anti-Semitism—or opt whole hog for Augustine, who, like his brethren Jerome and, later, Aquinas—all had their hidden agendas for which the notion of original sin fitted their playbook: the pursuit of power and the subservient status of women. Yes, male dominion. Just as the Gospels render all earthly power unto Caesar. I don't know about you, ladies—if Augustine ever had to carry a life to term and give birth, hold that precious life of your body in his arms, he'd think twice about taking up Paul's notion that we are born with a sinful nature. An original sin passed down from Adam and conceived by Eve in her thirst for knowledge—in the very act of conception, mind you—an act that is one of the greatest blessings for a woman, in which she partakes in the energy of the universe."

"Wrestle . . . ," sighed Annette, reaching out to the labial splendor of a saffron-gold rose with pink-tipped petals, nodding in agreement from a rigid stalk of razor-sharp thorns. Reprising Gini's flushed cheeks and flicker of panic and confusion across the luncheon table.

Spying a shaded corner of the garden, she wandered over to a bench beneath the drooping boughs of the firs, there to catch her breath, a repose for a galloping mind and Laureen's disconcerting pleas, even as she found herself confronted again with scores of nameless blossoms, as once upon a time, long ago, when Jake had taken her hand tenderly in his as he conducted her around the gardens of the All England Tennis Club (while her husband was being interviewed by the BBC after his loss in the quarters), when he proceeded to bestow names to flower after flower, like Merlin, calling each into life—as if to old friends to do his bidding.

"So, my friends, ladies, I leave you with this: like Jacob, who wrestled with his angel all through the livelong night, I hope you might want to do the same: wrestle with your faith as Jacob wrestled with his—his God—and wake up on the morrow to a new life."

"Oh, Jacob . . . ," she echoed (pierced to her soul by that young man's eyes). "Yes . . . energy of the universe." Startled by her outburst, she glanced guiltily around, relieved to find above the nameless panoply of rapturous color those chapel towers, just where she knew they would be.

CHAPTER 8

Gini knocked on her daughter's door. Finding it ajar, she tentatively—"Hello . . . it's Mom"—let herself in, carrying Erma's graduation dress in a Bergdorf garment bag, a stunning Akris sleeveless zip-front and seamed A-line number in dark blue that could easily pass for black, especially if highlighted with an orange scarf or even a tiger broach (she just so happened to have an extra). Perfect length to show off Erma's long legs and gorgeous figure. Her mother, a smile of nostalgia easing up her lips as she surveyed the cozy single room, laid the garment bag down on the window seat and glanced out the bay window at the familiar view, a quiet, grassy quad with its blooming dogwoods and lavender wisteria. How was it that she was only now visiting her daughter's room for the first time? "Ah . . ." She began a thoughtful tapping of the leaded glass as if those lemony-blushing dogwood blossoms might lend themselves to a tally. Of course, she'd been at a trade fair in Milan last September, and so Erma must have driven down and settled herself. Not that Erma had ever invited her to come by. And she'd been down for the Yale game and at least two swim meets that she could remember, if just for an hour or so to watch Erma dive. Disguised beneath a cap, manuscript open in her lap, tucked into the back row of the viewing gallery. (Erma always claimed her mother made her too nervous, spoiling her performance.)

It had been such an exhausting spring season of tight deadlines: but a banner start to the new year for her best-selling authors. If there was one thing she'd learned as CEO: delegating too much authority spelled disaster. Her reputation, like her father's before her, had been made by attention to detail; speaking of which, she turned to the unmade bed with storage bins beneath and sniffed the air as if for the telltale scent of any recent male presence. She then turned an admiring eye to the chestnut paneling and Erma's book-piled desk, where photos of her father—father and daughter sailing in regattas—took pride of place. She picked up one of the dusty, plastic-framed snapshots (convinced she'd taken the photo), her lips quivering as she inspected her late husband's intelligent face, thinning hair pasted back from sea spray, in matching yellow slickers. Holding his daughter close at the tiller. A science kid like her dad (who had edited science books for Tandem Press), an introvert too, happiest bird-watching in Riverside Park, hunting for shells and sea glass at West Chop, or curled up in a chair with the latest book on evolution or the new-new thing in genetics research.

She fished in her saddlebag for some spray lens cleaner and a couple of tissues, and proceeded to wipe down the photos and return them to the desk.

"Hey, Jake, she might as well have been yours."

Aghast that such an insane confession had escaped her lips, she flicked away a stray tear and shook her head, remembering how, even as a young girl, Erma had been so fascinated with living creatures. While little boys her age had their dinosaur toys and Batman action figures, Erma would be collecting specimens on the beach off the Vineyard's Lake Tashmoo. Like her horseshoe crab, Black Beauty, flipping it over to inspect its underside teeming with scaly little legs like something out of *Aliens* (how Erma totally identified with Sigourney Weaver's Ripley), insisting on taking it home as a pet, where it had lived in a child's blow-up pool that long-ago summer, as Erma, pail in hand, headed down to the beach each morning to bring up fresh seawater, worms, and mollusks to feed her living fossil.

"Dinosaurs," she intoned, looking up, as if trying to bring into focus something hovering just on the edge of her peripheral vision.

How many past Reunions, with Bill and Erma in tow, had her roommates cast skeptical or intrigued glances her way? Thinking, no doubt: she's married a man with Jake's brilliance without the alpha apex predator baggage. "Hey, she's got her father's brains, with all of Bill's scholarly apparatus and attention to the significant detail—just what a young woman needs today." Apolonia and Bianca could barely contain the ironic edge in their comments, while Annette just smiled that secret, faith-filled smile. "Listen, sisters, Erma and her kind will inherit the future; trust me, the humanities are dying." This cynical pose, something her Stoic resignation required, barely disguised Gini's secret pride in marrying Bill Cheshire, a Harvard physics major who gave up academia at twenty-eight when he didn't get tenure at Penn, becoming one of the top science editors in the business. Yes, of course she missed Bill, who always attended Princeton Reunions with his typical grace and humor, who'd be so proud of his daughter, especially now she was headed to Harvard, his alma mater, for graduate work in biophysics. Or was it biochemistry?

Studying the photos once again, she couldn't resist rearranging them in chronological order, the father-daughter team sailing their Vineyard 15 and winning the Edgartown regatta four straight years. And while she was at it, she straightened up the books on the desk as well, happy to find, mixed in with the biology and physics texts, well-thumbed copies of Shakespeare's plays and Penguin classic editions of *Middlemarch* and *The Wings of the Dove*. "No wonder the girl has no time." This possessive exclamation, as if to justify her prying eyes, had the odd effect of spinning her on her heels as if caught snooping, where, mystified, she discovered her four Carpaccios—reproductions from the Scuola di San Giorgio degli Schiavone—hanging over Erma's sofa.

"What the . . . ?" she sputtered, disconcerted, as she crossed the room to the handsomely framed Carpaccios, her face burning with bemused mystification to explain the presence of these familiar scenes out of the lives of Saints Augustine, Jerome, and George. Yet another Reunions ambush whisking her first back to college days, when the Carpaccios had been the centerpiece in their suite, then to her adolescent bedroom overlooking West End Avenue, and finally to those very first moments of discovery—the electrifying viewing of the originals in hand with her father, who had taken her to Venice when she was seventeen. She had to steady herself on the back of the ratty couch as she began an inspection of the images, while multiple layers of memory ferociously jostled in her mind—palimpsest merging with palimpsest as she raised a tentative hand to the glass and the face of Carpaccio's Saint Augustine turned to the window of his study.

"So," she began, tapping the picture glass, hoping to calm a racing heart, "there you are, old man, still seated at your desk, pen still poised as if something has caught your attention beyond that window." The pensive sound of her own voice did little to help settle her rattled mind. What mystery had so enchanted her? That omniscient bearded face, the rapt expression, the scholarly apparatus so tantalizingly displayed—everything bathed in an ineffable crystalline light? The jewel-like colors? What was the secret elixir that had stolen her heart at seventeen and set her on her present path: if not quite the writer of books, at least their scholarly editor? Now transformed into the embodiment of memory instead of a future foretold.

A wistful smile as a fingertip sought out a red-figure vase: "Thou still unravish'd bride of quietness."

Her fingers slid across the glass. Perhaps, like her daughter, she'd been charmed less by Keats and more by the cute little German spitz seated on the floor by his master, echoing Augustine's rapt stare in its eagerness for a walk.

She backed away, letting her reflection in the picture glass dissolve in and out of view, as if tempting her limbo self with her real.

"Yes, yes, I was seventeen that summer, ranked eleventh in the country in the eighteen and unders. And higher if only . . ."

For a moment, her spirits soared, latching on to this rediscovery of the Carpaccios (hidden away in her basement storage locker, where they must've been dug out by her daughter without any maternal prompting) as heralding the beginning of a new mother-daughter chapter. Exactly as had been the case with her own father, who, on that first morning of their arrival in Venice, the very first thing, had, like Virgil, guided her through the endless labyrinthian streets until, crossing a final bridge, they had arrived at those mysterious green doors in a crumbling marble façade, where two dolphins, tail to tail, presided as tutelary guardians above the lintel. Her father had remained unusually quiet on the flight over: no lectures, no explanations—nothing to prepare her. He had paid their entrance fee to an old bald-headed man who had taken the dirty lira notes and parted the heavy velvet curtains, ushering them from overcast sunlight into a shadowy oratory. A moment later, a switch was thrown, and the room came ablaze, the dazzling Carpaccios lit up at shoulder height on the surrounding walls. She had been captivated, speechless, as if entering upon some exotic realm of the senses, assaulted everywhere by the colorful details of these enchanted, ageless chronicles.

For each of the next five days of their stay, she'd insisted on revisiting the scuola and then sought out a bookseller her father knew who stocked high-quality reproductions of Venetian artworks, where she picked out four of the Carpaccios, carefully rolling them up and placing them in a cardboard tube for the flight back to New York. She'd spent almost a year's worth of her allowance to have them beautifully framed in dark oak moldings and hung in her bedroom.

"And now, here they are," she marveled, transfixed by a sense of familial continuity.

After all, hadn't she reprised that trip to Venice on Erma's sixteenth birthday, the year after Bill had died of pancreatic cancer, a chance to be mother and daughter once more, to get away from the tragedy and the fraught issues that had plagued Erma's adolescent years?

So maybe the trip had indeed paid off, even if Erma hadn't seemed to show a flicker of interest in the Carpaccios at the time (well, maybe Saint George and his dragon . . . and Jerome with his lion).

She nodded at these good omens—"critters"—and again reached a hand to the glass and the return of her vague reflection in limbo.

Freshman year, she had planned to hang the four Carpaccios in her bedroom, but as soon as her roomies had caught wind of them, they insisted the pictures be hung in the common area of the suite.

"We need more class," proclaimed Apolonia, from where she stood by her stringing machine.

"Tennis posters will hardly bring the guys running," Bianca added.

"Saint George slaying the dragon will certainly bring the boys running," said Annette.

"You mean coming," Bianca leered, her eyes narrowing.

She had been more than pleased to find her good taste (and breeding) elevated to pride of place on the walls of their suite. How the Carpaccios had in time become touchstones of their friendship and rivalry, each of the women drawn to a favorite: Annette to Saint George baptizing the Saracens; Apolonia to Saint George slaying the dragon; Bianca to the scene where Saint Jerome leads his obedient lion into a monastery, causing the monks to flee in all directions; while Gini remained forever entranced by the *Vision of Saint Augustine*, as she had on that first day with her father. Epitomizing some unspoken literary bond between father and daughter: the ideal of scholarly remove, of bookish hauteur, of rich traditions echoing between the lines of closely scrutinized texts. (And Venice, which, by the end of the fifteenth century, had become a center of book printing, with nearly four hundred presses. The finest, the Aldine Press, was headed by Aldus Manutius, a Greek and Latin scholar who originated the smaller, compact, and cheaper book for a mass audience. Her father had kept an etched portrait of Aldus over his office desk, as did his daughter.)

Over four years, the Carpaccios found their way into many of the roommates' most private moments, often subjects of delicious discussion with their boyfriends, bywords for aesthetic taste among the chosen, bespeaking an exotic destination for the well-traveled and intellectually adventurous, which, by the end of junior year, had prompted elaborate plans to visit Venice together: a girls' holiday, shopping for leather goods and fashionable Italian clothes, romantic affairs, trysts in gondolas by night, wine and cappuccinos at Florian. The kind of daring youthful escapades and high jinks deemed to be the stuff of enduring nostalgia (the Nude Olympics a perfect example). Until "viewing the Carpaccios" had taken on a meaning as ineffable as it was enticing, invoking an exotic and risky wildness unconfined to romantic trysts: magical, fabled, more dream than real, of the kind of daring risky business sure to keep their athletic fame, if not the glittering celebrity of the Shirelles, forever fresh in the minds of their contemporaries.

Had any of them succeeded?

The Carpaccios, whether symbol or imprimatur, had always seemed to confirm Gini as the indispensable player, even if Annette had retained her grip on the number-one spot and Bianca the dazzling lead singer of the Shirelles, while Apolonia's affair with John Proctor had kept them breathless with expectations of disaster. Prompting Gini's not entirely playful boast, when drunk or stoned, that none of them would even be able to find the Scuola di San Giorgio without her guidance, much less know the best rooms to reserve at the tweedy, academic purlieus of the Pensione Seguso on the Zattere: the best views overlooking the Rio San Vio and a king-size bed best suited for the randy couple. Not to mention that essential ensuite bathroom only to be found in twenty-one (the room frequented by Lady Duff Cooper, her son Viscount John Julius Norwich, and travel writer James, now Jan, Morris). Gini's sage advice included instructions to avoid the pensione's meal plan and so take one's lunch and dinner farther afield.

As to finding their way to the Carpaccios and the Scuola di San Giorgio: "Take one wrong turn, one wrong bridge, and you can spend hours wandering in the back-water of Castello."

She returned her gaze from the windows to Saint Augustine seated at his desk, the pensive, dreamy eyes touching some reticent and tender essence—something in the remembered expression of her father, half revealed to that precocious seventeen-year-old as if holding some clue to her ultimate destiny. Not that she'd ever been drawn to the *Confessions*, guilt-ridden anathema to her once rigorously held Stoic beliefs. Even if Augustine had originated the autobiography, now so much in fashion—memoirs of abuse and redemption—as to be almost a glut on the market. But then, hadn't Augustine first broached the idea that there really was no past or future: "a time present of things past; a time present of things present; and a time present of things future." Hadn't she once, dazzled by Jake's mind, found herself stirred by just such ruminations—or perhaps her father's? She reached, as if for an answer, to the familiar scholarly face turned enigmatically to that glorious Venetian light, seeing her long fingers poised as well in the picture glass. "All three of memory composed," she whispered, as if privy to more echoes out of her past.

Various tales concerning Augustine's vision came to mind: a deceased Saint Jerome calling out from the Holy Land, a ghost of a voice, a prophecy from the land of the dead warning of his own imminent passing. Such a sad prospect perhaps foretold by the empty hourglass (memento mori) on a shelf by the saint's writing table. As a precocious seventeen-year-old, infinitely removed from such morbid reflections, she had imagined scenes of Renaissance pageantry beyond that window, of gondolas drifting by, or imagined convocations of scholars and writers delving into the deliciously esoteric and mysterious. "Just the kind of thing," she chided herself, she always warned her authors to avoid: indulging sentimentality or downers, such as death coming a-knocking. Surely Carpaccio had nothing so depressing in mind, charming the eye at every turn with the vivid richness of Venetian reds and Tyrian aquamarine, a feast of sumptuous details to invoke that Aladdin's cave of a Renaissance scholar's study; doors and cabinets thrown wide, curtains drawn back to display a cabinet of wonders: sumptuous calfskin volumes, scientific instruments, Greek statuettes, red-figure pottery, the open pages of incunabula (the score of music so loved by Bianca), much less the cute little German spitz with those adorable black eyes pleading for its walk.

And the glittering armillary sphere hanging behind Augustine that had always drawn Jake's attention.

Could it be that Carpaccio's vision had something to do with her possibly rash decision to forgo the pro tour, and her equally rash decision to break up with Jake, and so embrace her true destiny (her nom de guerre, Isabel Archer, as her father and, later, Jake had adopted as a term of endearment).

"Oh," she exclaimed, feeling the kindling of her youthful ardor: yes, the glories of scholarship, the creation of imperishable works that deployed man's genius against the forces of entropy. Literary works that captured the eternal present—the quintessence of their life and times, as Augustine might have it (as had Carpaccio): when she—body and soul—burning with a keen, gemlike flame, had dedicated herself to just such a prospect.

That unwritten novel . . .

As she lingered still, longing fingers pressed against the picture glass, she found herself tapping, not with impatience but as if indulging some private Morse code, as her gaze lifted to the armillary sphere hanging above Augustine's left shoulder, a glittering brass instrument designed to calculate the position of astronomical bodies in time and space. The tapping suddenly stopped, as if a shock wave had traveled up her arm, interrupted by a voice in her head lingering from their luncheon conversation. She turned with a guilty look, first to the door, then to the bay window, and the familiar grassy courtyard, with its sumptuous array of blooming dogwoods.

"A thousand days . . ."

She moved to the window, as if to the hailing of a distant voice, where a slant of waning sunlight illumined purple whorls in the leaded glass, throwing paisley flares over the Bergdorf Goodman garment bag where it lay on the window seat. Again, she found herself tapping at the glass, admiring her newly done nails, the most subtle hue of pastel orange.

"A thousand days . . . ," she murmured again just above a whisper, brows knitted in concentration. "Bianca, you bitchy witch."

The night before the senior dance, she and Jake had returned to her room after seeing the Streisand-Redford film *The Way We Were* at a cinema out on Route 1. A desperate expediency to distract themselves from the impending doom of their breakup, only to find the thwarted love story in the movie an uncanny reflection of their own disaster. Drunk or stoned, they were casting around for some way out of the dead end into which they'd blundered, first blaming each other for the choice of film, then for each other's resentful mood, or the noxious weed they'd smoked. In days past, such a contretemps might have been cured by a round of raucous sex—breakup sex, as it was nowadays described. But no. They had finally washed up on the window seat, listening to the vague beat of music from parties all over campus, staring out at the dogwoods, flecks of white suspended on the gloom, or helplessly at the wall of Carpaccios over the sofa. And a line of Shelley had floated into her perturbed mind.

"I would dedicate my powers to thee and thine: have I not kept the vow? With beating heart and streaming eyes, even now I call the phantoms of a thousand hours each from his voiceless grave . . . love's delight outwatch'd with me the studious night."

"More like a thousand days," had been Jake's heartbroken retort.

"A thousand days?"

"Since I tracked that first Harvard match."

"Since visiting the Carpaccios," she countered, searching for the more apt phrase or felicitous note, finally standing and going to the wall over the sofa, where she sought distraction in the *Vision of Saint Augustine*. Perhaps it had been her way of asserting the scholarly ideal now that her tennis career was officially over (only the NCAAs still to be played), after accepting the publishing job at Knopf arranged by her father.

And he'd joined her there, their immaterial shadows haunting the picture glass, twin specters with bleary, tear-stained eyes. He had put an arm around her shoulders as if in solidarity, to set a marker, to fix them in time and space.

"Would we . . . could we . . ." His voice rising as he reached and tapped the glass to the Hamlisch tune, tapping the armillary sphere, rings of glittering brassy-gold hung on the liquid void, his hoarse voice failing. So rare for one never at a loss for words. His tapping finger slowed to a more pensive rhythm as he hummed along, as his confidence swelled, his eyes widening as he turned to her. "So, let's call it a thousand days from this moment."

"Your math or memory or both are wrong. We first met around the pool table at Cap. It was January, and we were both wearing green sweaters, and you regaled me with Lucretius, how the slightest swerve of an atom can make all the difference."

"Okay, let's make it a thousand days from last January. It should be fall by then, and I should have finished my PhD or pretty damn close. And you will have been beavering away at Knopf, or—who knows what random fluctuation—maybe decided to give the women's tour a chance after all. A chance to revise your first novel for publication with material from real life instead of out of books and your so-deprived childhood."

"Oh, thanks a million."

"And we'll meet in Venice at three in the afternoon—call it October 15, 1979—in the Scuola di San Giorgio. And if you show, if I show, we'll ask the blessings of Augustine on our immortal souls, on our marriage of true minds. Sound like a plan?"

How typical of Jake. Shooting from the hip, throwing out some wild idea, some far-fetched theory to mend a broken heart. A dare, a risk, a way of winnowing fate and so forever testing her loyalty, her resolve, the tattered banner of their love.

Had she been in love? Had she walked away from love?

"Not a random meeting at the Plaza like Redford and Streisand?"

"Too late for them, but not for us."

"A lot can happen in a thousand days. Armillary sphere or no."

"But that's the point. It's the same with any experiment. Years of lab work, perhaps a lifetime, everything or nothing, Nobel or nada. If this"—and he squeezed her shoulder—"meant anything, and we both show up . . . well, we'll know something for sure."

"Hey, on the way to curing cancer or my first Pulitzer. What's not to celebrate."

"Visiting the Carpaccios—Augustine without a safety net."

She wiped hot tears from her eyes as she heard the door swing open.

"Oh, it's you, Mom—you okay?"

Ermalinda Cheshire (she'd kept her father's name) swung into the room, one towel-draped hand raised, drying her long blonde hair, the other balancing a toiletry caddy, wearing only a sports bra and panties.

"Fine, fine"—she went over and kissed her daughter on the cheek—"just waxing nostalgic about the Carpaccios."

Erma stared for a moment with a look of mild disbelief. "I'd never have recognized you."

"Oh, the floral sundress," she said and waved dismissively. "Thought it was time for a change."

"So you met my friends," and she went over to the wall of Carpaccios. "There's *Dracorex hogwartsia*, the reluctant dragon, a little worse for wear; Mufasa, the cowardly lion, brought to heal; and Rosella, my friendly parrot with his patient pal, Borzoi."

"And don't forget Augustine's German spitz," her mother added as if scrambling to fully decipher her daughter's taxonomy.

"Fritzy . . ."

"And the armillary sphere, just your thing. Where did you find the Carpaccios?"

"Gathering dust in the back of the basement storage locker."

"Of course—like me." She smiled, dusting herself off. "It was just a surprise finding them here. We had them hung in our suite, where they were admired by one and all, especially our boyfriends."

"Hardly the stuff of Wimbledon legends." Erma returned to her desk, as if her eye had detected something amiss, setting down her caddy as she continued to dry her hair.

"I've been texting, emailing . . . if you care to join us—your godmothers one, two, and three—for dinner tonight. Arthur too, so I'm informed. Oh, and Bianca's Matteo is performing."

"I was on airplane mode—late night in the lab, parties till dawn. Not enough hours. So many next-to-last goodbyes, everybody so desperate to drink to the dregs. And I still have a couple of lab experiments running. And tonight's our swim-team dinner."

"Of course. You smell good." She gave her tall daughter an admiring gaze, the sleek swimmer's body, the lovely ropey muscles in her legs, the taut shoulders framing a longish oval face, with a small but kissable mouth, her father's brown eyes and delicate eyebrows—but the rest all female.

"It's my new hair conditioner." And she pulled a plastic bottle from her teeming caddy and handed it to her mother to smell. "Coconut and avocado oil."

"Mmm . . . What else do you have in that bag of tricks that might regenerate muscles in my old-lady calves and soothe painful knees? A plasma transfusion, perhaps."

"Hey, speaking of which—nostalgia, that is—I got your fine blonde hair; I can skip the waxing salon. Thank God; around here it's a four-week wait for an opening for your opening."

"Thank God for small evolutionary favors. Hey, in my day we had co-ed bathrooms; we were shameless."

"You're kidding. How gross."

"They hadn't been able to refurbish all the bathroom facilities. We always had the far end downstairs for showers, so we'd just waltz past the guys at their sinks shaving, often bare-assed, to our end of things; nobody gave it a second thought." She went to the window and gazed out a moment. "Yes, I remember the rush . . . I was in granny knots over whether to go on and play the women's tour that summer. I had an invitation to Nottingham, a warmup for Wimbledon, and then the US grass circuit—Essex and Orange, leading up to Forest Hills."

Her daughter eyed her with a steady, if bemused gaze while combing out her hair, then replied with a slow, pronounced cadence as if careful to disguise any hint of disparagement.

"You should've done the Virginia Slims, Mom; then you wouldn't have to keep talking about it for the rest of your life. Or better still, finish that tennis novel you're always talking about."

"Sorry, I didn't mean to be a broken record."

"I wouldn't mind a few difficult choices. But my competitive diving days are over, and my internship at the Harvard genetics lab starts week after next, with classes and teaching assignments starting first thing in September."

"Oh, I was hoping to have you home for a few days. But at least you'll be near the Vineyard and the big races for August."

"We'll see . . ."

"Well, my father got me my internship at Knopf; it was a tough job market in the midseventies." She picked up the Bergdorf garment bag. "Here, I bought you a dress for graduation."

"You shouldn't waste your money. I have plenty of dresses."

"Did I ever tell you"—spying a clothes hook on the back of the door, she went over and hung the garment bag—"that it was my father who took me to Venice when I was seventeen, like you, and first introduced me to the Scuola di San Giorgio and the Carpaccios?"

"You mean after Dad died?"

"Yes, I thought it might be a new chance for us."

"Without Dad . . ."

"You see, my father—Grandad—"

"I barely remember him."

She felt a flutter of repressed panic cross her face, and she edged nearer the Carpaccios, again seeking her reflection in the glass, and that of her watching daughter, as if the merging of the two might allow her an angle of repose, a reset.

"We had barely arrived at the Pensione Seguso—remember?—and we were off, charging through tiny streets and crossing bridges and passing wonderful shops, without so much as catching our breath until we reached that modest scuola with the two fierce dolphins—remember?—tail to tail over the door; and my father had barely knocked on that green door when a tall, bald-headed man appeared to take his lira notes, holding back a velvet curtain—crimson, wasn't it?—and we were suddenly engulfed, surrounded by these extraordinary paintings; and there was a smell—incense, candles, and brine and an indescribable feeling of age. The silence so alive, the barest echo of my father's voice as he narrated the scenes to me. Yes, they were all there: your tame lion, a curious red parrot, a patient dog, a dragon brought to heel—all the charming details. But it was Augustine who captured his fancy, surrounded by all his gorgeous books—enchanted; he was utterly enchanted as he related his theories about Augustine in a voice I'd never really known before: all his most passionate—perhaps most enduring—attachments. And he said something I've never forgotten, I think quoting Henry James, which he was wont to do: how the well-tempered imagination is drawn to certain spots—places, times, incandescent moments—where art and life have become so interfused as to become consanguineous. How all Venice was both model and painter . . ." She pulled up her most winsome smile for her daughter and straightened one of the pictures. "Yes," she said, glancing at her father's Rolex, "I've never forgotten that."

"You and Isabel Archer, creatures of overactive imaginations."

"Really? Well, I think my spellbound father saw in Augustine a portrait, perhaps in homage, of Venice's greatest printer of books, Aldus Manutius. We spent hours with booksellers as my father picked out a sixteenth-century volume of Greek odes for my birthday. His hands were shaking when he handed it to me."

Erma sat in her desk chair, an accusatory glance. "You didn't get my name out of Henry James by any chance?"

"Of course not—like my father, we wanted something distinctive, wholly your own."

"Great, what's not to like about Ermalinda: Ermoo, Ermy, Squirmy Ermy in middle school—and let's not forget, Linda, Linda Lovelace in high school. Lindy—Lucky Lindy seems to be what I'm stuck with on the swim team."

"Why Lucky?"

"'Cause three times I got a third place when the top divers at the meet were down with the flu. Like, when I'm diving, the opposition stars get sick."

"You're a beautiful diver—a beautiful woman and a hell of a lot smarter than your mother. And thank God you turned out to be a science kid." She looked away from her daughter's near nakedness, embarrassed at the longing looks directed at her muscular legs. "How come none of your brilliant classmates on the team or in—what is it?—bioengineering . . . have latched on to you?"

"Biochemistry. And I'm actually getting my degree in integrative genomics and biophysics, in case you'd forgotten, with a certificate in computer science."

"Summa too. I have to bite my tongue not to boast to my old roommates."

"Don't bother; nerdy women are the kiss of death around here. The guys want girlfriends like you, who can sweet-talk them about art and literature and music, fill their heads with splendid delectations from Proust, the ravishments of Degas, the undying bliss of Rilke."

"Ah." She smiled, waving toward the wall over the couch. "So, hopefully the Carpaccios helped then?"

"Hey, three years with my roommates hanging out with Michael Phelps Speedo posters—hardly magic for date night on the street."

"Yes, a touch of class—romantic Venice, as my roommates always assured me."

"Is that why you never went to Venice with Dad?"

She marveled at how deftly her daughter disguised her disapproval, countering with a gracious smile: "He was more partial to England—his idea for our honeymoon, the land of Newton, Rutherford, Darwin, Hawking, Francis Bacon." She stood from the door and unzipped the garment bag. "And don't forget Francis Crick, whom he wanted to publish in the worst way. Hawking was and still is beyond me. Black holes and such. Perhaps we'll be publishing you someday." She pulled out the dark blue dress and held it up in front of her, modeling it for her daughter. "You know how proud he was of you, and especially now with your Harvard scholarship."

"Hardly," she snorted. "It's a grant, and I'll have to work my buns off teaching undergraduates in survey courses and labs. And I don't want to end up the next Lynn Margulis."

Something about the name caught her unawares: "Lynn . . . who?"

"Your generation—Margulis, a molecular biochemist in the late sixties who proposed that eukaryotic cells did not emerge due to natural selection alone but through endosymbiosis. That's when a bunch of bacterial cells get together to form multicellular organisms. She was controversial in her day, but we now know that at least two components of eukaryotic cells got their start with endosymbiotic bacteria—mitochondria and chloroplasts, the energy transducers and photosynthetic machinery of cells."

She eyed her daughter pensively a moment (Margulis stirring a vague memory) and then removed the price tag on the dress and hung it up. "You've kind of lost me already, honey. But your Lynn—my father's generation—was right, then?"

"Nope, her serial endosymbiosis theory that eukaryotes were formed by multiple bacteria cells getting together over millions of years after the Great Oxidation Event kind of collapsed under its own poetic weight. Some derided it as a feminist view," she intoned with a deprecating, come-hither look and a thrusting of her bust. "Her take on the origins of life: a way in which evolution happens in a more cooperative, user-friendly networking manner rather than the dog-eat-dog playpen of natural selection: nature red in tooth and claw. Margulis—too bad for her—turned her back on the more computational nitty-gritty of phylogenetics, which tells a far different and possibly even more compelling story."

"Ah, compelling story—I like that. That can be your story to tell perhaps. At least your Margulis woman made a difference, if not quite on the right track."

"There are no second places in this game, not in the long run. As one biochemist put it: Life is nothing but an electron looking for a place to rest."

"Ah," she muttered, puzzled, trying to decipher the improbable echo of this conversation—desperate to get the drift. "How many runners-up or even semifinalists at Wimbledon do we remember."

"You see, genomes don't predict the future but only recall the past, like memories, like books. And it turns out that all eukaryotes have the same ancestor, that life as we know it happened only once. That's a little freaky, Mom."

"But I thought, like your father always said, the splendor of evolution was in its vast variety."

"Not for most of the millions of years of life on earth; it was very constrained—common as dirt, *bo-r-ring*, just bacteria all the way down." She went to her window and began a slow brushing of her hair, her gaze seeming to luxuriate in the elaborate candelabras of off-white blossoms, perhaps prompting the line of thought. "You see, bacteria changed their genes and biochemistry, but never their form. Only now, now that we can read DNA, we're beginning to understand the missing connections, those invisible steps to complexity. The sixty-four-million-dollar question is why complex life only happened once and not on more than one occasion. Once we have a handle on that answer, it will open all kinds of areas of research into aging and health and curing diseases."

Erma put down her brush and shook back her mane of hair, going to her desk, where she began rearranging her photos.

"Remember when I used to brush your hair before bed?"

"You recited poetry . . . hoping that something would stick."

"You remind me of your father; it almost makes me dizzy, the way you two always had so much to talk about."

"I remember visiting him in the hospital, in those chilly afternoons after school, his head propped on those robin-egg-blue pillows, face turned toward the light from the East River." Erma glanced up from the photos with an accusatory stare. "He had tears in his eyes: 'Maybe I was never good enough for your mother; maybe I could never love her enough—maybe I was never smart enough to earn her love.'"

"That's ridiculous—he never said any such thing." Gini lowered her face into her hands and shook her head. "Christ, half the time I couldn't understand what the two of you were going on about, like it was a secret language that excluded me." She began walking a frantic circle until she spied a wastebasket in which to deposit the crumpled price tag.

"I'm sorry. I didn't mean to upset you. I think Dad was just trying to figure stuff out—the way his mind worked."

"Hell, if anything, you're a chip off the ole block."

"Well, brains aren't everything."

"He was my first real boss, a senior editor. I worshipped the pages he edited."

Erma disguised her eyeroll by dipping her head and gathering her hair: "Now you run the place."

"I just have a knack for picking up on the current vibe—hardly rocket science."

"Your avocation and vocation . . . 'as my two eyes make one in sight . . .'"

"Ah, the Frost, you remember."

She picked up her hairbrush and brandished it like a hammer to mark the rhythm: "Only where love and need are one, and the work is play for mortal stakes, is the deed ever really done, for Heaven and the future's sakes."

"Yes . . ."

"You had it posted—framed on my bedroom wall."

"Oh," and she picked up the Henry James from her daughter's desk, "at least you're still reading." And she brandished the dog-eared paperback. "This is what allows us to return to the past, to breathe in the spirit of a great writer." She brought the novel to her nose and closed her eyes for a second. "Your twelfth-grade English teacher made me promise to keep you writing; she said you were a wonderful writer."

Erma only shrugged and turned to go sit by the window.

"Here, why don't you try on your graduation dress for me." She went and got the dress down again and walked it over to her daughter, who rose reluctantly from where she sat. "The saleslady told me this is the hottest thing going right now, especially for a young lady who's going to change the world with advances in genetics—gene therapy, right?" She held it up to her daughter's broad shoulders. "Perfect fit." She handed it off and retreated to the door to watch as her daughter got into the dress.

"Did I tell you?" she asked. "An amazing thing. I ran into one of your teammates managing our Reunions site. Jake—Jacob Burrage."

For the merest nanosecond, her daughter froze mid-zip, then looked up with a concentrated stare—zipped and abruptly shot a hip, head thrown back in ecstatic release, arms and leg extended in an electrifying jazz move.

CHAPTER 9

Annette sat with her son and husband in the stands, watching the end of the men's tennis practice. Arthur and Matt had just showered and changed. She found herself surveying the scene, the scattering of huge tennis bags, the detritus of towels, sweatbands, ball cans, socks and shoes (flip-flops), and grip tape and loads of racquets—tools of the trade. Women would have been a lot neater: they always are. In her day, it was just a wooden racquet or two.

"What's up, Mom? You look a little dismayed."

She turned to her son, seeing his profile next to her husband's, with all his height (thank God), sandy hair, and same bemused twinkle in his eyes. "Just dreading the charity event tomorrow. I don't know if I'm still up to it."

"You've—we've played hundreds of charity events," Matt assured her. "You'll do just fine."

"As long as I'm not matched against Gini."

The two men laughed. "That much can probably be arranged," said her husband. "Why not your old doubles combinations, Gini and Apolonia, you and Bianca. After all, you dreamed up this thing in the first place and lined up the sponsors."

"Mom, you're still a rock star."

"You know what's nice? I still meet people in my class who never knew me." She raised her eyes from the agile players on the blue-and-green tennis courts, checking the angle of the afternoon sun, and adjusted her broad-brimmed hat. And smiled, feeling the cooling northwest breeze. "Or worse, remember me as one of the Shirelles."

Matt patted her knee. "Try being remembered as a tennis shoe."

"A great shoe," noted his son, waving toward the courts. "Just look at all the guys still playing in your shoe, the immortal Matt Collins shoe."

"An old shoe that, if not for the Adidas sponsorship—well . . ."

Annette nodded dreamily. "A perfect fit." She found herself mentally rearranging the scattering of tennis bags according to color, the green Babolat with the blue Yonex, the black Wilson with the gray Head. How many abandoned tennis bags had she unpacked in her life, extracting smelly towels and sox and sweatbands and worse, doing the laundry, sometimes twice daily. And yet the smell of a laundry basket, of male sweat—honest sweat—had somehow been a comfort, the scent of bodies exalting in God's gifts of health and love, always reminding her of a favorite line from the Psalms: "The Lord is my strength and song, and is become my salvation."

"The saddest thing is losing friends along the way," said Matt. "Losing Arthur Ashe so early took a lot out of me."

His wife laid a hand on his arm: "The loss of such a gentleman, the kindest of kindhearted souls: such a loss would take it out of anyone. You did seem to lose your enthusiasm for Sunday service, though." As she spoke, she glanced at her son, who seemed absorbed in the play below where they sat.

"Hah—not with Laureen now stirring the pot. Watching the old geezers squirm in their pews is worth the price of admission."

Arthur avoided his mother's glance as he joined the conversation. "I feel as if I should've known Arthur better, my namesake, the way you talk about him, even if I only know him mostly from YouTube."

"Your godfather," his mother added.

Matt chuckled. "Not that I didn't hate losing to him. But if I had to lose to somebody, I'd rather it be Arthur."

"Amazing," she said, "how he snuck that Wimbledon crown past Connors in his prime."

"It's the gap they leave behind that is most troubling, which somehow ends up the something missing in you."

Their son asked, a hint of curiosity creasing his damp eyebrows as he turned to his father: "What was your lifetime record against Ashe?"

"Six and ten. I won more titles overall, thirty-eight to thirty-five, but he had the edge in Grand Slams, three to my two."

Arthur rocked back and forth with laughter. "Some things we never forget."

His mother took a deep breath, as if ready for the plunge. "Actually, it's nice when people take an interest in you just because of who you are as a human being. Like the Athletes for Christ panel tomorrow; you'll do just fine."

Arthur rose from his seat. "I'm off to my Reunions site for cocktails and then the tennis dinner: I meant what I said."

She reached for her son's hand but too late. "Try to make it over for our class dinner, or just dessert; there's a chance Erma might be joining us. Oh, and Bianca's Matteo will be playing."

They watched him go.

"What was all that about?" Matt asked.

"Oh, he emailed me this morning; for some reason, he's got cold feet on the panel and wants to cancel."

"You can hardly blame him, living in the fast lane: How do you explain that to such a pious crowd?"

"You say 'pious' as if it was an affliction."

"Well, mammon may even be more of one."

"I worry about his drinking. I don't think he even goes to church anymore—it's either weekends in the Hamptons or skiing in Aspen."

"Where the clients are." He returned his gaze to the match on the number-one court, a look of longing she knew well. "And the way things are going with Laureen, a one-woman demolition derby, you may lose the unenlightened half of your congregation."

"My congregation?"

"I, for one, love the fireworks and the squirming bottoms. Wildly attractive too, when she gets up a head of steam—better than the Sunday news shows."

"Great: pulpit porn, just what I need to hear. A tad aggressive, and the men run for the hills."

"Not that you would know anything about that."

"I long ago accepted my limits."

"That's why I married you: just keeping things simple."

"Unlike my roommates, who always overreached: three unhappy marriages."

"Not Gini . . . that was just a tragedy, like Arthur. Bill was such a gentleman; his sweet equanimity always reminded me of Arthur."

"No one could have lived up to Jake."

"Strange, I can't get it out of my mind, running into young Jacob, like he was our Jake of so many years ago, his face alight with fascination and joy, like when he was watching Chrissie play."

"Or you. For a while there, you were best pals." She laughed uneasily and took her husband's hand. "He could never hide what was on his mind—an open book. He'd let loose with the oddest things." For a moment, their eyes locked in the swarm of uneasy memories that flowed between then, until, with a squeeze of his hand, she returned her gaze to the incredibly fit young men moving effortlessly on the court. Realizing, as she did so, just how much she missed the old clay courts overlooked by that grassy hillside filled with spectators, where Jake would always sit with notebook on his knees, plotting her downfall.

"At the sign-in table," her husband went on, "I almost expected that fine young man to start lecturing me on how I needed to change my shot selection."

"You too," she murmured, nodding. "Something in the ease with which he chatted on, like the years meant nothing, winging me right back to those days after Rome, in Venice, at the Scuola di San Giorgio."

"Really, Rome, not Venice? When you saved my life?"

"God and prayer did that: such simple things."

He turned a searching eye toward his wife. "Unlike Jake and Gini . . ."

"Gini always likes to say they would have ended up hating each other."

"And you . . . such a brilliant and attractive guy?"

Annette gave her husband's hand a playful slap. "She always complained he was a control freak. She said it was like being a puppet on a string."

"I remember that string." He held up his long, callused right hand and made the motions. "For four months, I hung on his every word like the gospel truth."

"Do you remember our graduation dance?"

"How could I forget?"

"It haunts me to this day. The image never leaves me: seeing her dancing with Jake, her head on his shoulder, embracing each other like there was no tomorrow. She had tears streaming down her face—tears and more tears. In all our years, I'd never seen her cry, not once, not ever." She sighed. "After all those nights I'd been woken at two in the morning . . . gone to tears . . ."

"You're trembling."

"Am I? Well, running into that kid kind of exploded my brain. Like all the things left undone in your life—things, just things."

"Like what?"

"I don't know, just: maybe . . . we've been so lucky: having it all is never enough."

"Sounds like maybe you missed something about those two a.m. wake-up calls."

"Hell, she had all the physical equipment to go all the way."

"But not enough to get past you."

"Saved by the graduation bell. The last time I beat her, it took every last ounce of my strength, with Jake seated right there on the hillside, dissecting my weaknesses."

She gave a little snort of defiance, now following the arc of the yellow ball being rocketed back and forth by two young men in black shorts and orange sports shirts.

"What?" he asked.

"I often wondered, but, of course, never brought it up with Jake: if she'd dropped him and his tracking system, the whole package, the minute she decided against the Virginia Slims tour."

He laughed and put his arm around her, squeezing. "Remember how often Jake predicted the winner of a tournament, or who'd I be playing in such and such a round. The only times he was ever wrong was when he predicted I would win."

"I've sometimes wondered if she'd beat me in that last match, claimed the number-one spot for the NCAAs, if she'd have gone on that summer to play the women's tour and stuck it out with Jake. And written that damn novel she always promised us."

"Good Lord, you do go on (more maybes than a month of Sundays)—worse than me."

"She was like that, you know: once she made her mind up to do something, there was no turning back."

"Except she ran into you."

"Oh, worse. I even delayed having to play that second challenge match until I knew it would be on the worst day of her period."

His eyebrows peaked, and a smile eased up his lips. "All's fair—"

"Of course, I was the only one of the roomies not on the Pill."

"I guess there are predictions, and then there are *predictions.*"

"A regular armillary sphere."

"What's that?"

"It's in that Carpaccio painting of Saint Augustine—remember?" For a moment, she found herself spellbound by the arcing flight of the ball. "An instrument that describes the rotation of the planets around the sun, that predicts the summer and winter solstice."

A big smile broadened his long face: "Ah, there you go: that famous Princeton education."

"Jake always thought he could predict the future—like Gini's Wimbledon crown: anything was possible—by the numbers."

"Maybe we just met that future at sign-in."

"But I think those tears of Gini's convinced me I'd rather stick with God's plan for eternity."

He got up stiffly. "You mean that one on YouTube . . ."

She joined him, sighing. "My soul magnifies the Lord . . ."

CHAPTER 10

As she wandered in a half daze, Gini found herself repeatedly muttering under her breath "Jabberwocky," as if requiring a new mantra for whatever ailed her, some vaguely reassuring watchword bandied around between her and Jake in their student days. And, oddly enough, like so much else in the last few hours, a name that sparked memories of the risky business in which Jake liked to indulge, that, looking back, she had to admit, had been a big turn-on. Nor could she shake the feeling that young Jacob's sudden appearance in her life was a disconcerting reminder, a premonition—of what, she couldn't as yet fathom. But signs of her discomfort, her disequilibrium, now seemed to greet her at every turning. Even as she headed for her car and a nap at her hotel before dinner, she found familiar landmarks crying out to be more fully deciphered for clues to her failure, that failure of nerve to fulfill a stellar future first predicted by herself and then others.

She looked up suddenly, as if a voice had confirmed this creeping suspicion, only to find the gargoyle-encrusted battlements of Guyot Hall staring down at her: horned rhinos and trumpeting elephants, fire-breathing dragons and winged griffins, lions and tigers and bears—oh my . . . Jabberwocky!

She reached for the handle at the entrance to the Department of Geology and Earth Sciences, and the heavy oak door swung wide with a jarring bang, confronting her with an elderly member of the great class of 1966, a lined and fossilized version with a leering, sun-spotted face, prompting—how odd!—a spontaneous mimic of Erma's jazz move of just minutes before, a step reprised from her Jazzercize class.

"Ah, Fosse . . . ," exclaimed the wizened gentleman in his natty orange-and-black checkerboard jacket and threadbare geology department cap (*Take Nothing for Granite*), as if instantly deciphering this esoteric Princeton greeting, akin to a secret handshake.

"Bob's your uncle," she shot back, having no idea where this was headed.

"Fair maiden, I hope you won't be disappointed, as was I; for I fear the idiots in Nassau Hall got rid of most of this historic collection some thirty years ago now. Most of the bones and fossils went to Yale's Peabody Museum, as if they needed them. The Egyptian mummies to the Met. All sacrificed to the call for more office space! Office space replacing a famous historical collection, a time capsule of taste and discrimination going back to the eighteenth century, an attraction for schoolchildren and students, a spellbinding period piece."

"Oh dear," Gini quailed, immediately jumping to the conclusion she'd been on a fool's errand as she struggled to regain her dignity in the eyes of this sunbaked veteran sporting a collection of age spots that would've done proud the now seemingly lost Egyptian mummies of memory. "Not the dinosaur as well?"

"Oh, the allosaurus is now front and center. New office space didn't quite gobble him up. Were you in the geology department?"

"No, but I took rocks for jocks and oceanography for my science requirement and consider the allosaurus as something of a mascot to my misbegotten youth."

"Youth be damned. You don't look a year over thirty. While I've been weathered and hollowed out by fifty years of breaking rocks, unlike these office-bound academics. I cut my teeth in these halls, pored over the specimens as a kid, and am soon to be shoveled out the door as well—like the rest, headed for the boneyard. I wish you good prospecting, young lady."

"Gini . . ."

"Boris." He doffed his cap and bowed. "Well, off for my twenty winks before joining what remains of my class dinner."

"Boris . . . ," she intoned and swept past him and into the brightly lit atrium, only to be confronted by yet another of time's ceaseless makeovers.

Gone were all the dusty mahogany display cases of Victorian vintage, the hand-lettered, yellowed note cards describing the moth-eaten specimens, the display jars reeking of formaldehyde, the thousands of curated rock samples, the painted mummy cases with their gruesome residents laid bare. The great hall was transformed into an overlit postmodern confection of discrete exhibitions, with the allosaurus as a proud centerpiece, sole revenant of all that had been, still standing tall and proud, if less terrible to behold, lit up like a carnival attraction by overhead white LEDs. She paced out all thirty-five bony feet of him, from fearsome serrated jaws to his switching, lizardly tail. Tiers of offices now obscured the wonderful Gothic windows of her day. As she circled the allosaurus display, touching the taunt wire guide rail in places, she sought to recover something of the penumbral pathos of memory, of the chilly yet somehow engaging fear engendered by those once-shadowy scimitars of sharp teeth and dagger-arrayed forelegs, of an unimaginable primeval past now replaced by a spruced-up and petulant character out of a child's picture book. "The jaws that bite, the claws that catch . . . ," she murmured as if, by casting her own spell, she might yet return herself to the dim precincts of memory, where, lured by Jake's eccentric charms, like Saint George to his dragon, she'd regularly been drawn into the lair of this late-Jurassic killing machine. Once dismissed as a folie à deux, she now, again, detected the distant shimmer of a life foregone.

"Just act like you belong here, and nobody will be the wiser," Jake assured her.

"What, carrying pizza and incendiaries into this museum of horrors after hours?"

It always took a few minutes until their eyes adjusted to the ambient lamplight filtering through the long and narrow, sinuously carved Gothic windows (modeled on Triassic ferns, according to Jake), through which a moldy mustard light filtered inward, to be reflected and refracted by the three score antique-glass vitrines, arrayed like a labyrinth of spectral funhouse mirrors, where sinister glass eyes glittered in ambush. She shivered in trepidation until Jake managed to get his scrounged candles lit, affixed to paper plates, and set like watchfires around their campsite, a rickety wooden bench where they ate dinner.

"Why are we hanging out here in your rag-and-bone shop, this dingy dragon's cave, eating greasy pizza?"

"Well, let's try the Annex for pizza next time."

"When we could be having a perfectly convivial candlelit dinner at Cap with my roommates, who all adore you."

At this plea for sanity (repeated how many times), he had only offered that annoying but-I-know-better smile (a crooked front tooth), a puzzled crinkle between luxurious eyebrows as he busied himself with lighting a last candle, perhaps setting out a votive flame before the altar to his gods, while deftly sweeping back locks of stringy hair lest they catch fire.

"As your guest, no less. A scholarship kid who can't afford an eating club."

"Then pay me back the guest fees if that's what's bothering you. Use your poker winnings."

"When was the last time you had dinner with me at Commons?"

"Why would I want to have dinner with a lot of strange, pimply freshmen when all my friends and teammates are elsewhere?"

Again, he dug into his bulging jean pocket for a book of matches, scattering scraps of paper, napkins, bits of newsprint on which he'd scribbled cryptic notes to himself.

"There are friends—*and* there are friends." He sharpened his airy gaze, stroking a hand up her thigh as he bent forward to adjust two guttering candles at her feet. "What, you don't like the fascinating company we keep here—granted, absent gristle and flesh, but magnificent dinner companions who provide so many conversational gambits."

"They stink, have threadbare smiles, and no manners. Not to mention being mostly extinct. It's like communing with ghoulish ghosts." She waved a hand in the direction of the Egyptian mummies. "And Boris is the pits."

He grinned that ghost of a smile: "Careful, he might hear you . . ."

She detected a silent detonation of stealthy wickedness flickering across his face, reminding her of a stalking cat, ready to pounce the moment the prey lost awareness. Exhausting, how she had to remain constantly on her toes.

"Pizza's stone cold," she groaned, throwing back the lid with disgust. Her stare rose again to the surrounding clutter of Victorian glass vitrines, where she could just make out the dissected specimens arranged on shelves—coiled pythons, ostrich embryos, dinosaur eggs, and other indecipherable masses of lumpy green flesh preserved in tall jars, while elsewhere, various critters stared back, arranged in characteristic poses, their moth-eaten hides sloughing hair, glass eyes beady and bright when caught by the flickering candlelight, somehow reminding her of soot-blackened icons she'd once visited in an orthodox church on Cyprus while on summer vacation with her parents, where obscure nameless saints stared out beneath haloes of tarnished silver and gold.

"They help to settle my mind by posing essential questions. That all progress in science evolves from the chaos of what came before."

"Surely, this . . . progress?"

"The messy nature of life."

"Oh please, I've got Epictetus, Seneca, and Marcus Aurelius—even Saint Augustine, in a pinch, to expostulate on such existential matters, not ghosts of ghosts." And she looked up from her paper plate of runny pizza to where the bony forelegs of the allosaurus loomed against the graceful curves of the Gothic windows.

"That's just my point: our dinner guests are not philosophers spouting the claptrap of received wisdom but real flesh-and-blood creatures, sojourners like us on this tiny planet. Can't you feel their journey in us, the continuity that makes us all cousins, the miracle of how geochemistry gave rise so seamlessly to biochemistry, making us denizens of a living, breathing planet? What better company or more fascinating dinner companions."

"Even if they still stink of formaldehyde and dry rot. I still have bad memories of my tenth-grade biology class—pithing frogs and the like." She shivered. "It's like walking through a graveyard without the graves. And Boris and his ilk will never be welcome at *my* dinner table."

"Oh my," he intoned in mockery, sweeping his hands outward toward the glimmering shadows, his voice a low, gravelly plea in perfect imitation of Boris Karloff. "You have to think of life, even objects, big and small, animate and inanimate, as all interrelated—"

"Stop that," she ordered, clamping a hand over his mouth.

"Okay, call it shared information," he went on in his lecturing tone that simply drove her wild. "How any physical entity acts on another physical entity. It's the imaginative leap that's the thing. Nothing exists in splendid isolation. Every moment is made up of interactions. You see, it's the interactions that matter most, on the quantum level, the cellular level on up, not just us in the here and now." And as if to demonstrate, he bent and kissed her gently on the lips, urging out her tongue with his. "Without interaction," he whispered, "touch, smell, taste, light, sex, electricity, photons, there would be nothing: we wouldn't actually exist. In the end, we're all observers of the light."

She licked her lips and glanced up at Jabberwocky's cocked head listening in. "Okay . . . I guess."

"We exist," he paused, chewing thoughtfully, "only in as far as we influence others. Who we are is a coefficient of how we react to life in the here and now. This"—again he gestured with a slice of drooping pizza to the watching faces in the glass vitrines—"is a microcosm of a greater web of interactions, a net in which we are just nodes among nodes. And the way we love now, in this moment, can never be repeated or even equaled by future interactions."

Her heart leapt at the romantic notion of such absolute uniqueness, even as her mind registered a complaint at the inclusion of those in the peanut gallery.

"Like I said: formaldehyde and dry rot and God knows what else. I'd rather read all about it in books."

"But the feeling . . . the feeling of being part of a journey, the sheer hard evidence that connects everything, that makes us all cousins: it's thrilling."

"Just as long as we bring the pizza . . . to the party?"

"Listen." He hung his head for a moment, the merest flicker of criticism in his voice. "I think it's good for you to get your nose out of books, to hang out with a more downscale crowd, to contemplate, if not the moon and stars, the creatures who have paved the way to who we are. Your Seneca would appreciate—what was it you like to quote to me in one of your more loquacious moments? The importance of keeping your will aligned with nature, to acknowledge the impermanence of things, and so fathom what is under our control and what is not. To treat all things with equanimity."

Now annoyed at his poaching her territory and uncanny recall: "You don't think sweating my buns off playing Division One tennis keeps me grounded enough in the here and now?"

"You, Agrippina, buns and all, see a boneyard; I see a thousand questions crying out to be answered. They haunt my dreams."

"Do you suppose"—she nuzzled his cheek and waved, thankful for the scent of his Aqua Velva—"that this is a male thing: science, I suppose. I mean, poor Apolonia struggles, even with your tutoring, to somehow pass organic chemistry."

"She does struggle, but she has a big heart and the determination to be a doctor to see her through."

"Maybe she's more your type—a science babe?"

"She's scrappy, for sure. With ambition to burn—first in her family to even finish high school."

"Unlike me: self-centered, privileged, with her head in the clouds."

"You're a thoroughbred. In the race of life, I'd put my money on you. I'd risk all—what about you?"

"Mmm . . . *so*, you've come on to her, or she—I wouldn't put it past her—on to you?"

"You must be kidding. She's the human sphinx. Every good-looking guy on campus has found his way to her stringing machine. She sells more Adidas sneakers than the U-Store. And yet she refuses all offers for a date."

"Except you . . . of course."

He reached to her shoulder and bent as if to whisper an endearment. "Tell me, what's the deal with her? Is she a lesbian? She just exudes a wild sexual energy."

"Oh, wouldn't you like to know. Obviously, she must have rejected your charms, too."

He grunted, biting off a huge chunk of pizza, chewing pensively for a moment as if to return the conversation to a more useful wavelength. "Listen, I predict that women will one day dominate science, since most of the hard research takes focus and meticulous attention to detail."

"Yes, and don't forget Marie Curie. You need to add her to your pantheon."

"Done."

"Hate to tell you, but Apolonia is one of the world's great scatterbrains."

"In fact, there's a lady biochemist I interned with last summer at the University of Chicago, Lynn, Dr. Margulis. You'd like her, very no-nonsense, a mind very much like yours: curious, systematic, laser focused."

"Curious—Lynn—about you, needless to say."

"About trying to fathom the connections." And he waved as he took another bite of pizza, sending the candles at their feet flickering like distant heat lightning.

"How romantic!"

"Like, how did rocks and water and oxygen and CO_2 produce life? How did eukaryotes—large, complex cells—evolve from a bunch of single-celled bacteria?"

"An older woman no less."

"Dr. Margulis came up with a theory based on endosymbiosis, a kind of mating dance between bacteria: merging, swapping, and acquiring genes—pushed by natural selection, so producing multicelled structures. Just the kind of theory you'd come up with if you were a scientist: poetic, mythic, Demeter and Persephone, sort of Gaiaish."

"Gaiaish? Mother nature—like Apolonia."

"But I think I've detected a flaw in Dr. Margulis's theory—not that I was going to mention it to her, not yet. If the merging of bacteria was the origin of complex cells, why aren't there gazillions of various kinds of eukaryotes, which are basically all alike, all with the same fundamental components? Turns out, it's white bread all the way down." He paused for another bite, nodding, his eyes tight as if he'd glimpsed some inspiration in the surrounding gloom. "Diversity all around but running off the same battery cells."

"Whatever keeps your motor running—huh, Jake?"

"How come all eukaryotes have two sexes?"

"Well, for your info, Apolonia is no lesbian."

A flicker of delight at this data point flashed in his eyes, even as his mind was elsewhere. "In evolutionary terms, it makes much more sense for the female to pass on one hundred percent of her genes instead of just fifty."

"Hey, that's such a lesbo thing. And it sure beats indoctrination with table manners, piano lessons, and *The Little Engine That Could*."

"And then you've got to find the right mate and give up half your genes. Asexual reproduction—in effect, cloning yourself—makes, if you're a betting woman, much more sense."

"A clone, huh? Another Jake? Surely you'd never clone yourself, even if it was possible."

"In our lifetimes, cloning oneself will not only be possible but probably commonplace. And if Johnny von Neumann—along with Alan Turing, the father of computers—is right, we'll be able to download the contents of our brains as well, memories and all."

"No way." And she took his arm and cuddled for a moment. "By Jove, if masturbating could get you pregnant . . . who needs Zeus or Apollo to rape and inseminate when immortality is just a hand job away."

He nodded eagerly. "Precisely. Which begs the question: Why do we have to age at all? Why cancer? Why Huntington's?"

"Don't look at me. I'm sure Apolonia has an answer, what with all your tutoring sessions. Or why not just ask Jabberwocky; he's been around the block and then some."

He stuffed his mouth with the last of the pizza and chewed slowly, nodding as he pondered: "Roadkill on the way to life as we know it."

"Spit it out, Jake." She handed him a napkin. "Is it Apolonia who's got you so hot and bothered? Up from the streets of Philly?"

"From Manayunk . . . ," he mumbled, chewing.

"Oh, yeah . . ."

"You see, Dr. Margulis can't explain the explosive evolution of eukaryotes or how these multicelled life-forms are able to harvest energy, free energy from proton gradients. Somehow these early complex cells just appeared out of nowhere, out of some bacterial soup. Somehow, they were able to harvest power—somewhere, somehow."

"That gets me so hot . . . photons and protons and morons. I just love harvesting from your energy gradient."

"You figure evolution had to be a kind of competition between software and hardware—you know, computers."

"Computers?"

"Our brains. You figure our brains are a product of biology and culture, two systems of inputs: an internal genetic-biological input and a material-social-cultural input—your piano lessons harnessed to *The Little Engine That Could*."

"Don't forget tennis lessons. That's what gives me the edge over Apolonia."

"There you go: language, spoor tracking, probably throwing spears and lances . . ."

"They're all jealous of me, you know. That you won't share your tracking system with them. They'd do almost anything to steal you away."

At this, he wiped his hands on his shirt, even as she again handed him a paper napkin, picked up a paper plate with its flickering candle, and waved her over to a long display case.

"I'm not visiting with Boris," she said defiantly.

"Just to say hello; he's lonely after his three-thousand-year nap."

Grudgingly she made her way over to the mummy case, which contained a painted coffin and the blackened upper torso and emaciated head of a man bedded down in linen strips. She took a quick look and turned away, leaning on his arm.

"I think Boris is still napping; we shouldn't disturb him."

"What do you think he's dreaming about? What was he expecting? Where was he hoping to wake . . . the elysian fields, the fair isles, the paradise of river reeds ruled over by Osirus?"

"Certainly not at our dinner party."

"What a lot of time and effort they put into overcoming death—pyramids and monuments and grand tombs. Clearly, evolution has designed us to up our game and overcome death, or at least a too-precipitous decline."

"I sometimes think of myself as a dying breed—who cares about the humanities?—your thoroughbred put out to pasture. Or maybe it's just that hanging around with you makes me so aware of my inadequacies."

He gave her a reassuring squeeze and a kiss. "You're evolution's darling—the poster girl for what training by the numbers can accomplish. You're hitting with more and more power because of the weight work; getting more topspin on the ball than ever and so improving your margin of error. And your offspring may even be bigger and better, especially if you figure out how to reproduce asexually."

"Ah, clone myself—just the ticket." She stole a glance at the papery face of the figure in the glass case, sunken cheeks, a toothy grimace, and just as quickly turned away to nuzzle his shoulder. "But then there's the coaching, work ethic, competitive instinct—your opportunities."

"You've got to be willing to risk everything for a Wimbledon title and a Pulitzer for literature."

"Every day with you, I feel like I'm risking everything."

His laugh, more a cackle of pleasure, echoed like distant thunder out of the surrounding darkness. "And a bigger topspin shot will be your phenotype."

"Phenotype?"

"Like bears learning to catch leaping salmon, chimpanzees using sticks to prospect for ants: changes in behavior, habit, nongenetic markers that might well be followed later by genetic changes as those new habits prove beneficial to survival. A kind of evolutionary catch-up."

"Hey, just as long as I can finally beat Annette."

"I predict the top women pros of the future will all average close to six feet, like you."

"Ah, so that explains why we've been so busy practicing breeding. Apolonia may have the gritty street smarts, Annette the tenacity, Bianca the sultry sex moves, but I have the reach advantage."

"A crapshoot, of course, with both our parents and grandparents getting into the act. What if our kids got my backhand and your brains?"

She slapped his shoulder. "Would the phenotype of a writer be her first novel?"

"But then your mother was once a New England women's champion."

"Sure, but her phenotype is happy hour at West Chop."

"And your competitive instinct trumps your Stoic equanimity any day."

"Sometimes"—and she turned away from the glass of the vitrine, where she'd detected a troubling reflection of her spectral self, to the happier silhouette of a toothsome Allosaurus—"like Jabberwocky on a bad day, on my period, looking up to see that asteroid streaking through the atmosphere, my confidence fails me. Or even looking up from the court to see you on the hillside plotting my weaknesses—like: evolve, baby, or face extinction."

He studied her troubled face for a moment, holding up his candle so that her blue eyes shimmered with a dull iridescence, and bent, with the tip of his tongue, to lick off a bit of tomato paste at the corner of her mouth.

"You may live in your head too much, but your heroes, Epictetus and Seneca, would be proud to be your teammates."

"A living fossil with a finch's beak for a nose and a so-so backhand."

"The way your brain connects to your body is a textbook example of evolutionary selection happening in the very moment—every time you step onto the court."

"I don't know if I like your nature red in tooth and claw. Maybe I'm more my father's daughter, the scholarly thing, the bookish thing—just the world of ideas. Like Boris under glass, dreaming away in his ivory tower. Lacking the killer instinct: to risk it all."

Again, he cackled with pleasure. "Methinks the lady doth protest too much." And cupping her left breast as if scooping out her heart and soul in an offering, he kissed her deeply, knowingly, possessively. "And let me tell you: the science world is not for the shrinking violet. It's ambition's playpen: all sharp elbows and stealing each other's research."

"And writers . . . ?" she sighed.

"Artists are at the pinnacle of natural selection: they discover new worlds, new pleasures, that delightful illusion of order in the chaos of creation."

"Maybe Apolonia's street smarts, her doggedness, is more your blue-collar style?"

He turned and tapped the dusty glass of the vitrine so that her eyes met his in the murky blue of their reflections, twin figures staring down into an open crypt.

"This"—and he slid his spidery fingers down her spine to find a grip on her left buttock—"is the only truth that matters."

"Yes," she sighed, "your energy gradient. Or is it just plain, old-fashioned truth telling, as my father likes to say, if a bit hifalutin." She stared at their merged reflections and for a moment laid her head against his shoulder. "But I'm glad you love me best for my mind, the bookish-scholarly-classicist-aspiring writer in me."

"No, for your soul: It's the Wimbledon crown that will be the making of you. Or, as Boris would have it, your royal ka—the energy of personality."

"I didn't think you believed in souls."

"Maybe not Annette's kind of soul. But I believe in the unseen forces that rule the universe, the sheer wonder of discovery when you're on the verge of grasping some elusive detail of that hidden reality—like when you hit a perfect shot, when Bianca rings that perfect note in a Mozart sonata." He turned again to the glass of the vitrine, tapping out a silent tune, as if staring off through a dark window, cocking his head, glimpsing the imponderable. "Like the world of mathematics when I lose track of time and space: differential equations, Lucretius's swerve, tetrahedrons—crazy. Like you're surfing this perfect wave—standing at the pinnacle of Jabberwocky's and Boris's lost world, all the way back to the first eukaryotes, a wave of aspirations that finally allows us to break free from the iron hand of evolution and claim our own future."

"Stop that," she said.

"What—oh, I was just hoping Boris might perk up."

"Stop," she commanded, grabbing his hand. "Nobody lives forever."

"Dear Isabel, how do we know . . ."

CHAPTER 11

There came a distinct change in mood as Friday-night dinner got underway—portending since lunch, perhaps prompted by a lowering of the humidity (that tepid Canadian high), as if an elixir of eternal youth was being served up for the faithful, a loving cup silently passed among old chums, along with soft-spoken whispers of heightened expectation that something of their former glory still remained in reach. Such was certainly the case for the Shirelles, seated around their dinner table under the tent in the McCosh courtyard, cheek by jowl to the chapel and the collegiate Gothic halls of the history department, as if the immemorial clash of things theological and profane had found momentary resolution, a consoling standoff inspired by a celebratory scene where middle age and youth mingled as one. For the roommates, that cooling breeze also raised hopes that their once-exceptional lives still had room to roam, much less relief that the next morning's tennis event and then P-rade wouldn't be an exhausting steam bath.

The air was further sweetened with smiles of recognition among the faithful, redolent of freshly mown grass, sweating flagstones, and steam tables of boeuf bourguignon. Fairy lights twinkled along the sides of the tent like swarms of fireflies rising on the dusk, evoking childhood wonder and animated cheer. For most, if not all, the eternal question was posed: Can you believe we're really here? Are these familiar strangers milling about in the chow line, grown portly and gray, really our ageless classmates? How did time catch us so unaware? And what of these glittering table settings and candles, the fine wine contributed by some deep-pocketed classmate, the colorful and healthy buffet spread—here, here . . . how strange, in the very same grassy courtyard where once we lounged smoking and sunbathing and taking to heart Hermann Hesse's *Siddhartha*. Raggedy-assed students with barely two nickels to rub together who were dedicated to Martin Luther King's dream of a better America, where all God's children would be judged not by the color of their skin but by the content of their character. And how had that dream fared? And what had we done to further the cause?

The Shirelles were hardly immune from such ruminations, even as their joy in one another's company had them bubbling over with catty chatter to turbocharge their youthful ardor, now unleashed absent spouses and offspring or significant others. So animated was their charmed circle, so festive their pleasure in one another, their unfading celebrity, that few cared to intrude upon their conversation. A smoke screen of banter while each secretly kept an eye out for their Reunions manager, Jacob Burrage.

"Annette," protested Gini, "I thought we were going to have the pleasure of Matt and Arthur's company at dinner."

"There's a tennis dinner for the current men's and women's teams. Arthur was invited as an ex-captain, and Matt as an honorary member, as their guest of honor." Annette pulled a face of sad loss and then shared a fond giggle for her three teammates. "We got trumped by youth and beauty."

Gini sat back, her stare lingering on the Mather Sundial, a monumental column in the courtyard topped by a heraldic pelican standing on a globe, at the base of which she remembered gathering for precepts in Latin poetry. She often stood and greeted classmates, showing herself off, remaining defiantly open to the male gaze in her Armani black sable dress with a stylish orange-and-ochre silk scarf deftly tied around her long neck. Hair in a tight chignon. Her class jacket (orange-and-black shooting stars on a field of white) hung on the back of her chair. "No way," she now protested. "You're a captain. How come you didn't get invited?"

"I think the cutoff was ten years out." Annette looked up from her heaped plate and shrugged. "Besides, who wants to sit around a table with a bunch of gorgeous amazons, hearing about how they were crushed not getting into the eating club of their choice, when tomorrow, facing them across the net, is going to be difficult enough."

"Yeah," said Apolonia, "well, some of us couldn't afford an eating club, even if Bianca and I bickered for Cap and Gown."

Annette between mouthfuls: "You know Gini and I invited you two as our guests almost every night; and you guys were there for all the parties. Honorary members in good standing."

Apolonia, dressed simply in a white Reunions sports shirt and short skirt and their class Reunions jacket, shrugged this off and nodded knowingly at her teammate. "And speaking of bicker, I've already endured enough humiliation for one night, let me tell you! What a meat market Bianca and I just endured."

"Testosterone—somewhat aged with a hint of oak—on hyperdrive," Bianca echoed. "Billed as a discreet, single-alumni cocktails and mixer—a bicker meat grinder, more like it—for the assisted-living set. Worse than Tinder, although there was plenty more money and worldly success on offer."

"You do Tinder?" asked Annette, eyes pinched in disgust, having once detected the app on Arthur's phone.

"Hey there, Li'l Red Riding Hood," sang out Bianca (Sam the Sham and the Pharaohs), "not all of us managed to marry Troy Donahue at sweet sixteen." She bent over the table toward her captain, so that the delicious decolletage of her black vintage pencil dress showed to splendid advantage, and popped a lascivious thumb from inside her cheek. "And I was blackballed, as you know, when I bickered Cap because I was considered a down-market chatterbox, threatening to spill the beans on your preppy crowd of blue blood insiders."

"Maybe you should have gone strawberry blonde back then," retorted Annette, dressed in a simple blue summer dress. She gave her doubles partner a patented look of mild horror mixed with amusement and smoothly segued. "I scouted out the end of the women's practice this afternoon, and I can tell you, any one of their top three or four could have reached the finals of the US Open or Wimbledon in our day."

"Check that," said Gini, rubbing her right knee under the table as she refilled her wineglass and tried to remember that now-weathered Latin inscription on the base of the Mather Sundial. "How did we get roped into this?"

"Don't look at me." Annette shrugged. "I mean, I first suggested an exhibition match by the girls' team; then they countered with a cross-generational matchup with prize money—if I rounded up the sponsors and Matt would referee."

"So, how did the mixer go?" asked Gini, her distracted gaze (trying to put names to familiar faces, old admirers, at nearby tables) now returning to Apolonia and Bianca. "I just couldn't quite see myself as a needy single woman."

"There you go," Apolonia cried. "*You*, Agrippina, court queen, surely not. How undignified."

"I mean, what if Erma found me with a strange man?"

"For God's sake," said Bianca, "Bill has been out of the picture for—what, six years. What, are you supposed to remain celibate for the rest of your life? Married to your eroscillator."

"Eroscillator?" said Annette.

"Don't get her going." Apolonia raised a warning hand.

"Heck," shrugged Bianca, "my Matteo has no problem setting me up on dates with his musician friends. I have to practically plead with the busy kid to hang out occasionally with his father."

Apolonia laughed. "Hey, try dating when your grown kids are still living with you. And Christopher and Margie are both working for their dad; so, everything gets back to Tony. You'd be amazed how many of my patients email me for dates—male *and* female."

"What is it with you," said Gini, mildly amused, "with other women?"

Bianca sat forward over their table, her ample boobs lusciously displayed, an eager grin on her full lips. "Hey, not all of us have guys like Gareth hot on our tail. In case you haven't noticed, he keeps looking over at our table like a lost puppy, just waiting, after all these years, for a last-chance-last-dance to claim his long-lost prize. Hell, it's his own equity firm, now that his dad's passed; you'd be so set up for the golden years. He's probably as rich as the guy who nabbed me tonight."

"Do tell," chimed in Annette, wolfing down her boeuf bourguignon and contemplating another run at the buffet line.

"Jack, Jack Rambridge."

"As in Rambridge Capital?" Gini asked, mildly shocked.

"You didn't even have to google him. I'm much impressed," said Bianca, eyebrows raised in appreciation.

"Jesus, he tried to buy Tandem Press a few years back—a hostile takeover. He wined and dined me at the Four Seasons and tried to peddle me a series of mystery novels set in a French vineyard—bodies that turn up in wine casks and suchlike."

"Smart man, bookish even; all he wanted to talk about was the microclimates in his Burgundian terroirs." Bianca swished her wineglass, pondering. "Why do you suppose I've always attracted Jewish guys—this old-fashioned Catholic girl?"

"Plural terroirs?" exclaimed Gini.

"Six in the Côte de Beaune, by my count. He keeps an apartment in Dijon for harvesting season."

"And to think I ended up marrying a penniless Neapolitan chef," sighed Apolonia, a fork ruminating in her salad as she gazed upon the gray flanks of the chapel, where a white Avis rental truck was being unloaded by the catering service.

"A good one," assured Gini, who had dined at Tony's restaurant on many a Jackson Hole ski trip. She raised her fork in salute before poking at the litter of al dente haricot vert on her plate, her eyes wandering to the comings and goings under the tent: old friends, familiar faces from Cap and Gown, writing precepts, classics majors, some more familiar than others, all greatly changed, putting her in mind of the penultimate Guermantes reception in Proust's *Time Regained.* Another glance to where Gareth sat with his roommates (her freshman-year boyfriend and best friend of Jake Burrage).

Gareth (president of Ivy Club in their day) was checking his phone as if disengaged from the conversation at his table. Something in his darkly complected face, those intelligent mocha eyes, the crinkle at the corners, attracted her not-too-obvious stare. She suspected his quandary was her own: when a superior intelligence encounters the mystifying in the guise of a young man just too omniscient, too supremely self-possessed to be true. An intuition weighing on her mind since lunch. Along with a sneaking sense of things not adding up, things barely recalled but still touched with tender pain around the edges . . . fractured bits of memory lingering from student days yearning to be made whole in the guise of young Jacob Burrage. Her heart fluttered with barely repressed demonic desire as she again turned to Gareth. What a good sport he'd been, even losing out to Jake. A Black man with a rich white father who fought for social justice without wearing it on his sleeve. How she'd admired that . . . his stalwart equanimity, of which she herself could now use a good dose. And later his lovely wife, Ruth, a Jewish firebrand on every philanthropy board in New York.

"Oh, go ahead, invite him to join us," said Apolonia to Gini.

"Remember," chimed in Bianca, "when we were still dating—except little Miss Sunshine here—and Apolonia's Tony Soprano invited us all for dinner at his first restaurant in Trenton. What was that—our fifth reunion?"

"How could we forget?" said Annette. "You took over the piano and sang all those Sicilian songs."

Gini added, "You even got us to reprise our Shirelles routine for the whole restaurant."

"They—when in Rome—loved it; we brought down the coliseum."

Apolonia smiled. "Was that the last time we were all together—just the girls, before kids?" Her warm, steady expression deepened as a flicker of light brushed her eyes where she gazed at her upraised wineglass. "I was four months pregnant with my Christopher."

Oddly, this unguarded remark seemed to beach itself with barely a shudder, and Apolonia gazed around, while mentally noting the many older children in attendance with their parents.

"No way," Annette chimed in, distracted by a text as she buttered up her third dinner roll. "You weren't even married—"

"Enough," said Gini, turning back as Gareth's athlete daughter (with her mother's deep-set brown eyes and expressive mouth) now joined him at his table, noting the hint of pleasure and relief in her father's eyes. "Well, the lacrosse dinner got out, and we can't talk about our ailing sex lives all weekend, if this is where things are going, Big Mac Macaluso."

Bianca, a mysteriously knowing smile on her lips, again dipped her oar. "Helter-skelter, what fun we had, didn't we? Annette excluded, of course, not that we ever sullied the ears of little Miss Goldilocks." She made a face and grabbed the basket of rolls out from under Annette's outstretched hand. "Go on, girl, go for seconds before the boys eat us out of house and home."

"Thank the Lord for small blessings," sighed Annette. "Not that the paper-thin walls of our suite didn't provide me with a thorough sex education."

Bianca smiled deliciously. "Then I'll take all the credit for your successful wedding night, you lucky girl."

Gini eyed Bianca suspiciously, sensing her mood, the revelation being held back for the precise moment of greatest impact. "One thing for sure: whenever there was a strange naked man wandering our suite, we knew to whom he belonged."

"You should talk," piped up Annette. "Jake was hardly a shrinking violet on that score—talk about a sex education."

"Really," said Gini, intrigued, as if yet another obscure puzzle piece had dropped into place.

"Oh, nothing," said Annette with a dismissive wave. "I'm a veteran—what with four men, three of them teenagers, growing up in our house. Well, one learns to adjust. The laundry runs."

Apolonia winced. "I gave up changing sheets and towels and just parked a roll of Bounty, the quicker picker-upper, in my all-male bedroom. That and a box of Trojans." She nodded at her empty glass, which she then refilled. "What amazes me is how my patients, my younger moms and dads, never allow their kids any independence. Between baby monitors, minicams, and cell phones, their kids are forever under observation: a nanny state. Scary."

"What's scary is all the guns in circulation," Gini noted. "How are we to keep our schoolkids safe?"

Bianca, oblivious, drained her second glass of wine. "You three had it so easy. Already, by sophomore year, you had your futures so locked up, while I got left with the deluge, sifting through the guys madly in love with Gini or AP or Annette, having to constantly answer questions from men who couldn't figure out AP, who was turning down the hottest guys on campus while conducting a clandestine affair with Mr. Big."

"You were hardly dodging the incoming sperm donors," said Apolonia.

"What, me a cum-whore? I told them you were a lesbian and that if they made it with me, I might arrange a threesome."

"You pimped me?" Apolonia exploded in laughter, raising her wineglass in salute.

"I told them AP only makes exceptions for guys who buy at least two pairs of tennis sneakers. 'Two-Pair' was your nom de guerre."

"And to think we'd end up two needy, past-our-sell-by-date women haunting an octogenarian singles bazaar."

"Jack Rambridge can't be much past seventy," added Gini, sniffing.

Bianca snarled. "Hey—his fiftieth—I never put out in Prospect Garden like some sluts I know." A wagging finger. "Just as well you didn't make the scene, Gini. We didn't need any more competition from un-needy women, so your queenly dignity remains intact. And you"—she shot a look at Annette's mildly amused smile—"Sandra Dee, who plucked Troy Donohue's brass ring while still a teenager, with four homeschooled children and a Princeton tennis captain to boot, should have some respect, if not sympathy, for your lovelorn teammates."

Gini smiled pleasantly, the chardonnay beginning to make her a little giddy, even—was it possible?—a tad horny at mention of escapades past, their salad days. She saw herself before the full-length mirror at the Marriott, drying her hair with critical appraisal of the body she was about to daringly dress, checking the line of her chin for incipient sags, biceps nicely firmed. Just a touch of makeup, enough mascara to highlight her flinty blue eyes, a peach-rose lipstick for her too-small mouth but full lips. (Chrissie Evert had been commentating on the French Open in the background on the Tennis Channel.) She'd kept her hair short for the better part of a decade in inverse proportion as Erma had let hers grow out, only letting it lengthen over the last year down to her shoulders, but still serviceable, practical, businesslike for the first woman CEO of a major publishing house. Only a few touch-ups here and there to banish any creeping gray. Her hips still retained something of their girlish armature (for which she'd paid the price, giving birth to a near-ten-pound Erma), and her boobs were still perky, thank God. The gym three days a week with her personal trainer and regular workouts on courts at Sutton Place. Her legs, she always felt, were her best assets: just a hint of slackness at the back of the thigh—the merest shadow of cellulite, calves still robust in high heels. Knees, her weakest links—you're going to need them tomorrow, baby, so just a dance or two.

"Save me a dance."

"You say something?" asked Annette, sitting at Gini's right.

"I was just thinking that Erma's still at the swim-team dinner, so maybe she'll come by later and we can get her together with Matteo and Arthur."

"I'll text her," said Annette. "Maybe Arthur will be with us by then."

"I'll text her as well," said Bianca. "She seemed mightily impressed in high school when she heard my Matteo at Dizzy's."

"Hey, aren't I a godmother as well?" said Apolonia, texting (more annoyed at herself than ever for not having invited her Christopher).

Gini, now on her third glass of wine, found her troubled mind drifting off again (their class president was making announcements) to when she'd been debating in her hotel room if wearing her mildly sexy dress might be taken amiss by Erma. She'd been distracted by the panel of commentators, headed by Chrissie, who were reviewing the match highlights of the day. She'd paused every now and then with her dressing to watch the tall and powerful women whaling away on the red clay of Roland-Garros, many with unpronounceable Eastern European names. Their speed and agility, the godlike power, and the way they carved tight yellow parabolas with their shotmaking was mesmerizing. Thrilling. Everything that Jake had once predicted. Everything she'd feared to face. She'd turned up the sound to hear what Chrissie had to say about the women in the quarterfinals of the French, pleased that her might-have-been rival still looked pretty damn good, given her years in the sun. And why not . . .

"Boy, bet she's got one great dermatologist."

"What was that?" asked Annette.

"Nothing . . . ," said Gini. "Sorry, what were you just saying?"

"The thing is: Arthur seems at something of a loose end these days in the Manhattan finance world. He's been detailed by his boss to scout out recruits among the seniors, but I can tell his heart isn't in it, pumping the party line. Besides, I sense he's more inclined to be looking for himself, hopefully a good Christian woman."

"How about a good-great molecular biologist," said Gini.

"Ain't that the way of the world?" Bianca interjected. "Always looking to marry younger women so they can have their diapers changed by Marilyn Chambers in their dotage."

"Marilyn Chambers?" asked Annette.

"Behind the green door," suggested Apolonia, winking at Bianca with a sly smile. "The Scuola di San Giorgio, don't you know."

Bianca rattled on: "What fools we were, not having grabbed a great guy while the going was good, when the odds were five to one in our favor. Just look around. I count fifteen women who married classmates—and we were stars. And look at 'em, fat and happy with double incomes to go with their double chins. Their 401ks runneth over."

"Look at us," laughed Apolonia, raising her glass. "To the un-Spanx set."

"We were so spoiled—didn't know how good we had it," added Gini.

"Hell," retorted Bianca, throwing her dinner roll at Annette while turning to Gini, "you, our Amory Blaine, coulda married the spanking new biochemistry lab I've been hearing so much about."

"Okay." Annette raised her hands in surrender. "I'm off for seconds, and I'll bring back a dessert plate for the table."

"She could always outeat the three of us," said Bianca, her heart racing as she caught sight of a line of young women in black dresses, the Tigerlilies, an a cappella group taking the stage.

"The metabolism of an ocelot," laughed Apolonia.

Gini just smiled, following Bianca's gaze to where the Tigerlilies now broke into song. So young, so thin, so ardent with wonder as they gazed out over this gathering, witnessing what their future might hold in store, just as the Shirelles had once sung at Reunions.

Something Chrissie had to say about the women in the quarterfinals had registered with Gini, how so many had back injuries from the torque on their slingshot serves. And she'd turned again to the mirror and then the bed, where she'd laid out a phalanx of her favorite bras. Finally, deciding on a Simone Pérèle push-up demi-cup with delicate blue tulle, see-through but wouldn't show her nipples through her dress. A bra, according to her favorite saleslady at the Town Shop, that wouldn't embarrass her in front of a man. As she modeled the cute bra in the mirror, her eye was drawn to where a shaft of light gleamed in her perfectly trimmed pubic hair: still the same lovely reddish highlights that Jake Burrage had once loved.

"You're flushed," said Apolonia. "You okay?"

"It's nothing," answered Gini. "I was just thinking about poor John Ruskin."

"Besides," Apolonia continued, "your data sets are all corrupted: most of the failed marriages, or worse, don't show up at Reunions. We're the sad exception."

"I almost didn't show, but how could I not with my Matteo on tap for tonight? And the Shirelles tomorrow."

"Will you still love me tomorrow . . . ," sang out Apolonia.

"Hey," scolded Bianca, "that's my theme song."

"We really need to rehearse," Annette complained, handing around a plate of dessert selections, orange icing, all perfectly sliced and arranged.

"Do you think we can still get away with channeling a Black women's group?" asked Gini. "I mean, today people might take exception, white privilege and all that."

"Hell, I was a blue-collar kid from Queens," replied Bianca, indignantly. "I started the Shirelles with you guys as a way of paying homage to Black women, in solidarity with Black women. And now more than ever, sisters."

The four women turned again to the stage and the performance of the Tigerlilies, twelve young women in short black dresses and black high heels performing a medley of standards. In just moments, the dinner crowd was transported, exchanging wistful looks, as most were returned to student days and arch sings past, seeing in the young women all their own hopes and aspirations, some realized, many not. For their closing numbers, the Tigerlilies were joined by two alumni of the group in Reunions attire, merging their voices as one.

"Go on . . . ," urged Annette, giving Bianca's shoulder a shove, "you started out with the Tigerlilies."

"No, I'm saving my powder for tomorrow night with you guys."

After standing and singing "Old Nassau," led by the Tigerlilies, the four teammates settled back in their seats, for a moment overcome with helpless nostalgia, almost afraid to meet each other's eyes for fear of giddy tears.

Then Apolonia broke the spell. "At least Jack Rambridge has money: How much do you suppose a Harvard tenured professor makes?"

"So, you did meet someone?" purred Annette, holding up a forkful of carrot cake.

"Ridiculous, I know, after crying my eyes out at John's memorial service. Frankly, I was so depressed: the ones who knew him were ancient beyond belief, and the younger crowd couldn't have had any idea what he'd been like in his prime. It was all clichés, even from his kids."

"Well," offered Bianca, "you should have just marched up to the pulpit and told everybody how great he was in the sack—or was it the kitchen floor?"

"Fuck you, Macaluso."

"Ladies . . ." Annette grinned, savoring every bite of her cake.

Bianca tilted her head side to side: "Hey, he'd have been proud of you. You could've set the MeToo movement back decades: I fucked El Presidente at eighteen."

"Nineteen," Apolonia shot back. "What I regret is allowing myself to settle for less."

Gini, as if coming out of a daze: "What I always tell Erma: we can't always choose who we fall in love with."

Bianca leaned across the table, sloshing her wine. "Says she who stumbled back to our room at two in the morning with a rose thorn stuck so deep in her ass I had to get Dr. Kildare over there to do minor surgery."

"You were such a naughty girl," laughed Apolonia. "Always an acquired taste: cedar mulch and cum. Talk about risky business."

"Jesus, don't ever tell Erma."

"Listen." Apolonia gripped Gini's forearm. "My Christopher really enjoyed being Erma's ski instructor. Seems they talked one another's ears off. That's the thing about Christopher; he may be a sous-chef for his father, but he spends more and more time in my library of classics on Venetian art and architecture. A voracious reader, unlike his father, who only reads cookbooks."

Annette, sipping her wine, raised a curious eyebrow at this exchange, then raised her hand as if still in middle school. "As the mother of one daughter, Emily, I can attest that she was more difficult to raise than the three boys combined. Of course, her father always let her get away with murder."

"Which explains," said Apolonia, turning to Gini, "all those screedy memoirs on battered women you publish."

"Hey, whatever benefits the bottom line." Gini held up her hands in surrender.

Annette beamed around the table, always able to calm the waters. "We hired a new minister last fall, Laureen: a woman with more degrees than you can count. And let me tell you, she has shaken things up big-time in our congregation—talk about blushes on Sunday morning. It's kinda thrown me for a loop, to be honest."

"Speaking of cedar mulch and cum," said Bianca, sotto voce and ignoring this near admission. "Looks like our Reunions manager is back checking up on his charges." Their heads swiveled as one in the direction of the buffet table, where young, clean-shaven Jacob Burrage, sporting his class beer jacket, was chatting with his crew of servers.

This appearance electrified the table, not that any one of the four was going to let on, or at least not immediately. Annette was winged back to Sainte-Chappelle in the spring of 1980 when a locks-shorn Jake Burrage—her savior's face bathed in translucent tones—had arrived in Paris to take up his job tracking her husband's matches. Apolonia, prompted by a glint of waning sunlight on the upper windows of the history department, was, strangely enough, hurtled back to that terrifying moment when she was first confronted by the bald provost in his Nassau Hall office. Again, she recalled that scribbled notebook page on his vast desk: that Jake might have betrayed her and her lover. Gini, for her part, felt herself lifted yet again into a whirlwind of longing, a flurry of chances foregone, as if a sheaf of manuscript pages had been blown to the four corners of her office, pages without page numbers: a disorderly mind that refused to settle into a comforting pattern. And Bianca, strangest of all, found herself catapulted back, painfully so, to the Venice–Vienna overnight train and her reflection in the compartment window, the clatter of the tracks and the receding *campanili* of the lagoon city echoing the disarming voice of one greatly changed Jake Burrage, a voice that she had carried around in her head for over three months. A vanished soul mate who had suddenly stopped returning her letters. An agony of regret that poured out in a sudden confession, loosed on the table like a breached dam.

She threw out her bust and took a deep, conspiratorial breath. "I was so weirded out at sign-in when young Jacob addressed me in Italian."

"And just why would he do that?" shot back Gini, trying to hide the panic in her voice.

"Well, what was I supposed to do when our crazed genius, like a lost boy, washed up on my doorstep in Venice?"

"What?" exclaimed Gini.

"Oh, don't get your knickers in a twist."

"Venice? When?"

"Best three years of my life after I finished up at Juilliard. The Scuola Antiqua, studying seventeenth- and eighteenth-century performance styles. I was a star, ladies, playing two, sometimes three concerts a week. Not than any of you bothered to come visit me."

"Come on, sister, spit it out," urged Apolonia.

Gini hissed: "You met Jake in Venice, and you didn't tell me? You wait—what, almost forty years to tell me? What the fuck, Big Mac?"

"Take it easy, Gini." Annette reached out a hand.

"Oh, summer of 1979—or, let's see . . ." Bianca smiled serenely, a swaggering of her shoulders. "The leaves had changed in the Giardini, where we liked to stroll, so it must have been early fall, October."

"Jake . . . really?" asked Annette, curiosity mixed with a hint of alarm, since this would have been just six months before Jake joined them to tour—and not a word.

"It was like, 'of all the gin joints in all the world,' I run into him at the Scuola di San Giorgio. I was playing a concert there that evening, and I was rehearsing on the second-floor *sala*. And as I came down the stairs and headed for the door, who should I find, sitting there all alone, staring at the Carpaccios, his mind a million miles away: Jake, a Samson shorn of his locks. When I tapped on his shoulder, it was like he'd seen a ghost. The only time I've known him to be speechless."

Gini sat back listening intently, fingering her wineglass with her eyes fixed firmly on Bianca as if in ambush at the faintest misstep. "Did he tell you why he was there?"

"Of course: he was waiting for you."

All eyes at the table turned to Gini.

"For me—don't be ridiculous."

"A thousand days, that was the deal you had with Jake," replied Bianca, barely able to hide the proprietary tone of her voice.

"I never . . . we never agreed—never in a million years."

Apolonia interceded in a searching voice: "Well, that certainly puts a new spin on viewing the Carpaccios, huh?"

"Visiting the Carpaccios," sang out Annette, as if to tamp down this volatile bit of scuttlebutt before it inflamed the table, not to mention her own memories of the Scuola di San Giorgio. "Jake never mentioned anything about that over the summer of 1980 when he worked for Matt."

Bianca again preening, jousting her bust and shifting her muscular shoulders, eyes glittering with happy malice as she squinted at Gini. "Of course you did: Why else would he have shown up? He had no idea I was studying in Venice." She glared around the table, catching each of her teammates' eyes. "I sent postcard after postcard to all my sister Shirelles, inviting you, pleading for your company, and no one came to visit me."

"We were on tour," explained Annette unconvincingly.

"You fucked him," burst out Apolonia—fuel to the flame—with a sardonic grin.

"I did no such thing! He was totally lost on Gini."

Gini shook her head (parsing postcards) and sucked in her lower lip as she refilled her glass. "Oh, it was some vague outlandish idea he had—you know how he was. Yes, something about a thousand days. The kind of desperate craziness you put out there when you're breaking up—excuses, pretending there might be hope when there's not."

Annette protested. "But there's always hope. At the senior dance, all those tears: we all thought you two had decided to tie the knot."

"The old rope-a-dope, huh?" chimed in Bianca. "Well, you certainly still had him on the ropes. All he wanted to talk about was you—what news—any news—sightings. Good old Jake, twisting my mind into granny knots until I had a migraine just trying not to seem a total airhead. At the Rialto fish market, I got a whole lecture on the evolution of crabs and squids."

"Admit it," laughed Apolonia, "you jumped his johnson."

Bianca raised her right hand and fixed Gini with an impish look. "*Lo guiro su mia madre*, I never laid a hand on him. I had an Italian—talk about hands—boyfriend, who played viola da gamba to my harpsicord. Of course, he hated my Sicilian accent; his family was from Turin, very upper class. We performed all over Italy: Scarlatti, Vivaldi, Monteverdi, and Couperin. I might have married him if it hadn't been for an old girlfriend back in Turin his parents wanted him to marry—such a mammoni. Of course, her dad was a director of Martini & Rossi."

"Well," huffed Gini, raising her glass, "may you have better luck with your Daddy Warbucks tonight."

"Hey, he's on the board of Lincoln Center, not like my ex, who was raised on Mantovani; every time I opened the door to our home, it was like walking into an elevator."

"Visiting the Carpaccios," toasted Annette with a vague smile of relief.

"Visiting the Carpaccios," said Apolonia.

"Why not," Gini added, touching her glass to the others.

"Only thing," complained Bianca, "Jack's kinda short."

"They're always shorter than you, Macaluso," Apolonia laughed.

"Bianca," Gini leveled a malicious gaze, "you can hardly complain about your luck *dans le temps*: you had a different guy almost every night—a permanent wet spot; the dudes were stacked up outside our entranceway like flights into LaGuardia on a stormy night."

Annette giggled. "And who came up with the best-kisser prize, worst-hands-of-the-week prize?"

"And don't forget," said Apolonia, "spunk of the month selection." She reached over and patted Bianca's arm. "That's the thing about being a doctor: men are a little afraid of you, like you know too much about their MO."

Bianca chuckled. "Hey, girl god, who pimped for your girl-on-girl racquet-stringing business in hopes you might come to your senses and give up El Presidente."

"I had the highest-grossing student agency except for the hoagie man."

Wolfing down her third piece of carrot cake, on a sugar high, Annette let loose. "While trying to conceal from the world that you were cavorting with the human neutron bomb."

Apolonia snarled. "Sorry if Armageddon so upset you."

"Upset! Try traveling the pro tour with a husband whose career went into the tank the moment he married." Annette blinked rapidly. (How had she let that cat out of the bag?)

The three looked at Annette a tad astonished, guilty, resisting the glib rejoinder on all their lips.

"Oh, hell," sighed Bianca, "I so envied you three—the men in your lives. Mine was all a big act. Maybe I just need to stop going to Dylan concerts. That legendary genius has sung out his voice and worse. Like a lizard with a frog stuck in its throat, he keeps tinkering with his lyrics." She sang, gesturing to the crowd, now with more Reunions jackets being donned as the evening cooled: "Saw a shooting star, and it made me think of you."

"Well," said Apolonia, waving a kiss to Bianca, "we'll find out tonight how my bad boy of the Harvard History Department holds up—that is, if he shows up at our dance."

"Oh . . ."

"Oh . . ."

"Yeah, baby . . ." High fives from Bianca.

"Class of '66, academic, still teaches at Harvard, tenured, summer place on Martha's Vineyard, three beautiful, talented daughters by his beloved wife, who died years ago of ovarian cancer. Of course, being a doctor, he wanted to rehash all the gory details about her treatment, if they made the right decision around chemo and the like."

Opined Bianca: "Your problem will be the daughters; they'll never let you replace their mom."

"She's right about that," said Annette. "Daughters may be difficult, but they're loyal."

"Good Lord, we only just met an hour ago. And all he could talk about was his faltering career propounding a Marxist interpretation of the American labor movement, the proletariat that was supposed to cast off its chains and overthrow the bourgeoisie—"

"Us wicked capitalists who control the means of production," interjected Gini.

"But after the fall of the Berlin Wall, it seems his whole academic gig tumbled as well: once a titan of the historians' fraternity, with best-selling books read by thousands, now he's reduced to teaching Freshman History 101 and writing articles for journals that no one reads anymore."

Gini, astonished. "You got such a confession out of him at a mixer?"

"Must be AP's bedside manner," chortled Bianca.

"A branding problem," quipped Gini. "The Marxists don't sell anymore, relegated to the dustbin of history. Why don't you suggest to him that you're really a neo-Marxist. Better still: tell him you're a Trotskyite."

"I always liked Trotsky—such a sixties kinda guy." Apolonia looked around a tad sheepishly. "He probably won't show."

"Jack Rambridge promised he'd bring Trotsky along," said Bianca, always delighted to have the inside track. "They were roommates."

"No way," said Gini. "The lion and the lamb. What's his name?"

"Daltrey Assingham."

"Daltrey—oh my God, when I was a kid, his family had a house on West Chop not far from my parents' old house. And so-o Henry James—I love it."

Bianca, not to be outdone: "Jack's got his own Learjet and a place in Bermuda for winter getaways."

"Invite him to the charity match tomorrow and get him to contribute," said Annette.

"To watch us get humiliated."

"That's why I'm dreading tomorrow as well," said Annette. "Those girls on the team, these days"—sotto voce—"they're animals."

"Animals—really?" laughed Apolonia at this uncharacteristically crude remark.

"Just between us"—Annette bent closer over the table—"you see, Arthur told his father that, as part of the initiation ritual for both the women's tennis and squash teams, each member has to seek out her opposite number on the men's team and, well . . . *sleep* with him."

Such a tale coming from Annette's lips had the effect of quieting the table as each woman pondered the full implications of this bit of delicious gossip.

"Hallelujah," cried out Bianca, "how I lusted over the men's number four in our day. I'd have done anything to fuck him."

"I'll bet," said Apolonia.

Gini and Annette looked at each other and smiled uneasily. In unison: "The Colson brothers."

Annette's phone vibrated. "There you go: Erma will try to join us for dessert or meet us with Arthur at the fifth."

"And there's Matteo and his trio setting up on the bandstand," exclaimed Bianca. "My boy, my wonderful, talented son." She looked around, panicked, at her roommates. "Do you think it's okay if I run up there and give the big guy a hug and kiss?"

"No."

"No."

"No."

CHAPTER 12

A silence fell over their table as Matteo's jazz trio began to play, a respectful silence, an attentive silence, but a silence that had more to do with Bianca's cagey bombshell than the soft strains of Coltrane, as all were winged back—postcards or no—to the Scuola di San Giorgio, to moments of fraught silence and sanctuary, where once Jake Burrage had presided, in the flesh or otherwise, with consequences that still rattled down the years.

Annette for one, after Bianca's fireworks, found herself drifting under the spell of pealing bells, as she had before John Proctor's memorial service, transporting her first to the Zattere and the Pensione Seguso, where they had been serenaded by the bells of the nearby Church of the Gesuati as they unpacked from Rome and prepared to find their way to the Scuola di San Giorgio. Not that she dared mention her phone call the previous day to Jake Burrage at the Stanford chemistry lab. As they stood on the steps of the Gesuati, map in hand, trying to decide between a vaporetto or walking, she had breathed deeply of the scent of brine and sea wrack and diesel fuel from the supply barges along the quay. They'd walk it. She was determined to prove Gini wrong, that she was just as capable of finding her way to that elegant bridge that led to the green doors of the scuola.

And why hadn't Gini ever mentioned the hundreds of churches that seemed to greet her at every turning, a city overflowing with churches, spiked with tolling bell towers that rang out all the hours of the day? And then there were the story-filled church façades tottering on the narrow blue sky, porches peopled with the apostles and saints and the Virgin Mary, as if the Old Testament and Gospel scenes of her childhood, so vividly pictured in the books open on her mother's knee, had sprung to life. She could hardly contain her wonder and delight as she led her husband, still reeling from his humiliation in Rome at the Italian Open, past jostling crowds and into the soaring churches that proclaimed her two-thousand-year-old faith to the angel-filled heavens. Just wandering the winding streets—as if the wandering was the best part of their goal—seemed to raise their spirits as they paused to breathe in the cool, musty, candlelit interior of San Stefano, with its ship's keel ceiling; and then a jog to the right, winding their way until greeted by the marvelous if cluttered mélange of the façade of San Moisè and onto the expanse of San Marco (Gini: "If you pause to window shop, you're lost."), barely pausing as they hung a left under the clock tower in the piazza, and a right again until striking upon the intimate Renaissance rectitude of San Zaccaria, with a quick visit to the Bellini *Madonna and Child*, the otherworldly serenity bringing tears to their eyes, as their faltering faith seemed to gain airspeed by the moment (only days before on life support), and then off again to track down that elusive bridge (Gini: "You'll never find it without me."). And yet with only a few wrong turns and cul-de-sacs ending in the milky green of a side canal, they managed to stumble upon the right bridge. And there, a near-mystical presence in Annette's mind, the green doors of the scuola guarded by two glowering dolphins.

They lingered on the bridge holding hands. Partly it was just relief, to be strangers in a strange but enchanted city where no one had recognized her tall husband in his baseball cap and dark glasses, no one to remind them of Rome's slow red clay that had nullified his serve-and-volley game, while allowing that rude and sassy Argentinian teenager (a wicked topspin backhand to go with his acne) to prevail in three humiliating sets.

Map now stowed in her husband's pocket, she felt inspired, invincible, unerring in her sense of direction, knowing that God had called on her to make this happen: in two days, they had to decide whether to withdraw from the equally slow red clay of the French Open and either prepare for the faster grass of Wimbledon by committing to small grass-court tournaments in Germany, and then Nottingham and Bristol—or simply announce Matt's retirement, which he'd mentioned at least twice on the train from Rome. But as she stood proudly on the arch of the Ponte de la Commenda, lungs filled with a fresh sea breeze, she knew, with the help of the

Lord (His dispensation to call on Jake Burrage, who both scared and fascinated her), they might yet catch a second wind.

"There it is—see? Just like Gini said it would be."

They gazed as if not a little spellbound—lost even when found—at the white marble façade of the Scuola di San Giorgio in the humid spring air of late afternoon, a slant of golden sunlight on the uppermost octahedron window, columns set upon columns, three tiers like a slightly off-kilter wedding cake, the ground-floor footings, in deepest shadow, all worn and crumbling due to salt fretting. Stray cats slunk from the shadows. In the distance, two boys kicked a soccer ball back and forth.

"And look," said Annette, pointing, "there's the ice cream place Gini went on and on about."

Her husband seemed hesitant, as if only too aware his wife had something up her sleeve but was biding her time before springing it on him. He was still mulling over a sporadic conversation begun on the train from Rome, just as a nearby peal of church bells rang out. "When you lose at Wimbledon, especially an ex-champion, especially in an early round, it feels like such a disgrace. And my seeding will be so low that there won't be any easy matches."

"Come on," she said, squeezing his hand, "we came here to get away from all that. Why don't we just pray on it."

Dare she admit it, that she was of two minds: retirement would mean an end to ten months on the road, the grind, the logistics, the bad losses . . . and a chance to settle down, put down roots, children.

"Oh, look," she said as they descended the bridge, "there they are, the two grumpy dolphins above the green door, just like Gini described them." Still ascribing this folly of a road trip to another.

"I'm not sure I'd like to hook one of those characters, much less land them in the boat. But I'm glad you're feeling better disposed to your ex-teammate." (Had it been that obvious?)

Once inside the first-floor oratory—ushered in by an oddly attired, tonsured figure with a sun-weathered face who took their lira notes and then melted away into the shadows—they were met by an unworldly calm, only to be enveloped and then bathed in the magic of the Carpaccios. The cool air was scented with incense and beeswax. In the loosened grip of her husband's hand, she could feel all the pent-up tensions and bad losses of the tour melt away. Matt, not usually drawn to art, was so captivated by the stories in the paintings that his own depressing tale of a three-year fall from grace momentarily faded. She could see the tension in his face dissolve in his wonderful smile as they stood before the painting of the monks fleeing in the presence of Jerome's tame lion.

He'd squeezed her hand. "Heck, I'd be heading for the hills as well."

But the Carpaccio that stole fully into their imagination was not that of Gini's favorite, Augustine in his study, but the scene where a golden-haired Saint George baptizes two kneeling supplicants, a prince and his queen dressed in silken robes.

"Selenites," she said, "according to the guidebook. Don't you just love how that elegant white dog with the long snout sits so patiently waiting for its master and mistress to rise—born again."

"Imagine," he said, "so long ago, the very beginnings of our faith. Somehow, just as I'd imagined it, a time and place far, far away."

"And yet you've been to many of those faraway places."

"Not this far. Not outside the tour bubble."

She laughed. "And I thought you'd identify with Saint George slaying his dragon and saving his lady fair."

"And look how that princely fella has put a melon in his turban—there on the steps by the red parrot—to keep its shape while he's baptized."

"Do you suppose it happened five hundred years ago, or five hundred years ago it happened—what?—fifteen hundred years before . . . and in a way, I suppose, keeps happening, God's grace being eternal."

The quiet and seclusion of the oratory, where they lingered under the narrative spell of the Carpaccios, seemed to raise their mood by the moment, a sacred space reminding them of all the blessings of their life together, how that world's number-one ranking and those Wimbledon and US Open crowns would always be there, and maybe, just maybe, come hell or high water, that was plenty.

"How's the elbow?" she asked. He'd been rubbing it.

"Okay, it's really not sore. Just a habit, I guess."

"I think we need to get you a dog and maybe a red parrot."

"Ah, domestic bliss, huh? Just your everyday pro teaching snotty-nosed kids and rich widows."

"Serenity, like it really did happen only five minutes ago when we arrived and not five hundred years ago—two thousand even. A blink of an eye on eternity."

"It's an Ibizan hound, by the way."

"How do you know?"

"A friend of mine when I was a kid had one, more brown than white." He squeezed her hand. "Yes, a place where one's faith seems to matter. Where once Saint George had bagged his dragon—his claim to fame. Well, I guess it was all downhill after that—right, just baptizing the heathen? The reason you—or is it Gini?—brought me here."

She laughed and placed her other hand over his. Whispering in his ear: "Oh, you remember how Gini was: she always thought she had all the answers until she didn't."

"Because the real burden has always been yours. I get a chance to redeem myself every day, while you get stuck worrying about whether I'm going to fall on my butt."

"It beats struggling at the bottom rungs of the women's tour while being married to the number-one men's player in the world."

"Was I really such a rare bird—not a red parrot, I hope—once upon a time?"

"You were and are and will remain forever in the record books."

"Do you suppose Saint George is really going to pour that pan of holy water over the heads of those two and spoil their nice clothes?"

"He wants to make sure they're good and baptized."

"Well, no more shellacking dragons. A life preaching and baptizing the heathen wouldn't be the worst fate."

Thinking she had heard another voice, she turned for a moment from Carpaccio's Saint George to the Madonna and Child above the small altar, looking into the tender face and pensive eyes of the Virgin, the bright eyes of her son like beacons of love (the children she longed for), hesitating as she sought inspiration, or was it guidance, as if for something left undone that needed doing.

"I didn't mention it, but at the hotel in Rome, I put in a call to Jake Burrage."

His voice was barely above a whisper. "Ah, Gini's genius—boy wonder. How's Jake doing?"

She knew by the feigned nonchalance in his voice that she had his attention.

"He's just finished up his doctorate at Stanford. Looks like he's got a whole summer on his hands before he starts his postdoc at Chicago."

"The guy Gini ditched after losing to you in that final challenge match."

She took a deep breath, hearing that distant murmur of a voice again as she had by the window in the Rome Hilton, turning to find the nearly bald caretaker in the shadows by the stairs to the second-floor muttering to himself, seemingly oblivious to their presence. "The Lord forgive me, but maybe to your benefit."

"You think?"

"Remember how you once asked him to go over his notebooks, his tracking system?"

"Lots of numbers . . . I was a tad skeptical."

"You seemed pretty impressed at the time. Maybe he could work some of that same magic he did with Gini." Nervously, she now turned her guilty eyes to the painting of Augustine, where the saint was staring out his study window, his bearded gaze soft and distant, transfixed by some memory, the flicker of an angel's wing. And the thing came through her, the rapture of a timeless moment of certainty. "It's your main chance."

He had turned to the painting of Augustine as well. "I thought you were plenty steamed up he wouldn't track your matches."

"She was the best of the four of us—adaptable, tall, and quick: if I were Jake testing out a new theory, I'd have stuck with Gini too."

"Is that why you brought me here?"

"I find myself praying occasionally that you win, or worse."

"Is Jake Burrage the answer to *your* prayer?"

"Like you always said: all you can ask of the Lord is that you play up to your potential, and if the numbers are part of His plan, then so be it."

"What did he say?"

"Jake wanted to talk to you."

He gestured with his long hand to Carpaccio's Augustine. "What do you suppose the old guy's looking at out his window?" For a moment, she was at a loss for words. And he laughed: "Gini's ice cream place, where we can go over the numbers."

As Apolonia listened to Matteo's jazz riffs, his intent face bent to the fingerboard of his guitar, she found herself reminded of her own son, Christopher, her firstborn, with similar dark eyes and, if anything, a more pronounced Roman nose. A dreamy child, a bookish teenager, a scholarly soul, even if drawn to skiing and haute cuisine at the University of Colorado Boulder. Who liked nothing better than to curl up in the La-Z-Boy in her small library with one of her many art history books, compliments of her secret lover. How many mornings had she come downstairs to find him fallen asleep in that chair, returned home after a long night as sous-chef for his father, a book on Bellini or Titian or Carpaccio open in his lap.

Yes, she should have had Christopher come and hang out with Gini's Erma or Gareth's lovely daughter, Diane. If anyone, Christopher had a right to be here.

"Just tell Neil you're on vacation—a mini vacation, four or five days—make it six, just enough to relax and recharge, and that you won't be near a phone. Don't give Neil the number of the pensione. Say you'll be off hiking in the Adirondacks."

Apolonia'd had everything planned—yes, sparked by a postcard from Bianca (not that she was going to let her teammate know). She and John had taken separate flights and stayed at a modest pensione, the Pensione Seguso (Gini's ne plus ultra for the academic set), off the beaten tourist track on the Zattere. A name she remembered from Gini's novelist's description of the place, a cozy nest of writers and historians, and how she'd stayed there with her father when she was seventeen. The perfect fusty academic backwater for scholars (mostly Yale and Oxford), where they would be unlikely to be recognized, where they could fuck to their heart's content and take occasional breaks for meals and sightseeing. And so have the time—almost a whole week, a near eternity—to themselves. A final break, or no. Since, so she'd told herself, they couldn't go on like this. A crazy idea, but one that changed her life forever.

In the days before the internet and cell phones, John Proctor was paranoid about being out of touch. There'd been a big brouhaha just before he left when a trustee had leaked to the press that they were going to bestow an honorary degree on George Shultz, class of 1942, who had been secretary of commerce under Nixon, a president detested by the left. There had been rumblings of campus protests, outraged objections from the faculty. So, every morning he'd grab an *International Herald Tribune* from the kiosk by the Church of the Gesuati, half expecting something catastrophic—an occupation of Nassau Hall, a student riot—but after a few days, he realized, somewhat to his chagrin, that his august Ivy institution was still way down on anyone's list of newsworthy items. He'd even resisted calling Neil, her bête noire, his provost.

And then the sex was better than ever, long, casual, unhurried hours to themselves without fear of discovery, which was not a good omen if she really had hoped for a clean break. Of course, it didn't help that early spring in Venice—cool, sunny, no mosquitoes—was incorrigibly romantic, how the waves of the lagoon lapped urgently beneath their window overlooking the Rio San Vio. Glittering reflections off the canal pooling like airy windows in the ceiling of delicate acanthus leaves as they lay like sweaty, rutting beasts in one another's arms. If anything, their sex was deeper, more relaxed, more sweetly innocent, like honeymooners. But it was the silence that mesmerized her the most (no cars or scooters or trucks), the slow, unhurried pace of their strolls, and John's longing gaze upon the architectural wonders (the architect he'd once considered being) that only weakened her resolve to tell him her news. How to get it out when every turning brought something even more splendid into view than the last. The immemorial whisper of eternity that made her issues seem insignificant. And yes, it hadn't helped that he'd ended up being so smitten; he couldn't keep his long nose out of the *Blue Guide* as their lovemaking began to exhaust itself and the art and history—time took over. So, when, on the third day, she had suggested they go visit Gini's Scuola di San Giorgio and the Carpaccios—Geronimo, they were off.

Even now, she smiled to herself in wonder as she flicked glances Gini's way, where she was talking with Gareth in low whispers while he held out the screen of his phone to her, recalling how Gini had once insisted to her roommates that only she had the intrepid instincts of a pathfinder, got from her publisher father (a family of intellectuals going way back), to find, much less properly appreciate, that magical gallery of Carpaccios. How Gini had always insisted—like she did about so much else—that without her ball of twine they'd be lost like Theseus in the labyrinth. As if she'd staked out some odd proprietary claim on the Carpaccios. But she'd done Gini one better: scored her own bookish guide who turned out to have an unerring sense of direction, even with his map of Venice stuck defiantly in his back pocket. As in so many things, John had guided her true.

Suddenly, at a turning, there it was on the far side of the bridge, the Scuola di San Giorgio, a humble white marble façade like a tiny chapel, where a bald-headed, somewhat ambiguously aged man wearing a long green apron lounged in the doorway beneath the twin dolphins. Just down the canal-side *calle* was a small gelateria, where Gini had promised them the best ice cream of their lives.

John paid the entrance fee, and the wizened custodian, muttering in Venetian dialect, bowed and waved them through the double green doors, where, passing through a red velvet curtain, they found themselves enveloped in the artist's quattrocento world: luminous, crystalline, exotic, and utterly enchanting. The Carpaccios were more splendid than she'd dared dream, as if the ersatz reproductions that had once hung on the wall of their suite had come to glorious life.

And John was beside himself, going from one painting to the next, eyes aglow in the reflected light from the canvases as he bent to the pages of his *Blue Guide* to relate the adventures of Saints George, Jerome, and Augustine. He too seemed transformed, as if shed of any last remnant of the learned economist so adept at academic politics, able to finesse complaining faculty and students, reassure trustees up in arms—born anew, a convert released from bondage and possessed by a dream, a vision of something grander and more enduring than simply managing the affairs of a great university. And only adding to her chagrin, it was the pensive vision of Saint Augustine (Gini's Augustine) that so captured his imagination.

Not that she could be dissuaded from arguing her favorite, claimed years before, when she had instantly identified with Saint George slaying his dragon: that tough street fighter who'd fought her way up from the blue-collar streets of Manayunk, first mastering a gritty tennis game by winner-take-all jousts on public courts, managing just enough academic wherewithal to get a Princeton scholarship, and finally—finally, med school. He'd laughed at her going on about her princely, golden-locked Saint George leaning into his spear and sat her down instead before his patron saint to review the fascinating iconography of Augustine's study. And again, like so many times in her life, she had felt somewhat slighted for her lack of sophistication, that she had preferred the literal, the narrative to the less-than-narrative, the intrepid slayer to the more abstract philosopher and theologian. The mystery of a story untold. A failing brought doubly home to her as she gazed upon Carpaccio's Saint Augustine through her lover's eyes, only to have his ruminations result in a spate of soul-searching—trigging the same in herself—as he began a wrenching meat grinder of introspection: his job, his academic field, his marriage, the whole shooting match. So much so that her news, when she finally got a word in edgewise, seemed only timed to magnify his distress.

They had remained silent for a long minute.

"That's not why I wanted to bring you here," she scolded him playfully, nestled against his shoulder with his arm wrapped around her. The glittering, gloriously arranged precision of Augustine's sumptuous study seemed now a rebuke to the messiness of her life. "It was not an annunciation to trap you, to tell you I'm with child, to have you make an honest woman out of me—put up or shut up."

His arm tightened around her shoulders, a gentle, reassuring squeeze.

"You couldn't have picked a more, well, romantic place. How far along, did you say?"

"Six weeks or seven. I've missed one period, and I never miss; like Mussolini's trains, they're always right on time. And I'm not feeling the beginnings of the next. I changed prescriptions to a lower dosage to keep the ovaries fresh, and I guess they got too fresh."

"I'd never suggest an abortion."

"And I'd never press you one way or another."

"Do you get the feeling," he said, pointing to where Augustine's face was turned to the window, "that he's seeing us, perhaps reflecting on our dilemma, the man who, along with Paul, brought original sin into the world?"

"Oh, he definitely wouldn't approve of the likes of me, a home-wrecker." It was in that moment that she noticed John had removed his wedding ring. "Heck, a sin against God—and worse, old Nassau."

"Only those who would be harmed by our actions."

"Your wife . . ." She could never say her name.

He turned his gaze for a moment to the caretaker in the far corner bent to the inlaid paneling beneath the Carpaccios, which he was polishing with a bright yellow dustcloth.

"Good Lord," he whispered, "he looks just like Neil."

"Yeah, I was thinking the same. Wasn't Venice famous for its intelligence service?"

"Actually," he went on, "I'm feeling pretty damn proud of you, how you've handled yourself, even grateful at the thought of having a child with you, given present company." At this, he angled his dimpled chin at the Madonna and Child over the small altar, and then back to the corner by the entrance to where *their* Carpaccio hung, his large left hand lingering before her eyes (the pale circle of skin on his ring finger), as if contemplating this new reality that had so strangely found them in the company of a saint. Somehow, as if attuned to a transfiguring spiritual grace—spellbound by the crystalline light emanating from Augustine's study, she felt kindled with a kind of serene otherworldliness—a cosmic energy, hers only one of a thousand stories deep: there, safely harbored within the pages of the volumes strewn about the saint's study. "Say the word," he pronounced in that clear, unmodulated, firm voice. "If you want to have the baby, I will divorce Betty Anne and marry you. We'll have a family of our own."

For a moment, her eyes closed in pure bliss and gratitude. "Family? My God, I've finally passed organic chemistry; I've finally gotten into med school: family is about the last thing on the agenda." She looked to his craggy, handsome features, that distinctive beak of a nose, and tried to resist tears. And that insistent, if boyish, cowlick over his large, furrowed brow that she'd failed to tame.

He glanced up at the painted ceiling as if momentarily befuddled by the intricate hypnotic patterns. "The Rockefeller Foundation has approached me to run the place in a couple of years. But honestly, at this moment, here with you, I'm wondering about a professorship at some small but good college—and maybe I could even switch fields: architectural history or even art history. An economic history of Venice, why not? I'm told there are civic archives going back a thousand years. What do you think?"

"Being in med school for just three years is going to be hard enough."

"We could find a way, and that's a promise."

"I didn't mean this to be a downer, spoil the moment or anything."

"Hardly. I feel full of life—not the same as you," he laughed, his voice rich with possibilities, "but excited. I can't remember ever being so moved by works of art—something . . . maybe the place, the intimacy—not a museum, in situ, as the art historians would say. Or maybe it's the age, the history, the time stored up within these images, or the millions of eyes that have viewed our dear Augustine, been touched, like us, by the sheer immutability of his scholarly abode, the exquisite pleasure that all the world's knowledge might be compassed by one intelligence—the soaring humanity of such a thing."

"And to think, I brought you here to see San Giorgio bagging his dragon. Not to mention all the roadkill, which was how I always imagined an anatomy lab, cheerful soul that I am."

"That knight from the mean streets of Manayunk."

"Actually, I thought more the maiden in distress." She gave his arm a playful slug. "And Neil over there reminds me of how my mother always had me cadging cans of furniture polish when I was on the cleaning crew at the Merion Cricket Club—'the high and mighty will never miss it.'"

"We could have our own cricket court." He kissed her cheek. "Actually, I find myself rather taken by our friend Mr. Augustine, with his dreamy, scholarly face, turned to the last of the sunlight—a eureka moment after having assembled all the data available on the subject of the sack of Rome for his latest book, *The City of God*—like us, forgoing earthly pleasures for the eternal truths."

"While I'm just a slayer of dragons. A lust-driven maiden, contemplating the ultimate sin."

He'd squeezed her shoulder, slipping a hand over her breasts as he kissed the top of her head. "It takes two to tango."

"Sometimes, I wonder if that's all we have."

"You know it's not, and if anything, being here with you—absent the risks—proves it's not. But it's certainly changed the way I look at marriage. Without the jet fuel, a marriage never gains airspeed."

"So, you're not thinking of taking up holy orders anytime soon."

"Not as long as you're around, that's for sure."

"Me and orgasmic chemistry."

"Your pleasure in life—and aspiration to doctor to the needy—is an aphrodisiac in and of itself. No wonder God wanted to keep the good news from Eve."

She laughed and shook her head. "I can't help thinking how well you'd get along with my old roommate Gini. She too was a big fan of Augustine—definitely *your* scholarly type."

"You mean getting pregnant or getting the ball over the end line?"

"Consanguinity of minds. One of Gini's—your—two-dollar words."

"I thought—yes, young golden girl, your salutatorian. I once thought I had that with Betty Anne, certainly when we were in high school." He bent and lingered with a kiss to the back of her neck, and her eyes closed with pleasure. "But we ended up very different people. She would bow out gracefully, you know. She understands completely. She's just very low energy, a very private woman who would be happier with her gardening and a life on the sidelines. How we were able to breed as well as we did is a mystery."

"I'd never want to be what my mother called a home-breaker. And have the whole Princeton community hating my guts. Not to mention your kids."

"Oh, I think we're beyond that now. You've graduated, and I'm headed for the Rockefeller Foundation. Neil"—and he nodded graciously to the old caretaker taking a break in the corner—"can no longer plead the apocalypse."

"Did you ever figure out how Neil got wind of our extracurricular shenanigans?"

"Someone in your class, an anonymous letter—a grudge, he said, by the tone, an axe to grind about ROTC—threatening to make the accusations public if we didn't ban ROTC from campus."

"Only two of my roommates knew, and that doesn't sound like them a bit."

"What does it matter now? We're beyond the reach of those who would want to do us harm. Time heals most things." He had drawn her closer. "Like I said, the Venetian archives are a treasure trove of mostly untouched material. Perfect for a budding historian working down to bedrock on the story of who we are and how we came to be that way. We could even get a little dog, a German spitz, like Augustine's."

She wiped away tears and pointed.

"Hermann, why not, as in Goering."

"Ah, the Nazi propagandist and art collector. Who never got his hands on our Carpaccios? I wonder what—Henry James, wasn't it?—who could never figure out which was the greater artwork, Venice or the depiction of Venice, the theme or the rendering of it."

"There you go, sounding like my roommate Gini. Who liked to point out to us lamebrains the hourglass on the shelf beneath the desk—memento mori: past the two-minute warning with no more time-outs."

"Time suspended between past and future, like us: just the eternal now absent sins real or imagined."

"Except the little time bomb ticking in my belly."

"We could name him Christopher, after the saint in charge of the lost and found department."

"What do you really think our Augustine is seeing beyond his window?"

"Our Christopher. Who else?"

Gini was far from falling under the spell of Matteo's trio even as she was drawn to trying to interpret something of her own dilemma in the handsome young man's face, a face she'd known growing up on stages at the New York High School for the Performing Arts, then at Columbia, and most recently at Dizzy's nightclub high above Columbus Circle. All that might be detected in a face over time, in his soulful, compressed eyes, the undulating furrow of his brow, and the slight, flexing dimple on the chin responding to the pleasure of his playing . . . all—thank God—Bianca's, with barely a hint of her deadbeat husband.

Typical, really, that big-mouth Macaluso had kept that little bombshell (deftly gutting her in public) under wraps for so long. Not that she'd exactly forgotten, or re-remembered, that Venetian rendezvous meant for her. Hadn't she a mind like a steel trap? Or so her employees whispered behind her back; she could remember a comma edit five hundred pages and three weeks back. Just as she could perfectly imagine the lit-up oratorio of the Scuola di San Giorgio—even the creak of the green doors opening, the jingle of the caretaker's bag of change as he took their entrance fee . . . and the press of a hand on her shoulder as she looked around the tent in hopes of laying eyes again on that familiar face.

"You don't have to repeat yourself." Jake's face had been pale, distraught, hair drawn back tight with a rubber band. "I know, when your mind's made up to something, there's no turning back."

Yes, it had been late spring of their senior year, and there had been moonlight, Prospect Garden—an effusion of scent on a humid night. They had been on the verge of breaking up for weeks, ever since she'd accepted the internship at Knopf and so given up on the chance of playing the women's tour that summer (and the material that would transform her senior thesis novel into something gripping, eye-opening, commercial).

"Your majesty—Ginistrella Wingate, with your Carpaccio affectation in train, your brass-knobbed Henry James thing, your well-readness." He'd sat down on the garden bench and put his arm around her. "Don't you see, it all crimps and stultifies your mind, your talents as a writer; it's all over the pages in your senior thesis. It's not life: it's life—a book written from books—construed from the thinnest etiolated, moribund matter. A rare orchid that can't breathe, can't breed."

"You read my senior thesis?"

Jake rolled his eyes and reached to touch the tip of her nose. "For Christ's sake, baby, you asked me to help you type up your third draft. All about your childhood growing up summers at West Chop, with your alcoholic mother as the villain of the piece. And your noble, all-knowing, selfless father rescuing the situation. Your secondary characters—the White House adviser to the president stricken with guilt about Vietnam, the depressed novelist based on Styron, and the hard-drinking celebrity reporter from *60 Minutes*—are all stereotypes: quaint, half-drawn, cloyingly sentimental—hard to care about. What's more, there's a gaping hole in the narrative, something missing . . . the author's secret life: that underground woman."

"Just fuck off. Get your hands off me."

"You barely mention tennis or the ambition that burns in your soul. The woman drawn to risk."

"What ambition—and hardly a burning soul . . . And as for risk, it's a horrible job market out there, especially for the likes of me."

"Even Fitzgerald, in *This Side of Paradise*, drew on his Princeton experience to render some pretty interesting characters."

"So that's it," she shot back. "Obviously you want me to write about you, our relationship."

"Well, you must admit, it does have a fascinating dynamic. A blue-collar kid falls for an elite WASP girl. The counterpoint of science and the humanities—a risky affair in all the particulars. And then there are your quirky teammates—talk about risky business."

"*This Side of Paradise* is overwritten and tedious, messy in tone, wandering. No thank you: I'm no Amory Blaine."

"Well, writing about the Virginia Slims circuit, all those women breaking free, breaking out of gender stereotypes, the rough and tumble of tournament play, fighting with guys for recognition and pay—all the fascinating characters you'll encounter: Billie Jean King, Bobby Riggs, Chris Evert, Martina Navratilova—that's pay dirt. You could write the thing from your perspective as a privileged WASP woman who had to learn to be street tough, who finds she has to get along with women from very different backgrounds, who learns about lives—growing up behind the Iron Curtain, for instance—so different from her own. Just imagine the conversations your characters might have."

"Enough, please . . ."

"And your title: *Carpaccio Summer* sucks, does nothing. You're skating over surfaces instead of a deep dive."

How that criticism of her first novel, her senior thesis, had stung her. Tennis was one thing, but her writing—yes, her soul—was quite another. She'd been furious that he'd refused to see the lovely turns of phrase she'd learned from Cicero and Seneca, or the delicate atmosphere of mind that only James captured, things touching on enduring values, her father's values, and the moral ambiguities of human nature, much of it hovering between the lines. The unspoken, the barely apprehended, where science and logic couldn't penetrate.

It had been late, a gibbous moon hung between the chapel spires, seated on *their* bench, scene of so many midnight trysts, where the heady scents of the California lilacs and the balsam firs hung like smoky incense in the air. His hand again had strayed from her shoulder to her thigh as if oblivious, as if another round of sex, having his way, would mend things. On the cusp of the rest of their lives without one another.

Her own words were hardly convincing. "It's not just Venice or James; it's Virgil and Homer, Proust and Ruskin, a pean to memory that somehow survives three thousand years and insinuates itself in our present, a past come to life and so spurring on human imagination, which, try as you might, is a richness you can't fathom on your lab bench or grow in a test tube. Nor the likes of me, for that matter."

She'd grabbed his hand, as it had wandered into her crotch.

"Your inner egomaniac. Whatever happened to your tent pole, the thing you always like quoting to me from Frost: 'By countless silken ties of love and thought, to every thing on earth the compass round . . .' Isn't that the bond that strengthens how we feel about each other, the compass that points not just your way or the highway, but our way—true north? Your surety of soul?"

How she hated his flawless memory, how he quoted (rarely bothering to read the texts himself) back her most private and secret thoughts, expressed in those most vulnerable of moments, just before or after their lovemaking, as if not just riffling her mind but appropriating its contents.

Now, trying to distract herself, she gazed at the still boyishly handsome face of Matteo, eyes half closed as he deftly picked out the melody line on his electric guitar, a jazz version of "My Favorite Things." And in the notes, again, another young precocious and so seductive voice forever calling into question her amour propre.

"You're a writer first and foremost, not an academic, not an editor, not a modern version of Henry James—God forbid, Cicero or Seneca. Follow James's damn advice: be a woman on whom nothing is lost. The Virginia Slims tour would give you that chance. Not a clone bobbing in your father's wake."

"Admit it, you just want a way to be around Chris Evert."

"I want my thoroughbred to run for the triple crown."

"I'm hardly your three-year-old."

She looked askance to where proud Bianca sat glowing like a lighthouse, as if asking: *Hey, Gini, where the hell were you on that long-ago October 15th in Venice?* Probably at the London Book Fair, setting up the booth for Knopf, meeting with her British counterparts, and tending to endless editing chores. A thousand days and her senior thesis, her novel, still languishing. The necessary revisions to turn it into a publishable work delayed year after year as her brain, her voice, like a well-worn palimpsest, atrophied, overwritten by the voices of her authors, by her own critiques scribbled on manuscripts, her queries reverse-engineered in her attempted revisions of her ailing pages, now long gathering dust, until her own writing seemed insipid, derivative, her voice drowned out in white noise. So that marrying her husband, a fine and thoughtful editor of Tandem's line of science books, had seemed the safe thing, the smart thing. Something Jake had anticipated, like so much else.

"Working in a publishing house is like an artist working in a museum. You'll find yourself curated, castrated—neutered: you're always so careful to use the mot juste."

"Fixed . . ."

She turned again to Bianca's tear-streaming face—Bianca, who liked to say of her son (a neuroscience degree from Columbia) that he'd taken a vow of poverty just so he could spend every waking minute of his life making music. Poverty, like mother like son.

What had they possibly had to talk about in Venice? And yes, those flighty postcards had thoroughly pissed her off, going on and on about what a star—on her turf—she was in the city's music firmament. Enough to nix any thoughts of rendezvousing in Venice.

"Oh my God . . ." She choked back her outburst (under the applause) by downing her wine.

Of course, the cruelest irony was that it had taken her husband's tragic death to send her fleeing back to Venice, with sixteen-year-old Erma in hand, desperate to win back her daughter's love and respect. To find something of the connection she'd once had with her own father, that Erma had with her father, William Cheshire. Nothing of the dowdy splendor of the Pensione Seguso, nor the toniest shopping streets near San Marco (Erma forever immune to the splendors of Italian couture), nor, surprisingly, the critter thing—Bill's magic—when she had begun pointing out the menagerie of dragons, griffins, lions, and dogs depicted in the Carpaccios. Of all things (yes, she remembered it now so vividly), it was Augustine's study that had oddly sparked Erma's imagination.

"Don't you get it, Mom? He's surrounded himself with all the earthly knowledge of his age. Hey, that's an armillary sphere behind him, and the archaeological artifacts, the books—like he's just had a revelation, a moment of discovery, a deduction that has come to him as he stares out the window, a new construct that will change everything."

"Well"—she could hear her late husband's voice in her daughter's—"there you go, sweetheart, even if Saint Augustine was hardly a scientist and he died in 430 AD."

"You're missing the point. That brass armillary sphere hanging over his shoulder describes the paths of the planets and stars. And, back then, science and theology were kind of all mixed up, at least by the Renaissance. I mean, it's like he's really a Renaissance kind of guy, a contemporary of Galileo, Kepler, and Copernicus. So, it's like he's just realizing the earth is no longer the center of the solar system but revolves around the sun in an elliptical orbit. Or maybe he's sensing the operation of gravity before Newton."

"That's my girl. Your grandfather thought it might be a portrait of Aldus Manutius, the greatest Venetian publisher of his day. Anyway, I much prefer your narrative to the one in the guidebooks about Augustine's vision of Jerome's death in faraway Jerusalem."

"Dad would have called that entanglement, things unseen exerting a force on matter." Erma had glanced over to where the ancient custodian—bald, wrinkled face like a squeezed lemon—was staring at his phone. "That old guy kinda creeps me out, like he's pretending not to listen to us."

"Entanglement?"

"Entangled particles, what Einstein called 'spooky action at a distance.' Like Jerome in the painting leading his lion might be entangled with Augustine in his study. So that a measured electron, like Jerome's soul leaving his body at death, might have alerted a cell in Augustine's brain, causing him to turn to his window. Like the way Dad used to turn his head to the window in the hospital—and like: I knew just what he was thinking."

"And what was that?"

"That we were back on the Sound with the snap of the wind in our sails."

"How cool is that! So your entanglement might be something like memory, something that suddenly arises out of the past and captures our attention in a fleeting moment of discovery."

"Dad would have called it an imaginative leap, an inductive moment that leads to a workable theory."

"I like that, your imaginative leap. Someday you might even read Proust, who thought the souls of the dead awaited us in things—trees, rocks, even a madeleine dipped in lime tea, things we encounter in fleeting moments of sensation, like how the past first came fully alive for Proust when he tripped on a curbstone and was reminded of the uneven paving stones in the baptistry of San Marco—so setting him on the path to his masterpiece—which we can visit on the way back to the Seguso for dinner."

"Dad asked me to remember our time together each time I sailed our Vineyard 15."

"You know I couldn't afford the storage fees for such an old boat." She lowered her trembling gaze to the checkerboard floor of Istrian stone and porphyry and shook her head. "Dad is writ large in all the books he edited and gave life to."

"What about those he never lived to write?"

"You're what he writ—proud and free and unafraid of the future."

A voice behind them: "*Orario di chiusura, signora e ragazza.*"

"*Andiamo . . .*" The wizened caretaker was pointing to his watch and had pulled back the crimson curtain by the entrance. "Closing time, sweetheart. I promised you that ice cream, and the best gelateria in Venice is just across the way."

CHAPTER 13

The night was preternaturally alive, the campus lit up like a ten-ring circus, glittering, humming, jostling with expectant joyous voices, aswirl with memory-glutted revelers adorned in funky Reunions gear (tiger-themed nonsense). Old friends were suddenly espied—greetings, hugs, high fives, hearts aflutter, while a dozen bands and DJs at the various sites began to unload with guitar riffs knifing through the starlight as the wail of brass sections and solo saxophones drew in the eager dancers.

"Come on, Gareth, out with it," Gini demanded. They were walking together arm in arm like old pals in their white Reunions jackets of orange-and-black shooting stars, making their way back to the 40th Reunion site in the spired coziness of Holder courtyard. To their right, an underlit, ivy-clad Nassau Hall beamed out across Cannon Green; at their left, the Ionic-columned Greek Revival propinquity of Whig-Clio, a comforting if slightly anomalous presence, so beloved by the classicist-minded. "You've been distracted by that phone all evening." She paused a moment to fully take in the recently cleaned white-marble porticos of these nineteenth-century Greek Revival buildings, slender columns dramatically backlit, a pair of happy fixtures in her imagination from student days.

"Sorry, I shouldn't let it get to me."

"What's that?" She placed her arm inside his to help her balance in high heels (a tad too much wine) as they navigated the moving stream of revelers, now distinctly made up of younger classes. Far fewer Reunions jackets in evidence, natty if garish, than when she was a senior, certainly when she'd attended her father's Reunions as a girl.

Gareth chuckled as he waved his free hand: "You know what one of our classmates said to me tonight: 'First Reunions, you think you're still one of the kids; twenty years out, you're plotting: my kids could be here just like those kids; and forty years out it's like: I could have been one of those kids and married a brilliant Princeton woman instead of my airhead first wife.' Can you beat it?"

"Men," she laughed. Her ever-faithful Gareth, who had gone so far as to bring her home to his parents at the end of freshman year, to his disapproving African American mother (eight generations of African American Philadelphians going back to the Revolution), who expected him to marry an African American woman, even if she had married a white man (and paid the price with her people). How marrying Gareth and disappointing his gorgeous, raven-haired mother had once seemed so appealing, if only as a way of shocking her own parents. "How did you think of me when we were dating freshman year: a spoiled, selfish, privileged WASP bitch who only cared about writing and tennis?"

"None of the above. I was simply entranced." And he patted her shoulder.

"Strange, in those days, right after the civil rights revolution, I never really thought of you as Black, until I saw the look of horror on your mother's face."

"She should talk, God rest her soul." Gareth chuckled and tossed his head. "And I never thought of you as white, only as the most talented writer in our class. Who would go on to be our next Fitzgerald."

"Seems like I've disappointed everybody. Someone tonight even accused me of being Amory Blaine—a character, Fitzgerald's alter ego, I've always detested."

"Fitzgerald was smitten with Southern women who still exalted the glory of the lost cause, the *Gone With the Wind* thing."

"Yes, *The Ice Palace*—poor Zelda, too."

They showed their wristbands to the proctors at the entrance to Holder courtyard and made their way to a cozy table just off the dance floor as the band was doing sound checks.

"After that conversation at lunch, about Jake's son," Gareth continued, "I must say I found my curiosity piqued—about Jake, I guess. You know how it is: the guy—or gal—who was marked in our student days to be a world-beater, whom we couldn't help measuring ourselves by. And, well"—his brow furrowed as he adjusted his reading glasses and took his phone out of his jacket pocket—"maybe it's just too many years doing equity deals and looking for flaws in the data."

"His kid is hardly a data point."

"I got my best junior analyst to do a little digging."

"Oh . . ."

"I just had the oddest feeling. Found myself doing a little tour of the new Burrage Biochemistry Lab, just to get a feel for what two hundred eighty million and unchecked aspirations can buy. A spectacular creation, like a modern cathedral to a new religion, which, I guess, is the idea. Soaring glass and aluminum and granite—solar photovoltaic panels, sunscreens, gray-water collection tanks, you name it. A Swiss architect, and the place seems to float on an Alpine breeze. I mean, not just the money that it cost, but Jake endowed it to the tune of hiring away complete biochemistry teams from Caltech and MIT to man his spaceship of the future."

"Goodness, I had no idea the future had such a budget line." She found herself somehow attracted to Gareth's hands where they cradled his phone, long dexterous fingers, nails buffed and polished, still wearing his gold wedding band. "You seem a bit swept away by this naming opportunity—a monument, I guess, to our boy wonder, our world-beater."

"Oh—that's the thing, less a monument than a subsidiary of Burrage Pharma & Health. Or that's what popped into my head as I was nosing around, half in a daze, the ethereal light filtering down from this long, nave-like atrium, the labs all transparent walls. And who should be there but the young man himself, in his white lab coat, seated at his bench running some elaborate experiment. Let me tell you, it threw me, jolted me right back to the old Frick Chemistry Lab. And no sooner had I laid eyes on him than he turns and smiles—I swear, like he was expecting me—for all the world looking like his old man in that rumpled lab coat, excepting the haircut, of course."

She nodded dreamily. "Jogging, lab coat flapping in the tailwind, oblivious that he'd forgotten to take it off."

Gareth turned his gaze over her shoulder, as if distracted by the middle-aged soul band taking the stage under the tent. "It was just odd"—he tapped a finger on his phone in frustration—"uncanny, the way he leapt into every conversation—how Jake used to do, as if picking up on something you'd discussed the week or weeks before, as if he'd been mulling it over the whole time."

She dismissed this with a shrug. "Well, like father, like son . . ."

"You see, when I asked about his research project, he kept explaining everything in poker terms, as if that—risk-taking—was the only way I could hope to understand what was going on . . . as if I'd never left the poker table."

"Forever playing it by the numbers, huh? Even you, a physics guy."

"Almost dismissing the difficulties of basic research, as if with a wave of his hand, with enough money and energy, the future was in the bag."

"And your research analyst?"

Gareth shook his head and raised a hand to his face as if to examine the slope of his temple, the soft contour of his cheekbone. "Maybe it was Jacob's overfamiliarity, a kind of uncanny omniscience that froze my blood. Or the way he wanted to know which biotech firms we were investing in." He placed a hand on her shoulder and gently squeezed. "As if he came up to you and only wanted to hear about the competition you'd vanquished on the court, the other publishers you'd outbid for a bestseller."

"Oh," she sighed, "just what I need: the aging athlete thing." Avoiding his eyes, she turned to the band as the saxophone section launched their first set, the canvas overhead lit up with the class logo, shooting stars emblazoned with '76. And then to the nearly deserted sign-in table.

"Of course, given what great shape you're in . . ." Gareth laughed, his dark, graying hair neatly swept back off a widow's peak as he now slipped on his tortoiseshell reading glasses, turning again to the screen of his cell phone. "After one hip replacement, my serious climbing days are over. Your name came up too, your last quarterly numbers—amazing, in an industry under so much pressure to cut costs and consolidate."

"You discussed our numbers—with Jake's son?"

"I'm, sadly, in the numbers business—and the kid couldn't resist mentioning how much he'd enjoyed meeting you at sign-in. Like Dad had prepped him to keep an eye out for you. And, by the way, you should be damn proud: How many classic and English majors have managed to make a living working at their passion? I always point you out to Diane, my English major, as why the humanities still matter."

She gave him an uneasy smile. "Where is Diane?"

"Annette wanted her to meet Arthur, so she's off to the fifth-reunion site but promised me a dance a little later."

"Yes, talk about hedging her bets—always a steering hand. I think Erma agreed to meet them there too." She laughed a giddy laugh, watching as Gareth opened a bottle of Napa Valley chardonnay. "Isn't that the way of the world? The young fry off to the fifth, while the old harpies like Bianca and Apolonia are off big-game hunting at the fiftieth. Leaving us wallflowers in limbo—huh, Gareth?" He gathered in two glasses and began pouring. "Keeping a few worthy writers before the public, if barely making a living, poor souls. As for your numbers, the roadkill among editors is horrifying; the best have retired or been eased out into genteel poverty, while we take on mostly women from the graduate publishing programs who have read almost nothing and whose editing skills leave much to be desired. Keep Diane away from the likes of me. And Erma, the gods be praised"—she waved to the shadowy faces of the gargoyles peering down from the roofline—"won't be following in her mother's footsteps."

He raised his glass in a toast. "To our graduating girls—against all the odds. Diane's older sister, captain of her high school lacrosse team, sixteen hundreds on her SATs, had to make do with Harvard."

"Yes, a miracle; I never gave more than a few hundred bucks a year to annual giving." She smiled gamely, admiring his delicate grip on the stem of his glass, and drank deeply. "Why is it, Gareth, that daughters are so drawn to their fathers while giving Mom such a hard time?"

"Oh, quite the reverse with us. They were so close to Ruth, a stay-at-home mom when not doing her board work, that when we lost her, they were utterly crushed: their best friend, confidante, cheerleader." He sighed, swishing the white wine in his glass, his brown eyes indrawn (his Harry Belafonte eyes, as she'd once fondly thought of them). "While I just brought home the bacon. Thank God for their grandmother, who helped them through a lot of rough patches."

"I liked your mother a lot, the one time we visited her in Philadelphia. Although I'm not sure she liked me much."

"Oh, she gave Ruth a hard time too—Jewish to boot—when we married. I sometimes felt like a character out of Henry James who draped a cloak of invisibility around his shoulders so as to pass unnoticed in a world of white financiers—sold his soul to mammon and so misplaced his internal compass. True north guided by our better angels. Like one of your lost characters in that story you wrote for our writing seminar with Richard Ford."

"Goodness, I'd forgotten—but you spend half your time working with inner-city Black kids in Newark, funding charter schools."

He shrugged this off as of no account: "No one dared critique your stories, including Ford."

"What was it"—she sipped at her glass, eyes alert to the dancers merging onto the dance floor—"we once believed in? Books, wasn't it? Henry James's faith—do you think?—in the intelligent reader's lucid mind, the informed imagination. That ideal reader who would allow his characters to come alive between the lines, just enough to be worth writing about. Those tried-and-true virtues espoused by Homer, Dante, and Tolstoy. Of course, what writer today—what editor, for that matter—would dare assume as much in our brave new digital world?"

"I reread Anna Karenina recently (part of my project to prepare for retirement); I just loved the scene where Levin is out hunting snipe in the marshes and how Tolstoy goes into the mind of Levin's dog—reflecting the way a hunting dog looks at things: uncanny. And his descriptions of the changing light at dawn brought tears to my eyes. Like you say, I was glad that something of that ideal reader lingered in me after decades of poring over financial reports, much less the digital rabbit hole."

"I was just thinking along those lines as we passed Whig-Clio, reminded of all we've lost of the writings of the ancient world, those fragile papyrus rolls once housed in the Great Library of Alexandria."

"Ah, your informed imagination. You'd be amazed how it comes in handy reading the sadly fallible dreams of some twentysomething entrepreneur with tin cup in hand: the ones with the gift to visualize a product or service that the future requires but may not be quite ready."

"Like Jake . . ."

Gareth's phone vibrated on the table, and he reached to shut it off, only to flick through a few screens.

"There you go again—what, an important deal coming down?"

"No, like I said, my hotshot analyst doing her thing on Burrage Pharma & Health—BPH. Even if we sold out our stake years ago when my father ran the firm."

Her attention came firmly into focus where his thumbs were scrolling. "Something not on the up and up?"

He tapped his phone. "Oh, just the usual issues with FDA approvals and some of the claims for proprietary products. Run-of-the-mill stuff. But between the lines . . ."

An eager: "Yes?"

"You remember how he was. How Jake always had this way of concealing his true thoughts—not so much because he was hiding something or trying to sneak something by you, but because the thing, his idea—a revelation—might make you uncomfortable if he didn't lead you to it in the right way."

"So that," she laughed, pitching her voice over that of the band's lead singer as Gareth bent an ear closer, "you thought you'd come to it on your own: the new-new thing the world was simply not ready for." She reached for his wine bottle. "Like James (for my sins), who never wanted all the facts on the table, just enough to keep the reader turning the page."

His dark eyes shone with pleasure. "Hardly your Gilbert Osmond . . ." He shot his long eyebrows, as if in the retelling of some standing joke they'd once shared, and tapped his phone. "Here's the thing: while our boy's company has become more and more a leader in biopharma, Jake has made himself less and less available to his many fans in the press—missing in action, his investors complain. Jake still takes quarterly investor calls, but nothing in the way of live events, in-person interviews. His PR people claim he's too busy with research. When, in the early days, when I got my father's firm to invest, he was the face of the company, the salesman for BPH—Steve Jobs front and center. All underpromising and overdelivering. Now that he's made it, big-time, he's become almost invisible."

"Well, I hope you pumped young Jacob on that score."

"A charmed life until"—Gareth picked up his phone and adjusted his reading glasses—"eleven years ago, Jake's wife and son were in a terrible car accident. She was killed instantly, and young Jacob sustained serious injuries. In the aftermath, Jake moved with his son from Evanston out to Denver, where BPH had opened a huge new lab complex and manufacturing facility."

She reached a hand to his. "That can't be right; the kid told me and my roommates that his parents were divorced."

Gareth nodded and held up his phone. "A FedEx truck skidding on black ice."

"I feel terrible—the poor kid. And we had no idea."

"That we lose track . . . stop caring—maybe explains why he hasn't shown at Reunions, or even the ribbon-cutting ceremony for the new biochemistry lab."

"But"—she shook her head—"we're still here, his old gang."

"While he's on the cutting edge, battling aging and dementia"—he flicked impatiently at his screen—"computer-designed drugs and gene therapy to turn back the body's evolutionary clock, reverse-engineering entropy to preserve the body's machine from destruction. Hell"—and he tossed his phone on their table—"changing the world as we know it, the moon and the stars and then some." He waved a long hand toward the battlements of Holder and the gibbering gargoyles.

"But why would the kid lie when two Google clicks reveal the truth?"

He looked up, pondering. "Maybe that's what had me so spooked this afternoon in the lab, on my conducted tour of the future, when, all the while, he seemed more interested in me—and you too, for that matter—picking my brain for thoughts on this, that, and the next thing, rather than trying to impress me with the splendid state-of-the-art facilities at every turn. Even the landscaping collects rainwater. A tragic accidental death hardly fits that narrative, and certainly not at the sign-in table: hardly the place to explain a family tragedy."

"Yes, that must be it, I guess."

"Walking that soaring atrium of the Burrage Lab, as I prepared to head back to my hotel, the space alive with this soft, ethereal light, one felt that anything was possible: CRISPR gene editing—gene drive. Who's to say what Jake—or his son—has got up his sleeve. I was left with the feeling: like, what have you done with your life recently?"

"Oh, don't say that—you who've been funding charter schools for years! Not that I haven't been having some of those same thoughts as well." She patted his hand in solidarity. "And the way you put it, like father and son are a team."

"Isn't that what, as parents, we secretly hope for—the succession plan?"

She laughed, now almost giddy. "Not this parent. And gene drive?"

"Genetic changes moving through entire populations. Editing ticks for Lyme disease, breeding infertile female mosquitoes to eliminate malaria—that sort of thing. He's even got the Gates Foundation backing him on that, according to young Jacob."

"When did you say was the last time you saw Jake, Gareth?"

"Goodness, has it been twenty years, give or take, since we first invested? He arrived beaming and confident at my father's New York offices to pitch Burrage Pharma to our analysts. Blew everyone away with his total command of the science, product demand and competition, and marketing strategy—a triple threat in our business. We had lunch afterward, and it was like nothing had changed. Same old Jake, fit as ever, beaming about his wife, whom he'd recently married, a young son."

She winced as she caught his troubled stare. "A charmed life for a charmer, as if nothing could ever touch him."

"Yeah, still twisting my mind into granny knots. Like this afternoon, not even pitching me on what his lab was doing, just glad to have somebody to shoot the breeze with."

"I envy you that. I struggled so. Bill and Erma so often lost me in conversations across our dinner table."

He smiled as the band launched into the Temptations' hit from 1972, "Just My Imagination," his brown eyes deepening with nostalgic pleasure. "I remember bull sessions with Jake around the poker table, how he rattled and riffed, how the second law of thermodynamics didn't necessarily apply to human beings, as if we're somehow any different from steam engines, much less the universe. 'We're not a closed system,' he kept insisting. We're part of our human and natural environment, which means, at least to hear Jake tell it, that we don't have to accept the inevitable descent into decay—much less death. We can import energy from our surroundings and use that to either recycle, remove, or replace critical components that are prone to wear out. Ergo, we are not bound by thermodynamics to age."

"But that's crazy, isn't it?"

"Forty years ago—twenty years ago—it was crazy . . . now, not so crazy. Jake always liked to say: if salamanders can grow a new leg and bowhead whales can live over two hundred years, what's stopping us from deferring the aging process, just as long as we're willing to spend some of our energy on warding off the ravages of time and entropy."

"Hey, as the kids say: I'm down for that."

"And what I heard this afternoon at the lab had the uncanny feel of a 2.0 version of the original. All about focusing less on reproducing ourselves and more on what's termed negligible or even negative senescence. As young Jacob put it, aging is just an evolutionary oversight, in the sense that our genes are predisposed to maximize reproductive success in our youth, even as the accumulated mutations over time also foster aging—so removing us from the scene for our offspring."

"Just like us, here," and she waved to the dance floor, where scores of graduating seniors in their beer jackets were savoring seventies soul vibes. "Aren't reunions really about gently easing out the old folks—trumpeting annual giving, and so the young can take wing?"

"Do you think . . . ?" He refilled their glasses. "The odd thing, you see, was that, as we parted this afternoon, as he shook my hand goodbye, as he held my gaze for a long second or two, I had the impression that there was something he wanted to tell me . . ." He shrugged and clinked their glasses. "Just one of those uncanny feelings—déjà vu, huh? How we like to invest our brightest dreams in the young."

"And not let our overactive imaginations—a Reunions thing, yes?—run away with us."

"And then, standing there in the atrium in his white lab coat, he gestured majestically—a priest of kingdom come in his cathedral of aluminum and glass, floating walls of granite. 'CRISPR,' he said as if offering me a final tip, 'gene editing, gene therapies . . .' Where I should place my bets."

"Editing," she laughed, "our own stories before they end up on the obituary page." She closed her eyes for a moment and gently shook her head. "Everything seemed possible when you were around him. He seemed to have such a charmed life."

Gareth scrolled down on his phone and frowned. "Until . . . black ice and a FedEx truck."

"Thank God the kid is okay. When I mentioned his name to Erma, she almost swooned; they're on the swim team together, and she works in one of those labs in your cathedral of kingdom come. Says he's on the way to Olympic tryouts."

"Is anybody—after a tragic accident like that?"

He tapped a link on his cell phone and shared an old video of a young man in jeans and turtleneck walking back and forth on a stage with a huge company logo emblazoned above the words: *a healthier future now.*

She nodded, not a little entranced. "I still can't quite imagine him in perfectly tailored jeans and stylish haircut."

"A new product rollout, just before the accident, a sales conference, his last public appearance pitching BPH."

"So, Gareth, who knew our lives would all come down to marketing?" She swished the last of her wine and jutted out her chin to where he held his phone. "Dare I ask, did your analyst note anything about the woman he married?"

"A brilliant woman, a PhD biochemist out of Cornell, Harvard, and the University of Chicago. Hired for his Evanston lab. Ten years younger, tall—a basketball player at Cornell . . ."

"No need to tell me her name."

He glanced up from his phone. For an instant, his eyes burning into hers, his head canted, his neatly cropped, slightly kinky hair combed back, touched with blue highlights from the dance floor as the lead singer of the soul band, channeling Gladys Knight, began belting out "I Heard It Through the Grapevine."

"Ah, but maybe there's material here for the novel you were telling me about earlier, your revised senior thesis." And he tapped his phone. "Henry James—right: without a touch of bewilderment, without a sensitive intelligence, without stirring the deepest registers of the imagination, there would be no tale to tell. Something our Jake seems to have mastered, given all the media speculation about his whereabouts, much less his plans for BPH."

A dismissive wave. "He once told me my novel was solipsistic."

Gareth laughed. "Because it didn't include him coaching you from the players' box at Wimbledon. But now you have another character, a new character: the man who vowed to banish death and aging, only to have the fates deal him a mortal blow. Now that's a story for our writing seminar with Richard Ford, who always predicted great things for you. Or, as my analyst writes: 'Jake Burrage, for so many years the corporate face of BPH, presented an ageless face to the public, a face full of health and eagerness to embrace the future, an unbounded enthusiasm that held his investors and the business press spellbound until his wave-function collapse.'"

"Collapse?"

"A physics notion: how consciousness happens; all those entangled regions of the brain, which make up our perception of the world, arise simultaneously, all our neurocircuitry that constitutes experience: sight, sound, smell, taste, touch. Well, how our observations tend to blur the distinction between past and present, like memory—and so altering the thing observed. Although I think he probably meant chance or fate entering the equation, which even Einstein, though unhappy, accepted."

"How do I get that into a novel? The ghost in the machine. When I even missed that he was on the swim team freshman year."

"He quit, as he liked to say, because it took away from poker time, but what it really took away from was his work in the chemistry and biology labs, on top of his student jobs. And by sophomore year—you, of course. I remember him saying once how he found tennis much more fascinating than swimming, more multidimensional than simply busting your balls to swim faster from point A to point B. But I think his real reason—how did he put it: 'I've already peaked, Gareth. I've hit my limit.' Or, as we might say in economic terms, he'd hit his point of diminishing returns."

"You've got his voice down," she laughed, now giddy with wine, her eyes turning to where the band had launched into a rendition of "You Can't Hurry Love." "Do you miss it, Gareth, surfing the wave of love and ideas without a safety net? Careless of finding an angle of repose and certainty?"

He shrugged. "Mixing your metaphors."

She took his hand. "I'm sorry if I ever hurt you—ending up with Jake."

"The moment I saw him start tracking your matches, I knew he'd drawn an inside straight."

For a moment, her face went blank with wonder. "He was my Prospero," she offered in consolation.

He laughed: "And you his spitfire Caliban."

"Do you remember our Shakespeare course?" He nodded, smiling at a text, his face a vivid brightening. "I was always so chagrined to find that some thought, some complicated emotion that I considered mine exclusively had originally been thought by Shakespeare."

"Well, now's your chance to put some of those well-seasoned emotions to work and finish that first novel."

"Gareth, was I really such a bitch?"

He laughed, irradiating her with his joyous eyes as he reached over and pressed a comforting hand on hers.

"I mean, I remember scolding Jake, trying to hold my own, for never having read *Moby Dick*." She bowed her head. "Did I just chicken out?"

"Ah, there's Diane, back from the fifth. She promised her old man a first dance before she heads down to the senior-party site." He chuckled with pleasure and bent to give her a kiss on the cheek. "As Jake used to say: 'Stay tuned: the only future that matters is the one where the numbers don't lie.'"

CHAPTER 14

Gini, cruising on a wine high, surprised herself by a certain satisfaction, even pleasure, she took in watching Gareth dance with Diane, who reminded her of Ruth with the lush curve of her brow and warm, deep-set, adoring eyes. Such a handsome couple (as her father would have described them). Diane was almost as tall as Gareth, agile in her movements, her powerful legs shown off by striped orange-and-black shorts, her muscled shoulders filling out a lacrosse tee shirt and class beer jacket emblazoned with the de rigueur drunken tigers stumbling with tankards raised through a bamboo forest. Erma, she figured, instead of saving a first dance for Mom, was hopefully off dancing with Arthur or Matteo at the fifth. Saving her expensive new dress for tomorrow night's dinner and Wednesday's graduation.

There was so much to admire in her daughter's generation: averse to showing off wealth or relying on privilege, concern for others, community service, and embracing a diverse world. But then the tradition of wearing a funky Princeton class costume for Reunions had always had an element of classless tomfoolery about it, disguising the hugely successful and the moderately so, the Bezos and the lowly high school English teacher (a career she had toyed with if money had not been an issue). She was reminded again of eleven-year-old Erma dancing with her father ten years ago at their thirtieth: how crazy Erma was about Bill. And how he doted on her, the enchanted smile on his bespectacled face as they danced, knowing he'd produced one of his own. She too now found herself smiling and then laughing as the whimsical Diane began showing off her dance moves to her dad, moonwalking, a perfect Michael Jackson imitation. Gareth always had such a self-deprecating sense of humor, a shyness even as he fearlessly indulged his daughter's zaniness by trying to keep up with her antics. Yes, so she again assured herself, it goes with the territory: daughters are always a little in love with their fathers.

She felt the touch of a hand on her shoulder and turned to find young Jacob Burrage at her side.

"You promised you were going to save me a dance." He smiled that enigmatic oh-so-suggestive smile she remembered so well.

"Of course." She laughed, more loudly than intended. "My old boyfriend just got waylaid by his daughter. So"—and she stood, holding out her hand to her escort, using the moment to work out any soreness in her right knee—"I'm all yours if you can stand this retro-seventies band and retro girl."

"Gareth," he said familiarly, with a gracious tilt of his head. "It was such a pleasure to have a chance to show him around the lab today."

They made their way across the crowded dance floor close by Gareth and Diane. Young Jacob was wearing the same beer jacket as Diane, shorts, swim-team tee shirt, flip-flops. He and Diane paused to give each other a big hug, the significance of which Gini could only wonder at. Gareth flicked her a delighted glance and shot his eyebrows. Then they were dancing to an O'Jays classic, "Love Train," and for a few minutes, the years seemed to melt away. Young Jacob was about her height and, except for the short swimmer's haircut and Reunions garb, the very image of his dad, apart from the added, almost streamlined muscles in his arms and legs, the broad shoulders, a swimmer's build she recognized in her daughter growing up. For some reason, he'd shaved off the incipient goatee and mustache of the morning. She attempted to distract herself from such details by focusing instead on the twelve-piece band dressed in extravagant, silver-and-gold-sequined miniskirts and bell-bottoms that did little to disguise, apart from the young lead singer, the past-middle-aged performers. But what the heck, given the nostalgia-soaked occasion and her own over-the-hill gang.

Allowing herself only passing glances at her partner, she couldn't help feeling that he, like her, was more drawn to the current of jittering bodies that surrounded them, his eyes registering, if only for nanoseconds, hints of a recognized face, bodies filled out, backs bent, age lines disguised in the soft blue light filling the dance floor, while shooting stars played on the undersides of the tent above.

She couldn't help admiring, possibly envying, Diane's fitness, much less that of young Jacob. The rigorous training of today's athletes. Not that Jake had been a slouch in the muscle department—not in bed certainly, not coaching her in the weight room of the gym. "Your right arm and shoulder are overdeveloped compared to your left; so the bench presses will even out that imbalance with a compound movement that engages the chest, triceps, and shoulders—hey presto, a killer serve. And more perky breasts in the bargain." She felt a flush work its way up her neck into her cheeks, which she sought to disguise by revving up her dance moves, even as she resisted giving herself entirely over to the music. Better she had resisted finishing off that bottle of Gareth's delicious chardonnay. Better to resist anything that could be interpreted as inappropriate or weird, with all her classmates ogling their Reunions manager: the tepid smiles, the ache of wonder, the joy to be had in happy and successful children.

Why such maternal solicitude? Hadn't her executive coach always advised she needed to show more emotion, to open up more with employees, let a little more of her fun-loving self out, "let your hair down occasionally," enter into the spirit of the thing. Actually, she was feeling pretty damn loosey-goosey, figuring that any moment Gareth would do the honors and cut in. Then she could unleash her true seventies self, her Shirelles self. Or, given the charity tennis event tomorrow, a perfect excuse to beg off and head for the barn.

She settled on a warm, tender, possibly matronly smile, lest any of her classmates get the wrong idea, nodding cheerily to people she recognized as they in turn were, no doubt, reading all kinds of things into her dancing with this gorgeous young man who seemed totally oblivious of anything amiss: that half-dimple in his chin firming, jawline flexing, expressive thick eyebrows (the oh-so-tender cleft space in the right) rising and falling as he nodded at Diane, who seemed more than ready to pull the rip cord on her dad and claim her fellow student athlete. The prospect of which, oddly, now prompted her to dispense with her class jacket, throwing it over an empty chair just off the plywood dance floor—pretty damn warm, after all—and so let her Spanx-free figure do its thing, if not her tight-fitting dress riding high on her thighs, while her not-too-shabby long legs kicked up a storm.

"Christ . . . ," she exclaimed, swallowing the word before anyone could hear. What if members of her class were reminded of their graduation dance when she'd made such a fool of herself by bawling her eyes out on Jake's shoulder all night?

Surely it was time for Gareth to save her from such humiliating recollections (that and the neutron bomb her mother, Enola Gay, had dropped on her daughter at their graduation dinner) by cutting in and giving Diane a chance with this remarkable kid.

As if to repudiate that distant, life-altering disaster—prompted as well by the incendiary smile on Jacob's lips, the wicked glitter in his glance—she found her more daring, risk-loving self tempted out of retirement. Before she knew it, she was crying out ecstatically, raising her arms to the disco beat, pumping the air, taking Diane's lead to "Stayin' Alive" and doing her best John Travolta imitation: what any self-respecting CEO should be able to pull off—one of the gang, a trooper, a good sport.

And just as she'd managed to ascend to this careless state of ecstatic amnesia, the music segued into a slow ballad, and she found herself eased into Jacob Burrage's arms without so much as a yes-please and thank-you.

The lead singer, cornrows down the back of her white sequined dress, was crooning out a lovely version of "Love Hangover" in perfect imitation of Diana Ross.

"That's better," he said forthrightly, his sweaty hand enclosing hers, tender but resolute as he led her around the floor at a discreet distance apart. "I was hoping we'd have a chance to talk some."

"Yes, of course"—Gareth: "the kid likes to talk"—she panted. "I'm delighted, especially since my classmates, the women, are clearly green with envy." She laughed at her own joke and fully intended to mention her daughter, Erma, an obvious subject since they were in the same class, same department—on the swim team, for heaven's sake. But the sight of Bianca on the far reaches of the dance floor with an older man in a fiftieth-reunion garb (Jack Rambridge, she now recognized) somehow derailed this conversational gambit. She was suddenly delighted to be holding the inside track on all things Jake Burrage. Besides, so she now assured herself, Erma must be safely in the arms of Matteo or Arthur or both, dancing the night away at the fifth. "I was hoping that your father might still decide at the last moment to come to Reunions, or certainly your graduation. What can we do to entice him?"

"Oh, don't worry about him. I've gotten used to his no-shows. There's a bunch of particularly important new product lines being submitted to the FDA, and I'm sure he's reviewing the data with his lab teams to make sure everything is in order. The company lives and dies by FDA approvals."

"I can imagine. Fortunately, we don't have to get our books past a censor." She could smell him now, the sweet healthy aroma of male sweat scented with deodorant, perhaps a hint of chlorine. His large, liquid eyes brushed hers. "And your mother?" She scolded herself for her copy editor's instinct—prying into a tragedy.

"They're not speaking to one another. Which is a polite way of saying they're long divorced—messy, but money always seems to make things messy. If one of them threatened to show up for graduation, the other would feel compelled—well, the result would be an ugly cage fight."

Strangely, this admission, this rewrite, rather than first striking her amiss, contradicting the details of the tragic accident related to her only minutes before by Gareth, instantly recalled the trauma of her own divorced parents' grudge match at her graduation. "Sorry to hear that. But I know how humiliating *that* can be."

Jacob, unabashedly staring into her eyes, nodded as if fully appreciating this bit of shared history. Hardly appropriate for the crew manager of their Reunions site.

"Yes, for some, graduations can be a death-defying balancing act." His hand squeezed hers as if in full sympathy over that ancient trauma. "The only thing worse than a divorce is having two parents whose preferred way of communicating is screaming at each other as they itemize each other's perceived faults."

"Ouch," she heard her literary persona say (he could just as easily have been referencing her own parents), pondering this alternate narrative (Henry James's donnée?), as if this young man had unaccountably signed on to help her rewrite that languishing novel from senior year, eager to provide added material that cast her own dilemma in a possibly healing light. Yes, better (now wearing her editor's hat) than a stereotypical tale of a perfect love match sundered by fate, a love forever overshadowed by an irrecoverable past. Her mind was racing: Had the young man googled her? Had Jake briefed his son, concocted this story for her benefit? But that would be so unlike Jake—say what you will: without a fabulist bone in his body. Even as she detected in his son the same confident equanimity that had so frustrated her: never wanting to dwell on the downside: the early death of his father, the family's financial woes: never inviting her to Thanksgiving with his mother, his childhood home in Evanston—that sacred place close to his heart, unavailing to her probing.

While Jake had been privy to the wretched, blow-by-blow dramatics of her mother's venomous alcoholism on their flying visits to her Upper West Side home, and then big-time with his visit to West Chop the August before senior year. Trumped only by the Chernobyl meltdown of their graduation dinner, the memory of which caused her to press an apologetic hand on his shoulder and look fully into his blue-touched-with-olive eyes, where flecks of reflected light now reminded her of his father's eyes upon waking at their Lake Tashmoo camp.

"We—that is, my husband and I—had our moments, our arguments, mostly professional; we worked for the same publishing company, you see. But, as the saying goes: we always tried not to take disagreements home with us. When Bill died, we were at peace with each other." Aghast as she realized how she was now adding her own rewrites, she found herself focused hard on her hand in his, trying to tame the instinct to squeeze it as they glided gracefully across the floor. And that's how she made what in retrospect she considered her first fumble. "Especially not in front of our daughter."

"You have a daughter?"

Her heart skipped a beat. It was less a question than an observation—a prompting (Gareth had probably mentioned as much).

"Yes, just about your age." Her second mistake. How could she not mention the obvious? Even as she had a feeling—spit it out, Gini—that he already knew. "In fact, she's in your class."

His hand tightened on hers for the briefest of instants. "No kidding."

"Erma, Erma Cheshire—her father's name. Bill died when she was sixteen."

"Erma, oh, of course." He squeezed her hand again. An impulse to joy? "Sorry for your loss and Erma's. Lucky Lindy." He smiled (perfect teeth, unlike Jake's slightly unruly front incisor). "Such a graceful diver. Her dad would be—you must be so proud. And smart as a whip. She's a total star in the biochemistry department, not that I need to tell you that."

"It's always nice to hear." (Smart as a whip? No kid in her daughter's generation used that term.) She had the odd sense that he'd known all along and just wanted to give her the chance at bragging rights, about how she'd still managed to produce a talented science kid, something Jake might be pleased to know, or, as he might have thought of it: that she hadn't let her good genes go entirely to waste. Some protective instinct—or a leeriness of bragging about offspring in proximity to her classmates, many of whom harbored grudges because their gifted children failed to gain admission—caused her to change tack. "Talk about proud—your dad must be thrilled with your swimming records, Olympic trials, a guy who never said boo to me about being a standout swimmer as a freshman."

"Actually, I think swimming quite bored him. Too much time practicing, too tedious, not enough strategy—not like tennis. He lives to have his mind fully engaged."

She gave him a crisp, penetrating look, feeling the rewrite—that tingle down the spine, the narrative shift. "And yet you . . ."

"I've come to enjoy the way swimming relaxes the mind; call it meditation, the pure rhythmic movement through the water, almost becoming one with the water. I find doing laps recharges me to return to the lab fully primed. I keep my phone near the pool just so I can jot down notes, solutions that have appeared out of the blue. You'd be surprised how much of science happens like that."

Her eyes lit up, her breath quickening at such a delicious detail. "Oh, I know just what you mean. I often have my coach just do drills with me for an hour, and suddenly, after a hundred crosscourt backhands, the pages I've been struggling with in the office suddenly come clear."

"My father mentioned that he used to track your matches. In fact, he always likes to talk about the summer he spent tracking Matt Collins's matches and raised his world ranking almost a hundred places. He sold his system years ago, and its latest iteration is now available in a smart app, Smashpoint, the number-one tennis tracker in the industry."

"And to think I was his guinea pig." She laughed, delighted at yet another plot detail, that their roles had settled into a comforting groove, that Jake had, indeed, spoken to his son about her. "The lines of the court were once my little bubble of space, like a ballet stage I suppose, where I felt totally in control."

Young Jacob laughed knowingly, musing. "Yes, once an experimentalist, always an experimentalist: the comfort of playing the percentages with all your bases covered."

As if inspired by his prompting, a vivid fantasy suddenly possessed her, and she found herself stepping onto the grass of Wimbledon's center court, tennis bag slung over her shoulder, the crowd cheering. "At the highest level, the pros will tell you the difference between winning and losing is a matter, on any given day, of who is the most focused, confident—in the groove. There were years when I was addicted to winning matches, when I lived off that high."

"Erma," he now noted, pausing to reflect, "only lacks confidence."

She almost stepped on his toe at this shift of narrative back to her daughter, so vivid was the dream of glory in her head. "In New York, even in New England competition, Erma was a good swimmer, but given the level of the Ivies, she figured she wasn't fast enough, so she switched to diving, which she once loved. Until she got here."

Again, his hand tightened on hers for an instant, prompting yet more revisions.

He continued in a near-proprietary tone: "Like I said: confidence. She just needs to believe in herself, to see herself as others see her. She needs to visualize the dive before executing and simply allow her body to flow into the visualization. Diving is like Zen practice. Hey, same with tennis. I'll share with her my Vedic meditation practice; it can be life-changing. And I'll ask her to share my email with you as well about the practice, and my teacher. You'll rediscover the tennis player you were always meant to be."

His supreme confidence, his seeming mastery of such insightful details, affected her viscerally: a heated yearning to have her youth back—even a replay, feeling even now her body opening into a crosscourt backhand, the sensuous pleasure of the movement, prompting the need of a deep breath to suppress the excitement he might otherwise have misinterpreted in her voice.

"A little late now, but not for you." She paused—a frisson of panic at her mistake—until she realized: of course, she would have known all about his Olympic-caliber swimming from Erma, or simply by attending their swim meets. (So busy editing a manuscript that she'd paid no attention to anything but Erma's diving, if that.)

"Maybe, we'll see. I have a bunch of ongoing experiments here that I can't just walk away from. And then, they need me back in Denver at the R&D labs, perhaps more than ever. We're awfully close to several critical breakthroughs in bioengineering that may revolutionize medicine." He sighed, and she detected a peppermint scent—a Listerine tab perhaps, as if he might be checking himself: a proprietary product still under wraps. And the tone of voice? Not unlike that of an insider at Burrage Pharma. Prompting a vague, uneasy, indefinable suspicion, verging on science fiction—beyond crazy—prompted by Gareth's unease at his guided tour of the new Burrage Biochemistry Lab. And yet another hastily jotted editorial comment in the margins.

"How nice for you, following in your dad's footsteps."

"Oh"—an easy laugh (those perfect teeth)—"I wouldn't go that far."

Prompting a whimsical change of tack: "When Erma was a girl, she was a voracious reader—still is—and aspired to be a writer. I mean, poor thing, she grew up in a publishing family, what with her mother and father and grandfather. What else was she supposed to think? Even her English teachers in school fawned over her essays and stories. But I didn't want that for her—the uncertainty, the crushing self-doubt (Oh, the handholding I do with my authors!), and so I let her physicist father take her under his wing, left it to him to nurture her curiosity in the natural world, her numeracy, guiding her, if anything, to where her real talents lay. I sometimes feel guilty bringing up money worries in front of her, but I think it has worked out for Erma."

Such a confessional narrative! More than she'd ever confided in her roommates.

"Science, basic science, is hardly a money-spinner. And I don't think my father was ever in it for the money—only the necessary funding to fuel the research. More for the deep dive: God's foot on the treadle of the loom."

She unintentionally squeezed his hand, her body electrified by how the Melville image rolled so lightly off this young man's lips—the former version of herself (the first draft) just managing to resist hugging him with a shout of approval.

"Yes . . ."

"What he wanted was the resources to pursue the lines of research he was most interested in, that showed the most promise. And at some point, he realized that academic research wasn't going to allow him the speed—the one precious lifetime, as he always liked to say—to achieve everything he wanted in the promising field of antiaging research. As you must know, he is quite methodical about laying out his life the way a scientist lays out his lab table." Her radiant partner now eyed her with the certainty of the ages, as if making a perfect cast into the silent pool of her soul. A boyish grin: "Not exactly to everyone's taste—such single-mindedness." She felt the slight shrug of his shoulders, as if in apology. "But like you noted: at a certain level, it is all about focus and confidence in letting the data points lead to breakthroughs. Goes with the territory."

This veiled confession, touching on the very things that had once driven her crazy, now sparked a moment of panic, so that she glanced in the direction of the lead singer as a familiar tune began to register itself in her hearing. "Oh, that"—a little misdirection—"parents always seem to be about plotting and planning to their offspring."

"If you're an experimentalist—why women, Erma, for one, preside like queens in the lab. It takes patience, care, precision, ungodly curiosity—the patience of a saint. You've got to be in it for the long haul. And the money only buys time and infrastructure."

She nodded toward the lead singer and her Whitney Houston rendition of "I Will Always Love You," her voice rising to the lyrics as she mused: "Sounds like the guy I remember." A sigh, a nod: "If only I could've made your dad's numbers work for me, executed my shots according to his game plan—yes, played the percentages—I might have ended up center court at Wimbledon. Risk the humiliation of losing more matches than you win, which surely would have been my fate on the pro tour. Who knows?" She shook her head, as if momentarily aghast at such a confession to a near stranger, even as she found herself intrigued at the fictional possibilities. "Except there's always the kid on the other side of the net: bigger, stronger, faster, and more determined to make the numbers work for her."

He turned her in place, gently flinging her wide—dismissing such talk—and reeling her in with an exchange of significant smiles. "On a bad day, he'd complain he should have gone directly into cancer research, where the Nobels are to be had, instead of malfunctioning mitochondria, cleaning up senescent cells, epigenetic alterations, amyloids and adducts, and the length and condition of telomeres."

"Goodness, I think you've lost me there."

"Oh, I haven't even gotten to the nanorobots that will live inside our cells and constantly repair damaged genes, while seeking out mutations and other diseases to destroy."

"Nanorobots, yes, Tandem's science imprint has published books on them." She tried to dampen the excitement in her voice. "Yes, I remember Erma talking about nanorobots. Something about mapping the brain, wasn't it?—all those neural pathways translated into computer language and uploaded. Like a book, I always told her, except a great book is always somewhat strange, quirky, and, of course, scrupulously edited, ridding the pages of all the garbage and useless information. Perhaps that's what I need on the court tomorrow: nanorobots."

She grinned at this one certainty in her life: a great editor was loved by her authors for making them look good in print.

"Oh, we can do better than that; it's called CRISPR, gene editing, where we can literally snip out bad or dangerous genes that cause sickness and premature aging. It's pretty exciting stuff; we're transitioning from a future controlled by natural selection to a future determined by genetic engineering and design. No longer will we have to accept natural selection on *its* terms—or evolution as a process closed off to our intervention. We can set our own goals. Taking control of our own biology may end up being the future course of human evolution."

She smiled gamely, as if to fully give herself over to such a prospect, feeling rejuvenated within this young man's energy field, that something in the change of timbre in his voice, that passionate tone, that optimistic echo out of her past touching on her essential self. And as once before, long before, she found herself eager to embrace such wonders of human ingenuity, even while raising a caveat.

"And human choice? Surely, we still get to choose. I mean, I suppose every parent's hope is for their child to be better than themselves—smarter, stronger. Why not kinder and more compassionate?"

"That too is our choice, along with the right to live in a world where no child need be born with a genetic disease. That aging may be a thing of the past. We're right on the cusp: removing senescent cells that gum up the works, renewing what's broken or lost, repairing the damaged or out of kilter, and, most important, reprogramming our biology to slow or reverse aging. That's the beauty of the thing: now we're truly in control of our destinies." He drew her in close as if to impart a final intimacy. "My father's dream has become mine—and perhaps yours." With this suggestive note, he kissed her cheek and then seemed to laugh it all off. "Email me if you're ever tempted to write a book about where all this is going."

"Ah," she intoned, a tad spellbound, "sounds like you—or is it your dad?—do have a book in you."

"Yes, yours to write . . ."

And with this dazzling summation to the jury, and a reassuring squeeze of her hand, he turned away as the last of the slow ballads ended and the lead singer began introducing members of the band as they prepared to get things smokin' again. As she stood sweating, flushed, not a little unhinged, she became aware of a phalanx of seated classmates with tepid grins, either because they recognized Jake in her partner or were moved by the ever-poignant modalities of age disparities, which even ruthless memory might have somewhat softened, as elegiac images long lost to mind rose unsummoned in the picture of youth and age: mothers and sons, fathers and daughters. Or for others, a cautionary tale directed at the few foolish women among them who sought to thumb their noses at Old Man Time by wearing inappropriate clothing to go along with their flirting smiles.

Fortunately, Gareth saved her from further dwelling on these dispiriting scenarios by gallantly presenting Diane to young Jacob, and so happily exchanging partners, thus settling the world once more in its tidy orbit.

CHAPTER 15

The Shirelles, absent Annette and Matt, who had retired early to the Marriott, were huddled at a table just off the dance floor. Bianca and Apolonia sported pleased and even expectant, if slightly incredulous faces, not a little amazed that the over-fifty singles mixer had paid off in the guise of Jack Rambridge, CEO of Rambridge Capital Partners, and Daltrey Assingham, fading doyen of Harvard's history department. Jack, in addition to being on the board of Lincoln Center, was a great jazz aficionado and so had listened avidly to Matteo's last set, which he had praised to the skies, immediately cementing her son's prospects in Bianca's mind. Jack, who had graced their table with the last two bottles of Corton-Charlemagne Grand Cru 2005 from his class dinner, now sat across from Daltrey, comparing notes on the wine and the sad decline of certain beloved members of the class of 1966.

"Come on, out with it," demanded Apolonia, eyeing Gini slightly slumped in her chair. "You've got the whole class in a titter."

"And how," added Bianca, "such a touching sight, like old times, like you and Jake were reunited, like we were back at our graduation dance sans the waterworks."

"It wasn't my idea," retorted Gini in a half stupor, staring into her nearly empty wineglass. "He just asked me to dance, like it was—I guess—somehow expected of him. A kind gesture, I suppose."

Apolonia cocked her head. "Some gesture—I'll bet his old man put him up to it—for a student manager, the way he was staring into your eyes."

Gini swished her wine, casting an eye at Daltrey Assingham across the table, remembering him from childhood at West Chop. That fetching older Princeton boy with long hair and striped bell-bottoms. "Jake produced a wonderful son, smart, considerate, he even—of all things—encouraged me to revise my novel, my senior thesis."

"He did—really?" Apolonia drew back her head in a critical stare. "That's crazy . . . how would he even know?"

"Wow, I only hope this time we're in it," said Bianca, now gazing off to the thinning ranks on the dance floor, where a few longtime couples moved in soft ripples to a seventies love vibe. "Hey, whatever keeps your motor running, head out on the highway."

"Whatever happened to Gareth?" Apolonia asked, as if reprising a question often asked many years before.

Gini blinked and shook her head with a slight swaying of her long neck, detecting something troubling in Bianca's distant stare, an uncharacteristic hint of unrequited longing. "Off with his daughter to the senior site to meet the boyfriend." She reached a hand to Apolonia. "Erma never showed up."

Apolonia laughed. "Hijacked by Annette, who personally made damn sure Arthur and Erma teamed up at the fifth; she actually had them texting each other."

At this, Bianca smiled. "Yes, Matteo as well. What a talented and handsome threesome, our kids."

Gini again reached out to Apolonia. "I never feel like I know how's she doing."

"Doing—doing." Bianca gave a dismissive wave. "She and a thousand other sweaty bodies in Hawaiian-themed swag. The boys and girls were humping and pumping to the loudest techno music you ever heard. It was like walking into a Turkish bathhouse. Even Arthur and Matteo were overwhelmed. I've never seen Erma with such a heavenly smile, two wonderful guys vying to dive into her gene pool."

"She did have her freshman-year roommates with her," noted Apolonia, "so it wasn't entirely clear whose gene pool was on offer."

Gini caught herself staring again at Apolonia's date of just a few hours: Did she realize how Daltrey Assingham's craggy features, the close-set eyes, the dark hair of dangling cowlicks, could have been a greatly aged John Proctor? Right down to the slight bend along the ridge of his nose.

"Erma looked like a young Taylor Swift riding the breakers." Bianca swirled the wine in her glass for emphasis, spraying drops on the tablecloth. "But talk about shooting the curl—like I said, you've got half the class worked up into a speculative bubble. So, what's with his old man? Why is Jake such a no-show?"

Gini let her gaze now drift in the direction of the band, where the lead singer was belting out the Diana Ross version of "Ain't No Mountain High Enough" to the thinning ranks of holdouts. Avoiding scrutiny from Bianca, who just exuded some secret gossip bottled up, who never asked a question or brought up a subject to which she couldn't add some bombshell of her own, Gini drained the last of her heavenly Corton-Charlemagne and glowered at Bianca. "You tell me, Big Mac—no-show, my ass."

"Okay, spit it out, Gini: like I said at dinner, I did not sleep with Jake in Venice. Not that it didn't occur to me, but I had too much of a good thing going with my Italian boyfriend." She glowered and hissed. "But let me tell you, that kid of his sure knows his way around Venice—freaky, really."

"That never stopped you before."

"Okay, we fucked like Hurricane Katrina for over a week; he was just so devastated that you had stood him up in Venice that I figured a little sexual healing was in order. Oh, and I had his baby as well. Does that suit this revised novel of yours?"

Gini couldn't help smiling at Bianca, a little lost, not knowing what to believe, fact and fiction reeling through her mind.

"Just kidding, oh queenly one," assured Bianca, cocking her head to indicate where Jack Rambridge and Daltrey were still deep in conversation. "But you could hardly blame me for taking Jake in hand. For giving him free tickets to my performances. The best days of my life until I gave birth to Matteo."

Gini, struggling to keep her wits about her, forced a look of serene indifference. "To answer your question: it seems Jake has a whole boatload of FDA applications coming up. A busy man."

"I wonder," mused Apolonia, "if our Jake encouraged the scion of Burrage Pharma to work our reunion just to keep tabs on his old pals, put a juicy data point out there to confound us while gathering scuttlebutt on all of us. Somehow—huh, Gini? I wouldn't put it past him. Jake always had something up his sleeve, and that son of his—take it from a clinician—is almost too good to be true. Or he has second sight. At sign-in, something in his oddly plaintive stare made me feel like a crazy kid all over again."

Bianca's brow furrowed, as if her teammate's observations rang more than a little true, then quickly disguised her consternation by wildly hooting with pleasure as she clapped for the lead singer, golden cornrows spilling down her shoulders as she took her final bows. "Remember, AP, when we worked the fiftieth our senior year and how much effort it ended up being, how much lost partying time?"

"The pay was great, even if we were worried half the time about how to treat cardiac arrest and hoping we wouldn't have to perform mouth-to-mouth resuscitation."

Gini, bleary-eyed: "I was working on my salutatorian address, dreading the fireworks with my mother."

"Actually," mused Bianca, "I really enjoyed working that reunion; those old guys were incredibly nice to us. My God, they'd weathered the Depression and then fought in the Second World War. And I couldn't count the times they cornered me and asked what I'd been studying, what my plans were—giving me their business cards, practically offering me a job in their firms."

"They just wanted to bag you," laughed Apolonia.

"Says you, the expert in geriatric cases, bagging El Presidente."

"Shush," admonished Apolonia, with a nod to their male company.

"So, who got bagged?" asked Jack Rambridge, turning to the women with his keen brown eyes under extravagant brows, suddenly all ears to their conversation.

Bianca patted the sleeve of his natty, black-with-orange-trim Reunions jacket. "We were just saying how it seems like just the other day when AP and I worked the fiftieth our senior year, and everybody seemed so young at heart."

"Lucky survivors, like us," laughed Jack, "who just wanted to bag you."

Chimed in Daltrey, with a flickering amused smile on his lean, bony face: "Hey, I remember working the fiftieth in our day, and some of those fellows had fought in the First World War. I believe one hundred seventeen Princeton students lost their lives in that war—a higher per-capita fatality rate than the Second, even though combat lasted barely six months. I remember thinking, if it hadn't been for those old geezers—as eighteen- and nineteen-year-olds—and millions more like them, there would have been no Lenin or Stalin or Hitler, and no Vietnam War."

"How does that—and no Holocaust—follow?" asked Jack, white teeth flashing as he filled all their glasses from his last bottle. His white shirt cuffs displayed gold tiger cuff links to go with his perfectly pressed Oxford shirt and Ivy Club tie in kelly green stripes.

"If Germany had won the First World War, they would have finished off Lenin in no time flat and installed a puppet government in Saint Petersburg to their liking. They already occupied huge swaths of Russia and the Ukraine by 1918. So, no Lenin, no Soviet Union, no hyperinflation, no Hitler, no Second World War, no Mao, no Vietnam War. Instead of a century of unimaginable horrors . . ." Daltrey raised his glass and shook his head sadly. Unlike his classmate, the collar of his blue shirt was frayed, a button missing from his cuff, his Princeton tie faded and rumpled. Even his black-with-orange-trim Reunions jacket was wrinkled and missing buttons as well.

"'Imagine,'" sang out Bianca, "you and John Lennon."

The five clinked their glasses, just as another cooling breeze blew through Holder courtyard that had many remaining members of the class reaching to put on their Reunions jackets.

Jack bridled: "They should have shot John Maynard Keynes for writing that idiotic apology—what was it, Daltrey? *The Economic Consequences of the Peace*. Where he claimed that Germany couldn't pay war reparations; a Carthaginian peace, wasn't it, inevitably leading to another world war."

"Which it did."

"Not if Germany had been occupied and forced to pay. My God, the Germans planned to annex half of Russia if they'd won the war. That would have been a true Carthaginian peace and curtains for your boy Lenin. And all my lost aunts and uncles and cousins would have been spared the Holocaust."

Daltrey tapped a long, ink-stained finger on his wineglass. "I struggle to explain to my students the full catastrophe of the First World War, the death counts, the talents wiped out—lives never to be realized. I throw out, just for starters, the figure of two hundred thousand British boys whose bodies were never recovered, obliterated by shellfire, sunk without a trace in the putrefying mud, enough unidentified bodies to fill up Palmer Stadium four times over."

Apolonia reached a hand to her date's shoulder. "I never realized . . ."

"And twenty-four Princetonians who died in Nam," added Daltrey. "I headed up our SDS chapter protesting the draft and only wish I'd been more successful in convincing a lot of our guys to avoid the military."

"Like me," snorted Jack, holding his wineglass up to his crooked nose and closing his eyes a moment. "Neither your SDS nor counterfactuals saved me from the draft and three wasted years of my life." He nodded and ran a pensive hand through his full head of gray hair.

"You were in Vietnam, Jack?" asked Bianca as the band launched into a moving encore of the Jackson 5's "I'll Be There," hastening her back to her last year at Townsend Harris High School in Queens.

"Pushing papers in Saigon for two years, since I wasn't in a combat role. I met my first wife there, an army nurse. Our kids are both doctors, like you, Apolonia."

"Worst luck." Apolonia shrugged, saddened at the thought of how that cute little Michael Jackson had come to such a sad end. "I hope they're making more of a living at it than I am."

"Are you kidding, orthopedic surgery and dermatology? And"—raising a wriggling digit—"I get a family discount. That's why—can't you tell?—I look like such a spring chicken." And he smiled through his gorgeous suntan, again sweeping back a lock of silver-gray hair off his taut brow.

Daltrey, with the white pallor and gray-baggy eyes of the eternal academic, nodded musingly into his wine: "Anyone who had read Thucydides or studied the strategies of the world wars could see that LBJ and his asshole minions—don't get me going on McNamara and Mac Bundy, who I knew at Harvard—not only had no idea how to fight that war, but lied to the American people to cover up their total ineptitude. So I hid out in the Harvard History Department with a 4-F deferment—asthma, not that I'm proud of it. Sometimes I feel like I'm still hiding out."

Jack laughed and swirled his wine. "And still a true-believing Marxist to boot, even after the fall of the Berlin Wall."

"You keep the plastic surgeons busy; I teach Marxism to young clueless progressives—keeps us both young, Jack." Daltrey took a long swallow of his wine. "I should have stuck with Roman history, my major here. I even went to the library this afternoon and dug out my senior thesis in the stacks. It brought tears to my eyes, reading it, remembering how fascinated I had once been with all things Roman."

Gini, somewhat moved at this admission, perked up from her wine-softened swoon. "What was your thesis on?"

"The emperors Vespasian and Titus, the Flavians, and the origins of Christianity. I point out the odd parallels between the official Roman propaganda of their reigns and how Paul and the Gospels echo so many Roman imperial dogmas."

"Really?" prompted Gini, looking up from her glass.

"For starters," said Daltrey, eyes beaming at having an audience, "it was okay to keep slaves; you should willingly pay taxes—render unto Caesar and so on; skip kosher; keep your foreskin: peace, meekness, submission, obedience, and getting along with the Roman authorities all to be encouraged. Not to mention the portrayal of a suffering mystery-cult savior suspiciously modeled along the lines of healer gods like Asclepius and Serapis. Exactly the kind of mild-mannered millennial religious doctrine the Romans required when battling the Jewish revolt of the mid-first century. Hell, Seneca could have written a lot of what passes for early Christian ethics in Paul or the Gospels—the Golden Rule and all that."

"Seneca, really . . . ," mumbled Gini, trying not to sag in her chair.

"Just as well Annette has hit the sack," said Bianca, a quick head-lean into Jack's shoulder. "She'd be scandalized by such talk. Gini used to terrorize our fearless leader with pithy quotes from Seneca. Besides I'm a great fan of the circumcised—right, Doc, for all our sons and lovers?"

"You betcha," nodded Apolonia with a clinical half smile, patting Daltrey's arm as if only this minute recognizing something familiar about his face. "Just ask any attendant at an assisted living facility for their preference. Not to mention the communicability of AIDS."

"I never terrorized Annette with Seneca," retorted Gini, waving limply to friends as the few remaining dancers headed off the dance floor.

Jack raised his glass. "To 2005, a vintage year for my Beaune terroirs, perfect weather captured in a bottle. And it might interest you to know that, but for Christianity and the requirement for communion wine, the Roman art of wine production might well have disappeared into the Dark Ages."

Daltrey echoed the toast: "To the great class of 1976, our bicentennial year, and the admission of so many fine women." He tapped the label on the wine bottle. "Hard to believe but Charlemagne was illiterate; he could speak fluent Latin, but he couldn't write it."

"Yes," sighed Jack with a sour glance at Daltrey, as talk of his vineyards was waylaid, "we were just remarking how much better preserved your class is than ours and figured it must have been the admission of women that kept everyone looking so perky. A testosterone high—what say you, young ladies?"

"Yeah, right," said Bianca, "human sperm banks made us all that we could be. Until tomorrow, when we get to be teamed up with the young fry—you don't want to know what goes on with those hot chicks—and we're going to be made to look like a bunch of retarded jack (no offense) rabbits."

"Oh, dear," cried Daltrey in mock horror. "One of the many terms on our faculty list of forbidden words."

"A shame," noted Jack, "how more and more convivial discourse, even if controversial, is discouraged by today's overly politicized climate. Why I wrote my senior thesis on Shakespeare and the earl of Oxford. Why I quiz all my new hires on their knowledge of Shakespeare and the characters in his plays."

"Why would you do that?" asked Gini, intrigued.

"Because the secret of Shakespeare's centrality to our literary canon is his total disinterest in ideology, religious or otherwise: his strangeness. His greatest characters are free of ideology, as are his greatest wits: Hamlet, Rosalind, Falstaff. No metaphysics or theology or world-encompassing theories mar his characters being wholly human and free to be themselves. His wisdom filters through all the ages, asking only that we open ourselves to all possibilities. I treasure that in my partners, as I do in my friends." He tapped his raised glass like an alchemist of old. "On an evening like this, with youth and age a spirited farrago"—and he entertained his listeners with a significant half smile—"anything is possible."

"Here, here . . ." Daltrey toasted.

"Kids reading Shakespeare," Jack went on, "may not end up better or worse persons, but they may learn to overhear themselves when they talk to themselves."

"Well," said Apolonia, with a worried glance at Gini, subdued, distracted, who should be adding her own insights, "I must admit to struggling in my Shakespeare course. But I've always been partial to Dorothea Brooke in *Middlemarch*. Inspired by her good works and the fusion of what I guess you'd call the aesthetic and moral power of the novel, Eliot's subtle and deep exploration of the moral imagination. Only

Wordsworth comes close in portraying the downtrodden and needy. Something I try to keep in mind with all my patients, from hedge fund managers to ski-lift operators."

"And you, Gini?" asked Jack, as if quite pleased by this turn of the conversation.

"Oh, since I was a girl, I was always charmed by Isabel Archer for her imagination—so attuned to the vibrations of life—and her determination to have it her way and not accept the man, the traditional moneyed suiter, even as her judgment tragically lets her down in a disastrous marriage. But as I grow older," she nodded at Apolonia, "I too find myself drawn to the way James weaves the moral and the aesthetic. How did he put it? A fragrance and moral elevation rising from his pages—a love of justice, truth, and light. A generous way of looking at things. A torch held high in the dusky spaces of our conscience. Something like that. And yes, an ideal I try to instill in my editors and encourage in my authors." She waved an airy hand. "And, of course, I now need to get such wisdom into my unfinished novel, perhaps, like Isabel, a chance at a rewrite of a life half lived."

"Oh yes," exclaimed Jack. "Dear lady, you owe it to us and humanity, and like my beloved Shakespeare, my Falstaff and Lear, help us recover some of our literary individuality and poetic autonomy."

Daltrey raised a glass as he warbled: "To Lady Wisdom . . ."

"Gosh," exclaimed Bianca, breaking her silence for a foothold in the conversation, "I was aways drawn to Jane Austen's Emma for her love of matchmaking, which I get from my Sicilian grandmother, God rest her soul. I guess I've spent too many years reading Mozart and Scarlatti to run with this bookish crowd." She gave a little yelp of pleasure and nodded into Jack's arm. "Of course, was there ever a greater American poet than Hank Williams in 'I'm So Lonesome I Could Cry.'" And she sang the first verse for the table, beginning with hearing the lonesome whippoorwill.

"The rest," commanded Jack, clearly entranced.

Bianca stood and, with a dreamy, indrawn expression, sang for the table. When she finished and sat down, the others remained speechless.

Jack gave her hand an encouraging pat as Daltrey weighed in to break the silence. "I was always drawn to Jack Burden in Robert Penn Warren's *All the King's Men*: how he had to navigate his way between the class into which he was born and the political whirlwind of a thinly disguised Huey Long. The greatest political novel ever written."

"Good choice," and Apolonia placed her hand over Daltrey's. "And, Jack, our roommate Annette, who would have picked Salome or Bathsheba, or the Book of Psalms, was hoping you might see your way to contributing to our charity match tomorrow."

"Will a hundred thousand buy me a ringside seat?"

"You're down for the players' box, thank you." And Apolonia pumped her fist.

"Oh," said Gini, now in a near daze, "I just discovered this evening we can now be edited: CRISPR, it's called. Just snip out the bad genes and you'll live forever."

"I've invested in five or six biotech companies that are working with CRISPR," noted Jack. "That woman Jennifer Doudna is an absolute genius."

Daltrey stroked his long chin and leaned forward to toast their nearly empty glasses. "Oh, they're already CRISPRing away on Chappy, where I have a home. The idea is, if I have it right, by using gene drive to render the mice who harbor ticks sterile—well, no more mice, no more ticks, no more Lyme disease. Or, as Sylvester so aptly put it: I hate meeces to pieces."

"Oh"—Gini piping up again, in a wine-softened, complaining voice—"am I the only one at this table who thinks the humanities, much less Jack's Shakespeare, have gone the way of the dodo, that all the kids today are majoring in economics, computer science, and, like my good daughter, the life sciences. Daltrey, are we just aging antiquarians without a role to play, a gift to give, ready for the boneyard, as somebody suggested to me this afternoon at Guyot Hall?"

"My dear," assured Daltrey, "we are the institutional memory, the genetic repository; the past lives and breathes between our pages, just as long as we have the confidence to invest in the wisdom of the ages."

"Ah, yes," muttered Jack, "Lenin's progressive ravishments." He raised his glass. "I prefer to think we can drink in the past, to one glorious growing season in 2005 (warm with just enough rain), and to aged, deeply rooted vines, some of which were planted before the First World War. Just imagine the time stored within (fewer grapes but concentrated vintages); it rather boggles the mind."

"Oh, Jack, young man," sighed Bianca, leaning her head on his shoulder, "just wait till you take communion with my Scarlatti sonatas breathed into life beneath my fingertips, wafting you back to seventeenth-century Venice, where something of me still reigns like lost royalty."

Gini, now decidedly inebriated, caught something in Bianca's braggadocio that left her uneasy. While Apolonia, who had resisted more than two-and-a-bit glasses of wine all evening, found her gaze returning to the effigy of John Proctor hanging between the Gothic colonnades of Holder (strangely evocative of Daltrey, of that alternate life John so often mulled over after lovemaking). A transposition of souls that for an ecstatic moment translated her back to Venice and the tug of her lover's hand, as he had insisted on one more stop before regaining the Pensione Seguso, leading her through the doors of San Zaccaria, where he slipped a hundred-lira coin into the light box, and where, after a minute transfixed before the gloriously illuminated Bellini ("A sacred conversation . . . what do you think their subject may be?"), she had slumped crying into a seat. The hard-nosed kid from Manayunk utterly undone, even as she knew the answer and what she must do.

The table fell silent as the band launched into their final number, a rousing version of Stevie Wonder's "Signed, Sealed, Delivered (I'm Yours)." Bianca again rising to perfectly mirror the band's moves, echoing the refrain: "I'm yours . . ." in Jack's direction.

Gini, slightly aghast and staring through a drunken haze at Daltrey (what had caused him to abandon West Chop for Chappaquiddick?), caught a long-secreted glimpse from her early youth, where a Bolshevik charmer stood on their veranda overlooking Vineyard Sound—long-haired, angular, smoking, a Princeton man like her father—as he declaimed to her parents' scandalized cocktail guests on the evils of the Vietnam War and the progressive beatitudes of Ho Chi Minh and Mao.

Daltrey, picking up on her wistful gaze, placed a hand on her shoulder.

"Ah," he murmured, bringing his face closer with an intimate smile, touching his glass to hers, "West Chop, right? Our next Chrissie Evert." He wagged his eyebrows in a Groucho imitation. "Ginistrella . . . was it you or your mother who seduced the tennis pro?"

"Shush," she whispered, trying to make light of the thing with a playful slap of his hand. "Tell me more about how Seneca wrote the Gospels."

CHAPTER 16

Staggering—could she really be staggering?—back to her car after too much of Jack's Corton-Charlemagne, she halted at the entrance to Prospect Garden, a shortcut she'd already avoided twice that day. Scene of the crime. Where she and Jake had been caught in flagrante delicto at one in the morning by a campus proctor. The dean of students had let them off with a reprimand for destruction of university property (rose plants). Worse was the thorn embedded in her backside, for which she (mortified) had neglected to get medical help, relying on Apolonia's surgical skills, only to have the wound get infected, requiring a galling visit to the university health center and a course of antibiotics. A tale of youthful indiscretion spread to the four winds by big-mouth Macaluso until outdoor sex, illicit or otherwise, became known to the cognoscenti as "prospecting."

"Admit it," she confided in herself, "once upon a time you were drawn to risk, to Jake's daring, to the risk of losing every time you stepped onto the court."

She smiled and shook her head in sheer wonderment at such youthful candor, struggling to take a few deep breaths and so shore up her faltering dignity. Then, raising a power fist, she launched herself past the wrought-iron gates, the soothing crunch of the familiar white gravel echoing out above the distant wail of an electric guitar, while hovering in the lamplit shadows, congeries of bobbing, petaled faces bent an eager ear at her approach, each a throbbing dollop of muted color clamoring to be named, as once, long ago, her partner in crime had peopled her world with names: "geraniums, begonias, ageratum, impatiens, and, by my tally, at least four kinds of marigolds, and then the perennials—that's us: daylilies, hibiscus, and this lovely iris . . ." She felt again the pressure of his guiding arm around her shoulder, acolyte of the piping Pan presiding over the now barely spouting fountain, hand tightening as they paused to breathe in the intoxicating scents, as if to weave a chrysalis of enduring sensation and so halt time, that profligate so blindly rushing their lives forward—brutally so, to which an anchor to windward in the constant carnal possession of one another seemed the only antidote. For which marriage was already a long-spent token.

She paused along the lower path by the looming hedge of California lilacs, scores of nodding, inky-blue heads vying for her attention, yet she was fearful of their enticing spirit, as if one more hit of their soporific ether would take her under. A temptation to another life (just glimpsed in the eyes of Apolonia and Bianca, if not young Jacob's), a more forgiving story line that some broken part of her yearned to embrace. Had Erma been right? Had Bill, her husband, felt unloved? Had Jake spoiled her for the quotidian pleasures of a comfortable marriage?

Her eyes lifted in supplication, as if to a distant tallying cry (an expression, her watchword adopted by the Shirelles), anticipating what her legs already knew, where the shadowy balsam firs, tall and supple, lifted their pointed crowns against the starlit sky. Watchers over so much of their lovemaking, whether here on a secluded bench or at her father's camp at Lake Tashmoo: when profligate sex had seemingly sealed her fate. She mused: it wasn't just that Jake was a great lover but that his lovemaking was infused with the power of his mind, that incendiary to her heart.

Such a cascade of memory-glutted sensation only sent her head spinning faster, and she cautiously placed one foot in front of the other as she retreated to the concealing moon shadows of the firs and the sanctuary of a wooden bench, no longer its rickety old self but sturdily refurbished with a brass plaque proclaiming the generosity of some donor even more ancient than she. Relieved, she gazed out like a patient in an operating theater to the sloping terraces of the garden, waiting for the ranks of breeze-stirred buds to behave themselves and even, if she listened hard enough, rehearse their names in her lover's voice.

Carapaced in the cool, ambrosial scents of the firs, she pulled her Reunions jacket tighter, relieved to be screened from the distant clamor of rap and techno or the raucous laughter of passing bands of youthful revelers behind the firs, which, as she closed her weary eyes, she found translated into the voices of dissolute gods haunting some Virgilian grove, gods or even goddesses, whose once prophetic heralding of a golden age now seemed to fall on deaf ears. How she longed, even for just one day, to be young again and in heat. Fueled by risk.

She felt as if some essence of herself was rising upward, a vapor leaving her huddled body behind, her atoms spilling across Lucretius's fathomless cosmos, there, perhaps, to make a sudden swerve, and so rendering her free will paid in full, recalling in turn Shelley's sad truth: that the wise lack love and those who have love lack wisdom. Did she lack a loving heart, subsisting instead on the carnal indifference of her literary gods? She breathed deeply and opened her eyes (seeing herself from afar), as if to confront her embowered lovers, show herself immune to the siren call of those pestering heralds lapping at her breakwater. Nodding off, she again pulled her Reunions jacket tight, pulling up her legs against her chest, and closed her eyes to where the cooling breeze stirred the night, privy to yet further soundings of promise foregone.

"Don't pick it—we're in enough trouble with the dean as it is," she cried. "Leave it to forever scent the night."

"Forever," he laughed. "Such a long time. For us, there's only this moment." And his vandalizing hand had somehow retreated to her breast as he bent to kiss her.

"I'm exhausted, and we have a match tomorrow. Don't you ever think about anything except sex?"

"What, you who are in the business of salvaging dead languages, while I'm in the business of saving souls from the ravages of Huntington's?" He waved at the nodding lilacs, as if making concluding remarks to the jury box. "Whether your gods or mine . . . ," and he pensively swept back locks of his long hair, a motion, as she remembered it, like that of a woman: calm, deliberate, tidy like his lab bench. "I delve into the living future, while you're stuck in the unliving, unlivable past."

"Me, me—you have no idea how the past infuses the present and dazzles the future. To you, these are just lilacs, to me, they're Walt Whitman's eternal lilacs."

"Walt who?"

"'When Lilacs Last in the Dooryard Bloom'd.'"

"Yeah, I'm calling your bluff. Show me what you've got."

"'For the sweetest, wisest soul of all my days and lands—and this for his dear sake, lilac and star and bird twined with the chant of my soul, there in the fragrant pines and the cedars dusk and dim.'"

"So, clue me in."

"It's an elegy for the death of Lincoln, for all those fallen in the Civil War—for me, well, all the dead from the world wars, the Holocaust, the Vietnam War."

"Go on . . ."

"The point is: when you read, when you recite, when you put the poem to memory, it becomes part of who you are. Part of Whitman is speaking to me, reaching out from the past to the future."

"So, dear Isabel, teach me," and he pulled down a blossom to breathe in its scent.

"It can't be taught unless you're open to the mystery: the voice of my spirit tallied the song of the bird—the hermit thrush, the song . . . heralding the ocean of the night."

"Of course, it can be taught—anything can be taught. The brain evolved to instinctively project consciousness, agency, intention, and emotion onto the world around us. Like your gods with their sublime indifference." And he led her into the deeper shadows of the pointed firs, bending to kiss her, his hand moving to her crotch as his tongue swept deftly between her lips. "You're the goddess of my idolatry."

"That's your Zeffirelli version." She pushed his hand away. "You know how long it takes me when I'm exhausted."

"Not like Apolonia—girl god, huh, who needs, hardly indifferent, to come four or five times before she's through with El Presidente."

"Who told you that?"

"I fell asleep on your bed the other night, waiting for you to get back from the library, and woke at two in the morning to hear you three nattering away about how hot a sex life she has with him, and all the crazy places they've found to get it off. I was shocked—shocked: the details! I hope you don't go on the same way about us."

"Good Lord, no, even if they're always trying to get it out of me. But nobody is supposed to know about El Presidente."

"Frankly, I was so stunned by what I was hearing that I thought maybe I'd been dreaming. Except when you came into your room that night you were so hot to trot that obviously the thought of fooling around with Zeus on Mount Olympus thoroughly turned you on—talk about wet chemistry."

"Don't breathe a word—that's dynamite."

"Proctor should be fired. And so wishy-washy about ROTC. I've a good mind to go to the trustees and spill the beans—good riddance to both him and ROTC."

"Is that a threat?"

"Of course not, I'm just saying."

"You can be such a jerk sometimes."

Finding their bench beneath the firs, they sat in brooding silence until he delivered yet another hammer blow.

"Know what your problem is? You subsist on the imaginative works of others, while neglecting to live a life that would allow your own imaginative life to prosper. Otherwise, shut off from the real world—the women's tour, for instance—what will you ever have to write about?"

She was jolted awake as one bare foot slipped free from where it had been tucked up on the bench. Other voices now arrived out of her dreams, where her offstage character lurked in the wings listening, yet more reminders of that closed-off life. Could it be true . . . like the brilliant Isabel Archer, only lacking the imaginative reach to save herself from a disastrous marriage and so soar in her own right.

From within the scrim of firs at her back came the familiar scalding tones of an older woman in a too-too short tennis dress sprawled with her gin and tonic in a rocker on the piazza of the West Chop Club. Her hem bunched up to reveal her underwear and a few strands of leering pubic hair. Words tumbling. Words garbled. Or was it just Daltrey's malicious toast at the table, that old radical dismissing all the conventions: "To our days of wine and roses." Or had that been her mother's stab at what passed for irony. The snatches of dialogue she kept trying to remember, which she should note on her phone to be included in her languishing novel . . . languishing life. Or had it been Jack Rambridge going on about his terroirs? No, another Jack—Jack Lemmon and Lee Remick. Drunks together. "The bitter sweetness of days falling in." Who had said that? She again pulled up her legs, hugging her knees tight as her father's high, nasal voice whispered in her ear: "Dear, you never want to end up like Lee Remick in a disastrous marriage. Or saddle yourself with a partner who consumes your life—body and soul." That sad admission now led her down endless corridors, her mother's face on the hospital pillow, a brain hemorrhage, adding to complications from cirrhosis of the liver, after tripping on a curbstone while waving down a taxi at the Cos Club. "I guess I'm just bored, dear, bored with life."

She started awake, thinking she'd heard a cry, perhaps her own, only to see the shadow of a figure pushing a bicycle. The moon was riding wispy currents of cirrus clouds high above the chapel towers. There was something odd about his clothes: a cape? He stopped as if he'd been hailed, turned a curious face her way, a smile of recognition as he made his way down the path to where she sat huddled in shadow.

"Are you okay?"

A white linen coat hung open from his shoulders, like a young doctor making his rounds, except for the shorts and tee shirt and flip-flops. She lowered her legs and pulled down the hem of her dress, which had slid up her thigh, laughing into the watching face of a young Jake shorn of locks and holding the handlebars of a very up-to-date Trek Dual Sport.

"Oh, I'm just having my maiden-in-distress moment. You see, these two old roués from the fiftieth arrived with a third of a six-pack of very fine wine at our table. Truly, nectar of the gods. It kinda got away from me."

Young Jacob raised his eyes to the tall firs, as if to fully drink in their scent, and smiled a serene smile. "You guys seemed to be having the time of your lives."

"I never overindulge, on principle," she declaimed with mild amusement, struggling to hold her slurred consonants in check. "My mother, you see, was an alcoholic—a bad one—and I swore I'd never be like her."

He nodded as if this was old news, gazing at her with an expression that seemed to waver between mild intrigue and genuine concern, perhaps leaving the young man at a loss for words.

"What's the matter, Dr. Kildare?"

"Oh, this." He laughed, motioning with his free hand to his lab coat. "I was just on my way over to the lab to check on an experiment."

"And I was on my way over to Cap, where I'm parked. Got to get to my Marriott and sleep this off: a charity tennis match tomorrow morning."

"You can't drive like that. The state police have checkpoints—especially during Reunions—set up and down Route 1 to catch drunk drivers."

"I'm not *that* drunk." And she tried to stand and flopped back down on the bench.

"A BAC of 0.08 or over is enough to lose your license for three months, plus a whole bunch of other indignities."

She slipped on her flats and slung on her shoulder pack containing her high heels and again attempted to rise, wobbled, and straightened herself. "Can't have that."

"I can call you an Uber, but they're pretty busy around here at Reunions." He pulled out his phone and checked the app. "Yup, an hour and a half for the first available driver, if then. So, I guess I could drive you—except, how do I get back?"

"Lovely, my very own chauffeur . . ."

"How about we stop by my room and get you a cup of coffee until your Uber shows."

"That sounds like a plan . . . thank you." And she carefully stood and made her way out of the deeper shadows of the firs and steadied herself on his arm. They began slowly walking while he wheeled his bicycle. "I thought you had to get to the lab."

"It can wait until later."

"Is it just me," she asked, pulling up on his arm, "or are these California lilacs almost overpowering."

Jacob laughed as he effortlessly recited: "In the dooryard fronting an old farm-house near the white-washed palings, stands the lilac-bush tall-growing with heart-shaped leaves of rich green." Again, he laughed with gusto, a parlor trick, as if amused at his own conceit. Then, just as Jake would have done, he plucked a sprig of purple blossoms and presented it to her.

"Ah, so you know your Whitman," she said, dreamily burying her face in the blossoms, trying to recall the thing on her mind from moments before. "Jacob, you've already got me breathing out of the palm of your hand."

They continued out of the garden at a measured pace in silence, passed by gangs of stoned, yelling students and a few lingering reunion goers, mostly five and ten years out, dressed in various outlandish outfits. Barely taking note of this fine-looking couple, mother with her graduating senior. Her mind, she decided, was beginning to clear, even as she again felt like she was watching her character pretend an ambling sobriety from some distant roofline, spied upon by some demonic gargoyle, weaving her way along this circuitous route past the lit windows of these so-familiar, collegiate-Gothic dorms, where her tutelary gods stared down from the slate rooftops on this strangely familiar couple—years erased, the way they had walked many a night from the physics library to Jake's room in Pyne Hall.

"I feel like I've been here before," she offered, shaking her head. "But of course, I have—haven't I?"

"Stands to reason," he replied in an all-too-familiar tone. "I wanted a quiet corner of the campus away from the hustle and bustle."

Coming to a halt in the hushed, tree-shaded Pyne courtyard, Jacob walked his Trek over to the bike rack, while she waited, propped in his entryway. She found herself smiling idiotically at the familiar jingle of his key fob as she followed his exacting movements, unlocking his bike chain and carefully weaving the chain through the front tire and frame of the Trek, and then securing all to the metal stand. Not a little aghast to find herself the guest of a male undergraduate, she turned apprehensively to a stirring of wisteria above her right shoulder, leading her eye upward to where a pair of majestic London plane trees reached into the night sky, leafy arms gesturing to a roofline and a glittering moon silhouetting a phalanx of voyeur gargoyles—yes, she smiled, now acceding to her guardian spirits. There was music playing, something sad and somber, so it struck her, a saxophone riff, a Coltrane standard, perhaps a senior reflecting on the approach of graduation, of last goodbyes, tearful partings. A pang of loss flowing through her so that she had to stifle a cry. Then Jacob, with the touch of a key card, had the door open for her, gently taking her elbow and guiding her into the stairwell. Where the smell of beer and smoky dope hung heavy in the air and with it a longing that seemed to work itself up her legs and lodge somewhere in her solar plexus. The stairs were sticky underfoot with the acrid stench of spilled beer. Buoyed on the echo of their careful steps were other voices, other times, women's laughter, and soft music muffled by closed doors.

Again, the telltale jingle of his key chain and a door opened, and so she found herself inside this young man's room, a large room for a single, not unlike Erma's, with a compact bay window, wood paneling, and a view of the quad and plane trees. She breathed deeply of the sweaty scent of a linen laundry bag hanging on the inside of the door.

"Lucky you, to have drawn so high in room draw," she said.

"Very high," he laughed. "You probably think I gamed the system."

"Never," she laughed. "Made it . . ." She sighed as she collapsed into a black leather La-Z-Boy lounger next to his desk.

"I'll get us some coffee."

She watched intently as he flicked on a goosenecked lamp on his well-ordered desk chockablock with a pile of journals, pens, Sharpies, laptop, and, unaccountably, a familiar slide rule that had seen better days. He then switched off the overhead and busied himself with plugging in and filling a Keurig coffee machine that had been stashed behind books on a bookshelf.

"Ah," she noted, "*some* illegal things remain illegal."

"And the smoke detectors can pick up a mouse fart at fifty paces."

"Does that machine make tea? Coffee might keep me up all night."

"Green tea it is."

She settled into the embrace of the leather recliner, while taking in as much of the room as she dared without being obvious. The teak desk seemed almost antique, with a bay of locking drawers nearest where she sat and a burnished green-leather top, ink-stained, slightly scuffed, embossed in gold along the edges with a garland motif. Jacob was seated in a high-end Herman Miller desk chair that allowed him to shuttle between the coffee machine on the floor and his desk, where he'd placed two celebratory mugs emblazoned with *Ivy League Champions 2016* and the names of swim-team members. She squinted, thinking Erma's name might be on the list. As she did so, she noticed his long, agile hands, slightly puffy and reddened, the nails rough and broken, a somehow-familiar scar above the cuticle of his forefinger. But then so much of this day had seemed familiar.

She glanced away to make a further inventory: a couple of Navajo rugs, geometric patterns of brown, umber, and black, faded, threadbare in places, possibly authentic to her untrained eye. And then to a line of framed photos above three standing shelves, university issue, IKEA particleboard, packed with chemistry and biology texts and a scattering of paperback novels—a few happily recognizable titles: *Ulysses, Passage to India, Tom Jones,* a volume of Whitman's poetry, Henry James's *Portrait of a Lady*—all, except the Whitman, fondly remembered from her English novels course junior or senior year, which she'd shamed Jake into taking to fulfill his humanities distribution requirement. But only after he'd extracted a promise to use her extensive lecture notes for the exam.

And there, above the double bed neatly piled with pillows (where she'd resisted turning her gaze), a large and handsomely framed reproduction of Carpaccio's *Vision of Saint Augustine.*

"Good Lord, you too."

"What's that?"

"Augustine: it just seems my day to keep running into the old boy."

"Isn't it a wonderful painting? I still find it captivating after all these years."

"You've—how many years exactly?—been to Venice then?"

"When I was sixteen—seems ages ago. Two weeks, all expenses paid."

"Ah, yes, the magic number—sweet sixteen, I mean. That's when I took my daughter, after her father died: a mother-daughter, getting-reacquainted thing, you see."

He swiveled in his desk chair and poured out their tea into two mugs and handed her one.

"After the great divorce, my mother got the Sheridan Place house in Evanston, which she then sold, and my father got me. That's when he handed me a round-trip ticket from Chicago to Venice, or his executive assistant did—she made all the arrangements, the pensione, his credit card, itinerary, while he was busy with the new house and our move to Boulder, to be near the Denver operation."

"So, Augustine, Carpaccio was on your itinerary?"

"Yes, the Scuola di San Giorgio. He told me he aways regretted that at my age, before Princeton, he'd never had a chance to travel, to see the world, to savor the great art and architecture, not just the inside of a lab or the pool. He liked to say that if he had 'indulged myself earlier in art and literature,' things might have been very different in his life." Young Jacob shrugged and checked his phone, holding up the Uber app showing an hour still to wait. "The parallel universe, the what if . . ."

"Ah, those, but certainly not—hopefully not regrets? Not at your age."

"Oh, nothing he might admit. If we learn to follow our instincts."

At this enigmatic admonition, she smiled (attributing her confusion to Jack Rambridge's wine) and sipped at her tea, relishing the warmth spreading through her, and with it a curious feeling, an expansive tide bathing every nerve end, causing her to glance once again to Augustine's distracted face, as if for help as how best to navigate this extremely awkward conversation. She squinted again to where the desk lamp barely illuminated the Carpaccio, as if suddenly aware of a roomful of neglected treasures, suggestive, tantalizing, sparking a thousand latent sensations. Her imagination refreshed, indulged by fine wine, beginning to hum, she turned her gaze back to her young host (How could he be lying so convincingly—to himself—for her benefit?). The business about the divorce, instead of raising red flags, strangely emboldened further revisions of her own past, now that she had quite unaccountably found herself marooned in this confessional annex of Augustine's lair. She nodded her head, not a little amazed at how these new narratives could flow like freshets after a heavy rain.

"But how unusual in a divorce case, even at sixteen, for the father to get sole custody."

"Nothing so official, just a mutually arrived at modus vivendi." He put down his cup of tea and picked up the slide rule, moving the slipstick up and back. "They were not happy. She was a world-class biochemist, and they had worked together in their early years in the Evanston lab. At a certain point . . . well: she just wanted her life back, her career, not dealing with an adolescent, I guess. So, he gave her the house, a lab of her own, her independence. He was probably planning to move out to the Denver lab anyway." He shrugged, putting aside the slide rule to pick up a pen, tapping it thoughtfully on the desk. "Everybody got what they wanted. And I got Venice and Carpaccio's Augustine in the bargain."

"Umm . . . this tea is wonderful; I'm already feeling more like myself." She cocked her head (Could this revised text play into one of her own? After all, she could detect no aftereffects of that devastating car crash that killed his mother) and waved at the Carpaccio over the bed. "I'm trying to remember if I told Jake, your father, how it was I ended up in Venice in the first place—hey, another father-daughter trip at seventeen under less auspicious circumstances than yours." (When, in fact, so she noted to herself, divorce had been first broached by her father.)

"It's a special blend of green teas from a shop in Boulder, very relaxing." Jacob began to twirl the pen between his fingers. "I think my trip to Venice was his way of making up, compensating for his blue-collar upbringing. Maybe it's a midwestern thing, keeping up with Easterners who had such a corner on sophistication and savoir faire."

She laughed and reached to give his knee a friendly pat. "But of course we did, just like we had our own cultural cringe in the face of all things Old World. So aptly stated by one of my authors at Knopf, Lord John Julius Norwich, who, by the way, wrote a superb history of Venice, who liked to say: 'There are two kinds of people in this world: those who have been to Venice and those who haven't.'" Again she patted his knee. "You and Fitzgerald. And I bet your parents went to Venice on their honeymoon."

At this, his eyebrows rose with a repressed, possibly distraught smile, as he twirled the pen faster in his fingers. "Your cultural cringe obviously had my father so intimidated, buffaloed, that he provided me with a well-worn folding map of Venice from his graduate days at Stanford, which . . . here"—he swiveled around to a bookshelf and pulled out a decades-old map of Venice, which he unfolded for her—"he had carefully marked with a yellow Sharpie and annotated, and"—he held up his pen like an asterisk—"circled his must-see attractions. Along with extracting a promise that I'd stick with his map and not resort to Google Maps on my phone."

"How sweetly *retardataire* of him . . . a printed map." She carefully unfolded more of the map, squinting as she nodded upon recognizing some of the circled destinations, a route embedded like second sight in her mind's eye. "So, you were just following in his footsteps to the knee of Augustine."

"An old friend, really," he replied tonelessly. "After all, Augustine had been hanging in my parents' bedroom, and then mine, like a member of the family. He even made it as far as my bedroom in Boulder, and now here. A well-traveled éminence grise." The pen came to rest in his fingers. "I guess I'm hooked."

She drew in her bottom lip as her eye noted yellow markings farther afield on the map spread over her knees, some in the farthest working-class districts of Castello, well off any beaten track of hers.

"Castello," she murmured, "hardly a scenic part of town."

"Oh, he had an appreciation of the old Venetian crafts, especially stone carving, trades passed down through families, timeless artistry. His dad was a builder, a cabinetmaker."

Looking up, as if momentarily foundering in her determination to lead the conversation (no family photos anywhere in sight), she pondered the somehow familiar framed black-and-white photos on the wall above the bookshelves: Einstein and Marie Curie she recognized, the others not, or had she just forgotten?

"I'm sure"—she smiled as she fumbled to refold the map—"Carpaccio's Augustine is much admired by your girlfriends. He and his fellow saints were catnip for spirited, even romantic conversations in my day."

"Oh"—his face lighting up with what she took as gleeful pleasure—"he's all the talk around the pool and the lab."

"Looks like you had a full itinerary," and she put the folded map on his desk.

"Just the usual suspects: the Rialto fish market, the Scuola di San Rocco, Florian, the Fenice, the Pensione Seguso, and, of course, the Scuola di San Giorgio. Concerts almost every night."

At this, she found herself sinking even as she maintained a cheery smile. "Ah, so you stayed at the Seguso?"

"I thought that was your idea, the Seguso?"

Startled by this near accusation, she hid her consternation with a valiant effort to go with the flow, simply to allow her imagination free rein, to revise at will—if necessary, make it up as she went along. "Why, of course, like father, like daughter: my father swore by the Seguso. A dowdy haven for scholars and aesthetes, writers like Jan Morris and my very own Lord John Julius Norwich, whose parents Duff Cooper and Lady Diana Cooper stayed there as well—the great society beauty in her day. Who once lamented that all the boys she danced with at seventeen and eighteen had died in the Great War."

For a moment, his eyes brushed hers, a crinkle of recognition at the corners as he swiveled to a nearby shelf and took out a well-thumbed paperback. "James Morris—now Jan Morris's—*Venice*."

She ran a trembling hand over the cover with a photo of the lagoon in fog. "For a science kid from Chicago, you've certainly spread your wings."

"Evanston," he allowed. "And then there was an old waiter, Fauto, who demanded at breakfast whether one was going to eat lunch or dinner at the Seguso."

"Yes," she hurried out, "a dead ringer for Pavarotti . . . and the soggy salad and greasy ravioli and overcooked fish."

"And the lounge smelling of feral cats."

She took another swallow of tea and fanned her face. "It's warm in here . . ."

He stood and went and opened the bay windows to a night breeze stirring the plane trees. Nodding as if something had finally clarified in his mind, he seemed to adjust his position, his gaze, to a point that relieved the glare in the glass over the Carpaccio.

"Like you, he told me to first find my way to the Scuola di San Giorgio, make it my benchmark for everything else. How did he put it? 'If you can find your way there—truly find your way"—he paused, as if unsure of the voice he was channeling—"all the rest will fall into place.' I suppose like getting your first peer-reviewed paper published or winning that first match at Wimbledon."

"Yes, except, of course, one has to make it into the draw in the first place."

"You can't imagine," he went on, head turned to the window, eyes drawn inward as if spellbound by a vision, "my trepidation as I left my bags at the Seguso, pulled out my map, and began to make my way from the Zattere across the Accademia bridge, zigzagging all the way to San Marco, and then skirting the church and the Doge's Palace and all the crowds, diving beneath the clock tower and then following my nose until I managed to come out just at the right spot and the bridge over the Rio di Santa Augustin." He had seemingly been tracing his route along the window's leading with an outstretched finger, his voice rising in a diffident, searching tone. "It was cool, a late-October day, and with that map snug in the back pocket of my jeans, I felt a surge of confidence—that some instinct had seen me through, that I'd somehow managed to find my way back after all—waiting for me there. A second chance: the thing lost and found." He tapped the window as if catching sight of something tucked deep in the night, where the chattering roofline hovered against a silvery moon. "You see, he was a man unused to failure of any kind. Perhaps it was only in the aftermath of the divorce, or perhaps an intuition, something only a scientist would properly understand—the overlooked data point, the chips left on the table."

She had been intently following where his finger traced along the leading, seeing the shimmer of reflected light on the underbelly of that bridge, the green doors, the marble dolphins, even as the alteration in the tone of his voice sent a shiver of recognition down her spine.

"Funny." She closed her eyes as if seeking an inner light to see more clearly. "My daughter, Erma, was saying something just this afternoon, how whereas I always saw Augustine's study as the lair of a classical scholar (not a theologian)—a literary artist even—she saw him as a Renaissance scientist, surrounded by his library of all the world's existing knowledge. And the armillary sphere, of course, along with the works of Ptolemy and Aristotle at his fingertips. Even an astrolabe at his elbow. Such an intimate and comforting picture of human ingenuity, of the glories of civilization."

"We see what we want to see—what we half expect to see." He paused until she opened her eyes and nodded. "For a theologian, the relics; for a musician it would be those open scores—don't you think? The inspiration of the harmony of the spheres. For a scientist, a workable theory to guide his research."

"Something like that—yes, I suppose. Yes, the way the very greatest works of art reflect our deepest yearnings back to us?"

"Music for the harpsichord and viola da gamba . . . along with that ineffable luminous light that might seduce even the most hardened of researchers at his bench—secrets, tantalizing, mysterious—answers at the tip of the tongue for the prepared mind: Einstein"—and he waved to his power wall of Nobel laureates—"Johnny von Neumann, Kurt Gödel, Kip Thorne, Erwin Schrödinger, Marie Curie, Alan Turing—all, except Marie, worked within a mile's radius."

She laughed uneasily, her cheeks burning with fascination at this outpouring. "Ah." She raised a hand. "I believe I was responsible for Marie." She shook her head. "Wow, forgive me, but you truly remind me of your father: how he saw things that I always yearned, struggled, but failed to see."

He smiled with a tentative purse of his lips and returned to his desk chair, picking up the pen and again flipping it through his fingers. "Oh, I don't think even he would number himself among such immortals. Not yet, at any rate." He caught her eye and held her gaze as he continued in something of an apologetic tone. "Here's the thing: for a scientist, only the result matters, a result that is discovered but that has existed for all eternity. That's the grandeur, the power and beauty of science, the logic and precision, even if it can seem quite impersonal to outsiders. Not like your writers, where individual expression is everything. Maybe Augustine, at least for Carpaccio"—and his hands gently revolved between them—"somehow bridges that imagined divide?"

She nodded eagerly. "Yes, yes, but how odd, for I'm sure Augustine would never be my pick to hang out with for all eternity—or even stranded on a desert island. A saint with certain ideological bête noires, a penchant for sinful guilt that would make long acquaintance difficult, if not extremely unpleasant."

"Funny, my father used almost precisely those same words."

She thought she detected a flicker of uncertainty—even nostalgia—cross his face as he then swiveled once more to a nearby bookshelf to retrieve a well-used textbook, a history of science, which she thought she recognized. He placed it on his desk and opened to a page marked with a pamphlet emblazoned with the university crest. He fingered the underlined passage and read aloud.

"'There is another form of temptation, even more fraught with danger. This is the disease of curiosity . . . It is this which drives us to try and discover the secrets of nature, those secrets which are beyond our understanding, which can avail us nothing and which man should not wish to learn.'"

As his eyes rose from the text, she found herself staring intently at the pamphlet where he'd laid it aside: the much-faded program for her class's graduation exercises.

"Yes," she replied, now reaching for the program, "sounds like our man. And his trump card—curiosity killed the cat—was to propagate the doctrine of original sin. Banish sinful curiosity and the world stands still, an eternal present absent risk, or something, I suppose, close to the repose of a life everlasting."

"Or the Dark Ages," he offered. "And yet your Carpaccio has portrayed him as a Renaissance man, a scholar, a humanist, even as your daughter, Erma, suggested, a man of science, hardly the Church's enforcer of ideological purity, perpetrator of a theological straitjacket that stifled descent, much less the development of science, for over a thousand years."

At this thinly veiled accusation, this reprise of a thousand arguments from student days past, much less mention of her daughter, she looked up with alarm from the yellowed graduation program she had been leafing through. "How did you come by this bit of memorabilia?"

"The move to Boulder, the great divorce, in a pile of stuff to be thrown out—moved on."

"Why—no . . . and such a vintage year." She laughed uneasily. "I was salutatorian."

"Yes, and a remarkable address, even if it was in Latin. Your Augustine would have been pleased that you played up the role of Plato and his ideal state."

"Well"—struggling to gather her wits, material for the rewrite, she turned the page to her Latin text, smiling tentatively—"I thought it pretty good at the time, a counterpoint to the mess of the Vietnam War. Even if LBJ and Nixon were hardly philosopher kings."

His brows creased as he once more picked up his pen, tapping it on his desk impatiently, a quick, echoing tattoo as if to signal a battle properly joined.

"Even if Plato worked assiduously to undermine the mainstream tradition of Greek science based on empirical observation." His eyes now glittered defiantly before hers as if echoing long-ago bull sessions, erasing the years. "And our Augustine was a team member in good standing since Plato's ideas about the invisible and eternal world of Forms would be fatal to any scientific enquiry. No axiomatic foundations for research could ever be derived from such will-o'-the-wisps."

"Well." She smiled, as if now taking some comfort in the familiar sparring. "Even without my reading glasses, I believe I was trying to defend the classical tradition, the classical virtues—Stoic virtues, to inspire our class in the pursuit of the good, the true and beautiful. And yes, the empirical tradition that stands behind your fundamental axiom: the requirement that any data must be experimentally reproducible. We go to great lengths at Tandem not to publish junk science—my late husband saw to that—even when profitable." She brought the program to her face, breathing in the fusty smell of the yellowed pages, as if of a thing long banished. "Pulling on the same oar as you and the new Burrage Biochemistry Lab I've heard so much about, which, shame on me, I've yet to visit."

"I'll show you around, if you like. And yes"—he smiled, a deprecating wrinkle on his brow—"we are rather like worms grown in a beautiful petri dish on a perfect diet: a steady food supply, good hygiene, and health care—isolated from all the natural hazards we might face in a life in the wild."

"Worms?"

"Yes, worms, *C. elegans*, that can be bred to far outlast their limited lifetimes."

"Lifetimes?"

"Evolution . . . aging," and his face lit up with the air of a debater building to his central argument. "You see, aging is simply an evolutionary oversight, the result of mutations that worsen our fitness in old age, mechanisms that prioritize having children early to the detriment of our disposable somas."

She cocked her head as if very much attracted to the thrust of the idea, yet another narrative twist, even as she put her own spin on the idea. "Oh, we waited too long for our first child and then . . ." She waved a hand of dismissal at this too personal note, as opposed to a better fictional ploy, returning to where her finger marked the paragraph in the program, squinting. "Ah, I even got Madison into my salutatorian address, a worthy Princetonian who drew on the classical heritage to establish the Constitutional ideal of balance—checks-and-balances—and so prevent flawed humanity from spoiling a good thing." Another dismissive wave. "But enough of me. Tell me what you and your dad have been up to: Jake, who used to have me hang out in the physics library with him, who liked to say that just the brain waves flooding the place inspired him."

"Oh, yes," he laughed. "Maybe—who knows, maybe hanging with your Carpaccios did something of the same for me."

"And what is that, Jacob, exactly?"

"What always struck me about the painting, especially seeing it for the first time in situ, as the art historians like to say, was the hourglass by his desk that has run out. An archaic bit of machinery—a memento mori, I suppose—which in the quiet of the oratory of the Scuola di San Giorgio struck me as a kind of metaphor for the problem of the human condition: an hourglass at rest always runs out unless or until you turn it over. In effect, beginning again."

"'Beginning again,'" she mused, "has a nice ring to it. Like those revisions to my first novel. Was I telling you about that earlier? What you and Erma—children—are all about for Jake and me. Isn't that the point of it all: to have no regrets?"

He bent eagerly toward her as if his narrative was beginning to fully register. "Yes, yes, a revision. Just as I found a renewed energy—call it curiosity, how such a telling symbol of lost time, even the end of time, how, once upon a time, that image of an hourglass running out was such a foregone conclusion." As if to demonstrate, he flipped the pen between his fingers and held it upside down. "When it only requires a turn of the hand."

"Yes, if only . . ."

His voice rising, a barely restrained eagerness: "Think of it: viewing the Carpaccios, just you and I, like dipping into your Whitman, erases time . . ." His voice seemed to falter as if this concept might be beyond her grasp, a narrative twist that had turned in upon itself.

Yet this idea so deftly conjured was not entirely foreign to her, even as it had the odd effect of instantly returning her to the oratory of the Scuola di San Giorgio and the memory of her father's admonitory cadences to a young and wild seventeen-year-old on the values of sobriety and a more caring propinquity as the foundation for a well-lived life. She squinted in the lamplight to where his phone lay on his desk, an hourglass in the guise of a stubborn Uber app.

"You're tired," he apologized.

She raised a gracious hand to disguise a yawn, feeling as if her imagination had finally outdistanced what little remained of her energy, even if the young face above the lamplit desk, titled in half shadow, had gained a new maturity over the previous minutes, who now picked up a thick journal, a final piece of evidence, and handed it to her.

"My senior thesis."

She opened the journal, *Nature*, and squinted at the table of contents.

"Good God, already published—that's more than I ever managed."

He snapped his fingers. "Just a turn of the hourglass."

"Ah, now that you mention it, I remember a guy always a little obsessed with the lack of time, always trying to see how many hours he could pack into a day by cutting back on sleep."

"That's why he moved to Denver, to be closer to the research teams, to get away from the day-to-day administrative duties." He gestured to the journal she was holding. "We worked on this together, over summers, over the internet—a leap of faith that paid off."

She flipped the pages to his article, squinting to further decipher the précis. He opened a desk drawer and handed her a pair of reading glasses.

She laughed, taken aback, as if he'd thought of everything.

She placed a finger on the page and looked up. "I suppose that's why he quit the swim team after freshman year." She reached out and laid a palm on his bare knee, feeling the flex of a muscle, searching for an opening as if hopeful of more material for revisions.

"He quit because he realized he'd reached the limit of his potential as a swimmer—and because he saw more potential in you."

"I . . . oh well," she stammered, pleased even as she stole a furtive glance at her father's Rolex. "Perhaps you'd have been better off visiting Venice with a girlfriend."

Such a prompting, perhaps facetious tone seemed to spring a repressed admission. "Here's the thing: I met a wonderful lady there. She was studying music, playing concerts. Tall and athletic, like you. Her enthusiasm for the classics, for literature, inspired me to become a reader of James and Melville and Whitman." And he waved in the direction of his shadowy bookshelves, as if proof of his bona fides.

Somehow this didn't fit with the editorial suggestions she had in mind, her line of thought further disrupted by drunken shouts out in the quad. She pressed the reading glasses up her nose to focus on the précis in her lap. "Gene editing, gene therapy, AI, and the therapeutic uses of psilocybin: the potential to boost health and slow the aging process."

"My mind must be playing tricks on me." She pulled off the reading glasses, tapping the pages and fixing him with a plaintive stare as she nodded, desperate to collect her addled wits. "Why, this, this is exactly how I imagined things to be."

"You see"—his eyes widened, radiant, burning into hers—"we collaborate on everything."

"Ah, of course. I should have guessed."

"A partnership that reflects our R&D priorities." He reached to relieve her of the journal. "Burrage Pharma has been working on cutting-edge biotechnologies to rejuvenate aging cells, what is called regenerative medicine: remove, replace, repair where we can and then do a little reprograming of cells, hacking them, editing out the problematic and optimizing the good stuff. Using stem cells is the most obvious strategy for regeneration of many parts of the body. A geared-up immune system can also restore a more youthful state. And then there's our microbiome ecosystem of bacteria, viruses, and fungi, which can also be enhanced. Another promising field of research—and Princeton is at the forefront—is the scaffold of proteins outside our cells that are damaged over time and can be replaced, if not repaired. It's all about getting the right cells to the right place at the right time."

"But isn't it the natural order of things," she half-heartedly protested: due diligence even with a brilliant collaborator. "That we're born and age and sadly die. Seneca certainly thought so, even found hope in the natural order, that spring follows winter, that life renews itself season after season. Exiled to Corsica, he found great consolation just contemplating the great cycles etched in the night sky."

"It depends, of course, where you stand. How much you still need to accomplish in a limited lifetime. How excited you are to, well, stick around, to see what happens next." He placed an encouraging hand on her right knee, gently massaging the muscles. "To get that revised novel of yours published."

"If only we could write ourselves into our novels and have them come alive. Even if I still think of myself as the youngest person in the room. Even if tomorrow—I can't believe I'm still up—I must play a charity match with much younger women."

He tapped his cell phone, and the Uber app had barely budged for her ride to the Marriott. He shrugged, compressing his lips as if possibly exasperated.

"Who knows," he offered cryptically, patting her knee affectionately. "The trouble is, for a scientist, the velocity of information can be so overwhelming—especially as all the various disciplines begin to merge—whether on the scale of the cosmic microwave background radiation or a primitive eukaryote. Geology passes seamlessly into biology, as we are all descended from one event, from one eukaryote fused from bacteria—think about it: just once in four billion years, and all the plants, animals, algae, and fungi evolved from that founder population. The mystery of the thing keeps me up nights, fills my dreams."

She found this near confession—echoing her recent conversation with her daughter—daunting, if thrilling, spilling her backward, awash in long-banished recollections, and providing a tepid second wind. "No wonder you might want to stick around to find out what happens next. Like your heroine, Lynn Margulis."

His blue-gray eyes glittered softly, as if his words, like a net spread and drawn slowly in, had, indeed, caught something of her remaining wildness and wonder. "I guarantee you, Lynn would have grabbed the chance to stick around, even if her theory about eukaryotic cells being derived from endosymbiotic bacteria proved to be otherwise." As if to seal the deal, before she might protest his first-name relationship with a woman dead five years and retired for many more, he threw out even more evidence to boost his theory. "Even your Seneca, gazing at the night sky over Corsica, if he had any idea about the discoveries to come in cosmology, would have chosen to stick around too."

"How exciting for you, Jacob: to have your whole life still ahead of you—to stick around to see what happens next." She collapsed backward in near exhaustion.

He swiveled in his chair and gestured impatiently toward the Carpaccio. "Trust me, you'll be along on this ride." His voice rose, as she would someday describe it, like Virgil conducting Dante through the infernal regions to the uplands of paradise, where his Beatrice reigned, imploring her to follow his train of thought. "Our minds, the electromagnetic energy that flows though the fibers of our logical selves, our brains, our long-term memory—well, in our consciousness, space and time are a single construct, past and present mirroring one another. So that nothing"—he gestured with a spread hand, describing rising circles within rising circles, holding her eye—"separates us. Nothing is lost. Ever."

Somehow, this cri de coeur sparked a last reserve of energy. "How did Emerson put it? 'The universe is the externalization of the soul. Wherever the life is, that bursts into appearance around it.'"

"Yes, yes, the mystery, the sense of awe at what's unknown, even if we don't have all the answers—yet. And you," he now prompted her blue pencil with a curious tilt of his head. "If you had it all to do over again?"

She closed her eyes for a moment as if (rejecting the Hamlisch version) conjuring with the possibilities. "Perhaps, I should have taken that novel out of the drawer sooner, or tried to play the women's circuit for a few years, if only to gather material, or . . . I don't know."

"So, now you can."

"Don't tell me"—she tried to laugh it off as her hoarse voice rose to a near cry—"that it's all in my head, to be made up out of whole cloth." And she reached to her sore right knee as if to demonstrate. "Only as young as you feel—that can't be right. Oh, what does it matter?"

"Here," and he fumbled at the side of his chair, where a key fob was attached to a belt loop on his shorts. Unhooking the jingling keys while she watched, not a little spellbound, he sorted through them until he'd found the right one, tiny, antique, and unlocked a side drawer in his desk. Reaching in, he pulled out a large dark green plastic bottle imprinted with the Burrage Pharmaceuticals label. He popped the cap and shook out two oval capsules, also sea-green in color, and held them out. "These are in late-stage clinical trials, but all our results have been outstanding, with no side effects whatsoever—just the opposite. They will do wonders for your energy and put your metabolism into high gear. I take them myself every day. I can guarantee you will sleep like a baby and wake up feeling like a million bucks, like your old—or should I say—your revised younger self."

"A couple of Motrins might do the trick."

"Seriously, we spent over half a billion dollars and ten years developing this—truly a wonder drug." He tossed the two capsules in his mouth and swallowed them with the last of his tea.

She sat back in her chair, smiling idiotically as the room swam before her.

"When I was seventeen and first in Venice with my father, there was a gelateria across the square from the Scuola di San Giorgio, and we'd take a break from the Carpaccios and sit by the canal and eat ice cream. Those were the best ice creams I ever tasted. You see, my father had just confided in me about my mother's drinking problem, and how it had gotten to the point where he couldn't take her to publishing parties anymore for fear of her disrupting things. He was at his wits' end. And all I could think about was my ice cream: strawberry and pear with a touch of mint. The geology of my privileged life had so hardened that I was oblivious to his pain."

"The ice cream place is still there." He gazed at her with half-shut eyes, as if her words had tapped into some waking dream of his own. "And your novel"—he tapped the open drawer of his desk—"awaits."

A line from Tennyson sprang to mind: "'To follow knowledge like a sinking star, beyond the utmost bound of human thought.'"

She abruptly held out her hand. "I'll take 'em. What have I got to lose?"

He shook out two capsules from the plastic bottle and placed them in her palm.

She squinted and kept her palm open: "And one for the road." She swallowed them down with the last of her tea, gasped, and collapsed back in her chair. "Do you suppose these might help our Jabberwocky?"

"Ah, Isabel . . . you see, almost anything is possible."

CHAPTER 17

Ensconced in the luxury of Jack Rambridge's palatial penthouse suite at the Marriott, Bianca found herself lying wide awake while Jack snored blissfully beside her (dreaming, no doubt, of his ripening grapes snug in their Beaune terroirs). Her attention was taken up by a glimmer of light coming through the drawn curtains, a spectral presence that had insinuated its way and now resided within a long, V-shaped aperture on the ceiling over the bed. A colorless, barely discernible life-form seemed nestled within that V-shaped cavity, perhaps only the refracted emanation from a flickering streetlight in the parking lot, where Jack's dark blue Mercedes CLK-GTR Roadster was parked. Somehow this apparition made her uneasy, tapping into a free-floating sense of guilt that had plagued her since running into young Jacob at the sign-in table. This when she should be thrilled out of her mind to have landed such an astute wealthy gentleman, and a good lover in the bargain, already with two Viagra-assisted orgasms to his credit: the first lover she'd ever known who liked to speak his mind while giving head.

"These kids don't get it," Jack had opined, glancing up from between her legs. "It's not the biosphere that supports human life but humans, who by ingenuity—knowledge and problem solving—made life marginally supportable on planet earth.

This spaceship earth idea is just another one of the inanities these kids today get stuck with by their no-nothing professors. We aren't passengers or stewards or even a maintenance crew; we're designers and builders. Go ask the anthropologists, or even the paleontologists: there are very few fossils of old people."

"Don't stop, baby."

"Go ask the Vikings what they thought of Greenland and Iceland during the last period of global warming—or Vineland. I'm fully invested in Iceland, microalgae cultivation using geothermal energy."

"Yes, yes, yes . . . me too, I'm totally into geothermal."

She was tempted to get out of bed and just pin closed that pesky gap in the drawn curtains. Yet this eerie presence on the ceiling had her half hypnotized, as if the pulsing amoeba was insidiously connected to her heartbeat or, so she preferred to think, the rhythm of one of Matteo's signature Coltrane numbers, still playing in her mind. How proud she'd been to show him off to her class, proof positive that her life, her talent, had not come to naught. Walking on air as she accompanied her son, along with Annette and Matt, to the fifth to meet up with Arthur and Erma, leaving Matteo and Erma dancing to a jarring techno beat provided by a skinhead DJ, before he had to rush off to a late-night gig at Dizzy's. Just the sonic waves of youthful phenoms were enough to bring an older gal back into heat.

Maybe it was only that she was a little freaked out after again running into young Jacob. She'd been on her way back up campus to the fiftieth reunion, where she was to meet Jack Rambridge, when she was passed by a young man on a bicycle pedaling like mad, a white cape like a drogue chute fluttering behind. Suddenly, screeching to a halt, the biker turned to her with an endearing, if disconcerting, nostalgic smile.

"*Bella serata, senorina Bianca*," young Jacob proclaimed in perfect Italian as he hopped off the bike. And he held out his free arm to escort her up campus as he wheeled his Trek.

The kid's familiarity with her Venice years was more than a little bizarre. It was bad enough feeling guilty about Gini, who thought she had a corner on all things Venetian, when it was she, Macaluso, of venerable Sicilian heritage, who had actually lived there for almost three years while studying (her prize-winning dissertation on the music in Carpaccio's *Vision of Saint Augustine*) and performing two, sometimes three concerts a week. A minor celebrity in seventeenth-century music circles, not that her roomies gave a damn. Who had saved a distraught Jake Burrage, who'd arrived in Venice with little more than a map in his back pocket.

"You were so in a league of your own at Florian. Especially when you were belting out that rendition of 'Will You Still Love Me Tomorrow' while standing at the piano. You brought down the house."

"I was, wasn't I . . ."

She had barely been able to get that much out, given the disjunction of time and space invoked by young Jacob's nostalgic vibes.

"Nice, your dad still talks about me," she said, thinking she'd had way too much to drink at the fifth, or maybe it was the toke she and Matteo had shared on the way.

And yet she found herself clutching Jacob's arm just as she'd once clutched Jake's after a concert at the Scuola di San Giorgio or the Scuola di San Rocco, when they'd retire to Florian for late-night snacks and cappuccino and dolci. And when the café band (all great pals of hers) went on break, she would commandeer the white piano and play and sing for the Florian crowd of well-heeled tourists and strollers in San Marco, belting out standards, jazz, rock and roll, Carole King, greatest hits of the sixties—until even the returning musicians were clapping in appreciation. Days of mellow Amarone and yellow roses (Jake's favorite), when she had been so alive that she could barely catch her breath.

"You were such a star."

"Hey, the tips weren't bad either."

She'd gripped his arm tighter, as if unable to resist being transported back to those distant nights when they'd hurried back to her tiny Castello apartment over the bakery, struggling out of their clothes to exhaust themselves in extravagant love-making. She never would have guessed a science nerd could be such a technician of pleasure: nothing about a woman's body fazed him. Even his mild bondage thing was a turn-on. Something—not that she'd ever breathe a word—she couldn't imagine Gini putting up with. And irony of irony: she'd never liked Jake at Princeton. Not his brilliance, nor the way he had Gini smitten, the way he had Apolonia eating out of his hand as her student tutor, the way Annette was green with envy as Gini came closer and closer to grabbing her number-one spot using Jake's tracking system. Never, ever tempted to steal him from Gini: too damn cerebral and full of himself for her more artistic tastes in men. And yet, lying in each other's arms, Jake had poured out his insecurities and frustrations, his guilt at not somehow being able to save his dad from an early death from some terrible disease. Sparking her own doubts about a career as a performer, which made their ten days together that much more intense, fraught, combustible, foolhardy. Two improbable souls—Gini's name rarely passing their lips—in a leaking lifeboat.

Once, years later, at a girl's lunch with Gini at the Plaza, her pain still tender, curiosity had gotten the better of her, and she had brought up Venice and the Carpaccios, alluding to Jake, in passing, to see if Gini's memory might be sparked about their missed thousand-day rendezvous at the Scuola di San Giorgio. Nothing. Or nothing, at least, Gini was willing to share, even as she went on and on about her growing reputation in the publishing world.

For what it had been worth: Jake had been fair game.

Staring at the ceiling, she contemplated taking one of the marijuana gummies Apolonia had slipped her when they parted. "Better than Ambien and much safer." She reached into her purse-backpack, discarded in their rush by the side of the bed, and found the packet of gummies, popping one in her mouth as she closed her eyes to the ghostly homunculus overhead.

And then young Jacob had suddenly stopped wheeling his bicycle, his face rising as if to the familiar throb of some oldie but goody emanating from a Reunions site they were passing, his lovely, compact nose sniffing the air along the lamplit path, indicating with his turned shoulders the bagel man with his cart of still-warm bagels.

"Ah, the smell, Bianca, what does it remind you of?"

Dispensing with the Pensione Seguso and its ridiculous meal plan, Jake had moved into her one-room student flat over a bakery in the wilds of Castello, where they'd woken mornings in each other's arms to the cries of boatmen and the aroma of freshly baked bread. Had she really, once upon a time, fallen in love with Jake Burrage to the smells of focaccia and ciabatta? Or was she just exulting in powering her way out of the shadow of Ginistrella Wingate, dazzling Jake with her musical stardom, her sexual gymnastics—more ways of pleasuring a man than ever dreamt of by white-bread West Chop. By the time he'd had to leave to return to Stanford and finish up his doctorate, he'd been thoroughly cured of Gini, or so it seemed in letters he'd written to her, first in a torrent (vivid epistles about his hopes of revolutionizing medicine, a cure for Huntington's that had ravaged his father) and then a trickle and then no more.

"Huntington's . . ." Did Gini even know?

"How could I share such a thing with Gini—you know how she is: perfection is her middle name. And Huntington's is an inherited disease—fifty percent chance I'm afflicted, that I'll pass it on to any children I might have."

"Pasticceria Panificio . . . ," young Jacob had mumbled, taking a bite of his bagel and offering half to her.

"How is it, Jacob, that you're so up on things Venetian?"

"My father, who, by the way, wanted me to convey to you his fondest wishes: *la terra sancta nostra . . . la ragazza dei miei sogni.*"

"No fucking way, Jacob. Forgive my French, but I was such an interlude. What would your mother say?"

"They parted ways when I was a teenager. When he handed me a map of Venice with a route marked on it to the Scuola di San Giorgio. A destination where he'd found, as he put it, one of the most remarkable women in his life. 'So, go lose yourself; and, by losing yourself, see what lost part of yourself you may discover, with no thesis, no theory to guide you . . .' or something equally abstruse to that effect."

This had brought tears to her eyes, as once more she found herself a twosome wending their way through labyrinthian *calles*, taking delight at every turning in the simplest things imaginable: an unexpected slant of sunset light sprouting vesperal flames on a crumbling wall of red ivy, a fourteenth-century set of Gothic windows, sinuous, flickering, immemorial, at a turning in Campo San Margarita, a carved sparrow taking flight amid Istrian stone laurels by Pietro Lombardo on the lintels of the Scuola Grandi di San Giovanni Evangelista. The memory of those Italian names conjuring again their wanderlust, those precious hours: her glory days.

She had laughed, giddy as a teenager.

"If only you'd known me then, my best power-lifting days, when I could bench-press 198 and a squat of 302. Now I'm down to 150, and plenty of fish oil for the clogged arteries."

This ridiculous observation had seemingly broken the spell, bringing him up short.

"Oh, there's so much misinformation out there, so many false, even deceitful, claims, like the benefits of fish oil in large doses—totally bogus and worse, when you consider where the fish come from." Then he seemed to catch himself and grinned that lovely boyish grin as he picked up again where they'd left off. "Remember the Rialto fish market and all those fabulous sea creatures preserved on ice."

This broke something in her, shedding all inhibitions as she threw caution to the wind.

"We were something . . ."

"When you played that Shirelles number at Florian, 'Will You Still Love Me Tomorrow.' The bravos were like a tsunami sweeping San Marco."

There and then, close to losing it, she'd almost pulled this vision of her reincarnated youth into an embrace, tempted to kiss the young man right in front of all the revelers passing them by. Only saving her sanity and self-respect by erupting with the first inanities that came to mind.

"Here's to San Giorgio, the peacocks, the guinea hen, the red parrot . . ."

"The deer escaping from Saint Jerome's tame lion, and don't forget the griffin."

"You loved that griffin of Saint Tryphon almost as much as George's dragon."

"Wasn't it you who always said: life resided in the details—note by note by note, the essential truth, the hidden melody in the polyphonic weave."

"Did I say that? Yes, my beloved mother—God rest her soul. How did she put it? Look for that golden thread in the tapestry, that small truth that contained a larger truth, the imaginative truth that gives rise to the essential myths that lovers need to live by."

"Miraculous, ritualistic, ingrained, and so a life of purpose."

"Jesus, Mary, and Joseph—Jacob! Did I really go on like that?"

Okay, so maybe she'd lost her mind—who wouldn't, with all the dope and music, the revelers at every turning, the lovers reunited after years, the happy heat wave of craziness?

"Remember," he'd suddenly exclaimed, "the faces in Giovanni Bellini's picture in the Accademia?"

"Wrong Bellini—Gentile. Yes, the old graybeard with a scowl in his splendid robes, or the one with the receding chin and long mop of straw-colored hair—maybe his brother or even his son, and the redhead displaying that huge signet ring on his finger."

"The pageant of life, you called it. Captured all with their cares, their joys and sorrows—a sort of immortality on canvas, and so living on into our world and time . . ."

At this, she'd reached a trembling palm to his lips, as if to prevent the further appropriation of her words, her story—her unlived life.

"No more, Jacob," she pleaded, "no more." She was beyond mystification, her instincts less romantic than maternal, stranded in some strange borderland of unrequited yearning.

As if aware of her distress, he had simply grasped the back of her hand, pressed it gallantly to his lips, and hopped on his bike to disappear through the crowd. Leaving her stranded at the entrance to the fiftieth watching a Lesley Gore imitator sing "You Don't Own Me."

She sighed, now realizing that young Jacob had been hurrying back to Holder to grab that dance with Gini. Gini, who, as much as she tried, couldn't hide the expression of serene pleasure that sparked her eyes as she danced in the arms of Jake's son, looking for fleeting moments like the girl she remembered from forty years before, who couldn't help speaking exactly what was on her mind, who had a streak of wild risk-taking that put even Apolonia to shame.

Her phone vibrated on the bedside table with a text from Matteo: "On a break at Dizzy's. That Erma is something else, as brilliant as she is beautiful."

"What the fuck, you still awake?" mumbled Jack.

"Sorry, dear, didn't mean to disturb you."

"You were singing, just now."

"Was I?" She realized she was high as a kite. "Oh, just something I do in my sleep when I'm having a happy dream, probably a fifteenth-century little number I transcribed from a painting by Carpaccio."

"The Scuola di San Giorgio, or is it the Accademia?"

"You know it . . ."

"Days of wine and roses, huh?"

"I was dreaming about Venice."

"Well, then, how about week after next?"

"You're not serious." She nuzzled his shoulder.

"That's what you seventies gals are all about—right? Spontaneity. I'll arrange my Learjet 75 in the morning and make sure my suite at the Danieli is available—where Ruskin stayed with his wife, Effie, pussy hair and all."

"Yes, smart girl. She ditched John-boy for Rossetti."

"My two favorite restaurants in the world—Ai Mercanti and Tuttinpiedi—are just a ten-minute walk, or a tad longer if you prefer a gondola."

"Oh, let's walk . . ."

Like Bianca, Apolonia had found herself wide awake in her bed at the Hampton Inn, unsatisfied and cynically musing on the events of the day. How much she missed John Proctor, especially given Daltrey's vague resemblance. How John's letters, and then emails, then care packages of books, had proved to be the high points of her busy doctoring days. How she missed her children, Christopher, and his kid sister, Margie, especially Christopher, her favorite. Given that all her teammates had their kids in tow, Christopher would have fit right in, especially since Erma once had a crush on her handsome son. While her Harvard professor, Daltrey Assingham, her booby prize, had been more interested in hearing himself talk than taking care of business.

"That Ginistrella Wingate of yours is quite something. Did I mention I knew her as a kid, a gangly, plucky teenager who could outtalk most men and outplay them on the tennis court? A spitfire, an unguided buzz bomb, a mouth like Mae West."

"She's learned discretion since those days, and then some. More like her father than her father."

"Her father—brilliant, dignified, unworldly—was a legend in the publishing world, married to a woman who was an embarrassment to any male who got within ten feet. A disastrous marriage and source of endless cruel gossip."

"Yes, we got a good dose of the sad lady at our graduation dinner."

"The West Chop rumor mill—one of the reasons I moved to Chappy. How little Gini Wingate, a daredevil of a kid, survived all that is a wonder. But survive she did, turning my ear tonight on Seneca, as I shared with her some recent scholarship I've been doing on fifth- and sixth-century Ravenna, Galla Placidia, and Theodoric—those glorious mosaics, you know."

"She was known to us girls as Agrippina, court queen. She helped Bianca and me with our essays; even then, she had a brilliant editor's eye. Looks like you should have stuck with the classics."

"Julia Agrippina—huh, Roman emperor, court queen, and then some. Well, I was more drawn to the sixth century, when the vesperal flame of classical civilization flickers out, engulfed by the shadows of crumbling ruins, of mysticism and a fanatical faith, raising the question: How will our generation be remembered by our children? Will we be just the post–Second World War generation, Cold War warriors who survived the Cuban Missile Crisis, or the generation that brought about the fall of the Berlin Wall?"

"Hey, how about the civil rights movement or even the Summer of Love? My idol growing up was Billie Jean King, who made her way up in the rankings from the public courts of Long Beach, California. She fought the all-male bastions of professional tennis and put women on the path to equal billing and pay with the guys. She's still out there fighting the good fight."

"Yes, LBJ's Great Society legislation, voting rights, and school desegregation."

"Enough." She'd reached a finger to his lips. "Doctor's orders."

When she'd showered and slipped between the sheets, Chatterbox had actually fallen silent while diligently beginning to kiss her, first fondling her boobs with gentle foreplay, then a digital rumba on her clit, only to fall into a profound sleep, leaving her vaguely aroused and not a little perturbed. It was precisely the scenario of aging indignities, should they be so rash as to marry, that John Proctor had predicted for themselves all those years before in the oratory of the Scuola di San Giorgio.

Then Daltrey had begun to sweetly snore, a low, gurgling rumble in her ear, which found her inventorying her cheapo Hampton Inn room, desk chair and desk with her open laptop, microwave atop a small fridge, background hum of the window AC unit overlooking the parking lot, bringing to mind Augustine's melancholy stare (as John had once pondered its meaning) out his window (how distant his randy boyhood) as he contemplated a life dedicated to the inevitability of sin and death.

"The barricades on which you—and Billie Jean—will fight the good fight." And Daltrey had kissed her ear, nibbling the lobe, before passing out.

A long-ago sentiment strangely echoed by young Jacob as she moved off from the sign-in table.

"Doc, never forget, you and I are a tag team in the same fight." And he had gestured to Holder courtyard and the line of arriving classmates, his blue-green eyes flecked with a kind of mesmerizing curiosity or possibly longing, as if all the old folks passing his station in review were merely a carefully selected control group in some elaborate experiment, where the sorry effects of aging on the best and brightest might best be evaluated.

Young Jacob's off-kilter, cocky attitude still had her buffaloed. Dare she admit it? Jake had been John Proctor's only possible rival in her student days, less for his youth or looks than for his brains. She shook her head: how science-minded men had always been a turn-on, moth to the Bunsen burner. As if her glaring lack of numeracy required a near-Einstein to make her whole.

Case in point: her son, Christopher, back in Jackson Hole, who, as a schoolboy, had always aced his math classes, scoring 5s in AP calculus, computer science, biology, and physics, a voracious reader from day one, even as he idolized Bode Miller.

"Yes, my dear," she whispered in Daltrey's ear, "genetics do matter."

Hardly something to hold against her gentle bedmate, certainly by any measure intelligent enough, with Harvard tenure and a second home on Chappy, as he liked to refer to it, as if citing some snappy imprimatur that only the right sort of people recognized. Though, oddly enough, booked into her moderately priced Hampton Inn. A discovery that had sealed their liaison, prompting Daltrey to insist he sleep in her room. Most likely, she figured, because of a grown daughter, a professor at Rutgers, who lived just up the road, and an ex-wife living near Gini on the Upper West Side—both prone to drop in on their old man "at a moment's notice." Not that he needed chaperoning by his family, as far as she could tell. He seemed sound in body and mind, even if he'd fallen asleep with his hand firmly entrenched between her thighs. Probably just as well: his nails were a tad long. And the good news: her travel vibrator and THC gummies were just three steps away in her open suitcase.

And yet, there was something vaguely comforting about that hand between her thighs. Daltrey could hardly be blamed; he, like Gini and Bianca, had guzzled Jack Rambridge's fine burgundy, while she abstained (headaches and lack of energy on the morrow), and so had ended up the designated driver to the Hampton Inn—luckily so, given the numerous traffic stops out on Route 1 for Breathalyzer tests.

She found herself intrigued by a simple calculation: How old would she have been when John was Daltrey's age, which she assumed was seventy-two or three? Forty-two, about the time of her divorce from Tony, when her sexual energy was off the charts and no partner in sight. Her gaze wandered from Daltrey's craggy features—yes, unnervingly like John's—to the window, where a vague light from the sodium lamps in the parking lot filtered inward, recalling nights at the Seguso. There had been one night when a squall line had blown in from the Lido as they lay exhausted in one another's arms. Then, too, John Proctor had liked to keep a hand between her thighs (finger in the dike, he called it), pondering, like Daltrey (an older man's thing?), that fine line between past and future, ruminating on his Depression-era childhood, the Second World War of his teenage years, the atomic bomb dropped on Hiroshima and Nagasaki, and the Red Scare and early Cold War world that had marked his adulthood, that thin, invisible, ever-receding line of catastrophic events, that no-man's-land from which no one in his generation could escape.

"As much as I love you, I would hate for you to have to deal with another pessimistic Augustine, always wondering: Is that all there is? When you are the most fearless creature I've ever met. Because your great gift will be as a healer, just as now you make me feel like the young whippersnapper I once was with his whole life still ahead of him. I don't want you to wake up some morning aghast, disappointed, unfulfilled, and wonder how your life got hijacked."

"So, here I am, John," she whispered, "the antidote, the Erasmus to your Augustine." One of Daltrey's hearing aids beeped. "An aging lady doc with a disappointed academic and would-be lover."

She felt Daltrey's hand move on her upper thigh and squeeze down deeper as if in protest at her characterization. A surreptitious motion that prompted yet another memory, long banished, of an evening sitting at Jake Burrage's desk in his Pyne dorm room for her weekly tutoring in organic chemistry and calculus, when his hand too had strayed to her thigh as if somehow demonstrating how the motion of matter, from particles to stars, can be predicted, their movement and change tracked through time. His hand had moved up and back, up and back as if encouraging her to get the feel of the concept in her body: the beauty and aptness and logic of mathematics.

"Newton invented calculus to predict the velocities and acceleration of pendulums and planets, applied mathematics that makes possible everything from televisions to computers. But pure mathematics is pure mind, a weightless, gorgeous realm where the brain seeks comfort only in itself, free of entanglements. Along the lines of Einstein's free inventions of the mind, that feeling for mathematical beauty, of the harmony and elegance of geometric forms." He had then patted her thigh and gestured to his genius wall of Princeton greats. "Hanging out in the physics library, I find myself tempted to stray into these mysterious, magical realms but have to pull myself back to deal with real human problems. So, remember, no matter how exasperated or overwhelmed you feel," and his hand again came to rest on her upper thigh, "all your struggle and hard work—you do it for your patients, the ones you are going to save long years from now. All the lives you are going to change for the better. That will be your story—hopefully, our story."

She had been so turned on by his solicitous pep talk that his hand on her thigh might have been an electric eel, that—"our story"—infusion of gray matter connecting with her deepest aspirations, that she had barely resisted grabbing and kissing him wildly. Which, knowing Jake, was precisely the experiment he was running on her.

Instead, she had tried to make light of it. "Oh, everything is just so fucking easy for you, Jake."

"You think Huntington's is easy? You, me, we're two working-class kids in a three-legged race against time."

At that moment, that cry of solidarity against an uncaring universe had thrilled her, even as she wasn't going to further display her ignorance by asking what he meant by Huntington's.

"Good Lord . . . ," she murmured to herself as that night, that memory, came firmly into focus: Huntington's, a fifty-fifty chance of getting the disease and transmitting it to your offspring! Was that what she had seen in young Jacob's glittering eyes at sign-in—a triumph over the odds that, as a diagnostician, she might have guessed?

Again, she found herself returned to that long-ago night. A kiss that might have changed everything. Provided a cover for her affair with John Proctor or even an alternative, a way out, a very different life. A betrayal that, given Gini's cruel dumping of Jake at the end of senior year, might well have suited everybody. Gini, her doubles partner, whom she loved like a sister, might well have benefited from a good dose of humility.

Had Gini known?

She sighed and gently removed Daltrey's hand and slipped over to her suitcase.

Annette woke at four a.m., as she tended to do, with her husband fast asleep beside her. She'd been dreaming about Carpaccio's *Baptism of the Selenites.* Something about how she and her husband had been asked to bear witness at the ceremony, but since they couldn't understand the language or even hear the music, they were left dangling, uncertain of their role. Then she realized that whatever anxiety had prompted the dream had mostly to do with Arthur's refusal to take part in Saturday's Athletes for Christ panel discussion, Prosperity and Christ; she sat on the group's board, and so had volunteered to take Arthur's place. Their mother-son talk at the fifth had not gone well. Arthur just kept repeating that he didn't feel he was the right person for the panel, finally dismissing the subject by reminding her of the kind of question he was liable to get: "Can you be a good Christian and still work for Goldman Sachs?"

She checked her phone, somewhat relieved to find texts from her son.

10:45. Sorry if I was so abrupt, Mom, but sometimes I feel like that bone shaken by the dog!

1:15. Headed back to my hotel. You'll be a much bigger draw in the forum, you and Dad—what a team. Knock 'em dead, Mom, Luv u Art.

1:45. On Route 1 backed up in a line of cars flagged down by New Jersey's finest. Looks like they are Breathalyzing anyone under forty. I had two vodka tonics with Erma about three hours ago, so if I disappear into the county lockup, you'll know where to post bond. Erma is quite something. So grown up from the last time we saw each other at the Yale match senior year. Quite the lady, even if she's still very much a science kid. If I had her brains, I'd already be a Goldman partner. Her mind works in strange and mysterious ways; one minute we're talking about her thesis in biochemistry, rejuvenating aging cells, then the next we're on to original sin and birding. She fixed me with her dazzling blue eyes: "What will God do when we no longer die—or when we no longer fear death?" Try that one on for size! Here we go—wish me luck!

1:55. Passed with room to spare. All okay.

2:15. Another conversation with Erma that keeps playing through my mind. Somehow, we got on the subject of Venice, prompted by the Carpaccios hanging on the wall of her room. She was saying how much she enjoyed the art but found much of the religious stuff not to her taste. The portrait of Augustine in his study was her favorite, even as she found his views on "carnality" forbidding. How he'd propagated the doctrine of original sin, which is passed down through the generations like some terrible disease. "Disease," she exclaimed, "like Huntington's." Which one of her colleagues is working like mad to find a cure for gene therapies and suchlike.

I felt like such a failure, much less never having been to Venice—wasting all my summers playing tournaments—and so knowing diddly-squat about Augustine or Carpaccio. So I offered how I'd always been drawn to the epistles of Paul, especially his thoughts on contentment: whether well-fed or hungry, in plenty or want, as long as Christ is at my side. She looked at me with that musing smile of hers like I was the village idiot. And I thought, well, here it comes: she thinks I'm some nutty Christian out to convert her. Nope. Instead, she told me how she always found it strange how much of the New Testament was given over to Paul when he hadn't even known Jesus, not the way the apostles had known Him, who had witnessed His crucifixion. How Paul wasn't even from Galilee but from Judea. I countered that Paul may not have known Jesus personally but was filled with Christ's spirit. She laughed—quantum entanglement? But in the nicest way, as if I'd had one too many vodka tonics. She explained how one of her best friends on the diving team was a gay Christian and felt that Paul would condemn him as a sinner—the straight way or the highway. While Jesus was more inclusive, more forgiving of sinning, real or imagined. Jesus, she said, would have laughed off the idea of original sin—He was a healer of diseases, right?—even as it was not a little strange how He seemed to condone slavery. Like I said, amazing kid!

"Wasted," she whispered and put down her phone, taking a deep breath, contemplating the half Xanax on her bedside table. So, Arthur had been to Erma's room, visiting the Carpaccios, no less—how retro bizarre was that! Talk about original sin, at least on the part of her roommates, a notion that aggravated a guilty edginess that had plagued her ever since young Jacob had waltzed over to their dinner table with that engaging, if cat-that-swallowed-the-canary smile, as if somehow reading all their minds. And it wasn't just her imagination run wild. With Gini off at another table chatting with Gareth's roommates, she'd caught the eye of both Apolonia and Bianca, barely an instant, enough to exchange guilty looks, as if each knew something the others didn't. Bianca she could read like a book: she'd obviously had some kind of affair with Jake in Venice. As for Apolonia, any woman who could so blithely seduce (not too strong a word) the president of the university was quite capable of stealing Jake away from Gini, given half a chance. (Hadn't Jake been her tutor in organic chemistry?) But as to her own guilty feelings, maybe it was just her failure to ever tell Gini about hiring Jake to track Matt's matches. Not wanting to upset her—hardly an offense against man and God. Okay, maybe she'd been a little envious of Gini teaming up with Jake. What player wouldn't be? Hadn't Jake's success with her husband, moving Matt up in the rankings, justified her righteous envy?

Or maybe it was watching Arthur dancing with Erma at the fifth, after ditching his mom, that had left her vaguely out of sorts. Arthur, who had been so recently questioning his Christian faith. Not that Erma, her goddaughter, wasn't a wonderful girl and so different from her mother: sweet, soft-spoken, a trifle insecure—yes, a science kid to her dexterous fingertips. And brilliant—like her wonderful father, Bill Cheshire . . . like Jake.

"Dear God—Arthur visiting the Carpaccios!" she murmured under her breath.

Such evocations of sins, real or imagined, only got her more rattled, raising the specter of a score of barely remembered conversations with Jake in the stands of Roland-Garros, then Wimbledon and the US Open, over that magical summer when her husband had regained something of his earlier championship form. That summer, the best summer of their life, when astutely playing the numbers, savoring success together, had probably saved their marriage.

Had Gini's name come up in any of those conversations? When Jake had been moonlighting with Chrissie Evert, tracking some of her matches on the side. When she'd sat with Jake as he tracked Chrissie in the Wimbledon finals as she added yet another title . . . The question always and forever left hanging between them: Could Gini have played in her league?

"Gini always gravitates to where her advantages give her the most leverage—uncanny, don't you think?" Jake had shaken his head with exasperation. "All the instincts to go far in this life."

Had that been the comment of a jilted lover after Gini's no-show in Venice, what—six months before?

She closed her eyes to the dim outlines of their hotel room, trying to concentrate her focus the way she did on court, trying to hear the tone of Jake's voice as they sat in the stands—bitterness, relief, resignation?

"If she could have been as good as Chrissie, it would certainly have proved you right."

"Well, now Matt has proved me right. I rest my case."

"I think I'd have been tempted to give up my faith for her extra six inches: the height and reach and power I could never generate."

She remembered his laugh, that soft cackle and long indrawn breath ready to parry any argument.

"I could have made you a contender without the six inches. There are some things that even the numbers can't help, like hunger, like single-mindedness—a willingness to risk all. The tin woodsman without his heart's desire can only generate heat."

As she lay in the dark—hardly the comments of a jilted lover—listening to her husband's regular breathing, she felt a profound sense of gratitude for Jake's candor and possibly wisdom. Perhaps her faith would always require original sin, the friction of a healthy sense of free-floating guilt, the very dynamic to encourage self-improvement that she'd hopefully passed on to all her children. Except Arthur, her eldest, who always retained a healthy level of skepticism, of curiosity, something that remained tantalizingly beyond a mother's control, glimpsed for a moment in his eyes when she'd left him dancing with Erma. What a tall, handsome couple they made, with Erma's long blonde hair streaming down the back of her beer jacket, glittering and golden, as her mother's had been all those years before at their senior dance, when she'd dumped Jake. Gini's gleaming eyes molten with tears as she gave up on a chance at a Wimbledon crown and a best-selling novel—and a billionaire—that might have included her teammates and all the pathbreaking greats like Billie Jean King, a life that might have been hers for the asking. Hells bells, no regrets. Nothing she did or thought was going to change history. End of story.

And she had to hand it to Jake, loyal to his lights. When he admitted after the Wimbledon ball, after dancing half the night with Chrissie, that she'd offered him a "king's ransom" to take her on as a client. But he'd stuck with Matt through the US Open and then hung up his spurs, as he put it, heading off to Chicago for his postdoc.

"To save my life," as he'd so strangely put it.

Yes, Matt was his proof, as was Jake's talented son as he strolled up to their table, Olympic-caliber swimmer on his way to—who knows—a Nobel Prize maybe: all part of God's plan. That their lives, although conceived in sin, were not a one-way street down a dead end, but only one chapter in a never-ending story, where all God's children might find His abiding grace and eternal blessing in life everlasting . . . amen.

Erma hugged her pillow as she tried to dry her tears. Why she was being so emotional was a mystery when she'd had such a great time with Matteo and Arthur, both of whom she'd known as big older brothers since before she could remember. Maybe she was a little in love with both (she chided herself for her indecisive nature), yet another romantic brew concocted by her fairy godmothers, something of a Shirelles specialty. Or, more likely, she was just sad about leaving all her friends and moving to Cambridge, where her father had always wanted her to go, and where she would've gone if he hadn't died. Not that she could imagine the last four years anywhere else except Princeton and the diving team, especially the Burrage Biochemistry Lab, less a workplace—spectacular, intimate, inspiring—than a second home. After all, hadn't she been sucked in and groomed all her life in the Reunions game? At least Harvard would give her an easy shot to West Chop and getting some sailing time in, even if her father's beloved Vineyard 15 was long gone. Crewing for her father on Vineyard Sound, where his ashes had been scattered, had been the happiest days of her life. His looming absence at her graduation, she decided, had to be the real source of her tears.

A day didn't go by when she didn't ache to turn to him for advice or to share some fascinating fact or detail in her research, like how you could measure the song of crickets in the fall to get a reading on the outdoor temperature. There were still words that couldn't pass her lips—oystercatcher, common eider, coreopsis, close reach, luffing—without hearing them in his soft nasal tones.

"Quantum entanglement . . . that's us," he'd murmured to her on his hospital bed, gripping her hand, nodding into her tear-stained blue eyes with that funny, knowing smile he reserved only for her.

None of the teasing had bothered her: in grade school accused of being daddy's little clone, or a clinical and cool bitch in high school, the lab rat with an efficiency of warmth that froze out potential boyfriends. Not even the Shirelles dared praise her for being like her mother. A mother so lost in her various obsessions that she was blind to the needs of others.

How had her father once described his daughter? A curious herring gull happy on her solitary stanchion, missing nothing.

Surely not the kind of woman to impress a guy like Arthur, who had a worldliness tempered by a spiritual grace she found hugely attractive. And what not to admire in Matteo's musicality, playing with Wynton Marsalis and Bobby McFarland, a prodigy of creativity that her own analytical mind seemed to forever rule out. Proof beyond reasonable doubt, as demonstrated by her years of fruitless piano lessons with Aunt Bianca.

"She could use the income, dear—truly. Imagine having a PhD in music history and performance and being reduced to giving piano lessons, dog walking, and working with geriatric cases as a personal trainer. Stick with science and avoid cocaine—her ex-husband, you know."

Aunt Bianca had done her best when Juilliard had ditched her for younger, more celebrated talent.

"First, you have to feel the music in your inner ear, Erma, and then let the notes and your fingers lead you to that soft, gentle center of your being reflected in the music."

Gentle, gentle . . . that was Matteo in spades, even if their brief time dancing together had been to a super-loud techno beat designed to help you lose your mind along with any inhibitions. Matteo had only smiled with a soft inner radiance, one raised, scrappy eyebrow in her direction, the crinkled corners of his eyes going to crescents of bronzy gray, as if to offer a silent plea for a little Stan Getz or Coltrane, or even Red Garland, her father's favorite.

Oh, the pleasures of men unacquainted with her failures as a diver, the talented drudge of the biochemistry department, acclaimed for her patient, deft experimental touch and iron focus. "A natural curiosity combined with a passion for discovery" was how her Harvard recommendation began—translation: Erma's quite the studious lab drone and can be depended upon to run your experiments with care and precision, a sous-chef with a petri dish.

As she'd walked Matteo the short distance to the Dinky and the train to NYC for his late-night gig at Dizzy's, she tried talking a little neuroscience (his Columbia degree), mentioning Alan Turing, who had helped develop the first computer at the nearby Center for Advanced Studies, blathering on about the Turing test for the creation of AI, that constellation of attributes of the human mind that had puzzled philosophers since Plato and Aristotle.

"Nothing's going to replace the complexity of the human brain anytime soon," he'd replied, hefting his guitar into his right hand.

"Besides consciousness," she'd suggested, "how about free will, choice, meaning—subjective sensations like seeing the color blue?"

"Qualia," he replied with a chaste kiss on the cheek as he prepared to board the Dinky. "Trust me, we don't know—may never know—how creativity works. What's the reach of the DNA code? I've played with the best, watched Herbie Hancock at work, hoping to discover the clue, the secret sauce." Again, he had smiled, a grace note of curious serenity, and shrugged, the body language of one at peace with his innate talent, and a quest that enjoyed fulfillment simply in the joy of the journey.

How long a dry spell had it been between lovers?

She opened her eyes to the dim twilight flickering over the wall of her Carpaccios and sighed at these twice-told tales, as she had at her mother's despair at her early dating life: "Your own worst enemy, sweetheart—give the poor boys a break: let them go on about the Yankees and Jets." Forever attracted to older guys, postdocs, experimentalists, young married professors—all of whom had been excruciatingly indoctrinated and trained to avoid even the taint of sexual harassment and so wouldn't lay a finger on her, much less even joke about taking sexual interest in a lowly undergraduate.

She became aware of a tantalizing, if strange, melody she'd been humming under her breath, a thing haunting and melancholy that Bianca used to play for her years before when she'd taken piano lessons. "Oh, just a bit of polyphony I transcribed from a painting by Carpaccio; we were wild about Carpaccio when we were undergraduates." She turned on her pillow to the wall across her room; only now did she make the connection (quantum entanglement, just like her dad said) to those open music scores on display beneath Augustine's desk.

"Yes . . . ," she exclaimed, as if that perfect room held her spellbound. Surely just another example—songs, poetry, paintings—of the continuity of human feelings over time. Something, sometimes, she feared her logical mind was closed off from. The very thing, just an hour before, she'd detected in Arthur's delighted laugh as he'd rediscovered the long-nosed borzoi and red parrot. A laugh that sped her back in time as she tried to recover her first memories of Arthur at Reunions, of being a kid seated on her father's lap under a huge tent, watching the Shirelles perform, when an embarrassed teenage Arthur had been summoned to the stage by Bianca, who then sang to him their closing theme song, "Will You Still Love Me Tomorrow." Bianca had tousled his blond hair and kissed his blushing cheek. Years later, as a teenager herself, she'd watched tennis matches when he was captain of the Princeton team; she'd been dazzled by his effortless movement on court, his power and speed, more handsome than his famous father: What's not to fall in love with? (Even as her years of tennis lessons had been a flop, along with her social life.) And now an up-and-coming Goldman partner, duly noted by her mother, who always calculated the income potential of any prospective romantic interest.

When she had returned to the fifth from saying goodbye to Matteo at the Dinky, Arthur had been in a heated argument with his mother. Her arrival provided him with the excuse to break away and hustle her onto the dance floor. Later, still boyishly attractive at twenty-six, athletic, self-possessed, he had steered her away from his crowd of female admirers to an empty table where they could sit and talk. At first, she'd assumed it was just another arranged Shirelles playdate, only to find that Arthur seemed truly interested in her as he began to share his disillusionment with the fast lane of New York's finance world. The kicker was their discovery that both were avid bird-watchers, he in Central Park and Amelia Island, she along Lake Carnegie, Riverside Park, and Martha's Vineyard. Their intense discussion of avian sightings was interrupted by a succession of recently arrived women, all gorgeous and super fit and disdainfully scrutinizing her senior wristband.

He laughed as the latest wonder woman sashayed off to better hunting grounds.

"I'm cramping your style," she said.

"Friday night, it's our class for all the still unattached. Tomorrow, the guys will filter down to your class to seek out prospects, while the women will mosey on up to the tenth to do the same. Of course, I'm tasked to do a little informal recruiting for the firm."

"Not me, I hope," she said in mock demurral, taking in the crowd of midtwenties, class of 2011, swarming the dance floor in their jungle-themed outfits, safari hats, and camouflage sports shirts.

"God forbid, even if you're the perfect candidate for an analyst on Big Pharma." He smiled into her watching eyes. "You see, I've created a minor crisis by foregoing my place on the Athletes for Christ panel discussion. Mom is thoroughly pissed—relentless—since she's going to have to take my spot."

"Another recruiting opportunity?"

"Only my heart's no longer in it."

"Athletes or Christ?"

"Neither." He laughed. "I've taken up golf and worshipping at the nineteenth hole."

"You should talk to my mom. Right now, she's struggling to maintain her ranking as the top woman player in the seniors on Martha's Vineyard."

"Hey," he grinned, "don't knock it. Mom always said she was the golden girl on the team who could've taken on Chrissie Evert and a Wimbledon crown."

"She always likes to brag how smart she was to forego the women's tour for the higher calling of literature."

He bent forward and touched his plastic cup to hers. "Never forget how precious your time is here. Once you're out, the story changes. So much seems only a means to an end: work, money, status. It's hard to figure out God's plan for your life."

Erma, staring at her glimmering wall of Carpaccios, murmured aloud, "God's plan, huh . . . even Einstein never figured that one out." Who was it?—her dad, of course, who'd always told her that the greatest artworks reflect more about ourselves than the artist's intentions. Just as Arthur had seen aspects of an ancient faith, with which he was struggling, she saw, first in Venice at the Scuola di San Giorgio, and now translated to her own room—mythic stories, improbable events, miracles that researchers in her lab and others aspired to make a reality every day, dreams she daily pondered as she looked up from her petri dishes to the floating mobiles, armillary spheres, adorning the glass-and-aluminum atrium of the Burrage Biochemistry Lab.

"You're a scientist," he offered as they merged into each other's arms (finally a slow dance and a break from the deafening techno beat). "Isn't this just a law of nature, the mating game—natural selection and all that?"

"Perhaps we come alive in the mating dance, like the manakins, more alive to ourselves and others. And speaking of evolution, wait till you get a gander at the latest theory about how birds evolved. Well, it comes down to the feathers, how the planar feather evolved—not to facilitate flight, as you might expect, but to provide a spectacular canvas for mating aesthetics, complex color patterns: stripes, spots, dots, and spangles." She squeezed his shoulder as if to indicate where the wings grow. "Yup, a whole new way for the male to strut his stuff. Including, eventually, flight, as vane feathers came more and more into fashion, and so creating the aerodynamic forces to allow lift-off and gliding. Here's the crazy thing: feathers did not evolve for flight—flight evolved from feathers for display. I mean, who knew!"

Giddy, smiling, they both scanned the crowded dance floor, packed with as gaudy an array of weirdly adorned creatures as any tropical forest.

"So, that's it"—and he slapped his forehead in a comic show of stupidity—"why I sometimes feel so leaden-footed, like those exiled angels in *Paradise Lost*: having shed all my flight feathers."

"Try going off the high dive and struggling to levitate for just that extra split second before gravity does its thing." She motioned to the crazy mix of outlandish

Reunions outfits. "Well, it sure seems clear that aesthetic coevolution has a powerful, even innovative, and perhaps decisive impact on the diversity of biological forms."

He laughed and high-fived her. "Lucky you for picking the perfect field. God knows, if I'd spent my undergraduate years working in that splendid Burrage Biochem Lab of yours, instead of the economics department (that dismal science), I might be more of an optimist like you. Creating new knowledge, making discoveries in basic research, on the cutting edge of progress—like you said about original sin, curing terrible diseases and saving lives."

"Oh sure, I guess. But progress with a big P is such a long, tedious crawl, with many more blind alleys than even marginal successes. As for being an optimist, just waking up each morning in April or May—or strolling Prospect Garden, for that matter—to see what's on offer today is enough to make anyone an optimist. Or the song of a thrush on a July evening. Even if ten years of pursuing the perfect reverse two and a half somersaults with two and a half twists in pike position cured me of any dreams of perfection."

"As the saying goes: don't let the perfect be the enemy of the good."

"Life in a lab is just getting results, any results at all—good, bad, or indifferent."

"I thought I was pretty smart getting out of tennis when I did, instead of being ground to dust on the satellite circuit, only to end up in finance, where everyone cuts corners, lies, and steals deals from one another. What's not to admire?"

When he had insisted on walking her back to her dorm in Patton, seeming to relish their spirited conversation, or more likely indulging nostalgia for his student days, she found herself emboldened, perhaps reckless.

"Come up a moment—not etchings exactly, but I think you might enjoy visiting the Carpaccios."

She switched on the light and waved to the wall where the reproductions were hung.

"These are wonderful," he exclaimed. "I would never have guessed."

"Oh, I was just clued in today that these hung in the Shirelles' suite all their four years together. Avidly admired by their male suitors. So you can consider yourself fairly warned if prompted to romantic rapture."

"Strange, they seem so familiar."

"You mean," she laughed, giddy from her third vodka tonic, "you haven't been to Venice?"

"Worse. Until I was twenty-one, there wasn't a summer when I wasn't playing tournaments."

"After my father died, I was dragged off to Venice kicking and screaming by a guilty mother. The Scuola di San Giorgio . . . not that I was going to let on."

"How much you missed your father?"

"Oh, well—only the best of all time." She sighed, shrugging her broad shoulders as she stared up at his curious face, a note of longing sparking his porcelain blue eyes beneath a neatly cropped thatch of blond hair.

"Now I remember," he said, going over to the *Baptism of the Selenites*. "Mom had a big picture book on art where these were illustrated, which she used in one of our Sunday school groups when we were kids." He laughed self-consciously and pointed. "The dog with a long snout was a favorite, along with the red parrot, always a big hit."

"Yes, the Knopf borzoi, says my mother. For a while, I was really into the poor dragon brought to heel and Jerome's lion freaking out all the brothers. But Augustine's cute little spitz gets the prize—Fritz the spitz, I call him."

"And where, I wonder, would we be without Augustine and original sin."

"Oh, I just drowned my sins in this fabulous ice cream parlor across the square from the scuola, apricot and lemon sorbet to die for."

"Lucky you, to have a mom who loves you enough to see that you had a guided tour of Augustine's study."

"Oh, not for me; she only does stuff that either benefits herself or soothes her bad conscience—or adds to the bottom line."

He had laughed, as if to say, "Don't we all?" and then held out his hand to say good night.

"I've a better idea. The chapel fellowship is having a reunion after Sunday chapel in Murray-Dodge—or keep it simple, just Sunday chapel to admire the light through the stained-glass windows, all those angels up there strutting their flight feathers, maybe not evolved for flight exactly, or in the league of your Burrage Biochemistry Lab, but an aesthetic experience to lift the soul. Almost as good as a perfect dive."

She felt her eyes wavering, sleep overcoming her, as a last vague memory of the oratory of the Scuola di San Giorgio filtered back, of her mother's tear-stained eyes as she pleaded with her daughter.

"You see, I married your father for you—the best, smartest, most beautiful, and perfect daughter in the world, sweetheart. And it was the best choice I ever made."

CHAPTER 18

Gini's eyes popped wide to the chiming of a Bach cantata on her cell phone alarm. An abrupt if luxurious awakening from a fleeting dreamscape where she was once again a teenager, or more likely a Princeton student entwined in the arms of her lover. She felt energized by a flood of morning light—leafy, vibrant, vivifying—poured like an offering of ambrosia and nectar from the gods above. She blinked and blinked again. Something almost transcendent, rising from a dwelling veiled in mauve tones, as if refracted through various glazings of lapis lazuli and jade. A room, a sanctuary, a place of eternal scholarly repose. She felt more than wonderful—ecstatic, an inner radiance that had her in a tightly sprung crouch, ready to return a hundred-mile-an-hour serve. And such a refreshing sleep . . .

As she reached to silence her phone, which had somehow found its way to the desk across from her bed and so out of easy reach, she took note that something wasn't right. Where, in fact, was she? A Proustian quandary. Her eyes sought to inventory the compact room, familiar and not: the antique desk and high-tech office chair, the black La-Z-Boy recliner occupied by her spiffy Yonex tennis bag, back of a door hung with her . . . new tennis dress? She blinked, startled by the glare in a mirror over the bureau, where, of all things, Carpaccio's Saint Augustine was reflected back to her, as if one room had simply elided into another, as if she had somehow wandered into the saint's resplendent study and nestled down on a comfortable divan to catch forty winks. Only, like her mentor, to suddenly find herself under the spell of a visionary moment, her aging body released from gravity's tyranny, while her spirits soared aloft, veins throbbing with ichor. Could the hope of redemption possibly be on offer—there, unveiled, delicate as a dragonfly's wing, suspended in the crystalline light refracted between mirror and picture glass? She sat up, quite mystified by this epiphany, this rapture once confined for her to the pages of Joyce, Keats, and Shelley, or possibly Sappho, as if falling under some sibylline spell. Spurring forth some long-forgotten lines from Ovid's *Metamorphoses* . . . "on the wings of love, he who pursues is swifter and gives no respite . . ."

"Oh my God!"

She flopped back on the bed and scrambled to pull up the bedclothes to cover her distinctly Ovidian nakedness. And yet the sensation of sheer aliveness, both profound and novel, was such that she could forgive whatever failure of her internal GPS had brought this improbable, possibly irredeemable folly to pass. Turning to the pillow beside hers, she was relieved to find a comforting dent. Of course, she must've simply passed out. But who undressed her? She bent and sniffed the pillow. "Oh, no . . . no, no, no . . ." Horror at the distinct scent of sweaty sex. She pulled back the sheet and thin blanket but could detect no telltale stains. Relief was now added to the stubborn persistence of her indwelling joy, not unlike the afterglow of a weekend spa treatment. Or had she forgotten the transformative effects of great sex? God forbid! But yes, yes, she could now smell it, even taste it on her lips, along with whatever caused that lingering effervescence in her pubes, nothing like what solo ventures with her faithful pocket vibe had managed to produce in the dry spell of recent years. Had they had sex—sex-sex? With that brilliant, spellbinding young man? Could it be true, even if she couldn't quite remember the details? Could she be accused—by her daughter, teammates, her board!—of having seduced an undergraduate? A Mrs. Robinson on the prowl in cougar territory! Thankfully, not one of those benighted high school teachers seducing fourteen-year-olds. Nor would being seduced fly anymore, or even drugged by a younger man, not in this MeToo age. A man young enough to be her graduating son. A Jake transformed . . . son of Jake, Jacob Jr., a Jake cloned.

And yet, her endorphin high, her steamy, blurred memory, the lingering erotic thrill had all the hallmarks of Jake's lovemaking: his distinctive sex moves, his patient, unhurried caresses connecting every erogenous zone in her body—or at least that was the story her fast-retreating dream state wanted to tell.

What, was she now contemplating science fiction—a techno-thriller?

Of course, if she'd been in her right mind, she would never have let any of these scenarios happen. A mind that was clearly playing tricks on her. Abetted by a pleasure woven so deep in her nervous system that she found her fingers had been fondling her flushed erect nipples, as if seeking there a refutation of all accusations of a sinister nature.

So fucking alive she was about to levitate off the mattress.

Her hand strayed to the dampness between her legs, where a slight ooziness of yore was detected, which, bringing her fingers to her nostrils, she could only detect a young woman's randiness, nothing of the distinct odor of male seed. Hardly conclusive proof in the age of AIDS, or DNA testing, when all the kids used condoms as a matter of course.

She kicked the bedclothes free: let the world feast on this body, come what may! She sat up and surveyed the scene of the debauch: the desk (her car keys, phone, Marriott key card) stacked with journals and a dog-eared paperback copy of Ray Kurzweil's *The Singularity Is Near*, the La-Z-Boy recliner now occupied by her tennis bag and nifty backpack, the packed bookshelves, tennis outfit and dresses on a hook on the back of the door. What, had she moved in? Clearly, she'd been seduced by an expert: picking her up in Prospect Garden, the tantalizing bull session, the scintillating notes touching on halcyon days, a veritable cavalcade of Nabokovian spine tingles as first her mind and then her body was masterfully hijacked.

Yes, indeed—what a subject for her novel! A twisty plot that defies all reason.

And wasn't this . . . exactly Jake's MO?: earnest optimism about cutting-edge discoveries that might unlock a boundless future, juicy ideas du jour, a dollop of praise—then bingo. She held up her wrist to check her father's trusty art deco Rolex, finding the blue hands stopped at 12:16. She tapped the crystal, brought the silent wristwatch to her ear, then tried the crown but found it fully wound. She closed her eyes, palm over her heart, as if to check for a tick there: better to rewind her brain, if not recalibrate her dignity. Again, she glimpsed Carpaccio's captivating painting in the mirror—now imprinted in her imagination, radiant and luxurious, a numinous presence that indeed fully animated her imagination, prompted her fingers to yet further soundings. Perhaps the same fife-and-drum call to arms that had once swept open another door, through which an obnoxious seventeen-year-old had marched as she plotted her escape into adulthood.

That long, hot summer of 1970, hotter than Hades, with lingering riots and antiwar marches and sit-ins (still simmering at Columbia just up Broadway from their Eighty-Second Street co-op) across the country, about which she'd remained stubbornly oblivious—disinterested, truth be told. Two years before Princeton, when she'd scored just about every academic accolade: top in her class at Brearley, captain of the debating team, captain of tennis and field hockey, president of her class. The academics came easily, Stoicism her métier, but tennis—when her nose wasn't in a book—was her controlling passion, some said her obsession. It had begun years before, first summers playing with her mother (a New England women's champion in her own right) at West Chop, and then training indoors at West Side Tennis, junior tournaments in the city during the school year, and then July and August around the Vineyard, then off-island to claw her way up in regional age brackets, first in New York and Massachusetts, then in New England and the Mid-Atlantic. She played the nationals in the sixteen-and-unders at Kalamazoo, Michigan, where she reached the quarterfinals in 1969 and her first national ranking: tenth in the nation, prompting a front-page article in the sports section of the *Boston Globe* touting this talented Bay Stater (even if she lived in New York City), who was taking the junior ranks by storm, compared by some to 1962 Wimbledon champion Karen Susman for her power game and speed around the court. Every women's college was recruiting her, even as she had her heart set on Old Nassau (not missing a single one of her father's Princeton Reunions since age five), which, the gods be praised, had taken in its first women undergraduates in the fall of 1969.

By that summer at West Chop, she was insufferably full of herself, already a minor celebrity on the island and turning down dates from college boys, too busy preparing for another shot at Kalamazoo, now in the under-eighteens, and a possible number-one national ranking in the juniors. Her problem was finding competition. She could beat all the women on the island and most of the men, except for a couple of twentysomething ex-Harvard tennis team members, who, having careers and families, were only available on weekends, if then. Even her tennis coach, West Chop pro John Chandler, could only spare a couple of hours a day from his other duties. And then there was her overbearing, big-mouth, sarcastic mother, who insisted on co-opting her talented daughter to play ladies' doubles, along with various demands in the kitchen, marketing chores, and crewing duties with her father.

Only adding to her annoyance and mortification, John Chandler had become the prime object of her mother's flirting and unwanted attentions. She mercilessly pursued the handsome and affable Colby College grad, especially in her alcoholic fits of bravado, brazenly propositioning him in front of her daughter and others in her ladies' doubles crowd, partly to show off her disregard for convention and razor-sharp repartee, but mostly a crude means of disparaging ("Am I alone among you ladies in not getting any in a month of Sundays?") her marriage to a busy publisher husband, who, even on vacation, rarely had his nose out of an author's manuscript. Once looked upon with wry smiles, if not pity, then exasperated censure, her mother's long-standing outrages had made her the laughingstock of West Chop and an albatross for her husband and daughter. A pathetic case who could still manage a decent game of tennis half-potted on whiskey sours, even as her tennis togs had the sly habit of sliding disastrously up the crack of her flabby ass.

Somehow the steam bath of early August, the pressure of training for the nationals, her intensely competitive nature, and the terror of humiliation at the hands of her mother, put it into her head that the best solution for all that weighed on her ambitious, daring soul was the seduction of her tennis coach, John Chandler. This justified, even extolled, by her Stoic practice as erotic love directed by reason toward a mentoring friendship: Cicero's *conatum amicitiae faciendae*. Besides, it was high time to lose her virginity, now an added check mark on her life's to-do list (Princeton, Wimbledon, and a Pulitzer). And who more appropriate than the adored John Chandler. She'd been training with him for three summers, pleased and proud to be his top protégé, as she had dispatched all her rivals. John was drop-dead handsome, tall, with dark curls and a prominent nose to complement cheekbones to eat dessert off (her mother's phrase); he also had a wry sense of humor (how he dealt with her mother's advances), was a talented classical guitarist, and a serious scholar to boot. John taught classics and ancient history at Deerfield, while coaching the boys' tennis team during the school year.

The way she would one day narrate this risky affair in her magnum opus was a story of frustration due to her ambivalence toward boys her own age (whom she humiliated on court and outsailed on race days), who were clueless around a girl's body in late-night make-out sessions on Big Pier, whose conversational repertoire rarely strayed beyond drunken opining about Carl Yastrzemski and Carlton Fisk and the World Series prospects of the Red Sox. Most of her peers, especially the girls she knew in the junior tennis ranks, were little better: when not smoking dope or drunk, pathetically indulged and pawed over by their boyfriends out of sheer boredom. Such indignities she refused to suffer on principle, even as she delighted in showing off more and more of her cleavage as the summer wore on, scoring push-up bras from one of her mother's mail-order catalogs and strutting her magnificent breasts, of which she was justly proud.

"Gini, for Pete's sake," warned her mother, "if you feel the need to compete with every male who comes within ten feet of you, you'll end up an old maid. Men want a companion and helpmeet, not a woman who constantly reminds them of their inadequacies, and believe me, the male sex is rife with inadequacies—your father excepted, of course. By the way, you might want to crew for him occasionally; I think he gets quite lonely out there without his manuscripts to keep him company."

Not that she didn't consider herself exquisitely sophisticated for a seventeen-year-old going on twenty-seven: supremely intelligent, engaging, funny, and well-read, reserved, when need be, proclaiming herself to John Chandler and a few other sophisticates to be a modern-day Stoic, able to discuss equally well Greek philosophy and the novels of Virginia Woolf, while arguing Simone de Beauvoir with illustrations from the most erotic passages in *Lady Chatterley's Lover*. Confirming, all the while, her conviction concerning the superiority of her sex, although finding little sympathy with bra-burning feminists and their lamebrain sisters, the flower children and hippies run amok on Boston Common and Washington Square. Their vapid pleas to make love, not war, left her cold.

As her confidence and sheer exhilaration on the court mounted day by day, as Princeton and even Wimbledon beckoned on the horizon (Karen Susman had been nineteen), her contemplated seduction of John Chandler now gained the added rationale of providing the delicious epiphany for her first novel, the crucial wellspring from which her literary fame might blossom: a tell-all tale of a young woman fighting her way up the rankings with lovers left sprawled in her wake. Hardly a heroine out of Virginia Woolf (a little too cerebral; no wonder she committed suicide). Possibly Edith Wharton, since they shared material from upper-crust New York and Boston. Or, more to the point, Henry James's *Portrait of a Lady* (her father's favorite) and the energetic and enigmatic ardor of Isabel Archer in pursuit of her destiny. Anything to trump her mother's taste, which ran to Mickey Spillane and *Peyton Place* (not that she hadn't read it twice, fingering herself to her first orgasms at fourteen). And the more she read in Zeno and Seneca, the more convinced she became that her loss of virginity had to be a shared act of love with an older, wiser man, a mentor and soul mate, who might instruct her in Ovid's erotic arts. A rapturous celebration before the temple of her body, and so illuminating mind and soul. And just possibly serving double-duty as a vivid character in that same long-contemplated coming-of-age novel.

This crazy plan soon became a psychic compulsion, or so she would one day write, less an emotional desire than an idée fixe: the poignant moment of lost innocence that would ballast the rest of her life: a store of creative energy, of imaginative insights—the more uncertainties, the riskier, the more dangerous (hadn't John Chandler praised her nerve for pulling off risky shots under pressure) the better. To love but not fall in love. The natural extension of her on-court workouts with John Chandler, especially her beloved backhand drills: that dynamic exchange of energy—the grunting, sweating, sweet precision of a body in perpetual motion. An affair that surely would be the making of the soon-to-be author. A woman on whom nothing was lost. And who better than John Chandler, just engaged to be married, and so—now or never—out of the running in summers to come. She did draw the line at being a marriage-breaker, something she'd witnessed her mother do at least once, possibly twice (sneaking back to the house at three a.m., disheveled and drunk, from an assignation with a prominent Boston attorney who had a summer home on the Chop). And in her most bizarre plot twist (an outlandish conjuration never to make it into her text), her fevered mind rationalized her act as a heroic service to the West Chop community of upright Boston, New York, and Washington intelligentsia: by seducing John Chandler, she'd put the kibosh on her mother's depredations and embarrassing flirting. "Stop it, Mother: he's taken."

But how to get the thing done discreetly, under her mother's radar, in a beehive of gossip and watchful eyes?

She stood for a moment longer on the rickety, wraparound veranda of her family's cottage overlooking Vineyard Sound, gazing out over the moon-swept sea where it glittered with soft purple highlights, sharply silhouetting the ragged planking of Big Pier, the club's swimming hole. She was summoning forth all the previous hours and days of that long, hot summer, victory after victory under a blazing sun, to steel her nerve. John Chandler lived alone above the small post office on Iroquois Avenue, a tiny attic room with bathroom and shower, copper sink, and one-burner stove, for decades reserved for the summer tennis pro. The apartment could be steamy hot in high summer with only two windows, fore and aft, and an industrial-size fan to circulate the air. Her excuse for an after-dinner visit was the notebook she carried that contained pages of elaborate daily practice routines (the urtext, so she would eventually write, for Jake's elaborate tracking system by the numbers) in preparation for the nationals at Kalamazoo in two weeks. Notes (including brief reflections on opponents and various other characters for her novel) that needed updating, things to work on, drills to master, challenges to overcome, weaknesses to address and compensate for as she faced the eighteen-and-unders and girls a year older and even bigger and stronger than she, all heavy hitters with no apparent weaknesses, whom she would probably have to outlast from the baseline and finesse with steady, slow-paced, looping returns to their backhands, where they couldn't hurt her.

"Power, power . . . ," she whispered like a mantra to herself, pressing an outstretched hand to and fro on a weathered column of the veranda, as if by just saying the word, fantasizing being held in John Chandler's strong arms, she might transfuse something of his strength and so increase her pace on the ball. She and John had discussed switching to a more powerful, two-handed backhand, the coming thing in the fast-evolving women's game, but she loved her one-hander (good enough for Billie Jean King and Margaret Court and Karen Susman), the purest pleasure in the opening of the body and the long reach, the exquisite almost mystical sensation of a deftly hit slice, as when a sail perfectly captures a following wind. (If she hadn't been a tennis player she might well have opted for ballet.) But, as John Chandler had judiciously determined, it would take her a year or more to make the switch to the two-hander: so stick with the tried and true.

"Yes . . ." She threw her arms wide, like a good Stoic embracing the promptings of the moonlit universe, and leaped the wooded stairs to the sprawling lawn. Sweat-stained notebook in hand, she glanced back at the lighted windows of the dun-gray clapboard house on the bluff, dormers and gables in green trim, a single conical turret with a witch's-hat roof: the place (my Tara, as she always put it to the Shirelles) she loved most in the world, room after winding room stuffed with long-abandoned novels, signed by their authors to her father and grandfather, many going back to the turn of the century, cluttered closets and cabinets spilling over with bric-a-brac and stored time, summers collected and curated by a bookish family now hard pressed to pay the upkeep and taxes. Her father had only recently bemoaned that he might have to rent out the fine old place, Waverley (long-winded, like Scott, her father liked to say), for July and September.

She made the turn from the gravel and dirt road onto Iroquois Avenue, breathing deeply of the scents of vagabond cedars and freshly mown grass on the lawn of the West Chop Club, the whispered slap of the rope against the tall flagpole on the nearby bluff jostling the song of cicadas as she contemplated the lighted window in her coach's bachelor quarters two hundred yards farther on, above the white clapboard post office. She felt her pulse quicken as she paused to savor the smell of the freshly watered clay courts, her nerves fairly humming in anticipation, as if about to take the court in the face of an opponent whose game she knew well enough to effortlessly dismantle—certain that all her godlike powers would surge to her aid and so confirm her mastery of the moment. Could it really be some subconscious yearning: by seducing her coach to appropriate something of John Chandler's sweet backhand? This absurd thought barely registered, but enough to again pause her steps and possibly reconsider the notion of a frenzied maenad on the prowl? She shuttled her jaw judiciously and checked to see if the coast was clear (dog walkers, kids larking about), her steps waylaid by the airy shelter of the West Chop Casino, where once upon a time, as a child, she'd played endless games of checkers and chess on rainy days, where her mother played bridge and mahjong, where the club membership met for a nondenominational Sunday service—chatty uplifting talks and hymns—before retiring for sticky buns and coffee.

She entered this gray clapboard sanctorum of raw-beamed walls and high fanlight windows, hung with ranks of bright red plaques listing the names of illustrious tennis champions going back to the nineteenth century, a pantheon of memory, of family names linked through time, names she knew like an arcane vocabulary, names invoking faces old and young, homes grand and not so grand, names spoken of in awe, while others, failures in life's race, were only whispered about in catty gossip. These lists of names bore the imprimatur of the eternal summer season. The world as she'd known it. Lists of champions that now, numbered among the immortals, included one Ginistrella Wingate among the pantheon of ladies' singles winners. Here in this modest temple that honored, more in the breach than the observance, the most cherished and enduring WASP virtues: continuity, prudence, forbearance, tolerance, tenacity, honor and faithfulness, sobriety, and—yes, even kindness. And last but not least, good sportsmanship. Values passed down generation by faltering generation, on the court and off. Which she would one day describe, not without dismay, even sadness, as white privilege. A code of honor she had co-opted in the peculiarities of her Stoic practice, which now extolled in matters of the erotic life an embrace of true fellowship between men and women as the highest good.

With consequences lingering far beyond John Chandler.

In the near darkness, her gaze strayed upward, where a mysterious half-light filtered through the high windows, crystalline touched with sapphire, bathing the blood-red plaques (a sheen of softest violet) honoring the valiant. She sometimes liked to imagine them hung like the captured enemy shields on the Pantheon, which, in turn, put her in mind of the *Iliad*'s catalog of ships or the honor role of heroes fallen on the plains before Troy. Her eyes welled with a precocious romantic sensibility: *sic transit gloria mundi*! How many of the brave and blessed contestants were fated to fall by the wayside, their lives unrealized. How few would endure against the bitter odds, to be numbered among the elect. She sat for a moment in one of the red Windsor chairs that lined the wall and scribbled down these and other sentiments in the back pages of her notebook. Standing, throwing her chest forward, nerving herself up, she again located her own name in black letters on the Ladies' Singles plaque, *1969–Ginistrella Wingate*. Surely the beginning of a run that might well break the streak of Sarah Brightman (two plaques over and now an old lady), who had won seven titles in a row in the 1930s. She took a last deep breath—her period conveniently ten days behind her, nicely regulated by the Pill—and strode on, an intrepid Diana, to embrace her well-considered destiny, erotic and otherwise.

She flung open the battered screen door that led to John Chandler's lair on the second floor overlooking the teaching court. The creaking stairwell was lined with faded, oak-framed, black-and-white photos of West Chop's tennis pros beginning in 1912, bandy-legged, sun-ravaged faces wearing long white ducks right into the forties. Mounting the gritty, gray-dusted stairs (clay residue from the Har-Tru courts), she encouraged the budding novelist to minutely absorb everything about this moment, to be the canny author of her own life. There, at the top of the staircase by the half-open door, she confidently smiled as she breathed in the delicious all-male scents of unwashed dishes and neglected laundry, sweaty socks and jock straps tinctured with hints of damp mildew and creosote—and, as she reached for the knobby brass-handled door, that most aromatic of essences, freshly opened tennis balls.

"Hello, Coach, I'm here," she called out in a guileless greeting, with a quick glance at the rolls of catgut hung in bunches on wall pegs by the stringing machine, bunkered by boxes of tennis shoes that occupied an entire corner of the pro's modest digs.

John Chandler was stretched out in his one easy chair, wearing only tennis shorts and a tee shirt, while airing out his bare callused feet propped on a book box labeled *Allied Van Lines–When a Move Is in the Cards*, a half-full wineglass and nearly empty bottle of red wine at his elbow. He was reading Gibbon's *Decline and Fall.* Captain of Colby's undefeated Division Two tennis team in 1965, an English and classics double major, summa cum laude and Phi Beta Kappa, he now coached tennis over the summers at West Chop while teaching classics and ancient history at Deerfield the rest of the year.

He sat up. "Gini, did we have a meeting scheduled?"

She stood at the top of the stairs and held up her notebook to his inquiring, finely featured face, merest hint of a five-o-clock shadow, dark curly hair damp from a shower, and those glittering, sensitive hazel eyes—this agile creature with such a smooth and effortless backhand that watching him play still brought a lump to her throat.

"Nope, but I thought we'd get a head start on strategizing for our training sessions for the next couple of weeks."

She began a deliberate reconnoiter, drawn to the legions of Jack Kramer racquets hanging on wall pegs, those to be re-strung or waiting to be picked up. She stopped to sniff a jam jar of shellack and then inventoried the half-dozen open paperbacks abandoned on piles of shoeboxes, others on an antique oak writing desk, where they weighed down stacks of invoices from various sporting goods purveyors, stacks that fluttered uneasily in the gusts of cooling air from the rotating fan by the back window. Serving as well as paperweights were a brass handbell (a rich jade patina) with intricately carved handle, a chipped conch shell displaying a lustrous pink interior, and an antique cherrywood hourglass containing blue sand. She fingered these oddments, as if they provided vague clues to her unfolding destiny, until moving on with a sigh, then kneeling, as if about to cross herself before an altar, to examine the low plywood shelves that displayed John Chandler's small lending library of classics. Yet another excuse for an impromptu visit, so she let it be known, even as her own home contained thousands of similar volumes. As she rose, chattering on about nothing, her damp blonde hair blew about as the large standing fan in its metal cage made another purring pass, momentarily drowning out the wavelike chorus of a moon-shimmering summer night beyond.

In the tiny galley, she caught sight of a gravy-stained aluminum Swanson's TV dinner tray abandoned on a full trash bin. About to offer to take out his trash, a daily duty at home, she quickly dismissed the idea from the plot she saw herself as unfolding. Instead, easing up a fetching smile, she proceeded to inspect the Fernando Sor etudes open on a music stand, beside which a classical guitar lay in a felt-lined case next to a stool and small footrest. Sadly, the music notation put her in mind of her failed—one of her few failures—attempt at piano lessons, aged eleven, with a brilliant Juilliard student who took piano (this a revelation by thirteen) as seriously as Gini did her tennis. There had been moonlit nights when, walking past the old post office, white clapboard aglow like burnished ivory, she had heard John Chandler playing his guitar, the gentle, sometimes brittle thrumming wafting out his window like enchantment itself, stirring in her heart a perverse mix of longing and resentment, something along these lines: instead of listening in the road, she'd rather be serenaded between his sheets.

"I thought," he interrupted her ongoing stream of consciousness with a bemused if slightly troubled tone, "we usually went over your training schedule on the front porch of *your* cottage."

"Not with my mother prowling about . . . lest she snatch you away. Besides, I need something new to read." She sashayed over wearing a freshly laundered and ironed Fred Perry pleated tennis skirt with a pale green trim of laurel wreaths (what Karen Susman wore in her Wimbledon victory) and matching sports shirt, her long, just-washed hair stirring across her broad shoulders. "Any suggestions, Coach?"

He held up the thick volume of Gibbon (the Heritage edition, she noted, illustrated with Piranesi etchings). "Fourth century, the emperor Julian, who tried to wind back the clock on Christianity before it became the established religion of the Roman Empire. You might say Gibbon was the first Enlightenment fan of our Julian the Apostate."

"Yes, Julian was also a fan of Seneca and the Stoics." She picked up the folding chair by the writing desk and brought it over to seat herself in a teenage sprawl, with knees spread, notebook in her lap, near enough to smell the wine on her coach's breath and closely examine that sexy white scar—an accent mark above his upper lip. "He tried to be a moderate emperor by not persecuting Christians, just trying to roll back their privileges. But in good Stoic style, he also attempted to be just one of the boys when the people only wanted him to act like an exalted emperor."

He laughed uneasily, nodding. "Ah, how could I forget, your passion for Seneca."

"Roman history AP," she corrected, scooping the book off his lap and flipping through the pages, pausing to gaze upon a few of the Piranesi illustrations, in which tiny, animated figures gazed in awe upon the moldering ruins of a still-imposing past.

"Anyway," he went on, scissoring his jaw, barely dusted with fine whiskers, "last I heard, you were planning to be the next Virginia Woolf, not that it wouldn't hurt you to familiarize yourself with Mr. Gibbon's mandarin style, a rather lovely, mellifluous prose, both stately in cadence and in his use of apt metaphors, while ringing the changes in his commentary on the disaster that was Christianity." He reached for his wineglass, perched on two cases of Wilson tennis balls that served as a side table, the ratty easy chair protesting, and drained what remained. "A subject not to be broached among polite society in these sacred precincts."

"I've decided I don't like Woolf or her characters—too negative, always depressed. I don't like negative people, do you?" She sat up straight, pushing her bust forward as she reached for his bottle of Almaden Napa red and filled his glass, then taking a deep swallow herself before handing it back. So appropriating something of the femme-fatale body language that she imagined Allison MacKenzie had employed to good effect in *Peyton Place*. She arched her thick eyebrows to emphasize her sea-blown eyes, along with a soft, aching compression of the lips, wet, expectant, enticing.

"Well," he continued, pausing to drink, "your Stoics, full of renunciation and refusal to look on the bright side, are hardly paragons of optimism."

At this, she relaxed and smiled, knowing she was now on firm ground, tapping her notebook where she'd left it on the boxes of Wilson tennis balls: the script she had memorized.

"'No one is deserving of love who is incapable of bestowing it upon others. Love is an undiluted emotion conferred with magnanimity.'"

He laughed uneasily at her recitation. "Never did I imagine a sixteen-year-old quoting Seneca to me."

"A love"—she sang the line about being seventeen going on eighteen—"steadfast, unspoiled by time and circumstance, and now, more than ever, looking for guidance and inspiration from my longtime mentor."

"Okay, Gini." He clapped his hands together and sat up. "I think you've made your point, and it's late, time you got going."

"But I only just arrived. It's barely after dinner; surely there's more to Gibbon and poor Julian than you've let on."

John Chandler shook his head in unamused exasperation, his long, straight nose rising as if to the possible smell of danger, his wineglass balanced in his callused right palm as he seemed to reconsider—eyeing her with his golden-brown eyes—by launching into a more comfortable scholarly mode.

"He was schooled in Athens on Greek philosophy, so he was prone to questioning the quarreling Christian sects, each with their different understanding of the nature of Christ, a subject on which Gibbon deploys heavy sarcasm."

"Go on then . . ." She leaned forward like an avid student, the unbuttoned collar of her sports shirt falling open.

He laughed uneasily, as if by lengthening his gaze, this provocative vision of his young protégé might somehow be defused. His leg spasmed when her knee strayed against his thigh. She noted the blackened toenails (battle scars) on both his long, callused feet.

"Julian," now in a lecturing distant tone, "was a brilliant guy, not only steeped in Greek philosophy but totally familiar with the Christian Gospels, and so was able to astutely question many Christian concepts, like the virgin birth, for which, he noted, there was no prophecy in the Old Testament. And then there's the Old Testament, with an all-too-human and even resentful God. And why did God create Eve, whose only role seemed to be to thwart his plans for creation and bring sin into the world? And why deprive Adam and Eve of the knowledge of good and evil? Why did God neglect the world for thousands of years, passing by all the brilliant Greek thinkers, and suddenly spring Christ on a small group of Jews in Galilee?"

"More questions than answers," she sang out, barely able to contain herself. "I, for one, always thought Eve was perfectly justified at her bite of the apple. I could never figure out exactly what knowledge of good and evil amounted to, or, for that matter, original sin. How about you, Coach?"

"You and Edward Gibbon, who might be considered the sworn foe of Augustine's City of God and his doctrine of original sin, which the Enlightenment dismissed as a perverse and damaging interpretation of scripture. Not that we should dismiss notions of right and wrong—like you showing up here uninvited and putting me in a compromising position."

She licked her lips, aware of her father's astringent Listerine, which she'd gargled for a good three minutes until the roof of her mouth had been numbed.

"But evil has got to be in the mind of the beholder, don't you think?" She stood and walked over to the fan, letting it blow her long sun-bleached hair, as she'd once seen Olivia de Havilland's fiery locks blow in *Gone With the Wind*, and, for a few long moments, casting longing looks at his bookshelves, a furtive glance to the corner and his perfectly made bed. "Just think, if Julian had survived, everything might have been different. We might still have all the plays of Sophocles and Euripides"—moving from the fan, she let her fingers dance along the top row of the bookshelf—"Virgil and Cicero, with Seneca and Epictetus and Jesus all hanging out together, a great big love fest." She cocked her head. "You know, reading the Gospels in Sacred Studies class, I could almost swear that some of the ethical admonitions—the Golden Rule and all that—are cribbed from Seneca."

"Good night, Gini. I've enjoyed our chat."

She sauntered around, almost giddy, as if overburdened with some great surfeit of life that needed relinquishing. Her deepest enjoyment, like her father's heroine Isabel Archer, so she liked to think, was "to feel the continuity between the movements of her own soul and the agitations of the world." Again, she ran her fingers over the titles on his bookshelf, picking up an abandoned paperback for quick perusal, then rattling the racks of tennis racquets. "But surely . . . we've got world enough and time." She returned to her seat and notebook and began fanning her face as if oppressed by the heat.

"Sorry, it's always tropical at night in here even with the fan going. You're lucky not to find me in the nude." He chuckled and made a devil-may-care face, draining his glass. "Like one of Mr. Gibbon's revelers in Nero's Rome."

"Fine by me." She peeled off her shirt and tossed it in his lap.

"Hey, Gini"—flustered and tossing it back at her—"please put that back on."

"You don't like the way I look—my body . . . my *soul*?" Said with a facetious giggle.

"It's not in my West Chop Club contract to have such an opinion about an underage minor."

She got up and walked across to his door and closed it, sliding the dead bolt.

"No one needs to know. Just"—another sly glance at his narrow bed in the corner—"us. We're just working up a game plan for the Nationals. Check out my notebook, the last pages; I've already dated the entry with two pages of notes you've dictated to me covering plans for next week. Just like we always do."

"Please put your shirt back on, unlock my door, and say good night."

She came over and slid off her bra and tossed that too.

"Good night kittens and good night mittens, good night socks and good night"—she went over to a stopped Timex wall clock and tapped the glass—"clocks . . ."

"I'm engaged to be married next spring."

She glided back to where she'd left his Gibbon on her chair and carefully slipped a subscription form for the *New Yorker* between the pages, placing it on his makeshift side table, and, picking up his bottle or wine, took a long swig. She then maneuvered onto the armrest of his chair so that her breasts nodded hello to his crinkled squint.

"So, you need to stay in practice, and I need to get in practice. It's the perfect doubles partnership or, if you prefer, love's attachment."

"Do you have any idea what could happen to me—or you—if I so much as touched you right now?"

"I'm the soul of discretion." And she bent and kissed him, her right breast pressed against his arm. "And, unlike all the good little West Choppers, I'm not into sharing, so I'm hardly going to go around blabbing to all your women admirers."

He grabbed her shoulders roughly and then gently shook her backward and forward.

"I actually believe you—worst luck." And he bent her breasts into his face, her left nipple firmly between his lips, running his tongue around the tip until she feared she might faint for the pleasure.

She reached for her notebook: "Mind if I take notes?"

She had kept her word to the letter. And John Chandler had proved himself as good a lover as a tennis coach, better even than his down-the-line backhand, if such a thing were possible, finishing out his season at West Chop before returning to Deerfield, where he taught for three decades, a beloved fixture on the faculty, married (to a different woman from his fiancée) and father to three girls, and years later returning to West Chop as a member, when he and Gini would renew their friendship and happily rally together while alluding in gleeful smiles to that long-ago August and their spirited trysts, beginning above the old post office and transferring to the farthest reaches of the Mink Meadows golf course (beneath the tall, pointed firs) and along Lake Tashmoo's scrub-oak shore in her father's camp, where, five years later, she and Jake Burrage would spend two blissful weeks in late August before the start of senior year. But John Chandler would forever remain her first lover—tender, sweet, caring, proficient—almost as proficient as Jake Burrage, whose connoisseurship for giving head had taken things to another level and left her addicted to slow-burning lovemaking, if not forever imprisoned by her own entitlement to the limitless pleasures of mind-embodied flesh.

Not that all had quite gone to plan. Despite all their elaborate precautions and secrecy, somehow her father had gotten wind of the affair. Perhaps because of his sensitive radar for his wife's infidelities, or from her mother, who had an expert's nose for scandal, given her own history of subterfuge. Who might have detected her semen-stained panties in her hamper even as she carefully did her own laundry. Or even the visible chemistry between coach and player on the practice court, the exchange of knowing smiles, the banter, the briefest touching—who knows. Whatever the case, her father upended her life by canceling her flight to the Nationals in Kalamazoo and booking her on a father-daughter trip to Venice (canceling, too, his own annual sailing trip up the coast to Bar Harbor). There was no reprieve, no chance for a possible number-one national ranking in the under eighteens—missing the Labor Day West Chop tournament as well, just the kind of punishment her mild-mannered father would dish out when pressed. Probably, looking back, saving John Chandler from scandal and a career-ending catastrophe as a high school teacher and coach.

The affair also had the salutatory effect of ending his long-running engagement with his college sweetheart, who lacked Gini's intelligence and playfulness; eventually, he married a professor of English at Smith, an independent woman, tall and blonde and accomplished in Gini's mold. In recent summers, when they played friendly matches against each other, Gini had decided that what had probably given her away was, indeed, the joyful pleasure she took from working out with John as a teenager: the look on her face while doing crosscourt backhand drills, grunting, sweating, crying out with the pure pleasure she took as her body glided through space: a sexual act in all but the particulars, which anyone with an iota of suspicion could not have failed to notice.

"Galla Placidia," she still liked to whisper under her breath in moments of reverie. What John Chandler had called her all those years ago in postcoital afterglow as they lay panting and sweaty in his narrow bed, he propped on an elbow, staring into her insatiate eyes. A very cautious lover, he had first suggested mutual masturbation (absent condoms), which she had nixed with assurances she was on the Pill. Remarkably, she'd actually orgasmed during first intercourse, with only the lightest touch of self-help, seeing yellow butterflies flitting against a dark blue sky: the first and last time that had ever happened.

"Galla" (before "Isabel") was the lover's nickname bestowed, honoring her fair eyes of "lapis lazuli," her namesake the once-upon-a-time empress of the Western

Roman Empire, a wily and determined woman, a revenant of her noble class, an alter ego that had remained a secret to Jake Burrage and the Shirelles, a tale still untapped. A character thoroughly disguised and downplayed in the pages of her novel and senior thesis, even as she had scribbled out John Chandler's endearments word for word in her notebook upon arriving home that first night.

"My fierce Galla . . ." He'd stroked her cheek, wiping away a tear of joy. "Must be the alliance of virtue and fortune that ran in her blood—fortitude smiled on by fortune. That's you. And her passion for commissioning wonderful mosaic programs. Her mausoleum in Ravenna will take your breath away—your namesake, especially—an arched ceiling patterned with star-like, jewel-like white orbs against lapis lazuli that will make your eyes ache with the wonder of it." (And it was all true. Only weeks later, she and her father made a day's excursion to Ravenna, and all she could think when she saw the archivolts of her patron saint's mausoleum: yellow butterflies against lapis lazuli.)

CHAPTER 19

She opened her eyes, marveling—how odd—that the vividness of her memories of lovemaking with John Chandler should have found her under such bizarre if not compromising circumstances, but nevertheless providing crucial fresh material for that revised novel in the making. Even more oddly, her memories seemed, if anything, more real, more compelling, more visceral than whatever had happened the night before, as if the old palimpsest was rewriting itself over the new. Could the vibes emanating from a young man's disheveled bed cast such a spell? Not to mention a scolding Saint Augustine glaring down over her shoulder, not unlike when her father had sat her down in the Scuola di San Giorgio to elicit their mutual confessions, gently probing for signs of sanity and contrition in his wayward daughter while his faults as husband and father came tumbling out.

Hadn't her life been ruined by missing Kalamazoo and that number-one ranking?

If John Chandler, that sweetest of souls, had been wrong, what could ever be right?

Willing partners and nothing like poor, abandoned Ariadne of Naxos (her father's take) pining away on her enchanted isle.

The thing—first things, first tallies—only re-created in part five years later in her lovemaking with Jake Burrage lying under the stars in their camp by Lake Tashmoo, when her body came alive once again under the spell of his ravenous tongue, tenderly, slowly, searching, opening her to the song of the cicadas and the call of the hermit thrush, there beneath the fir boughs where the stars burned into a summer's sky, until his tongue roved upward to her begging lips, and then her ear lobes, there imparting another song, a different leitmotif from the original, but drawing splendor from the first, if not its primacy. So filled that she felt emptied out, spilled out into that star-streaming night where her invisible namesake, Galla Placidia, roamed in all her imperial splendor.

Why had she failed to include that secret rapture—a young girl's awakening—in her first attempt at long fiction? Nor Kalamazoo, nor her father's enforced visit to Venice, nor even the mausoleum of Galla Placidia. That and her mother's venomous secret blurted out in a drunken rage at her graduation. Love and abject misery intertwined in her heart like serpents of the caduceus, never to be spoken of, much less written down.

Had Jake Burrage somehow thwarted her fictional candor? A guy who positively reveled in risky escapades and so overrode her own temptations until transformed into an overly cautious drudge. Thwarting her essential wildness and so giving up on her Wimbledon aspirations for the safety of a job she could master in her sleep? A marriage as comfortable as it was predictable.

"For God's sake, Gini, get a grip . . ."

She huffed as if to free her body from the constraints of an overactive imagination, raising one long, muscled leg, toes pointed to where Augustine might properly appreciate the full wages of sin.

Her breath tumbled inward: "By George" (her father's expression), but that leg looked very fine—fine indeed, sleek, tightly muscled, not a hint of flab or cellulite on the undersides of her thigh.

Tapping again the crystal of her father's stopped Rolex, she stood to properly survey her young seducer's room, spotting her car keys and Marriott key card on the desk by her phone. Her car keys had been in her backpack, which stared at her from the La-Z-Boy along with her green Yonex tennis bag. "Oh my God . . ." She grabbed her phone and saw that it was 8:35, still over an hour before the start of their charity match, but hardly enough time to get all the way out to the Marriott, shower, and change, and be back in time—much less sneak out of Jacob Burrage's room and entranceway without being detected.

Then she noticed her tennis dress hanging on the back of his door, still in the clear plastic bag from her dry cleaner. "What the fuck?" And what was her tennis bag with a white terry cloth bathrobe on top and a note doing here anyway?

"6:00 a.m.—didn't want to wake you, so got your tennis gear from the Marriott. Parked your car in same spot behind Cap. Off to my lab, a busy day, see you courtside! Jacob."

"I'll be damned." She parsed the note in her hand, shaking her head at the sheer audacity, even as she instantly recognized the familiar MO, as she did the young man's writing, the same loops in his o's and the slashing, crossed t's. Considerate—like father, like son, anticipating her every need. "Like father, like daughter," she muttered, turning to Augustine's bearded face as part of that long-ago confession came to mind, yet another discordant, possibly perplexing note.

"I fear I haven't been much of an attentive father to you, Gini. Truth be told, I'm rather intimidated by women today, like your mother, and you as well—quite a shock to the system since the day you were born . . . in a good way, you understand. Somehow, I've managed to let your mother down and now perhaps you as well. But your behavior with Mr. Chandler put both that man's life (and yours) and livelihood in jeopardy, as well as our membership at West Chop. Can you even begin to imagine . . . ?"

Yes, yes, perhaps it had been there, the Scuola di San Georgio, where she'd lost her nerve.

Jerking her head in stupefaction, she suddenly realized she'd read Jacob's note without her reading glasses; in fact, everything around her had a crystal clarity, including where her clothes of the night before had been carefully folded and placed on the top of the bureau. Even her sensible walking shoes, along with her high heels, had been neatly paired on the floor. Had she so carefully undressed herself, not in some frenzied rush? Yes, she was sure she could summon forth that first kiss, but after that . . . things became blurry, as if she'd drifted off into some dream of her wild, unencumbered youth. Although, for some reason, that name he'd mentioned came back to her, von Neumann and something about computers and critical mass, how knowledge of complex molecular machines had deepened our understanding of life, while our understanding of technology had faltered as computers approach the complexity of living things. She tentatively reached a finger to the well-worn paperback cover of *The Singularity Is Near,* placed next to her car keys, perhaps the owner's manual left for her edification.

"Our brains, you see, turn out to be less logical and sequential than we might have imagined. The past haunts our present in ways we have no idea about and, under the right circumstances, is fully recoverable."

She shook her head and blinked rapidly: Yes, he sure had that much right.

Neatly lying across the back of the Herman Miller desk chair was the white cotton lab coat Jacob had been wearing the night before. She picked it up to find *Burrage Biochemistry Lab* inscribed in green letters over the pocket. She raised the coat to her face, as she might to check for the past indiscretions of a wayward lover, reacting with an exclamation.

"Bleach . . ."

Momentarily at a loss, she tried sorting the confusing signals emanating out of "space-time," a neologism that seemed to have been bandied around a lot the previous night, like how the hell had she gotten into this mess and how best to extract herself. She unzipped her bulky green Yonex tennis bag and discovered not only her racquets and gear, but that young Jacob must have riffled through her suitcase for fresh panties, bras, her makeup and toilet kit, the black dress she was going to wear at the publishing forum, including an orange-and-white blouse and Hermès scarf. And her Crest toothpaste and toothbrush!

"How . . . what a fucking operator!" She shook her head in wonder at the meticulous care that had gone into all this, this—what? An open invitation to shack up with him over Reunions?

"You see, Gini, our ability to take general, organized advantage of local, haphazard processes is what distinguishes information processing in living organisms from information processing by digital computers."

She had to smile (the very idea!)—couldn't help smiling, her eyes lighting up as she took down her recently purchased Thom Browne sleeveless orange tennis dress (picked out for the charity event) from where it hung on the back of the door, holding it up to her body as she inspected herself in the full-length mirror. As she was about to re-hang it, she froze, blinking, disbelieving at the upgrade confronting her in the mirror. She reached first to the glass and then to her face, her breasts. Her deep blue eyes, flecked with teal green, stared back, absent any disagreeable crow's-feet.

She raised her face to the new firmness in her jawline, to the taunt tendons in her throat, where any incipient hint of a double chin had vanished, her skin soft and supple and glowing.

Had it been that good? Such an endorphin rush. Could anything be that good?

As her curious gaze moved lower, she noticed a similar tight rigging in her upper arms, elastic muscles that extended across her chest, where her boobs stared insolently back without a sag, upturned, her pale pink nipples like nobody's business. And then there was the added miracle of the lovely compact plane of her belly descending in a smooth arc to wisps of reddish blonde pubic hair. Like a model on a runway, she adroitly stepped back and turned side to side for the full effect, relishing the lithe molding of her powerful thighs rising above her ropey calves. Better than a figment of her imagination. Better still, her knees felt positively buoyant, an exhilarating springy lightness as she now bounced on her toes, ready for liftoff. Even her butt seemed to be defying gravity, perfectly compact and happy-go-lucky.

She cocked her head.

"There's good sex . . . *and there's good sex.*" And something to do with green tea and Boulder.

Her half smile faded to an expression of confusion verging on panic. She spun around as if she'd missed something or some voyeur had glassed her bare, complacent pride, only to find distant gazes emanating from the collection of framed black-and-white photos hung above the standing bookshelves. Somehow more penetrating—insistent, given her nakedness. She reached a searching hand to the watching face of Einstein, then, bending to read the signature, "von Neumann," and those of Curie and the others, as if possibly canvassing an opinion on her intimate event horizon. As she touched again the glass barely containing the white, unkept locks of Albert Einstein, her eyes fell on the volumes of Whitman and James on the shelf below—now, in the morning light, more familiar than ever.

She lovingly removed the two volumes and slumped into the desk chair, first examining the Whitman, which she now realized was the expensive, beautifully printed Modern Library "Death-Bed" edition, with an introduction by William Carlos Williams, she'd given to Jake on his twentieth birthday. Inscribed by her (and a cute drawing of a hermit thrush) with a not-so-disguised plea to diligently explore the text within, as if in hopes of bridging some unbridgeable gap, countering his talents, his inspiration with hers. Even to the extent that she'd carefully noted poems to read, lines to be put to memory, which, as she thumbed the well-worn pages, she could tell Jake had diligently done, often with multiple underlining and marginalia to himself.

"What a pushy, full-of-yourself bitch . . . ," she muttered, turning to the dog-eared Penguin paperback of James's *Portrait of a Lady*, the same copy she and Jake had used for their English novels course, James having been hijacked into a tradition only tangentially his own. This volume too had been underlined in yellow Sharpie and annotated in the same familiar hand, passages describing Isabel Archer's motivation and state of mind. "The union of knowledge with liberty," she read in a marginal notation, words that sparked a guilty wince as she first glanced at *The Singularity Is Near* on the desk, only to swivel in alarm to where, above the bed, old Augustine sat in judgment on her choice of reading matter. His scrutiny of what, by any account, had to have been two extraordinary scenes of seduction had the odd effect of clarifying the critical moment of the night before when, the veins in her temples suddenly throbbing with jet fuel, she had ended the agony by reaching across that lamplit space and grabbing his face in her outstretched hands. "Forgive me my no-show . . ." More to hold fast the look of recognition in his adoring eyes than to steal a kiss (taking advantage of that local, haphazard instant). By any stretch, an act of pure, unhinged possession: a second chance at a life unlived.

She found herself captivated—if not terrified—by an outrageous notion, a notion that would only grow, hour by hour, over the next few days: that she had been—somehow, some way—brilliantly seduced by none other than Jake Burrage.

A thing so beyond even science fiction that she spun in desperate alarm away from Augustine's absent stare to the desk and made a grab for the handle of the side drawer, only to find it securely locked.

CHAPTER 20

Years later, when poised at her word processor, trying to sort fact from fiction and which to indulge for the sake of a believable narrative, she found herself puzzled at the coincidence of the repeated appearance of the Carpaccios at her fortieth reunion, first in Erma's and Jacob's rooms, then in the vividness of memory, viewing the originals with her father and, years later, her daughter. She began to feel—to save her sanity, or the integrity of her text—that the less-familiar twilight zone of science fiction might better suit her purposes than literary fiction. The story, which had begun as a reasonable and true account, kept taking unnerving turns, an otherworldly swerve as she tried to make sense of the enigmatic character of young Jacob Burrage, who seemed haunted as well by a visit to the Scuola di San Giorgio, as had, so it seemed, his father, glimpsed not only in his son's eyes but also, oddly, in Bianca's guilty dismissals. As if all had, once upon a time, come under Augustine's pensive spell.

Posing yet another tantalizing question: What had come over her at seventeen to seek out and purchase the expensive Carpaccio reproductions in the first place? Sparking a chain reaction that seemed to circle in upon itself, circles within circles, not unlike an armillary sphere or astrolabe. First hung on the wall of her bedroom overlooking West End Avenue, then in her dorm to beguile male visitors, then her first apartment, only to be dispensed with in various storage bins until resurrected some forty years later by Erma. Should she treat the captivating images in the

Carpaccios as telling symbols of some deeper truth? Omens? Afterimages in a retrospective mind? Harbingers of Proustian memory? Or simply straightforward tokens of her father's good breeding and connoisseurship—of the intellectual distinction admired in her family for generations. Or—keep it simple, Gini: let the reader take delight in such charming narratives for their own sake. In her rewrite, she marveled at how these esoteric stories of three saints' lives, first associated with missing Kalamazoo and giving up John Chandler, had been transformed into a new intimacy with her father: an alliance against her mother would not be putting it too strongly. An alliance confounded by her mother at her graduation dinner.

Or—dare she admit it?—telltale reminders of a faithless life and her failure to rendezvous with Jake Burrage. An alternate life that would finally come alive, first in young Jacob's bed and then beneath her fingertips.

How wonderful to once again indulge a young woman's rage at being hauled off like one of Dante's lustful sinners to Venice by her father. Missing Kalamazoo at seventeen might not have exactly ruined her life, but she lost a season of momentum and the spark her lust for John Chandler had imparted to her game. For the first time, she began to doubt herself. And her taciturn father had only made it worse by first giving her the silent treatment, refusing to name her crime, even on the ferry to Woods Hole and the taxi to Logan airport, only advising her to sleep soundly on the overnight flight to Milan, barely begrudging a peep on the early-morning train to Venice, where, the light rain and threatening squalls notwithstanding, he splurged on a gondola to carry them to the watery steps of the dowdy Pensione Seguso (reeking with cat piss), only later allowing a few scholarly observations as they wound their way through the damp and gray back streets of Venice, just enough backstory, as she too would later deploy it, to provide context to their arrival at the Scuola di San Giorgio, when suddenly the clouds parted as sunlight brilliantly illuminated those welcoming green doors presided over by a tutelary pair of dour, if lovable, dolphins. Where, upon entering this sanctum sanctorum, her father had been transformed as he poured out his heart in the agonized confessions of a penitent who'd failed his wife and daughter.

"Gini, dear, sometimes we need to remove ourselves from one world"—a wave to Augustine's crystalline chamber—"to properly enter another in hopes of finding ourselves again: the road not taken."

Not that such an admission arrived in so many words. Rather, it was couched in a detailed explanation of Carpaccio's iconography (first time she'd heard the word used in a sentence), which, much to her consternation, she found both revealing and fascinating—that hidden world aswirl with delicious symbols and arcane knowledge available only to the properly initiated, even more intoxicating as her father segued into a distinctly confessional mode, as if the artist's subjects mirrored certain agonizing, if obscure, moments in his own life.

"My own father brought me here when I was a boy, a powerful man, a paragon of the Princeton classics faculty before he went into publishing, whose lectures were always filled to capacity, with faculty wives adding to the overflow. His effect on women was quite stunning. I was forever in awe, even as I felt quite diminished by his celebrity. I was headed for a life in scholarship before certain unfortunate . . . well, let's say misunderstandings ended that little experiment after my PhD. I felt a little like Jerome over there, leading his lion, only to find the confraternity of brothers fleeing his presence: a good man but out of step with his time. And slaying dragons or converting sinners was never my line. Studious Augustine was more my ideal, even though university life turned out not to be for me. Your mother was the daughter of one of my father's admirers."

Still wearing his tidy seersucker jacket from the flight over (they had the musty-smelling first floor of the scuola all to themselves), he had nodded sadly to his daughter as he gestured with a delicate hand to where Augustine sat in contemplative reverie at his busy desk, face turned to a window.

"You see, my father had an idea, a fantasy really, that beyond that open door at the rear of Augustine's lair was a vast library containing many of the long-lost volumes from the great library of Alexandria, Hippo and Alexandria being not so far distant. For years I entertained my father's whimsy as my own, wondering what unknown classics of the Hellenistic world might be shelved behind that door. But then in time, I dreamed up my own take on what lay beyond that open door; I started to think that Carpaccio's Augustine might be a secret portrait in homage to the great Venetian printer and publisher Aldus Manutius, and that through that door was a printer's workshop or a wonderful library of rare first editions from the Aldine Press, rediscovered classics from Lucretius and Marcus Aurelius and Seneca. Aldus's reputation was such that the compassionate humanist Erasmus came to stay with Aldus in Venice and spent time writing in his workshop. So, I, when I was not much older than you, preferred to believe that Augustine (my beloved Aldus) saw, not a vision of Jerome beyond his window, but the approach of his great friend and fellow scholar, Erasmus, who so eloquently called for tolerance and the end of cruel and pointless wars."

Her father shook his head as if in wonderment at such youthful folly.

"You see, Ginistrella, the life of scholarship is not just about picking up arcane details for their own sake, perhaps to be trotted out at cocktail parties to burnish a reputation or woo a lover, nor even to furnish a well-tended mind by an acquaintance with the lives of Saints Augustine, Jerome, and George, or the denizens of Dante's inferno that once upon a time provided the stories that men lived by. What matters is how these stories allow us to enter into the flow of time, pulling an oar, so to speak, so that one feels the weight of the past when one leans into the stroke, when our glide forward is buoyed on the thousands of past lives that have brought us to this place. That is what great writers do as well."

Drawn to the cute little German spitz yearning for its walk, she had at first resisted her father's importunate lecture, impatient to head out and make for the promised nearby gelateria. Yet something in her father's searching tone struck a chord.

"Literature and history and art—why I followed my father into publishing—bring the past alive so that we can enter not only into the lives of these paintings but appreciate the succor they provided for the members of this confraternity, the Dalmatian community of Venice, mostly poor dockworkers, galley oarsmen, shipbuilders in the Arsenale, for whom these images provided meaning in a life of hard labor, danger—good Lord, the vicious wars against the Genovese and Turks—and early death. A sense of identity, loyalty, and pride—a larger sense of themselves. By such a close appreciation of Carpaccio, we catch a glimpse of the individual humanity of these lost souls, to share in their simple faith, their hopes and joys, their prayers for meaning in this life and glorious repose in the next. Without this place, these paintings—in situ—spared by the depredations of Napoleon, I ask you: What would we know about these people—or, more to the point, even care to know?"

She remembered how her father shook his long head of closely cropped gray hair, half smiling in wonder, tears in his bloodshot eyes as he wiped his glasses and shifted gears from the general to the particular, all perfectly gauged to persuade his bookish daughter. How his voice always lowered partway through his sentences, as if challenging her to listen all the harder for the key points, even as she found her attention gravitating again and again to the saint's desk, sprawling with open volumes, that telltale conch shell and handbell, the hourglass run out, invisibly registering in her imagination like a fate foretold.

"I fear that, ever since my days at Princeton, when I first fell in love with scholarship, I have lived too much for the life of the mind. It's not that I'm a prude or entirely unaware of the sexual needs of the human race, but there is a time and place for such things, as I learned the hard way collaring my lion." He smiled uneasily at this reference to his wife and plunged on with a sigh and raised eyebrow. "Nor am I unaware that your mother has not always provided an appropriate example in this age of Kinsey abetted by Dr. Freud. Even as my work and—shall we call it my admiration for Carpaccio—my delight in the abstract world of ideas and aesthetics often distract from the here and now. Quieter pleasures—sailing our Vineyard 15 with you, perhaps steered away from the more practical pleasures of a marriage. Of course, the ironies of this moment haven't entirely escaped me either, that Augustine originated—popularized, as we might say today—the doctrine of original sin, while Jerome was obsessed with virginity as a sign of holiness, of the complete renunciation of carnality. Augustine—not that anyone reads him much these days—in his *Confessions* is a tortured soul driven to a renunciation of the world and its many pleasures, carnal and otherwise."

"Carnality," she had finally blurted out, a raised eye to the left, where San Giorgio was spearing his dragon amid a litter of body parts. "I guess that's why we're here."

"We are and we aren't. I, believe it or not, was never really taken much by asceticism—nor aestheticism, art for art's sake, in the Oscar Wilde mode, if you take my meaning—that preoccupation with our bodily state, specifically our fallen and sinful selves, from which only God's grace might deliver us. The hard Unitarianism of my grandfather, rest his soul."

"You always made such a point about Seneca, that although he wrote about the division of body and soul, he never made it a fetish."

"Ah, Seneca. Well, I hardly think we're here due to a fetish." He passed a hand over his jaw and reached under his tortoiseshell glasses to wipe his eye. "But as I—or you—were saying, our Stoics certainly never considered what we might call goodness as an insurmountable challenge, even in a fallen world. Perhaps a degree of serenity is the best we can hope for in this life, along with the power to think for ourselves, as does Carpaccio's rendition of Augustine, recasting his dour personality in a more lustrous, perhaps forgiving light. A Renaissance scholar, no less."

"Is that what you and Mom have—serenity?"

"Well, as you've clearly anticipated, I was about to get around to that. Perhaps it's my fault—your mother and Mr. Chandler, I mean—that I didn't take a stronger stand."

"At least I never embarrassed anybody."

"And I'm sorry if it's made your life . . . well, confusing."

"He told me she actually grabbed his crotch at a tennis clinic, in front of everybody."

Her father shook his head.

"A family's reputation, especially at West Chop . . . well, that's why I think we're here: Your mother and I have decided on a trial separation."

"Divorce?"

"More than likely. I've suggested she seek professional help or at least enter a program to get her drinking under control." He placed a hand on her shoulder. "I'm sorry, but it seemed that stepping back from our normal lives was the best way to break it to you. Not that a little of Augustine's confessions might not be in order as well."

"She actually accused me the other day of competing with her, as if I'd moved in on her turf."

"How did Seneca put it: whatever is in your power—no, whatever can make you good is in your power."

"Yes—what do you need to be good? To will it."

He put his arm around her and gave her a tentative hug. "Something—willpower. That and the power of metamorphosis you seem to have in quite an abundance, dear." He stood and nodded to the old custodian in his green apron, whom he seemed to recognize from previous visits. "Now, how about that ice cream I promised you."

And strangely, a huge load—even as that seed of self-doubt was planted—seemed lifted off her mind, and just possibly her soul, and instead of a punishment meted out, their week together in Venice and a day in Ravenna (to meet with her glorious namesake, Galla Placidia) had proved an awakening, a true turning point in her young life. Instead of being cast down, she found herself triumphant and fully allied with her father against her mother. Through the looking glass of his gaze, a kind of metamorphosis had, indeed, taken place, prompted by the rare and exotic beauty of the Carpaccios, intimations of a secret door opened wide to reveal a hidden chamber available only to the elect, where the aesthetic and esoteric mingled, where the beauty of ideas lived resplendently—that eternal past, that secret code available only to those possessing the keys to the kingdom. Keys to a different and not so different kingdom that, three years hence, would be rattled before her frustrated eyes by Jake Burrage.

And then there was the storybook nature of the city itself. Who could have guessed at the plenitudes to be read in those elegiac traceries and carvings adorning the Doge's Palace, distilled through the writings of Byron, Ruskin, James, and Browning. All quoted to her by her father from memory, who deigned to reference a map or guidebook. Or his description of the uneven, mosaic-tiled floor of the Baptistry of San Marco that had inspired Proust to unlock his past and so find his way to the masterpiece he was born to write.

"Not that you are quite ready for Proust, or even your first novel, but in good time you may be able to look back—keep a journal, why not—on a full life, full of incident and insights, and like Proust in a moment of reverie, when a figment of the present reminds you of something formally lost (perhaps this very moment or the like), a sensation, a fleeting glimpse, the scent of brine and incense, which in turn triggers an extratemporal insight, where you will discover the essence of things, that lost self, your essential self existing outside of time." He had bent to examine the baptistry of San Marco's uneven inlaid floor of porphyry and marble, while she gazed around at the dazzling gold, greens, and blues in the mosaic arches, identifying the saints as her father had taught her. "Or as James would put it: be a woman on whom nothing is lost. All material for the great novel you will surely write someday."

Over that one incandescent week, her father had played Virgil to his impressionable daughter, waving her on from one obscure turning to the next, with an uncanny sense of where hidden gems beckoned the astute eye. And then, farther afield, as they made a flying visit to Murano's Basilica dei Santi Maria e Donato and the pinwheeling hypnotic beauty of the mosaic floor, before moving onto Torcello for lunch at the Cipriani (where a bottle of Amarone della Valpolicella, '62, provided her a first lesson in wine connoisseurship), capped by an inspection of the mosaics in Santa Maria Assunta and a Dantesque vision of the damned emblazoned on the rear apse that would haunt her for the rest of her life.

"How horrible," she shuddered, still reeling from their wine, at the mounds of skulls with snakes slithering in and out of the eye sockets. "The Stoics, the Greeks, never had to resort to such terrifying threats of damnation to encourage virtue in their followers."

"Yes, virtue for its own sake, whether in a family or community—the stuff that binds civilization, the past to the present. Even our dear John Ruskin in his *Stones* found these scenes of the harrowing of hell unpleasant to his discriminating eye." Her father had gently taken her arm and returned her gaze to the dazzling gold apse at the front of the nave, where the Virgin and Child were assumed into heaven above the saintly host. "Why, what a band of saints and apostles she has for company where she reigns in the imperium—a dozen; you should be able to name them now by their attributes . . . there's Saint Peter with his keys . . ." He paused in this litany, sweeping his hand upward as his eye was caught by an inscription running above the apostles' heads. This he began to translate from the Greek, when he paused yet again as if struck by a thought more propitious for the moment at hand. "I'm reminded of something Ruskin wrote: 'When you come upon a text that quite baffles you at first, you may have to struggle a bit because the author, on purpose or otherwise, has hidden away, in parables or a discursive style, the gold that glitters—to make sure you really desire what the author has to offer.'" Her father chuckled and nodded, a nod she would one day read as an invitation to interpret the hidden text of her life and his, if not the parable of her fate as fashioned and told by one Jake Burrage. "Emerson too panned hard for such nuggets. So the struggle for meaning, you see—curiosity being its own reward—requires the tapping into some deeper strata rich with elusive ideas. Ideas that will be the making of you as a novelist."

If she was transformed by that week, her father was as well, his reticent laconic persona washed away by the sea breezes (oh, to be sailing their Vineyard 15 on the Lagoon!) and the bright near-autumnal sunshine after the rain that had first greeted them. Time and time again, his long face frozen in memory-softened wonder, pale blue eyes blinking in sudden recognition, he would suddenly break off from the beaten track on the way to the Scuola di San Giorgio to hunt down some miraculous survival of genius once pointed out to him as a boy by his own father: a marble gorgon head with wide, lolling tongue embedded in a wall behind San Giovanni e Paulo; the ravishing subtle tonalities ("Gosh, just the richness of their cassocks, the somber blue, the eggshell white, and those modulations of gray like a moonlit cloud—who would have thought such a ravishing color scheme possible?") in Piazzetta's *Three Dominican Saints* in the side chapel of the Gesuati; the fanciful dolphins carved in gleaming white Istrian stone by Pietro Lombardo, spiraling tails transformed into laurel blooms; and the sumptuous marble inlays of Santa Maria dei Miracoli when glimpsed in just the right slant of late-afternoon light.

"Good Lord, the marble is almost translucent, the purple veining like something of Clyfford Still's!"

Secret moments of impassioned awe (she still had visions of his raised seersucker arm waving her on, wearing his beloved gray Hush Puppies oxfords) shared with his daughter as if he were still a young student roaming abroad with his sweetheart.

So much so that, in years hence, when stumbling upon certain color combinations of pink and mauve and off-white, she would find herself transported back—"Yes, yes, oh yes"—to her adolescence and the labyrinthian streets of Venice in the neighborhood of the Miracoli, all parsed in her father's sibilant tones.

And yet, with so much to see, they still found themselves, as if by unspoken assent, gravitating, bone-weary, each afternoon to the Scuola di San Giorgio to visit the Carpaccios, where the scholarly Augustine seemed to prompt her father's most revealing reflections.

"It seems, don't you think, to always begin with this image of reverie, which inspires one to take up the names and places that properly situate us in space and time, and from there, shimmering in the haze beyond, the ideas upon which our true sense of self rests." She remembered listening intently as her eyes wandered that magical chamber within a chamber where the armillary sphere glittered like a twisting road map, its counterparts in the Burrage Biochemistry Lab one day hurrying her on to her appointed destiny. "As a writer (or these days mostly an editor of other writers), one must revere words, their qualities, their etymologies, their beauty in and of themselves, but resist the temptation to make a fetish of beautiful words—mere wordplay, as Proust would have it. The art may be in the arrangement of the words, as musical notes (see how apt the display of music manuscripts there beneath Augustine's desk) are arranged—the orchestrator, the mosaicist, if you like—but the writing is only as good insofar as it provokes sensations or feelings—wonder—in the reader." The balding, gray-haired custodian, in his forest-green apron, had appeared from the stairs, examining his watch as he caught her eye, prompting her father to check his beloved art deco Rolex with the blue hands. "Which is simply another way of revealing one's true self undisturbed by the appetites and distractions of the moment, as here beholding a supreme work of the imagination. Proust liked to call it a *resurrection*, as when—remember—he, as an aged man, stepped on an uneven paving stone on a visit to the Guermantes in Paris and found himself translated back to the cracked mosaic floor of the Baptistry of San Marco, where, as a young man, he had once been fully alive—even if in thrall to the memory of his insipid Albertine. And so transformed, he—or at least his character, his alter ego, Marcel—was able to embark on his life's work: I suppose no more can be asked than such a miracle."

"And Albertine?" she queried, a fetching smile directed to the waiting custodian, a plea to give them another minute.

Her father had sat back with a sigh, blinking back weariness. "It was a terrible mistake (and what a terrible admission for a father to have to make) to marry your mother. I felt, perhaps more an idea than a feeling, that our differences would prove our strength, my failures made up in her and hers gainsaid by me. An idea of matrimony gone so wrong. Just as Isabel Archer in the *Portrait* marries for the wrong idea, a complete failure of imagination." He had looked at his watch again and nodded to the custodian, placing his hand over hers. "Somehow, you have always reminded me of Isabel; you have all her beauty and wit and dynamic intelligence, an intelligence in search of the beau ideal, to imagine your way to a brilliant destiny. Or, as James wrote: 'Her notion of the aristocratic life was simply the union of great knowledge with great liberty; the knowledge would give one a sense of duty and the liberty a sense of enjoyment.' But beware, as I say, the trap of marrying for what you lack—letting your imagination run away with you: it is a recipe for disaster. A woman like Isabel Archer—or you, for that matter—needs to be the mistress in a marriage, not an acolyte." He gestured to the empty hourglass beneath Augustine's desk. "Yes, the sands of time forever slipping away."

With that, her father had tipped the custodian ten thousand lira for his kind forbearance, and they were off to a last dinner. "Shall we make it Harry's in honor of Ernest, or Florian, or even that snappy chartreuse evening dress—sky's the limit—in the window on the way to San Marco."

Walking the narrow *calles*, up and down endless bridges, she had been happy again to swing on her father's arm like a little girl, avidly listening as the city came alive in the tones of a young man, who had once himself been led by his own brilliant father (who in turn had been schooled on Venice by his father, an editor under William Dean Howells, American consul to Venice during the Civil War), as she in turn would lead her daughter, remembering to recite like a mantra the names and places and so resurrect the abiding traditions of their family. Along with a careful selection of her father's admonitions. An act of fidelity, even love, and possibly caution that had kept her from truly loving, inoculating her imagination against a mate who would truly challenge her worth—expand her imaginative grasp, whether Jake Burrage, or, for that matter, her late husband, Bill Cheshire.

A failure sprung from the seeds of doubt first passed from her father's lips during their Venetian sojourn and, six years later, her mother's explosive accusation at her graduation dinner.

CHAPTER 21

The young lady, showered, hair pulled up tight and neatly tucked away under a Princeton tennis cap, deliciously attired, slung her heavy tennis bag, packed with all her gear, slipped discreetly out of her paramour's entryway in Pyne Hall, and made her way toward the new court complex. The first thing she noticed, after what she assumed for the record was a night of illicit bliss, was how little the bag weighed—and it was not a short walk. Could sex with a younger man actually flip that hourglass: the plunder of a succubus? She laughed out loud, thrilled at the sensation of walking on air! Not unlike that wide-eyed seventeen-year-old traipsing about Venice on her father's arm, or the student on the way to practice, even to the point of finding her eye attracted to every passing gargoyle (D. H. Lawrence's dark gods, a cautionary voice whispered in her ear) and collegiate-Gothic tracery—mauve grays against the vivid blue of a June sky. That pesky breeze at yesterday's lunch was indeed a true harbinger of lowered humidity and just possibly resurrection. Better yet, she was strangely at peace, confident, almost blasé: a woman still desired by the universe. That is, until she reached the courts and the displeased expressions of her old teammates: her regal aplomb momentarily deflated at the need of a convincing white lie—and pronto.

Exclaimed Bianca: "The prodigal Agrippina arrives. We've been texting you all morning—and Erma, who didn't get back to us either."

"Yeah," added Apolonia, "calling your hotel room didn't do it either."

"I knocked on your door this morning to see if you could give me a ride over," said Bianca, not bothering to note she'd actually been shacked up with Jack at the same flossy Marriott. "And there was no answer—nada."

She smiled with perfect equanimity as her sister Shirelles gathered around in their rather matronly (except Bianca) no-name tennis attire, with a nod to the huddle of the current women's team nearby, less dressed than sheathed in orange-and-black spandex.

"Oh," she sang above the milling crowd entering the stands, "I had a little too much of Jack's burgundy, couldn't get an Uber, so I passed out on Erma's sofa under the Carpaccios." A careless, even stupid lie, since Erma could easily blow her cover.

"Carpaccios?" asked Annette, with a quick glance to where Arthur was seated in the stands.

"No wonder, at five hundred bucks a bottle, it's a miracle any of us are here," allowed Bianca, with the merest note of proprietary pride as she reached to Gini's bare arm as if to make sure of her corporeal presence, then giving her bicep an admiring squeeze. "And I thought I was the only one lifting weights."

"We were a little concerned," scolded Annette, now staring hard at Gini as if something didn't quite add up (perhaps her overstuffed tennis bag, which she jettisoned as if it weighed nothing).

"*Noli me tangere*," she sang out, with the sweetest smile she could muster. "After all, I can hardly be the only one who didn't have great sex last night to prep for our match?"

"Old guys," muttered Apolonia, hiding her late-night frustrations behind a tetchy squint at Gini. "It's always afternoon delight." She too reached a hand to Gini's shoulder. "My eyes must be deceiving me," she went on, "or was I too distracted yesterday. Have you had plastic surgery, Botox maybe?"

Bianca oblivious: "Do you remember when our coach made us vow not to have sex the day before our match, to save ourselves—our precious bodily juices?"

"Fluids," corrected Apolonia. "And that has been thoroughly discredited as an old husband's tale. Along with roommates all getting their periods together."

"One of the few advantages of age before beauty," sighed Bianca.

Apolonia, still perplexed, continued to examine Gini. "I'm either losing my mind or my eyesight or both, but I could swear—sure you didn't go to some local dermatologist? Is that why you're so late?" She bent closer to her teammate's face, squinting, as she pushed her dark glasses down her nose.

"What you see is what you get," laughed Gini, striking a pose. "It's his latest."

"Hah," said Bianca, strutting her own outfit, "pretty in pink for the virginal sacrifice."

"So," Annette sang out, as if to end the funny business, "they figured we'd be more comfortable playing against our former doubles partners, so they've split us up. Gini plays Apolonia—and you guys get Matt to umpire your match (not that he'd favor me); and I will play against Bianca and her partner. And to make things more even, I play with their number-four singles; Gini plays with their number three; Apolonia plays with their two; and Bianca gets their number one, already a two-time All-American who got to the second round of the US Open last year."

"Numero uno—yes," gasped Bianca, pumping her fist.

"Zowee," cried Apolonia, giving Bianca a fist bump. "I always wanted to play against Gini in doubles, to see if her crosscourt return was really as good as she always maintained."

Gini looked up, prancing in place like a filly released into the paddock as she went through her pre-match warm-up, breathed deeply of the crisp spring air, and exclaimed, "Better."

"Or maybe not," said Apolonia, now more curious than ever as if she detected more than a little bravado in Gini's voice. "And talk about legs"—she slapped her opponent's ass—"get a load of the legs on this amazon."

"So," murmured Bianca as if weighing the percentages, "I get to play against our number one, paired with," she looked over at the women's team in their sleek spandex black-and-orange uniforms, huddled as if conspiring among themselves against their mothers, "their number one: I like them odds."

Annette, asserting her captaincy, motioned them into a tight circle: "Now, ladies—"

"Now, girls," interjected Gini, as if all her heavy breathing was making her giddy. "And I prefer to think of us as girls once more, maybe for the last time."

Apolonia motioned over her shoulder to where the women's team was preparing a Princeton cheer for the great class of 1976. "They could all be our daughters—or granddaughters, if we'd reproduced early enough. No doubt the brilliant overachievers who are the bane of their mother's life—huh, Gini?"

"Notice," said Bianca. "They've all stored their cell phones, no social networking, no likes—no anxieties: they're all business."

"As I was saying, *girls*," said Annette, smiling and flicking a glance at Arthur in the stands, now joined by Erma. "Ladies, women, girls, once-upon-a-time daughters, the point of the charity event is to total as many games as possible, with each game worth ten thousand dollars to the charity supporting research into girls' eating disorders. So, our job is to check the killer instincts of the young fry: it's not about winning or losing but racking up as many games as possible (before we collapse). *And* there's no sudden death at six-all."

"Slow death," noted Apolonia. "No tiebreakers?"

"Yes, every set is like the fifth at Wimbledon—no tiebreakers. So, remember to remind your partner, who probably wants to win at any cost—she's programmed that way—that the name of the game is to accumulate as many games as possible. In fact, the two teams that total the most games win an extra forty thousand dollars, split four ways, to give to the charity of your choice. Thank you, Rambridge Partners."

"Jesus," exclaimed Apolonia, "that's a recipe for cardiac arrest."

"Hey, how about *this* charity," said Bianca mugging, looking for Jack in the stands.

"I guarantee you," assured Annette, "your partners will probably want to get the thing over with as quickly as possible: they've got better things to do. So our job is to keep things chugging along."

"Hey, Gini," laughed Bianca, "your partner, the gorgeous blonde (the Erma look-alike) seems a little stoned or hung over. You figure—good luck to you—they were all out partying until late last night."

Annette eased over to Gini, motioning to where their children sat in the stands. "Arthur texted me this morning that he and Erma danced the night away at the fifth"—a hard-eyed protective chin flex—"and visited the Carpaccios—of all things. I hope they didn't disturb your sleep."

Gini looked up from where she was stretching. "I was out to the world . . . and yes, Erma dug out those four Carpaccios from our storage locker and hung them in her room. I had no idea."

"So here we go, girls," shouted Annette. "Let's give a locomotion cheer for the reigning Ivy champs, Princeton's twelfth nationally ranked women's tennis team."

As they went into a huddle, holding hands, Gini found herself distracted, giddy with weirdly quixotic expectations—that she dared not even name—as she scanned the crowd entering the viewing stands for a familiar face.

Entering the court for warm-ups, Gini checked the program for the stats on her partner, Grace, the number-three player out of Newton, Massachusetts, a sophomore ranked number one in New England, and forty-seventh nationally when entering Princeton, with a 32–5 overall record going into the NCAAs in a week's time. Grace too had her lovely blonde hair pinned tightly under her cap, her brilliant blue eyes just level with Gini's as they went over strategy. Given Grace's powerful two-handed backhand—"my go-to shot"—it was quickly agreed that it made sense for her to hold down the add court. There was something about Grace—her fitness, her beauty, her youth—that both inspired and disconcerted Gini, a mirror image of her own past glories that made for some very odd moments during the match. For one, her muscle memory, as they began to rally, reprised her long-discarded eastern game, the forehand and backhand grips, the flat strokes she had, with such great difficulty, abandoned some twenty years before for the modern topspin power game. These antiquated strokes had emerged like specters of a previous life, dance steps learned at her mother's knee. So queer was the thing that she had to walk to the green tarp at the back of the court, close her eyes a moment, and re-situate herself in time and space.

She took two deep breaths and reminded herself: "Gini, you're a veteran with an upgraded game."

A moment later, she was back to her new/old self, her topspin shots flowing like second nature. Better yet, she was moving with speed and agility, seeing the seams of the ball as if they were basketballs, her shots rocketing off the dead center of her racquet with such singing beauty and pace that it almost brought tears to her eyes. Perhaps it was her young opponent, Michelle, a brunette even taller than Grace, with the most gorgeous suntanned legs and muscular upper body, who hit the ball with such power and pace and deep topspin that the ball was bouncing up around her shoulders. Prompting her to return the ball, power with power, leaping to generate each return. Her knees, her fragile knees, buoyant like the suspension of her Mercedes: resilient and tightly sprung—not a hint of pain—and on a hard court, no less! Instead of being hammered by Michelle's shots, she was absorbing her energy and using it to generate her own—an energy transfusion indulged with some very unladylike grunts and cries as she sailed through space like a mortal touched by the hand of a god.

Apolonia finally motioned her to the net as she went to pick up balls; her roommate's eyes crinkled in the warning expression of the experienced diagnostician, one who'd had to pick up the pieces of more of Jackson Hole's masters-of-the-universe glitterati than she cared to remember.

"What the fuck's with you?" Apolonia whispered. "Are you on speed or something worse? Keep this up and you'll have a separated shoulder or a torn ACL in nothing flat."

Gini shrugged. "I'm into it, I guess. Maybe it's Jack Rambridge's wine: the most expensive drunken binge of my life."

"Thank heaven you didn't try to drive last night; they were stopping cars on Route 1 left, right, and center." Gini glanced up in the stands to give Erma a wave, only to find her and Arthur in eager conversation . . . and, a moment later, joined by young Jacob Burrage.

As if suddenly struck by performance anxiety, Gini turned to her partner, Grace, and placed a steadying hand on her shoulder. "What's with Michelle? What are her weaknesses, her strengths, her comfort zone?"

Grace laughed, toweling off her sweating face and wiping down her arms.

"She doesn't have any weaknesses unless you consider hitting everything harder than her opponent a weakness. Maybe not laying off some wide shots to give herself enough time to recover the center of the court. But then she hits more winners off the angle, so she rarely even needs the time to recover. If I were you, not that we're actually trying to win or win big or anything, I'd just slow the pace; that way, she will do the same, so you're not running more than you're comfortable with. She's got a killer's instinct, so we don't want to goad her on. And I won't serve hard to Apolonia, so Michelle won't serve hard to you; otherwise, you'll end up with your back against the fence on returns; she has a wicked second serve that can jam you high into the racquet shoulder."

This was as much as Grace seemed comfortable offering in a friendly match against a teammate. Then, cocking her head: shy, reticent, searching for the words: "Ms. Wingate . . ."

"Gini."

"I just want you to know I'm so excited to be your partner, and believe it or not, I'm an English major as well, and taking Joyce Carol Oates's writing seminar; she has encouraged me to think about writing a first novel that would give readers an inside look at women's professional tennis. And well, I'm so-o looking forward to your talk at the forum on the publishing industry."

"Yes . . . let's do it," exclaimed Gini, a tad freaked out at the very idea, high-fiving her partner. "Now and forever . . ."

In later years, writing in her novel about the match (and the main character's early years on the Virginia Slims tour), Gini was never able to quite explain to herself or her readers what had come over her protagonist, or how she'd played at the level she did—or people said she did—because she couldn't explain the feeling of a wildfire rushing through every vein in her body, because such feelings couldn't be put into so many words, even as memory of those glorious sensations infused her writing, bursting like champagne bubbles at the back of her throat—the sheer exhilaration, the sheer life force, which, like a flame, burning bright and brighter, must soon consume itself. Feelings first invoked, so she would write, hitting backhand drills with John Chandler.

But what she did remember was how well she and Grace played as a team, matching each other shot for shot, as if reading off some intuited game plan, the way twins, mothers and daughters, sense the thoughts of the other. They barely spoke—had to speak: the simple joy in the snap of a well-hit tennis ball launched into inner space: the controlled energy that creates a perfect parabola, that gorgeous margin of safety, as if all life was amenable to such margins.

They slowed the pace to Michelle as long as she remained in the backcourt. Slower still when hitting to Apolonia or returning her serve. They left it to Apolonia to hit winners when she could, picking off easy volleys at the net. But Michelle made few unforced errors, and so, statistically, the majority of the errors came off her partner's racquet. Gini simply wasn't missing shots, blistering returns to Michelle, matching her stroke for stroke. Before they knew it, they were up 5–2 in the first set, with Gini serving for the set. On the changeover, Apolonia shouted out to her old teammate: "I don't know who you were sleeping with last night, but I'll take a dose of him."

Grace, perhaps thunderstruck, turned to Gini as if she didn't quite recognize the woman she was playing with. "You're so totally in the zone."

"Listen," said Gini, "I'll serve to their forehands, and maybe you can poach and flub a few volleys, or I'll pop up my first volley to Michelle and set her up for a passing shot."

"Not a problem."

And so they managed to gracefully lose four games, allowing Michelle to hit a bevy of passing shots by them. Then it was back to plan A, and within minutes they blew off three games and took the first set 7–5.

On the changeover, Gini resisted the urge to look up into the stands, where Arthur and Jacob Burrage were engaged in a spirited conversation with Erma: she was too alive to herself, an aliveness that youth can never know, an aliveness that allowed her to move effortlessly on the court, to meet every ball with perfect balance, to execute with controlled precision and absolute confidence. Running on pure instinct.

Gini and Grace had their strategy down pat: taking two games, losing two games, always letting their opponents creep back, and when necessary, setting Michelle up for the put-aways, losing the second set 8–6, while taking the third 6–4—mercifully so, since Apolonia was clearly losing steam. But they had accumulated thirty-six games, four more than the second doubles pair of Annette and Bianca, so earning a grand total of $360,000 for the charity event, and ten thousand each for the charity of their choice.

As Matt, joined by Arthur, posed for photographs with the eight players, Gini kept glancing nervously to the stands, where Erma sat in intense conversation with young Jacob Burrage, too preoccupied to be photographed with her mother and godmothers.

CHAPTER 22

If her performance on the tennis court had been exhilarating, cathartic, a death-defying highwire act, as she would one day describe it, her appearance at the publishing forum had an uncanny, almost occult power.

A mind on fire.

A mind racing so far ahead of itself that, as she sat confidently at the dais in the well of jam-packed McCosh 41, she was seeing around corners before there were corners. Never had her superpowers been more in abundance. Without her notes, left behind at the Marriott, she managed to rattle off her presentation with barely a pause for breath. All the while finding it harder and harder to believe she was actually seated in the well of McCosh, and not where she belonged, somewhere high in the back rows amid the rafters, often in the company of Jake Burrage, who bowed to her guidance in choosing his humanities distribution requirements. Even more disconcerting were the distractions of a mind preoccupied with vivid memories of the many lectures she'd attended in McCosh: Shakespeare, Homer, the English novel. A cavalcade of lectures peppered with the most exquisite ideas—whole pages of texts appearing before her eyes, including her elaborate lecture notes and fierce arguments with preceptors.

So immediate were these memories that when the forum reached the Q&A period, she panicked about being asked anything for fear she'd launch into an exposition on the father-son relationship of Prince Hal and the King in *Henry IV*, or Molly Bloom's sex life in *Ulysses*. Or worse, that her 1.0 version, her unfettered badass student self, would belt out some impolitic remark, bringing scandal and shame down on her and Tandem Press. One had to step so deftly these days. As if to escape such a looming catastrophe, her brain seemed to be playing tricks on her, visualizing herself—a transmigration of souls!—at the dais from a reverse angle, safely perched high up in the shadowy hinterland of the "gods" (as the back rows were known in her student days), where once she'd hung out with Jake and a scattering of inattentive, stoned, or slumbering students and athletes, where Jake might reach over and deftly rub her thigh if she was nodding off at a particularly boring lecture, where, even now, she thought she could make out Erma seated next to a well-behaved and attentive young Jacob Burrage, yet another haunting, if not vaguely threatening, flashback to her own day.

Only the frantic signaling of the moderator, a dreadful middle-aged, already-graying-haired woman professor, latest English Department wunderkind, a Virginia Woolf scholar who pandered to the worst instincts of her students (axes to grind, crosses to bear), alerted her that the last question had been for her.

"Could you repeat that?"

"Ms. Wingate, as one of the most prominent women in the publishing industry today, don't you feel that publishers have a duty to address issues of women's rights, along with the wider issues of inequality and racism in society?"

She peered up into the shifting shades, past the colorful middle-aged reunion goers (hard of hearing) gathered in the front, where teammates Bianca and Apolonia were seated (absent Annette, a last-minute replacement for her son at the Athletes for Christ forum), and Gareth, faithful Gareth, then to the middle rows, from where the complaining voice had emanated. Instead of her pat answer, something to the effect that publishers, like newspapers, like great universities, the guarantors of free speech and discourse, must always bend over backward to make sure all voices and viewpoints have a say . . . something else flowed from her lips, as if she had simply taken down a book, one from that infinite shelf of volumes now at her fingertips, out of which her thoughts flowed like a spring freshet.

"I often think of how my father, or even my late husband"—roping in Erma—"a classicist and a scientist, publisher and senior editor at Tandem Press, would have answered that question. And even though these times are different from their times, they are, and they aren't." She raised her eyes to the shadowy gods and nodded. "True art is too complex to follow or even echo any party line. Art that seeks to reflect the truth about our life and times is never easy or comforting, often expressing unpopular, even offensive opinions. Our heroes end up faltering, our convictions are trashed, our notions of good manners and fair play litter the gutter. Nevertheless, we still find ourselves moved, our souls touched, hopefully identifying with characters we enjoy while sympathizing with those we don't, because we understand them better for having walked in their shoes."

A woman questioner, another graduate student she figured, by the tone of grievance, jumped to her feet in the middle distance and waved an angry hand.

"But don't you think art should attempt to right the wrongs of history, to make judgments about the past and so help in the fight against inequality?"

"Oh." She smiled graciously and sat back to hide her exasperation. "Don't you think walking in another's shoes—whether Raskolnikov or Dorothea Brooke's Casaubon, even a chauvinist pig like James Ramsay." She saw an entire page of *To the Lighthouse* appear in her mind's eye, after recently publishing the definitive biography of Virginia Woolf. "Even if Woolf suffered, and maybe worse, at the hands of an overbearing father, who draws our sympathy in Virginia's prose—is worth the journey? And so softens the past's painful bewitchment of our souls? That the best humankind has created is always life-affirming, even if we might not fully agree? My father called it the dichotomy of Plato and Aristotle: that all of life comes down to an interplay between the Platonic and the Aristotelian modes, between theory—ideas, forms, imaginings—and concrete facts." She gazed out at her audience, hoping to find a sympathetic look on her daughter's face . . . if not the young man at her elbow to whom she addressed her next remark. "As my father once described it: we are like the scientist at her lab bench, testing out a hypothesis, looking to our literary lights to ask the right question that will lead to a demonstrable answer, a result that is proof positive. Even if it means having to dig deeper than deep, to challenge the existing paradigm, challenging the very values that have been handed down to her, until finding herself in the clear, she can publish her results to the world: a thing good and true and beautiful in its own right, touching our hearts with its glittering elegance."

(Had she not heard such a proof the night before?)

Not surprisingly, the moderator took immediate umbrage, so she thought, with her rather poetic metaphor.

"Isn't that a bit self-indulgent, leaving it to science to tell us what to believe—even worse than a discredited artist, a flawed but captivating artist who may well lead the gullible astray?" The professor turned to her student constituency in the middle ranks of the lecture hall as if in hopes of support or praise.

At this, she could barely suppress a knowing smile, the trap well sprung as she scanned those many volumes tumbling through her mind to launch her refutation. She saw Bianca and Apolonia scowl with glee and give her the thumbs-down: *ditch the bitch*. And her father's magisterial face rise before her.

"Well, Plato in his *Republic* would certainly agree with you. And since he probably considered himself a scientist of the unseen, that ultrareal realm of perfection behind all delusional phenomena, Plato would allow very little leeway for the arts lest the wrong ideas do irreparable harm to young minds. But I think, if I recall my father's thoughts on the subject (a classics major from the great class of 1931, who helmed Tandem Press for over thirty years), he always said, when in doubt, better to side with Aristotle, who took a more commonsense attitude on these issues, who liked to describe the artistic process in terms of *energeia*, in effect allowing the potential inherent in certain striking characters, possibly based on real people, to actualize themselves through their acts—the plot—thus setting them on a narrative path to triumph over hardship, or even to ruin and tragic waste, when doing the right thing might lead to disaster, and so demonstrating the real-world outcomes of a moral law in action. The greatest writers, like Homer, Dante, and Tolstoy, managed this by letting their characters discover a better path by virtue of feeling, seeing deeply, considering how their actions might affect others. In a sense, discovering what God or an existing moral law might rightly expect of them."

Her eyebrows shot up, intrigued, maybe even inspired to start that languishing novel of hers. A hand was raised in the first row, and she was pleasantly surprised to see Grace, her young doubles partner of the morning.

"But surely for today's authors, for those contemplating a writing career, the world is a lot more complex, the pitfalls more real, the vital issues more burning. That's a lot of responsibility, a lot of weight on the shoulders for those of us just starting out."

"Ah"—and she had to restrain herself from rushing over to plant a kiss on Grace's flushed cheek: a put-away at the net—"I imagine every time and place sees its moment as of special, perhaps cosmic import. Even in a world without a God or gods, in a time of political turmoil, Wordsworth's lines still ring true and offer consolation and hope: 'Whose dwelling is the light of setting suns . . . A motion and a spirit, that impels all thinking things, all objects of all thought.' It is unfashionable today to even suggest that art instructs, given the twentieth century's history of propaganda and today's distortions of fact that now fill the internet and social media. And no decent writer—or publisher—should blatantly offer instruction per se. But neither should we forsake the responsibility to broadly educate the young, to at least suggest more noble ideals: that truth, of a kind, does actually exist even if it must sometimes be panned for in fast and chilly flowing streams. That the greatest literature expands our experience of the world and humanity and so requires us to delve into the most hidden corners of our hearts."

A middle-aged African American, a male alumnus in a gorgeous Reunions jacket, stood and gestured broadly.

"Ms. Wingate, you mentioned your father was a classicist, as were you, salutatorian no less. I too was a classics major and am now a professor of classics. What if I told you that Classics with a capital C was a cheat code for mastering whiteness, a cheat code—the mastery of damaging and distasteful suppositions, which was a way of marginalizing my own personhood (where I came from)—and constitutes a history of oppression that extols Western authority in its subordination of other races. Some of us now in the field are dedicated to the struggle of overturning a historically proud and elitist discipline built on a Eurocentric conception of intellectual inheritance. What can you do as a publisher to help remake the discipline for a changing world?"

She stared for a moment at her handsome interrogator, her eyes drawn to counting the tigers rampant on his jacket, a perfectly pleasant face but with a hard, unyielding look in his eye. Her gaze then shifted upward to the gods as if in appeal for help, to her younger self seated with her boyfriend, that young woman who was now, oddly, the center of attention on the dais. But her younger self didn't even understand the question: hell's bells, she was the first woman to graduate from the Princeton Classics Department, summa cum laude, no less—and yes, salutatorian. She'd broken down the ramparts of this all-male bastion of patriarchal authority—first at Princeton, then in the publishing industry—and had demonstrated, beyond a shadow of a doubt, that a woman could not just master the field but set an example of intellectual excellence while extolling the value of the Stoic tradition as something worthy of the modern woman. Hadn't she published women scholars—African American women who brought attention to the lives of women of color, of women in the ancient world, the horror of slavery? Was she now to allow herself to be lumped in with some disagreeable idea of white male privilege—whiteness—and so have everything she'd achieved and fought for—racial equality, the great strides in women's studies—dumped in the wastebin of history?

Perhaps a little misdirection was called for.

"Goodness, my days in the classics department were many moons ago (did I hear rumors of dropping the requirement to learn Latin and Greek?), and I'm not sure I'd much like to be a woman in fourth-century-BC Athens or first-century-AD Rome, even if they could be educated and own property and served as priestesses. But then, they were a hell of a lot better off than their contemporaries living elsewhere at the time. Academic subjects have always been influenced by the larger culture of which they're a part—and sure, classics have a toxic history; so do nuclear physics and anthropology. As a publisher today, all we can do is try to publish the best voices, wherever they come from. Words are difficult and tricky things . . ." She paused her mind's Daytona 500 at a blinking warning light as she considered mentioning her father's reference to Proust and the fetish for beautiful words, only to raise her blue pencil. "There are lies, damn lies, and statistics, and marketing is the lingua franca of the internet. I like to think that books are our last and best hope for sanity as we seek for enduring values—a moral stance, a moral center that is as good for us as it was for Homer, Dante, and Cervantes, and yes, Twain's *Huckleberry Finn*, where Huck discovers his own racism and finds an innate moral center that accepts Jim as a flawed yet generous human being like himself. Books written from the heart, but where the author resists the temptation to endlessly rehash the crying injustices of the moment—or even the past, which a hundred years from now will no longer so engage the reader. Or reinvent the wheel to satisfy the critics and her peers of the moment, who tries for stunning effects, or scintillating texture, or finally falls in love with her own mastery of intricate language and so loses her reader in a pyrotechnic display. When all is said and done, do we not still feel some warmth when sitting by a crackling fire with Nestor's truth telling?"

She gave her best convivial smile and rubbed her chilly hands to demonstrate, even as her interlocutor continued the chase.

"It is not simply a matter of rehashing the crying injustices of the moment. The classics have been embraced by white Eurocentric colonialists and even now by white supremacists. It's not a question of change or even inclusivity, but of a systemic, entrenched privilege, both white and socioeconomic privilege, Eurocentric intellectual privilege that adjudicates how we think and what we learn."

Again, her face rose to the gods in supplication, or possibly to enlist her younger self, the intrepid woman she was to become, feeling the energy of all her days course through her, along with a thousand-thousand memories, millions of pages of text spilling through her mind, as if a great library had opened its door, familiar landscapes and windswept seas, all in hopes of bolstering her once-fearless gaze upon the male of the species. The *energeia* that could take on challenges old and new. And so, she dialed up her patented enigmatic, if patient, smile that could be depended upon to throw off her most tenacious pursuers.

"Tolerance, I think; it really all comes down to tolerance." And she swept her arms like a high priestess over the dais. "Picture it, if you can, a young girl sitting by her father in front of a lovely painting by Carpaccio in one of the smaller scuolas of Venice, an enchanting painting of Augustine seated in his study—an Aladdin's cave of a place filled with books and antique art objects and even an astrolabe and armillary sphere, where our good saint, deftly disguised as a Renaissance scholar, stares out his window lost in memory. What we might think of as a *Kunstkammer* or *Wunderkammer* or cabinet of curiosities, so popular among the well-to-do in the Renaissance. Now this is really my father's store, even as I am about to represent it as mine and so make it yours, which is what the best writers do. My father was a man of the old school, of Boston Brahmin stock, whose scholarly grandfather moved from Boston to New York with William Dean Howells. The way he explained Carpaccio's Augustine to me was as if we were staring into a glass darkly, a mirror that reflected both our world and the many worlds of the painting. 'Funny thing is,' he explained to that diffident seventeen-year-old, 'I don't really like Augustine for beans, and I doubt you would either, if you knew how he deprecated women as the bearers of sin and temptation.' Augustine, according to my father, made a virtue out of intolerance. He pushed Christian rulers and magistrates, not just to persuade heretics to join the church, but compel them, and by all means, including execution if they refused. He claimed that it was God's order to compel allegiance and that, by such compulsion, the will to conform would arise and they would be saved from the danger of damnation." She paused and gave her head a doleful shake in uncanny imitation of her father. "Later, I remember my father turning to me as we viewed a particularly gruesome harrowing of hell—a terrifying mosaic in Santa Maria Assunta on Torcello—saying with a mystified nodding of his head: 'Hah, maybe this puts our Augustine in perspective. Persecution driven by such charitable motives once seemed beneficent: it was no kindness to indulge people in error lest they end up in the Gehenna.'"

She blinked rapidly, a little aghast (the slithering serpents), less for having revealed such a private moment than for so effortlessly reproducing the speech patterns of her father, and a moment returned to her with such wrenching clarity.

"'And yet,' so my father went on, 'such intolerance is nowhere to be found in Carpaccio's vision of Saint Augustine. In fact, just the opposite; we sense a man of letters, possibly a man of science—or even a depiction of the great Venetian printer, Aldus Manutius, who was an admirer of Galileo—certainly a kindly and compassionate gentleman, hardly a rabid ideologue.'" She nodded, a thousand-yard, trance-like stare. "Was this the more sympathetic personage Carpaccio saw fit to depict? Perhaps in the artist's imagination a compassionate, even worldly scholar, steeped in the classics, at home in a tolerant Venice—even on the very cusp of the Reformation, an oasis of intellectual freedom and learning and, yes, book publishing. Did Carpaccio have any idea what a monster Augustine—or Augustine's ideas—had helped to create, that saw the destruction of countless pagan temples and works of art and Lord knows how many ancient texts of philosophy, literature, and science? Not to mention, in Carpaccio's day, the wars of religion brewing just over the Alps, wars that would wipe out a third of Germany's population. And don't get me going on the Spanish Inquisition. But of course, Carpaccio couldn't have known all that was to come, or even all that was past. Perhaps the artist was simply deluded, living in an eternal present—like we here today—and had no idea how Augustine, drawing on more Plato than was good for him, had derailed Greek science. After all, Aristarchus had hypothesized as early as the third century BC that the earth revolved around the sun—that fact, so explained my father, 'would probably have been confirmed in ancient times, but for the insidious misdirection of Platonism—instead of taking another eighteen hundred years until Copernicus finally worked it out from the data he'd so meticulously accumulated.'"

She paused, on a roll, reluctant to reduce speed for the off-ramp, when a score of new vistas opened before her fervent eyes. A glance to her small cheering section in the first row, the delighted, encouraging smiles of Bianca and Apolonia and Gareth, now joined by Annette, blew a following wind in her sails.

"So maybe we should simply settle for Carpaccio's happy myth and leave it at that? A lovable old Augustine, a true Renaissance man, perhaps, as my father conjectured, a portrait of the Venetian publisher, Aldus Manutius, a humanist and scholar of Latin and Greek, who published textbooks and the classics in affordable editions for a growing readership. 'For Augustine'—I can almost hear my father's richly cadenced voice—'can hardly be held accountable for the crimes done in his name: How could he have guessed to what ends his words would be put? Nor would our saintly subject have objected to such useful myths, the stories we make up in families, communities, and nations, not unlike Venice, for example, which constructed an elaborate communal origin myth by stealing and translating the bones of Saint Mark from Alexandria to Venice in the eleventh century, or in its civic ceremony where a gold ring is cast into the Adriatic to symbolize the city's marriage to the sea—the kind of mythology that offers emotional support and promotes loyalty to a shared tradition and history.'" She touched a knowing finger to her eye. "But Plato, who inspired so much of Augustine's thought, would not have been pleased: myths, stories, fables distract from the unseen world of the Forms. Plato would rather we disfavor the senses for purely intellectual beliefs in the existence of the perfect—to the detriment of the good or even useful. This amounted to an attack on the mainstream scientific tradition of the Greeks, which relied on empirical observation."

She could sense the moderator's growing alarm, perhaps an uneasy shiftiness in her audience, and so began seeking that off-ramp, even as her mind was eager to explain Plato's fundamental flaws as a thinker, how untethered ideas wreak havoc on humanity, how Aristotle (hadn't Jake said as much?) provided the best model for a life at peace with itself: *eudaimonia*, as the Greeks called it—a life drawn to one's natural talents and proclivities, a life lived to the best of one's abilities. And she hadn't even gotten to the Enlightenment and the arguments for toleration from Spinoza, Bayle, Lessing, Goethe, Voltaire, or the example of William Penn's Quaker experiment just down the road.

She raised her hands in self-mocking surrender at her breathless torrent of words and gave a mighty laugh of sheer audacity.

"So . . . I'm sure you're just dying to know where this seventeen-year-old daughter and budding classicist came out on the matter before us: tolerance in the academy. Did she embrace the artist's—Carpaccio's—vision, or his subject's? Did she find sympathy with an old theologian's reverie on the death of his friend Jerome in faraway Jerusalem, anticipating his own? Or did she listen to her Unitarian father and—yes, a lily-white classicist who had a big axe to grind against the depredations of Augustine and his ilk, whom he blamed for the destruction of Greco-Roman civilization—a civilization more inclusive and tolerant than any other until our own day? I see him even now seated in the oratory of the Scuola di San Giorgio (speak to me later if you require directions to visit the Carpaccios), sighing gravely as he shook his head and quoted to me Saint Jerome's glee in a letter to Augustine, where he'd reflected on the city of Rome he'd left behind, where the old temples were being abandoned to decay: 'The gilded Capitol falls into disrepair; dust and cobwebs cover all Rome's temples. The city shakes on its foundations, and a stream of people hurries, past half-fallen shrines, to the tombs of the martyrs.'"

She shook her head as if in sadness at such a scene.

"An empire of toleration, sporting gods and goddesses, priests and priestesses, scores of religions, and thousands of works of literature, science, and philosophy—the greater part all lost to us. A tragedy translated to me at seventeen in my father's voice, and passed on now from me to you . . ." She paused either for effect or captivated by the notion that perhaps that very same letter from Jerome had been lying on Augustine's desk, to which he was replying, pen poised with a heavy heart. "A letter, a voice, a description of a crumbling, degraded, and lost world that my father, once upon a time, evoked for me at an impressionable age in a sigh of despair when he recited the final words of the oracle at Delphi, as he was prone to do when we were out sailing: 'Go tell the king Apollo's lovely hall is fallen to the ground. No longer has the god his house, his bay-leaf oracle, his singing stream. The waters that spoke are now stilled.'"

Again, she paused, as if she might have been listening for the last echoes of that singing stream, just barely controlling the reins. Her face lifted to the gods and another face, her father's voice faded in hers to be replaced by Jake's wagging Groucho Marx eyebrows as his irrefutable logic had the last word, as it had the night before.

"Tolerance, for all . . . I suppose—the only saving grace that is available to us in this troubled, uncertain life, this imperfect world. And, oh yes, enchantment in this disenchanted digital rat race we lead. That is the true role of the publisher, the writer: to re-enchant our small corner of the universe for our children and our children's children."

CHAPTER 23

The four teammates lounged on the maple- and elm-shaded grass of Cannon Green (the butt of an ancient revolutionary war cannon planted at its center) while waiting for the start of the P-rade, that long-standing Princeton Reunions tradition where the oldest classes to the youngest march in procession through the campus. A gaudy, high-spirited, crazily attired affair of communal nostalgia accompanied by precision-stepping, trumpet-blaring high school bands and befeathered, fantastically attired (think Aztec gods or birds of paradise) Mummers from nearby Philadelphia. Occasionally, an antique fire engine or orange Model T put in an appearance, and even more rarely, at least in the living memory of the Shirelles, a "tame" tiger, somewhat ancient and threadbare, led on chains by professional handlers.

Reminded of this by someone in the waiting crowd and accusations of "cruelty to animals" leveled by the ASPCA, Bianca raised a paw to the cooling shade of the stalwart elms: "That's me . . ."

The Shirelles were in a titter, having just been informed by their class president that they were to lead the class in the P-rade, carrying placards on long poles emblazoned with their grainy *Nassau Herald* freshman photos and captions touting their "firsts": first women's tennis team, first women's Ivy League champions, first Princeton woman to play Wimbledon (Annette in mixed doubles with her husband), first woman to run a major publishing house.

"Hey," said Bianca, inspecting their signs and squeezing Apolonia's bicep, "first Princeton woman to shag a Princeton president."

"Shush," exclaimed Apolonia, "someone might hear you." She had been staring off at the ivy-clad walls of Nassau Hall, remembering her terrifying moments with the provost.

All, except Gini, were exhausted by the charity match of the morning and, like most of the marching multitudes, caught up in nostalgic ruminations about their student days, precisely what the P-rade was designed to do, a seasonal, recurring, communal affair not unlike, so it occurred to each of the four women at various times that afternoon, the sumptuous parade of Venetian notables so famously depicted in Gentile Bellini's *Procession in Saint Mark's Square* in Venice's Accademia. Gini had this and much else on her mind as she gazed around, distractedly taking feverish notes on her iPhone: all grist for her mill.

"What's up with her?" asked Bianca, still in her tennis gear and in clear earshot of Gini.

"Taking notes for that novel she never completed," said Apolonia, an ironic tilt of her head. "The one that was going to be about *us* and her days playing the women's tour."

"Which she should've done long ago," said Annette in a scolding, if friendly, tone. "Just think, she could've immortalized our years here, our championship days, all leading up to her Wimbledon crown—at least in fiction."

Gini cocked her head at this spirited banter, a little wild-eyed, as if spurred by the sporadic drumbeat of a nearby marching band warming up the sticks. She'd been remembering the last time she'd seen Jake, right here on Cannon Green, standing with his mother after graduation. The only time she'd seen him in jacket and tie. Something she'd said, or meant to say, that might have changed everything, which even her supercharged memory refused to reveal. "Oh, there's time yet," she retorted to the gentle ribbing of her teammates, "all the time in the world . . ." And she'd waved airily, pausing to apply Annette's sunscreen to her nose and cheeks and tuck loose strands of hair under her Reunions cap. "I was just thinking, what if one were able to visualize"—and she gestured again to the jam-packed upper campus, where thousands waited to march and thousands more to watch—"all the memories of all these folks summoned forth by these all so-o familiar scenes. There are moments when I feel like I'm reliving my student days like yesterday."

"You'd blow a circuit—that's what," said Apolonia, squinting over her dark glasses at her doubles partner. "You're not tripping on something, are you? I mean, your performance on the court and at the publishing forum was freaky enough—channeling your father like that. You even had his intonation and hand gestures down pat."

"Here comes the Old Guard," interjected Bianca, standing now and stretching. A procession of tiger-striped golf carts began passing, conveying the oldest alumni, some from the thirties. "Class of 1936, his eightieth! He's got to be well over a hundred. And God bless Methuselah. What must he be thinking, seeing the likes of us?"

"Wishing he had the likes of you around in his day to jump his bones," offered Apolonia, keeping an eye out for Daltrey, for whom, even after a one-night stand and performance issues, she found she had developed a vague, even nostalgic fondness. "Talk about memories, born during the First World War, probably fought in the Second. And get a load of that gorgeous granddaughter marching by his golf cart—genes to die for, huh."

Gini, whose mind seemed permanently in past-recall mode (partly inspired by the cooling breezes of that Canadian high), picked up her sign pole and examined her black-and-white freshman photograph blown up to near life size, her hair down past her shoulders, eyes a brilliant sheen, a pleased smile that she'd checked off that first, possibly second, item on her life's to-do list. Tempted now to unleash her chignon tucked firmly underneath her baseball cap.

"Just think," said Gini with a hint of wistfulness, "he could have known Fitzgerald at Reunions, read *The Great Gatsby* in a first edition as a teenager, hobnobbed at the Princeton Club with Fitzgerald's editor, Max Perkins."

"He could have seen Ellsworth Vines and Alice Marble play," said Annette, passing around her SPF 100 sunscreen and wondering if she might bring up the subject of Arthur and Erma.

Among the multitudes marching and waiting to march, such memories were hardly in short supply, stirred to life by the names and aging faces of classmates and those no longer with us, whose military service was commemorated by the scattering of folded triangular flags, white stars on blue, carried by their comrades. A panoply of memory, as Gini had already detected, a thousand layers deep. A theater of memory, of on- and off-stage voices, of heroines and villains, of tragedy and comedy.

Where the old marchers gaze upon the youngsters lining the parade route, gazing out at the youths they once were, while the young, waiting their turn, get to contemplate the future they will inherit—the shoes they will try to fill, the aged masks of their predecessors that will soon enough be theirs.

If such a collation of stratified memory could, in aged oak barrels, be stored, they would fill Jack Rambridge's wine cellars for an eternity and some. Not that there weren't moments when Gini felt there wasn't yet more to be drunk to the dregs, the half-full glass tightly grasped and held up for inspection, which she was loathe to set down. The thing she had failed to do when first spying Jake and his mother on Cannon Green after graduation: the instinct denied or thwarted.

"Oh, there's Jack," shouted Bianca as the fiftieth began to parade by. She scampered out to give a lumbering Jack Rambridge (holding aloft a sign: *In Vino Veritas*) a big kiss on his sweaty cheek, while he whispered something in her ear as she swung on his arm before returning to the fold of her own waiting class. She high-fived her teammates with a cryptic, "Lear's all fueled to fly."

Apolonia yelled and waved to a lanky Daltrey Assingham, who, dignified and professorial in mien, was accompanied by a frisky daughter, a tall, attractive brunette who had a firm grasp on her father's arm, as if he might escape. Daltrey blew Apolonia a kiss and doffed his broad-brimmed orange hat, his large brimming eyes just visible behind his sunglasses. She gave him a thumbs-up even as her heart suddenly ached at her cowardice in leaving her Christopher back in Jackson Hole.

"We're on, ladies," shouted Annette, pumped from her triumph at the Athletes for Christ forum. She gave her husband a hand up from where he'd been napping on the grass of Cannon Green. "Fall in, mount up, and let's head out. Who's got my sunscreen?"

And like Bellini's scarlet-clad grandees of five hundred years before parading San Marco Square, the Shirelles took their place at the head of their class, just behind the two standard-bearers holding aloft their class numerals, less in pride at their accomplishments and more in gratitude just to be around for their bit parts in this ritual moment, suspended in time between those older and younger, as if buoyed on an ardent, singing stream of memory. For the power of ritual lies in its rhythmic repetitions through time, the enchantment of the transcendent when past, present, and future merge as one: shimmering, resplendent, a window onto a momentary state of grace. Yes, a *Wunderkammer.* Along with the promise of a recurrent springing forth, of godlike immortality, if not as individuals, then as part of an extended family—that outward spiraling galaxy of glittering, gaudy promise and affection passing in review in a little over two hours.

Gini could barely control herself, a mare champing at the bit (spooked by tiger masks, tiger tails, tiger mascots—tigers, tigers everywhere!), seething with uncanny, indecipherable sensations, her energy still fresh and yearning to be spent, on what exactly, she would be hard pressed to say. She felt intoxicated with life, if still in a mild state of shock after her performance on court and at the publishing forum; her mind now shuttled in a feverish feedback loop between the present and her student days as they wended their way down campus past so many familiar scenes (the white, marble-clad Greek Revival faces of Whig-Clio once again bringing a lump to her throat), as the waiting classes poised to join the P-rade got younger and younger, now with recalcitrant teenagers bobbing in and out, now parents holding the hands of young children—giddy with awe at the spangled and befeathered Mummers—now harnessed with baby carriers and pushing strollers. It was orange and black to the Gothic rooftops, where the leering gargoyles peered down from the rooflines of buildings carrying the names of rich donors lost to time, names seared into memory, names that might in years to come draw scrutiny for their ill-gotten wealth, possibly derived from slavery or the exploitation of immigrant workers.

Gini squinted behind her sunglasses, as these names kept eliding into more recently recollected names on the wall of young Jacob's room—Johnny von Neumann, for one, Alan Turing another. And then there had been that book left by her keys on his desk, Ray Kurzweil's *The Singularity Is Near*, yet another key to an unexplored *Wunderkammer*, the futurist contents serving as plot points for her novel in the making, if not her new life.

As she marched, things seemed to further merge themselves, as if the book talk of last night, the spirited ideas tossed between them, as she reclined in her La-Z-Boy and Jacob in his Herman Miller, could just as easily have been a bull session out of their undergraduate days. Every memory adding to a creeping, unimaginable sensation that she'd really been with Jake the whole time, while the near blackout of what must have been a night's extravagant lovemaking, was instead filled in with a hundred sexual escapades of their student days. As if time itself was coalescing and compacted into an eternal present, a singular explosive act of nuclear fusion, even now fueling her present high. There were moments when she felt as if she'd slipped her mortal bonds, surfing space-time, living a glorious dream frontloaded out of their lovemaking and her soundest, most restful sleep in years. An endorphin rush to end all rushes. A sleeping beauty woken to a renewed, more creative life where she'd finally become the author she always knew herself to be.

Had she been drugged? She kept seeing those two gleaming green capsules in her outstretched palm, and the third proffered with a wry, devil-take-the-hindmost shooting of his eyebrows. But she didn't care; all that mattered was that most potent of aphrodisiacs, that shimmering masked figure of a beckoning Fortuna in the shadows, James's donnée, the idea, the plot point to launch a thousand ships. She was bewitched by the possibilities, turning over names like cards in a tarot deck: keys to a destiny still within reach. Yes, it was Alan Turing, as in the Turing test. She could barely restrain herself, holding her banner high as if it read: First Wimbledon crown and bestseller. Crazy! Had she just possibly slipped over some invisible event horizon and so found herself spinning down a black hole, a nostalgic orange-and-black hole! She skipped a step or two, like a young girl thumbing her nose at the improbabilities, goaded on by the cheering members of a younger class draped in Hawaiian shirts and leis, raising her placard high and so aptly emblazoned with her gorgeous freshman-year photo. She could hardly be held responsible for her actions of the night before, not in this exuberant din of locomotive cheers and the constant echo of names called out between the marchers and those lining the parade route, waiting to march in turn.

"Teller," she announced (another name on young Jacob's power wall) with an incantatory wave of her free hand. "Edward Teller . . ." Of course, she'd edited his autobiography. Teller still spoke with a strong Hungarian accent, even after so many years in America. But the voice she heard in her head was not Teller's.

"Extraterrestrial intelligence, if it exists, would have to communicate in unintelligible code. Globular clusters . . . too far apart to communicate." She'd been watching his hands, spellbound . . . something about young Jacob's hands—his father's hands—as they danced before her as if struggling with an invisible foe.

"Penuel."

"Penuel?"

"The face of God, like you, the face of my angel."

"So, that's where you've been . . ."

"Swinging birches, yes."

But there the transmission ended—her bonds loosened—like everything else about her seduction in young Jacob's room, with a delicious, if slightly scary, question mark. As if the more vivid her memories of the distant past, the less clear those of just hours before—sensuous avatars that slipped her attempts to waylay them.

She murmured the Frost half in hope of elucidation: "I'd like to get away from earth awhile, And then come back to it and begin over."

"Yes, yes—yes . . ." She screamed to the cheering crowd, pumping her fist.

And where had that young man got to, and where was her daughter, for that matter? Neither, slipping away together, had congratulated her after the tennis match and publishing forum. As she gazed around, with a fixed, serene smile to hide a vague panic now touching the spiral arms of her galactic mood, she caught sight of the quatrefoil windows of the art museum, their steadfast presence invoking again the voice of her father, in whose company she'd marched in the P-rade as a little girl holding on to the tiger tail attached to his orange-and-black-checked jacket. Ritual moments whisking her back half a millennium or more on the wings of her father's voice.

"Look how Bellini has so perfectly captured these gentlemen here in their white robes. They're members of the confraternities. You can see how they're eyeing—a tad uneasily, don't you think?—the noblewomen on the sidelines all decked out, the sumptuary laws being suspended, dressed to the nines in their crimson gowns embroidered in gold silk, trimmed with furs of ermine and fox, bedecked in glittering jewels and pearls from the exotic East."

And oddly enough, Apolonia, marching next to Gini, whose memories, though more circumspect and bittersweet, had found herself transported as well by those same quatrefoil windows, and the kindness and astuteness of Daltrey Assingham, who reminded her not a little of John Proctor in his more reflective moments, as he had once pointed out the parallels in the Accademia's Bellini to their beloved P-rade.

"Whereas ours is a thoroughly democratic celebration befitting a great American university, with no distinctions of either social or office rank: no functionaries of the chancery, nor clergy leading their patriarch, nor members of the Scuole Grandi jockeying for pride of place."

How they had laughed, given the unbridled ambitious souls that made up the Princeton community.

"And you, the doge, pretending to be university president, standing in his viewing box at the end of the P-rade, decked out in sumptuous robes of orange and black, throwing me a big kiss."

"I throw every pretty undergraduate a kiss—thoroughly democratic."

Bianca, even with Jack Rambridge's fueled Learjet, was feeling a bit low. Unusual for this larky eternal optimist, whom she always prided herself on being. Surrounded by successful life stories on every hand, she felt as if hers hadn't lived up to early promise. When, once upon a time, she'd been the real star among her roommates, pulling out that fourth or fifth clinching point in match play, easily the most lusted after (the only one unattached), when she'd played the Rachmaninoff piano concerto with the university orchestra to a cheering audience of thousands in Alexander Hall (whose dowdy Romanesque visage they had recently passed as the P-rade wound along), and was well reviewed by the *New York Times*, toasted to the skies in the music department, leading the Shirelles in arch sings, and bringing tears to the eyes of her contemporaries. What a future had been predicted for her!

And now, to add insult to injury, her bizarre conversation with young Jacob Burrage on the way to the fiftieth last night had her more than a little spooked. Not just her failure to land a devastated Jake Burrage in Venice all those years ago, then at the very pinnacle of her powers (after which her life had seemingly tipped into a downward spiral), but the lingering sadness of that overnight train journey to Vienna, haunted by the face of a young man that might have been hers.

Thank God, her beloved parents had not lived to see their daughter reduced to dog walking (more remunerative than she dared admit) and piano lessons.

"Oh, girls"—she fought back tears as she lowered and raised her sign, emblazoned with a blurry photo of a gangly young woman with pigtails and glasses—"I feel like that's my head on a spike up there, like my whole life has been nada since teaming up with you guys on the court and the Shirelles."

"Oh, Bianca," cried Apolonia, "you're the best doubles partner a girl could ever want, and the best preserved of any of us—well, who knows about Gini? And with a handsome and supremely talented son who got it all from his mother. You just need to meditate more and say your gratitudes."

The two embraced and high-fived with their signs.

Annette, marching hand in hand with her tall husband, immediately rode to the rescue. "Bianca, you played beautifully today, better than me, and remember how many times you clinched that fourth point for us, and how we always gathered around to cheer you on."

"Yeah, because you guys had wiped out your competition and I was always struggling to win my matches."

"Yes," weighed in Gini, "but you won them; you never gave up. Not then, not now."

"Oh, you guys: that pressure to come through almost killed me."

They surrounded Bianca and hugged her, high-fiving their signs.

"And speaking of then and now," said Annette, "we shouldn't forget the other girls on the team. I feel badly we don't celebrate them in some way."

Their number five had died many years before of breast cancer. Their number-six player had ended up in an abusive marriage and had mental health issues, and, for whatever reason, had completely disappeared. The remaining members of the team had been mostly freshmen when they were seniors and so belonged to other classes and Reunions cycles.

"I say prayers for Sheila every Sunday in church," said Annette. "Remember that funny laugh she had coming off the court, like she was a little embarrassed, like she couldn't believe she was really in the game."

"I've tried reaching out to Sheila over the years," said Apolonia, "but she's lost to the alumni office, no forwarding address or email."

"Do you suppose we were such a tight crew," ventured Bianca, "that we made them feel—I don't know—unwanted, unappreciated. I've been there, now . . ."

"It had to be tough on them," said Gini, "what with Bianca always winning the four singles and the rest of us the doubles point."

"The Shirelles, forever young," sang out Bianca, figuring better to be a survivor than the alternative.

As their class in the P-rade finished, marched past the historic buildings of the old campus, and turned downhill toward the newer dorms and the expanded science facilities, Apolonia found herself overcome with helpless nostalgia. Every Princeton cheer summoned up another fraught moment of her student liaisons with John Proctor, if now assuaged by happy memories of all his letters and books arriving in recent years, loving missives written after his wife's death, poetic lines about aging and loneliness in which he questioned his marriage, his legacy, all the while chastising himself for not divorcing and marrying her.

"Your pregnancy should have been enough to give me the courage to break with one life and embrace the one that beckoned in your unsatiated smile."

She waved off this memory (the truth never told), as if fearing for a split second that she'd mistakenly spoken out aloud. Sparking a reprise in the same gravelly voice as she lay in John Proctor's arms, nearly hypnotized by oscillating plum-green spates of canal-reflected light on the ceiling of the Pensione Seguso.

"Bricks and mortar are easy; it's just a matter of money. It's the people, the faculty, the researchers, the students—yes, athletes—who matter, their values and aspirations that make a great university. Talented women like you, my one and only . . ."

She and John Proctor had never really lost touch, even in her medical school and residency years, her disaster of a hasty marriage and motherhood, establishing her Jackson Hole practice, her divorce. His thoughts, later in his Rockefeller Foundation days, began to find her again in his beautiful handwritten letters (such good penmanship for a guy), then in emails, and then in recent years, his last years, reverting to letters again, letters and postcards slipped between the pages of books, book after book after book, all his favorites as he began downsizing after Betty Anne's death and his move to assisted living. Then boxes of books on Venice, monographs on artists and architects, dog-eared, underlined, annotated: Bellini, Carpaccio, Titian, Sansovino, Tintoretto, Veronese, Codussi—just saying these names brought back their Venice days. It was as if he'd actually consulted with these artists and architects as plans for the university's modern expansion went forward. In those long, rambling letters near the end, as his heart was giving out, she could sense his mind reaching back to that elixir of a lagoon city, when a life together beckoned, just beyond their window in the smell of the Lido-girt sea, when she carried his child. A child she'd lied about. And the abortion she'd never had. Because she refused to use it to trap him—what people would have always thought. Letting her pride overrule her love. A love child instinctively, uncannily drawn to the books once in his father's library. As if by sending along those books, John knew all along. Why the books kept arriving week after week until just a few weeks before his death, as if insisting on proof positive of that alternate life they'd fantasized about: he an art history scholar and she a doctor, living a simple life at some small college in the hinterlands.

But she had saved him from that fate, borne out by all the new dorms and science buildings now lining the parade route, planned and funded on his watch, proclaiming to the skies the rightness of her choice for him: that of a builder rather than a disgraced scholar.

And yet, and yet, as the beauty and fitness of the new buildings began to overwhelm her, crowned by the latest addition, the glittering towers of the Burrage Biochemistry Lab in the distance—oh, the wonder of such a thing—her eyes began to soften with tears, remembering other wonders found between the pages of those books (the art and architecture that helped a community cohere and prosper), wonders that had drawn her bemused son, Christopher, to her miraculously growing library, a transplanted library, itself reflecting a microcosm, the splendor of a parallel universe—there, where she had carried her firstborn; there, where some part of her still dwelt, beyond setting suns over the lagoon city. There, as well, in the very smell of the volumes when she brought her face close to the well-thumbed pages, inhaling the scent of damp and stored time, of art that survived the ages, and just the faintest hints of his aftershave. And an old office memo—a note to the files just in case—recovered from John's personal papers that had somehow found its way as a bookmarker in a volume on Sansovino and the building of the Marciana library in Venice.

A student, a senior in the chemistry department, *Jacob Burrage*, came by the office today ready to chew my ear off about something—ROTC, most likely, but after a few minutes of spirited discussion, and hints that he knew more than he was letting on, the entire tenor of the conversation seemed to shift—the architectural drawings spread out on my desk?—and he proceeded to describe to me in cogent and convincing details how the life sciences were about to evolve exponentially, how in the coming decades the various fields of chemistry, biology, genetics, physics, and computer science would be integrated and expanded as one field merged with another. Quantum mechanics, he boldly stated, will revolutionize all the sciences. He made a compelling case that the university needed to anticipate and invest heavily in new infrastructure to accommodate the advanced technologies and engineering know-how required by these new, evolving fields. Computers, he kept repeating, as if frustrated by his lack of access to the computer center, computers, the speed and precision to crunch numbers: modeling, numerical analysis and simulation, process dynamics, and a host of other things I didn't quite understand. But a very convincing case indeed! A scholarship kid headed for greatness.

A future nudged ahead by Jake Burrage. And embraced by John Proctor.

She was tempted to ask Gini if she had any inkling of that long-ago conversation of Jake's with John Proctor. Had he been contemplating a demolition job on their clandestine affair as a way of having her for himself? But this tantalizing, if vaguely unsettling thought, an alternate to marriage to an alcoholic, first glimpsed in the flickering, empathetic glance of young Jacob Burrage at sign-in, she now dismissed as quickly as it had arrived, inundated by the inland sea of young, eager faces that now lapped the parade route. Thousands upon thousands of members of recently graduated classes, Princetonians who, so she assumed, wouldn't even know the name John Proctor, the man who had been instrumental in expanding the life sciences and engineering and computer sciences, along with the new residential colleges. So did once-mighty reputations fade down the wind even as their achievements gave back thousandfold.

She laughed as that vibrant voice came back to her out of the din of locomotive cheers.

"A life without feeling, without a ruling passion, is a life running on empty. And you are my tank full of ruling passion, you are the living, breathing, twenty-four-carat foundation of any institutional loyalty I may have left. If I was a B-17 pilot in World War II, your image, rangy tits and all, would be on the nose of my ship: Apolonia, goddess of light and safe returns."

She whooped with pleasure, wiping her eyes as she screamed out a return cheer for the fifth-reunion class. Loving all those young, clueless faces in all their wild diversity of colors, shapes, and nationalities—a million shades of pale from the four corners of the globe, John's legacy as well. A powerful and good man who could equally lust after a lowly undergraduate as after life itself. A man willing to risk everything to be fully alive—an aliveness that lived on!

Approaching the fifth reunion, Annette and Matt were on the lookout for Arthur, who had seemed in much-improved spirits after his parents had deftly fielded many probing questions at the Athletes for Christ forum—how good men and women of faith might handle fame and power and the temptations that came in the wake of success. Gini too found herself sidling up to Matt and Annette, her eyes peeled for a glimpse of Arthur after rumors of a late-night visit to the Carpaccios, a possibility that now, more than ever, she found congenial, even easing her mind.

Arthur emerged from the throngs of twentysomething reunion goers wearing an orange safari hat and tiger-striped sunglasses. Long and limber like his father, with his fair hair and easy smile, he embraced his parents and quickly got out his phone for a family selfie. And then spotting Gini, his godmother, gave her a lingering, heartfelt hug as well, whispering, "Erma's such a fantastic woman." Music to her ears. Arthur then insisted she stand between his parents for a group selfie.

Annette laughed, always pleased when her children were happy, and turned to Gini, who still had her arm around Matt's shoulder, with an expression of mildly shocked pleasure. "You never know . . . ," she sang out above the din of cheers.

Gini, more eager than she knew to second the sentiment, nodded her assent and laughed, even as she feared not having covered her last night's tracks, playfully flirting with Matt.

"Well, this is about as close to a Wimbledon championship as I'm likely to come. So how is it returning to Wimbledon each June, you and Annette sitting in the royal box, presenting that silver cup with your name on the roll of champions, hanging out with Federer and Chrissie Evert?"

"Chrissie's always in the commentary box," noted Annette dryly.

Matt laughed at the hint of jealousy in his wife's voice. "Yes, peace of mind and relief that I don't have huge regrets like the other fellas—finalists who never made it. But then, like I said in the forum this morning, there's the business of dealing with the envy of those—Federer and Nadal and Djokovic—who've won Wimbledon multiple times, that flip side of the equation: that I should have done better, that God had expected more of me. If only I'd been able to talk Jake Burrage into another year on tour with me."

"Hell's bells," cried Annette in an unusually strong outburst. "Jake turned down Chrissie's offer to track her matches for five times what you could've paid him. And then there's the Borg factor: you'd have had to change your antiquated game to deal with the wonder boy and his spawn."

Matt seemed momentarily abashed by his wife's stridency. "Actually, I beat him in 1973 at Gstaad, 7–5 in the third set. He made too many errors. The next year he was fitter, faster, and a human backboard with a killer instinct, and he won the French Open."

"He was seventeen at Gstaad," noted Annette, peevishly.

"Is that what it takes, do you think?" asked Gini. "The killer instinct."

Annette gave a dismissive laugh, as Gini caught her glance and held it. "She's asking, Matt, because Gini did have the killer instinct, and she was so terrified it might run away with her that she turned down the chance of joining the tour and playing Wimbledon. Remember, Matt: Didn't Donald Dell tell you once that he tried to recruit Gini after she won the NCAAs, that June after we graduated?"

"The Don, my old agent . . . ?" Matt said, a little dreamily.

"Hey, Donald only landed you the Adidas tennis shoe endorsement—remember old shoe?"

"I'd forgotten about that," said Gini, somewhat disconcerted. "I . . . I was rushing to take up my internship at Knopf."

"Forgotten?" cried Annette in disbelief. "You won it all, and without Jake there tracking and coaching you. Your highest national ranking, and you finked out on us all."

Apolonia, overhearing the conversation, rode to the rescue. "She was the perfect gentlewoman this morning." She gave Gini a hug. "She knew better than beating up on the old doc."

"You were incredible this morning," said Matt, giving Gini's shoulder a squeeze. "If I didn't know it was you, I would've had a hard time differentiating your play from the youngsters."

In the commotion of cheers from the younger classes, Gini and Apolonia drifted off together, arm in arm, holding their placards high.

"And thank you again," said Apolonia.

"For what?"

"For not ripping me to shreds this morning, not making me look worse than I was already."

"You were playing great."

"You were—I don't know what you were, what terrible things you've injected, snorted, or swallowed, but if you ever want to share your secret, I'm down."

Gini smiled as if as much an enigma to herself as Apolonia.

"Oh my God," she exclaimed as this lost memory of such a glittering prize now hit her full force. "Yes, yes . . . he slipped off his Ray-Bans, squinted under that expensive haircut, and tapped the table with his glasses to make sure he had my attention." Apolonia gave her a curious look. "Donald Dell did try to sign me up for ProServ. He cornered me at the courtside snack bar and patiently explained how he'd already got me a wild-card pass into the first round of Wimbledon, based on the NCAAs."

"No way, José—you never told me that."

"Oh, AP, I felt it this morning, all the power, the ambition, the love of the game—I don't know what happened."

"Must have been the great sex."

"Great sex . . . ," echoed Gini, her mind in a whirl as she searched for Erma's face in the crowd of seniors now coming into view, and just possibly young Jacob's. "Yes, of course, does wonders for body and soul."

Gareth now moved up in the procession and threw an arm around Gini as he kept an eye out for his daughter.

"What's this about great sex?" he asked.

"Us, last night," hooted Gini. "Don't tell me you've forgotten already."

"Hah," said Apolonia, punching his shoulder. "I should have known it—you two, and after all these years."

"Better late than never," he cried over the din of cheers, as if quite tickled and game for anything thrown his way.

Gini felt a wave of guilty relief. "I was so drunk on Jack Rambridge's wine that I couldn't remember if it was your room or mine."

"My room, of course. But I was the perfect gentleman not to take advantage of a woman after Jack Rambridge's Corton-Charlemagne Grand Cru," he pronounced in perfect French.

"Not—I hope—that much of a gentleman," laughed Gini, relieved at such a convenient apocryphal narrative to cover her bold-faced, stupid lie of the morning.

"Well," said Apolonia, "you two couldn't have done any worse than my Harvard historian who fell asleep during foreplay."

"Better to stick with tigers—law of the jungle and all that jazz," said Gareth, now taking Gini's arm. Their two classmates in tiger masks, carrying the class banner between them, turned with loud growls of ascent. Two world-famous heart surgeons who had performed surgeries for months at a time in the Third World for their church charities.

Gini gave Apolonia a big hug. "Amiga of mine, I know how much you miss him."

"Hey, it's like we're reviewing the troops, his living legacy."

"There you go," said Gini, now turning again to Gareth as the P-rade slowed, as more and more sons and daughters of Old Nassau dashed into the ranks for selfies with parents. "Does the name Johnny von Neumann mean anything to you?"

"Sure, a legendary mathematician and statistician, and just about everything else, who worked at the Institute for Advanced Study, just down the road, before the Second World War and later. He developed the codes and the engineering for the first real computer using vacuum tubes, housed at the Institute, that was built to do the calculations for the hydrogen bomb."

"Did you and Jake ever talk about him?"

"Who didn't, when we were students—a genius among a pantheon of early Princeton geniuses, along with Einstein and Turing. Besides designing computers and hydrogen bombs, von Neumann and his circle sketched out the concepts of computers reproducing themselves, and even our ability to upload our genetic code to a computer and so gain a kind of immortality, and even the possibility of that code being downloaded into a replicant—you know, the *Blade Runner* thing."

"Computers can do all that?"

"The power of computers derives as much from their ability to copy as from the ability to compute. And once AI, artificial intelligence, comes online—who knows what disasters might be possible?"

"I'd never thought of it like that."

"Sounds like you and Jake's boy had a lot to talk about last night."

"Oh, sure"—her mind raced, scudded, sailed—"a little hard to hear over the band."

"And you were fabulous in the publishing forum, going on about your father like that—well, it brought tears to my eyes. I remember him so well from graduation, and now I feel as if I almost know him."

"Oh that, I was faking the whole thing."

"No."

"I mean"—she glanced at her still-stopped Rolex strapped to her wrist—"I heard his voice like it was mine, channeling his mind, speech patterns, as if I could no longer differentiate the two. To be honest, I'm at a loss as to what's gotten into me today." She squeezed his arm as if for support. "The odd thing about that conversation on the dance floor, not that I pressed him on the subject: the accident, young Jacob's mother, his injuries . . . well, I could swear he almost insisted it was all just a messy divorce."

Gareth turned away from the massed ranks of the senior class, holding her arm tight as if she might blow away.

"You know how kids are. Half the time my daughter speaks in the present tense about Ruth, as if nothing happened."

"Yes, yes, of course—Erma too, that must be it. Who knows if someday . . ."

Gareth picked up on her paused thought with spirited aplomb: "We'll have the ability to transform ourselves and loved ones into digital copies. Like some advanced form of extraterrestrial life transported across space and time. Now wouldn't that be a fine thing?"

His riff instantly registered in a fragment of conversation she reiterated from the night before. "The ability to create and use explanatory knowledge gives us the power to transform nature and ourselves."

"What was that?" he asked, above the rolling wave of cheers.

"Swinging birches . . ."

"Come again?"

"Just a little scary: such a chip off the old block. And so much better read."

"Read, you say, better read!" he sang out. "That's your takeaway after only a few swings around the dance floor." Gareth laughed, as if happy to find himself able to give his old flame a hard time. "Ginistrella Wingate's sole criteria of worth. Well, you look"—he was searching for the right word to describe her somewhat abashed reaction—"I was going to say, to coin a cliché, like a million bucks, but I'll amend that to: I wish I was as well read as you look."

She flinched, waving a dismissive hand: "And then there's that book by Kurzweil."

"Ray Kurzweil, you mean, the futurist author and computer engineer. Yes, I've read it, *The Singularity Is Near*, a future where people will live forever—trust me: I deal with pitches like that once a week."

"Sounds like Jake, doesn't it?"

"Dismiss something long enough and it'll come true. Just a few decades back, biochemical organisms began to assemble digital computers, right here in River City. Now digital computers are being programmed to create biochemical organisms. Next it will be AI. What do you think? Are we looking at the beginnings of a life cycle? Or are we at the larval stage of digital computers? Or are computers the larval phase of living organisms? In my line of work, we face the likes of Kurzweil—like Jacob, his angel—all the time in our investment portfolio meetings."

"Thank God, I managed to hire a great science editor to replace Bill." Like Gareth, she was now searching for the comfort of a familiar face among the teeming sea of seniors. "I have enough paradoxes on my hand as it is."

"You and Niels Bohr, the father of quantum physics, who thought the crazier an idea, the more chances of it being correct—that when we encounter a paradox, it's a sure indication we're on the path to something true and real." He caught sight of his daughter working her way through the crowd in his direction. "Ah, and again, speaking of ageless, you were fabulous on the court this morning: every inch the young woman—not a little mind-blowing, actually—Jake and I fell in love with. Treat yourself, give the Burrage Biochemistry Lab a look-see. What our boy dreamed up. A mind-altering drug in all but name."

At this, with a peck on her cheek, he broke away as Diane, his daughter, rushed up to give her dad a hug.

For a moment, Gini was left alone, swimming in the backwash of spirited adulation as the senior class, now led by the women, cheered their placards of "firsts" (paying special homage to the banner *Nude Olympics Begins*), revenants, antediluvians who had graduated before the dawn of the digital age. With Gareth's parting words still reverberating in her ears, her gaze lifted from a copse of approaching maples to where the spires of the Burrage Biochemistry Lab glittered in the afternoon sun. Yet another paradox beckoning her embrace, perhaps offering solace, if not answers, of a kind. Along with another familiar voice causing her to return her gaze earthward as she spied her daughter breaking free from a group of swimmers garbed in their distinctive tee shirts and beer jackets. She found herself almost shocked at Erma's radiant, happy face, hurrying with all speed to intercept the passage of the P-rade, as if hastening in pursuit of time itself. Then her undemonstrative, laconic daughter did something even more un-Erma-like and flew into her mother's arms as if they hadn't seen each other in ages.

"Oh, Mom, you were so wonderful on the court today—just fabulous. And you brought tears to my eyes in the publishing forum when you talked about grandad and tolerance."

With that unheard-of fulsome praise, Erma locked one long arm around her mother's shoulder and drew her close, her other arm outstretched for a selfie, to be joined, only moments later, by Annette and Matt, and then Apolonia and Bianca, with Gareth and his daughter squeezing in. As this brief interlude ended, as Erma scurried back to join her teammates, her mother glanced across to the gathering of swim-team members under a young maple, only to lock eyes with their captain, who gazed back at her with a serene, even affectionate smile, slowly nodding as the P-rade, that river of life, moved on. Bringing to her mind the only term of art that seemed to apply: "Yes, swinging birches . . ."

CHAPTER 24

To say she could barely believe her eyes may have been a cliché, but one from which she withheld her blue pencil and embraced like the Second Coming. Standing awestruck before the Burrage Biochemistry Lab, she yearned to make sense of this looming glass-and-granite outcropping of the sky, curtain walls of polished, dove-gray slabs and translucent panels that seemed to hover in space as if breathing of the very elements—light and air—that buoyed them. Again and again, waylaid by the entrance, she found herself reaching to the delicate graining of the stone, to the tiny, pale blood vessels immured beneath her fingers, as if to better articulate her feelings, this brilliant integration of the practical and aesthetic, of living, breathing cosmic-reaching aspirations . . .

"Yes . . ." She breathed deeply of the lush landscaping round about. "It's you, Jake: the future incarnate, just as you predicted." Speaking his name so forcefully gave her pause: What had come over her daughter?

She got out her iPhone and began feverishly taking notes, delving into memories of Jake's ramblings, how one day he wanted to build bigger and better labs—labs open to the sky, labs that were as beautiful as Sansovino's Marciana Library in Venice. Yes, a true *Wunderkammer*. Yet another memory along these lines hovered just out of reach, somehow lacking the right associations or sensations to be summoned forth.

She dismissed this absence with a wave, laughing out loud, dazzled by all the fictional potential of such wonderful material on invention and reinvention.

She entered the vast atrium that ran the length of the building and rose unimpeded to a blue, nearly cloudless June sky. Yes, Gareth had it right, an open-air nave, a twenty-first-century Chartres vibrant with tones of soft azure and cobalt, where natural light poured in from a thousand sources, a river of light fed by another thousand crystalline freshets from the tiers of labs, bespeaking a temple of science and human ingenuity. She was reminded too of Sainte-Chapelle in Paris and wondered if Jake had ever seen it.

She tried to take it all in, take notes in the precious moments of inspiration, give voice to her senses, filled with an optimism and lightness of spirit, surrounded everywhere she looked by nearly invisible walls that pronounced the clarity and precision of scientific research: labs rising upon labs into the blue, floors connected by spiraling stairways and diaphanous skyways crisscrossing the atrium like some futuristic vision first conjured in Piranesi's phantasmagoric Carceri, though hardly doom and gloom: faith, hope, and charity—and yes, love.

"Yes, Jake, love. I can feel your inveterate optimism here."

After such an oracular pronouncement, as if Jake (a conducted tour) had his arm around her shoulder, she felt compelled to seek out the naming opportunity, where, just inside the door, barely visible, discreetly carved into the granite in hand-sized letters: *Burrage Biochemistry Lab*. She traced an admiring finger over the name.

"Yes, yes, it's really you . . ." She glanced up to where security cameras panned the atrium, as if he might be there with her, watching her every move.

Whispering his name like a Pythian priestess, her wonder was tinged with a vague sense of guilt and possibly loss, even shame at how once she'd derided such a prophecy foretold. And how could she conceivably have failed to visit this stunning addition to the campus? The lab where her daughter spent much of her time. And practically cheek by jowl to the fabulous new swim-team natatorium, a mere two hundred yards away, although parking for swim meets was in the opposite direction. How many times in casual conversation had Erma noted how she rolled out of the pool and into the lab? Given a CEO's busy and distracted life, where was a mother's natural curiosity? So jaded by the proliferation of cutting-edge science facilities that she'd simply waved it off, walked away, turned her back, as she had on the man she'd once loved. Or had she?

"And to think, you still managed to produce such a brilliant science kid."

"Oh, just hedging my bets."

She turned on her heels at this sounding of voices out of a past as recent as the night before, as distant as the spiraling arms of the Milky Way—fiction or fantasy. That so-familiar voice and her flippant reply brought her wandering to a halt before a flickering panel of yellow and green lights monitoring the mechanical systems, the integrated brain controlling all the louvers and shades and arrays of solar panels that harnessed the energy of a distant star, calculating the perfect mix of sunlight in winter and shade in summer to provide the perfect atmosphere conducive to inspiration. Intrigued with the beauty of the thing, she found herself fingering the panel of blinking lights, so very like a heart monitor, touching one amber LED and then the next, until she lay her palm flat against an adjoining wall of gray granite, richly seamed with those enticing capillaries of coppery green, as if by taking a sounding of the heartwood she might even detect a few more of those fading echoes from the night before where they sat huddled by young Jacob's desk, or even further back, dispensing with time, conspirators against time's betrayal, when he'd suddenly shot back in his chair, a revelatory smile of promise creasing his lips.

"You and me and time are all apiece"—and he'd joined together his interlocking fingers—"like granite aggregate."

Had they simply been carried away by such impassioned conversation? Seduced by some stray echo out of her youth? His just a flippant retort to her equally flippant boast, her drunken admission of subterfuge, her genetic sleight-of-hand, a coup de main, appropriating a life without his father's genius: her nemesis and savior. Yes, she had won the NCAAs in 1976 without his tracking and coaching, liberating herself.

She stared at her hand against the granite. "Really, Gini?"

Concentrating all her powers, she thought she could indeed detect a slight hum, a rhythmic vibration, as if indeed from a great throbbing heart, causing her to press and then withdraw her palm, leaving a sweaty imprint on the stone, a vague approximation, so she marveled, of those ceremonial Lascaux hands.

She laughed out loud at such a conceit, though somehow it was apt, and began again to reconnoiter this enchanted realm, perhaps to better confront her invisible, near present quarry, whether human or in the guise of a marvel of human engineering, bathing her eyes in the transfixing tinted light as if from the inside of a prism. Never for a moment could she admit that she might be looking for her daughter or

Jacob, presumably off at their eating club, Ivy, celebrating the finale of the P-rade. Yes, she now remembered her daughter's words: "Jacob's only relaxation is fleecing his Ivy Club mates at the poker table. Even on the bus trips to and from meets, he's busy on his laptop."

Floating way above, she noticed diaphanous whirligigs of air, mobiles hung from the transparent ceiling of the atrium in various sizes and colors, bronzy blues and golden-jade, bobbing against the sky like so many fishermen's nets, the *cogoli* she remembered from Venice: delicate, fanciful, airy spirals, as if she was underwater staring up at these creations; galaxy clusters was another image that came to mind. These enticing apparitions and the inner workings of the labs now drew her steps to one of the circular staircases, just as she detected a slight diminishment of her superpowers of the morning, a quiver of discomfort in her right knee, a hinted trickle of sand slipping through the hourglass, which hurried her steps in avid pursuit of the answer to her mystification—the thing, the data point wrapped in some elusive memory that still escaped her. Or just the faltering residue of postcoital bliss from the night before? No, she told herself: it wasn't about any specific act of love but a love manifest in the marriage of true minds. Less an alternate life than a parallel universe where newly created knowledge not only confirms the existence of a truth that has been there for all eternity, but one that alters both past and future, so exiling would-be lovers to an eternal present.

"The source is not empiricism per se. The real source is theory, ideas, the conjecture alternating with criticism. Taking ideas, reformulating them, rearranging them, modeling and adding to them with the goal to improve the initial concept. Don't you see? Not just good explanations, but better explanations are the key to progress, to everything we are as human beings."

She paused on the steps, scolding herself for being unable to remember if those inspiring words had been spoken last night or forty years before.

And then, with a laugh, rising, peering through one window and the next: "Don't you see, don't you get it—Gini, you ignoramus."

Moving slowly upward, drawn to those shimmering airy crowns, she searched her mind for any corrective to the growing danger of regret. How, when provoked by her obstinance, her obliviousness, Jake had sometimes shaken her in frustration, rattling her teeth! Even in their lovemaking, he liked to wrestle her arms to her side, pinning her, scaring the daylights out of her as she lost control nearing her orgasm. When losing control was precisely the experiment he was running: the bonded truth her body craved.

Now those same constraints proffered another truth, once so obvious to him and only dimly grasped by her—until now, made manifest everywhere she looked in this temple of enlightenment: ungodly curiosity, risk, patience, indefatigable exactitude, and thinking outside the box. What she was witnessing was nothing less than a physical embodiment of Jake's quest to extract knowledge from a parsimonious universe: for mastery over nature—over her!

Not that she wasn't tempted—proof positive—by the sublimity of the thing to give way and become a believer! Hadn't she assigned her daughter from day one as a vestal virgin? And now, like some awed supplicant in the presence of the sanctum sanctorum, she found herself eagerly climbing, drawn upward into the luminous dynamo of light and energy, curious in precisely the way Jake had always accused her of being negligently incurious, where those honeyed blues and bronze spirals floated in pure space, changing tones and even dimensions as she climbed, filling her with an untethered longing, which, she suddenly realized, was beginning to finally take on shape and substance in the glittering complex arrays of beakers and flasks on the lab workbenches lining either side of the atrium. Each a window on a future-into-being. She paused her climb, breathing of outdoor scents as if the lush green landscaping beyond was being breathed in by the building. She turned to yet another window where intricate arrays on the workbenches were lit up like Tiffany lamps, a spectrum of hues dancing in the miniature scaffolds of ongoing experiments: the fever of discovery—of breakthroughs!

"Tashmoo," she exclaimed, glancing to where the treetops cast shadows across the highest reaches of the atrium wall—the thing, the very quality of light reminding her of their Martha's Vineyard camp and just possibly that elusive memory she sought. She paused in her climb, struggling, faltering; her powers began to fail her, fascinated just to linger and watch some lab technicians at their patient tasks.

"Don't you see, there is no alternative to optimism since all evils are due to insufficient knowledge or its corruption. For there is no limit to the creation of knowledge, only limitations imposed by those who refuse to seek good explanations. Problems are hard, that's a given, but every problem can be solved with enough time and energy and resources. Just like your tennis game; as long as you're willing to innovate, to first detect and then eliminate errors. Innovate, that's what your body, your glorious orgasms, is trying to tell you—your tighter parabola on your shots, so that risk becomes second nature."

"Christ, what do you think I am? Some kind of experiment that only you have the God-given right to run, to tweak a muscle here, a tendon there—much less the mush inside my head? Much less getting clobbered by your period in the middle of a match."

"Tashmoo," she again repeated under her breath, as if now intent on casting her own spell. "Yes . . ." She took out her iPhone to note down that long-ago exchange. Yes, it was all coming back to her: how they had finally managed to find peace—a truce, and tranquility—there, under the pointed firs, beneath the stars.

She'd talked her father into letting Jake spend the last two weeks in August with them at West Chop before the start of their senior year.

"You can use our camp at Tashmoo. I'm not going to have you two shacked up in Waverley and setting off another round of rumors and innuendo."

Jake had just finished up a summer internship at Princeton in the Frick Chemistry Lab. She'd been playing the women's circuit all summer and had lost in the third round at Essex, so hadn't made the cut for a first-round berth at Longwood or Forest Hills, even as she'd taken the sixth seed, Susan Barker, England's number one, to three closely fought sets. It had been a grueling summer season. She'd done better in tournaments than any of her teammates (way better than Annette), but she was finding it harder and harder to squeeze out wins against the better players and make it through to the very top ranks without Jake on the sidelines tracking her matches and sizing up her next opponent. The women's game was rapidly changing, with Chrissie Evert leading the charge, as the powerful, two-handed, topspin backhand was coming into vogue. Wimbledon, without Jake, was looking out of reach. She was exhausted, slightly depressed, just wanting the respite of West Chop and Jake, who she'd barely seen all summer.

The camp at Lake Tashmoo (a tiny clapboard cabin of two rooms), where she'd "camped" out as a little girl (scene of at least two trysts with John Chandler), had unexpectedly become free when their last renter of the summer had to leave for a medical emergency. Waverley too now had to be rented for July to make ends meet (galling for her proud father) and so was only available for the family in August. Their idyllic days at Tashmoo unfolded gently, slowly, filling with the waning summer light filtered through the towering firs and scrub oaks, shimmering off the placid surface of the lake, as they woke, morning by morning, to the lapping water along the shore, when they'd make love at full tilt before the fifteen-minute walk to Waverley, overlooking Vineyard Sound, and breakfast. Then she would go off for three hours of tennis training, while Jake would go for a jog, watch her practice while assiduously taking notes, or hang out in her father's library reading, while on Saturdays and Sundays, race days, they would take turns crewing for her father in their Vineyard 15. Most afternoons they would read and relax on the porch, occasionally looking up to catch sight of the ferries gliding past, clockwork white ships against the blue making for Vineyard Haven and Oak Bluffs and Falmouth. And after dinner (she and Jake cooked for her now-divorced father), they returned to Tashmoo, barely able to keep their hands off each other, bathed in silver moonlight, alive to the hum of the crickets, where, smoking a joint or two, they would talk after lovemaking, long into the night, about the life before them. Lulled on the waves of such plans, they would fall into an exhausted sleep.

She gripped the railing, shaking her head as she began climbing once more. "Bliss . . . pure bliss."

And in the early morning, woken by birdsong and first light streaming across the calm water, she would watch where he still slept, where the first spates of glimmering, oscillating, enchanted light played in the stickwork rafters of their tiny cabin, then whispering its way to caress the shelves of ancient moldy paperbacks, only minutes later setting fire to the patchwork of faded postcards tacked to the wall, mostly European scenes sent back by children in the twenties and thirties. She was always happy to be the first to wake, to have those precious peaceful minutes alone, staring into her lover's face on the pillow beside her, more like a sleeping child, sweet, soulful, than the sex-crazed male who woke up with a hard-on and even more ideas than the day before: new drills to master on the court, more ways to tax her brain to its limits, until she wanted to scream in frustration, even as she so needed that morning orgasm or two to get the day off to a brilliant start. Bathed in transfiguring morning light, piped to by wrens and vireos, she felt torn between peace and desire, childhood and adult pleasures, drawn both to that demon lover of the night before, that nonstop, relentless mind endlessly pressuring her, and the desire to simply indulge the song of a red-winged blackbird that frequented a scrub oak by the door—startled by the sudden call of a gull, until silence enfolded her again in the patient, soft, crepitating walk of a great blue heron that stalked the lakeshore where their yellow kayak was drawn up.

Oh, the freshness, the innocence of those Tashmoo mornings before sex had quite done her in, tinctured with scents of brine and sun-yellowed shellack, mildew and the foxed pages of thirties' editions of Conrad and Hemingway she kept by the bedside, and the mint that grew by the lakeshore, a world held in suspension, in the glorious minutes before he woke and reached for her. Even as something in her—pride, her competitive nature, her desire for mastery (her mother's child)—had always known it couldn't last, really couldn't imagine it lasting, even if their sex might have been somehow preserved, so she liked to think, like fine comfiture to be spread on buttered croissants at her leisure . . . that same slow lapping of his rhythmic tongue between her thighs that stirred her into near delirium, another dimension.

"Oh my God!" The lost memory now unleashed . . . how one of those postcards tacked to the cedar paneling of the bedroom, color faded to the sepia of Carpaccio's Augustine in his study, had so caught Jake's eye (only a shadow of the original, much less the reproduction hanging in her college suite): the merest whisper, the faintest echo of something grander still to be beheld, a rare, sunstruck artifact of her patrimony that he was determined to make his own. He had carefully removed the rusty tack and taken down the postcard to read those few scribbled lines by the young boy her father had been in 1925, writing to his grandmother. Prompting, it now occurred to her, the first mention of a trip to Venice to visit the Carpaccios, to the Pensione Seguso where, seemingly light years before, she'd lain in bed staring up at the reflected light from the Rio San Vio in an olive-green Murano chandelier, fingering herself and thinking of John Chandler.

The urtext of Jake's mad plan for a thousand-day rendezvous.

She found herself waylaid on the stairs, pondering their Tashmoo days as she stood, head turned to yet another window of glass, intently watching the back of a woman lab technician seated at her workbench. Her exacting, precise movements.

Gone, all of it: her mother, her father, the big, gray-shingled house on the bluff, and even the simple camp at Tashmoo—all gone when the upkeep and taxes made it no longer possible. As the tech millionaires moved in and slowly took over from the old families. Even as she'd just managed to hold on with a downsized rental house in the Mink Meadows woods so that Erma could have something of the childhood magic as hers of long ago.

And yet—her eyebrows pinched in wonder, yes, the light remained—just as Jake, waking, had put all her fears to flight, her doubts swept away on his flood of optimism, his pep talks, his praise, his delicious lovemaking.

"Lucky I didn't come from all of this," and he'd laughed as he stroked and kissed her breasts. "I'd be hard pressed to lift a finger or fearful of lifting the wrong digit. Much less change things for the better."

She saw her pensive face reflected in the glass wall of the lab, for a moment eliding into that, or Jake just waking on his pillow, staring at her, as if at an apparition, her dream lover.

Springing up to pee off the open deck, he proclaimed to all who might hear: "Oh, it was always me and my dad camping every summer, just the two of us, a couple of sleeping bags and a tent and our fishing and cooking gear—on the Osage River in the Ozarks. It was heaven on earth, if hardly as fancy as this."

Why had he been so reticent to talk about his own father? Why had she never asked more about those camping trips along the Osage? Why had they never visited Barbara, his mother in Evanston, whom he adored?

Her gaze kept drifting beyond her reflection in the glass wall, as if the young woman, a high priestess in a white lab coat seated at her bench, might hold some answer.

But no, it was Jake's face she saw again reflected in the glass, a lover's face as his lips moved down to her belly button, tongue swirling there until she begged him to move lower, the soft morning light shining in his laughing eyes, making her beg.

She held on tight where she stood on the stairs as more details came into view, seeing Jake wave that ancient postcard of Carpaccio's Saint Augustine, minutely examining the image as if a rare specimen of her good breeding, then holding it up again to rattle off the news in a telegram.

"And we'll go to Venice."

"Of course."

"And you'll marry me—there?"

"Yes, oh yes—where else?"

"And I will build you a wonderful room, a huge room of glass windows"—brandishing the postcard like a preacher his Gospel—"a tower of glass to reach to the heavens, containing all of mankind's discoveries. Maybe a research center—a lab, why not?—that will reveal the secrets of the universe, cures for terrible diseases!"

She now reeled, gripping the railing with all her might: What had she missed?

A promise foretold . . . Had he built the Burrage Biochemistry Lab for her—her daughter?

A moment of sheer audacious enchantment and terror that would one day find its way into her resurrected novel.

She took out her phone, desperate to get these details down, even as she sensed her supercharged memory beginning to falter as doubt crept in. Did he really say all that, or was she just imagining things, making it up, revising their story as she went along?

She pressed her hand against the glass, as if in a plea for sanity.

The lab technician, seeming to sense her distress, turned on her stool and smiled, waving this stranger to the laboratory door.

Shaking off her fever dream, she flicked back some stray locks of hair and gathered her wits as she introduced herself to this woman (so unlike Erma) with her white, sunless face, sculpted black eyebrows, and raven hair tightly wound in a chignon. A serious face—midthirties she guessed, with a professional demeanor she instantly recognized as her own when in the office. Searching to provide an explanation for her slumming (a ditzy interloper way over her head), she rattled on—proud parent—about her graduating daughter and how she felt overcome with guilt at failing to tour the lab where Erma had spent so much of the last four years.

" . . . besides the pool and her eating club, of course."

"Oh, Erma Cheshire, you mean?" the woman surmised, her probing eyes examining again this mother's face and then her Reunions name tag hanging on the lapel of her spiffy Reunions jacket, as if the data points on the name tag didn't entirely match up with her daughter's pedigree.

"Yes, of course, she kept her father's name."

"Erma is a fabulous researcher and a very fine experimental technician—good hands, a patient soul."

"You know her?"

"I was her lab preceptor in the integrated science course, maybe her sophomore year. And even though she doesn't work in our lab, I've heard from many of the other postdocs that she's been—'meticulous attention to detail'—a brilliant addition to their labs."

Relieved, her bona fides duly tendered, she drifted over to the lab table with an admiring expression at the array of elaborate equipment, drawn to the vivid colors of various beakers, flasks, test tubes, and trays of shimmering pipettes, like a child discovering a drawer full of marbles.

"Oh, I guess I can take credit for the meticulous attention to detail, even if her father was Harvard physics. Only I wish I could say I was responsible for her departmental thesis . . ." She looked to the woman for help as the realization dawned: she'd forgotten what Erma's thesis was on, if she'd ever known in the first place.

"She works in Professor Bialik's lab, so it probably had something to do with biological systems."

"Ah, but doesn't that just about cover everything? Forgive me, I was an English and classics major, so I've been trying to catch up with Erma most of my life as a clueless parent—and wife, for that matter."

"Bialik's research is about how the functional behavior of life-forms differs from inanimate matter. The difference seems obvious, but it is sometimes difficult to quantify this functionality in the same way we describe other physical systems. We're made up of the same stuff, after all, so most of the same rules do or should apply. But how we differ begs a lot of fascinating questions."

"Evolution and such like."

"Sure, if you like." The woman smiled easily, searching for the intelligent layman's language. "We pretty much agree that evolution sets some baseline limits on physical principles in terms of size, speed, longevity—that sort of thing. Even to the point that evolution designs the biosphere based on developmental compromises to achieve optimal performance for the most crucial tasks in terms of survival. I believe Erma's thesis was attempting to calibrate the performance of biological systems against theoretical systems, an ideal versus a real system, showing how the interaction of theory and experiment can, in some cases, lead to the observation of new phenomena, and so prompting future research."

"Horseshoe crabs," Gini declared, looking up from the lab bench and laughing. "Like new ways of understanding the limits of physical performance."

"Yes, or the enhancement of physical performance. Whether on the level of a single molecule or the interaction of cells, or possibly even neurotransmitters in the brain: how we see and perceive and think."

Feeling pumped at such marvelous thoughts, she felt free to make disparaging noises. "Enhanced neurotransmitters . . . I could certainly use a tune-up."

"Erma's a star performer. You know she won the departmental prize for her senior thesis."

"Yes, of course," she lied.

"In today's job market (as I'm sure you'll be delighted to know), analytical skills and communication skills rarely go together so neatly. We may be in the idea business, the proofing business, but if we can't go out and sell our ideas"—she shrugged and gestured with empty hands—"who's going to know or care? Much less provide the funding."

"Well, I'll certainly take the credit for communication . . ." She paused, the colored liquids in a row of flasks casting rose and lemon-yellow highlights on her face. "She was so curious as a little girl, whether digging around in the sand on the beach for shells or exploring the woods for wildflowers and bird nests. Her room was a regular zoological garden between goldfish, salamanders, turtles, and whatnot."

She gestured to the stacks of petri dishes, trying to put names to more of the equipment. Finding her vocabulary ill-equipped, pressed her lips into a quiet smile and went on.

"I just can't get over how spectacular this place is. It's not just the light but the way everything is so deliciously exposed to view."

"Our fishbowl," the woman laughed. "Only the toilet stalls have proper walls."

"And crazed parents wandering in here like lost souls interrupting your work."

"Oh, the pleasure is all mine, to meet a mother capable of producing a woman like Erma. In our line of research, one always wants to put a face to the gifted—a pedigree, I suppose." She laughed, as if to make light of such curiosity. "Besides, the lab is designed to promote just these kinds of spontaneous-serendipitous interactions: the social world on hyperdrive, making us all into busybodies poking our noses into everyone else's work. Like bees flitting from flower to flower, we are reprogrammed to cross-fertilize. Superefficient hybridization is the idea: our research maximized at every turning, the heat turned up on human potential."

"It sounds exhausting, in theory."

"And relentless, in practice."

She spotted a dog-eared paperback on a corner of the bench, now a familiar title and author's name: Ray Kurzweil, *The Singularity Is Near.* A curious smile crossed her face as she picked up the book and flipped through the heavily lined pages.

"Yours?" she asked.

"One of our interns, probably. My copy is at home. Everyone who works in the lab gets a copy with their first paycheck. You might say it's our bible, or marching orders from our fearless leader and benefactor."

"Not Jake Burrage?"

"Invisible as he is omniscient and ubiquitous."

"Yes, only last night, his son was talking to me about the author Ray Kurzweil. Of course, Jake Burrage was in my class."

"Ah, I was wondering about that," and the woman shifted her eyes to Gini's name tag with a nod. "So, you knew Jacob Burrage, our benefactor?"

"You sound surprised."

"Let's just say, like Erma, one is fascinated to know. In his case, the parents of Jacob Burrage, who rarely says boo about his father—our lord and master—and yet echoes, in a convivial way, directives from Burrage Pharma and Health."

"Oh, yes . . . omniscient and ubiquitous, though not quite invisible." Gini's stare moved from a security camera high on a corner wall to rest on the curious face of the younger woman, her pale complexion setting off her deep auburn eyes, a female affinity that seemed to encompass something of that dream state of just minutes before, the flickering light from above like a freshening breeze launching her voice, or merely another faraway echo. "Yes, Jake, his father, was, even when I knew him, something of a loner. Private is the wrong word; let's just say a man on a mission. So busy with his studies, student jobs, tutoring—and late nights at the poker table—that there were never enough hours in the day. Something, call it single-mindedness, I greatly admired, even if possibly hard to live with."

"Oh my . . ." The woman sighed, as if catching something of that same distant echo in the older woman's voice, or perhaps more clarification of the circumstances of their meeting.

Gini nodded, more to herself, eyes narrowed in recollection, seeming to weigh the paperback in her hand. "The maximization of human potential, by the numbers."

"And you, a test case, no doubt," the woman noted, placing a palm on Gini's shoulder. "I'm Pauline, by the way."

"As you—Gini—like it," she heard herself reply, shifting her stance so that her shapely legs showed to good advantage in her sport tights. "On the tennis courts, no less—tracking my matches, coaching me." She held up the cover of the book, reading: "when humans transcend biology—huh."

"Strange . . . the moment I saw you . . ." With that mysterious half note, Pauline turned to her lab bench with an expansive gesture, as if to properly pose the question: "No expense was spared, four hundred million, including an endowment for five departmental chairs and free food in the atrium café."

"As you might expect, well, I was quite startled when, only yesterday, I learned that Jake had a son in my daughter's class. Managing our Reunions site, of all things, a scholar athlete—and looking more like his father than his father. It was quite a shock to the system."

The woman squinted as if trying to fathom the hint of panic in the voice. "I see, yes, yes—well, one doesn't know Jacob as much as one breathes in the atmosphere, the weather that blows in with him. The only undergraduate more promising than Erma. In fact, you just missed him; I saw him leave less than an hour ago dressed in one of those strange jackets."

"Well . . . beer jacket. Late for the P-rade."

"He even turned down the departmental prize for his research—already published in *Nature*, no less—into the effects of aging on mutations in our cells, and how new therapeutics have the potential for reprogramming or dispensing with problematic genes. 'Knock down and replace,' as he termed it: silence the aging genes, the disease carriers, and replace with healthy new genes." Pauline reached out a congratulatory hand and again patted her visitor's shoulder. "So the prize went to your daughter."

"Why would any gifted kid turn down a prize in his field?"

"There are full professors and senior researchers who would give their eye teeth to be published in *Nature*. Given how much he circulates among the labs, soaking up others' research, he may have felt less deserving. He even cites his father's work and proprietary research at BPH, patents already applied for. Jacob strikes one as a very private person, but a person on a mission with the clock ticking. Even if he can be quite candid at times about frustrations with progress in the fields of CRISPR, gene editing, somatic versus germline editing, which hold the promise for cures of rare but devastating diseases like Huntington's."

"A man on a mission . . . ," she echoed, even as mention of Huntington's somehow struck a dissonant chord.

"There's something slightly mysterious about him, a maturity beyond his years, the shadow of—what to call it?—a personal tragedy."

"His mother was killed in a car crash."

"Oh dear, I had no idea." She put a hand to her face, a tiny mole at the corner of her lips, as her eyebrows arched and crinkled with doubt. "Still, there's something—how to describe it?—sui generis about him. When he won the Pyne Prize for his junior work in nanotechnology, the president of the university had to personally twist his arm to get him to accept it before the gathering on Alumni Day. Even then, he just gave a few innocuous remarks as if to avoid drawing attention to himself. What I hear around the fishbowl is that he's turned down offers from Stanford and Harvard and right here to go back into his father's firm and make more millions."

"My sense of young Jacob, the way Erma (she's on the diving team) tells it: money is hardly on his mind."

"It never is," she noted with an appraisal of her lab, "when you don't have to worry about funding."

"Shareholder value," shrugged Gini, now going to the transparent wall of the lab, which offered a spectacular view over the atrium, where those huge, basket-like mobiles hung suspended, orbed, organic, gently swaying like jellyfish in an invisible current. "Armillary spheres," she gasped to herself and turned. "Who knows what motivates people these days. What expectations we saddle our kids with."

"None of us are immune. The university incentivizes us as part of the hiring package; they get the patents, but we get a percentage when they're licensed. Valuable, too. There are people around here hardly out of their thirties who are already millionaires many times over. Who would tell you, if they dared, that they'd happily give up the cash for a Nobel."

"I couldn't help feeling, wandering in here, how difficult it must be for young Jacob to have"—and she turned in place, her hands outspread—"all this weighing down on his shoulders, with brand name attached."

"Perhaps that's it—you may be right. I sometimes wonder if he ever sleeps. I have to be in here at all odd hours. He was here this morning in the lab next door when I arrived at seven. Sometimes he'll come in smelling of chlorine, check on something, and it's back to the pool. And even for a private person, he's always chatting people up on the fly, sharing ideas, solutions—all for the good of the cause. He's waltzed in here on occasion and plonked himself down and, before you know it, come up with a solution that had been hanging fire for weeks, if not months. A lot of researchers will hold their cards close, never a peep until publishing, especially if there are commercial applications on the line." She tipped her head from side to side, like a balance wheel. "Cool customer though he might be, Jacob is a breath of fresh air."

"Promoting the modus operandi, the point of all this, this—this transparency?"

"And not unlike his old—forgive me—man, our benefactor, your classmate, who never makes a peep, never shows his hand. I've never even heard Jacob mention Burrage Pharma—or his father, for that matter—even if we're practically a subsidiary. Strange, how nobody has laid eyes on your classmate for years and years, as far as I can make out."

"Decades."

Pauline smiled and shrugged with a wicked chuckle. "Another Howard Hughes—who knew?"

"Well, we can hardly blame his offspring. And it's true for a lot of kids today, don't you think: your sui generis. My daughter, for one." She smiled uneasily, her lips thinning. "The penalty box for us slackers who haven't lived up to our potential or, worse, cut a few too many corners."

"Oh," Pauline now offered a sympathetic smile as if she too (thick as thieves) was privy to the strained modalities of the generational churn. "I think our Jacob would say it's simply about asking the right question. And if you pressed him, I believe he'd tell you, as he told me once, right at this bench, that inspiration is simply a matter of fine-tuning, speeding up the neurotransmitters."

"I used to think it was simply a matter of a double latte."

She laughed. "Oh, we've gone way beyond memory and the various interactions between short- and long-term memory."

"And love—will we ever have a cure for love, do you suppose? It seemed like when I was the age of Erma or young Jacob, or younger, I was falling in love again every month or so."

"No love without memory." Pauline broke into a wide, gracious smile. "They've actually done brain scans displaying the areas of the brain activated when one falls in love. Turns out to be like a drug, an addiction, a hunger that takes us over and turns us into a very different kind of person from who we were before."

"Ah, you see, words, ideas were my drug of choice. My love potion number nine." She tapped the glass wall of the lab as if to indicate the hanging mobiles, which she now fully grasped were intricate representations of armillary spheres, concentric circles, modeled on various solar systems, heliocentric and geocentric, and constructed out of delicately painted ribbons of wood and steel and wire (including archaic images of moons, stars, and planets)—almost alive, vibrant with blues, purples, and a patina of bronze-gold, gently turning as if breathtaking in the sunlight. "You don't suppose Burrage Pharma has a cure for that as well?"

"A cure or an elixir? But surely you," she laughed, possibly out of wonder or curiosity, "are better placed than any of us to put that question to your classmate: the first—was it on the court or off?—of his clinical trials. Our first singularitarian . . ."

"Oh, yes. So"—and she picked up the paperback—"I'd better borrow the user's guide."

CHAPTER 25

Saturday night of Reunions always arrives—certainly by the fortieth—with pangs of giddy joy touched with sadness, an admixture of nostalgia with relief for having at least made it this far, along with moments of creeping retrospection about paths taken and not, challenges met and unmet, aspirations long jettisoned—the silently departed years. Yes, joy to be still alive and kicking and mingling with old friends and new in a place so seeded and saturated with youthful ardor (otherwise, why would you be here?) that the onslaught of recalibrated memory can exhaust the heartiest of hearty souls. And yes, relief that one had got through most of the weekend without being uncovered as a fraud or being overwhelmed with regret at having to explain about ditched (or abandoned by) husbands and wives. Or plagued by second thoughts about the many stupid life decisions made on the spur of the moment that resulted in nada. So, even for a Princeton grad, maybe batting only .330 on life's to-do list wasn't so bad. And yes, sadness at missing friends who either didn't show (whose foresight was even worse than yours) or who are no longer with us, whose absence casts a flickering shadow over our own mortality: how five or even ten years hence, given the actuarial tables, much of this crowd might be celebrating without you—and would anyone notice or care?

And then there is the battery of intemperate stares that must be endured. "My, he hasn't exactly aged gracefully." "What a figure she once had—to die for." Like the aging actress who retires from stage and screen before her looks go, many prefer to forego Reunions and so leave their youthful splendor unspoiled in the mind's eyes of their classmates.

So, better to pretend that life has pretty much gone to plan, thank you very much. While wondering all the while if this or that old friend is really on the level or doing half as well as they make out (since you've been so expertly lying through your teeth much of the weekend). Or worse, the captains of industry, Nobel and Pulitzer winners, senators and congressmen who have proved your long-ago snarky prognostications of their chances so wrong. Prompting sneaking suspicions about your own early promise and soaring ambitions: How could your parents and teachers and mentors have gotten it so spectacularly wrong? But what the heck, it's Saturday night—last dance, last chance for love, and so one might as well put on a sporting face, for tomorrow you'll be back in your very ordinary, unglamorous existence and nobody the wiser.

The Shirelles and their guests, Erma, Gareth and his daughter, Diane, Jack Rambridge and Daltrey Assingham, were hardly immune from musings along these lines, though inoculated by the comforting pleasure of the young and each other's company, buoyed as well by the siren song of fresh starts and prospects of a happier future—given the wisdom of age, if not second, even third acts.

Though none would dare admit as much, something of the retrospective giddiness of the occasion had been prompted by the incandescent presence among the diners of a smiling and convivial Jacob Burrage. For Bianca, Annette, and Apolonia, it had only taken an ambiguous phrase, an odd reference, a mind-bending, all-too-private familiarity to send their thoughts spinning back in timeless reverie. For Gini, covering her tracks with aplomb, mildly flirting with Gareth—given that both their daughters were in attendance—young Jacob was fast becoming an obsession. She was barely holding panic at bay, even as she furiously took notes on her phone. Possessed, more like it, with the notion that Jake had—somehow, some way—actually shown up for Reunions. Crazy, of course, something out of a bad techno-thriller, but made all the more credible as she felt her jet-fueled high of the morning slipping away, her knees and back aching, the vividness of her memories dimming by the moment, as if her very youth was deserting her. Nor was she unaware of her roommates' furtive glances—Erma's as well—directed to where their Reunions manager, now dressed in jacket and tie, was making the rounds of the festivities, checking the buffet, the bar, glad-handing and chatting up members of her class as if evaluating participants in some drug-trial control group. Hardly the retiring private soul described to her by Pauline in the lab.

She couldn't resist the feeling that young Jacob Burrage actually belonged among them—might pull up a chair at any moment and slip on his Reunions jacket, even if only as an exemplar of their youthful aspirations, his spirit imparted too by the cooling evening breezes, wafting on the hickory-smoke currents of their candlelit barbecue (sacrifices to the nattering gods peering down from the roofline), filtering and invigorating their fellowship, now accented by the piano player's spirited rendition of Cole Porter's "You're the Top." His knowing, optimistic smile echoed in every toast of their raised glasses under the canvas of billowing white stars that adorned the tent's underside. While the intimate charms of Holder courtyard's quatrefoil arcades, so evocative of Carpaccio's Venice, only added to the spell of eternal youth on offer.

She looked up from her phone, where she'd been furiously taking notes, spotting her protagonist at a nearby table, clearly charming his avid listeners, as if offering them—handing out Burrage Pharma prescriptions right and left—a safe passage through the realms of time. "Crossing to safety," she wrote, "along that winding, upland path, and so securing a place of rest—a Virgilian grove, for their weary souls, there amid the Olympian heights."

Not a little aghast at such fevered conjuring—excuses to assuage her guilty secret—Gini felt her cheeks blaze. Nevertheless, she was intent on recording all these potential plot points—her backstory, as she thought of it—before she completely lost her mind. The crack-up she sensed coming: a mature woman in heat and seated across from her daughter.

And desperate for another fix!

What, indeed, had possessed her—she finally holstered her phone in her sleek purse-backpack—to think she could get away with wearing her fifteen-year-old Manolo Blahnik stiletto heels, even if they went so perfectly with her racy orange-and-black, tiger-striped evening dress from Bergdorf's. Continuing to scold herself, she reached for one of Jack's bottles of Burgundy Grand Cru—Salomé Beyle (how odd a name)—with the admonishment that, unlike last night, she would drink moderately, just enough to calm her raw nerves and fully enjoy Erma's presence at their dinner table. Besides, having neglected to bring her Motrin in her rush to leave the Marriott and be on time, a little wine might do medicinal wonders for the ache in her right shoulder and slight pain in her right knee, which she had foolishly failed to ice after her match. Such minor concerns to be dispensed with by tapping into her daughter's excellent mood: so animated, so sparkling, so talkative—like her old/younger playful self, her father's playfulness, when not distracted by a stream of texts on her unmuted phone—all so un-Erma! Even the ever-attentive Annette, matronly attired, and scatterbrained Bianca, a slutty crop top and fishnet stockings, had noticed Erma's glow and high spirits. Could it be they knew something she didn't? Hopefully, Arthur or even Matteo?

For their part, Bianca and Apolonia, tittering like schoolgirls as they side-eyed their dates, were pumped to the skies. Jack Rambridge and Daltrey Assingham had gallantly exiled themselves from their fiftieth dinner to dine with their fair ladies. Gareth too had gamely invited himself and his lacrosse-captain daughter, Diane, to Gini's table, no doubt encouraged by their rumored assignation of the night before that had quickly made the rounds during the P-rade and so become an established fact. Gini, having so deftly covered her ass, kept telling herself she should be thrilled to still be wooed by Jake's best friend. And basking in her daughter's love and affection, who—the fashion gods be praised—was actually wearing her hugely expensive (not that she'd breathed a word) graduation dress to such spectacular effect.

And yet, as the evening unfolded, as she caught glimpses of young Jacob amid the crowd of diners, she found her head spinning with still more fantastic scenarios verging on science fiction, which her ailing body (she was having a hard time holding her fork steady in her stiff right hand) now yearned to believe (certainly in those green capsules), not that she would ever breathe a word of her crazy suspicions to anyone, especially Gareth, who was best placed to put such absurd ideas to rest.

If she'd heard it once, she'd heard it a dozen times over the last thirty-six hours: almost anything was possible. She could almost swear—call it woman's intuition—to Jake's presence circulating the tent, expecting at any moment for him to come up behind her chair, squeeze her shoulders, pin her arms as he liked to do when she was about to climax, which had caused her to gasp with a pleasure so intense that it verged on an out-of-body experience. Yet another delicious detail for a semi-autobiographical novel.

Nor was her plight helped by the way the table conversation seemed to gravitate to the subject of Jake Burrage. Even Jack Rambridge dipped an oar, going on and on about seeing Matt play in the semifinals of Wimbledon, that stirring comeback season after those disastrous years following his Wimbledon crown and marriage. Jack, big-swinging-dick Jack, ever the equity-turnaround guy, wanted to know how, exactly, Matt, with Jake's tracking system, had managed it. And why had he faltered after reaching the quarters in the US Open three months later?

"Yes, yes"—acknowledged Matt, shaking his head, a hint of reluctance in his voice as he stared into his wineglass—"that one spectacular summer when I seemed to round back into form, when Jake Burrage debriefed me before and after every match, tracked my winners and errors, scouted my opponents for weaknesses, gave me five takeaways to focus on—well, my confidence simply soared. Such a wingman. Like I could do no wrong."

"I had no idea Burrage had worked for you—and in such a capacity, how extraordinary," said Jack. "A genius, a triple threat—who knew."

"Totally news to me too," said Gareth with an uneasy glance at Gini by his side.

"And I have Annette to thank," said Matt, raising his wineglass with a retrospective twinkle in his eye. "Without her recruiting Jake—and in a moment of near despair—it would never have happened." He bent and gave his wife a peck on the cheek. "I only wish I could've bottled Jake's secret sauce. But it was enough to put that one great summer of wins against all the rising stars in the record books."

Annette, a curious glance at a distracted Gini, waved this off with peevish sarcasm. "Oh, sweetheart, Jake just wanted a chance to watch the women play. He was quite fixated—remember—on the evolution of the women's game, how Chrissie dominated with her two-handed backhand until Martina came along and dethroned Miss Goody Two-Shoes with her ultra-power game."

Gini hoped her face hadn't flushed, even as all her teammates and Gareth kept turning her way for a reaction to this now-dated scuttlebutt, which only reflected on her stubborn idiocy (something she noted in the shark-eyed squint of her fellow Shirelles), in addition to the ridicule, revealed during the P-rade, for turning down Donald Dell's offer, not only to represent her but also to hand her, on a silver platter, a bye into the first round of Wimbledon. She closed her eyes in a silent scream of regret as those immaculate green lawns lined with chalk swam before her: that stubborn streak, that misbegotten calculation that equated Dell's offer with her having to swallow her pride and crawl back to Jake and so take up his offer to delay the start of his

Stanford PhD and coach her on the women's tour. Again, even in absentia, she felt his strong hands pinning her arms, holding her fast—once again having his way with her!

She twisted in her seat as Erma returned with a second helping of steaming, hickory-smoked New York sirloin fresh off the grill. Red meat, not the delicious tuna. Since when did Erma eat red meat?

Nor could she fail to notice her daughter's rapt attention—how well she read her mother's mind—as more bits of ancient gossip trickled out, nuggets of fascinating lore about young Jacob's father, her mother's lover! Not to mention those pregnant pauses in the conversation, a gap, a royal highway for her to add her own delicious two bits on all things Jake. But not tonight—holding her cards close, ladies and gentlemen: she was a hunter-gatherer, a fabulist, a scribe, poised on the cutting edge of the possible.

"Without Jake's inspired tutoring, I'd never have passed orgo, never had the wherewithal to make it to med school. He wrote me postcards from Stanford to cheer me up while I gave tennis lessons to bratty kids and studied for my MCATs."

"When I ran into Jake in Venice"—crooned Bianca, not to be left out, eyeing the quatrefoil arcades of the courtyard, and winking at Jack as she wolfed down her grilled tuna—"I began to see the city, the Carpaccios and so much else, the way Einstein might have seen them. It was like the proverbial scales had fallen from my eyes—Charlie the tuna's, that is."

Such conversational gambits Gini chose to ignore, preferring now to simply admire her radiant daughter in the candlelight, transformed from the scruffy naturalist and lab rat, the bleary-eyed pool girl, into an elegantly attired goddess, upon whose broad shoulders that sleek, dark, blue-with-white-trim Akris dress hung to perfection, as if made for her newly confident straight-backed superstar. A crazy splurge that only twenty-four hours before she'd despaired of ever seeing Erma wear. Goodness, how that honey-blonde, reddish hair simply shimmered against the dark silk, full of streaming highlights that returned her for a moment to those translucent tones that had danced before her eyes while mounting the spiral staircase in the Burrage Biochemistry Lab (not that she'd ever mention such a crack-brained observation, lest her daughter accuse her of spying on her workplace). Hair so lovely (she shook back her own as if looking in a mirror) she almost wanted to cry. She drained her wineglass and reached for a refill, only to wince at the pain in her right shoulder.

"You okay?" Apolonia asked, picking up on this moment of distress.

"Oh, it's just my shoulder acting up. Did you bring any Motrin?"

"Thank the Lord. At your service—you're only human," assured Apolonia, looking radiant in a pale orange dress, Reunions jacket, and discreet pearls (a gift from John Proctor), scrounging in her fanny pack as she scrutinized her roommate's face, faintly relieved to find again the crow's-feet she remembered from the day before.

"I don't know about others seated at our little gathering," Jack continued, delicately, wiping his mouth to catch a ruby tear of wine, broad, full-eyebrowed face taut and tanned, "but knowing intimately the history of the vineyard, the *goût de terroir*, from which each of these bottles came—well, it almost does me in, enough that I can even smell the air and the earth"—and he swished the dark crimson Pinot Noir in his wineglass, grasped so delicately at the stem in his large hand—"that gave birth to this baby. I could, but I won't bore you with the details about that marvelous day when I first laid eyes on my starter vineyard (which our fund now owns), the purple grapes swollen, fit to burst, the yellow leaves in the trees, even the cool fall weather—the elegant dress and scarf that my then-wife was wearing. For me, it comes as close to actually capturing—lightning in a bottle—time and memory and the earth from which we take our life."

Jack patted Bianca's hand and raised his glass to the gathering.

"To the land, the very earth, from which my people had been run off, first by the Spaniards, the English, then the French, then the Germans."

Daltrey, gathering Apolonia's hand: "And thank you young and younger ladies for inviting us old folks to your gathering: no country for old men—the fiftieth, I mean."

"Praise the Lord, not Anton Chigurh," exclaimed Bianca, with a sidewise lean of her head to Jack's reunion-jacketed shoulder. "Nectar of the gods, Jacko. I don't think I've had such great wine since my student days in Venice, when our concert season was sponsored by a local vineyard, and the master of the *vigneto* would provide vintages from his private reserve for the annual dinner at the Palazzo Grassi. And speaking of Jake Burrage"—she glanced across the tent to where young Jacob was hobnobbing—"he was my guest at one of those affairs, and I remember how he and the wine master got into a spirited discussion about the difference in fermentation using oak versus steel casks. Within five minutes, the guy wanted to hire Jake for his vineyard."

Gini, knowing Bianca's taste for one-upmanship, chose to ignore her and, instead, as the pianist launched into Gershwin's "Embraceable You," raised her glass with a knowing look at Erma. "'Caught in that sensual music all neglect, monuments of unageing intellect' . . . Yeats."

"Ah, the Delphic oracle and our class salutatorian," intoned Apolonia. "Who graciously spared me this morning on the court."

"To Tandem Press," added Gareth, "and the young lady who still publishes great books, while turning a handsome profit."

"Modest . . . ," sighed Gini.

"Just look at that knowing smile." Bianca nodded at Gini. "Talk about the cat that swallowed the canary, as she plots to sweep us all into her forthcoming Pulitzer novel."

Gini, noting the merest quiver of pain at the corner of her roommate's lips, knew for a near certainty that she and Jake had been lovers in Venice . . . and been left in the lurch—*tant pis*. "I wouldn't dare. I'd get a triple-X rating."

Matt eyeing Gini from across the table with benevolent eyes: "There were moments out there on the court this morning when I could almost swear I was seeing the young woman I remembered playing Harvard."

Annette raising her glass: "And thank you, Jack, for your generous contribution; a lot of young women with eating disorders will benefit."

"Yes," laughed Jack, nodding and turning to Gini. "A Pulitzer: 'To lords and ladies of Byzantium, of what is past, or passing, or to come.'" He nodded on each downbeat, eyes a smoky agate. "Gini, dear, you should have taken our buyout offer; the cash infusion would have made you more competitive with Random House and HarperCollins."

Gareth chuckled and raised his glass. "To the well-read. And may Tandem Press long prosper and remain an independent voice in publishing."

"That's you, young ladies," spoke their historian Daltrey Assingham, motioning graciously in Erma and Diane's direction, "the 'to come' bit."

Chimed out Gini: "While we, in Edith Wharton's phrase, ladies of ripe but well-cared for middle age, salute the younger generation, daughters as wise as they are beautiful."

"Yes," echoed Jack, "another pleasure we lack at the fiftieth, although there were a few class members' daughters who made it into Princeton and so to our reunion, and plenty more granddaughters." He raised his glass again. "As I was going to say: here's to the bicentennial women of seventy-six, pathbreakers, pathfinders to a kinder, gentler Princeton, to a Princeton more alive and vibrant—and yes, loving, God only knows." He drank deep and sat back. "Too many damn men in our day—no wonder, Daltrey, our marriages soured. If we'd had talented and forceful gals like you in our class, we'd have been properly trained and housebroken to be better husbands."

"Housetrained, lovers—what more could a gal want in life," offered Apolonia, laughing as Erma and Diane caught each other's eye (Can you believe he said that?).

"What, three marriages between us," noted Jack, "you'd think plenty of housebreaking along the way."

"You needed daughters," offered Daltrey. "My daughter kept me in line during the P-rade, just like she has since she was five years old. Along with her younger brothers, my two wonderful boys, both in computer science. Not that it got them into Princeton and so disinclined to attend Dad's Reunions, worst luck. But you'd get along like a house afire with 'em, Erma. In the Boston area as well, so I'll provide you with their emails, if you like."

"Two sons, whom their mother spoiled rotten," said Jack. "But it didn't stop them being great doctors, even if they have zero interest in our family's past, much less the history of anti-Semitism, or couldn't care less about what happened to their grandparents. Still, maybe they're happier than I was at their age, listening for incoming rockets in Saigon." He turned to Gareth, whom he knew professionally. "Gareth, do you suppose we sold out? Physics majors who went to the dark side, lured by filthy lucre?"

"Oh, I was all set to go on to teach high school physics—or even English, right, Gini? We talked about becoming teachers."

Gini gave a quick, distracted smile as she noticed her daughter take in this stray remark (had she really been so crazy freshman year?).

"But I knew I didn't have the brainpower to make significant advances in the field; besides, my father talked me out of any such thoughts. Claimed he needed help with his investment firm, what with all the quants coming into the business. 'Let's put all those expensive math and physics skills to use.' So, I ended up designing the first computer programs for his investment firm. The thing is, I kind of got hooked on designing algorithms, seeing how well they functioned in the marketplace—fascinated, to tell the truth. The money came easily; I never really thought about it—just how well my algorithms functioned." Gareth shrugged with a devil-may-care grin at his watching daughter. "Why Diane's dad spends his weekend tutoring math to kids in Newark."

"While I"—piped up a somewhat disheveled Daltrey, with a grandiose wave of his hand to the Gothic traceries of Holder courtyard, bathed in a soft blue haze from the lighting of the tent—"made the fatal error of going into American history, after doing Roman history here."

Apolonia's eyes lit up at the prospect of stirring the pot: "Yeah, Annette, you'll be thrilled to know Daltrey's senior thesis demonstrates how Seneca might well have written the Gospels."

"Hey, why not," exclaimed Gini. "I'm beginning to believe almost anything is possible."

"I noted the parallels between Seneca's moral teachings on treating your neighbors—and your slaves, for that matter—as you would want to be treated: the Golden Rule in all but name."

Annette bristled and then calmed. "Maybe it was Seneca who was influenced by the teachings of Christ."

"Well," nodded Daltrey, "later Christians even forged correspondence between Seneca and Saint Paul. All we know for sure is that Saint Paul and Seneca lived and wrote at precisely the same period, writing in Rome about the same time as the Gospels were conceived; even their death dates are approximately the same."

Gini raised her hand like a schoolgirl in class and intoned, with a glance at Annette, first giving the Latin and then the translation: "'Treat your inferiors as you would be treated by your betters. And as often as you reflect how much power you have over a slave, remember that your master has just as much power over you.'"

Annette smiled sweetly, wiping her plate with a roll. "'And, masters, treat your slaves in the same way. Do not threaten them, since you know that he who is both their Master and yours is in heaven, and there is no favoritism with him.' Saint Paul's Epistle to the Ephesians." She folded her arms. "I rest my case."

"Slaves," and Gareth shook his head with a nod toward his daughter. "All that justification of slavery in the New Testament—slaves, obey your earthly masters with respect and fear—was used by Southern slaveholders to justify their peculiar cruel and inhuman institution."

"I'm with you on that score, Gareth," said Jack. "Sorry, folks, but your Gospels, much less Paul, are full of the most inflammatory anti-Semitism—the source of centuries of oppression, suffering, and death for my people, culminating in the Holocaust. And let me tell you, before the Nazis came along, the French in the modern era were the worst anti-Semites of all; my grandparents, my aunt and uncle, and their two daughters were rounded up by French gendarmes and shipped off to Auschwitz in 1944."

"Good Lord . . ." Bianca grasped Jack's arm in an almost protective grip.

"The Holocaust," Jack continued, "don't you agree, Daltrey, has to be seen as the central fact of our history, reflecting back thousands of years, and informing how we see human nature in the present." As if to demonstrate, Jack blew out the candle nearest him and watched the smoke rise from the blackened wick.

"Yes," echoed Daltrey, "even if Stalin and Mao and Genghis Khan might have had a higher body count."

"Why, I will share with you, I take such joy in buying up my terroirs, little spots of earth high on a hill with the perfect drainage and sunlight, age-old vines rooted deep, places that the French treasure above all things." Jack reached and relit the extinguished candle from its neighbor. "It does my heart good to reclaim this territory, if not in compensation, in memory of those lost souls. I've even renamed some of our vintages"—and he tapped the nearest bottle—"after my aunt and uncle and their daughters: Salomé, Jeanne, Yaëlle, and père Abraham. Not that I've mentioned the circumstances to my French staff; they think it's merely the whim of a rich American Jew, a marketing gimmick. But I like the idea of these bottes appearing on tables all over France and worldwide: a reminder, memory in a bottle, and, as you see, a subject"—he wiped a tear—"for table talk. I tried to express to my sons as they grew up something of the grief and emptiness that filled my parents' lives, but to no avail. Perhaps it is just as well that some memories expire with the passing of a generation—who can say? Now, if only I can interest one or two of my sons, or even my grandsons (whom I invite to help harvest the grapes each fall), to take over the operation, I will go in peace."

"Ah, yes," sighed Daltrey, reaching to place a hand on his classmate's shoulder. "How our earliest memories fashion who we are. My mother took me as a little boy to visit the mosaics in Ravenna, Theodoric and Galla Placidia, the palace church of Sant'Apollinaire Nuovo, and her mausoleum. I was dazzled; I was hooked; I wanted that place and time to come alive in my mind."

"Really," said Gini, as mention of Galla Placidia sparked a memory that seemed, oddly, more recent than past, and possibly useful in distracting her daughter from a troubling, if not ardent, fascination with her phone. "My father took me there when I was seventeen, a day trip from Venice. Remember, Erma, I took you to Venice for your sixteenth as well, and we drove down to Ravenna to visit with Galla Placidia and all her court."

Erma looked up from the carcass of her steak with hungry eyes: "Justinian and Theodora, Mom."

"Quite right, young lady," Daltrey hastened to acknowledge.

At mention of Venice, all the Shirelles came to attention, Bianca especially, who had been mulling over, for much of the day, her disturbing, if enchanting, conversation with young Jacob Burrage of the previous evening.

"Visiting the Carpaccios—'in me prime,' according to Miss Jane Brody," sang out Bianca with a wistful look, crossing with Gini's in the direction of where young Jacob Burrage was in animated conversation with classmates.

"Yes, indeed, talk about memories," added Annette with an adoring smile, dipping her head against her husband's arm as she eyed the cheese platter. "We were there with Saint George, our saving grace, right, honey?"

"Yes, dear, at the Scuola di San Georgio, where you first mentioned the idea about enlisting Jake Burrage at Roland-Garros."

"No way," exclaimed Bianca, mystified, just as an image of Jake staring up at Carpaccio's Augustine was returned to her like an echoing chant out of memory. For an incandescent moment, she felt her steps on the stairs from the upper chamber of the Scuola di San Giorgio with her score of Scarlatti etudes in hand—and again Jake's expectant face turned to hers. She now bristled, even as she managed a carefree smile: "You were in Venice, and you didn't let me know."

"It was a flying visit," Matt explained, "on the way to the French Open."

"I just mentioned the Carpaccios, and it was a done deal," lied Annette (she'd made the first call to Jake from their hotel room in Rome), "since he'd just completed his doctorate at Stanford and so had the summer free before his postdoc at Chicago."

"We paid him a king's ransom at the time," noted Matt.

"And a ringside seat in the players' box," added Annette, deftly spearing a wedge of Camembert while studiously avoiding Gini's eyes, "to watch Chrissie steamroll Wendy Turnbull in the Wimbledon finals." She nodded apologetically at Bianca. "We didn't have your address or phone number."

Added Matt, barely catching Gini's eye: "After my loss at the US Open, Jake seemed to have his heart set on other matters that fall."

Apolonia, though reticent to gush, found herself as well spirited back for a shining instant to the Scuola di San Giorgio, then in the company of another older man (not that she was about to mention any names in front of Daltrey and Jack), but just as quickly returned to monitoring the amount of Daltrey's wine consumption, figuring that their chances of successful lovemaking back at the Hampton Inn, after the morning's disaster, might be crucial to future prospects. Blue pill or no, she'd had to rush off to their morning charity event. After the P-rade, at Ivy, she'd gotten an earful of how for twenty years, Daltrey had taken his family, his boys, his daughter, skiing in Jackson Hole; so the prospect of future co-habitation was potentially in the cards. While mention of Galla Placidia gladdened her heart as well, mosaic programs emblazoned in how many volumes on Ravenna sent to her by John Proctor.

"Yes," continued Daltrey, "my dear mother, a Radcliffe art history major and notorious snob (right, Gini?), dragged me around to see all the mosaics, patiently explaining all the various building programs, how the style of the mosaics, or rather how the depiction of Christ varied from one ruler to the next, from Galla Placidia to Theodoric—a Goth, you see, and an Arian—to the orthodox Archbishop Agnellus in the 560s, who then erased, banished, chipped away at the mosaics of the heretics, Theodoric and his wife and counselors, leaving curtains in their place and a stray hand or two."

"Curtains for them—huh," cried Bianca, already a little high and wondering if maybe she'd drunk too much wine the previous night and just imagined half her conversation with young Jacob. Only barely restraining herself from revealing their Venetian affair, much less its sad aftermath.

"'Canceled' is the term of art, I believe," suggested Gini, wincing with pain as she rubbed her right knee.

"Air-brushed away," corrected Jack, with a broad sweep of the hands setting the candles aflutter. "A specialty of Stalin—right, comrade Daltrey? Destroy your enemies, destroy memory of the past, and we are forsaken souls."

His classmate, palms raised, long fingers intertwined: "Iconoclasts—it never really ends, from Edward VI to Charles I, how many sculptural programs or stained-glass windows were destroyed. Even today, their successors are out trying to lay the ghosts of the past—blowing up Buddhist shrines, wiping the slate clean of sins real or imagined."

For the first time that evening, such talk seemed to tempt the attention of the two young women.

"I remember those hands on the columns in Sant'Apollinaire," noted Erma. "Kind of creepy, remember, Mom?"

"Goths or ghosts?" asked her classmate, Diane.

Daltrey in professorial mode: "Yes, clinging to the columns, spooky, like the dead hand of the past clinging on for dear life, or memories of Samson, perhaps, still intent on bringing down the temple. Ghosts behind the curtains of the rulers and ruled whose ideas inspired past builders."

"I remember," said Apolonia, reminded again of that stray memo of her lover's noting Jake Burrage's advice to invest in the future of the life sciences, "John Proctor"—she nodded to the two young women—"Princeton's president in our day, telling me how hard it was to 'visualize into the future,' as he called it, to figure out what of the old—memorials, places, names—needed keeping and what required upgrading with the new. The right balance, I suppose, in the churn of history."

Gini patted her teammate's hand sympathetically. "A master of time's arrow. Something, I daresay, we deal with every day in the book-publishing business."

"The Borg phenomenon," laughed Annette, "the younger players always moving up the ranks." She gave her husband's hand a comforting pat, feeling somewhat immune to such dolorous concerns after her triumphant talk at the Athletes for Christ forum, the lovely cordon sanitaire provided by her ironclad faith in the immortal soul.

Matt grinned. "The record books, the names on a trophy—that something of you passed this way . . ." His voice fell off with a shrug.

Apolonia, still a little amazed at her teammate's performance on the court, was about to praise Gini's eternal youth when her clinician's eye noted the tremor in her upper arm and a slight sag in her chin to go along with the reappearance of those crow's-feet, and so held her tongue.

"You see, the Goths were heretics," said Daltrey, now directly addressing Diane's question, as if seeking to bring alive his fascination with the past for the youngsters. "As heretics, barbarians from the wooded hinterlands beyond the Danube, Theodoric and his kind were much frowned upon by the Romans, even as they were drawn to his valor and toughness as a fighter. Why, when I was an undergrad, about your age, ladies, I was so drawn to the Goths—a real Goth, mind you, not the play-acting kind with black getup, purple hair, and piercings—and King Theodoric, who captured Ravenna and much of northern Italy in the mid-sixth century. Theodoric was hardly an uncouth barbarian; he'd been brought up in the court of the Eastern empire at Constantinople, knew Greek and Latin, philosophy and literature. But the extraordinary thing about Theodoric was that he allowed all factions of Christianity, his Arian church, and the Orthodox church to coexist and do their own thing. He even allowed what was left of the pagan cults to pursue their ancient ways. Drew up laws protecting the rights of free speech—or at least on the most burning issue in his day: free speculation as to the true nature of Christ."

"There," proclaimed Jack, raising his wineglass to his classmate, "you should've stuck it out with Theo instead of Marx. Theo, the freethinker, instead of Marx, the ideologue. Instead of the tragic century we've left in our wake, we might have fared better with a Goth like your Theodoric or with Gini's Seneca. Sure beats the likes of Roger Williams, that most absolutist of Puritan perfectionists—a spiritual guide to Cromwell, wasn't he, Daltrey?—before setting up his heaven on earth in Rhode Island. Truth in advertising, I have a splendid place along the Cliff Walk in Newport—to which you are all invited in August, when I take up residence."

Gareth rolled his eyes at his daughter across the table. "Roger Williams ended up selling the surrendered Narragansett and Pequot tribes into slavery, while condoning slavery in New England."

Daltrey nodded sadly, sagely. "Another case of an ideological stance drawn from scripture to back up a hideous system of exploitation—why I was originally drawn to a Marxist interpretation of history: a way of overcoming America's original sin. And your Roger Williams, Jack—yes, Gareth, in his pursuit of the ultimate apostolic purity—ended his days with his poor wife worshipping all alone in the bitter cold, their spiritual utopia gone with the wind. Theodoric was a piker compared to some of those crazy millenarians who eagerly awaited their predestined end of history."

"Wasn't the fall of the Berlin Wall supposed to be that?" offered Gareth as he opened another bottle. "The end of history, I mean."

Jack's eyes flared eagerly. "Not according to your classmate Burrage, along with Bezos and Musk and their like; Larry and Sergey are in on it too. I get funding emails all the time from those biotech geniuses, these technocratic gurus: how aging is plastic, encoded in our genes; and if something is encoded, all you have to do is crack the code and, hey presto, live forever. These dudes would still have us believe in the possibilities of human perfection: ageless, free of want or disease, ever awaiting the Bridegroom—when and if He should show—all the while contemplating their magic algorithms and esoteric symbols, pondering eternal truths concealed from us ordinary folk."

"'Brigadoon, Brigadoon, where my heart forever lies,'" sang Bianca, playing sommelier for Jack as she poured the next bottle around the table.

"Speaking of the Second Coming, I took Gareth's advice and toured the new Burrage Biochemistry Lab after the P-rade." Gini offered a delighted smile for her daughter, figuring that, by bringing Gareth into the picture, she'd defuse any criticism about invading her daughter's privacy by nosing about in her workplace. "I don't know when I've been so moved—almost to tears—by such an enchanted palace of a building. Just the quality of light! Even Galla Placidia would be pleased. Or Johnny von Neumann—right, Gareth?—that numbers genius who helped design the first computer. And so sped us on our way—exponentially—to the new singularity."

"*The Singularity Is Near*," echoed Erma, a seeming ironic commentary on her mother's newfound enthusiasm.

"Just look at us, the perfect test case," mused Gareth. "When humans transcend biology."

At this, Jack bent eagerly across the table. "As a student, von Neumann was the prevailing deus ex machina of the physics and math departments, right, Gareth? The man who single-handedly brought together the team who invented the first computer at the Institute for Advanced Study, and then executed the critical math around the development of the hydrogen bomb. I remember the most brilliant professors who spoke about him with awe. His work, his team of mathematicians and physicists and engineers influenced a dozen fields, changed the world. And how many of us can say as much?"

"A genius's genius," noted Gareth, "who had figured in the development of the first atomic bomb and so had the blood of tens of thousands on his hands—Hiroshima and Nagasaki—even as he set the stage for transistors and silicon chips."

"Including genetics," added Erma, looking up from her phone and avoiding her mother's curious stare, as if the conversation had finally veered to a subject on which she could weigh in. "The same way primitive self-reproducing life-forms adopted self-replicating polynucleotide symbionts as the carriers of hereditary information from one generation to the next. We might even adopt computers as carriers of our genetic code."

"Oh, great," said Bianca, flashing a goofy smile at her goddaughter. "Next, we're going to be mating with our cell phones. Tinder was bad enough."

"Oh, much worse," said Gareth's daughter. "There are women in our class selling their eggs and guys donating sperm."

Erma looked up with a delicious smile from her phone, just catching the eye of her mother aslant. "Pretty soon, we'll be uploading our memories to the cloud and downloading libraries of memories from others—a cross-generational thing, why not?"

Gini gasped inwardly as if ducked underwater, a shooting pain in her right shoulder.

"By Jove," said Jack, "and to think, Daltrey, once upon a time we donated for free."

Daltrey, musing as he finished up the last of his tuna, seemed intent to ease the conversation around to his favorite subject. "I was just thinking about that—copying, that is—as I was visiting the history department today, walking down the corridors of McCosh and finding all my old professors gone—yes, erased—and young men and women with new names and very different, newfangled fields in their book-lined offices: gender studies, African American history, queer studies, and so on. And I was reminded about my fascination with Ravenna in the fifth century (and how my adviser had told me to stick with the Flavians: not enough primary documentation). You see, as the classical world faded"—he raised his near-empty glass and swirled his wine as if to illustrate—"well, no government, no civilization could survive without recordkeeping, as we humans wouldn't be human without a brain to store up memories. And municipal authorities like those of Ravenna were dependent on scribes to complete in triplicate, as was the Roman custom, all the necessary documents: laws, legal decisions, military orders, financial matters about who owned what land. But the number of skilled scribes, the educated and literate in Latin and Greek, was dwindling fast; and to make matters worse, the precious supply of papyrus from Egypt faltered as Mediterranean trade was cut off by pirates and the barbarian invasions. So recordkeeping, the duplicating of documents, fell off, as there were no longer paper or scribes." Like Jack before him, he blew out a candle to illustrate his point. "A whole world, year by year, going blank."

"Good Lord," erupted Gini, mysteriously affected as if Daltrey's tale touched on her worst nightmare.

"Yes," he went on, as if pleased to have everyone's attention, "just think about it: the cultural memory of a people, a civilization, slowly fading year after year, as if our Dropboxes were slowly winking out one by one. Not until the Renaissance and the recovery of the few remaining documents from the classical past did the world begin to remember again who we were and where we came from. And I couldn't help thinking, as I wandered the halls of McCosh, seeing all those new and unfamiliar names on the department doors—where once giants in their field had held court—that to remember, to properly remember, you have first to forget."

"When the wave function collapses," offered Gareth, catching Jack's eye, since they had both been physics majors.

"Wave function?" queried Daltrey.

"Ah, but perhaps we're on the verge of a new Renaissance," Jack suggested. "The world you young ladies"—catching the eyes of Erma and Diane—"will surely inherit. As we move toward that transhuman future advocated by your boy Burrage—right, Gareth?" Jack waved a hand to Holder's immemorial cloistered arcades. "Banish aging and cognitive shortcomings, much less suffering and pain. What the hell, even confinement to planet Earth—why not?"

"Far out." Apolonia handed the basket of rolls to Annette. "There goes my practice, yet another receding contrail on the horizon. Yet another dawning of the Age of Aquarius. Seems like I've heard this story before."

"The problem with the exponential rate of growth, whether in science or quantum computing or even fusion energy," said Erma, the last of her steak poised on her fork, "is that the technology to fully exploit the new discoveries develops only in a linear fashion." She made a chopping motion with her fork. "People keep looking for a magic bullet, when aging, like everything else, is a combination of interrelated factors—like falling dominos. Like restoring tissue suppleness, replacing cells that have stopped dividing, and removing those that have become toxic. It's not as easy as these grand theories would have you believe."

"Right on." Gareth placed a fond hand on Gini's shoulder as if complimenting her for her daughter's acumen, while perhaps tempted to a provocative remark, the testing of certain waters. "Oh, Elon Musk and Bezos will take you to the stars, but our very own champion of the future, Jake Burrage, my roommate freshman year, has his feet, by all accounts, solidly planted on terra firma. From what I can make out from Burrage Pharma quarterly reports, they are, indeed, working on all those problems simultaneously. Even if it's a game of Whac-A-Mole. But it's only a matter of time—right, Erma?—before the breakthroughs occur. After all, the collapse of the wave function is really just the birth of a new object, a new age, Daltrey's Renaissance—right, ladies?" And he withdrew his hand from Gini's shoulder as his eyes lingered fully on Erma's, wide, intent, and glittering blue.

"You knew Jacob Burrage, donor of our fishbowl?" asked Erma, a little high from the great wine, which may have had something to do with her proprietary tone.

"Did I know Jake, Gini?" Gareth smiled graciously at his dinner partner. "I was his poker piggy bank, then his backer. Maybe that explains my fall from grace. But your mother knew him better than any of us."

Erma shot a glance at her mother's pensive, possibly disbelieving, even guilty face, until, a moment later, she was distracted by the whispered vibration of another text.

"Knew him . . . ," echoed Gini, turning to the table, as if for help. Then, switching to cruise control, she recited the first thing that came to mind. "His voice was propertied as all the tuned spheres, and that to friends." A sloshing wineglass to toast her rhetorical flourish. A wince of pain. "But when he meant to quail and shake the orb, he was as rattling thunder. For his bounty, there was no winter in it; an autumn 'twas that grew the more by reaping. His delights were dolphin-like; they showed his back above the element they lived in."

This riff of bard-quoting subterfuge brought the table conversation to a brief standstill, as all were drawn to Gini's dreamlike voice, possibly stirred by something left unsaid or unsayable between mother and daughter. Erma now blinking, refocusing, perhaps trying to fully process the image of a swimmer doing the butterfly, until the spell was broken by yet more vibrations of her cell phone.

Bianca broke the ice with a cackle. "Goodness, Agrippina, not as in Richard Burton and Liz?"

"Careful," said Apolonia, "you're dating yourself, Big Mac. I'm sure Gini had *National Velvet* more in mind."

Gareth laughed and made eyes at his daughter. "Only the well-read need apply."

Jack looked at Daltrey, then Gareth, as if a little lost, as if their train had suddenly been shunted to a siding, embarking on a trunk line with uncertain stops. "Well, Gareth," he sighed, "I leave the mysteries of the quantum level to the youngsters. I find myself more concerned with how climate change impacts my vineyards, the cost of new sprinkler systems to keep my thirsty babes plump and happy."

Gareth, now nodding at Erma, whose attention had clearly been piqued, offered his own take. "Jake would have agreed with Johnny von Neumann's prediction that we live in an age of probability. Call it connectedness encompassing space and time." He sent an air kiss toward his daughter. "So much so, at least I like to think, that our observation of phenomena actually makes us central, perhaps indispensable, to existence. As someone put it, we"—and he motioned to the table—"are a way for the universe to know itself. Like all of us; our lives are entangled with one another's in how many spooky ways—ways we can barely imagine."

"Carl Sagan," said Erma with a gracious, even excited smile.

"So new agey, Gareth," laughed Apolonia, now nodding to his daughter. "Your dad was always such a sweetheart. We were all a little in love with him."

Gareth blushed, saved from having to correct the record by Erma's intervention.

"Hands and feet, across space and time," Erma now proclaimed as she held up her cell phone and then passed it across the table to Daltrey. "Just like you said, hands still on the columns."

Daltrey, in rumpled tie and threadbare collar, put on his reading glasses and inspected the close-up of the mosaics in Sant'Apollinaire, smiling broadly as he handed the phone over to his GP. "Yes, splendid, aren't they, enchanting to me first as a little boy and later here, contemplating my future in light of the past."

The cell phone vibrated as Apolonia was about to hand the phone on. "It's alive . . . ," she cried, spying the text, which caused her eyes to illuminate with a repressed radiance and a knowing glance when she held the phone up to Gini's curious eyes before returning it to her daughter. "Hey, girls, the 'flush of lush,' as we called it whenever love came knocking on our dorm-room door."

"Yes, love, the new messiah . . . ," ruminated Daltrey, as if reenergized by Erma's enthusiasm. "At your age, Erma and Diane, I was possessed by curiosity at the process of change, the slow winding down of the old clocks before anyone had thought to wind the new. How Christianity managed to slip into that gap and take hold, thus my senior thesis on the Flavians and the creation of Christianity. Like your boy Burrage—have I got it right, Gini?—whom I've heard so much about, your Anthony straddling the world, the new messiah for our day, perhaps not unlike the healer gods Asclepius and Serapis, promising eternal life."

"Now that sounds like the ultimate wave collapse," toasted Jack. "And maybe a messiah who didn't bring anti-Semitism in his wake."

Gini stared around the table with a brave smile, even as all the conversation whipped up her wildest fantasies, possibly nightmares.

Daltrey relit the candle he'd blown out with a delighted grin, as if an offering to the goddess Mnemosyne, possibly pleased that he'd touched a chord in his listeners. "And, you know, there's even a mosaic in Ravenna where Christ is depicted as a Roman emperor."

Apolonia cackled: "Jake our messiah—who'd have thought it?"

"Ah," said Gareth, as if sensing Gini's growing perturbation, giving her arm a gentle squeeze, "why publishers are our modern-day scribes, because any information we gain, whether on the subatomic scale or around this table, means that photons or at least bits of electromagnetic energy have registered on our retinal cells, an energy exchange lighting up—at least, hopefully, enlightening our brains. And so inspiring writers, like Gini, who dazzled us all in Richard Ford's writing seminar."

Erma looked up from her phone—eyes lit like flares—as if she'd been totally on top of the conversation from the get-go. "Wave function decay is very much like faltering or misfiring DNA, just another delivery method for information about likelihoods and probabilities. It tells us where to look and where not to."

"Imagine a time," said Daltrey, as if to put paid to this pesky subatomic scale, "where you lived in a landscape littered with the ruins of a past for which you had no information, even if you could read or write; part of a family with no memory of your ancestors going back more than a generation or two; where everything you knew was rumor, or gossip, or pure fantasy perpetrated by the local priest."

Annette, fed up and having a bone to pick, now broke into the conversation: "How do you know that those people in such a time of darkness, as you put it, weren't comforted by the stories of the Gospel as related to them by their local priest? Or even inspired by the stories so beautifully illustrated by your mosaics, and later in the windows of Chartres?"

"Sweet lady, of course, you're so right. One must be careful not to paint too dismal a picture of ages past or project our prejudices onto a world so very different from our own."

"And on the DNA thing," said Erma, eyes dancing with blue light, seemingly enchanted, as if the dawning of a new age was drawing nearer than anyone knew, "meiosis is always rolling the dice in terms of what DNA you inherit, whether you get more from your father or mother, or even more from one grandparent or another. We're studying violations of the laws of heredity—you might even call it fixing Mendel's dice—violations we call gene drive, in which a gene can be supercharged to spread itself across generations, kind of like a super epidemic. We know it happens in fruit flies, plants, and mammals—and probably humans. But we're not sure. And until we have more accurate and detailed DNA sequences, we won't know if gene drive rampages through humanity, bringing in its wake both good and bad things—diseases or immunity to diseases. Probably a battleground that littered our DNA with scars going right back to the Middle Ages and the Black Death. If we can figure out more about gene drive, we can potentially harness genes, by way of gene therapy, to cure diseases and even prolong life—clone ourselves. Hardly the stuff of a new messiah, but—who knows—enough to get you out of bed in the morning."

"Can I hire you as my analyst, Erma?" asked Jack. "Seriously, I'd like you to head up our team on biotech and Big Pharma."

"What, a shrink?" said Bianca with a sly smile. "I don't think so."

"Now, Jack, don't go throwing your money around like it's a busman's holiday," scolded Daltrey, with a twinkle in his eye. "Harvard has already pledged Erma for the fruits of her labor."

"The hell with Harvard. Erma, you would be instrumental in picking winners and losers, funneling resources to the best and brightest—accelerating the discovery of lifesaving biotechnologies."

"Hopefully somatic gene editing, not germline gene editing—Pandora's box," Gareth said in a warning tone.

Erma smiled graciously. "Who knows what the Chinese geneticists are up to. But yes, winners and losers, pretty much what we've been doing for the last four years, trying to explore new ways of understanding flexible design in cells, how they relay information, manage waste, and respond to stress. You see, cells achieve this flexibility by a process called liquid-liquid phase separation, aided by these little droplets called membrane-less organelles or condensates, which play a key role in a cell's nucleus, where genes are stored and direct cellular activity. These droplets help genes communicate in the cells, and so we're exploring various ways of manipulating this process and thus uncovering new ways of gene regulation."

"Holy cow," said Jack, leaning across the table so as not to miss any of this insider information. "The crown jewels."

"And how," laughed Gareth, shaking his head at his daughter, herself perhaps a little in awe of how her classmate captured the attention of the adults.

"Some of the other labs are using light to control cellular activities and gene editing—you've probably heard about CRISPR—so that by studying the biophysics of the droplets we can understand how certain genes are activated, and how to turn them off if they are causing diseases like cystic fibrosis and Huntington's." Gini couldn't help noticing how Erma's eyes seemed to be following a moving figure behind where her mother sat. "A colleague, a guy in my class, Jacob Burrage"—she paused for just an instant as if sensing the utterance of the name was sure to spark the interest of the adults—"is especially focused on the causes and cure for Huntington's." Her daughter's face, much to her mother's consternation, now lit up like the Second Coming, as if her very words were taking on a life of their own. "Jacob would be the first to tell you that gene editing and gene sequencing are on the cusp of revolutionizing biotech; software, hardware, data science, and lab science are coming together to reinforce each other. Most of my professors and senior researchers are licking their chops at the prospects—the patent registrations, for which they get a cut. Of course, AI will be another game changer."

"I see it all the time in my practice," added Apolonia. "Designer babies—and worse, unwanted babies."

"Did you say Jacob Burrage, Erma?" asked Jack. "Not the son, the scion of Burrage Pharma & Health?"

At this, Bianca, her voice a fluty octave higher, unloosed a torrent of gossip. "Yes, the one and the same. But get this, I've spoken to a bunch of folks in the chow line tonight, and they're all quite mystified by our Reunions manager, Jacob Burrage. Seems he'd been seeking out all his father's old cronies at dinner, his poker, swim team, and chemistry department pals, and chatting them up, recalling escapades, regaling them with fond memories of their student days as if he'd been there in person. Freaky, huh? All of them nonplused by how well he seemed to know them from years ago, like he was channeling Jake himself—at once charmed by his familiarity and not a little dumbfounded that this kid seemed so genuinely eager to reconnect with—well, complete strangers."

Annette turned to Matt: "We too were flummoxed at sign-in. Ever since, I've been reliving those glorious days of summer with Jake in the players' box when Matt made his comeback."

"Crazy," added Apolonia. "I had the strangest sensation that I was being evaluated as to how well I'd managed all the years since I knew Jake. Almost as if Jake had been running some kind of experiment and he'd sent the kid—his alter ego—on a mission to evaluate the data points, the proof of his theory."

"The hell with theory," Bianca chimed in with a delicious cackle. "I ran into Jacob last night, and it was like being regaled with memories of Jake's time with me in Venice. So vivid, I found myself practically living out a daydream of the best years of my life."

"Which begs the question," offered Gareth, "why his son and not Jake himself—why is he hiding from us?" He tapped his phone as if for an answer. "When young Jacob conducted me around the lab this morning, I kept having these moments of déjà vu. Perplexing as they were charming . . . the feeling of continuity."

By this time, all eyes were on Gini for a reaction, but with her detached stare (even as her head felt like it might explode), she, so she prayed, was giving nothing away. Prompting her daughter, who had been avidly listening to this exchange between her godmothers, to weigh in once more and so return the conversation to safer, if possibly more mind-bending topics.

"Jacob and I are on the swim team together," Erma said, with a toss of her head and a whimsical laugh, as if the consternation expressed around the table was easily explained. "His head is filled with so many ideas that you never know what's going to happen next. One moment he's explaining to our swim coaches how a certain team member could improve with just a tweak to his technique, and the next moment he's speculating on the impact of Dolly the sheep and the future of cloning—designer babies and all that." She laughed again as if under the spell of just such a future. "Trust me: cloning oneself is the next item on the hidden agenda of our budding Frankensteins in the field."

Gini stared off in horror at her daughter's comments, only further seeding her growing panic.

"Erma, I'll double my offer," said Jack, seeming to enjoy the casino-like atmosphere of a bidding war. "You'd be such a terrific addition to our team."

"Jack," scolded Daltrey, "your promotion of blind ambition and greed in the young is hardly appropriate for a gathering like this, besides being counterproductive by creaming off the very talent that provides the critical breakthroughs in the first place."

Apolonia was stirred to add her two bits, less to preserve the peace than make sure to give credit where credit was due. "Wasn't it John Proctor, in our day, who made the decision that the researchers—the worker bees—should be properly compensated and incentivized for their discoveries? And more importantly, to expand the role of the life sciences?"

"You should know," exclaimed Bianca, and then held her tongue when she caught Apolonia's narrowed, possibly homicidal squint.

"A brilliant, farseeing president," added Jack. "Whenever John put the squeeze on me for a university project, and later in his Rockefeller Foundation days too, I was always happy to chip in, knowing the funding would be spent wisely and well.

A prince among academic paupers. He had a way about him of making you believe in the best about yourself, that loyalty and generosity were the coin of the realm."

Apolonia had to restrain herself from reaching over and squeezing Jack's hand.

"Yes," added Gini. "We were lucky. *You*"—a sparring of eyebrows at her doubles partner—"were lucky; we shan't see his like again."

At this, Apolonia bowed her head and then rose a little shakily from her seat to address the table, holding her glass high in one hand, her phone in the other, face quivering, lustrous brown eyes tearing up under an unruly bang of auburn hair. "I have a confession to make. People think doctors are fearless, but I was a coward yesterday when I didn't march up to the podium during John Proctor's memorial service and tell everyone what a wonderful man he was. I had my words ready to go on my phone, with excerpts from his unpublished memoir, which he shared with me—what he valued most in Princeton." And she raised her glass and quoted: "'Great universities thrive by allowing disparate groups of scholars and scientists to band together in pursuit of higher purposes. Universities allow for continuity between the generations that can't be achieved otherwise, especially allowing the individual to thrive. Success also requires accommodations that academic affiliation make possible. And so allowing the ardent individualists to strike out on their own, to cooperate and collaborate when necessary, but in the end allowing their genius to flourish. This, the saving grace of our civilization.'" She raised her glass. "A toast to the man—a genius in his own right—I loved."

The table rose to echo the toast, with Jack and Daltrey, Erma and Diane exchanging slightly baffled looks.

"You'd think he was talking about Jake," Gareth noted with an insider's smile.

Then Erma weighed in with the perfect rejoinder, with a conviviality her mother hoped she'd learned at her knee. "Oh, that's something we experience every day in our labs: cross-fertilization. A principle that is now applied to the very architecture and design of 'Burrage Biochemistry, Inc.,' as our profs call it. We work in a greenhouse so that we, hybrid plants, can properly thrive, with free eats in the café. The only thing they haven't done, yet, is create multisex bathrooms so you can chat up the sixty-year-old bearded prof in the next-door stall while you change a tampon."

"That's my girl," laughed Gini, her moment of terror at her daughter's wandering eye momentarily quelled.

"Oh, Erma," said Bianca, "your mom and godmothers have so been-there-done-that—right, girls?—back in the good-old-bad-old days when we had co-ed bathrooms."

As her three teammates launched into a greatest hits collection of raunchy, twice-told tales of co-ed bathroom encounters and deftly parried sexual advances by faculty, Gini found herself fixated on her daughter's face, as their eyes seemed to meet in flashes of recognition, as if exchanging long-withheld secrets of the heart. There were moments when she felt—for the first time in their lives—allied to her daughter's aspirations and joys, somehow brought on by the festive occasion, even as a dark, unspeakable foreboding began to haunt her.

She had never thought of herself as her daughter's pathfinder (a role left up to her husband, Bill Cheshire), and certainly not a competitor for love, and yet her daughter's furtive glances past her shoulder, her incoming texts, spoke of something she now dreaded, something almost as bizarre as Erma's conversation with young Jacob in the tennis stands that morning (as odd and quirky as anything discussed around the table), which, one day, Erma would blithely share with her mother. A conversation that would find its way almost verbatim into the pages of Gini's novel.

"Don't you think Gini is playing like she's nineteen again?" He bent forward in his seat, eyes riveted on his protégé as she was about to serve. "She's even adapted her strokes to the modern game."

Erma struggled to pick up on the proprietary vibe in Jacob's voice: "Sure, except I wasn't exactly around."

"If you just focus on the arc of the ball"—Jacob had motioned with his finger like the beat of a metronome—"you can almost feel the paradigmatic forces that drive everything in life, that beautiful engine, fueled and flowing in fluid motion: the ball captured on the humming strings for an instant, its direction reversed—oh, was there ever such beauty in a parabola cradled in its gravitational field?"

Not a little mystified by this sudden outpouring of appreciation for her mother, Erma had just managed a semi-intelligent reply.

"You mean the S-curve, the slow increase in speed, faster and faster until it slows and its energy becomes exhausted."

"Like traffic patterns in the city, or oxygen transport in the lungs, or fast and slow thinking in the flow architecture of the brain."

"Oh," she said, trying to keep up her end with a snatch of memory from organic chemistry, "those twenty-three levels of branching air tubes in the human lung."

"You see how your mother's height—how she holds her own with the younger women on the court—gives her that slight edge in terms of both the speed and the power coefficient."

She had turned for the briefest of instants, as if needing to gauge the heated enthusiasm in his voice, a lab partner intrigued by findings in his petri dish. Realizing, as she returned her gaze to the match, that she'd never seen her mother playing so well or looking so good, like just another one of the girls on the Princeton team.

"She's like a Chrissie Evert in her prime, in the perfection of her movement to meet the ball at the optimal moment," he went on. "Newton's second law of motion encompassed by the laws of thermodynamics. Evolution, self-organized, self-optimized, an example of natural selection at its finest, well"—the merest quiver of a well-pleased smile—"given a little boost."

"I suppose," she countered, a tad baffled, if intrigued, by the way his voice went up on 'little boost.' She struggled to keep up her end of the exchange by moving from the particular to the general. "True, at least, I guess, on the cellular level. But like you said, living things are mostly about freely changing flow configurations or different rhythms of interaction, which then allows them greater freedom of movement across boundaries."

"Every generation—don't you think?—must outgrow its past, exceed those boundaries—or else. Gini," he nodded, now again musing on his subject's performance, "is still quite the inspiration to us all. You should be proud as hell to be her daughter."

If this last observation—certainly the tone—had thrown Erma off her stride that morning, by evening she too found herself somewhat transformed by young Jacob Burrage, even if half amused to observe a Jacob Burrage, Reunions manager—almost unrecognizable to her. Gone were the shorts and tee shirt, the Nike running shoes, the cap worn backward, the stained jeans, the sleek bathing suit, much less the lab coat and protective eyewear. Here was a Jacob Burrage dressed in khaki trousers, a button-down blue shirt, blue blazer, and Princeton tie as he made the rounds of the festive dinner tables, checking, like a solicitous maître d', that all was well with his guests. Was this un-Burrage simply duded up for the occasion, part of his duty as manager of the Reunions site—to gallantly blend in with this over-the-hill gang? Hardly the case with any of the other student managers she'd run into. Even more fascinating, to her researcher's eye, her view framed by her mother's right shoulder and gold tiger earring, was how many of the ancient faces that rose to meet his greeting did a double take: surprise, bafflement, then vague recognition with a sprinkle of incredulity, displaced, only nanoseconds later (long- and short-term memory coalescing), by a fond, even humorous smile to go along with a lingering handshake.

Or, as her mother would one day write in Proustian mode: she glimpsed her future, when a glance, a scent, or touch—and the unremembered rises again.

But for the present, at the sound of his voice (after a deluge of texts), Erma was practically levitating in her seat.

"Hey, folks"—young Jacob, his voice clean and ringing, had come to rest in his wanderings behind Erma's chair—"I hope everything's okay with the dinner."

Bianca gushed with girlish enthusiasm, figuring that, if anyone did, she had rights to this updated incarnation of Jake.

"Hola, Jacob, *ciao, come stai!*" And she threw the young man a big kiss. "You and the rest of the crew have done such a fantastic—more than fantastic—job. So much so that we even managed to attract two defectors from the fiftieth." She motioned to Jack and Daltrey with an added yelp of pleasure.

Young Jacob laughed at the admiring, not-a-little-curious smiles around the table.

"I have something to confess to you good people: I had my pick of Reunions crews, and I picked you guys—and not just because you're my father's class, but because the word on the street was that your class revolutionized Old Nassau. Hey, the first to graduate a significant cadre of women and so prepare the university to face the twenty-first century. Of course, having the world's number-one-ranked player as an honorary class member was the clincher."

Jacob reached over and shook Matt's hand.

"Kind of you, Jacob," said Matt. "And far be it from me to contradict your failure to use the past tense. But honorary class member?"

"Yes," said Annette, "we brought you in by unanimous vote at the end of senior year, before our wedding."

Jacob glanced serenely around the table, just catching Gini's eye with a tilt of his full eyebrows, before turning again to her roommates. "Pulling off that fifth set against Metreveli was one of the great achievements in the game. Only equaled a few years later when you made that gallant comeback against all the odds, adapting your game to changing circumstances and coming within a few points of reclaiming your Wimbledon and US Open titles."

"To gallant comebacks," toasted a bemused Jack, raising his glass high to the others.

"YouTube forever," Matt echoed as he clinked Jack's glass with his own.

Jacob reached for an abandoned water glass, waving his free hand as if to encompass the quatrefoil arches of the courtyard, bathed, as night settled on the encampment, in a haze of blue light from the tent, and toasted: "To the Scuola di San Giorgio and visiting the Carpaccios."

In the ensuing moments of somewhat puzzled silence, Jacob seemed to put any possible consternation to rest by placing his hands on Erma's shoulders.

"But I too have a confession to make—not as profound as our good Saint Augustine—and one close to my heart, especially in this auspicious moment of celebration, which as captain of the men's swim team, I failed to make mention of last night at our team's dinner together with the women's team—the diving team. That is my admiration for Erma, who, until yesterday, I had no idea was practically a member of your class. Her brilliant accomplishments in the lab go without saying. But there is something much more important. Over the last four years, Erma and I have been on far too many bus rides together, to and from meets, and although we never got to know one another well, I did notice how in countless instances she selflessly gave up her time to help one of her teammates, both men and women, with their math or organic chemistry homework to prepare them for tests. All those long, weary miles after an exhausting day. Helping to settle so many already anxious minds made a huge difference in their performance, allowing them to swim some of their best times and against tough competition—and so contribute more than I think she ever realized to our success. 'Lucky Lindy'—'Lucky,' as she was known to many of us was because so many felt her to be their luck. She was an inspiration to me and a super tribute to you, Ms. Wingate, and her godmothers three." He had been massaging Erma's shoulders and now gripped them for a moment. "And I've let her know that when she's done with Harvard, there will be a research post waiting for her at Burrage Pharma." With that, he gave Erma's blushing shoulders a final squeeze. "Good night, ladies and gentlemen. Enjoy yourselves."

"My God," said Jack, "I believe I've been gazumped."

"By a fortune made on Liracil," said Gareth. "Why we invested all those years ago."

"Guilty," said Bianca, raising a hand, her beaming face now intent on a member of the band's tech crew setting up their mics at the front of the bandstand.

"Don't believe what you see advertised," said Apolonia. "There's no such thing as an antiaging cream or formula. All the best treatments can do is hydrate and plump up the skin using hyaluronic acid and glycerin to promote the production of more collagen and elastin, or provide more retinol and vitamin A, nutrients or whatever."

Gini, who had had to resist staring at young Jacob's possessive grip on her daughter's shoulders, smiled through her shell-shocked silence.

The band's roadie arrived and informed Bianca that they were ready for the Shirelles.

"Girls, we're on."

"At least she didn't try to stick with the wigs," Apolonia exclaimed. "Today, we'd be lynched."

And so, the four women took the stage, perhaps for the last time—lead singer Bianca, at one microphone, backup singers Gini (favoring her right knee), surrounded by Apolonia and Annette, at the other. "Please welcome four girls from New Jersey," the band leader announced, "the Shirelles." A hush fell over the tent as the musicians launched into "Will You Still Love Me Tomorrow" and Bianca bent to the microphone with her most sultry, come-hither smile and purred out the opening lyrics, "Tonight you're mine . . . ," while her backup singers harmonized in perfect sync, their bodies turning side to side, fingers pointed at their rapt audience, only to fold palms back across their hearts, right arms bent at the elbow pumping the beat, their yearning, teenage voices banishing the years. Magical moments that found many of those gathered under the tent infused with tears of youthful ardor.

CHAPTER 26

Her imagination, as I say, now hung back; there was a last vague space it couldn't cross—a dusky, uncertain tract which looked ambiguous and even slightly treacherous, like a moorland seen in the winter twilight. But she was to cross it yet.

—Henry James, *The Portrait of a Lady*

Gini lay wide awake in her bed at the Marriott. Too wired, too exhausted, too anxious—too confused to sleep. Consumed by the oddest and most terrifying sensation that she was being robbed of memory—if not losing her mind: that Erma was in dire danger. She had somehow managed to get through their set of Shirelles' greatest hits with almost effortless aplomb, a climber on a rope line with her sister backup singers, joyously guided by Bianca's resonant contralto. This imitation of an imitation, this homage to four Black women and one white, Carole King, had a momentarily calming effect, a return to the known and true, buoyed on the heartfelt applause and the proud face of Erma beaming at their table. She had thought herself home free. Happy to depart from Reunions leaving this afterimage in her wake, perhaps the last fading image of her youth in the eyes of many of her fellow travelers.

But then there had been the dance with Gareth, her last dance, when her new superpowers began to drain away along with the last suppleness in her knees.

She now shifted the bags of ice on her aching knees, adjusting the one on her right shoulder, and closed her eyes once again, and once again a picture of possession came to her of a smiling young Jacob, hands on Erma's shoulder, as if pressed on her very heart.

"You brought tears to my eyes," said Gareth, squeezing her hand as the band segued into a string of slow ballads. "It took me right back . . . I was going to say to the early sixties, when those feelings first stirred the heartstrings, but it was really to an arch sing our freshman year when I first fell for you."

"Not because I reminded you of a talented Black woman? I always wondered about that." And she squeezed his hand in return as they danced, resting her aching right arm on his shoulder.

"No way," he laughed and sighed. "Maybe that was part of my problem; no Black woman could have lived up to my mother's persnickety Philly standards. Why, she married a white man from the South, Faulkner's Major de Spain; and I ended up with Ruth, a hardheaded, softhearted Jewess whose grandparents and cousins had all died in concentration camps. My family . . . as if the marriage of opposites could redeem all the horrors of the world. Jack Rambridge's as well."

"But you did. You and Ruth produced Diane and her sister."

"You're shivering—you okay? You were awfully quiet at dinner."

"It's nothing, just my knees. I forgot to ice them."

"Shall we stop, and I'll run down some ice?"

"Look at our girls dancing away. Do you suppose they'll cut in on us?"

"There's always hope."

"Did you notice young Jacob's right hand, the scar on his index finger just above the cuticle?"

"Scar?"

"Like the state of Florida, an acid burn."

"I guess I missed that."

"Jake had the same scar."

"Did he? I don't remember. Then I, well . . ."

"He was your best friend."

"Best . . . I wonder. He could be pretty ruthless in pursuit of his quarry. I was probably more in awe of him than you were."

"Quarry—like father, like son."

"Come on—out with it. What's bothering you?"

"Oh, it's nothing, nothing . . . just a graduating daughter, empty-nester thing."

He nodded as if suddenly struck by a memory: "Funny, how Jake always spoke of his father as if he was still alive, as if their camping trips to the Ozarks happened only the summer before. As if, when you love someone enough . . . well." He shook his head, his lips aquiver as he blinked rapidly.

"Oh, lucky you, Gareth—lucky you." And she kissed his cheek.

"Still, something's extremely odd, even unsettling, about that business of him lying to you about his parents being divorced."

"Hadn't we chalked that up to the young needing to un-remember—to overwrite the tragedies in their lives, to adapt, as my darling daughter would have it? Even if young Jacob seems . . . almost unreal—overadapted."

At this, Gareth seemed to stiffen, and she sensed his head lift and then nod with a sigh in her ear. "You see, I ran into an old friend in '74, the CEO of Pfizer, and I broached the question: how a bunch of us in '76 were wondering whatever happened to our brilliant Jake Burrage: how he'd never shown at Reunions, much less the ribbon cutting of the new Burrage Biochemistry Lab. Well, she just laughed and noted that we were not alone, that all the folks in Big Pharma were wondering too. Nobody's seen our boy in the flesh for twelve or fifteen years."

"Good Lord, in this day and age, is such a thing possible?"

"She and others in the industry figure he's gone to ground anticipating some drug trial disaster or some FDA investigation or even an SEC probe. Or holed up, getting out the kinks on some game changer that will astonish humanity. Except they've been taking such bets for over two decades: irregular clinical trials, rush to market, search for the Holy Grail, or even the 'God pill,' as she put it. And BPH just keeps getting a clean bill of health as it beats out the competition at every turn."

"God pill," she mumbled under her breath. "Sounds like Jake, doesn't it? Always taking chances, always skirting the rules, opening doors he had no business opening—like he's immune to the reality, the limits that govern all our lives."

"Defer entropy indefinitely."

"It's just"—she squeezed his hand—"I keep wondering if it's just my imagination running away with me."

"Running away from what exactly?"

"How about the unknown."

"Yeah, it can be a little scary out there on the cutting edge. Goes with the territory. How the scientist, the researcher, the entrepreneur must first sustain that blind faith in a proof of concept, and then double down—break down your doors, sometimes with inhuman ruthlessness. But most of the longevity scientists are health spanners, not immortalists."

"Immortalist." She winced as her right knee radiated a sharp pain. "That's a new one."

"Yeah, most settle for a healthier life followed by 'compressed morbidity'—translation: a quick and painless death." He snorted. "The jargon, the pitch decks, the eager young faces."

"Painless, huh?" She tried to laugh it off.

"Sure you're okay?" She nodded (fine). "Jake always left me feeling like I lacked some essential ingredient—imagination, I suppose. The imagination Faulkner extolled in *Absalom, Absalom!*: how art and literature offer us another way of entering the past, another path to truth, one closed off to scientists or even historians (facts, data), a path between dream and reality. I always thought maybe you'd provide that balance in his life, why he was so crazy about you."

"Hmm, imagination, which my killer instinct, or my healthy skepticism, my inbred risk aversion seems to confound at every turn."

"It's never too late: the novel you need to write—for Erma, for me." He laughed and spun her slowly around under the billowing blue canvas of the tent, flecked with white stars. The oldies band was playing the Temptations' standard, "My Girl." "I always thought of you as heir to the romantic movement, Jake to the Enlightenment—a heady brew."

"I just have this weird feeling, like I need to save Erma."

She glanced into his nodding, possibly apprehensive face, those deep-set, critical eyes, the burnished bronze of his mother's, as she'd once thought of them, and then to where their two daughters were chatting as they danced.

He shook his head and swiveled one hundred and eighty degrees: "As the father of two motherless daughters, I've borne witness to more broken hearts than I care to remember. Diane's crazy about a junior boy whose internship will take him to the West Coast for the summer, while she's starting a job in New York."

"Ruthlessness, you said," and she squeezed his hand as if needing reassurance. "That was hardly what I saw in the Burrage Biochemistry Lab this afternoon. Maybe I was just dazzled by the splendor."

"Trust me, splendor is the perfect camouflage for all kinds of outrageous scams. And the young Silicon Valley billionaires hardly have the patience to wait eighty years for human clinical trials to finish. Or the customary serial-specialist approach to aging, which treats the problem symptom by symptom. To quote our Pfizer CEO: they think that all their money can buy immortality, but it didn't work out so well for Asclepius or Tithonus."

"He . . . it's just, he did seem a little possessive." And she glanced toward her daughter.

"Well, he would."

"What's that thing about a spectrum—invisible light, the singularity?" she asked, as if trying another tangent. "Books—the afterlife of genius, I suppose." Again, she squeezed his hand. "Well, at least no one accused us of parodying a sixties Black-girl group, that we, with our white privilege, have no right to do."

"My mother thought the Shirelles a disgrace to the race, Black teenage girls singing about one-night stands and the like."

"Four Black girls from Passaic, New Jersey. I sang in the choir as a teenager, but Bianca had to coach both Annette and Apolonia, when she could have had her pick of prospects. And, of course, she did all the brilliant arrangements."

"On fire for her new patron, the brilliant Jack Rambridge (Jack, who buys vineyards, while I invest in Newark's charter schools). Not that our young Jacob wasn't quite taken with your performance as well. I could have sworn I saw tears in the kid's eyes."

Over his shoulder, she glanced around for any signs of their manager.

"The last time, maybe the only time, I saw Jake in a coat and tie was our graduation."

"A last time for everything, huh? The last time we'll see our girls graduate."

"The last time we performed the Shirelles was ten years ago, when Bill was still okay, and Erma was eleven, holding her father's hand, dancing with him all night."

"Daughters: it's complicated."

"Tears, you say . . ." She closed her eyes a moment to disguise another wave of pain rising off her right knee. "Jake was such a sucker for soppy nostalgia."

"Listen . . . first thing, I'll get my research analyst to do some more digging on Burrage Pharma. There's got to be more there—there always is."

"I remember the last time Erma spontaneously took my hand walking the beach at Tashmoo."

"I remember the last time you kissed me."

She smiled as she posed the question: "Did you ever cheat on your wife?"

"What kind of question is that, even among old friends?" His hand had relaxed in hers. "Only at the end, when she'd been confined to bed at the hospice, with her best friend. Less sex than comfort for losing all that she'd been."

"Yes, yes, the fear of being alone . . ." She sighed. "But then we have our girls to think about." She squeezed his hand on sudden impulse as some uncharted terror again seized her. "You don't think . . ."

"What?"

"It's possible . . . I mean, to hear Erma tell it, almost anything is possible."

He laughed: "Had we but world enough and time . . . nobody wants to be a late-adopter and a left-behind."

Now, alone in bed, sheltering in the indifferent dark of her corporate hotel room with curtains drawn, she could not banish the anxiety she felt at the seeming slippage of her sanity, as if some life-enhancing essence was slowly draining from her body. She'd only been saved from making a complete fool of herself with Gareth when Diane cut in on them and reclaimed her father. Erma had simply drifted off into the night, as if laughing at her mother's fears.

"She said she had an experiment in the lab she had to check on," was Diane's cryptic note.

Why couldn't she have saved just one dance for her mother? And no sooner had Mom returned to their empty table with ice packs for her aching knees than she discovered that Gareth and Diane had left the dance floor as well, probably off to meet up with members of her graduating class or her junior beau, while Annette and Matt had long headed for the barn. Departed as well were Apolonia and Bianca, closing down the fiftieth with Daltrey and Jack, and then, no doubt, off to their hotels, where success in the sack might confirm hopes for the future. She watched as the rest of her class thinned out, slowly giving ground with tearful waves and smiles, hugs and kisses, as she tried to keep creeping panic at bay.

Worse still than her fear of loneliness was how that vast event horizon, that spectrum of shining memories, which had so buoyed her spirits since waking, now seemed dust in an empty cabinet. Just hours before, during the P-rade, she found herself remembering each and every one of her Reunions with total clarity: where she and others were in their lives, the ages of their children, even the progress of her authors, the very pages she was then editing. While at the publishing forum, it felt like she could visualize entire chapters of books she'd read, while effortlessly synthesizing the key points to make her argument. Now that library too was closing its doors, her mind blurring like early-onset Alzheimer's. And she'd had no more than half a bottle of Jack's wine.

Then there was Erma, so responsive all day, who, after leaving the dance floor, had suddenly stopped returning texts. Complete radio silence. She couldn't quite decide if her instincts were that of a mother or jilted lover: to warn her daughter or run down her dealer and bum a few more of those green capsules—anything to recover her youthful spirit, her buoyant knees. That almost weightless joy at being alive. Had she been a one-woman clinical trial? She was even tempted to throw the ice packs aside and chat up the student bartenders to see if she could get Jacob's phone number (a lost article of clothing, an email address for his old man). Like an addict, she rehearsed this approach over and over in her mind as the band played to fewer and fewer dancers, until finally the last shreds of her dignity kicked in and she gave it up as insanity.

Struggling out of her chair, she found her lower back too in a knot of pain to go along with her knees and right shoulder. She hobbled off barefoot, carrying her stiletto heels, waving to any lingering members of her class, allowing hugs when required, still in brave celebrity mode as she blew kisses in her wake and held her head high, back straight, very much the aging athlete ready to head for the jacuzzi, bed, and Ambien oblivion, if necessary.

Except her bare feet (she'd neglected to bring her flats) seemed to have a mind of their own, navigating her down campus toward the twenty-first-century Reunions sites, as if the sights and sounds of more youthful gatherings might serve as a booster to her fading glory. Alas, mocking every weary step, the carousing, high-energy faces she passed only exacerbated her dilemma. As the decibels of the bands grew louder and more cacophonous, as the music segued from fifties and sixties oldies-but-goodies to disco, to various unintelligible if unlistenable flavors of rap and techno, she found herself increasingly unnerved. The slippage of decades, instead of an elixir, only added chaos to injury; her mind, far from being soothed by the river of time streaming past, was rattled by the fleeting glimpses of twentysomething revelers deliquescing (so Henry James) out of the night, outlandishly costumed, cantering along the shadowed pathways in pairs and groups, while she navigated step by careful step, on the lookout for broken bottles. She found herself searching faces that barely registered hers—a smile, the merest vague curiosity at this aging, limping interloper (with the foxy tiger earrings), or just possibly discerning enough to register a nodding acquaintance with what was in store, since their parents were disqualified from the generational churn.

Her phone vibrated with a text from Bianca, who she'd last seen swinging on Jack's arm like a pole dancer.

"Not to worry, Mom: Matteo invited Erma to his gig at Dizzy's next Saturday night after graduation—Jabberwocky or no. We'll be Learing it off to Venice. Wish me luck (the fiftieth is like a geriatric ward), amiga."

"Arthur," she exclaimed hopefully, clawing her way forward through the throngs entering and exiting the fifth-reunion site in Little courtyard. She heaved herself into an abandoned folding chair—a lifesaver—just off the dance floor, the perfect blind from which to observe the mating mayhem, hoping against hope to scope out her daughter and godson.

"Jabberwocky?" she intoned above the melee (when had she ever mentioned their mascot to Bianca?). She wracked her brain to remember anything about her own fifth reunion.

As she gazed across the sea of enviably fit and attractive bodies animated by a jarring rap beat, the briefest snatches of her fifth did, with effort, filter back, when only she and Bianca were still on the prowl, Annette long married, and Apolonia just married with a newborn, Christopher, and still the not-so-secret mistress of John

Proctor. Yes, she'd been vaguely intrigued by Bianca's regular checking of the sign-in register of returnees as if hoping to find a familiar name, until finally going off in a huff. "We've used up the hotties, and all the decent men are off to the graduating seniors in search of admiring women. Fuck it, I'm sick of being used and abused—tenth reunion, here I come."

She closed her eyes—*once a slut . . .*—to the maelstrom for a moment, trying to remember what Reunions Annette had first brought Arthur to, and Bianca, Matteo. Why had she delayed so long becoming pregnant with Erma, until she was almost forty, when having that second child became more and more problematic? Or had they just given up after a couple of miscarriages? Not that she'd ever admit to how hard it had been to get in the mood for sex with her husband, while procreation sex had left even Bill cold.

Her waking ecstasies of the morning now seared her memory like a wasp sting.

Forever ruined by Jake Burrage, who had gotten under her skin and stayed there.

As her eyes swept hopefully over the beehive of a dance floor, she criticized herself for failing to be the author she should have been, even as she groped for those last snatches of telling detail before their early years might be completely lost to her, summoning forth the Shirelles' disdain for so many of the men they'd first known in their student days, when, given the juicy ratio of five guys to every girl, they—celebrities of a kind with a short sell-by date—had their pick; how at that long-ago fifth reunion—or had it been their tenth?—they'd spent so much of their time cattily upwardly revising their estimates of the men who showed, guys upon whom they once wouldn't have wasted two minutes, unkissed frogs who now, on closer acquaintance, had turned into if not princes exactly, certainly passable cavaliers, transformed by a good haircut and shave, a clean, button-down shirt and pressed chinos (anti-war protests a forgotten chapter), fresh out of med or law school or, even more alluring, deep in the toils of the finance world, with the first taste of wealth sparking their conversational gambits: the glittering prizes that obscured their various upbringings, whether the Upper East Side or blue-collar Wilkes-Barre.

"And what about that novel you regaled us with in one of our precepts—a Shakespeare course, wasn't it, junior or senior year?"

Even back then, at their fifth or tenth, Gareth was still holding a whip hand to her early promise.

"Hell, I've got better things to do, like the two Pulitzer-winning authors I'm proofing for Knopf. You know, the thing about Shakespeare, so I find, is that his characters never really listen to anyone else except themselves, as if their brains are stuck in an eternal, if brilliant, feedback loop."

She watched, distracted, a young woman grinding her pelvis against her partner's, eliciting thoughts of the electric feeling of Jake's hard-on, that most comforting of sensations on the dance floor, the deep pleasure of being desired purely as a physical body.

"What a fool . . ."

This confession had seemed to shatter something inside her, prompted too by the disconcerting feeling that every time she accessed a memory, it changed on her, shifted in the same way this divine multitude on the dance floor shifted gears (such an exotic hybrid of gorgeous, mixed-race features flashing in and out of focus). Now here, now there.

Ah, a blessed moment of relief! There was Arthur's familiar face poised above Erma's left shoulder, her lithe back and tight butt on steamy display in her new Akris dress, her long neck, almost as tall as Arthur, allowing her sumptuous cascade of blonde hair to flow, barely concealing Arthur's right hand on the small of her back. Arthur was smiling (as well he might), saying something amusing in her ear. From the shadowed obscurity of her seat, she noted his father's powerful dimpled chin and firm mouth, set off by Annette's lustrous eyes, aglow with what could only be an inner strength, the glorious gift of a confident faith (did her Stoic faith fare as well?)—or that of a seeker discovering the perfect mate, there hiding in plain sight ever since they'd been children together at Reunions decades before.

"And a Wimbledon champion for a grandfather." What their comingled genes might produce in terms of a tennis prodigy.

She felt angry tears welling in her eyes at such pathetic schemes and bowed her head in penance, fearful of discovery or that her brash behavior might spoil the moment for these deserving lovers.

Relieved, preparing to slink away, she had raised her face to the dance floor, ready to leave this embryonic power couple to their private joys, only to find a different woman in Arthur's arms! There, staring off with a dreamy gaze, was Grace, her tennis partner from the morning, an NCAA All-American, a graduating senior already graduating to older men. Gorgeous, legs to die for, with the same long, reddish-blonde hair as Erma, her muscled arms clutching possessively at Arthur's broad back as if to warn off any competitor who might dare steal her prize.

She hastened away as if ashamed. All she wanted to do was stagger back to her car and the Marriott and ice her knees and raid the minibar for a half-dozen Glenlivets and so end this crazy, incoherent day. And yet she knew she couldn't, not without making sure Erma was safe and sound. And, though she dared not admit it, possibly score a handful more of those green capsules (could they be prescribed? she furtively wondered).

Dragging herself down campus while madly texting Erma, she felt as if she'd gained twenty pounds in the last hour. She scolded herself for her decrepit body, incensed that her legs, which had provided her with such speed and agility only that morning, might let her down at the final hurdle. She kept stopping to raise her smiling, game-on face and straighten her back as she was engulfed by a tide of drunken, possibly underage youngsters passing in review before the proctors guarding the lit-up gate of the senior site. Waving her Reunions wristband (proud mom of a graduating senior) to the security detail, she let herself be sucked into the vortex of the jam-packed enclosure reverberating to the techno-rap of a blue-haloed DJ presiding over the packed dance floor. If the fifth was a scene of relatively well-behaved mating mayhem, the senior class was a sweaty mosh pit, a melee of psychotic energy that verged on a primal scream. Just to make it to the dance floor, she was forced to squeeze by crowds of half-clothed sweating bodies smelling of cheap beer and dope, liberally applied deodorant, and just-shampooed hair. Many of the kids were clasping hands in pairs and groups, hugging, crying, full of drunken laughter as the clock ticked down on their college days, desperate to hold on to their final moments together—while she, parent-interloper, class of '76—yes, the bicentennial year—might be considered a poor specimen, if not a sad reminder of what disasters awaited them down the road. And yet, breathing deeply of this talented sea of humanity—if for only for a moment—something in her rebelled, and she yearned to find herself born again as she had been that morning. Ready to absorb all this youthful energy—why not, inspiration and details for her novel sure to come.

And so, trying for the authorial equanimity she did not possess, as the minutes seemed like hours, she struggled to reach a tent pole by the side of the throbbing dance floor (not a chair anywhere in sight), to which she clung while panting for breath, a mast on a pitching deck during a tsunami. Where, oh where was Erma? Where was Jacob? Yearning to see the scene through young eyes, she found it harder and harder to quite formulate the warning (or was it a plea for another fix?) that some obscure part of her had been intent on delivering. After all, couldn't it truly be said that she was part (by affiliation, if not blood) of this marvelous undulating din of beer jackets, these jarring daubs of orange and black that raised the temperature to sauna levels, sweet like the sweat dripping from her brow and gathering in salivating foam on her lips, even if the eyes that bothered to meet hers might find something little better than what the cat dragged in. Strobe lights blurred and jarred her view. What was this nameless thing she sought, this near-fantastic fear she yearned to dismiss and yet embrace—this stab at eternity? What place of peace and repose lay just beyond her reach? Even if only a pharmaceutical haven for the ache in her knees, her back and shoulder—her dulling brain! Every time she tried to give this tempting terror a name, it snaked away in a slithering mass of youthful ardor. She kept repeating a mother's mantra: just as long as Erma was happy, nothing else mattered. As this convenient cliché of maternal solicitude was expunged from her addled brain, she finally managed a tepid, even introspective smile, allowing her the nostalgic grace to find herself once again aged twenty-one, back in the fray, back in the game amid the bacchanalia of jostling, hugging, flirting bodies, flowing here, there, and everywhere, and so possibly granting her immunity from any dark thoughts about some lurking future. Hardly a late adopter or left-behind.

Oh, just for a moment of that insistent hard-on nudging her thigh.

Suddenly, she found herself screaming, joining the unintelligible cries of the ecstatic young women, many of whom seemed almost catatonic. She closed her eyes to better feel the drumming of the plywood flooring, the din of a thousand feet, hastening the out-of-body experience—the freedom—to which she yearned to give herself over, so much so that she found her spirits momentarily lifted by the rattle of her teeth, rattling to the pulse of the techno beat, rattling as they had when Jake used to shake her in frustration, as if by shaking her, or pinning her arms on the verge of orgasming, something of his fantastic hopes might gain traction in her dim-witted brain. As she screamed louder still, she grabbed tighter to the tent pole and a guy rope to steady herself, while scanning the pistoning bodies, feeling less and less a discarded part of this glorious human tumult, as she tried and failed to read tee shirts in hopes of detecting any members of the swim team and so consult as to her daughter's whereabouts. Or her drug dealer.

In just seconds, the last reserves of energy seemed to drain from her body, and calling upon what little remained of her dignity and strength, she pushed off from her trusty tent pole and wove her way through the converging mass of seniors until she reached the exit. There she found a friendly student worker delivering kegs in a golf cart who was more than happy to drive her back to her car. An old lady in need of a lift. A writer who had assiduously gathered her material, if not quite fact-checked it. Then, looking up from her phone as they made a wide swing across the new pedestrian bridge over Washington Road, connecting the science campus, she saw the Burrage Biochemistry Lab looming up before them like a temple of crystal light, a beacon mirroring the star-studded night. "Stop," she suddenly ordered her driver, catching sight of a single illuminated lab high up in the otherwise lustrous blue-gray dimness of the building. She squinted, bleary-eyed and exhausted beyond words, almost sure she could make out two silhouetted figures bent toward one another in eager conversation as they gazed out at the night sky from their Olympian heights.

And in a flash of addled memory, she recalled something of the night before, those godlike hands pressing her arms tight as her body exploded in ecstasy.

Yes, almost anything now seemed possible.

CHAPTER 27

Annette, awake, restless, stuck in review mode (a mother's burden), found herself still perplexed by Arthur's musings as Erma had gone to get them drinks at the fifth. How, in Saint Mark's Gospel, Jesus seems so strangely, so puzzlingly enigmatic, so unsure of who He is or what He's about—the way He keeps asking His disciples if *they* know. "Do you suppose any of us know who we really are, Mom?" he asked with a friendly hug. "Are we the same as the little boy of five, or fifteen, or twenty-five? Do you suppose we are changing all the time?"

"But that's the beauty of the Gospels, Art: they remain unchanged and unchanging, forever there for you, no matter what."

Had Erma planted that seed of doubt? Was that the kind of thing two young people today discussed on a first—or was it a second date? Viewing the Carpaccios, for Pete's sake. Arthur had glanced over at the bar line where Erma stood, a quick smile and that comic twist of his upper lip (oh, so like his dad), his eyes softening with ironic pleasure, as if to say: Who knew? A woman who talks theology as well as biochemistry—pretty awesome. No doubt an uber-girl: like mother, like daughter. And a helpmeet—could they actually end up as a couple?—who would relentlessly undermine Arthur's already wavering faith at every turn. Just as Gini had on some of those long (yes, young Jacob had that much right), interminable bus rides to and from away matches. Not that Gini had ever attacked her faith per se; she did it more insidiously, gnawing around the edges—the way she had disparaged Augustine with faint praise at the publishing forum (she'd slipped into McCosh for the last fifteen minutes of Gini's tirade), whether it was the existence of a God who tolerated the evils of Auschwitz and the gulags, or a Jesus, at least in Paul's telling, who provided the grace to transcend the taint of original sin. And then Seneca—teaming up with Daltrey, always and again Seneca, that great moralist. Somehow, her faith had survived Gini, the same faith that had sustained their marriage over that first arduous decade when Matt was struggling to regain his prenuptial form ("While you lost your virginity, I lost my confidence"), when she'd been reluctant to make love, to make babies, for fear—idiotic as it was—that his performance on the court might further suffer.

And she was hardly a slouch when it came to Augustine, whose *Confessions* she'd avidly read cover to cover with extensive underlining in her fellowship reading group. Augustine, who so movingly warned against rejoicing in our individual successes, "which are bound up with ephemeral things . . . instead, cast aside all attachment to times and places and apprehend that which is always one and the same."

"The unchanging . . . eternal," she intoned in a searching whisper.

And now that she thought about it, "one and the same," she was reminded of another perplexing thing Arthur had mentioned: "That guy in Erma's class, Burrage, who sat with us at your charity match—what an odd duck. He just kept on and on about Aunt Gini's playing, almost as if he was coaching her, almost like she was his—I don't know—creation, his protégé."

A touchy subject, young Burrage, a subject she was hardly going to bring up at the dinner table if Jack Rambridge hadn't opened his big mouth. Then, speak of the devil, that larger-than-life future—or was it the past?—had arrived in the guise of young Jacob, positioning himself behind Erma's chair like some prophet of the new age. A laying on of hands, more like it. Another Silicon Valley whiz kid come to bestow grace and healing, and thus, like so many of his kind, glibly dispensing with Paul's asinine (Gini's word) notion of original sin. Though hardly the next Steve Jobs in that button-down shirt and tie and clean, pressed khaki slacks, a dead ringer for the Jake who had toured with them over that magical summer season, from Roland-Garros to Queens to Wimbledon to Longwood to Flushing Meadows, when day after day, match after match, tournament after tournament, Matt was again moving up in the rankings, playing better and better, conferring every day with Jake, going over the figures—just playing the percentages, those relentless numbers, which thankfully added up to a new lease on life. And yes, a ritual blessing every morning after breakfast and around beers before dinner. "Just letting the numbers work for you," Doctor J called it. That one glorious summer, that charmed season first conceived looking out on the dome of Saint Peter's in Rome, announced in the Scuola di San Giorgio viewing the Carpaccios, then birthed on the red clay of Roland-Garros, had generated enough positive energy to sustain their marriage: those glowing milestones to be happily referenced in the bleakest of winters. A run that had finally come to an end in the semifinals of the US Open in a close match against Jan Kodeš (precipitating Jake's departure for his postdoc at Chicago), but enough for Matt—for the first and last time in their marriage—to again be ranked in the world's top ten. That evil incubus of doubt lifted from her shoulders.

Except sin lingered.

"When did Donald Dell tell you that he'd offered to represent Gini?"

Her husband was about to turn off the light for bed. "The Don . . . I told him that he should try to get Gini to play the tour and sign her up, that she was the best young player coming up in the ranks of American women."

"Oh really? You never told me that."

"Didn't I? Yeah, right after my Wimbledon win, when Donald reneged on the Converse deal to sign me with Adidas. I told him he'd have to offer her a wild card berth at Wimbledon to close her."

"Did he really offer her a wild card—could he do that?"

"The moon and the stars and then some. Yes, it was an old boy's thing back in the dark ages."

"Tell me about it. You were hardly a big supporter of women's professional tennis in the early years when Billie Jean King was sounding the charge."

"I made my amends for those sins when I married you. Billie Jean and I laugh about it now."

"I could have used a wild card into the main draw; it would have made my career."

"We played two rounds in the mixed doubles, wasn't that enough? And you got to carry that sign in the P-rade—still the only Princeton woman to play Wimbledon."

"Gini, Agripinna, our court queen . . . such a waste." She sighed and lay back on her pillow in the darkness. "You know, it always bothered me that I was the only one on the team without a nickname." Her husband was already sleeping soundly.

The thing conveniently forgotten, excused, excised from life's playbook with no living soul the wiser, including Matt. In the second week of the US Open, Jake, a tad sheepishly (what were those long talks with Chrissie about in the Carlyle bar?), had come to her and asked if she would contact Gini, invite her to the semifinals to watch the match with them from the players' box. "You don't have to mention that I'll be there, that I'm working with Matt—let it be a surprise." Of course she would, she'd be delighted: a mini third reunion! Instead, she'd lied straight-out, telling a disappointed Jake that she'd telephoned Gini's assistant at Knopf and been told that Gini was at a sales conference in San Francisco. When, in fact, Gini had picked up her phone on the first ring (her assistant at lunch), and Annette found herself frozen at the officious tone of her roommate's voice, almost hanging up, and only just managing to offer Gini a ticket for the semifinals. A seat about as distant from the players' box as the Flushing Meadows stadium allowed, where Gini wouldn't spot Jake. At the time, she had justified her lie, her betrayal of trust, as simply bowing to the practicalities: Jake didn't need any distractions during a crucial match: the stakes were too high.

Besides, she'd been duly punished for her little subterfuge: two match points on Matt's serve gone for naught. And just for keeping two onetime lovers apart (what with that horrendous breakup!). Hadn't they been spared a galling reunion, an impossible reconciliation? Didn't Gini's no-show the following fall in Venice prove as much? Wasn't Jake just hedging his bets on his thousand-day wager with destiny? As God was her witness: their lovemaking at three in the morning sounded more like they were in a death struggle ("Let me go, damn it; let me the fuck go!"). And their fights, their constant verbal jousting, forever vying for supremacy . . . something she had gamely endured and forgiven for almost three years with barely a complaint. Admittedly, as Augustine would have advised, she'd freely confessed her jealousy over Jake's coaching Gini in their student days, and later wanting to keep Jake exclusively to herself—team Collins, that is—even as Chrissie relentlessly tried to win over Jake and hire him in pursuit of a boatload of Open titles to come. She who had been regularly spurned by Jake in their college days—too brilliant, too charming and sophisticated for the likes of a good Christian woman who lacked the intellectual stardom of Gini, her perfect tennis body—much less having to deal with the pressure of Gini's relentless improvement under Jake's tracking and coaching, holding on to the number-one spot by her fingernails as Jake, day by day, week after week, dissected her weaknesses and plotted her demise.

Anyway, the whole sorry business could have been consigned to oblivion if young Jacob hadn't appeared and Matt let the Cheshire cat out of the bag. Almost spoiling that lovely equilibrium of more recent years enjoyed by the roommates, their competitive days long retired. Why stir up any possibly painful memories?

The unchanging.

Again, the image of young Jacob standing behind Erma presented itself: hands draped on her nearly bare shoulders (what a gorgeous dress), just as Jake used to come up behind Gini seated at dinner and grab her shoulders, pretending to massage her muscles, even as he pinned his protégé and so claimed his prize. And yet . . . there had been something in the kid's voice, in the liquid depth of his eyes when speaking of that long ago summer on tour, echoing his father's warmth, as if somehow thankful for the gift of faith she and Matt had offered to share.

"And get this, the moment Aunt Gini blistered that winning backhand past the Princeton girl, Burrage clapped his hands in triumph and muttered: 'If she'd only stuck it out with me, she'd have had both Wimbledon and that Pulitzer.'"

"No way, Art."

"Erma was sitting next to him, and she heard it too. She just laughed."

One and the same.

And Gini, of the four of them, had a chance at that Wimbledon crown. Or at least that bestseller about the women's tour, which might have featured her teammates, who all helped her on her way. About Jake Burrage as well—surely a fascinating character for any novelist.

She listened to her husband's rhythmic breathing, still, after all these years, relishing his certainty of faith, a faith he neither questioned nor explored. An easy thing with your name etched into a closet full of silver trophies, even if now mostly relegated to a brand name on the heel of a shoe. But what a shoe—such a lovable old shoe!

Forever young.

She buried her face in the back of her husband's neck, as if to hide herself from young Jacob's probing smile as he stood behind Erma, his eyes flickering over hers as if to say: you see, some things never change, God's plan is what we make of it.

Had Gini somehow found out about Jake's invitation to join them at the US Open—her white lie? Had Jake seen through her subterfuge?

Prompting a line out of Augustine's *Confessions*: "Great is the power of memory, exceedingly great, O my God, a spreading limitless room within me . . ." With room to spare for the confession of sins . . .

Did she owe God a confession? Didn't original sin really translate into God's grace and Jesus's sacrifice? Gratitude for all the blessings of this life.

Had she been imagining it, or had there been a certain longing, too, in young Jacob's voice describing Matt's winning ways, a low, searching tone that had a timeless quality, the wistfulness of something experienced as if only yesterday, not usually found on the lips of the young so distracted by digital ephemera and the brave new world of endless tomorrows?

Yes, a laying on of hands, she thought, like Saint George in Carpaccio's *Baptism of the Selenites*. Perhaps a new beginning for her goddaughter Erma (better Jacob than Arthur!). Two exotics of the age to come, a prince and princess, with their faithful silver-white borzoi, set in a sumptuous biblical landscape where time stands still and the lost are forever found. Like those surviving hands pressing on the columns of Sant'Apollinaire, where the invisible Theodoric and his court stand their ground against the ceaseless tides. Strangely recalling Jake's beautiful hands, long and sinewy, hands she'd observed for hours on end, sitting beside him in the players' box as he entered every point in his match notebook. Numbers, symbols, data points detailing that magical logic beyond the reach of her faith, things she dared not admit or confess. A man racing against the clock as if pursued by the Furies.

She squinted at the digital clock on their bedside table counting down the minutes of her life, telling herself to just let it go and allow sleep to take her. She who had always prided herself on an instinct for the truth—doing the right thing. A mother's duty in the face of a threat to her firstborn's future happiness. How when Erma had returned with their drinks, her love-stained eyes beaming, she'd bent and whispered in her goddaughter's ear in praise of young Jacob: "What a brilliant and talented young man. You must be so pleased."

Oh, what a smile!

And then, like a miracle pronounced, gorgeous leggy Grace to the rescue, Gini's young partner had shown up, full of tennis talk and idolizing eyes for Matt and Arthur, allowing Erma's graceful bowing out as she claimed to have to get back to her lab for an hour or so to monitor an ongoing experiment.

And listening to the soothing, rhythmic breathing of her husband (always a good sleeper through all the ups and downs of their marriage), she found herself returned to that fifth set at Flushing Meadows, seated next to Jake in the players' box, his jaw set, pencil poised, intent, whispering commands, hand signaling as if to his creation: get a tighter parabola on the forehand, more speed and penetration into the backhand court, jam him on the serve, as if he was whipping his stallion down the homestretch. And she had grabbed his free hand on match point (lowering her eyes to where his hand, with pencil poised, was going to mark the point won or lost), their fingers clutching, intertwining—like two souls in toilful embrace, his commands just rising above a raspy whisper, still confident in the outcome if only his orders were carried out to the letter, a perfection that might have got Matt into the finals and a chance at another major title.

"Redemption," she whispered, feeling again the pressure of Jake's hand in hers, so near, so far. And when he had released his grip, marking the error column, he had given a piteous sigh, as if the defeat had been his and God's alone.

"Oh, Gini . . . I'm so sorry."

And she turned and pressed her face into the warmth and safety of her husband's shoulder.

Apolonia lay happily awake, luxuriating in the afterglow of the unsuspected skills of her new lover, who, though a tad talkative (hey, no senile dementia), had proved his worth around a woman's body. He'd not only managed to stay hard long enough to come inside her but had finished her off with his tongue, not just once but twice, as if pleased to intimately revisit his vintage semen. As a doctor, she should have insisted on a condom, but then she didn't exactly have one either. Nice to have her reproductive organs lubricated once more. How both had laughed at their mutual embarrassment and the pleasant surprise of "bareback" sex, as her young women patients called it. The only man who'd ever regaled her during lovemaking with such pensive wonderment, reprising how as a child he'd been held spellbound by the mosaics of Ravenna, the lost majesty of Theodoric's court, the death-defying splendor of Galla Placidia's mausoleum. While she (not a little weird, AP) found herself tantalized on the run-up to her second orgasm by visions of Carpaccio's Jerome narrated by John Proctor's prophetic words: "Apolonia—my girl god, the thing I'd never want for you is to be stuck with an old guy like me in a wheelchair at your fortieth reunion—or, God willing, your fiftieth. When I'd be like the ancient mariner at the festivities or, like Jerome there, with his long beard and walking staff, leading his pet lion—a lion, mind you, not a tiger. Can you imagine wheeling me out for the P-rade, drooling down my front in a golf cart, and you, doctor—what a fool everyone would think that such a brilliant diagnostician had failed to diagnose the obvious: age differences do matter. Unless you're a saint with a seeing-eye lion, of course, in which case God is your wingman."

So, irony of ironies, she'd now managed, at her fortieth, to possibly land her old man at his fiftieth, when the age difference barely mattered, even if she was just as happy to remain the scrappy younger woman—a role she seemed fated to play (with her ex as well) in this vale of tears. Daltrey's regrets oddly echoing John's: for picking the wrong horse, a Marxist historian fated for brief stardom in the seventies and then to fight a rearguard action for the rest of his career, a regret that blighted his marriage while he struggled to hold on to the affections of his children, battling with abstract theories about inequality while remaining oblivious to the needs of his own family.

"You'll like Rosa—she goes by Lux—and Frederick. Can you take August off and join us on Chappy?"

"Hey, Theodoric the Great, if they're skiers, they can come join my crew in Jackson Hole over New Year's."

She had been moved by a confession from her lover just before he nodded off: "People don't realize that it can sometimes be tough being a professional historian. There are nights I can't sleep, just thinking about the ten million young men who died in the pointless slaughter of the First World War, what the world would've been like if all those talented boys had lived out their days."

Given the constraints of a doctor's schedule, she prided herself on never (well, almost never) neglecting her family—her talented Christopher, something she mightily pondered, their table graced by Gini's and Gareth's daughters at dinner. Missing her own two. Not that putting up with an alcoholic was ever part of her marriage vows. Even if she did introduce a cowbird into the nest, John Proctor's son brought to term and passed off as Tony's child. (She'd lied about her due date, and so gave birth all alone in a Boulder hospital during med school.) A necessary subterfuge that had saved one family and started another, while she finished med school and her residency at Boulder's Foothills Hospital, where a solid income from Tony's first Jackson Hole restaurant allowed for childcare and interminable bus trips home for mommy-doc, as young Christopher had first and forever called his mother. All had gone perfectly until genes did their thing and Christopher began to look exactly like his father, precipitating moments of doubt and then recrimination in their marriage. Her Tony began to down a bottle of amarone after closing, and then two. Yes, a self-serving subterfuge to keep something of John Proctor for herself, but not without benefits: a brilliant young man, even if his passions ran to skiing and playing sous-chef to his father's sometimes extravagantly impractical creations, a passion for order (never had to be asked to clean up his room) that brought sanity to Tony's chaotic kitchen, not to mention award-winning menus and exotic, cutting-edge dishes that challenged his traditional Italian father, who had grown up throwing pizzas in Trenton.

Young Christopher, though never Princeton material (with a ski scholarship to UCB), cookbooks being his métier, had hardly been averse to coming to Reunions, a curious soul always on the lookout for occasions to broaden his experience, especially the New York-Philly restaurant scene. But she'd always managed to finesse the prospect for fear that her roommates or other members of her class might notice the broad brow and delicate set of cheekbones, those luxurious eyebrows cradling his lovely, intelligent brown eyes. The Roman nose a dead giveaway. She figured that Gini had probably noticed when she brought Erma to Jackson Hole for skiing but had enough common sense—and class, unlike blabbermouth Bianca (or a shocked Annette)—to leave such observations to the silence of a ski run.

And so, she had quietly settled for the serene pleasures found in enjoying her good-natured, bookish son strictly on his own terms: gainfully employed by his father (she'd fudged the genetic test by surreptitiously swapping some of John Proctor's DNA with Tony's—both, thank God, having Italian ancestry), a championship skier, along with his sister, and a creator of sumptuous Sunday brunches that she anticipated from Mondays on. Into whose curious hands she would occasionally press a dog-eared volume on art or architecture from an old Princeton friend, partly to remind him of their visit to Venice (just mommy-doc and the kids) in the year after the great divorce, when they had savored the cuisine and wine of the Veneto, and, of course, visiting the Carpaccios, which Christopher had relished, while his sister had been more interested in the nearby gelateria.

"Did I mention," yawned Daltrey, a hand cupping her breast before nodding off, "that your roommate Ginistrella Wingate—well, Gini and I grew up at West Chop on the Vineyard. I thought she wouldn't remember me since I was ten years older and ran with a prep school and then a college crowd. Her mother was a disgrace, a bad alcoholic—not that there's ever a good one. We all felt sorry for the poor kid: it was everything she could do just to live down her mother's pathetic affairs and abject flirting."

"Yes, mommy dearest almost blew up our graduation dinner by repeatedly falling out of the top of her dress. I don't think Gini ever really got over the trauma."

Thoughtful . . . kind—that Daltrey didn't bring up West Chop at the dinner, since Gini obviously had plenty else on her mind, what with young Jacob showing up like the cock of the walk, the eerie familiarity of that penetrating stare as he patiently caught everyone's eye around the table like some insouciant maître d' at Le Cirque, while, like the evil count in a fairy tale claiming the firstborn as his due, he clamped hands on his prize—at least to go by Gini's and Bianca's shocked faces or Annette's unconcealed joy. What a picture of youth—a polished, clean-cut version of Jake *dans le temps*. Sporting the same salesmanly swagger that all the Burrage Pharma reps displayed as they hawked their wares. She knew the type: in thirty years, how many broken legs had she set for hotshots who thought nothing of taking double blacks at terminal velocity. Silicon Valley start-up gurus who thought they were invulnerable, who bent her ear about new drugs to target senescent cells that produce "zombie toxins," treatments that would delay cancer, prevent cardiac hypertrophy, and extend life spans by thirty years or more. To make the disabled walk again. She'd heard it all.

But to give Wonder Boy his due, young Jacob touted an even more potent drug—youth and hope—claiming Erma even as he cast a spell over the table, clearly relishing the effect he was having transforming the Shirelles back into the flighty girls they'd once been: a necromancer of nostalgia: a living presentiment of time past, present, and future. That most fervent of hopes vested in our children that something of us remains behind. The very thing she so loved in her Christopher. Her drug of choice to mend a broken heart.

And who could say what must have been crossing Gini's mind? Gini, who'd played that morning like an Amazon on speed, a Botoxed bitch on steroids. Something, surely, had changed hands, given Gini's crazed stare at young Jacob—she knew the look, as if her dealer had arrived in the nick of time with her next fix. Then, any mother might be a tad jazzed to find her daughter anointed as one of life's winners in a world where science now makes all the rules, even if, sooner or later, we're still bound to lose.

Such reflections, cocooned in the air-conditioned darkness, marinated in the warmth of a new lover's ardor, now brought to the fore a long-ago conversation inspired by that flicker of recognition in young Jacob's eyes as his bemused gaze brushed and held hers for a millisecond longer than necessary. A good forty years' worth.

"Don't you find it infuriating how the textbook takes so much for granted, as if time's arrow is irreversible. That we're—all life—stuck because of the second law of thermodynamics."

She could see, as if yesterday, his hands shaping the air by his desk, his eyes lit up like flares, his eager voice drawing her in.

"Second law?"

"Heat flows from high to low and so finally reaches an equilibrium—death. But here's the thing: we don't have to be constrained by physical laws. We have the freedom to change and adapt with a purpose. Evolution opens more doors than it closes, on both a molecular level and a human level. In the same way, geophysical systems tend to self-organization—call it self-optimization with increased complexity (like the Mississippi Delta). We're on the same path, even in cosmic terms. We too strive for more order, building networks and scaling, which results in more body mass to retain heat, better bone structure to distribute stress: healing, heart transplants—replacing the ailing parts."

"How does the song go? Something about not tugging on Superman's cape, and not spitting into the wind . . .?"

"Don't you get it? Time's arrow doesn't have to be all one way, as long as we have the brains to create the technologies to evolve better-designed systems. Faster computing power sure would help."

"I guess that's why I'll never make Team Gini, our queen Agrippina, or make it into her novel. Not that I'd ever ask you to share your proprietary tracking system with a kid from Manayunk, PA."

"Oh, don't be so sure. Why not? We're more alike, you and me—science kids. And wrong side of the tracks, as my mother likes to remind me. We've long had to make ourselves up as we go along. Hardly material for Gini's novel—if she ever manages to break free of her father and the Vineyard."

"Speak for yourself. Or as *my* mother would put it: queen of the dirt pile."

"That's the beauty of pursuing scientific truth: all the ideological bullshit fails to compute. All the stupid dogmas, class distinctions, Marx and Freud, capitalism versus socialism, the whole rotten mess falls before the beauty of the scientific method and demonstrable truth."

"Listen, Einstein"—and she blew a kiss to the nearby photo—"I'm just trying to pass orgo here and sweet-talk my way into any med school that will have me. And a tennis scholarship is hardly in the cards."

"Don't disparage your calling. You belong to an elect confraternity trying to make the world a better place. I'll never forget the helpless look on the face of the doctor who treated my father for an incurable disease. I vowed I'd never show such a face."

"Really . . . You never—"

"Forget it." He waved a hand and fiddled with his slide rule a second. "The real mystery is your absent sex life . . . or is it your underground sex life?"

"Tell you what, Sherlock: you track my matches too, and I'll fuck your brains out right here, right now."

That had been the moment. He'd been holding her hand.

"*Ipsa scientia potestas est.* Gini gave me the Latin—Francis Bacon: 'Knowledge itself is power.' The greatest aphrodisiac of all."

"I'll bet she did, since you track her matches, lucky girl."

"Give me a kiss, and I'll think about it."

She turned to Daltrey's disheveled profile on the pillow. Maybe she'd always had a thing for older men—men way smarter than she—out of which had come new life, just as Jake had predicted. In the near darkness, a slant of light from the cracked bathroom door, she brushed back a lock of Daltrey's long gray hair and stared for a moment into his not unhandsome face, as if seeing beneath his fleshy eyelids, where those mosaics in the mausoleum of Galla Placidia still glittered, reminded of something else he'd mentioned about West Chop, that Garden of Eden where he and Gini had grown up, where she'd spent a glorious two weeks in August between sophomore and junior year.

"Even in my day—my misbegotten youth, that is—the old WASP monied elite was under threat, having to rent out their big cottages for most of July and even part of August, or downsizing. Like your Gini. I remember her as a little girl with golden hair playing carelessly on the piazza of their huge cottage overlooking the Sound, with a lovely green lawn sloping down to the yellowing beach plums and scrub oaks, where a bracken-filled beach lapped by gentle waves beckoned the old ladies who still liked to ride the current down to Little Pier. But one of my most vivid memories was of a late-afternoon cocktail party at the Wingates' Waverley, when all the West Chop gentry tied on their school colors and the women their Lily Pulitzer dresses, while I—sniveling little revolutionary brat that I was—pondered, not without some relish, the demise of this ruling class, this upper bourgeoisie, that I, the Robespierre of the coming revolution, would decry for all its ill-gotten wealth and pretensions. And that young girl, she couldn't have been more than fifteen or sixteen, since I was a Harvard grad student. Well, she must've spied my bell-bottoms and long hair and disdainful ardor for our surroundings. She fixed me with an imperious look, cocked her pretty little head, and said: 'Yes, quite the boring scene. Why don't we grab a bottle of Jimmy Beam and head for Big Pier?' At which point, her mother came around the corner of the piazza and handed her a plate of hors d'oeuvres and told her to get hopping passing the shrimp."

"Jimmy Beam?"

"Jimmy Beam, I might add, was our West Chop code for making out. Poor girl, what a horror for a mother. Or, as my mother once put it: some women live for risk; it's their only way to get through life, as long as they're the center of attention—and relishing the damage in their wake."

"You don't know the half of it." Apolonia stared up at the vagrant shadows on the ceiling of her Hampton Inn room. "Her mother arrived at our graduation dinner potted and screaming curses at her divorced husband. She wore this obscene strapless dress that she was falling out of all during dinner. And Gini would have to reach over and pull it up and try to quiet her down. Her father remained oblivious, utterly unable to deal with the situation. A lovely man, but hardly one for the women, if you know what I mean. I've tried to get Gini to talk about that graduation dinner—her dad, and her breakup with Jake Burrage, but in all the years she's come to ski in Jackson Hole, not a peep. Like a clam. I think, if she hadn't been so humiliated, so traumatized—well, she and Jake might have gotten back together, certainly after winning the NCAAs without him. Proof of her power, as if she ever needed it. But what do I know, I'm only a doctor."

As Daltrey began snoring, yet more memories drifted in on the tide, from that long-ago August on that same narrow pier overlooking the Sound, when she and Annette and Bianca were training with Gini at West Chop, working out on the tennis court by day, on the prowl for men and boys each night at various clubs and bars. The Shirelles singing a capella on the dock they called Big Pier as they passed around a bottle—yes, of Jimmy Beam. Even Annette let her hair down. And she remembered thinking what a fine thing it must have been for Gini to grow up in such a gorgeous place over all the summers, summers when she had been ball-girling at Marion and stringing racquets and filling in on doubles with old matrons. And yet for Gini, it seemed never enough, as if something more or better might be found where she waved their bottle at the horizon, where the soft pinpricks of light over Falmouth merged with the stars. Never enough. Not even Wimbledon or being the next Mary McCarthy on her horizon . . . and she had taken another slug from their bottle and pointed to the near shoreline, where the Wingates' huge clapboard cottage was lit up against the night, all golden, leaded-glass windows, and looming gables, and round, turreted roof, where shadowy figures stirred on the wide piazza. And Gini had held up an open palm, as if taking an oath, and declaimed in that high, cadenced, slightly tipsy voice: "My father thinks he's going to have to sell our house—taxes—but I told him not to even think about it: that in a few years, even without Jake, I'd have a sponsorship deal with Wilson: so there." Sounding more like her mother than she'd ever dare admit.

Yes, when you've come from all that, you spend the rest of your life in mortal terror of losing it. Even if all the Shirelles were green with envy for her summers at West Chop, for her Jake of all trades, a lover and coach and confidant to steer for true north. And what a perfect subject for her novel: blue-collar kid to big-pharma billionaire. Whose offspring had defiantly claimed his own behind Erma's chair at dinner, fingers leaving ghostly shadows on her sunburned shoulders—yes, a claimant on that future Gini had once declared was hers and then let slip away. Or if the distracted expression of dismayed wonder on Gini's face was any clue: a tough if queenly broad (like Daltrey's Galla Placidia) who might just have been willing to sell her soul to the devil for a second chance at what she considered her birthright.

And she put her arms around her soundly sleeping lover, as if reclaiming something of a birthright of her own.

Bianca woke suddenly from a troubled dream. She had been wandering along shadowed byways, lost, distraught, even as she seemed to be following a shadowy, if beguiling figure, while close on her trail, stony-faced gorgon heads leered from pitted brick walls. She had been hurrying either to catch up or escape, wandering into dead ends or what seemed a cul-de-sac, brought up short by a watery abysm where the pavers abruptly turned to an undulant milky-green, a canal side pungent with crumbling plaster and sewage, where she found no reflection and cast no shadow, even as that enticing figure waved her on from the far shore.

"Venezia," she murmured reassuringly to herself—soon to be Learing—so as not to wake a soundly sleeping Jack, breathing in the scents of male sweat and aftershave. She scolded herself for allowing such a near nightmare to spoil her triumph at Reunions, such acclaim for her beloved Matteo, a decent showing in the charity match, her triumphant Shirelles revival, and landing the big Kahuna, Rambridge Capital, who turned out to be as great a lover as a braggart, hastening her on in Viagra overdrive to delicious orgasms with only a slight boost from her trusty travel vibe.

She chalked up blame for any dreamland terrors to the dark baggage of her Sicilian roots, where any gift of the gods came with penalties attached. Or as Gini would have it, the rule of nemesis: that vengeful Greek goddess meting out rewards and punishment for deeds naughty and nice. Was penance called for? Her unholy attraction to rich men (so allowing her gift of music to flourish during her marriage), her real estate baron ex who had gone bankrupt in 2008 and vanished with his mistress. Not even taking phone calls from their son. Had that been the unsettling accusation—selling out to the highest bidder—she'd detected in young Jacob's penetrating stare, when, for just a fraction of a second, their eyes had met as he stood behind Erma's chair? Or her unconfessed sin?

She turned on an elbow in guilty supplication to her claimant and Jack's well-earned slumbers, squinting in the near dark to scrutinize the neatly shaved cheeks and crisp locks of gray hair setting off that powerful, so distinguished Jewish nose—Anthony (thank you, Gini) to her Cleo. With an uneasy sigh and glance at the ceiling, where she'd almost succeeded (pinning the curtains closed) in banishing that pesky amoebic light form, she slumped back onto her pillow.

How slickly young Jacob had staked *his* claim, a lover's deft fingers on Erma's shoulders, as if about to sweep aside the straps of that wickedly beautiful dress, or a masseur ready to tweak those diver's muscles where her swan-like neck merged into her collarbone, just as Jake used to massage her shoulders as she rehearsed on the harpsichord in the upstairs salle of the Scuola di San Giorgio, fingers that had quickly, expertly found their way to every nook and cranny of her body, as if to say, as indeed he had once said: "It's really just the logic of the thing: she fails to show and here you are. If you're playing the percentages: we're just two kids from blue-collar tribes, two scholarship kids who had to work student jobs to make ends meet, who've devoted their lives to music and science—a shared calling, don't you think? Yours the eternal felicities of art, mine the lifesaving potential of biochemistry: both requiring self-sacrificing devotion and a risky wager on immortal fame or forgotten penury. There it is . . ." And his fingers had paused in their exploration, holding her firmly on the piano stool. "No such thing as halfway for the likes of us."

"So, here we are."

"So, here we are."

The comfort, the longing in those fingers, could not entirely displace the disquieting flicker of light peering through the pinned curtains, or that younger version of Jake as he would often rush ahead of her along the byways of her Venetian neighborhood, when a bit of sculpture by the Lombardi caught his eye, the geometries of a stack of artichokes in the corner grocery, or when the flower seller had opened her kiosk on the *campo* and he'd blow out the door of her room above the bakery, only to return minutes later carrying a bouquet of yellow roses (his mother's favorite), as if to bless their coupling. Or the way he was drawn to a stonecutter's studio just off her *campo*, where he liked to linger in the late afternoon while breathing in the scents of worked marble, watching the artisans at their work, carving replacements for damaged or weathered sculptures around the city, or funerary monuments for San Michele. When he liked to point out Michelangelo's words carved over the doorway: "The sculptor's hand can only break the spell to free the figures slumbering in the stone."

"That's what I hope to do: free the knowledge withheld by the universe, and so find the cures that await discovery." He'd fixed her with that breathless look once reserved for Gini, as if she might indeed have been transformed—spellbound, too, by the call of such ambition.

She'd swung on his arm and sung out: "And I to reveal the music of the spheres and so raise the spirits of mankind."

"Time," he intoned with a sigh, fingering the worn-to-a-nub head of a figure with windblown hair and acorn-shaped hat that took pride of place at the entrance to the stonecutter's shop, "waits for no man."

As if that working-class neighborhood, so appealing to the loyal son of a construction guy, where she could barely afford to live with her scholarship stipend, was yet another data point confirming the couple's aptness, where they got their daily cappuccino and breakfast rolls, where she . . . the little *farmacia* where she bought her Tampax and tried to get her birth-control pills refilled once her six-month supply from the States had run out. And the old chemist with the crooked gold teeth and leering grin had looked at her New York doc's prescription script and just laughed in disgust, waving the piece of paper and letting it drop to the floor as if she'd just handed him a sheet of soiled toilet paper. And the thought of enduring a pelvic exam from a similarly unsympathetic Venetian doctor was just too much to endure.

And again she saw Jake's turned face as he glanced over his shoulder and signaled for her to follow, reaching out a hand to take hers, as if they'd traded places and he was now the one anointed to conduct her around Venice, just as Gini would have done, sparking the realization that he'd spent months, if not that entire thousand days, mastering the intricacies of the city, its history and art—wolfing down literary novels, feats of learning displayed at every turning, less a boast in deploying his new erudition than an assertion of his dominance (if not over her then the absent Gini), and so powering to the heart of her expat life, as his expert lovemaking had nudged and electrified her brain, the moon and stars imploded behind her fluttering eyelids. Even his mild bondage thing got her off. How different from their college days of just a thousand days past, when she'd been a neglected sideshow on court four (fat chance he'd ever track her matches); when she'd listened awestruck as Jake and Gini went at it in the wee hours, dueling to the death; when fast-talking Jake's Einstein imitation seemed to come from another planet.

Her musical soul knew instinctively how to play second fiddle to such a man, confining her competitive spirit to her celebrity performances, while opening her veins to share in the sorrow and pity that spurred Jake's genius. An empathy (surely unknown to Gini) that prompted sharing of the deep trauma of his father's early death from Huntington's, and the fear that the disease lurked in his own genes as well. And his gallant quest for a cure that should've inspired Gini's unfinished novel.

"I realize now just how much I miss him . . ." And he'd waved from her narrow bed to the window over the *campo*, where the boughs of a stunted plane tree clutched bunches of amber leaves in the early-morning light. "How, as a kid, you take it all for granted."

"But how lucky for you, that you have it within your power to make a difference, to find a cure, to honor your beloved father."

"To save my life and my children's," and he motioned with his fingers of a thing going up in smoke. "Death—even now, I can't quite believe in the finality of it."

Ten days, ten enchanting days in which their pasts, rather than falling away, had electrified their embraces, as Jake took delight in her celebrity in the lagoon city they made their own. Just as her nightly gigs at Florian had celebrated a kind of timeless allure, bathed in the afterglow of time itself, in the lit arcades and glittering mosaics on the hoary brow of San Marco as they danced on the gray expanse of the piazza. When once Jake had quoted Melville—of all authors—to her, staring into her lamplit eyes as Ahab had stared into Starbuck's on that clear moonlit deck on a vast, imponderable sea.

"Close! stand close to me, Starbuck; let me look into a human eye; it is better than to gaze into sea or sky; better than to gaze upon God. By the green land; by the bright hearth-stone! this is the magic glass, man; I see my wife and child in thine eye."

"*Santa Maria, madre di Dio,*" she exclaimed and turned to sleeping Jack, fearful of having woken him. "Almost as if he'd had a premonition," she whispered. And yet it was not Jack's face she saw, or even Jake's face in her waking dream, but that of Augustine's turned to her, turned to Jake, as they sat before the painting on their last day together: a thousand days plus ten and counting, as if Jake had been prepping himself all along for the moment, steeping himself in art history and philosophy—clearly not for the likes of her, even as she had claimed the benefit.

"You see, from Augustine we get most of our original notions about memory, and this painting seems more about memory than anything else, don't you think?"

"Yes, memory, even if the old guy kind of creeps me out."

"A Platonist to his fingertips. For cognition and love both depend on memory. And reading is simply an adjunct to an understanding of God—our invisible scribe, do you suppose?"

"Oh, Jake, you're almost sounding like Annette . . . or is it Gini? Who always made me feel like the class dunce for all the books I haven't read. You and all this should be in that novel she's never going to write."

"You, too, the god of my idolatry," he laughed, and placed a reassuring hand on her shoulder. "I never realized how much books can nourish memory, in the same way our brain cells retain a conversation. I suppose from Augustine's perspective, or at least Carpaccio's version of the old guy, it's more a rare moment of spiritual enlightenment. What I think he described as the 'thrust of a trembling glance.' What we—was it Joyce?—like to think of as an epiphany."

"There you go. I feel like you've been preparing to hang out with this old guy for quite some time, and I must be a bit of a letdown. A second-stringer, a benchwarmer."

"Oh, you're hardly junior varsity. If anything, you're the living embodiment of Augustine's epiphany." And he took her hands, kissing the palms as he stared deep into her eyes. "Just think about it, in your hands lie the notes inscribed on those pages of music—there and there and there, just as Carpaccio painted them, just waiting for you, so that you can simply sit down at the piano and re-create those same moments of inspiration that occurred to our invisible composer centuries—or eons ago, and so move audiences to tears—tears of joy at the melodic interweave of harmonies, re-creating a long-ago inspiration that has come again to life in the very moments of your playing. You are the vessel for the transmigration of souls, of Mozart and Scarlatti; your playing makes the very air come alive, a timeless realm, a mirror and sounding board of life everlasting. Don't you think that's what Augustine and Carpaccio are trying to show us? That God is in the notes as well as the numbers."

"Go on," she had said just above a whisper, as if now truly transformed, turning their hands over to kiss the back of his. "You know how it turns me on when you talk dirty to me."

"I think the trick, the magic—like us—must be rediscovered, found, stumbled upon (when all theories fail) or even be forgotten and rediscovered, possibly against our will, defying our best intentions. Well, being both fortuitous and yet inevitable. A flash of insight into a law of nature that has existed for all of God's eternity."

Yes, yes . . . inspiration for a lifetime. Had something of Annette's and Matt's spiritual grace rubbed off on Jake the previous summer season on tour?

At this query, her eyes flew open, as if seeing Augustine's sad eyes for a final time as he pronounced her sin. She reached out a penitent's hand to that fading pulse of silvery gray on the ceiling, that phantom sonogram, as she had to that figure standing in the shadows with his bicycle and bagel, or that very evening, eyes gleaming with tears as the Shirelles reprised their signature number, "Will You Still Love Me Tomorrow." A figure she'd once followed to the *ferovia*, whose face she'd seen reflected how many times in hers in the window of the overnight train to Vienna, where a cruelly sympathetic specialist took her cash and got the deed done with Teutonic efficiency.

Too proud to call or write after the letters stopped coming. And dare she admit it: terrified of the odds: fifty-fifty.

And she nuzzled in close to Jack's shoulder, as if to atonement's gristle and bone.

CHAPTER 28

Chicago Sun-Times, November 23, 2006

"Evanston, AP. The board of Burrage Pharmaceuticals & Health (BPH) announced today that founder, longtime CEO, and president Jacob Burrage will retire from day-to-day management and become executive chairman of the board while overseeing the expansion of the new Denver lab to focus on cutting-edge genetic research and biophysics. The reclusive CEO will retain his present role until a new CEO is hired. Investors and the business press have complained in recent years that the Burrage Pharma CEO has been less than forthcoming about new product development. He has been described as laconic, brusk, and dismissive of critics, rarely communicating with shareholders or press except by phone on regularly scheduled conference calls reviewing quarterly results.

"This move comes after last year's tragedy when Mr. Burrage's late wife, Elizabeth Farrand, was killed in a car accident while driving their young son to school, leaving the boy with severe injuries. Burrage Pharma press releases have long described Mr. Burrage as primarily a conscientious researcher, happiest in a lab setting, where he spends most of his time, including nights and weekends, often pursuing challenging projects based on his own research—'moon shots,' as described by his critics—many of which later go on to FDA approval as proprietary products. Often portrayed as a visionary in the mold of Steve Jobs, he is the sole owner of twenty-three patents.

Burrage Pharma's latest cancer drug, Promeset, came directly out of Mr. Burrage's pathbreaking work on human antibodies. In a press release, Mr. Burrage wrote: 'I have long thought this move made sense since I'm fundamentally a theory guy and a scientist, while running day-to-day operations requires a very different skill set. Now, as we push for expansion into even more cutting-edge areas of research, as knowledge in the areas of genetics and biotech expands exponentially, I will be better placed in overseeing the Denver operation and keeping my eye on the broader picture, and so contribute to and guide the future of BPH.' The press release further detailed plans for the new, state-of-the-art lab in Denver while the company will keep most front-office and administrative functions in Evanston."

Ginistrella Wingate woke from a dream as vivid as it was disturbing. She'd been mounting a spiral staircase in a crystal tower where faceless figures in white lab coats turned as she passed, climbing higher and higher, only to suddenly feel pressure on her arms as if the staircase was narrowing, the passage closing in, darkening at each step, the thing alive as if wrestling her to earth, her knees buckling . . . "I will protect you wherever you go and will bring you back to this land."

"Oh my God . . ." She struggled through an Ambien haze to read her father's Rolex—miracle of miracles, the blue hands seeming to show a late hour in the morning. Then, grabbing her phone off the bedside table, she found, to her horror, that it was indeed past twelve and she'd missed a farewell breakfast back at the Reunions site. Not that anyone was exactly missing her: no frantic texts from her roommates, who, so she hoped, were lying abed as exhausted as she.

A text from Erma at 10:06 a.m.: Back in the lab. Thanks for the dinner. Thanks for everything! Shirelles such a hoot!!

As if all her panic and desperate texting and searching of the evening before, now ebbing like another fantastic nightmare, had only been the demented folly of an overly protective, out-of-touch, aging mother. Checking her emails, she found a *Chicago Sun-Times* article from Gareth's diligent research assistant. This she read twice and then a third time (the badly injured son) before, with a groan, sitting up and staggering into the bathroom to pee.

"Lab . . . dinner . . . everything! . . . Shirelles . . . ," she repeated to herself (editing out the second exclamation point), a brittle gaze at her reflection where she sat on the toilet. What kind of corporate interior decorator placed a mirror across from the john, she snarled, staring into her bloodshot eyes and drawn face, her knobby, inflamed knees sticking out and feeling like rusted hinges, and the soles of her feet a muddy avocado green: What had she stepped in? She wiggled her besmeared orange toenails and sighed. Erma never thanked her for anything (the dress?). And yet, did she detect joy, possibly even inner bliss—the "everything" had her spooked—in that less-than-laconic text from her ever-reasonable offspring? Oil on the waters: a calming response after a stream of hysterical cris de coeur from mommy dearest.

Downing a couple of Motrins, she showered and finally collapsed into the office chair of her Marriott business suite, where she faced her closed laptop, fearing to open yet another Pandora's box, which, she sensed, lay only a few keystrokes away.

As long as Erma was safe and happy . . . "Nothing else matters."

She grabbed her phone and texted: "You looked stunning in the dress. My brilliant girl, luv u Mom xoxo!"

The graduation dinner (the very thought still made her quake) was the day after tomorrow, so she assured herself, trying to calm the nagging doubts that seeped in around the edges of that expanse of blue, which her mind escaped to in moments of doubt and anxiety: Vineyard Sound, as she'd known it from her childhood while writing stories on the piazza of their sprawling cottage, a sunlit blue where the white ferries (*Naushon* and *Islander*) passed like the clockwork of a well-ordered summer girlhood, like good manners and respect for the feelings of others, so described in the drawn-out nasal cadences of her father's voice as he carefully explained the rigging of their Vineyard 15, as he first let her take over the tiller and summoned an offshore breeze to spur them over the waves.

She closed her eyes, repeating her mantra, thinking that a good dose of Vedic meditation would be the cure, or possibly summoning forth the Stoic virtues along the lines of the wise Marcus Aurelius, who appealed to her more and more, in advancing age, than the Seneca of late adolescence: the essence of happiness is tranquility, the entering into and enjoyment of a day-to-day routine, indulging life as an indeterminant dream state. "Kenosis," she queried, remembering something her life coach had recommended for a burnt-out CEO: "Try gratitude, that emptying out of difference—quashing the impulse to self-elevation that fueled the competitive instinct. Meditate more on the wonders of this life."

Her eyes flew open. Had it really been her competitive mania that had ruined them, her lack of a true spiritual dimension?

"Jacob's dream," she exclaimed, as if a shadowy figure out of her unconscious had suddenly come alive in her soul. Rudely jarred to a fully waking state, she flipped open her laptop to explore more about this Old Testament story that her emerging authorial voice was convinced fit her developing narrative.

"Wrestling with an angel . . . a ladder on which angels passed from earth to heaven's gate and back again."

Yes, yes . . . how Jake liked to surprise her by easing up behind her at Cap and Gown or the physics library and clamping his hands on her shoulders, as if claiming his prize, daring her to resist, holding her in place as he bent to kiss her brow, and only then relaxing his grip to sometimes massage her shoulders, especially her right after a hard match or workout. Just as he'd done with Erma, grasping her shoulders, and then as he finished up his BPH job offer, giving her a brief massage, where his right index finger became fully visible, revealing that pink scar running from just behind the nail and over the first joint. A scar, like the "Sunshine State," Jake had liked to joke, an acid burn that had landed him in the health center junior year.

"No fucking way." The demonic panic of the night before again loosed upon her pumping heart.

Staring for a moment more at her blinking cursor, she took the plunge and began the hunt for one Jacob Burrage, founder of BPH, starting with the links provided by Gareth's research associate, which brought up an array of images, the wildly successful biotech entrepreneur—all, so noted the associate, after scores of iterations, at least ten years out of date, before the 2005 accident that killed his wife and critically injured his son. There he was, very much the Jake of memory—or even more like young Jacob—shorn of locks, a Willy Loman with his pitch deck. He'd been in his thirties and forties at various sales conferences and benefits, hobnobbing with the likes of Bill Gates, Steve Jobs, and Steve Wozniak, a much younger Elon Musk, and a slew of other venture capitalists and entrepreneurs. Peter Thiel and Google's Eric Schmidt (fellow Princetonian) were the only names she recognized.

"How young and fit, Jake—even in your late forties." A face, a body, a résumé, a brand name.

Just as she feared, scanning these familiar faces had the unhappy effect, like a partially effaced palimpsest, of returning her again to the sweaty dread of the evening before, first prompted by aches and pain and then young Jacob's appearance, where he had moved so confidently among the shades of youthful exuberance, an invigorating antidote to Lethe—something almost feminine in the softness of his expression that made for a consoling presence among the gathered. Then drifting over to suddenly preside at their table, staking his claim with those controlling hands on Erma's shoulders, as if they'd all been summoned by their lord and master. A demonstration . . . a proof positive, his long-lashed eyes agleam with a flickering rapture betoken of some esoteric knowledge carefully locked away. A kind of test (guinea pigs)—hadn't Apolonia suggested as much—a control group, as if seeking FDA approval, whether his latest creation (those green capsules) or the wooing of his newest helpmeet, spellbound under his not-so-delicate caress, passed muster.

She worked her shoulders up and down, feeling those hands sliding south and pinning her arms, closing her eyes to the sweet agony, the purest of pure pleasures.

"Back in the lab . . . ," she moaned. Hardly the sentiments of the morning after.

"Get a fucking grip, Gini," she scolded and flicked again through a slew of earnest images from sales conferences. "Oh, Jake . . . Jake," squinting at her screen, as if to compare and contrast, to either invoke again—stickler that she was for the right word—or explain away her frenzy of the evening before. "Novitiate . . . ," she whispered tentatively as she returned to the Old Testament story. A laying on of hands—no, more like a priest presenting the host of memory, the hope of eternity or eternal youth to his congregation in the guise of a young woman. Clicking back to Wikipedia: a young Jacob staking a claim to his two wives, Leah and Rachel, after stealing his father's blessing, along with God's promise of land and descendants as the dust of the earth.

She moaned again at the pain in her right shoulder as she tried to make sense of the story coming to life in her imagination.

Something too about the oddness of how he sought eye contact among his celebrants, that smooth evangelist pitch while pressing his blessing on her daughter, who in turn seemed quite overwhelmed by his ministrations: that demure bowing of her flushed face, like a virgin bride, perhaps embarrassed by his ringing pronouncements and the voyeur-like glances of her godmothers. Yes, something that had come over Erma at his touch, as if at the bestowal of a spiritual grace that reminded her all too vividly of their midnight walks in Prospect Garden, the scent of California lilacs mixing with that of the firs, his voice yet another of night's incantations, naming names as he brought his myrmidons to life, when Jake liked to call her "my lost angel," fallen from heaven's gate.

"I have seen God face-to-face, yet my life has been preserved."

The prophetic voice, the cursor blinking on her screen, brought on yet another frisson of memory from the night before last, as young Jacob, when she had suddenly cried out in blissful wonder, had quickly risen from his desk chair and circled behind her to place calming hands on her shoulders. Her exhausted, inebriated body seemed to quiver back to life, her mind ignited with what seemed a starburst of cosmic energy, disconcerting as it was delicious, as she had gripped the arms of her chair to keep herself from flying into his arms. Until his assuring hands calmed her, his fingers beginning with her shoulders, massaging slowly into the gaps around her collarbone, working out tensions and cares, and then to her neck, even counting out loud the seven vertebrae, until straying behind her ears like vesperal flames whispering a luxurious melting ecstasy, flowing downward and then up again until her spine, ladder of the soul, crackled with electricity.

Getting out all the kinks, their euphemism for making love, when he'd religiously brought her first, even on her period. Desperate to remember more of that night before last, she found herself feeding off their thousand student days, hope and curiosity calming her anxiety, the Motrin kicking in as she indulged herself with another hour of Google search, as if she was indeed that angel transfigured in the mirror of her mind, safely musing on the foibles and calamities of overstriving mortals.

She poured her way through press articles, big-pharma industry newsletters, savvy investor reports—many after 2005 headlined along the lines: "Who's Running Barrage Pharma? Your Guess as Good as Mine." She pulled up an Excel spreadsheet and entered data and dates, until she had an almost perfect bell curve: the first twenty-five years out of Princeton full of accolades from Stanford and Chicago, patent filings, successful fund-raising as Burrage Pharma grows exponentially; until 2000 and a plateau of feverish press coverage on the rollout of one new revolutionary drug after the next, with Jake Burrage the visionary poster child for biotech's new century. Then a family tragedy in 2005 and a move to Boulder, precipitating a sharp drop-off in detailed press coverage and subsequent investor complaints and speculation about the disposition of the founder (not unlike the questions surrounding Steve Jobs's health of the same period) even as Burrage Pharma goes from strength to strength, including the building of the two-hundred-million-dollar Princeton biochemistry lab in 2013.

She shivered with nervous energy, pulling her bathrobe more tightly around her shoulders, and scrolled her way back in time, hovering over an article in *Forbes* from 2004, on the brink of personal disaster. "The Visionary Behind the Biotech Revolution Promises an Ageless Future." Jake is pictured in his lab in a white-linen, knee-length coat with the Burrage Pharma Health insignia stitched in green on the breast pocket. The reporter presses him on the latest research and future plans.

"There is no reason a lot of age-related diseases can't be treated early on—anticipated and proactively dealt with based on a family's health history. We bring a holistic approach to medicine, managing lifestyle, nutrition, and medications when necessary. People are living longer and longer. No reason this trend can't be sustained to well over a hundred and who knows how much more. The dream of antiaging medicine consists of treatments that identify the root causes of dysfunction as we age and then reverse them entirely—preventive rather than palliative strategies. The trick being to stop people from getting ill and infirm in the first place. Every disease we eliminate will add a few more years to the life span. We're already at work on drugs that could rejuvenate aged blood vessels and restore blood pressure to safe levels, which, in turn, would improve outcomes for kidney disease and dementia. What we're really talking about is negligible senescence, lowering the risk of death, disability, frailty, and illness so that our biological age would be irrelevant and no longer define us. Something that, as a species, we should be aiming for. For scientists, quality of life is the gold standard, even as a well-spent life has more to do with matters of the spirit, something we in the lab also need to keep in mind."

"Aging is an evolutionary oversight . . . ," she read out loud, smiling, as the sound of the voice in the interview echoed the one she remembered while dining with Jabberwocky. "You see, it comes down to a bunch of mutations accumulating over time that damage fitness as we age, which evolution can't dispense with: antagonistically pleiotropic genes that maximize reproductive success in youth but which have an unfortunate impact on old age: prioritizing having children while dispensing with parents. Not a trade-off we, as scientists, need to accept. If we baby boomers—as Ray Kurzweil has written in *The Singularity Is Near*—can make it to our seventies, we could potentially live for another hundred years or more. And just possibly upload our memories to computers to be stored for posterity, or even downloaded into our offspring, providing a kind of immortality."

She raised a fist and shook it in horror at the very thought of being saddled with the memories of her mother's infidelities—the horror and humiliation of that graduation dinner: "No way, José."

"And then, once we've managed the best we can with strategies of repair, we are turning to replacement therapies to reinforce our ailing defenses—broadly: stem-cell therapies to spur regeneration, supercharging our immune system, enhancing our microbiome, and suchlike. Of course, of much more immediate import is the curing of devastating diseases like Huntington's—something I have a personal interest in, and which the new gene-editing techniques on the horizon should allow us to eliminate, through both somatic and germline gene editing."

"Huntington's," she murmured. Was this an oversight, an overlooked plot point? Unshared with her and Jabberwocky?

Then there was an unfamiliar, unforeseen shift as the young woman reporter pressed him on his private life.

"I was influenced a lot by my father, a construction guy, a master carpenter who loved to work with his hands, to build things. The only thing he loved more than building kitchen cabinets was camping out in the Ozarks by his favorite stream, where we would go fly-fishing. Where my wife and I still go, where we snuggle up by Cripple Creek and catch up on our reading. Often, we will read to one another, most recently from Augustine's *Confessions*: 'Moreover, love itself, which binds us together in the bond of unity, would have no means of pouring soul into soul, and, as it were, mingling them with each other, if human beings never learned anything from one another.'"

Asked to explain the quote in his own words, he replies: "Oh, I guess that's Augustine telling us that our ability to love one another depends on our capacity to learn from one another. A little lesson for which I have my wife to thank. We honeymooned in Venice, and she became quite enamored of a painting of Augustine by Carpaccio."

She moaned softly and bowed her head, reaching a quivering palm to the screen.

The interviewer pressed on: "And what about Ecclesiastes: a season for everything, a time to live, a time to die. Doesn't death provide a meaningful end for the well-lived life?"

"Well, if you go back to Genesis, God (who often seems of two or even three minds) kind of hedges His bets, initially granting Adam and Eve—created in His own image—eternal life in the Garden of Eden. And then when they partake of the apple, the tree of knowledge, all bets are off, and they are exiled to a life of painful childbirth and difficulty making ends meet. Even so, Adam lives to a hundred and thirty, and God settles on a human life span of a hundred and twenty years. Later to be reduced further to four score and ten: 'for dust you are, and to dust you shall return.' Even if my namesake, Jacob, lived to a hundred and forty-seven. But as I like to think of it, that tree of knowledge was God's way of hedging His bets, so allowing us to claw back a bit of eternity by using our brains, spurred by curiosity (Eve's sin) to find better solutions and so extend our lives and, at the very least, banish debilitating diseases. The problem is, speaking of time, that unlike Silicon Valley's measure of success, creating killer apps in a few years, what we do in science is slow, painstaking research; however, all the new technologies—from computers, the internet, and the coming dawn of AI—are upping our pace of discovery, testing, and bringing new products to market."

She tapped her keyboard and smiled: "Jake, you've been doing your reading."

This prompted another slightly disgruntled search. "Jacob Burrage Marries Elizabeth Ferrand. Nuptials Celebrated by Hundreds of Admirers." Jake, aged forty-three, marries Elizabeth, aged twenty-six (oh, the younger woman, the fresh eggs!), Cornell undergrad, Harvard PhD in biochemistry, Chicago postdoc, and an employee of BPH. The *Evanston Gazette* (local boy makes good) covered the wedding in some detail. The wedding ceremony was held at Saint Mary's Catholic Church. (A full mass and communion! Had Jake converted?) The reporter noted that no expense was spared, as the couple celebrated their nuptials with two-hundred and fifty invited guests at the Four Seasons Hotel in Chicago. The bride's family was in attendance, the father giving away his daughter. Sadly, the groom's parents had passed on some years before. "Mr. Burrage gave an impassioned toast to his late father, describing, in sometimes funny and often poignant anecdotes, their camping trips—the 'Cripple Creek Hilton'—as a child to the Ozarks with his dad." Besides friends and family of the bride, the paper noted that most of the groom's guests were employees of BPH, all of whom were put up for the night at the Four Seasons by their employer.

"You married a woman of faith."

She stared at her laptop screen, a hinted pout, flipping through a few marriage photos, crushing the regret of a jilted lover. "Why did you never talk to me about your father, Jake?" How was it—maybe high-powered Princeton—he seemed so sui generis that she'd never quite imagined him having parents. Or maybe it was those painful memories of her two brief meetings with his tall, prematurely aged mother at graduation, first at the disastrous graduation dinner with her own mother on the warpath, and then those few awkward moments on Cannon Green after graduation, his mother standing with Jake, tears of pride for her son streaking her heavily made-up face, wearing a dumpy black dress, which she now recalled as something cheap from JCPenney. That had been her last glimpse of Jake, as she left mother and son in the humid sunshine to join her parents, her father relishing every moment with his salutatorian daughter, even as he had to deal with his tipsy and belligerent ex-wife.

She turned her attention again to the lithesome beaming bride (the doomed woman, in her writer's mind) standing next to her husband as they held a knife together in preparation for cutting the cake. There was much to admire in her long, flowing white dress of silk and tulle, her gleaming brow and doting gaze directed to her new husband. "Totally in love," she murmured, examining her rival's intelligent large eyes; she was not exactly glamorous perhaps, but handsome and quick-witted (she'd have to be to handle Jake), projecting a certain wholesome quality, a spiritual reserve with her small mouth and steady gaze and strong cheekbones. "A healthy specimen, full of smarts, and a fertile Catholic to boot, guaranteed to produce a brood of wonderful children . . ." She struggled to check the note of sarcasm and wounded pride as she scrolled down to Elizabeth's parents: father an electrician, hometown Syracuse, her mother an ER nurse, blue-collar, three daughters (a younger sister, Samantha, also a biochemist at BPH), steady working people, upwardly mobile, admirable in every respect. "Good for you, Liz. All the way from public school to

Cornell (three-time All-American in basketball!) and Harvard and Chicago for your postdoc and marriage to BPH—sky's the limit, girl."

Even confronted by this worthy competitor—and the tragedy to come—she found her mind racing, trying to be a good sport as she searched for the thing left undone, overlooked.

"Cripple Creek . . . ," she pondered, letting the words dissolve time.

And there the great expanse of blue rose again before her eyes, but now narrowed to something more intimate, their camp at Lake Tashmoo, and Jake's laugh at the very idea of "camp," given her family's sturdy, two-room shack with hot water, bathroom, electricity, and only a few minutes' walk to some of the fanciest homes on the Mink Meadows golf course. But it had been theirs for two weeks, as the August renters had abandoned it due to a medical emergency. How impressed she'd been that Jake had been able to repair the ancient Amana refrigerator by replacing some wiring chewed through by mice. And there, at night, with the moon and stars blushing on the lake, she had indeed heard about Cripple Creek and camping-fishing-hunting trips to the "far hills," as his father had called them, where they would leave the Ford pickup and hike into the wilderness and set up their tent and sleeping bags and live off the land for a week, fly-fishing for rainbow trout in the summer, hunting in camo gear in the fall, stalking deer, dressing and cooking venison on an outdoor fire.

She shook her head and rubbed tears from her eyes, as first apologies and then excuses cantered through her mind: between the tennis training, the sailing, the sex—when had there been time to listen, to truly listen? What kind of novelist . . . who—lacking empathy—can't even listen?

And again, she detected that revenant voice next to her ear, soft and low and searching, perhaps a note of loneliness, so at odds with her demon lover, who only moments before had launched arrows of lust through every vein in her body. Not unlike the lapping of wavelets against Tashmoo's grassy shore, where the undulant backs of otters passing on the prowl invoked tales told by his father about the Osage Indians and the Ozarks, a handsome people, peace-loving but fierce warriors when attacked, wily hunters, who, once, long ago, had built great palisaded communities along Cripple Creek, in a time before time, before the murderous rampage of de Soto and his killers who had enslaved those left alive, all for the sake of the fabled silver and gold mines that had proved an illusion.

He had been kneeling between her legs, massaging her thighs, his searching voice barely above a hush, as if not to disturb the lapping moon shadows.

"We fished every morning in that luminous blue light flickering though the trees, my dad's line like a silver thread breathing in the soft air over the stream, where he cast his fly into distant pools with deadeye accuracy. And every afternoon, we'd walk the riverbank searching for Osage arrowheads."

Had she ever asked, ever known what had happened . . . ? Was some spiritual dimension lacking in her Stoic practice?

"Kenosis," she whispered again to assure herself, as if hearing an echo, clicking back to her previous search and a description in the *Evanston Gazette* of Jake and Elizabeth's marriage service: Saint Paul's charge to the Philippians:

"Let each of you not look to your own interests, but to the interests of others. Let the same mind be in you that was in Christ Jesus, who, though he was in the form of God, did not regard equality with God as something to be exploited, but emptied himself, taking the form of a servant, being born in human likeness."

Born in human likeness . . . She bent intently to her screen: Jacob Ferrand Burrage Jr., born in February 1994 on the leading edge of her parabola of press attention directed to BPH. A year later, the complaints of the CEO's aloofness would begin, even as FDA approvals started to roll in by the dozen.

"A dedicated family man," explains one 2003 BPH press release, as journalists and analysts grumble about a lack of access. It seems Jake Burrage is working more and more from home, or as he sheepishly admits on one investor call: "Oh, I tend to go into the laboratory late at night after my son has gone to bed to check up on ongoing experiments. We're now doing the basic science once the preserve of universities. There's nothing like the quiet of night in a well-run lab—my sanctuary, my hermitage, if you will; gives a man time to reflect and plan—focus on the things that really matter in this life."

A *Chicago Magazine* piece, more photo spread than substance, from the fall of 2004, shows the young family ensconced in their lovely, ivy-clad home on Sheridan Place, Evanston's toniest neighborhood. There was ten-year-old Jacob posed with his parents, already looking a lot like his father. She squinted. Perhaps something of his mother's lithe height, her long, slim, elegant nose, pictured in the backyard lap pool, standing in the shallow end, water sliding off an already muscled torso.

His father's eyebrows and same long-lashed, light blue eyes. Aglow with a confident half smile. A young man happy and secure under the doting gaze of his proud parents. And Liz Burrage touring their splendid home, dressed in autumnal colors, fawn slacks and forest-green sweater, hair in a tight chignon to best show off her long neck and lovely set of cheekbones, photographed in their Arts and Crafts–style living room—mahogany shelves lined to overflowing with books—where she was pointing out, according to the caption, the Indian design motifs in the tiling around the hearth, the architect a protégé of Frank Lloyd Wright. "We love the way the interior flows so effortlessly out to the exterior and vice versa. Even the intimate sense of privacy is expansive. So allowing the mind to wander, to explore, to dwell in the fecundity of the universe. A place full of nooks to curl up with a book or the latest research paper."

"Fecundity . . . ," she murmured, finding herself drawn to the glossy photo spread, flicking again and again through the pages describing the wonders of Sheridan Place, following in the footsteps of the doomed woman through room after room, bringing her face closer to the screen as she thought she detected—could it be?—an array of California lilacs through the French doors sheltering in the shade of a line of balsam firs: "Oh, Liz, as articulate as you are beautiful."

In the early spring of 2005, tragedy strikes. Elizabeth is driving her eleven-year-old son to school on an icy road when, passing through an intersection at a green light, the Chevy Suburban is hit broadside on the driver's side by a speeding FedEx delivery van skidding on black ice. Elizabeth, six months pregnant with their second child, is killed almost instantly, while her son suffers broken bones and lacerations but "miraculously" survives. The death of Jacob's wife and badly injured son brings an outpouring of shocked condolences from the BPH community and beyond.

"Mr. Burrage is taking some badly needed leave from BPH to spend time with his recovering son. He will remain in seclusion for the immediate future while his son is treated and undergoes physical therapy."

"Oh, Jake, I'm so sorry."

How, she wondered, could she not have known—not Gareth or nosy Bianca—when all this information was only keystrokes away. Or cared . . . Grimly, aghast, she closed her eyes, desperately trying to remember something of that young body from two nights before—surely there had been scars? But then, she'd failed at first to even notice that scar on his index finger. And what prodigies of physical therapy for an Olympic-caliber swimmer to come back from such injuries?

She stood up, stretched her stiff back, and limped to the window of her Marriott executive suite. In the parking lot four stories below, a trickle of reunion goers began to head for their rental cars.

How could young Jacob have so guilelessly lied about such a tragedy, tossing off some clichéd story about a messy divorce, when only a few clicks away on the internet was the glaring truth? Unless, unless, the kid had wanted to be caught out in a lie, wanted her to be intrigued (encouraged?) enough to dig into his past—a way of drawing her in, drawing her back, drawing her closer. To what? To whom? A chance to flush out her self-satisfied life that had resulted in her never having been tempted (at least a temptation foregone) to check in on Jake's life until now. A stellar life she might have shared, that at the very least might have provided material for her unwritten novel (her first attempt, her senior thesis, lying moribund and gathering dust in Firestone Library). She tapped the window, her vague reflection layered over neat lines of waiting rental cars to speed souls back to their very ordinary or possibly extraordinary lives. Divorce, like Apolonia's and Bianca's, might signal early failures but at least leave open hopes of future recovery and fresh starts. Tragedies like hers and Gareth's mark stark endpoints that can never quite be dismissed, reimagined, or gainsaid. Grief everlasting.

"Why, Jake?"

She nodded, following a line of distant stratus clouds, harbingers of smoky humidity for Erma's graduation in three days, as she weighed the narrative possibilities.

Perhaps a superior mind, a mind obsessed with the science of aging, could not admit the workings of blind fate to spoil so perfect a marriage of like souls. Or, as Jake had put it in that *Forbes* interview: "This is not about Silicon Valley billionaires throwing a hissy fit about having to grow old; this is about a *Star Trek* future, where no one dies of preventable diseases, where life, if not fair exactly, at least evens out the playing field." How unfair is black ice, or the disaster of the human condition, that he simply couldn't admit to being liable to what James called, in his last words, the "distinguished thing." She shook her head in dismay at the ease with which she'd begun equating father and son. Could a father really cast such a shadow? She tapped the window glass as her eyes withdrew to her troubled stare. "A shadow of a shadow." Or did it have more to do with what Gareth had noted: how so many in the life-extension community—Ray Kurzweil, for one—had lost fathers early, lost some essential loved one and so had a visceral incentive to try to put right what they saw as a glaring wrong.

"They're in denial," she'd offered to Gareth.

"Well"—raised eyebrows and a pat on the small of her back as they danced—"*God* doesn't admit His mistakes."

Wearing her editor's—or was it her novelist's—hat as she sat again at her desk: "Elizabeth's untimely death—a woman of faith—just doesn't fit the brilliant game plan, the branding strategy. Or God's plan."

Then in late 2005, Jake hires a new CEO from Johnson & Johnson to run the day-to-day operations of BPH, becoming executive director on the board. The new CEO arrives at Princeton in 2013 for the ribbon-cutting ceremony to celebrate the gleaming glass and blue-granite-clad Burrage Biochemistry Lab.

After another half hour of more or less fruitless searches, she sat back, exhausted, her eyes aching, and then got up again, needing to work her bad right knee, and so returned to the window, gazing out at the parking lot, where families were streaming to their rental cars, some with young children in tow sporting tiger tails dangling to the pavement.

"Jacob, Jacob, Jacob . . . Jake." The thing nagging at her mind.

She returned to her desk and began googling around, using search terms "Evanston" and variations on "Jacob Burrage Jr.," including "swim team" and "high school" and came up with nothing.

"Where did you go to school, Jacob? You must have been a standout swimmer."

She pulled up the Princeton swim-team site and the stats for Jacob Burrage: four-time All-American, four-time All-Ivy, and in four different freestyle events and relays. Hometown, Boulder, Colorado, and Fairview High School. "Of course, Jake, you moved out to Colorado, to be near the new lab in Denver, abandoning Sheridan Place and all the terrible memories." Using the new search terms, she immediately found exactly what she expected. "And Jacob, yes, of course, you were everything your father meant you to be: captain of an undefeated swim team at Fairview High . . . summa cum laude . . . head of student council . . . captain of the chess team . . . captain of the debating team—just another smart kid headed to Princeton."

She sat back for a moment, done in by the dogged perseverance she was noted for, always turning over the last stone. Clicking around the Fairfield High School site, she found a picture of the 2012 swim team with Jacob posed, front and center, holding a sliver cup. She squinted, looking for scars. "Where's your mother's nose, her height?" Not that Erma hadn't changed as well, at ten and eleven sporting her father's dimpled chin and broad cheekbones, his quick smile, only to have adolescence erase much of the evidence.

"But, Jake, why are you not here? Why did you never come back? At least for your son's graduation, for Jacob's sake? Surely, Elizabeth would expect as much."

Her plaintive questions sparked a final spasm of wary curiosity, a hope that the thing could finally be put to rest. She googled around, entering a Boulder street address for young Jacob Burrage that had made it into his high school newspaper. Zillow took her to a grand, modernist home on a cul-de-sac overlooking Boulder, a dazzling confection of wide plate-glass windows, soaring views of gray mountains and billowing clouds, a majestic, cantilevered terrace reaching to the horizon, a place of peace and repose, all the seclusion that worldly prosperity might buy; it had been on the market only three years before and sold for eleven million dollars: "Cripple Creek, touching the clouds with some of Colorado's finest skiing and hiking only minutes away."

How un–Sheridan Place. A hermitage in the sky.

"How perfect for bringing over your school friends, your swim-team buddies, your chess-team sweetheart . . ." Taking the virtual tour through one glorious room after the next, one spacious view of blue skies after the next, she found herself listening to her version of a concerned parent. "Why, Jake, why would you sell your son's home less than a year after he graduated from high school? A refuge from Evanston and memories of the accident, his mother, your wife, Elizabeth? Why? Just because your son goes off to Princeton and you're left an empty-nester, working late in the Denver lab, fading from view . . . an out-of-touch parent."

She shook her head, gasping at the returning ache in her right shoulder: "Working late in the Burrage Biochemistry Lab."

She kept scrolling—scrolling and scrolling—through the virtual tour of Cripple Creek (same Swiss architects as the Burrage Biochemistry Lab), wandering through room after room in search of her quarry, breathing in the sprawl over the vastness of a weightless blue, an Olympian blue, her steps seeming to glide along through rooms and more rooms, each more spacious than the next, palatial, with floor-to-ceiling windows embracing the sky, the limitless horizon, filled with a celestial light gleaming on hardwood floors and marble kitchen counters, where gleaming silver appliances and perfectly arrayed glass beakers of pasta and rice, cereal and grain, and—what?—pomegranate seeds were arranged with the meticulous care demanded by an ordered mind. A lab bench. But so lacking a woman's touch, the coziness and warmth of Sheridan Place. She felt her heart lift at this observation as she continued, led on like Persephone from the underworld by a soft, ineffable, sapphire light, as if she had only recently inhabited such rooms, as if her refined taste might add some homey touches to the clean lines of the furnishings, perhaps fruitwood tables and chairs in modern updates of Arts and Crafts style, done up in pale fabrics of soft indigo, mango, peach, and lemon—infinitely restful, yet warm.

The master bedroom and guest rooms were immaculate, like high-end hotel rooms—no sign of life, nothing to indicate a personal touch or whimsy. Only the single child's bedroom displayed signs of ever having been lived in, with its wall posters, crammed bookshelves full of what looked like textbooks and novels, some displaying silver trophies, and . . . (she enlarged the image) display cases of rock samples or possibly arrowheads.

She flung herself back in her desk chair and let out a stifled scream of frustration, immediately surging forward again to further blow up the image hovering on her screen.

There, on the wall over the double bed, hung an all-too-familiar framed image: the figure of an old man seated at his scholarly desk, pen poised in midsentence—seeing now, for the first time, a writer at work on his autobiographical novel, curious face turned to his window, as if there, in the crystalline light of late afternoon, his yet-unfathomed, unimagined material still awaited.

What had she missed? Or forgotten? Or even blithely dismissed? What key unturned?

A line of Shakespeare's Hamlet came to mind: "Blessed are those whose blood and judgment are so well commeddled that they are not a pipe for Fortune's finger to sound what stop she please."

She began a furious Google search for Jake's father until she found the obituary. "Jacob Burrage, wife of Barbara, succumbed on Friday to the ravages of Huntington's disease . . . he was just forty-six years old."

"Oh, dear Lord . . . Agrippina exiled to the Pontines," she cried. How could she not have known? Why would Jake hold that back from her? Fearful she'd chicken out with such a genetic disease lurking in his family? Or had she known—half-known? Huntington's had been mentioned by Jake—yes, she was sure of it, in passing if nothing else. And by young Jacob, the other night, perhaps in hopes of prompting her curiosity. Was that the black hole, the event horizon from which she'd shied away at the last?

For minutes, she stared at her blinking cursor. The day before, she had seemed to have perfect recall. Now her memory was its usual blur. She sighed and clicked on her Expedia account to search for air tickets. One day, Monday, between now and Erma's graduation dinner and dance on Tuesday. Chicago or Boulder? She clicked back to Zillow and the address.

"No way . . ." Sheridan Place was back on the market.

She returned to her window, tapping the glass as she heard herself say: "He lied so that I'd try to find him and find the inspiration to finish my novel—write the novel that needs to be written. Find my way to the faith of a better person."

CHAPTER 29

She circled her Ford Escort rental around the adjoining streets to kill fifteen minutes (trying to nerve up her inner imposter), stopping to view the teal-blue expanse of Lake Michigan, hoping to get the feel in her bones for Evanston's toniest neighborhood: what with spacious parks to the north, the vastness of the lakeshore to the east, the dazzling talent pool of the University of Chicago's biotech labs just fifteen minutes south on the freeway, less than ten minutes from the executive offices of BPH, five minutes to the best schools, half an hour to O'Hare. What's not to like? With precious minutes to spare, finishing notes on her phone, she circled back to 2878 Sheridan Place, seeing it now afresh in her mind's eye as perfectly plotted to shelter a demanding life like hers—why not! She gazed avidly upon the wrought-iron gate beyond which she could make out a gravel drive leading to a rectilinear red-brick, ivy-clad home that seemed serenely at one with its setting. Pricy yet modest. Extensive yet intimate gardens, where the half-light of midmorning was gently filtered by a backdrop of closely packed—oh, so familiar—balsam firs. She craned her head as if quite pleased by her sleuthing, even relieved at this bucolic picture, and not a little tantalized by how the familiar tapering, conical shapes of the firs, nodding to the slight breeze, drifted silvery shadows across the gravel drive and grounded her expectations. An expectant flutter of her heart, as if the very air was deliciously alive, reminding her once again of her heroine, Isabel Archer, of whom James had written: "She carried within herself a great fund of life, and her deepest enjoyment was to feel the continuity between the movements of her own soul and the agitations of the world."

She took courage in such a pedigree (surely a claim to spiritual grace), even as she grimaced and sighed at near-memories of that Chevy Suburban that never returned.

As if to provide the necessary counterfactual relief, a white Mercedes, a most practical SUV, promptly drew up to the front gate. She sounded the horn and waved. An arm with gold bracelets returned her wave from the Mercedes as the wrought-iron gates slowly swung inward, a yellow bike lock dangling from a lower rung. Yet another frisson of pleasure diffused through her chest, listening to the welcoming crunch of gravel on the drive, the damp scents from the freshly mulched flower beds, the aching pleasure of early-spring colors. By habit more than design, she slipped on her high heels, since being the tallest woman in a room always played to her advantage. The real estate agent was still fumbling with a lockbox by the front door, and so she took the additional seconds to sample the stately lines of the portico, girdled with neo-classical concrete urns, spilling over with red begonias, while along the path to the front door purple foxgloves (a dangerous plant!) nodded as if hard of hearing, little devils with a such a lively head start on summer. Shadows flickered across her expectant face, and she turned abruptly with a pleasure she couldn't quite divine to the mature pointed firs. Yes, such a strategic picket line of privacy guarding the eastern perimeter of the property.

Again, she surveyed the compact, ivy-clad brickwork (already familiar from Zillow), hardly ostentatious at an asking price of three million compared to the pricy real estate of sea-view homes on West Chop running to the tens of millions—or Cripple Creek's eleven-million price tag overlooking Boulder. She smiled from the path as the agent got the recalcitrant front door open with a huffing laugh and shoulder bent to the brass knocker. "We are the words; we are the music; we are the thing itself," she heard herself recite, a bewitching refrain from her early years as aspiring novelist before life without Jake tumbled her in a different direction. She paused a moment more on the steps as she caught the slurred warbling of a purple finch among the firs, the song that had once put her in mind of Sappho's verses: she and Virginia Woolf.

"Yes . . . ," she murmured, breathing deeply of the comingled scents saturating the air. "I can see you here."

"It's the darkest space in the house, but fortunately I've managed to dissuade the previous two owners from painting the woodwork, though not the banister railing—sadly. You can't get carved chestnut paneling like this anymore for love or money."

The long, narrow entrance hall was indeed dark, even as it emanated a pleasant smell of tea roses and beeswax and spend-thrift time, their high heels tapping out the lingering seconds on the checkerboard floor of white and black marble: queen to h5.

"Good bones," and she smiled into the younger woman's soft hazel eyes set off by terse but full eyebrows.

Again and again, she had to rein in her nifty athlete's heart that yearned to gallop along the long hallway, to seek out the sources (the lap pool in the back garden) of light streaming from distant doorways, rooms where she half expected the quietude of the artist's model, there bathed in the luminous atmosphere of a Vermeer. She returned the gracious, soft-spoken, worldly-wise smile of her raven-haired host, probably yet another useless humanities degree that required the financial boost of dealing in high-end real estate.

"Hard to believe seven bedrooms walking in the front door."

"Yes, pleasantly deceiving, don't you think? Plainspoken modesty—yet with room to spare. Fortunately, none of my clients even contemplated fooling with the layout since the architect was a Frank Lloyd Wright associate who went on to build a thriving practice. And there are plenty of Wrightian features and details, from the long hallway retreating from the entrance to the organic rhythm of how one room merges into the next, the simple patterns of ample windows, and the Indian tiling motifs, which provide a unified vision throughout."

"You said, your third sale . . . why would anyone want to leave this place?" she queried facetiously as she raised her eyebrows and edged farther down the hallway.

"Children grow up, and job descriptions change. But how perfect for young children, who can simply lose themselves in a place like this, and the gardens, which are miracles of tiger dens and hideouts beneath the California lilacs."

"Ah, grandchildren, may they materialize in their plenitudes on holidays."

"Always hope that one's offspring may prove more prolific than their busy parents."

"My God, a spiral staircase, how *Gone with the Wind*."

"Like I said, all original, hand-carved railings and newel-posts, but the present owner couldn't resist having them painted white, thus covering up the wear and tear of young sneakers battering down the banister."

"Goodness, not too young, I hope—that's quite a drop."

"Oh, I remember a daredevil little boy spilling down in his pj's during a Christmas party, in anticipation, no doubt, of a stocking to come—a previous client plus one."

"I remember it now, many years ago, a quiet gathering, the then-owner was in my class at Princeton."

"Ah, I thought I detected an air of déjà vu. So, you knew Jake Burrage?"

"*Knew* is a loaded word. A brilliance so dazzling that *knew* got lost in the shimmer of whimsy and references beyond my pay grade. I was on a business trip, a publishers' sales conference—like this one tomorrow. And one of my authors—actually, my husband's author—was doing a book on the brave new world of biotech. And I thought: Why not have a few drinks with Jake at the Four Seasons and get his take on our brave new future? But he insisted I come over. It was the fall, the leaves were down, windy and wet, and I believe, yes, over there in the living room, a crackling oak fire, and his wife, Elizabeth, joined us, tall and striking. Jake hadn't changed much—a better haircut."

"Oh yes, but you know Jake Burrage (note the tiling surrounding the hearth) was a legend around these parts. Evanston born and raised. My husband is a biochemist at BPH, and in the early days, they were hiring by the score every month, bringing in complete research teams from all over. I couldn't resist the inside scoop I got from HR. Sadly, I got Jake in and out of Sheridan Place. One hopes for the perfect match in this business, that a client will stick, even as circumstances militate against it. Good for business, perhaps, but not the soul's aspiration."

"Oh, the soul—goodness gracious, but why sadly?"

"You hadn't heard? Elizabeth was killed in a traffic accident over ten years ago, just six blocks from here, his son severely injured. Black ice, a FedEx truck just skidded through a light."

"How terrible. I had no idea. I don't think anyone in our class knew either. Jake was never much one for reunions. Or staying in touch." She placed a hand on the back of a green leather sofa, staring into the fireplace, with its decorative border of tiles, chocolate brown on buff—Navajo, according to *Chicago Magazine*—drawing her closer to inspect the interlocking geometric patterns, where Elizabeth had been photographed for the magazine spread.

"My husband and I were at their wedding—an event for the ages. Before then, Jake lived in a nondescript, one-bedroom condo—which I also sold for him, hardly the digs of a biotech titan. This place was really Liz's; she picked it out. Jake took off an hour from the lab, came by, walked the grounds, sniffed the air—a done deal. But I think, with a little time, he came to appreciate the age and the craftsmanship that went into it. For scientists, both Liz and Jake were more knowledgeable about architecture than one might think. Both their families had been in the construction trades. I remember how thoroughly Jake checked out all the mechanicals before closing and then paced out the backyard to make sure there was room for a lap pool."

She went to the line of windows where coruscations of limpid light streamed off the pool surface. "Yes, I can see how that would be a necessity—swim team freshman year."

"I've always been fascinated by how properties end up changing the people who buy them. That wasn't the case with Jake and Liz. At Christmas parties, you'd see pickups and BMWs parked cheek by jowl. Professors and electricians standing around the spread on the dining-room table. We all felt like we had a piece of Jake; he made everyone feel like the sky's the limit. Especially with Liz at his side to keep his feet firmly on the ground."

"She seemed—I mean, I barely knew her—like the perfect foil to his brilliance." Straying from her post by the window, she went to the nearly empty mahogany bookshelves and ran a finger as if testing for dust, hints of a long-gone library.

"I never heard them talking shop—and trust me: at the highest level, scientists bring their curiosity home. At Liz's funeral, it was as if the whole city turned out. She was a good Catholic, you know—not what you'd expect. Bookish, too, for a woman in biochemistry, not exactly the kind of woman a biochem guy would think to marry: a teammate. Let me tell you, I had to start reading *Scientific American* from cover to cover . . ." The agent laughed to herself and shot her dark eyebrows cradling knowing eyes. "A breed apart."

Gini returned to the window, the cool light sparkling in the blonde hair of her chignon, like a tight fist against the back of her head, pressing for answers.

"I married—I know the drill—a Harvard physicist." She bent to a crystal vase of brown-tipped yellow roses. "They do have a certain way of looking at the world."

"Ah, I often wondered if Liz tried to change him—no earthly restraint, I mean. Good luck to that. When he spoke at her service, you could've heard a pin drop: a lot of would-be Jonas Salks wondering how he would deal with a limit on the limitless.

That was my husband's take: when men of science find themselves run aground by the randomness of the universe."

"Didn't Jake's father die of some terrible disease—Huntington's, I think?"

"I never met his parents. Fortunately, I guess, they were not around for Liz's service. Poor Jake, how he struggled, as you can well imagine. He praised her as a mother, barely mentioning her achievements in the lab. Preferring to talk about her days at Cornell as an All-American basketball star, relating how she'd dreamed about playing pro basketball, before there was such a thing in the women's game. He talked about how she challenged him to go deeper into the realm of the spirit—how did he put it: 'where God and the unknown join as one,' and he bravely put on a tepid smile. Liz's kid sister, Samantha, a biochemist with BPH as well, had to help him down from the pulpit."

"'God's mysterious ways' was the boilerplate trotted out in the memorial service for my husband."

"Oh, the priest who presided struggled mightily, given the crowd of mourners: that God"—she winced—"had so loved Elizabeth that he found it necessary to recall her home early."

"Oh, dear."

"We were sitting only a few rows back, and that clearly didn't sit well with Jake, the way his face fell, shaking his head as he put his arm around his injured son. Then he suddenly looked up, teary eyes imploring the archivolts of Saint Mary's, the universe—as my husband put it: a man betrayed."

"The rib volts," Gini corrected and then laughed off her indiscretion. "Betrayed . . . but then, time betrays us all."

"Oh, there's no accounting for love, is there? Some in my husband's crowd thought Jake was hedging his bets marrying a woman of faith, a crack scientist. In the end, she gave him a beautiful son." The agent shrugged and pressed back the wide wings of hair off her brow. "Everyone reacts to tragedy differently. In this business (death, taxes, and divorce), let me tell you: we see the whole gamut of the human condition. Take it from a psychology major: it keeps you guessing."

"I remember"—Gini returned to the hearth, reaching again to the tile surround as if to some talismanic object visible only to her—"the boy, Jacob Jr., coming in and throwing his arms around his mother. A handsome, bright, inquisitive eight-year-old who, when I was introduced as a publisher, immediately wanted to know all about how books were made, from the writing to the bookstore shelf. You could tell Liz doted on the kid; she couldn't keep her large hands from the boy, who had her long slender nose and dimple, and Jake's flashing sea-stained eyes. But that may have been a kind of optical illusion—you know how it is: how kids tend to look like the parent you know best."

"Oh, a dead ringer for Jake at five or six, a bit more like Liz at ten, but children change, of course, beginning to look like one parent and, years later, the other—then like neither, or someone's grandparent. My husband and I went Dutch on our two: split the difference."

"How was his son—poor dear—after the accident?"

"How is any child—after something like that? Seated next to his mother in the front seat . . . not something one wants to even think about. I still see a FedEx truck and I'm spooked. Funny, how we can imagine our own death but not that someone of our own flesh and blood will die."

"I remember her face, the way she hung on the boy's every word as I explained the editorial process, protectively stroked her son's hair . . . well. It was a chilly day with a fire going." She reached again to run her fingers over the tiling with the Navajo motifs and turned to the windows. "Firs—balsam firs, aren't they?"

"Splendid, as old—1905—as the house." The realtor smiled and patted the pleats in her Armani trousers. "The clincher, in my book, even if Liz seemed more drawn to the Wrightian motifs, the sense of continuity. Oh, and the three Navajo rugs go back to the original owners as well. I love that, when owners pass on what they've loved as tokens of respect. I remember Jake laughing at Liz's enthusiasm, and teasing her: 'Not Osage . . . well, I don't know.'"

At this, she looked up as if just catching sight of two large landscapes in teakwood frames on the wall across from the windows. The oils depicted a woodland clearing by a narrow river or stream—one at sunset, one in moonlight, both with a pronounced atmospheric quality, feathery soft, blue-tinged, as if a fine mist had overspread the shadowed riverbank.

"These are gorgeous. One thinks of Blakelock. Do they transfer as well with the house?"

"Oh, yes indeed. These were Jake's addition to Sheridan Place—besides the lap pool. He had them painted by a famous Indian artist, Shonto Begay—Navajo too, since the Osage are pretty much extinct. But Jake explained exactly the scene along Cripple Creek as he remembered it as a boy. No Indians or fake nostalgia—just the land, the spirit in the land. He unveiled these two as birthday presents to Liz. Quite the happy occasion."

She recited as if the words had been there hovering on her lips: "Smile O voluptuous cool-breath'd earth!" She reached a tentative palm to the canvas. "Earth of the slumbering and liquid trees! Earth of departed sunset—earth of the mountains misty-topt! Earth of the vitreous pour of the full moon just tinged with blue!"

"Gracious, were you there?" The agent's stare deepened with a long crease above the prominent nose.

"There? No, but I think Walt Whitman was."

"He had Liz read that, or something like that from *Leaves of Grass*, where he had marked his well-thumbed edition. She had tears in her eyes—you've never seen a woman so in love. Yes, the realm of the spirit—God's grace I suppose."

She shied away from the canvases, perhaps to disguise the hint of pain compressed in the blue of her eyes. "And yet—you'd think . . . they're still here?"

"The pair were painted for this room, to go with the house and gardens, so Jake explained when we went over the list for the movers, when the home in Boulder was finally ready. They took very little with them. Hardly anything, really, as you can see. None of the Arts and Crafts furnishings Liz had bought." She sighed as her hand explored the leather cushion of a Stickley easy chair. "A new house—a fresh start, all very modern, built to his precise specifications: functional, spacious, simple, and elegant."

"The books are gone." She noted the empty shelves.

The agent, with an indulgent undertone and lowering of the eyes: "Oh, yes, all the books went to Boulder."

She nodded, a guilty shrug. "The Jake I remember always believed in the purity of numbers. Something about—how did he put it?—how the laws of nature existed for all eternity—numbers—only waiting to be discovered. Inspirational, in a way, for us dunderheaded literary types. I think I took exception when he added that nature's laws, along with the greatest novels, are simply there for the discovering."

As she spoke, she found herself drawn again to the windows, as if her eye had been caught by something, perhaps the way the long, green, sinuous shadows dappled the pool.

"He had the lap pool put in, sparing no expense," the younger woman now noted. "I oversaw the construction and got it in under budget and in record time. Jake was a beautiful swimmer. I remember watching him—testing it out, moving with such power and speed. Hadn't lost any of his trim. Unusual for guys in his field, when so much of your life is spent cooped up in the lab on a bench, lots of coffee, lots of late nights with pizza. My husband refers to it as his lab belly."

Gini moved to another of the windows overlooking the garden. "He was on the swim team at Princeton, like his son, Jacob—and my daughter! She's a diver—a beautiful diver."

"That's wonderful about young Jacob. I mean, what a miracle. You see, I was always over here when I was selling Sheridan Place. And Liz's sister, Sam (Samantha), would be out there in the garden by the pool, overseeing the physical therapist and young Jacob. Trying to regain a full range of motion. His left shoulder and arm were a mess of scars—one operation after another. You could see the pain on the boy's face standing in the shallow end—and his determination when he tried a few strokes and then had to stop." She nodded and her lips tightened at the memory. "Tough on the kid, with Sam tall and lanky like Liz, maybe not as beautiful, lacking something of her sister's spiritual repose, but close enough."

The agent moved to join her client at the window, turning with a quivering smile as she continued. "You see, Frank Lloyd Wright believed in a continuity between the interior and the landscape setting, a feeling for flow, for seamless transitions."

"Yes, I see." Gini nodded. "He may go to the Olympics in Rio."

"You're limping."

"Oh, it's nothing. We played a charity tennis tournament at Reunions, matched up with the young women on today's team. Pushed to play harder than was good for old ladies."

"Tennis, well, Jake would sometimes regale us with stories about how he coached Matthew Collins one summer and almost won the US Open. We always thought he was just pulling our leg."

"Imagine, such a thing." She laughed and gave the younger woman's shoulder an affectionate pat. "Matt is married to my teammate, Annette. I was a bridesmaid at their wedding."

"I was struck by something Jake said about them: how their faith, their marriage, inspired him even more than the experience of working with such a great player."

"Well . . . do you see much of Jake these days, when he's back in town?"

"Moving to Boulder, you'd think he was taking up residence on the back of the west wind in the wilds of Tibet. We get—my husband and others in the lab—plenty of emails from the Denver operation, and one hears him on the investor phone calls, but I get the sense he now keeps a very low profile—too busy to do much handholding with the press, so it seems."

"What, a man running against the clock?"

The realtor shrugged and wiped an eye. "Or running it out . . ."

"I've often wondered why people like Jake Burrage never show up at Reunions. Some say that only the halfway successful bother to come. While those who see themselves as failures, or at least failing to live up to their early expectations, can't bring themselves to confront their earlier selves, especially in the jaundiced eyes of their contemporaries. While those who have been super successful, like Jake, simply can't be bothered; returning to the place of their first triumphs doesn't, I guess, fit a sui generis narrative. Loyalty to an institution and all that." She tapped a double-glazed windowpane, her eyes narrowing. "Or maybe life has just caught up with them in ways they don't want to admit or share."

The realtor turned from the window to her prospective client with a curious smile and then a note of sighing wonderment.

"Certainly not the case with those two sisters, Liz and Sam; they loved to relive their Cornell basketball days, standout stars, captains, always dragging Jake off to a Chicago Bulls game. And as for loyalty, who can say? Sam's now back at Chicago with her own lab. But she never gave up on her sister's kid—like he was one of her own—family, you know."

She turned again to the window and the garden concealed behind a parapet of purple lilacs basking in the dappled shade of the tall firs, where the long lap pool glittered in a wedge of sunshine, while along its entire inner length, a long decorative border of terra-cotta aquamarine dolphins skimmed the surface, rising in diving leaps. In one corner, a fountain shaped like a pink conch shell spouted a steady stream. On the surface of the pool, a child's blow-up beach ball floated, a pale green orb with yellow-ochre overlapping stripes rotating slowly in the breeze. An abandoned paperback lay open on the pool deck.

"Kids from next door sneak in," the realtor noted with a soft liquid smile. "There's insurance in case someone manages to drown themselves. The pool is so long, a hundred meters, that the neighbors always referred to it as the Erie Canal."

Nodding in recognition while making more mental notes, she found herself again pondering the fate of her rival. "I always wondered what kind of woman would take on Jake and not be, well, overshadowed, or is it overawed, by such a larger-than-life personality."

The realtor laughed as she raised a palm to the glass. "A woman who met him eye to eye, with a faith that enlarged his—that's who. Even Sam couldn't . . . well, who knows?" She gave an expiring wave, a judicious tilt of her jaw. "I mean, you never really get over something like that."

Again, Gini placed a consoling hand on the younger woman's shoulder.

"Usually, vanity burns itself out before such brilliance—a fall from grace, as the Stoics would have it."

"Unless you're too busy running experiments. According to my husband, after the tragedy of Liz's death, Jake threw himself into his job as never before, taking over Liz's lab and cordoning off all their ongoing research—joint research, as if he didn't want anyone else to get their hands on Liz's proprietary results. Very much against the protocols of BPH, which encourage the sharing of research. I think, for a time, Sam took over some areas of her sister's lab, but by the time of the move to Boulder, it seems she and Jake had a falling-out, and she moved back to Chicago as a full professor. Like you said, it would take some kind of woman to hang in there with Jake. And as to vanity, the only thing I—actually, my husband—ever detected (they went to the same barber near the lab) was that he'd have his hair streaked with a little gray over the ears. A more august look for the board and his investors."

"Gray?"

"Over the ears."

"Well, always a burden, don't you think: a name brand?"

"As an employee, my husband, Dan, has a full discount on the Burrage line. Not that it's done his waistline much good."

"Perhaps, if you or your husband can spare Jake's office email, we can coax him into attending his son's graduation day after tomorrow—why not his aunt Sam, as well. And I can get his thoughts about my relocation to the Chicago area."

CHAPTER 30

Never, ever, in her whole life had she managed such a lie, such a seamless stretching of the truth that she almost had the novelist in her convinced, as if some part of her had once resided at Sheridan Place—still resided. But it went beyond that. "Way beyond," she muttered in her Ford rental as she sluiced down the highway toward Chicago and the headquarters of Burrage Pharma & Health. Something to do with the compression of time, as if that chilly fall day at Sheridan Place by the fire could have been the day before yesterday, possibly last November, or a November still to come. Reminding her now of what Jake had once said to her about his home ground, perhaps standing by the tiled hearth of Sheridan Place: "Chicago was built on a coral reef, ancient accretions of time, tiny layers upon layer—a stopped clock, and the days were shorter back then, hundreds of millions of years ago: maybe that's why I feel like there's hope for us, that the planet is slowing, that we will have more time, not less."

So distracted by her instinct to timeless subterfuge, she almost missed the last Evanston exit for BPH. A world headquarters that the years had not been kind to. What had once been standard-issue, post-modern munificence now looking dated and down-at-the-heels, a messy hybrid of red brick and brutalist concrete, with arbitrary excrescences: blind arches leading nowhere, decorative pilasters without function, decorative at best, confusing and overly busy at worst. None of the spectacular rigor and simplicity, form following function, of Princeton's Burrage

Biochemistry Lab or the Denver operation. Even the lush landscaping of the parking area seemed somehow lacking, here and there a tidying up of past oversights with immature maples and less-than-stately poplars offering meager shade to cohorts of shiny new Lexuses, BMWs, and Mercedes, the preferred rides of what she figured was a largely white-collar biotech work force.

Waylaid at the entrance as she struggled to slip on her high heels, she noticed a nearby bike stand and a strangely familiar chrome yellow Trek Dual Sport, handlebars draped with a white lab coat. She tottered over, staring down at the breast pocket inscribed with the BPH logo in blue. Strapped to the handlebars was an inexpensive-looking Swatch watch.

Note-taking on her surroundings, she bent quickly and sniffed the lab coat.

"Jacob . . . ," she exclaimed in the facetious yet half-serious tone of someone who was now prone to make it up as she went along. "Well, you certainly made good time."

The reception area of the twenty-year-old complex was cheery, if threadbare, compared to photos she'd seen online of the soaring glass-and-steel spaciousness of the Denver lab. Security was tight. She had to show a driver's license and sign in with an address for her scheduled meeting before being given a visitor pass and being closely escorted by friendly security to the top floor and the CCO's office. The chief communications officer, a woman of medium height in her late thirties, was dressed in fluid Armani (draped Milano was her best guess), full of efficient corporate briskness, offering her visitor a cappuccino and a comfortable leather chair catercorner to her paper-strewn desk. Beyond the windows of the corner office, the skyline of Chicago glittered to the south.

After a few minutes of friendly chitchat and a quick survey of the walls chockablock with framed magazine and newspaper articles, including photos of the founder shaking hands with President Clinton in the oval office, she cut to the chase.

"I didn't mean to barge in on such short notice, but it just seemed like too good an opportunity to pass up since I was scheduled to be in Chicago at a publishing conference. And I've tried to get in touch with Jake any number of times through alumni circles, but no luck."

"Oh, but you couldn't have," she protested, fanning her perfectly manicured nails as her dark, shoulder-length hair bobbed over her ears. "Everything of a business nature must come through our office."

"Yes, I'm sure. We do the same; keeping our authors' privacy is rule number one. But here's the thing, a book proposal came across my desk a few weeks back focusing on—what to call it: a movement with religious dimensions, a battle between health spanners and immortalists, a contest between the power of nature as ordained by evolution and the potential power of evolution as directed by man. Working title: *Is a Transhuman Future in Your Future?* And the author wants to feature Jake Burrage, founder of BPH, structuring the narrative around his life along the lines of the biographies of Gates and Jobs. My editor pitched it to me as a hot topic. How did she put it? 'In our transhuman future, at least for those in middle age, we have a fair chance of never dying.' Well, that, sadly, probably excludes me, but for our younger readers—hey, bingo." She offered the CCO a wicked but friendly smile. "Lucky you, Linda. You more than qualify, with years to spare."

Linda laughed and joined in the frolic. "Of course, we have free access to all BPH products, and immortality comes with the employment contract and nondisclosure agreement." She waved at the limitless spring sky in the window behind her desk. "And most longevity experimenters have their favorite mice videos, one of scruffy fellows, timid and shuffling, the next sleek and energetic rodents headed for the treadmill. Trouble is, we've cured cancer in mice a dozen times and made them live twice as long, but mice are mice . . . and lab mice at that."

"As one of my colleagues once said about a history of the Mormon Church: the thought of meeting up with Mother again is enough to make me quit smoking." Her glance flickered to a shadowy wall by the window where the framed drawings of a child whispered in reply. "It really is a terrific-sounding project. Like I said, along the lines of Walter Isaacson's biography on Steve Jobs. And, of course, we would approach it as a serious work of scholarship: exploring the science, the upsides and downsides, the challenges, the long-term implications for society. And Jake really would make a fascinating central character to pull it all together. We were all just a little in thrall to his intelligence as undergraduates."

At this, she noticed the CCO's gray-green eyes, for just a moment, widen and then narrow in a protective squint, with the barest hint of crow's-feet above a glaze of pink on her cheeks.

"Steve Jobs died because he fell for junk science."

"Strange, isn't it, how some of the most brilliant people can be taken in by quacks."

"Ms. Wingrave—"

"Wingate. Gini, please."

"I love the idea, and I can certainly run it by my colleagues, and even Mr. Burrage, but we get these proposals probably once a month, and in ten years in this job, I've never known Mr. Burrage to agree to such a proposal. I believe the expression he uses in his emails: 'In case anyone's interested, I am still very much a work in progress.'"

She laughed, adjusting her posture just enough to sneak a peek at a grouping of family photos on the desk. "Ah, that sounds just like the Jake I remember. I've got to tell you, those of us closest to him at Princeton have sorely missed him at Reunions. Lucky you, hanging out with such a superstar."

The CCO canted her head, sweeping a strand of raven hair behind an ear, paused, as if desirous of saying one thing but perhaps saying another. "As you probably know, since the opening of the Denver lab, when I was hired for Chicago, Mr. Burrage has stepped back from all day-to-day operations to concentrate only on cutting-edge research. It's all we can do to rope him in on quarterly investor calls."

"Hah, that sounds more like the guy I remember, who could barely be bothered to take the time to change his shirt." She leaned forward as if to impart an intimacy. "And in that spirit, I'd be even willing to offer myself as editor—hell, I might even be convinced to write the book myself. Jake knows me—would trust me to tell his story, especially the early days, with nuance and sensitivity, while respecting his privacy."

The CCO, as if drawn to something in her petitioner's voice, bent her bony, narrow face forward, pressing papers back, as her tone gained something of the quality of a stage whisper.

"Tell me, what was he like as a student?"

Noting the whiff of curiosity, she spent ten minutes regaling Linda with the kind of frisky tales that might appeal to a younger woman, finally sighing with a faintly nostalgic look. "What fun. I really am almost tempted to take on the project myself."

The CCO nodded warily, yet not unsympathetically. "It's an odd thing; there's not much of an institutional memory around here. I mean, Chicago is pretty much left with upgrades and improvements to existing product lines—not the new-new things. A few of the older researchers—the old guard, most on the verge of retirement—tend to keep to themselves, many with incomes from patents, a few holding out in hopes of a Nobel. And Denver was all new hires, mostly young researchers, freshly minted PhDs and the like, and a few more established scientists from major university labs. I think Mr. Burrage wanted not just the best talent, but people familiar with, or more comfortable with, the latest research."

"Ah, the transhuman future, the new-new breed?"

"I'm not sure I'd characterize it as such . . . more"—her gaze wandered to a more indeterminant space—"a certain wild and wonderful optimism. On the cusp of curing uncurable diseases."

Gini's eyes lit up with repressed alarm even as she confided with a sigh: "Young blood. Most of my editors (the industry, alas, pays so poorly) are barely out of undergraduate English programs or graduate publishing degrees, and even those—the good ones, well-read booklovers—are in shorter and shorter supply."

"Yes, talent to burn, and who don't need to be retrained? Flying back from the Denver lab—the energy and optimism—I sometimes feel like I'm returning to a geriatric ward."

"And hungry, I'll bet, for Nobels and the like."

"Oh," Linda sighed, again flicking back a dangling lock of hair (gold, spiraling earrings flashing like beacons) and adjusting a photo on her desk, "having a piece of the patents doesn't hurt one's bottom line either. We on the public-facing end of things sometimes feel like second-class citizens."

"You mean not being in the business of editing triremes and such."

"Oh, telomeres, you mean. Editing or enhancing telomeres as a way of inhibiting or blocking senescent cells." Her eyes danced with the pleasure of esoteric knowledge. "Keeping one's hair from reverting to its natural white."

"Goodness, I'm always getting my shipping mixed up with those pesky bits of DNA."

"Trust me," and she bent and pulled a heavy textbook from a desk drawer and turned it to her guest. "My college biology text, just so I can keep abreast of the next press release."

"Hey, tell me about it. Jake was the most curious man I've ever met—and I mean, about just everything. Life was more a tag-team event. What I tried to liken to Stoic virtues, he saw as congenital pessimism. I often wondered if that made the difference."

"Oh my, you, you were—"

"A classics major for my sins—double major in English. My first love was Seneca, the great Roman Stoic and statesman who embodied the deepest contradictions of the life of the mind (the inner life—the spirit) and the practical responsibilities of dealing with the cutthroat politics of Rome. You might say I was fascinated about how one navigates between the public and private spheres, something I suspect Jake—and you too—must have to face every day. Although I sense that he seems to have come up with his own perfect solution: public invisibility. Perhaps that's where you come in, the outward-facing . . . a religion major, you said."

Linda tossed her shapely head from side to side, soft, brown-now-green eyes deepening with a hint of dismay. "For us in Chicago—well, just emails and a voice on quarterly investor calls . . ." She tapped the scuffed cover of her well-thumbed biology text. "Odd, though—hard to explain, working for such a phantom presence, yet one can almost feel his enthusiasm, his commitment to a future free of debilitating and killer diseases that shorten life: cancer, Parkinson's, Huntington's . . . a kind of electricity in the air—a mile high." She laughed as if to cover up the hint of mystification in her tone. "I guess you could say it's nice being part of something bigger than yourself—your religious thing, I suppose."

"Yes, Jake spoke of Huntington's—his father, you know."

"His father?"

She let this quickly slide by. "Oh, infectious optimism, even back in my day. You see, the Stoics did believe in God, one perhaps closer to Einstein's God: a nature at once awe-inspiring and fathomable by reason. We shared that much, I think, a happy and meaningful life, even if at least mine seemed more attendant on our flesh-and-blood reality." She shot her brows knowingly to cover the slightest hint of embarrassment. "The least squeamish man I've ever known."

"Oh, lucky you."

She stared at a splash of spilt coffee on the desk, a comma reflecting the pale purplish light from the window. "In the end—for my sins—if I remember rightly, I argued the point with Jake in the geology department, of all places, that I preferred what the Stoics refer to as *ataraxia*, the fitness of a moral life, one of tranquility of mind. Honored more in the breach, I fear." She laughed to herself and nodded, as if possibly perplexed. "Good Lord, how we argued into the night, barely restraining ourselves from mayhem." She laughed with a dismissive wave, as if to make light of an exaggeration.

"He keeps us plenty pumped, on the edge of our seats—especially over third-stage trials or pending FDA approvals. I don't know, a corner kick maybe (my daughter's a soccer fanatic) as the team presses around the goal for that winning header."

"With the coach on the lab bench, or is it the skybox?" The two women's eyes brushed one another as if slightly mystified at the exchange of such confidence. "And"—the cords in her throat strained outward—"the God pill?"

"God pill?" Linda laughed a deep, throaty laugh. "Oh that, take two every morning with breakfast, don't you know. Trouble is, your immortalists view aging not as a biological process but as a physical one."

"Ah yes, entropy screwing around with the machine."

"And if a machine, why not liable to the same rate of progress as computers and semiconductors."

"Exponential rather than linear . . ."

"Except aging seems to be more a set of rules rather than a program that can be so easily debugged."

"Oh well." She glanced to a dissolving interchange of contrails that backdropped the figure of her intent listener, a change in the wind that prompted a tiller to port. "You see, the Stoics even esteemed the study of physics and logic as ways to living a worthy life. I remember Jake walking me though Prospect Garden on a spring day like this, and stopping to smell some California lilacs; it was his way of defusing whatever it was we were arguing about, suggesting how the garden was a kind of metaphor as to how we need to lead our life, how things of the mind and the spirit require the right nutrients, light and air—that and a fencing out of what is destructive and distracting. Maybe, if I'd been a better disciple, took it more to heart, only believed—"

"How could anyone believe—what, forty years ago—the stuff happening today? My father was an Episcopal minister, in Minnesota of all places, who believed to his dying day that three score and ten was the most anyone should hope for. Today, in this job, it's all about how to stay in the game—stay healthy into your nineties. And then who knows?"

"Oh, we struggle in the publishing world, even as physical books seem to be making a comeback—along with my aging telomeres, my life's antidote to digital nothingness. Not that it ranks up there with a cure for cancer—or Huntington's . . . but heck: I like to think we are the caretakers of the tree of knowledge, allowing Eve and her sisters another bite of eternity's apple." She prepared to leave her seat and handed a business card across the desk. "I've written my private email and cell number on the back. If you'd be so kind as to let Jake know. I'm hoping against hope he'll attend graduation the day after tomorrow, when my daughter and his son, Jacob, will be getting their diplomas—or even the graduation dinner and dance tomorrow night. We could discuss the book proposal, of course."

"Yes, his son is quite the brilliant scion of BPH. A charmer, son of a spitfire, so I hear from some of the old guard around here."

"Goodness, yes. Did I mention that young Jacob was managing our Reunions site last weekend, and he had all of us in his father's class in a dither of wonderment at the resemblance to his dad—uncanny, really. Surely, that handsome kid reminds you of your fearless leader?"

At this flurry of enthusiasm, a flicker of unease, cheekbones tensing, replaced by professional grace: "Well, I can never forget a big rollout in Denver for the launch of a new cancer drug. The kid flew in from Princeton as a last-minute substitute for his dad who, again, was indisposed. Didn't miss a beat in his prepared remarks. Gave me and the PR teams a personal tour of the incredible gym—pride of the Denver operation, with an Olympic-size swimming pool."

"According to my daughter, our multitalented boy may be on his way to the Olympic trials for Rio."

"Hard to believe someone so young could be so accomplished."

"And too bad Jake missed the ribbon-cutting ceremony for that fabulous new Burrage Biochemistry Lab at Princeton. I was so hoping to see him."

"He was all set to go, including room reservations at the Nassau Inn, but some FDA clinical trial blew up on a drug in which the company had invested over a hundred million. But I thought our CEO and young Jacob did a super job representing the founder."

"Ah, if you'd known Jacob's father when I did." She gave it a beat or two to see if she'd get a bite and then stood to go. "Sounds like BPH has a seamless succession plan in place."

"You know"—her voice rising, a quiver of girlish amazement, gold, spiral earrings glittering in a beam of spring sunlight—"even in high school, and more recently in college, Jacob Jr. worked summer vacations in the most cutting-edge of the Denver labs—nanotechnology and nanoparticles, and something called nanoprecipitation that involves the encapsulation of drugs into nanoscale particles. The idea is to revolutionize the delivery and effectiveness of medications—a matter of seconds, or so we hear around the watercooler."

"A legacy if there ever was one."

"Do give Jacob my congratulations if you see him at graduation."

CHAPTER 31

Evanston's Memorial Park Cemetery and Mausoleum:
Serving Chicago Families Since 1915.

She stared at the sign by the entrance—the novelist's unflinching eye—only to smack the steering wheel with a wince of frustration that she hadn't pursued her interrogation into the decidedly invisible Jake Burrage more relentlessly. ("Tell me something, just for the record: Have you ever actually laid eyes on the founder of BPH?") To hear it, young Jacob Burrage had replaced Jake as BPH's standard bearer in Linda's wide, olive-green eyes, even if she'd dare not admit as much.

Moments later, finishing up her notes, barefoot, she luxuriated in the feel and scent of freshly mown grass as she tracked her quarry on her iPhone app (Find a Grave), more attuned to the haunting shapes of the aged cedars and the directives offered by the breeze-bent poplars, while here and there leavings of vivid if arbitrary floral notes amid the alabaster and gray headstones seemed to sum up her mood: just one damn life after another. Or even more prosaically, seeking out a past that might just as easily have been hers. A thing confirmed by the ease of locating her rival's resting place, which, to her jaded eye, seemed to rise like a presentiment out of the sea of green, twin undulating shapes of lustrous pale pink backed by a lavender cloud of lilacs.

"Ah, fair Anthony's consort."

She paused a little way off, fearful of falling in love with her facetious musings, her white lies, or, just possibly, given her overactive imagination (attuned to the vibrations of the universe), an unsheathed wildness. An infinitude more threatening than comforting (especially given the pain in her right knee) as she reeled in her quarry, finally settling an outstretched palm on the sleek dorsal fins rising from the antique weathered porphyry. "Be all my sins remembered." The stone was warm to the touch, as was the inscription below, the translucent lettering bathed in waning afternoon light. She dropped to her left knee, her rump, startled at the overlooked bouquet of yellow roses lying in the grass between the graves. She picked up the still-dewy roses, holding them to her nose to inhale their hopeful, abiding scent mixing with the lilacs. Then, as she replaced the flowers, she spied her gossamer reflection in the smooth stone overwritten with lines from Whitman. Yet another wanderer in the realms of time.

> I bequeath myself to the dirt to grow from the grass I love,
> If you want me again look for me under your boot-soles.
> You will hardly know who I am or what I mean,
> But I shall be good health to you nevertheless,
> And filter and fibre your blood.
> Failing to fetch me at first keep encouraged,
> Missing me one place search another,
> I stop somewhere waiting for you.

The final line was repeated on the pair of headstones, a pairing of texts in the form of an open book (the two dolphins leaping from its pages), bracketed in delicately carved intaglio by a feathered pen in the left margin, an armillary sphere in the right.

How many times had she recited those lines to Jake, deep in the night, tucked into their camp on Lake Tashmoo, after he'd plucked raw every nerve in her body, when she'd lain there sweat- and semen-soaked, and so swept back into the current of life, so alive to the starry firmament that she'd burst into tears of joy, weeping as if to sound the depths of her yet underspent mortality. "Oh, Jake, didn't we have it too—that spiritual dimension?" And now the poet's words, as if in answer, had found her once again—or was it a plea, a cry of anguish against the fading of the light, of life's sad betrayal. Of a promise unkept? Or even a mocking riposte to her unfaithfulness.

She recited like a mantra: "Missing me one place search another, I stop somewhere waiting for you."

She sat back, propped on her arms in the grass, pondering the death dates of Jake's parents—Jacob and Barbara—on the left and his wife, Elizabeth Ferrand, on the right. A span of some twenty years and yet sheared to a gap of mere inches, as if three fates stranded by the same improvident current. Impelling her to crawl forward and reach hungry fingers to the sides of the carved stone: *Giovanni Ducati fecit—Venezia, 2010.*

"So, Jacob, you *were* sent there at sixteen, on a mission."

Her voice recalling images recent in the telling, nestled between sleep and waking, about a small workshop of Venetian stone carvers in the farthest reaches of Castello—"rooted in an age-old tradition, heirs to Michelangelo." Where such craftsmanship, passed down from father to son, had miraculously survived.

"The sculptor's hand can only break the spell to free the figures slumbering in the stone." She echoed the voice of three nights before as if a spell had finally been broken, looking up to the nodding sprays of lilac as she fingered the name and dates of Barbara Burrage (BB to all who knew her), only to have Jake's mother come alive in her.

Standing in the thick spring grass of Cannon Green, she, class salutatorian, had finally broken away from the congratulatory throng, and spying her parents in the distance, already arguing, her mother screaming at the restraining hand of her ex-husband, she'd desperately turned for help, for escape, and, seeing Jake with his mother standing nearby, had scampered over, and in an instant, a moment of utter clarity, had been about to throw her arms around Jake and, if not beg forgiveness exactly, to tell him how much she loved him and how she never wanted to leave him. A complete reversal of her headstrong, bloody-minded breakup folly of the weeks before.

Dead on arrival—shot down in the sharp, protective glare of Barbara Burrage (after the cataclysmic scene with her mother at the previous night's dinner), who turned upon this tall, begowned young woman in ridiculous high heels and a pencil-thin, orange-and-black dress as she ran up to her son. A mother's instinct—fierce, glittering eyes beneath a golden helmet of hair, reducing her to a fraudulent imposter upon her son's affections. Struck dumb, she had beat a hasty retreat without so much as a kiss goodbye.

She keeled over, a heaving mass of regret, clutching at the soft earth between sobs, as if the sweet fistfuls of sod and dirt might provide some surcease from her betrayal.

The ring of her phone jolted her back, her heart a rapid throbbing against her breastbone as she tried to remember where she was.

She fumbled, staring at the screen, not quite understanding why a Samantha Ferrand might be returning her call.

"Oh, I'm sorry, of course, this is Ginistrella Wingate. Samantha, thank you for getting back to me. I'm sure you're very busy in the lab. I'm a classmate of Jake Burrage from Princeton, your sister's husband, and I was wondering, if you had a few minutes, whether maybe we could meet for a drink."

"About what exactly?"

"I just happened to be in town for a publishing conference. I'm the CEO of Tandem Press, and we're considering a book proposal on Jacob Burrage and the transhumanism movement. And I was hoping you might be able to shed a little color on your sister's husband."

"I don't think you want to talk to me. I'm hardly a fan of all that."

"Of what exactly?"

"Transhumanism or, for that matter, Jake Burrage."

"Your brother-in-law?"

"You said you knew him at Princeton, Ms. Wingate?"

"Gini, please. And yes, we were close for three years. But I haven't laid eyes on him since."

"You too."

"Sorry?"

"Our benefactor seems to have gone to ground."

"Yes, not even attending, so I hear, his son's graduation."

"Jake hired me away from the biochemistry department of Chicago, and now I'm back. Maybe that tells you something."

"You're godmother to his son, Jacob Burrage, who just happens to be in my daughter's class at Princeton; in fact, they're on the swim team together."

"Really . . . wow—now, that is truly astonishing."

"Yes, my daughter says he's been invited to the Olympic tryouts." She held the phone to her ear, watching a breeze steal across the landscape, stirring the lilac boughs as if impatient at the silence on the line. "Hello, Ms. Ferrand . . ."

"My God, they're not going out together?"

"Oh, I wouldn't say that—at least not as far as I know."

There was another long pause on the line. "I've, I've got to tell you: I've been waiting for this call for some time. Where are you staying?"

"The Hyatt Regency."

"I can meet you there in the cocktail lounge—it's called the Big Bar. Where us big girls hang out."

CHAPTER 32

She recognized her immediately—indeed, gazelle-like, tall, rangy and leggy, late-forties, early-fifties, sweeping up to the expanse of the Hyatt's Big Bar like a pedigreed athlete ready to dominate the court, even if unrecognized by her fans. Hardly elegant in her rumpled gray slacks and equally gray Chicago Bulls sweatshirt—menacing red horns. Sporting Nike Air Jordans, so she speculated. A bench scientist to her latex fingertips was the term of art that came to mind from her conversation at Sheridan Place. Something even dangerous, certainly aggressive, about the way her shoulder-length, brassy blonde hair was moussed straight back from her brow and brushed the air as she swiveled her head, pawing the dirt in search of her date.

Gini rose from her banquette in the farthest corner of the sprawling bar, where she had been nursing her glass of chardonnay, and waved to her appointment. A woman taller than she! Samantha Ferrand returned the wave, for an instant her figure backlit by the floor-to-ceiling windows behind the bar, detaching herself from the well-dressed crowd as if appearing out of the opalescent shadows of the Windy City's skyline, the gleaming bronze tints on the tallest buildings matching the flickering highlights in the woman's hair as she swept forward.

After introductions, first pleasantries, and orders given to their waitress, the two women settled across from each other in their cozy corner, sizing up one another for the substance of their meeting, but, failing that, falling into long pauses when more sensitive matters blew in, not unlike twin archaeologists squatting across from one another in an excavation trench, a tad leery of brushing off the last bits of dirt as the dazzling object between them glittered with a lethal sheen.

"Like I said," said Samantha, "you're about the last person I ever expected to be having this conversation with." Her broken and reddened fingernails tapped out a rhythmic counterpoint on the granite tabletop by her glass.

"Wrong sort of person, or just uncomfortable subject matter with possibly the right sort of person?"

"Oh, I don't know. Probably because I expected someday to be having this conversation with a young postdoc, a lab head—someone, unfortunately, like me."

"Hopefully not a disgruntled BPH employee dropping the dime on Jake?"

"No, that would probably come from the FDA, if it was ever to come. But the company's legal team would've been way out ahead of such a disaster, keeping it neatly under wraps."

"To tell the truth, I'm not really sure why I asked to meet with you. Except that college reunions sometimes have the unpleasant habit of turning up painful, perhaps even dismaying memories."

Samantha shot her a vaguely sympathetic, if skeptical glance, as if the admission of uncertainty oddly mirrored her own, as yet unbroached. Her dark eyes, slightly bloodshot, turned back to the twentysomething crowd on the make by the bar and she cocked her head to the soft, piped-in music. "Or mistakes—yours or your daughter's—Erma, right? That's the hell of it; we never stop worrying about our kids. Makes a lot more sense than the book proposal on Jake and the transhuman future."

Gini, a guilty shrug, felt a little helpless to disguise her motivations, not that she'd dare reveal them even if they were clear in her own mind, just as the source of the flashing red lights (a quick glance or two at the picture window) reflected in the glass exterior of a building across the street remained an annoying imponderable. "I'm not normally so imprecise as I seem to be at present. And yes, I do run Tandem Press, so I suppose I have no excuse for being so inarticulate about what might be a fascinating book. Even if biology was my worst subject in high school, something that Jake made me painfully aware of each and every day for nearly three years."

"Ah"—a knowing look, long lush eyebrows peaking—"so you got the full treatment too."

"Well, I'm hardly a whistleblower, if that's what you had in mind."

"Strange, it's almost as if I know you, or about you—around the edges, I mean. Perhaps from my sister, Liz, or even Jake in his salad days—is that the right term? I'm just a basketball jock like poor Liz."

"What a terrible thing; such a tragic accident."

Samantha looked up from her wineglass where her reddened fingers left smoky imprints. "Randomness is as deep as our genes, encoded in the cosmic microwave background radiation and the formation of galaxies. Everything is an accident, something Jake knew better than most, tragic or otherwise"—the crease in her full lips hinted at sarcasm—"just like it's no accident you're here. I mean, you hardly strike me as a seeker after truth, even if I get a sense you know a lot more than you're letting on."

"Would a jilted lover better fit your theory—not even invited to your sister's wedding?" She smiled as if some random truth had indeed escaped her lips, followed by a brittle raise of an eyebrow at the aggressive bull's head on the well-worn sweatshirt.

"Hah, that wedding—our lovely little Cinderella story. Sorry for not being as well-read as I should be. But for a kid sister, a biogeneticist, it was like I'd been invited to the palace, where every prince was smarter than the last. The minds, the brilliance on tap—and since I was bridesmaid, everyone figured I was just as smart as gorgeous Liz." She tossed her head and blew out a weary sigh. "My closest friend (unusual among female siblings, don't you think), my pathfinder, my inspiration, who got me out of Syracuse—Jesus, Mary, and Joseph, how we once schemed under the covers, flashlights blazing over the pages of *Cosmo*, worlds we were going to conquer. With the exception of going to Mass with Mom every Sunday, I followed, like the obedient benchwarmer, in her footsteps to Cornell and then straight to Chicago (she told me not to bother punching the Harvard ticket) and BPH, and afterward . . . back to Chicago. So, here I am—what: a sorry case, a walk-on in your fiction or mine?"

"A tough act to follow, especially Jake's handpicked mate."

"Yes, a twofer"—she raised her empty glass to the waitress making the rounds—"who wanted to both break the spell and indulge it, just a tiny nibble on the wedding cake." She handed over her glass and that of her drinking buddy. "I mean, why become a real doctor with patients to care for? Why"—and she pitched her voice down a register—"do you want to just watch folks die, like Mom died, and not be able to do a damn thing about it?"

Gini shifted her weight so as to draw a little nearer as another story began to unfold in her mind's eye. "Then, Jake and Liz shared that, losing a parent early to some terrible disease?"

At this, Samantha eyed her interlocutor with wary eyes. "Mom died of uterine cancer. I get my innards checked every year; both Liz and I had the gene marker—one of five genes with the potentially fatal mutation."

"And I complain of a mother who died of alcoholism." She waved a hand in a theatrical flourish, as if to further her point. "Jake never mentioned, in so many words, that his father died of Huntington's."

"Why would he? It's an arbitrary and cruel death sentence. His mother didn't as well, just like my mother could never admit she had cancer."

"At least your mother had two extraordinary daughters to take pride in."

"Oh, unlike Liz, I rebelled at the Catholic thing—I thank the stars: at least Mom didn't have to grapple with that FedEx delivery."

"Jake didn't convert, did he?"

"Are you kidding. Liz's faith was more mystery than dogma, more literary than theological. I think Jake took comfort in that, even inspiration."

"And Jake's mother, Barbara, she must have been thrilled with Liz. A practical, down-to-earth woman who would stand by her son, keep his feet on the ground, through thick and thin."

A faint knowing smile. "Barbara—Barb, BB—was as tough a broad as they come. Loyal to a fault. Gave a touching and funny toast at their wedding: 'At how many Catholic weddings is the priest wearing a lab coat and the communion wine comes in a test tube?'" A wild cackle that verged on a snort of pleasure. "A good Catholic mom who always insisted on Thanksgiving and Christmas meals at her modest home, even as Jake offered to set her up in something grander and more spacious. 'Grander' was Barb's expression for a lifestyle she found excessive."

She nodded and just managed to check herself from lying about that fall visit to Sheridan Place years before. "Yes, that's just how I remember her from graduation. I was at the cemetery when you called, paying my respects—to your sister too, of course."

Samantha flashed her a querulous look and shrugged. "I'm overdue to visit with BB and Liz. Work and family ever the no-excuse." She winced and raised her glass in salute.

"Yes, lovely—and how appropriate, yellow roses and that pair of headstones from Venice." She touched glasses and sighed. "Hard to believe that, once upon a time, we were still using typewriters and slide rules and landlines. Except Jake barely seemed to inhabit our hidebound life back then. Eyes set on some invisible horizon—your biotech revolution, I suppose, even as he vainly tried to get me up to speed on his dizzying future."

"Hopefully, this"—and Samantha motioned between them—"isn't just about regrets?"

"What, 'a prophet is not without honor save in his own country'?"

"There you go, sounding like Liz. You see, we were eighties kind of girls, me and Liz, surfing the potential of recombinant DNA, in vitro fertilization, and genetic-sequencing technologies. Hey, what's not to like about safe abortions to go along with designer children screened with pre-implantation genetic diagnosis? We lived the cutting edge both on and off the basketball floor, in the lab and out." Samantha swallowed and raised her glass. "Hey, big sis set the benchmark for the three-pointer in the women's game. She liked to say that the sound of a swish shot was like God had tapped her shoulder."

"I was nationally ranked at Princeton—tennis." She laughed uneasily, unused to the pursuit of bragging rights. "Jake wanted me to turn pro, coach me, and I chickened out."

"Oh"—and she thrust forth her chest so that her small breasts gave the red horns on her sweatshirt a hint of menace—"you're not the one who married Matt Collins?"

"Married to my teammate, Annette."

"Did Jake really track matches for him? It only came out when we were a little high around the pool, so it always seemed a smidge improbable. I remember Jake staring with lovestruck eyes at Liz and saying how much he admired the faith that saw Annette and her husband through all the ups-and-downs of the pro tour."

"Yes . . . a lovely couple."

Samantha leaned in, intrigued, as if detecting an unusual anomaly in a petri dish. "Ah, so you let that bad boy down—you, you didn't buy into the game plan?"

"I'm not sure whose game plan—well, exactly. Maybe that was our problem."

"Hell," Samantha exclaimed, reaching to place a hand on the forearm of her drinking partner, "we've come a long way, baby. The top women athletes today can regulate their menstrual cycles—six months on, six off. The curse of Eve a thing of the past—take it from a soccer mom." She blinked rapidly, her brow furrowing. "Liz was pregnant with her second when the FedEx man came a-knocking. Jake rushed to the hospital, but they couldn't save the baby."

"Good Lord," and she shook her head in horror, even as her forefingers were just itching to enter this rich material on her iPhone. For a brief moment, she searched the deep-set brown eyes in the narrow-angled face. "Well, and to think they were colleagues . . ." Her voice fell off as she checked any hint of regret. "I always wanted to be married for my brains."

Samantha seemed to float back in the plush banquette, gathering herself in. "So, to hell with transhumanism and their devil's spawn, the likes of Humanity Plus and the Extropy Institute."

"You disapprove—the health spanners, the immortalists? Jake's a founder of Humanity Plus?"

"You mean the safe and ethical use of technology to enhance and prolong human life, to mitigate disease and repair injury—to go beyond what we consider normal." Her voice had risen in pitch as she indicated quotes in the air. "Hell, they want to upload and download the contents of their brains, like a Hallmark card: share the happy memories. And while they're at it, why not a performance enhancer—Viagra for body and soul."

"Yes, the dream of all us aging athletes."

"Yeah, baby." And she held up a flattened palm for a high five.

"I guess he and Liz just had so much in common, fathomless curiosity, unlocking the secrets of the universe—a way to honor the memory of their parents. Like I said, he really never talked about it, but, looking back, I think it weighed on him. I guess I feel a little dismayed he couldn't have shared more with me." She swallowed deep from her glass to cover up her half-truth (a writer's prerogative), turning to the huge expanse of glass, where the city slipped, floor by floor, into night. "Years back, my then-young daughter dragged me to this film, *Gattaca*; she had posters of Ethan Hawke on her bedroom wall. She used to grill my late husband on a future in which genetic selection is used to enhance a child's function, in conformance to the best hereditary traits. And, yes, eliminate diseases."

"Hey, my kids too. But here's the thing, Ethan spawned two kids with Uma Thurman, and both, boy and girl, are the spitting image of Uma. How uncanny is that?"

"Fucking good for her."

"Hey, there's a guy out there today who sells gene-editing kits from his garage for building super Arnold Schwarzenegger frogs."

"No kidding."

She waved a hand as if dispersing an unpleasant odor. "When you've been on the front lines of all this—children made to order—as I was during my brief stay at BPH, as was Liz, taking our marching orders from biotech's Patton; well, let's just say it can be a bit unnerving, not to mention discouraging or even disorienting."

"What—exactly?" Her eyes widened, itching to get at her phone, to mine this rich material.

"Yes, what, you may ask. I mean who said this race had to be run in a single lifetime. The real scientists will tell you that advances happen in tiny steps—not leaps and bounds. That's what we spar over: who exactly made those baby steps possible. I mean, why not keep the patent lawyers busy."

"Baby steps . . . not exponential?"

"All depends how much money you're willing to throw at the problem."

"So that's why you retreated back to the relative sanity of Chicago."

"Oh—with my tail between my legs, I don't think so. There's no less competition in the academy, even if the money's not pushing as hard. Just look at the polite pissing match over CRISPR—talk about cutthroat politics, with Jennifer Doudna and her crew scurrying to steal the gene-editing prize. Very unladylike. But as we ladies take over the field from the boys, we're learning to be just as self-promoting. 'O brave new world,'" she sang out, pausing, staring off at the fading sunset over the city, a sheen of silver-blue coming into her eyes. "That was the strange thing about Jake; the money, recognition, even the prizes meant nothing: only results—and like yesterday. Liz liked to share with me the unpublished papers he couldn't—so he said—be bothered to submit! Lest it hold up progress."

"You speak of Jake in the past tense. When was the last time you saw him?"

Samantha turned suddenly from the fading sprawl of the city, as if catching something in the inquiring tone of the older woman. "Oh, you too. You mean: Where's that elusive character of yours lurking now? Seems like yesterday when he pulled up stakes and headed for Denver." She raised her hand to their waitress and signaled for another round. "Ten years," and she snapped her long fingers like a firecracker going off, her voice a honey drawl. "I can see why Jake would've been so-o drawn to you."

"We were hardly a match made in heaven. We were kids blinded by our passions—who didn't know better. He was such an inveterate optimist, while I was eternally cautious, yet drawn to his curiosity, the mystery of the new-new thing. The key that unlocked a hidden door. A Jane Eyre thing—who knows? He was a sleight-of-hand artist; he kept you so dazzled with his indirection that when the rabbit appeared from the hat it was—well, like magic."

"C'mon, you protest too much. Not into risky business? I don't think so. C'mon, you mean he didn't slap you around some—tie you up, the way he did Liz. And she slapped right back. Their sex life—why am I telling you this?—was no-holds-barred, rocked their gentle neighbors on Sheridan Place. Calls to the po-lice, baby," she laughed with a gleeful smirk. "Ambition—call it what it is—is ambition. You remind me of how Liz, when asked by the other gals what it was like being married to BPH, would just smile demurely and only admit that he was the best lover known to womankind. And she'd had the best of 'em, from Cornell to Harvard and Chicago."

"Tied her up—really?"

Samantha's eyes glittered with dark pleasure. "I remember at one of our intimate pool parties, just sisters, Liz turning to me with that lost-innocence smile of hers as she struggled to explain Jake to me, the DNA of their marriage. Liz, who was fascinated with religion—never a true believer per se, but the majesty of a tradition that reached so deep into the past. 'Here's the thing,' she told me, barely above a whisper, as we gazed up to where the stars seemed to filter out of the firs, as if we were kids again beneath the sheets with a flashlight and a forbidden book, 'he's like his namesake, Jacob, in the Old Testament.' I only laughed but she actually seemed serious. 'And so unlike Adam and Noah and Abraham, who were all screwed by a jealous, all-powerful God, master of His creation, willing to destroy the whole shebang as easily as He creates. But Jacob turned the temperamental old guy around, seized the initiative from God, so that God—his God, his wingman—elbows the path forward, sets the screens so that Jacob can take his shot, seizing other people's shit and fathering offspring like there's no tomorrow.' Liz guffawed and swept her hand across the sky. 'Countless as the stars. You see, Sam,' she went on in a trancelike, searching voice, 'God speaks to Jacob in dreams and visions, unequivocally—no paradoxes or beating around the burning bush. And that's how Jake is; he makes me a part of all that: when he's making love, when he holds me—wrestles me down, ties me up, like he's communing with something larger than the two of us, as if we're both plugged into some otherworldly source of power and inspiration. Better than a three-pointer at the buzzer. It fucks with your brain, let me tell you.'"

She peered across their table, where the flickering light of the onrushing dusk was reflected in the dreamy eyes of the other woman, now mesmerized, tongue-tied, taking in every word as if to hide them deep, secured in memory. Hiding her terror, she blithely swished the wine in her glass. "And he shared with her about his father's Huntington's?"

"Of course—it was why he married her. They were the perfect team to find a cure for Huntington's and every other plague of mankind. That was their bond—their endless love, their crazy ambition. When anything seemed possible."

Nodding, trying to resist the unseemliness of a knowing smile. "He almost had me convinced"—she held up her calloused right palm—"I could win Wimbledon and write a best-selling novel. Leaving me with a lifetime to dissect—you know: coulda, woulda, shoulda . . ."

"Ah, you were his first replicant—the discarded early model."

"I—"

"Just kidding." She laughed and reached a reassuring hand then, helping the waitress unload the next round. "Liz never gave the pros a second thought, not that the women's game was there yet, but you dream nevertheless." Now nodding as if fully grasping their conversation: "So, you were just his first girl genius, the one who got away."

"Oh, sure, living at fever pitch: the possibilities untapped."

"Until the FedEx man comes a-knockin'."

"Do you even blame him for that?"

Tears welled in Samantha's eyes, and her cheeks narrowed to the sharp line of her nose, translating into a pensive canting of her dimpled jaw. "That's how he ran BPH in the early days—still does, as far as I know, before he cleaned house in Evanston and hired all the top guns for the Denver operation. No seat belts—hold on, people, for the bumpy ride." She tried a weak smile, nodding. "Liz would've liked you."

"Do you suppose the sex can be so good that you mistake it for love—or, worse, that you fear his becoming indispensable?"

"Oh, lucky you—love, that old devil, that souped-up Corvette?"

"Good Lord, it's been forty years."

"She was tall—taller—and blonde like you. The Michael Jordan of women's basketball. Ten years younger than Jake, an exceptional specimen. She should have had plenty of mileage in the tank even for a Formula One jockey like Jake. But as you've alluded to more than once, the clock was always ticking in sudden-death overtime."

"But at least she had a brilliant and talented son."

"And just how is my godson doing?" Samantha propped her chin on palm and elbow in an exaggerated pose of rapt attention.

"He ran our reunion last weekend. He simply took all our breath away—the resemblance to his father."

"You betcha: spitting image of his old man. Didn't even have her height, nor her nose or dimple, her laugh, her dumb jokes . . . her spiritual grace."

"The Uma Thurman thing, huh." She flinched at the bitter edge in her voice. "What's the bottom line: Did he cut corners, steal research, tamper with trials—what sins are available in your world? You see"—she paused, careful now, as if fearful of giving something away—"young Jacob seemed almost too good to be true for a kid his age, like he knew more than he should—about our college days, among other things. Kind of had my old gang on edge—his sheer uncanniness, his savoir faire."

Samantha glanced away at a noisy gaggle of drinkers by the bar, their shadows telescoping across the floor, a hint of tension in her right cheek, even as she took a deep breath and returned to the fray.

"I love your Gucci outfit—did I tell you? Trolling for some kind of techno thriller, are you? Where hubris takes a fall. But how would you write about success beyond your wildest dreams? What if you develop a process for gene editing, CRISPR—what then? Do you draw the red line at germline editing and inheritable modified traits? Or restrict yourself to somatic editing, fixing the targeted cells of a living patient, beneficial for the patient but not the species? Can we hold the line at the treatment of terrible inherited diseases like Huntington's, Parkinson's, genetic abnormalities, or is it the slippery slope to enhancement designed to improve human traits and capacity? Where do you hide from the consequences? How many lifetimes are you willing to wager?"

"You mean Denver, or is it Boulder?"

"I feel like you've been on this ride before—or was it a pool party with you, too?" Samantha took a couple of deep breaths, nodding to herself, and then raised her outspread long fingers. "Large hands are better for ball handling, but Liz had two inches of height on me. You see, there's no end to it when you play in the big leagues for all the marbles; the closer you get, the harder you push. When Genentech launched in 1976, it shifted all the commercial focus from chemistry to biotechnology, and Liz was canny enough to realize where the action was—and Jake too, of course. But the manipulation of living cells is one thing; the editing of genes is another. Jake saw it coming before all the big-name players. He figured out that RNA was the key when most of the science community was still focused on DNA and the double helix, that spiral staircase to the future."

Samantha lifted her gaze, as if tempted to free solo the fading skyscrapers beyond the vast window, aglimmer with ambient light, her eyes burning with studied concentration as she continued.

"But he liked to keep it quiet, under the radar, as Liz would tell me in candid moments when the kids were in bed and we were lying around the pool at Sheridan Place. Didn't like anybody breathing down his neck. He figured why do original research when the trick was to be so geared up to quickly replicate the research of others—a matter of weeks in many cases, not months or years—and then apply it to real-world needs. He had all his labs set up to jump-start the next breakthrough. He was all over the research—not just his, but everyone else's. And Liz's, of course, attached at the hip—and if something promising or new emerged, an important discovery in the making, he'd become super involved. Liz often said she could literally feel the pulse of their progress in their lovemaking—that's not for your book, not the bondage either. He'd have his lawyers grab the patents and allow his people to publish, carefully cherry-picking this and that, but didn't care if BPH got the lion's share of the credit. He was just on to the next problem to be solved. When I joined BPH after Liz's death, I was younger, outside the charmed inner circle, but I could feel it, the pulse, the pace, the heated conversations in the luncheon bar, in the local restaurants. Jake never pushed others as hard as he pushed himself. Liz used to laugh about it because she found herself so fascinated by how his mind worked—and she was as smart as they get, way smarter than me. I keep seeing her standing in the pool, arms crossed over her tits, when she'd give me that sly look of hers and laugh: 'Nothing fazes him; he's tireless; he has the energy of a sixteen-year-old kid in the sack—and half the time I think he looks and acts the part.'"

Samantha took a long swallow of her wine and signaled to the waitress for another round. She reached to Gini's hand as if to prevent her from grabbing the consolation prize by the tail, bringing her lips close as if to whisper in her ear.

"What woman doesn't envy that, eh? I was happy for her. We were close, but there are always some things about a relationship, secrets that can't be shared for fear of hexing the thing."

She nodded as if with occult insight, an encouraging tilt of her chin: "Or because you bought into a shared ambition, or is it obsession?"

"Maybe that's why they liked having me around, sharing their lap pool at Sheridan Place—their backup, their benchwarmer: pool parties for three."

"Of course—what else, pool parties . . ."

"It always felt like tryouts, a test: feedback from outside the inner sanctum—or maybe just to see just how much the kid sister could be shocked."

"What, a good Catholic, you said—spiritual grace? Hey, for me, on the outside looking in, it looks like Liz got the big Catholic wedding with all the bells and whistles—a Mass and communion no less." She guffawed. "A well-read woman, I'll bet."

At this near accusation of simpering self-pity, Samantha seemed to bridle, with a glance at her wedding band and sapphire engagement ring, which she delicately adjusted. "Yep, Liz had a spiritual side—a fifth dimension, I always called it. Not unusual in scientists but rarely going the way of traditional religion. I think it was her way of staying in touch with her roots even with an Atlas rocket up her knickers. Dear me, I'm mixing my metaphors."

"You're doing just fine."

Samantha smiled wickedly as she bent forward, eyebrows arched, as if to relay some indelicate truth. "You know what they say about us good Catholic gals in the sack, if not a boatload of kids. I was the pesky kid sister whose soul always needed saving." She drained her glass and shook her head as she seemed to throw a changeup. "But here's the thing: it's always—the devil, that is—in the crucial details. Like tracrRNA in the gene-editing process, which Jennifer Doudna's team mastered first, but got beat out in the application to human DNA by at least two other teams, including Jake's lab, who never bothered to publish BPH's success." She thanked the waitress, who was now regularly showing up with refills. "Sorry, I don't mean to get so deep in the weeds. But you need to understand—your book, right—that scientists, the real ones, the great ones, are all consumed by curiosity fired by ambition to spare and driven by results: questions, puzzles, patterns, the unsolved riddles, the pieces that don't fit, the anomalies that are staring you in the face but won't give up their secrets. And we're pathologically competitive, even when we know how much the advancement of scientific knowledge comes about by collegiality and teamwork, in small, incremental steps."

"Yes, baby steps," she offered in encouragement, "even when you're competing like mad."

"While, at the same time as you're glued to your experiment, picking apart RNA molecules, you've got to see or at least be aware of the big picture, where the field is headed and where gaps exist that you can fill. And here's the thing: there's a delicate balance between basic and applied science, between the theorists and experimentalists. What we do is not necessarily linear, progressing from one triumph to the next. Sometimes it's a leap"—she raised her glass and drank deeply—"into the unknown."

Gini watched, blinking, noting the changes in tone, of other conversations struggling up from memory, the voice of a dead sister, a beloved competitor—a character coming to life.

"Pool parties . . ." She touched her glass to that of the younger woman, a clouded look coming over her face. "Are you telling me that Jake was none of those things or all of those things? Or does love, even sex, the ultimate catalyst—enzymes, right?—speed up the process to such a frenzy that almost anything is possible? There were times, well, I wondered if the sex could be almost too good, that it could blunt your better judgment, scare off your better angels."

Samantha laughed with a cackle and then caught herself. "Actually, I think I may be warning you—or is it your daughter? Of what, I'm not actually sure I can put it into words. Words fail me: Is that the proper expression to explain *your* young Jacob Burrage?" And she threw out her chest as if to better display those rangy red horns.

"Besides, after running Liz's lab for a year, before departing back to Chicago, I signed an ironclad nondisclosure agreement as part of my generous separation package."

"Oh, now you've got me hooked, pool parties and all."

"You see, in the early years, I used to babysit young Jacob, when Liz and Jake might be kept late at the lab, when I was finishing up my postdoc at Chicago, spending weekends camped out at Sheridan Place. Lavish tips and a leased BMW. And one evening, late in September, with young Jacob in bed, they returned after eleven, and I'd fallen asleep on the living room sofa. I heard their voices in the garden, their laughter, their war whoops, and so I wandered out to find them skinny dipping in the pool. I'd gotten used to that; my once-demure sister had become increasingly uninhibited as she, like her husband, scented the fountain of youth, the Holy Grail to banish aging bodies along with insidious disease—curing souls in the bargain, I suppose. And I'd increasingly become their sounding board—see if they could shock the kid sister."

Samantha sighed and lowered her eyes to her empty glass. In the background on the sound system, a Frank Sinatra standard, "Just One of Those Things"—"a trip to the moon on gossamer wings."

"Yes, aren't we all suckers for Ponce de León's mirage?" She attempted a half-humorous pose, her voice lowering, searching for how to phrase the question, to keep her characters on track. "So, Jake kept his youthful demeanor, his looks, his energy?"

Samantha eyed her sharply: "Liz too, like she'd just graduated from Cornell. A little freaky, huh?" Looking up with an uneasy, lengthening gaze, the younger woman continued in a low, edgy, somewhat troubled voice. "I was going to leave, but they waved me over, waved me in; they had a bottle of champagne on the poolside. Another celebration, another FDA approval: they were on a roll. It was one of those wonderful September nights, still warm but lower humidity, the last gasp of summer by the great lake, with the stars spread overhead, just peeking through the fir boughs like a glittering tiara. Even the fireflies were hanging in there, glimmering above the pool, as if trying to catch their reflections. All part of the magic to come. I was reluctant but tempted by their laughter, the sweet smell of balsam and chlorine—of success. Liz was three months into her second pregnancy. So I stripped and dived in and swam a couple of laps, and then they corralled me, hugging me, both of them kissing me, from in front and behind, laughing the whole time like children on a dare. Then, filling a glass, the last of the champagne, they bid me 'take communion'—Liz's words. But before I could take a sip, Jake stayed my hand and checked with a gloating Liz, who wordlessly nodded her assent. He grabbed a plastic prescription container next to the champagne bottle and shook out two green capsules and handed them to me. Liz was grinning: 'Take two before bedtime and you'll wake up refreshed to the world.' I was hesitant, but the mood was infectious. And so I chased them down with the champagne. And again we were in a huddle, just kissing and fondling and carrying on. My little piece of Jake. I felt so happy for them that nothing surprised me anymore, the moon and the stars and then some. We were just fooling around . . . and then something weird and crazy magical started to happen. I felt like my head was expanding into the night sky, that I was levitating, rising out of the water, walking on water . . . I remember yelling, screaming with this burst of energy flowing through me, like an electric current, and I sprang lose and began wildly swimming laps like Katie Ledecky, moving like a Jet Ski, until they finally flagged me down."

"A clinical trial of one?"

"The three in one. If we'd been on a basketball court, I would've tried to dunk myself."

"And sex, does that enter into the equation at Sheridan Place?"

"If we did—and it sure felt like it, a thousand orgasms deep . . . I couldn't remember any details—zero. The next day, I woke under a blanket on the sofa. Except for that whole day, it was like I was seventeen, with elbows out and ready for the roller derby. I've never forgotten that day, the intensity of every precious moment; every problem in the lab seemed to have an easy fix. That night by the pool is how I'll always remember Liz . . . just months before the accident."

"Did you ask what was in those capsules?"

"The moon and the stars. I thought maybe mushrooms, psilocybin, LSD, but no. According to Liz, not quite ready for prime time."

"Surely, you must have pressed her—I mean, as a scientist. The God pill . . ."

"Hey, queen for a day." An oddly troubled look dimmed Samantha's eyes for a moment, only to be dismissed with a shrug of her broad shoulders. "When I took over Liz's lab—like I said, a nondisclosure agreement."

She tried to make light of her eagerness: "Hell, can you write me a prescription?"

Samantha held up a flattened hand and then raised a forefinger to her sealed lips. "The second-string sister—life's side effects—who struggled just to be half the player she was at Cornell. Phi Beta Kappa, who had her own lab at Chicago as a postdoc, who finally met a mind who remained one step ahead of hers, who could finish her most personal and passionate thoughts—the erotic charge, as she liked to tell me. Boast more like it, like a depth charge to your clit." She waved a hand, fanning her face. "Sorry for the locker-room bullshit."

"Hardly, you've got me hot and bothered just listening to you."

Samantha looked away, sighing, searching. "I ask myself every day if it was just a case of—perfect subject, right?—blind ambition. Something that just got away from her—us. What I found, to my horror, when Jake had me leave Chicago and take over Liz's lab for a year."

"I'm not following you here. Is this about Liz or you?"

A moment of silence as Samantha bristled, her brows knitted. "I mean, what woman of science wouldn't want to wake up on the other side of the bed with Jake Burrage, to share pillow talk with such a mind? Or am I mixing my metaphors since you seem to be the editor in chief—or even the author—of our depraved little saga."

"Hardly depraved. It seems you were the faithful godmother to your sister's injured boy. All the physical therapy and emotional scars . . ."

"Preserving something of her, you mean?" Samantha smiled bravely and lowered her brow to her glass. "Even as he began to take on more and more of his father's traits. Against my better judgment—was that your word?—I moved into Sheridan Place for the last two years before the move to Boulder, until the new house was ready." She nodded. "And then, when Jake had me properly groomed, taking over Liz's lab at BPH, before it was all moved out to Denver."

"And so you turned down the opportunity to move with them?"

Samantha wiped tears. "Liz was so looking forward to her second child—'something of mine,' she liked to say."

"Mine?"

"You tell me."

"Boulder, or is it Denver, might have been something of yours."

"It's in your eyes: like you've been there."

"What, I wonder, might I have done in your place, the ambition part? Such a refreshing change from stories of unhappy childhoods or spousal abuse."

"We—women will take over the sciences; men don't have the patience and focus."

"Tell me about it—same in the publishing world."

"Thank God I met my husband, the man who would become my husband, before I totally lost my mind—what was left of my soul."

"Kenosis," Gini offered.

"Kenosis?"

"Augustine—the renunciation of the divine."

"Augustine . . . why, who else? Liz used to go on about him, about their honeymoon in Venice—paintings by Carpaccio. The good saint presiding on their bedroom wall. Liz kept a copy of Augustine's *Confessions* by her bedside table—confessing each night her sins, real or contemplated. I was never sure which." She raised her eyes to her confidant and shrugged. "Besides being a godmother to young Jacob, overseeing his rehab and PT, I basically ran Liz's lab, the clinical trials, everything she'd done while he drifted off into his own special projects—away for weeks at a time, getting Denver up to speed."

"Sounds like you've got an insider's book in you, Samantha."

"Not the one you're trying to write?" She held up her hand, thumb and forefinger barely held apart. "In our world: sin and salvation are kissing cousins."

A judicious, sympathetic smile: "But you saved Liz's boy. She has you to thank for such—what?—devotion."

"Did I?" Samantha bit down on her lower lip for a moment, puzzled, a lost flicker in her distant stare as she again seemed to ponder the pickup scene by the bar. "It took almost an hour to extract him from the wreckage of the Suburban. Can you imagine? Scars that run deeper than any physical therapist can touch. Much less the trauma psychiatrist for his weekly sessions. And then to catch him looking at me, all the time, with that distant glimmer of hope in his eyes."

She handed her cocktail napkin across the table to the younger woman.

"When my husband died of cancer, some part of my daughter never forgave me."

Samantha nodded and reached out to squeeze her hand. "Somehow, the kid got through it . . . and to hear you tell it, better than new."

"Like father, like son, and knowing way more than any kid his age should know about . . ." Her voice faltered as she leaned forward with fevered eyes. "And here's the thing: I chatted with the director of publicity at BPH today, and from what I could make out, she's never laid eyes on her lord and master."

A spark of recognition, perhaps panic, was quickly replaced by a studied air of recollection tinged with sadness. "I offered to help out with the new Boulder home, help get Jacob settled, but suddenly I seemed more an impediment than help. After a few heated arguments about the stuff going down in Liz's lab, I was suddenly persona non grata (how's my Latin?)." An icy smile compressed her long lips. "I was presented with a golden parachute, a separation package that included a new house, a BMW, a huge cash payout and BPH stock, and, of all things, an all-expenses-paid vacation to Venice . . . the works." A curious cant of her long face, a wedge of moussed hair framing her right ear. "And, no—thank you for not asking—I never slept with Jake."

She held up the glass of the red Bordeaux she'd switched to on their last round, swishing the crimson liquid like an alchemist of old as she noticed the lights in the skyscrapers framed in the purple dusk. "Venice, huh? But that's not why you said 'expecting my call.' Or is that in the nondisclosure agreement?"

"Of course, a nondisclosure agreement is standard (including a clawback of the house my kids grew up in), and Chicago welcomed me back with open arms. Jake always insisted Jacob needed a fresh start in Boulder, fresh faces, a change from the 'stifling confines,' as he put it, of Sheridan Place. For almost six years, I was ingeniously fenced out—no Christmases or Thanksgivings—before I finally demanded that I be allowed to see my godchild, my flesh and blood. I had my own children by then and felt I owed it to Liz, that Jacob's emails, the news Jake sent along about his brilliant son's high school career—well, it wasn't enough. So, Jake, finally, arranged everything, conveniently picking a weekend when he'd be away, off at an important CRISPR conference at Cold Springs Harbor. I figured he was just as happy—my inveterate caution, my skepticism, my foolish agnosticism—not to have to see me (an older Liz) again."

"What—a witness to playtime, to partner swapping at Sheridan Place—Liz's lab at BPH? Or something more?"

Samantha shook her head, her large, still muscular shoulders hunched over as if trying to harbor her failing energies, avoiding her drinking buddy's hard stare.

"It was the strangest weekend of my life, not unlike that strange day after our little pool party at Sheridan Place. My eighteen-year-old godson picked me up at the Denver airport; I almost didn't recognize him, even as I totally recognized him."

"Ah . . ." She offered an airy laugh as she touched her glass to Samantha's, as if toasting some inescapable convergence of their lives, or an intriguing narrative arc falling nicely into place.

"I was hugged by a grown man wearing a tee shirt and flip-flops. A body like Michael Phelps, with those top-heavy swimmers' shoulders (and no worse for wear—the left, that is—crushed by his mother's skull) and lean thighs and calves, who relieved me of my carry-on like it was a handbag. Of course, I was hoping to find something of Liz, something of her willowy height, her fearless eyes, her long nose, shadow of a dimple, maybe even her no-holds-barred confidence—oh, that much he had in spades. 'Aunt Sam' had always been Jacob's name for me, and so I was once again as I was whisked off to the parking lot and that navy blue BMW 740e—'safest car ever built,' Jacob laughed, as if that FedEx truck was just a speck in the rearview mirror. And then he gave me the once-over tour of Denver and the new lab complex—all exposed steel girders and blue-gray granite—on the outskirts in Thornton, hurrying me through the busy labs as if just conducting around another out-of-town colleague. Where, I must say, I found it kind of odd: he barely turned a head, as if they were used to seeing their"—her eyes snapped wide to encompass her avid listener's—"lord and master in a tee shirt and flip-flops. I mean, after a while, I just kept having these déjà-vu flashes, when I thought I was conversing with a young, ageless Jake."

Gini reached a hand across the tabletop as she might across her office desk, as if to steady the shaking hand of a nervous author. "Yes, so . . . you too."

Samantha seemed to take no notice, her voice lowering in pitch, dreamlike. "And then we headed west to Boulder and the Rockies. Of course, I'd seen all the plans when the house was being built, but nothing prepared me for the stunning marvel of engineering and design that greeted me, cantilevered on huge steel support beams off a sheer cliff, as if floating over immaterial space. Tasteful, simple, floor-to-ceiling windows that had you walking on clouds, a Mount Olympus that left the claustrophobic, ivy-clad shades of Sheridan Place in the dust. The first thing that struck me: they could've moved in the day before yesterday, instead of six years back. The place was just so clean and neat and spanking new, from kitchen appliances to the blinking control panels that monitored the louvers that let in or kept out light, that controlled the solar panels on the roof, the security system, and God knows what else. As if gravity too had been banished, if not the second law of thermodynamics, along with any lurking unhappy memories. A different planet, I guess, a parallel universe, you might say, not that more earthly pleasures had been entirely neglected. Jacob pointed out the large landscape paintings by Alex Katz and Fairfield Porter, a rearview nod to Cripple Creek and maybe—I don't know—Martha's Vineyard, or is it Maine? All I could think was, So this is where it was all heading, the plan B, the non-Liz option, this mountain-top all-male Elysium. And as we took in the view from the huge patio, with its hot tub and outdoor firepit, Jacob took my hand for a moment, perhaps on impulse, a spontaneous memory out of childhood for his adoring aunt, or just maybe a shared sense of our beating hearts paying homage to Liz and those agonizing months together with the physical therapist. Or, as it seems to me now, a moment of solidarity in the face of a past that was never meant to be.

"Jacob did his best to get me settled in the guest room, while I tried to make light of the awkwardness by making jokes about altitude sickness and agoraphobia. He showed me his father's room, the master's bedroom, joking in turn about the mess: the king-size bed was unmade, clothes dumped in corners, closet doors ajar—the only hint of chaos in the whole place, as if Jake had left in a rush to get to the airport and that CRISPR conference in Cold Springs Harbor, where two of my Chicago colleagues were giving papers. I remember making quite a point about Jennifer Doudna, who was scheduled to give an important paper, how I'd given up my place to a colleague. 'I'd much rather be here with you,' I told him—and I meant it. Which provoked a peal of sweet, assuring laughter—just like his father—from Jacob as he again took my hand and led me to his bedroom."

"What, six years? Kids change a lot. Even take on the habits and mannerisms of their parents—or the opposite."

Samantha seemed not to register this author's query. "Oh, the comfort of the pressure of his fingers in mine as we stood in the doorway of his room as if we both needed to adjust to that troublesome absence." She fell into a pensive silence as if grounded on that threshold, the wine having its way.

"Yes, go on . . ."

"He walked me to his window, if you can call a wall of glass a window, where he proceeded to point out his high school in Boulder, and then the nearby university, noting the various labs and departments—biomedical engineering was high on his list. How BPH was partnering with the department to develop better delivery systems for medicines. Somehow his tone seemed at odds with this kid's room—perfectly arranged, I might add, nothing out of place. What with the posters of Olympic swimmers on the wall, along with The Band and Bob Dylan. A little retro compared to what my kids were into. And the shelves full of swimming trophies and medals—his dad's collection of arrowheads from Cripple Creek. And, you'll be pleased to know, a Princeton banner, class of 2016. He'd been given early admission. I couldn't help feeling that the whole thing was being staged for my benefit . . . or maybe that only seems the case in retrospect. I mean, not a single photo of Liz, his mom—anywhere."

"Books," Gini prompted, just above a hoarse whisper, trying to repress her vivid if not desperate imaginings, on the verge of hyperdrive.

"Books? Yes, now that you mention it. Shelves full of books, textbooks, novels, Liz's and Jake's." She shook her head as if groggy, trying to pin the thing down. "Yes, lots of books. Impressive, to say the least."

"Jacob, well, from the little I could tell, seemed well-read for an athlete and scientist."

"Yes, Liz never liked to be thought of as just another jock, a lab rat; she always wanted to be the more exalted thing: a woman who could talk literature and philosophy. As a woman in science, not that I need to tell you, one is endlessly seeking the respect of male colleagues who feel threatened."

"Yes, like Augustine, a higher calling."

Samantha bent closer, as if to catch some fleeting wisp of memory in her co-author's blue eyes. "It's like you know all about us?"

"Yes . . . I was taken there—Venice—at seventeen by my father for indoctrination."

"Yes, of course you were. Like Jacob, who had this lovely reproduction of a painting by Carpaccio hanging over his bed: Augustine at his lab bench, he joked. Augustine caught in a moment of visionary inspiration. Of course, it had been on my itinerary—Jake's itinerary—in my separation package. Or as I'd come to think of it: Liz's Augustine." She smiled icily. "Or . . . yours—was it yours all along?"

"Venice, the Scuola di San Giorgio."

A pained, uncertain quiver of her lower lip as she pulled apart a soaked cocktail napkin on the table. "But so anomalous—there, along with the posters and such, when it had once hung over Jake's and Liz's bed at Sheridan Place—hardly something to find in a boy's bedroom. Even a kid on the way to Princeton. As if their kid had made their patron saint his own. And when I pointed this out, he was quick to explain about a recent trip to Venice and his introduction to a room full of Carpaccios."

"Yes," she confirmed, "he told me the same, a sixteenth-birthday present from his father, perhaps to celebrate his miraculous recovery—why not? Or even his parents' divorce—"

"Divorce?"

"Kids, don't you think, sometimes make up the strangest stuff."

"Yes, yes . . . they do, don't they."

"Kenosis . . . a renunciation of the divine—Augustine's take."

Samantha waved this off as if an irrelevancy, now struggling to keep her focus. "What touched me, the echo of Liz: how he found the image somehow 'comforting'—his word: how there'd been a time in human history when just a single room, a single mind could comprehend all of human knowledge." Samantha tapped her glass, brow furrowing. "His voice—so full of longing, nostalgia, even sadness."

"Yes, yes . . . he would, wouldn't he?" She took a deep breath, closing her eyes for a moment as if needing to take it all in. "I mean, imagine that, a single room or even a great soaring structure of glass and steel and stone—a temple of science, harbinger of our future. As time is embodied, going back five hundred years to first creation, then a thousand more to the saint himself, who, in turn, drew on the learning of Seneca and the Greeks, filtering the prophesies of Isaiah and the Gospels through a Platonic haze. All to write books that would change the world as we know it."

"Ah," Samantha exclaimed, eyes fixed on the rapt face across from hers. "You've got me hooked, echoes of dear Liz as well. And I can still see his insatiably curious blue eyes as he went on to explain to me about some of the instruments and manuscripts in the painting."

"The astrolabe and armillary sphere, the codexes and artifacts—all the knowledge of humankind compact."

"Yes—how well you know it."

"Young Jacob seemed quite taken with its subject."

"Really . . ."

"And there was a workshop of Venetian stone carvers he visited, so he told me, which explains, I guess, his mother's and grandparents' gravestones. How splendid the Whitman that honors not just the lives lived but offers such comfort to the living."

"He mentioned a young woman he met there, tall, leggy, musical, literary, artistic, who showed him around—someone like you."

"Perhaps . . . it was."

Samantha gave her a sharp look that then turned into an accusing squint. "It's almost like you're writing your book as we talk."

"Oh," Gini waved this off, "reunions always invoke second thoughts, even dark ruminations—goes with the territory."

Samantha shuddered, as if possessed for a moment by just such shadings of gray, pulling at the sleeves of her sweatshirt, fiddling with a necklace of lapis lazuli, checking her phone as if trying to visualize the thing that even now defied her analysis. "The strangest thing about that painting—or is it that room within a room?—as you said, how it echoes, at least in my memory, the light of the Denver lab or Jacob's home in the clouds, its ethereality, that eerie calm and exactitude as if strangely mirroring a brilliant lab setup. Where time stood still, as Jake liked to say when he caught sight of a new discovery—at least for an hour, a day or two."

"You must have been thrilled, how well Jacob turned out. Healed and happy."

Looking up bleary-eyed from where she'd been staring at her glass, Samantha bulged her cheek with her tongue and popped her lips. "Kids do, of course. They start out as babies, with one parent's hair, another's eyes, and then a few years later the nose, the mouth, the sneeze; and then ten years later like nobody at all, perhaps a grandparent no one ever knew. Life: a crapshoot, just like Liz always assured me."

"My daughter, Erma, stuck to her father like crazy glue, a tomboy helping him repair our vintage sailboat, crewing—a total father-daughter thing. Resenting the way she looked, which, according to our West Chop crowd, was the spitting image of my mother, whom she never knew."

Samantha, on some impulse, reached across and gave the shoulder of her confidant a gentle caress. "Lucky girl."

"Yes, she got her father's brains." She tapped her iPhone and slid the proof positive across the table. "That's her at our Reunions dinner with Jacob."

Samantha picked up the phone, squinting, her jaw trembling as she slid two fingers across the screen to enlarge the photo, staring until Gini placed a hand over hers and squeezed gently.

"You must," she repeated, "have been so pleased to find him safe and sound and all grown up."

Samantha shook her head vehemently as if fending off an accusation. "You've got me thinking about those books."

"Books?"

"They once lined the shelves of the living room at Sheridan Place. Liz used to encourage me to borrow, laughing as she ran a finger over the spines, choosing for her kid sister's edification."

"Was it the Whitman? Perhaps Seneca or Boethius. Even Henry James, *Portrait of a Lady*."

"She called it the rapture."

"Rapture?"

"Lying out by the pool at Sheridan Place under the stars, the water lapping as if to the spinning of the earth, her belly bulging, she liked to ponder—you know the kind of thing: if you had it to do all over again: coaching college basketball, not the next Madame Curie."

"The rapture . . . reunions."

"Their honeymoon in Venice, where the past is still alive, as she put it, the churches, the saints, the flickering mosaics, everything she'd neglected in a life of accomplishment, that gave life meaning—at least, in her book. Yes, the rapture, she called it, the splendor of the human imagination set free in all its glory."

"Yes."

"Why I always take my kids around the Art Institute, hang out at the local Barnes & Noble on a rainy Saturday—you know the drill, so they don't sit in front of screens all day, even if my eldest, Elizabeth, ended up in computer science and engineering."

"Is that what you found in young Jacob, too? Things a busy father would hardly impart to his son?"

"Jesus, Mary, and Joseph"—Samantha drained her glass—"did you—your daughter—sleep with him as well?"

Gini laughed with an added dismissive toss of her head. "Don't be ridiculous."

"Then why else are we here?"

"For that retrospective view: Liz's rapture . . ."

Samantha fixed her with a sarcastic, if uncertain smile. "Of course, of course—well, Jacob cooked me a wonderful pasta Bolognese dinner, frying up the veal, carrots, onions, and mixing in the sliced tomatoes, the seasonings, all fresh from a farmer's market we'd gone to on Saturday morning. And a bottle of superb Napa Valley Bordeaux."

"I forgot how much he liked to cook."

A spasmodic laugh escaped her lips. "And when we took a spin in the hot tub that afternoon, he explained how he'd had the best orthopedic surgeon in the country, the guy who patches up the Broncos. Barely a scar, if that."

"Except for that nasty little burn scar on his right index finger."

Samantha's flushed face, eyes burning into hers for a long moment, as if in a plea for help, and just as quickly looking away to the creeping darkness that had overspread the Windy City.

"There was a moment when Jacob turned to me with this most wistful look and I expected he was going to open up to me about his mother, but no: he asked me about myself—was I happy with the career I'd chosen. The kind of question you expect from an older colleague. I guess I'd mentioned once that I'd thought about becoming a regular doctor, helping people one-on-one, until Liz talked me out of it. And he told me about a girl in his class he was tutoring in math and biology, with the hopes of being a doctor one day, even though her quantitative skills were sorely lacking. And how inspired he was by her dedication, her passion—her humanity."

She reached an encouraging hand to her fellow traveler. "Oh, you should come to graduation on Wednesday, or the graduation dinner and dance tomorrow—someone from the family, don't you think? It's been four long years: Jacob would be so pleased."

Samantha stood suddenly, grabbing her purse and phone, her breath catching in her throat, her eyes losing focus as she planned her escape.

"Your daughter is a treasure. Keep her safe."

Gini made a grab for her hand. "Wait . . ."

Samantha looked her straight in the eye, as if finally allowed to read fully what was written there. "If you must know, that conference at Cold Spring Harbor, the CRISPR conference on the future of gene editing—Jake wasn't there, a no-show. I had two colleagues from Chicago attending, ex-BPH researchers . . . and they saw no sign of him, nada."

CHAPTER 33

She lay sleepless, propped on pillows in a terrycloth bathrobe after her shower, staring out her hotel window twenty-three stories above the glittering sprawl of Chicago. Dutifully, she kept lifting her phone, dictating notes on her conversation with Samantha, checking for messages—wondering what excuses she might give for texting Erma about tomorrow night's graduation dinner and dance. A warning ("Keep your daughter safe")? A cautionary note . . . the inexplicable, the impossible thing? All the while her racing mind was flooded with memories of her own last days before graduation.

And the thing ignored, dismissed, half forgotten.

She realized she'd been dreading the graduation dinner for weeks, maybe months or years.

She pulled open her bathrobe, running a palm up and down her body as if the friction, the warmth of her touch, might elicit that nearly transparent shadow of a reality snatched from the wildest of dreams. Her gaze was increasingly drawn to the homing beacons beyond her window where aircraft were descending off the expanse of Lake Michigan. Floating high above the night, she found herself returned again and again to Sheridan Place, transmuted into the poignant tones of Samantha's diffident voice (noting on her phone the telling details: the fireflies reflected in the lap pool, starlight in the firs . . . ageless bodies), where two sisters stood in the shallow end of the pool exchanging confidences, waiting for "the fittest forty-year-old you ever met" to join them.

Her hand paused on her left breast, perhaps taking a sounding for a heartbeat, or testing whether the sensation across her nipple might summon forth that same offstage specter, a fragment of her past raised from her mortal flesh, a voice possibly altered from the original when Jake had stood in the half-light from her dorm window, gazing at the Carpaccios, pondering, as was his wont, a corrective to the unaccountable failure of a carefully formulated experiment—that near sure thing. A catastrophic playing of the percentages that required a no-less-brilliant reset strategy.

"No, no, you don't get it. Our first thousand has obviously ended in disaster, a botched job. The whole point of the next thousand is that we *don't* keep in touch—or check in on each other's life. That way, when we meet again—if we do—it will be as near strangers, so we can start afresh and see what we've become without the distraction or expectations of the other. A new beginning, a new chapter in your revised novel, a control group to test my theory. A taste of what our lives would be like without the other. Showing up out of the blue is the perfect test of the original hypothesis."

"Out of the blue," she now repeated to herself as she followed the beacons descending to O'Hare, tempting as those fireflies on a September night over the lap pool at Sheridan Place . . . to be swept up in a young woman's eager hands.

She held up her phone once again, as if needing to monitor the full effects of this latest missive touching on her mortal soul (remaining out of touch for forty years), scanning her face and breasts as she recorded Jake's hopeful words, lest they flicker out like those distant landing lights. She smiled at the face in the glass, without makeup, her hair still damp, harrowed blue eyes, but still the person she'd always prided herself on being. Who, from her Olympian heights, could handle anything that the gods dished out. Hadn't she proved as much over forty years of editing some of the finest writers on the planet? And yet those pesky landing lights, sailing in from the isles of the blest, just kept on coming, like the fleeting hours and days, the very thing a tipsy Daltrey Assingham had so gone on about across the table as Erma kept turning her distracted gaze to her vibrating phone.

"Our lives, don't you think, gentle people, are simply another of time's artifacts, as we pass from youth to old age—hah, ain't that the cure for all things, as our memories turn into vague, long-forgotten yearnings, like that gaseous cloud of random fluctuations out of which matter forms—exoplanets around the distant star of our birth, as did those glorious mosaics of Galla Placidia's express their patroness's hopes for eternity, at the very moment when, in faraway Byzantium, the plague was on the march and jihad soon to follow. Well, my dear friends, speaking as a historian: so do our memories compose themselves into the residue of the glittering ideals of our youth, who we think we are, what we came here to do; as each time we pause to remember, share a glass with friends, we too emit a few sparks of reflected glory, until, sadly, they fade into mere words recorded on a cuneiform tablet, oracle bones and bronze inscriptions, perhaps a bit of parchment or illuminated manuscript, a book or scribbled letter—oh, and just possibly a stray footnote or lost email, mere impressions to be passed down to other sojourners as yet unborn. And born—yes, thank you, Erma and Diane! Until, until . . . some patient archaeologist or Bedouin boy exploring a cave full of shards, sifting the detritus of the past, stumbles upon that shimmering lonely papyrus fragment, and something of us springs back to life."

"Yes, you old motor-mouth," she exclaimed, realizing how he'd been cribbing Milton: "Those thoughts that wander through eternity, to perish rather, swallowed up and lost in the wide womb of uncreated night, devoid of sense and motion?"

At this little triumph of sleuthing (a wave of her copy editor's wand), exhausted, perplexed, confused, and anxious about getting enough sleep before her morning flight back to Newark, she popped an Ambien and returned her gaze to the window, as if in search of lost time.

Instead of a Proustian reverie, she soon—how strange yet almost expected—found herself being conducted into Augustine's study as if she'd bodily entered Carpaccio's painting, where she began a perusal of artifacts: fingering the glittering armillary sphere, the pink cone shell and brass bell, an Athenian red-figure vase, and, of all things, a delicate Naxian marble figurine of Venus, the sensuous carving turning her eye to the emptied hourglass at the foot of Augustine's desk, which she then, in a flurry of daring, picked up and flipped over. Caught in flagrante, she looked up with a quiver of guilt at her distracted host, only to spy, long overlooked, a bunch of keys hanging in the lock of an open door at the rear of the study, this leading to an inner chamber, sanctum sanctorum. She had to duck her head as she entered, there to find herself in an immense marble hall with mosaic floors and porphyry columns and racks upon racks of papyrus scrolls stretching as far as the eye could see, surely the great library of Alexandria as she'd always imagined it. And as she walked, the racks began to change, now shelving rare calfskin volumes as if in a monastic library, the echo of Gregorian chant leading her on, until she came upon a busy printing workshop in sixteenth-century Venice, where Aldus Manutius stood from his composing rack and beckoned her forward, holding out a rare volume: Hers.

Her phone, set to vibrate, nagged steadily in her palm, enough to finally wake her, even if she couldn't remember exactly what room she was in, or the time. Her only thought, if it was even that, was the name of her daughter.

"Hello . . . Erma?"

"Gini?"

"Yes . . ."

"It's me, Jake."

"Jake, is that really you?"

"I got an email from our PR people that you were making inquiries about some kind of book, a biography—something crazy like that."

"Jake, Jake . . . it's so good to hear your voice . . . it's been so long, but you sound just like your old self."

"Hey, a thousand days, give or take—but who's counting. You sound a little spacey, a little out of it. Have I called too late?"

"Of course not, I was just dozing, reading a rare book about our youthful selves in the old days."

"You seem to like that word *old*."

"Do I? How terrible. But I wasn't that in my dreams. I was reading a rare volume about our time teaming up on the tennis courts, with you tracking my matches, on our way to Wimbledon—and walking in Prospect Garden and hanging out in the physics library, of all places. And, of course, Tashmoo."

"Ha-ha. You have been time traveling."

"Oh, Jake, how are you?"

"I'm getting on, Gini, the years are catching up, the machine is wearing down some, even if I'm fitter than ever. And the new research just keeps coming on faster than ever, an express train you try to catch lest it runs you over."

"Surely not, Jake. I still think of you as somehow indestructible."

"Well, that depends on which day of the week you find me, or even the hour of the day or night."

"But where *do* I find you, Jake? And why haven't you made it back to Reunions? We've all missed you, the old gang, the Shirelles. Even Gareth, after you stole me away from him."

"The pace of the journey is just so rapid that, before you know it, you're further down the line than you realize."

"But you're okay? I mean, we're all getting on. Oh, we would love to see you, Jake. Can't you make it to the parents' dinner and senior dance tomorrow—and graduation? Oh, I know how our senior dance was such a disaster—and all my fault. Even if my mother's outrages spoilt things. But we can still celebrate that journey, even take a walk in Prospect Garden, find our favorite spot beneath the balsam firs—why not catch up with Jabberwocky, or breathe in the infinities of the physics library. What say you, young man?"

"You almost sound like an optimist in your second youth. Hardly the determined if overly cautious woman on the tennis court who had vowed to take a Wimbledon title and win a Pulitzer by thirty."

"Well, two of my authors have Pulitzers and I'm still ranked number one on Martha's Vineyard in the seniors. And yes, I haven't forgotten about the novel—our novel. That's why I'm so eager to catch up."

"Tashmoo said it all . . ."

"Yes, even though, sadly, I had to sell Tashmoo—taxes."

"It was to be a novel about the women's professional tour in a sport dominated by the male players and their abettors in the USLTA. Now, in retrospect, you can just make it all up."

"Yes, recently I've been doing a lot of retrospection with pick and shovel. I guess I'd . . . but listen—you were right. I changed my strokes to the modern game some years ago: tighter parabola, more margin, just like you predicted."

"You were marvelous, like you hadn't lost a step, and your power off the inside-out forehand was a work of art."

"You were there?"

"Your thousand days . . . perhaps I was slow on the pickup."

"My no-show at the Scuola di San Giorgio? It seems you and everyone in the old gang went there without me."

"Ah, just the music of your pronunciation returns me there."

"Visiting the Carpaccios—wouldn't that be something, with Saint Augustine looking over our shoulder?"

"How jealous I always found myself of that fabled past that seemed to reside at your fingertips in every conversation. How many books you'd read."

"That Puritan antediluvian . . . forever trying to slow time."

"My Isabel Archer, making time—forever in search of her destiny."

"So fearful of that imaginative leap, to risk it all."

"A Stoic if scholarly Jabberwocky—the skeptic's job description, as you once called it, combining rational empiricism with a dash of intuition."

"Goodness—did I go on like that . . . well, you always called opinions you disagreed with women's intuition, like marching against the bombing of Cambodia."

"If the bombing was wrong, it was wrong because of a whole series of reactive decisions flowing from a defective policy."

"See what I mean? You always hid your emotions behind that mask of omniscience, as if science was the only cure for what ailed the human condition."

"Oh, I'd certainly include the engineers who designed the roads and aqueducts and sewers, the civilization that allowed your Stoics to flourish. Even if one lifetime is never enough."

"Even if we use it as well as we can?"

"You see, it's the temptations of Tantalus, that's the problem: the new data, the theories that spark one's curiosity and so lead ineluctably into the future, that new civilization just aborning over the horizon."

"But isn't it enough that we love our children? Leave the world a better place—a few books? You must be so proud of your son."

"I keep seeing a world where sickness, aging, and death have been banished. Including such killers as Huntington's. So close . . . so close, so . . ."

"Jake, but the percentages worked out for you, I hope."

"My superpower, so I've been told."

"Did I ever tell you—well, I'll tell you now: how sorry I am about your father. It must have been difficult for you at such a young age."

"It inspired me to imagine a world absent the fear of death or debilitating disease, where we'd have the time to be better human beings. Not unlike your Stoics—a brotherhood of man."

"Yes, well, *oikeiôsis* is the Greek term; it means the familiarization with or appropriation of other people's concerns as if they were your own."

"There you go—how I always envied your scholarship."

"Or as Socrates would have it: a citizen of the universe. Surely enough for one lifetime."

"Precisely how you ended your salutatorian address."

"Hah, you remembered."

"How could I forget."

"Even if your mom didn't approve of me."

"She was crazy about you—overwhelmed more like it, to hear your speech in Latin. 'Just like the priests at mass,' she exclaimed. You astonished her."

"Oh, but I was such a wreck at the parents' dinner and graduation dance. And my mother, even worse—the scene she made—so mortifying. If your mom hated me, I could hardly blame her."

"I had prepared her—everything you confessed to me at Tashmoo: your mother's alcoholism, and your determination to be the best mother of all time: the un–mommy dearest of all time."

"Oh, if only my mother hadn't been there at that moment in time: it could've all been different!"

"Remember our walks on the beach, sailing on the Sound, chasing those white ferries over the blue, when you told me how you used your mother's disease as an excuse to reject her, as a justification for all your bad behavior—something about your tennis coach."

"Strike that from the record, counselor."

"But a perfect backstory for your novel. Chrissie Evert once told me something similar."

"Annette intimated you might have been having an affair."

"Only with her backhand, her grit—how she reminded me of you."

"Do you think I could have beaten her?"

"You could have beaten Virginia Wade, who won Wimbledon in 1977, our first year out."

"Using your tracking system, of course."

"Goes without saying."

"Come . . . you'll meet my daughter, Erma, a science kid no less, with my late husband's brains. You two would have so-o gotten along—as the kids say."

"Hey, rumor has it she works in a lab with my name on it."

"Where are you, Jake? I need to picture it in my mind."

"Oh, everywhere and nowhere—look for me wherever new discoveries are being made. There's no time for laurels. Just a room with a view—huh? Like our dreamy Augustine . . ."

"Dreaming of all our sins, real or imagined."

"Could be . . ."

"You didn't have an affair with Bianca when I did my no-show?"

"What no-show? . . . You were there big as life; I'd been reading up, getting up to speed for a thousand days and nights. That thousand days—Venice—made all the difference in my life."

"Well . . . what do you suppose Augustine saw beyond that window? Your future or mine?"

"He had decided that the past and future don't exist, just temporal mind-states of the eternal present that flicker out as soon as they arrive."

"You don't say," and she laughed.

"You've forgotten your *Confessions*."

"Well . . ."

"Augustine obsessed over the nature of time, right? A present of things past, a present of things present, a present of things to come—mind-states, right? Memory, immediate awareness, and expectation."

"You *have* been reading up."

"I had to if I was to have any chance with you, Isabel."

"Oh dear, my thousand-day no-show."

"You were there in spirit, the map in my back pocket."

"So, our thousand days was not for naught?"

"Just Ginistrella—Isabel, for short—ever in search of her destiny."

"If only I'd had the courage to risk that imaginative leap. Or the spiritual grace to truly believe in something greater than myself."

"I see a room, a vast library filled with books, memories, emptied of distractions—and a view onto eternity. Oh, so tempting, don't you think?"

"Yes, I was just there. Carpaccio's—or is it Augustine's—vision of the soul's flight from multiplicity."

"Yes, yes—you see, the higher one climbs, the more the details fall away. The more we forget, the more the enduring truths behind the veil come into view."

"Yes, of course, a room full of books and music and your armillary sphere—even a figurine of the goddess Venus, such an alluring humanist vision that floats the only world that really matters."

"Gini . . ."

"Yes . . ."

"Do you remember once in Prospect Garden—it was a night like this, the stars a flicker of rising sparks from a well-tended campfire in the pointed firs, and you said something that has stayed with me. Jacob—you called me that when you wanted to impart an intimacy—sometimes I feel that I'm that angel you're forever wrestling with."

"Did I say that?"

"Some say that it was God that Jacob was wrestling to a standstill all night."

"Well, thank goodness. For a moment, you had me worried."

"I wrestle with that angel every day and every night. I see her face everywhere."

"Like those crystalline armillary spheres afloat in the cosmos . . ."

"Do you think Augustine would have been partial to our Jabberwocky?"

"Sometimes, I think it's forgetfulness that opens the door to our past and present."

"Our madeleine . . ."

"Goodness, not Proust as well."

"To catch up."

"Jake, I'm so sorry about your wife, Liz. I know that must have been devastating for you, and such a wonderful mother. A woman of faith: I probably could have learned a lot from her."

"Ah, so you did do your fact-checking. Brilliant like you, a world-class athlete. A helpmeet—one of your famous two-dollar words. I miss her so much that I find myself making up stories, easy lies to avoid the truth. As if I could simply write a better ending. Your department, don't you think?"

"Oh, I have my own revising to do. I lost my husband, Bill, to cancer some years ago, and my grief felt tepid, like I owed him more love than was in me. A brilliant man, Harvard physics, a doting, attentive father to my daughter, Erma. You two would have gotten along famously."

"Perhaps I can meet him in the revised version."

"Come to your son's—to Jacob's—graduation, to the parents' dinner and dance. And you can meet Erma."

"Last dance, last chance . . ."

"Yes."

"Do you remember what you always recited to me in Prospect Garden—or was it our sojourn at Lake Tashmoo?"

"You will hardly know who I am or what I mean . . ."

"But I shall be good health to you nevertheless . . . Missing me one place search another, I stop somewhere waiting for you."

"So, you'll come?"

"There, waiting for you."

CHAPTER 34

For as the rain and the snow come down from heaven, and return not thither but water the earth, making it bring forth and sprout, giving seed to the sower and bread to the eater, so shall my word be that goes forth from my mouth; it shall not return to me empty, but it shall accomplish that which I purpose, and prosper in the thing for which I sent it.

—Isaiah (55:10–11)

She half wakened from a profound and dream-filled sleep, as close to a soulful embrace on eternity as her fiery spirit dared, buoyed, so it seemed, on tender lovemaking, on the most inspiring texts discovered in a vast library of calfskin volumes, those delving into the nature of love, human and divine, when even God, somewhere in Second Isaiah, has discovered His creation to have a mind of its own, as much godlike as human, subverting His intentions at every turning: unpredictable, unknowable, when only reciprocal love remained other than complete surrender.

The warming sunlight on her flushed cheek, flowing across her nakedness against the plush Hyatt counterpane, finally eased her up to tentative alertness. There too that joyful flutter of refracted sunlight on the ceiling, seeming to echo that in her loins, if not the assurance that all was well and her daughter safe and graduating on the morrow. She tapped the blurry crystal of her father's Rolex, trying to read the blue hands, holding it up to her ear: seconds now passing in a comforting rhythm.

Finding her phone abandoned at her side, she raised the glass (as if she might scope light years) to her bleary eyes as if for a final glimpse of that timeless realm beyond her study window from which she'd woken, where past and present so seamlessly merged into the immediate future, only to find she'd failed to set the alarm and so missed her early-morning flight to Newark. No matter, the next was only a flick of a finger away. All the time in the world to make that parents' graduation dinner and dance. Somehow her dread of the event had passed, as if harmlessly translated to pages in her forthcoming novel.

She checked her messages, skipping those from her office, and listening to the one with a Chicago area code.

"Hi, Ms. Wingate, this is Linda from Burrage Pharma. Just to let you know that we've tried to get through to Mr. Burrage and relay your message and contact information but have yet to hear back. Probably on his jet here, there, and everywhere. We'll keep trying. It was great to meet you, and have a great day."

She checked her recents and found a call from an 800 number at 3:18 a.m.

No wonder she'd been so spacey, so out of it. Even as Jake's voice, Liz's too, flowing out of her sister Samantha's vibrant if cautionary tale, echoed as if from some infinite star carelessly suspended high amid the fir boughs. Yes, yes, surely yes, a homing beacon from the blessed isles, filling her now-fading dreams as once her body had opened to a perfect down-the-line backhand, a spinnaker tightly billowing in sight of the finish line. Echoing in turn those haunting lines of Whitman flowing down the wind, sea-blown, blue on blue, spinning joyously through her mind: "The past and present wilt—I have filled them, emptied them, and proceed to fill my next fold of the future."

She tried ringing the 800 number.

"The number you have dialed is not a working number . . ."

With a knowing smile, she turned to the sweet smell of her underarms, touching the luxurious dampness between her legs, and headed for the shower.

Settling into her seat on the afternoon flight to Newark, she decided she was just as happy to have missed the packed early-morning shuttle: a window seat, a row to herself, time to herself. She smiled: "a room of one's own." Normally, she'd be so deep into a manuscript, editing away with demonic concentration, that she'd only be jolted into awareness by the wheels touching down. Now she was simply pleased to get out a pen (the old-fashioned way) to jot down a few notes on a JetBlue cocktail napkin for a dinner toast to her daughter, and just watch as Lake Michigan sailed by beneath the wing, a flat expanse of silver-gray fringed by olive green in the distance, until a deeper spring green swam into view, neat rectangles of farmland, falling away, falling behind as the 777 reached cruising altitude. She found herself recalling those ancient stone walls out of her girlhood, running across the overgrown meadows of Chilmark on the Vineyard, dotted with Queen Anne's lace, goldenrod, virgin's bower, and how she'd always wondered about the generations of farmers who had once worked the soil, long lost, even then, to present memory. Now gone to sprawling homes for the rich and famous.

Her gaze at times retreated to her reflection in the window against the blue, thankfully vague, the imperfect oval of an aging face, the glint of her large eyes, wisps of hair on her forehead, a face gone unnoticed by the inattentive male figure across the aisle. "Just as well, just as well, just as well . . ." She smiled. Like Augustine, looking up with pen poised, perhaps distracted by a vision of blessed Jerusalem or a misspent youth, she yearned for something of that peace and serenity, the certainty of a soul offering, as the ambitious lusts of the body cooled and were left far behind.

Sighing, she sat back and closed her eyes, luxuriating in the desireless feel of cloud soaring, a spotted hawk scanning the horizon as the years fell away, even as she found herself reviewing that phantom phone call at three in the morning. Reassuring in its way, but still inveigling her canny editor's eye to seek out contradictions, along with other troubling snatches of her characters' memories so deftly gleaned in the previous twenty-four hours.

"If you and I make it to seventy—what with the rapidly evolving breakthroughs in the field of aging research, we should be home free."

Whether forty years back or just hours before, she took comfort that Jake's optimism remained undiminished, blood still full of fight and fiber—that same cagey, if caustic humor and hope for the future, which, with the effortless retreat of immaterial time beneath her wings, seemed only a promise fulfilled. She tapped her looking glass, now in the guise of one fleet-footed Hermes tempting the realm of the gods, where the long-forgiven Isabel mulled her fate. Just as forgetting, even eliding the truth, she now determined, allowed one to fill in a new narrative. How a quicksilver trace of another's memories could be so quickly translated into a vivid image, like that of a traumatized eleven-year-old standing waist deep in the Sheridan Place pool, his atrophied shoulder and arm out of its sling, a broken wing that the therapist gently moved through a normal range of motion. All under the watchful gaze of his beloved aunt Sam. And later too, snuggling with his godmother on the green damask sofa beneath the landscapes of Cripple Creek, where his mother had once liked to sit and read to him. Yes, James's donnée, offerings of the gods.

"Sometimes," Samantha had winced, a glance to where the reflected red lights of an emergency vehicle flashed out a warning in the plate glass, "to hear Jake go on, injury was just a glitch in a lab experiment, something that could be rerun, and with enough application—a problem to be solved. But eleven-year-old bodies, much less minds, don't heal like that. A miracle he didn't end up addicted to OxyContin.

"And then there were moments when I felt Jake blamed Liz—even me. That she'd somehow let down the side and all their plans. That she'd somehow slipped his half nelson. I guess they had had a fight that morning or the night before, and Liz might have been distracted. She'd written something odd in her diary the day before, from Isaiah: 'As one whom his mother comforts, so I will comfort you; you shall be comforted in Jerusalem.' Just another of Liz's crazy ideas: how women were closer to God, or God was a woman—how, when women take over things, the world won't be so fucked up. Something . . . but—hey, they don't call it black ice for nothing.

"You see, here's the thing, that pasta Bolognese dinner Jacob cooked me in Boulder, with all the vintage wine—I found myself struggling to even keep up with the conversation, as if I was being carefully debriefed about the latest results in my Chicago lab, as if he couldn't help himself, his mind, his curiosity getting the better of him. Half the time, I couldn't understand the basic science—nanorobots living inside cells to repair the damage from aging—that kind of science fiction. And a senior in high school! Hell, I'm a full professor at Chicago. And then that immaculate conception of a home, that all-male paradise, started to weird me out—the complete absence of Liz (not a mention of his mother, not a snapshot), my flesh and blood, as if this child of God, healed in body, had become so weaned of memory, tragic or otherwise, as to have lost his soul in the bargain. Jeest, the way he squeezed my arm. It was just a little scary—nanorobots, my ass."

She reached into her jacket pocket for her phone and instead found a sprig of balsam fir from the garden at Sheridan Place. A pleased smile eased up her lips as she brought the aromatic needles to her nose and breathed deeply and, in an instant, found herself once again safely strolling in Prospect Garden—or was it swimming laps at Sheridan Place—with Jake's strong arm gripping her shoulder.

Her mind careening between memories past and present, she barely had time to fasten her seat belt before the 777 swooped down like some great bird of prey upon the New Jersey Turnpike's southbound traffic. The jolt of the wheels rattled her equanimity, her mind elsewhere—where faces familiar and not beckoned to her, hurrying her on through endless airport gangways, while her drogue chute of a carry-on impeded every turning. Even the comforting smells of her Mercedes's all-leather interior failed to disperse her forty-year-old panic, the days around her breakup with Jake and the imminent descent of her estranged mother for their graduation dinner and dance. Dutifully, Jake had marched her around Prospect Garden, trying to calm her, where the last scuds of hazy blue daylight dispersed among the balsam firs, their Virgilian grove where they had so often wandered as temporal outcasts. Even then, her onetime lover had encouraged her to good cheer, no matter the oppressive duty with her mother that awaited her.

She eased into the southbound entrance of the turnpike. Running late, she no longer cared that she'd have to abandon a pit stop at the Marriott and her gorgeous new Jovani, V-neck, split-sleeve evening gown, orange florals on black.

That forty-year-old dread again had her in its teeth: the calamitous threat of a mother on the warpath, five years divorced and out for blood.

Her father at his wits' end: "I take no responsibility anymore. You'll have to deal with your mother as best you can."

And again, she eased off the accelerator at the comforting embrace of Jake's arm in Prospect Garden. "Just be a daughter to her, talk to her . . . let her be a proud mother."

"How the hell your father actually managed to breed me—if he did—is a miracle (a frightful closet homosexual, did I ever tell you?). So, consider yourself lucky to even be around."

Traumatized, she found herself, again and again, forced to walk her mother to the ladies', holding her left arm in a death grip as she tottered precariously on high heels, her breasts falling out of a strapless, impossibly low-cut, blue satin dress, as she sputtered out curses at her ex-husband (while dismissing all the pointy-headed Princeton professors), who sat safely at the far end of the dinner table bunkered by her roommates' parents.

"Don't sass me. Where else did you get that nasty sex drive, dearest? Risking your reputation and John Chandler's livelihood. If not your addiction to beating every woman who ever took the court."

Throughout the evening, her father had nimbly ignored his wife's seething disaster at the far end of the table, somehow maintaining his distinguished, unflappable poise, impeccably dressed in his best gray pin-striped suit and Ivy Club tie, his large hands gesturing for effect as he engaged Jake's beaming mother ("Dear Barbara, your son is a most excellent second mate") and Apolonia's and Bianca's parents, keeping them laughing and comfortable with his arch penchant for puns and wickedly funny stories about the pathetic foibles of his best authors ("to remain nameless") and the high jinks of drunken classmates on the eve of graduation "eons ago."

Bianca, realizing the desperate craziness of the situation, embarked on even crazier tell-all fables to regale her ancient grandmother, who was nearly deaf and barely spoke a word of English. Tall tales about how the four roommates had to gallantly fight off leering advances by the most brilliant, if randy, professors on the planet. This all narrated in the most grandiloquent terms (employing obscene hand gestures that only her grandmother understood), while making goofy faces for the benefit of Apolonia, who quivered with apprehension: her lover and his wife presided at the president's table only yards away.

John Proctor had stood smiling, tapping his glass for silence, microphone in hand, catching Apolonia's eye for an instant, before launching into an eloquent welcome to the thousands gathered in the sprawling Jadwin sports arena. Then concluding with a humorous blessing of the graduating seniors and their "long-suffering parents" who had just paid their last tuition bill.

Bianca's grandmother, white-haired, dressed in black with lace trim at her sleeves, gold teeth aglint, became more and more agitated as Bianca continued her recounting of the ghoulish crimes of passion inflicted on the roomies, only suddenly to launch into a string of Sicilian curses that could be heard throughout the vast auditorium. The old crone held up a crooked finger as she knocked over her glass of wine, warning off any of these monsters—"*Andare a puttane*"—who might dare attack her granddaughter. In the ensuing shocked silence, Giuseppina shrugged and clutched Bianca's hand: "Even if the girl only talks fluent Florentine (bigshot) Italian." At which Bianca's scandalized mother, an ER nurse who sang opera, broke into peals of laughter as she began mopping up her mother's place, helped by her lawyer husband who, Bianca liked to say, kept half the Cosa Nostra out of jail on bail bond. "Oh, he does this for a living," his wife said, grinning, handing her husband an unbloodied napkin.

She found her mind calming as these remote memories took their allotted place in her text, preparing her reentry, looking forward to seeing Erma, even as the bumper-to-bumper traffic was delaying her further.

As the green exit sign finally loomed: *17A to Hightstown and Princeton 12*, her dashboard screen lit up with an urgent text from Erma: Mom, where are you? Her heart surged with gladness. With a yelp of pleasure, she texted: 11 miles.

Yes, how marvelously her father had engaged Apolonia's parents, probing lightly, as was his wont, to hear more about their blue-collar enclave of Manayunk, nestled on a craggy hill above Philadelphia, where her father worked as a roofer, her mother a beautician, the couple at first remaining impervious to his attempts to draw them out with wicked tales about his wartime years working in Philly's navy yards. But once the Phillies and Eagles were broached, they were off to the races, speculating on the chances of a Yankees-Phillies World Series. Annette's parents were a cinch, her father also a Princeton grad, her mother a tennis coach at a girl's prep school; they lived in Oyster Bay, where her dad commuted to his seat on the New York Stock Exchange. He was an avid sailor on Long Island Sound, so these two tigers had much to discuss, whether how they'd always supported co-education at Princeton, or the performance of their respective sailboats—and, of course, Annette's forthcoming marriage to the number-one tennis player in the world (now in the third round at Roland-Garros).

Talk of tennis, for a few blissful minutes, seemed to subdue her mother, who had once herself been a junior champion, ranked number one in New England before the war, and losing to Alice Marble in two close sets in the third round at Longwood in 1939. "Most of the European gals couldn't make it after the Nazis invaded Poland," she declared, staggering to her feet and asking which way to the ladies'. Once again, her daughter had deftly caught her arm with one hand while pulling up her bulging bodice with the other. (In the toilet stall, her mother had enlisted her aid in pulling down her tight panty hose and control panties.)

A scene long banished to memory's oblivion and now received with the gratitude (her panic a receding tide) of a novelist's love for the telling detail. She smiled serenely as she sailed through the yellow light at the intersection of Route 1, eyes lifting to the evening twilight as she picked up speed in the homestretch, remembering Jake's calming voice in Prospect Garden as he squeezed her shoulder: "You're the only daughter she has—all she has left, so just indulge her."

Throughout the excruciating dinner, on the verge of tears, tears that would flow copiously on the dance floor, she had turned again and again to Jake's amused face, admiring his calm as he lovingly attended his plucky mother, who clearly missed her husband beyond words. Halfway through the meal, Barbara Burrage had extracted a folded piece of paper from her purse, stood with shaking wineglass, and read her prepared toast.

"Jacob, my late husband, had always dreamed of sharing this moment with you, Jacob, and your treasured friends. Coming home every night from the construction site, he would take such joy in Jacob's news from school, not just the prizes, the swimming trophies, but the way his son made learning—well, like he always said—an open window on a better future. Jacob had hoped to be an engineer, but the Depression, the war . . . he made the best of the shortened life God granted him."

Jake had leaned over and kissed his mother, then, presenting her with a bouquet of yellow roses, raised his glass as he stood and turned his gaze upon the table.

"Somebody said we can't pick our parents, but in the crapshoot of life, I rolled snake eyes. My mom was always there for me with a warming cup of cocoa when I came home from school in a frigid Evanston winter. And Dad, what can I say? You never stopped dreaming about how to tie a better fly or how to make the perfect cast on Cripple Creek, as if the sky was the limit." He fished out his Phi Beta Kappa key, shook his clenched fist, and threw the gold charm down on the table. "Snake eyes, for the best dad a guy could've ever wanted."

"Unlike some at this table," her mother had screeched, sloshing her upheld wineglass all over her dress as her right breast popped free.

"Well," cried Bianca, "time for us girls to powder our noses."

Bianca had kept radio silence: a huge surprise for their parents. Somehow, she'd even managed to rehearse the twenty-piece band, including a violin section, which proved the perfect backup. As the dinner wound down, the roommates disappeared into the ladies', where they donned bouffant black wigs and heavy makeup ("Thank God we didn't do blackface!" echoing down the years). For most of the parents not in the know, for a few glorious moments, the Shirelles, in person, lit up the vast auditorium.

As she sang out the final bars of "Will You Still Love Me Tomorrow," the glittering face of the Burrage Biochemistry Lab rose up ahead off Washington Road, blue on towering blue against the amethyst dusk, a homecoming celebrated in the eager grip of Jake's hand on her shoulder, as they again sought the shadowed firs in Prospect Garden, where his delighted voice sang out the profusion of spring blossoms sprinkled on the humid evening, their scents now a heady cocktail mixed with that of the California lilacs and balsam firs, whose conical shade hid them deep from prying eyes, merging with the scents of jasmine and rose, elixirs of eternal youth, infused—could it be? was it possible?—with the rubbery smell of freshly opened tennis balls! She laughed uproariously at the stray cans of used balls that littered the passenger well, which only sped her winged heels up Washington Road as effortlessly as, once upon a time, her legs had on court. She opened all her windows to the following wind, seeing again the array of bowed spring blossoms, while overhead the first pale stars of evening rang celebratory changes.

Parking at Cap and Gown, she took a few deep breaths, glanced in the rearview mirror to make the necessary adjustments to her disheveled hair, a dash of lipstick, and an exclamation mark texted to Erma. A workaday pants suit it was. Only forty minutes late. Her knees felt almost back to their old scrappy selves as she made her way past the physics library (scene of how many crimes?) and the Burrage Biochemistry Lab, now a centerpiece of her bestseller to come. At the door of Jadwin, she searched a moment in her purse for the invitation she'd left on her desk at the Marriott, only to feel again that hurrying pressure on her shoulder (crunch of gravel along the garden path), staying her rush for a last look skyward at a pale moon just rising above the stadium, Jake's familiar laugh in hers . . . and the pledge of faith given in return.

"Only the future, huh, the one our children will one day inhabit and wonder if we had simply lost our minds."

"Yes, we did," she whispered in reply as the attendant checked off her name on the guest list. "'I effuse my flesh,'" she sang out, "'in eddies, and drift it in lacy jags.'"

"Surprise," Bianca shouted.

"Better late than never," smiled Annette, her voice rising as she presided at their table. "And look at her—unrecognizable, not a stitch of orange."

She couldn't get a word out, dazzled by the lovely candlelight as far as the eye could see in the vastness of Jadwin, as she hugged her old roomies. And then Gareth.

"I . . . I'm sorry I'm late; I had to be in Chicago for a meeting and only just got back and the traffic was awful. But I thought—where's Erma?"

"So, what's new? I told you she'd be late," laughed Bianca. "Chicago bear, my ass—you wicked girl."

"Ah, our author arrives," purred Apolonia in a facetious yet loving, even hopeful tone.

"Forever late if not forever young," noted Annette, gesturing to her seat next to Gareth. "But we kept your now-cold pumpkin-curry soup and chicken marsala, and there's plenty of dessert if you need a sugar high."

"Just for the record, Mom," Apolonia now explained, "Erma wanted this to be a surprise for you. We were going to be here for her graduation tomorrow, of course, for our favorite goddaughter, but Erma managed to cadge the extra seats for the parents' dinner-dance by saying we were all her aunts. She lies almost as well as her mother."

Gareth touched her arm. "Sit down, sit down, your fan club awaits you."

"And you won't believe who's here," sang out Bianca, "who showed up to join us. That was Erma's doing as well." And she held up a bouquet of yellow roses, as did the other women at the table with giddy smiles.

"Yes, guess who's here—like old times was new times," said Apolonia.

"We've just been having the most fascinating conversation, even if it was over my head," said Annette, bending to smell her roses.

"Good Lord," Bianca chimed in, "some things never change; it was like déjà vu all over again."

Apolonia shook her head in wonder: "You never heard such conversation—life-extension research, nanorobots, genetic engineering, and AI. Yeah, I guess we're all health spanners and immortalists now. What's to lose?"

Gareth added: "Negligible senescence—that's the new-new thing. Biological immortality. At least a dozen start-ups we'll need to take a look at for seed capital."

"Holy moly," sang Bianca with a tittering smile, "we're all going to live forever: it's a cinch, said the Grinch."

She waited, a little dumbfounded, behind her chair, quietly smiling as she eyed the bouquet on her seat, hearing and not hearing, trying to make sense of the awkward situation. Gareth, seeing the lost look, took her in hand.

"I was going to save the first dance for my daughter, but she's already beat me to it. So the honor passes to you."

"Yes, a spin around the dance floor to work up an appetite."

"And we'll seek out Erma so she knows you made it safely."

"Yes . . . ," her voice eager as a teenager. "Let's dance."

Gareth led her out onto the sprawling dance floor, where an inland sea of couples lapped the far recesses of the huge sports arena, young and old moving to the delicious nostalgia poured forth by a twenty-piece band, golden oldies spanning the generations. The lighting was dim, blue-misted, pricked by a thousand flickering candles on the dinner tables, which spiraled off into the shadowed recesses of the auditorium. The geodesic dome draped with orange-and-black banners heralded a near-century of NCAA and Ivy championship teams, including four of her own. She was happy, relieved, to let herself be led by her partner, whom she remembered as always a good dancer, certainly better than Jake: kind, considerate, letting her take the lead when she chose, something she always appreciated in her husband, Bill. She merged herself deep into Gareth's arms, which had once served as placeholders for his friend, Jake, so often indisposed by lab experiments and student jobs.

There, safely, she indulged the lovely view of the generations over his left shoulder, of parents with their sons and daughters, many younger than herself (why had she waited so long to marry and reproduce?). Oh, she sighed inwardly, the different faces, from the four corners of the earth—a veritable multitude of diverse rainbow colors, of hair and eyes, many with gorgeous, exotic, unplaceable features. Even as these graduating seniors, so she thought, looked so much older and cleaner-cut, taller, more handsome, athletic even than the motley, long-haired crew she remembered from her day. Not easy to pick out her tall daughter in such a multitude, her own flesh and blood, especially as more and more dancers filtered onto the floor.

For a brief moment, she found herself aware of a haunting, lilting melody wafting across the vast dance floor, a woman's voice, the band's lead singer, echoing down the years. She closed her eyes in recollection, the lyrics rising free and clear: "memories . . . of the way we were."

Her eyes opening as if on some figment of the past, where, in the near distance, she thought she caught a glimpse of Erma, or at least a tall blonde wearing a short black dress that looked a lot like the graduation dress she had bought for her daughter. This moment of recognition had the odd, almost dizzying effect of compressing the huge bubble of space around the dance floor, as if all of time was merged in the moment, one dazzling instant of acute vision conflating a lifetime's memories. So much so that whatever Gareth was saying to her seemed to be echoing harmlessly across time and space. A gentle nudge of her partner now brought her quarry closer, refocusing her gaze through time's aperture, where there appeared a face very much like her own, a young woman's face nestled peacefully on the blazer-jacketed shoulder of her partner.

She smiled with relief when she saw, indeed, that it was Erma. Never had she seen Erma looking so happy and serene, her eyes shining with a kind of resplendent light, a rapture withdrawn into an inner radiance. So much so that she feared drawing too near, as if she might break the timeless spell, as if her appearance might transform her daughter back into the moody, insecure young woman of recent years. She wanted this to be her daughter's moment, to preserve forever the happiness somehow snatched from life's capricious journey, celebrated on a thousand candlelit altars, a resplendent joy that had prompted her to invite her roommates to the senior dance.

And then Erma's eyes brushed hers, a twinkling recognition, less than a nanosecond in cosmic terms, but enough—yes, the rapture—to want to shout out her love and pride and gratitude for being blessed with such a daughter. A mother's prayer, which seemed to bring a knowing smile to Erma's face even as she turned away, swiveled with her partner as if to accede to love's claimant, but slowly, slowly, rhythmically, tucked safely within the spell of the music until her partner's face came fully into view, at once so familiar and not, so striking that she almost drew a blank, her throat so tight she found it hard to breathe. As if the vastness of the arena had narrowed even further to that single couple, framed by a single window to which she now reached out her hand, as if to tap the glass at catching sight of her own reflection, or to alert a lover, just as that familiar face seemed to recognize hers, call out to her as when he had pressed her shoulder in Prospect Garden only moments before, where a smile of deepest affection, if not gratitude, now met her blurry gaze (as her breath fogged the glass)—yes, of unalloyed gladness, prompting a telling nod of pure pleasure, or as she would forever remember, as she would one day write it: bespeaking less of resurrection or even reunion than possession against all the odds. While a quick turn—swish of a magician's cape, revealed again the fullness of her daughter's bliss—the untranslatable thing that remained forever sealed in her heart: a yawp over the roofs of the world.

THE END

ACKNOWLEDGMENTS

To my early readers, Sally Arteseros and Patricia Fogerty, my heartfelt thanks for your thoughts and encouragement, and to Jason Booher, our talented cover designer, who came up with an image that was tantalizing and suggestive of the story within. Thanks, Jason, for the fourth cover we've done together.

And an acknowledgment note to my editor Erin Brown for all her superb editing skills and help in bringing the novel to where it needs to be, and to Pam Nordberg for her copyediting skills, which were exceptional. And to the whole Greenleaf team who are great professionals and always a pleasure to work with.

ABOUT THE AUTHOR

MS CLEVELAND is a novelist and art historian. His previ-
Deception, was described by the *WSJ*'s Walter Russell Mead as
nd compelling novel of enormous ambition . . . the author is a
list whose ear for language, eye for both artistic and natural
ship, understanding of human character, and feel for Ameri-
es him a national treasure. *Gods of Deception* was a 2022
finalist for historical fiction. His third novel, *Time's Betrayal*,
) was awarded Best Historical Novel of 2017 by Reading the
ning author Robert Olen Butler called *Time's Betrayal* "a
rbing novel engaging with the great and enduring theme
for identity." Bruce Olds, two-time Pulitzer-nominated
etrayal as a "monumental work . . . in a league of its own
ge-hearted American epic that deserves the widest pos-
f readerships." His second novel, *Love's Attraction*, was
ly saga moving between Concord and Venice—a twisty,
old, about love and creativity, grief and pain, family
uk included *Love's Attraction* on its list of top novels
th a Gemlike Flame, drew wide praise for its evocation
lost masterpiece by Raphael. His most recent art his-
rican Tonalism, won the Silver Medal in Art History in
s, 2010; and Outstanding Academic Title 2011 from
ation; and the 3rd edition from Abbeville Press has

gone on to be one of the best-selling books in American art history standard reference in its field. David was a regular reviewer for *ARTne* written for *The Magazine Antiques*, the *American Art Review*, and *Danc* For almost a decade, he was the Arts Editor at Voice of America. He a split their time between the Catskills and Siesta Key.

ABOUT THE AUTHOR

DAVID ADAMS CLEVELAND is a novelist and art historian. His previous novel, *Gods of Deception*, was described by the *WSJ*'s Walter Russell Mead as "an accomplished and compelling novel of enormous ambition . . . the author is a major American novelist whose ear for language, eye for both artistic and natural detail, cultural scholarship, understanding of human character, and feel for American social reality, makes him a national treasure. *Gods of Deception* was a 2022 Indies Book of the Year finalist for historical fiction. His third novel, *Time's Betrayal*, (*Booklist* starred review) was awarded Best Historical Novel of 2017 by Reading the Past. Pulitzer prize–winning author Robert Olen Butler called *Time's Betrayal* "a vast, rich, endlessly absorbing novel engaging with the great and enduring theme of literary art, the quest for identity." Bruce Olds, two-time Pulitzer-nominated author, described *Time's Betrayal* as a "monumental work . . . in a league of its own and class by itself . . . a large-hearted American epic that deserves the widest possible, most discriminating of readerships." His second novel, *Love's Attraction*, was praised by *Booklist* as "a family saga moving between Concord and Venice—a twisty, atmospheric tale, leisurely told, about love and creativity, grief and pain, family and identity." Fictionalcities.uk included *Love's Attraction* on its list of top novels for 2013. His first novel, *With a Gemlike Flame*, drew wide praise for its evocation of Venice and the hunt for a lost masterpiece by Raphael. His most recent art history book, *A History of American Tonalism*, won the Silver Medal in Art History in the Book of the Year Awards, 2010; and Outstanding Academic Title 2011 from the American Library Association; and the 3rd edition from Abbeville Press has gone on to be one of the best-selling books in American art history—now the standard reference in its field. David was a regular reviewer for *ARTnews*, and has written for *The Magazine Antiques*, the *American Art Review*, and *Dance Magazine*. For almost a decade, he was the Arts Editor at Voice of America. He and his wife split their time between the Catskills and Siesta Key.